METLAKATLA

KEN TOMILSON

Map designed and created by Jackie Friesen using resources provided by Native-Land.ca. This map does not represent or intend to represent official or legal boundaries of any Indigenous nations, and is not meant to be used as an academic or legal resource. Native Land data on indigenous territories is an ongoing process created and updated through the support of local communities, and precise information may be considered inaccurate by indigenous communities, officials, or individuals.

Cover designer: Edge of Water Designs, edgeofwater.com
Interior Formatting: Jackie Friesen

ISBNs:
Paperback: 978-1-77374-078-2
eBook: 978-1-77374-079-9

TABLE OF CONTENTS

◇◇◇◇◇◇◇◇◇◇◇◇◇◇

ACKNOWLEDGEMENTS

With every step we take, we walk in the footprints of those who came before. We are made up of stars become earth and sea and sky and the People; people of all manner of living and all manner of loving. We live carrying hope forward for the people yet to come, and in friendly welcome for the people seeking to share the becoming-truth of our freedoms. With gratitude, humility, and no little sense of wonder, we acknowledge that the land on which we gather here on Canada's western coast is the unceded and traditional territory of the Metlakatla and the many other indigenous peoples of this land. Before the Europeans, the Coast Salish people described in this book lived in a harmonious and inclusive circle within the abundance of the land. It is our hope that this volume carries the message and spirit of that abundance forward.

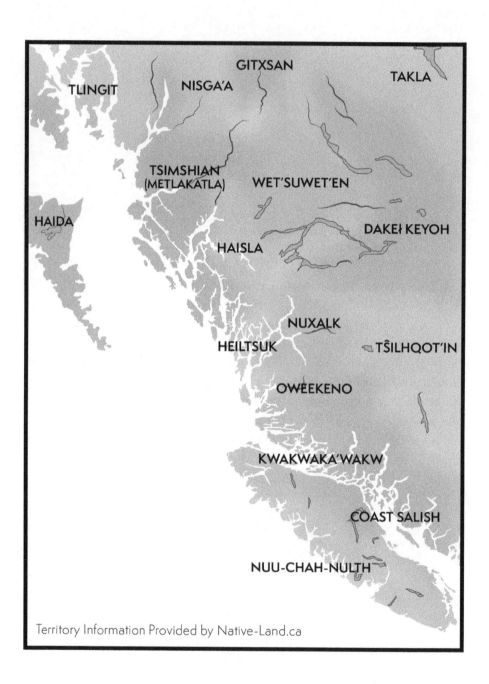

TLINGIT

HAIDA

NISGA'A

GITXSAN

TAKLA

TSIMSHIAN
(METLAKATLA)

WET'SUWET'EN

DAKEɫ KEYOH

HAISLA

NUXALK

TŜILHQOT'IN

HEILTSUK

OWEEKENO

KWAKWAKA'WAKW

COAST SALISH

NUU-CHAH-NULTH

Territory Information Provided by Native-Land.ca

GITKA'ATA

ONE

The Cannibal Spirits abducted me from my village early one morning near the end of the winter ceremonies. I was fifteen.

I rose from my bed that morning before the sky was light. I dressed with pride, for I knew this was the last time I would wear the clothes of a boy. I sat near the fire in the centre of my father's house and waited alone for the Spirits to arrive. The others in our house were awake but they pretended to sleep in their chambers. They too waited for the Spirits.

When I was dressing I found a small piece of dried salmon my mother had hidden in my clothes when no one was watching. I was grateful for her concern, but I could not eat it. My stomach was too nervous. I had prepared for this day for many moons. The Spirits had been expected two days earlier, but a great storm arrived first. My great uncle Silgitook, the Chief of my mother's Clan, announced that the Spirits would wait until the storm was over. He said they would not have me killed by falling trees or branches after so much preparation. This morning the winds had stopped. I waited anxiously in the darkness, watching the fire and listening to the silence.

My heart jumped suddenly at the sound of soft footsteps on stones. I saw the glow of their torches through the deerskin that covered the entrance. Six of them burst into the room, howling and waving their arms. They were both frightening and beautiful. Their naked bodies were painted red and the shapes of their ribs and skulls painted white over the red.

These were the bodies of men I knew, Hamatsas dancers I had practiced with, but at first I did not know them. The Cannibal Spirits filled their hearts and bodies and gave them strange movements. First I recognized Hahkwah, with his heavy stomach. Then young Doolyaks, with his strong chest and arms. My eyes were captured by his large tsootz. It was painted white like a bone and it swung back and forth between his legs as he ran.

I turned to watch them as they ran deeper into my father's house, wild-eyed and frantic, peeking into each sleeping chamber as they passed. They pretended not to see me sitting in the light of the fire in the centre of the room.

"Where is the boy, Ts'uwaas?" they cried in their strange, high voices. "We must take him far to the north, where he will be given supernatural powers and taught to crave the taste of men's flesh!"

The people of my father's house came out of their chambers already dressed. My father appeared in his ceremonial clothes that he wore on special occasions.

"Please leave my son alone," he cried. "Take me instead, Cannibal Spirits!"

"The Spirits do not want you, old man," answered old Jaksukjalee, the leader of the Hamatsas. "We want Ts'uwaas!"

My mother and the other women held out furs and raw meats to the Spirits as they passed, but they only laughed and pushed them out of their way. I watched their performance with amusement as they moved around the room.

Suddenly they turned and saw me sitting in the centre of the room. The first Spirit howled and led the others down the steps to the fire. I stood up and backed away. They circled me slowly, making terrible faces as they stared into my eyes. These were faces I knew but they had never looked at me like this. The smile left my face and my heart began to pound in my throat.

They chanted loudly, "He is the one! He is the one!"

I dared not look away as their hands reached for my face. My mother panicked and tried to pull one of them away. He turned and snarled. She squealed and leapt back when he tried to bite her. The other women pulled her away to protect her.

The Spirits closed in around me. Doolyaks pulled me to his chest. His strong arms lifted me off the ground with ease. Then he followed the other Spirits through the door, two in front of him and two behind, carrying me under one arm. The last Spirit stayed by the door to stop any who might try to follow them.

◇◇◇◇◇◇◇◇◇◇◇◇◇◇◇

The fear has left me, but my heart still pounds with excitement. The Hamatsas are taking me away! My life will never be as it was before. I belong to them now. I feel like their brother already. I want to be naked, painted red and white and running freely beside them. But I am also happy to be carried and that it is Doolyaks who carries me. I do not want to let go. The muscles of his chest are large and firm. I hug him tightly, pressing my face against his smooth skin. It is moist from his sweat and I slide against him as he runs.

Many faces peek out of the doors of the other houses. All the village has risen early to watch my abduction. I hear them calling to others to come watch us and I hear their words and their laughter as we pass. Only the bravest dare step outside for no one knows which way the Spirits will turn. The Spirits will bite the flesh of anyone who steps into their path, for that is their right.

The Hamatsas do not stop at the edge of the forest as I expect. They carry me up a trail and along fallen logs for a great distance. The morning light is dim. It is difficult to see but they know their way. I close my eyes and hang on tighter as the ferns and branches slap against my skin.

They stop at a secret spot they cleared and blessed only a few days before. This is where they planned my abduction. It is here they gathered in the dark and called to the Spirits to fill their bodies. I sense their sacred presence in the air around me. I feel soft cedar branches under my feet as Doolyaks sets me down. He looks into my eyes.

"Are you all right?" he asks with concern in his voice.

He wipes the red paint from his chest off the side of my face, then strokes my shoulders and arms with his large hands to soothe me and give me courage. I nod my head. My tongue cannot find the words to speak my thoughts. I feel my tsootz beginning to swell.

Jaksukjalee, the leader of the Hamatsas, chants a prayer to the Spirits and brushes hemlock branches up and down both sides of my body. He tells me to take off my boy's clothes. I will not need them again. He will offer them to the village as proof that the Spirits have taken me to their world. I slowly fold my blanket of mountain goat wool and take off my shirt that hangs to my knees. I am praying that my swollen tsootz will soften, but it does not.

The Hamatsas laugh when they see it. For a moment they forget their roles and make jokes about me eating men.

Hahkwah says, "I think he likes you, Doolyaks. Maybe we should leave you here so he can practice eating you!" They all laugh again.

I feel the heat of the embarrassment burning in my cheeks, but Doolyaks just grins. He reaches out his strong arm and pats my head playfully. He gives me a sweet smile to tell me that everything is fine.

Jaksukjalee clears his throat and hushes the others with a stern look. He brushes both sides of my naked body with a hemlock bough again to purify me. The tips of the hemlock brush my tsootz lightly and I shudder. The Hamatsas struggle to hide their smiles, but Jaksukjalee ignores them. He opens a ceremonial blanket and offers me a long, beautiful woolen vest and a blanket made of cedar and wolf fur.

"These clothes will keep you warm. Leave them wrapped in this sacred blanket under this log when you return." He folds the blanket and places it carefully under a log on a bed of cedar strips. "Take this dried fish and salal berry cake. It is only enough for one day. You must be hungry when you return." He places the small package of food in my hands. "We must return to tell the villagers to purify themselves and not to lie with each other for the next four days. You must remain pure too. That is why I cannot leave you with Doolyaks." He winks at me.

The others laugh again and poke Doolyaks. He smiles broadly.

They quiet themselves before Jaksukjalee speaks again. His voice is very serious, the voice of an Elder, wise and careful.

"Remember what you have been taught and what you have practiced, but it will be the Spirits who guide you from this place and show you the way back. They will come to you in the forest in different shapes. You must be brave and receive them with respect. If you run away in fear or come back too early they will curse your forever. When you come back to this sacred spot, you must summon them again before you return to the village. We will know then if you are worthy of being a Hamatsa dancer. Now you must walk north, as far into the forest as you can before nightfall."

There is only one way to go. Our village faces south to the water and the Hamatsas have taken me to where the mountains rise steeply to the east and the west. I must follow the valley north to go further into the forest.

I set out as soon as they leave. I walk part way up the side of the mountain to avoid the dense bushes and muddy ground by the river. Most of the winter snows have melted. I walk along fallen logs when I can. Even on the mountain slope my progress is slow, for the forest is thick with bushes here too.

The fear has returned now that I am alone. I have prepared with the Hamatsas for four moons. I know what I must do when I return but I am not prepared for the next three days. I thought they would give me more food. Perhaps they are playing a trick on me, I think at first, but then I realize they want me to prove myself worthy to be a Hamatsa. What if I am unworthy? Will they let me starve to death?

I crouch in the bushes to listen. They are not following me. They have left me to die. The child in my heart wants to cry. I wanted to be abducted, not abandoned. I think of the dried salmon my mother placed on my bed and I wish I had eaten it. She will worry for me when she finds it uneaten. I think about my bed and I want to be safe and warm in my family's home.

The villagers must know I have not been given enough food. I am angry with them too, but then I remember that the Spirits can sense what I am feeling. They will abandon me too if I insult them with my self-pity. I must prove to them I am brave.

I walk for three hours up the river valley. I cross seven streams angry with winter rains. The valley begins to climb steeply into the mountains. I am tired. I have walked far enough but I wonder where I will sleep. I could find a cave at the foot of mountain walls but I do not want to disturb a sleeping bear or mountain lion.

Instead I find a large fallen tree on the mountainside. It is caught between two other trees and there is a small dry space beneath it. I find a bed of hemlock boughs and cedar bark there. My heart is filled with joy! The Hamatsas have prepared this bed for me. The Spirits have not abandoned me. They have guided me to this place. I gather tree moss and ferns to make the bed softer. I find a sharp stone to cut more cedar boughs to make walls to keep out the wind.

I check around the log and other places nearby to see if they have hidden any food for me. I find nothing. I climb to the top of the log to look at the forest around me. From the top I can hear the roar of the river below, but the forest is too thick to see it. The sun has come through an opening in the trees. Its warmth blesses me. I am so hungry from the hard walk that I eat half of the dried oolichon. I pass the rest of the afternoon on top of the log. It is peaceful here. For a short time, I think the next three days will pass easily.

The winter sun does not last long. It disappears behind the steep mountains in the west and the cold wind finds me. Rain begins to fall. I wrap my blanket of wolf fur around me and crawl under the log onto my bed of cedar and hemlock.

I feel the loneliness again. I am not warm enough in the dampness. I pull my blanket tightly around me. The rain falls harder as the darkness grows. Soon it is hard to see the trees through the holes in the cedar bough walls. Then there is nothing but blackness and the sound of rain dripping on the bushes.

I want to save food for the morning but I think about the women preparing the evening meal in my father's house and I want to eat. I finish the last of what I was given. What will I do now, I wonder. Will I starve to death lying on these branches? How will I find food if it rains until then? I decide not to think about these things, but the thoughts will not leave me alone.

I lie there a long time before I fall asleep, imagining that Doolyaks was holding me, keeping me warm. I don't remember falling asleep, but I wake from a dream. In my dream I was playing with my brothers and sister around the brightness and warmth of my father's fire. But the dream is over and my family is gone. I am lying cold and alone beneath a log in the depths of the forest again. I cannot stop the tears of self-pity that burn down my cheeks. It is then I hear a sound that makes my heart freeze!

Did I hear a branch snap on the ground, not far away? It was not the sound of a falling branch but the sound of someone or something stepping on a branch. I forget about my family and listen hard. I listen for several minutes but I hear nothing. There is only the rain dripping on the bushes. I think I must be mistaken, that I imagined it, but I continue to listen. I hear nothing but the rain for a long while.

I just begin to relax when I hear it again clearly. The snap of a branch and the crunch of bushes. Footsteps! My heart screams in my chest. There is no mistake this time. It is much closer now, perhaps the length of two men away. It is large, but what is it? It is much too heavy to be a wolf or a man. It cannot be a bear for they are sleeping at this time of year. Would a moose climb so far from the safety of the river? Could it be the giant Sasquatch foraging on plants? I cannot hear him eating. What will he do if he finds me? If it is Sasquatch, I pray he does not take me to his mountain cave as my parents have often warned. I do not want to be abducted twice in one day.

Then a cold thought rushes through me. It must be Sonoqua, the great cannibal woman of the forest! She is hunting for meat. She will not care that I am the son of a Chief or that I will be a Hamatsa soon. If she finds me she will take me back to her lair. She will run a pole through my body, down my throat and out my bottom, to roast me over her fire. If she is hungry she might even eat me alive! I will not live to be a Cannibal Dancer.

The heavy rain hides the sound of her movements. I do not dare peek through the cedar branches to see the fire of her eyes. I close my mouth tightly so she cannot smell the fish on my breath. I lie silent, barely breathing. In a short while the footsteps move away. There is only the rain and the sound of my pounding heart.

I thank Great Spirit and beg for his protection. I promise Him I will not distract myself with self-pity again. I will not think of my family or the fire in my father's house. I lie quietly on my bed, listening for a long time before I stop shaking and my heart stops pounding. Finally, I can stay awake no longer.

The rain has stopped by the time I wake. I am safe. Sonoqua did not return. My blanket of cedar and wolf fur disguised my smell. The Spirits are still protecting me.

My legs are scratched and aching from my walk through the thick forest, but I am too hungry to rest any longer. I crawl out from under the log cautiously. There is no sign of danger now. I thank Great Spirit and I walk to the nearest stream to wash myself.

The food I was given is gone but I do not starve. While I am washing my face I see a moss that my mother taught me to find near the water, a moss that I can eat. I remember when she asked me to help her gather forest plants just before the winter ceremonies. I was angry for this was woman's work and I needed to prepare for my abduction. But she insisted her back was too sore to carry the basket and that the other women of our Clan were busy. She promised not to tell the men I had helped her.

I had never heard her talk so much as she worked. She led me from one place to another, explaining to me what she was looking for. At first I was impatient and did not care to listen, but she did not stop explaining. I thought this was her way to apologize for taking me away from my practice. Perhaps she missed my company. I had been so busy that we had not talked much in several moons, so I listened out of respect.

She asked me which plants I liked most, though she knew my answers. She showed me where to find the mosses, leaves, bark, mushrooms and roots I could eat, and how to tell which ones were not safe to eat. Her eyes watched mine to see if I was listening. I listened carefully because she would start again if I looked away.

I did not know so many plants grew in winter, or why she had to look for so many different ones. She told me she would not take long, but she kept me with her all afternoon. Now I realize she was helping me prepare for this time, that she did not want me to starve.

There are many plants I remember, but they are not easy to find in winter. Some I find in the wet ground beside the stream, others on higher ground or on logs and the sides of trees. I am lucky there is not much snow. I want meat most of all. I catch two small frogs sleeping in the cold mud on the side of a stream. There is no fire to cook them. I try to eat them raw but they taste terrible! I think it must be awful to be a real cannibal.

In the afternoon I cut more branches and make thicker walls around my bed to keep in more warmth. I clean the plants I have gathered in the stream and eat them. As it grows dark I crawl under the log onto my bed and block my doorway with more boughs.

There is no rain or wind. I hear the forest clearly and it is peaceful. I am still hungry, but I feel safe. Tonight there are no footsteps, no breaking branches. Only two more nights and one day must pass before I return to my village. Again I think it will pass quickly without problems. I fall asleep peacefully, not knowing that my real troubles have yet to begin.

When I wake it is morning. The forest is still. It smells fresh and inviting as I crawl out from under my log. I stretch my legs and breathe in its beauty. It is not sunny, but the air has a strange yellow glow. I walk until I find a pond where I can bathe. I take off my clothes and test the water with my bare toes. Suddenly the air turns cold and dark. I feel uncertain, like a deer stepping into an open meadow. I look around but I see no danger.

As I kneel to take a drink, I see the fires of her eyes reflecting on the water. A great chill races through my body. I hear her low growl and I look up. Sonoqua is staring at me from the other side of the pond. At first she does not recognize me without my clothes. She sniffs the air loudly with her large nostrils and licks her lips. She is twice my height. Her eyes flicker like red flames. Her skin is black and covered with a thin fur. The hair on her head is long and matted. Her naked breasts sag down to her belly. She makes a horrible scream that stabs my ears. I see her teeth as sharp as knives and smell the rotting flesh on her breath. She purses her lips. Her cheeks are sunken and her long arms reach out for me.

I turn and flee. She screams again and makes a great leap over the pond to chase after me. I run like a rabbit. I am amazed by my speed. I have never moved so quickly through the thick forest. I am sure I have escaped her but then I hear the pounding of her huge feet behind me.

She makes one long stride for every three of mine. She breaks through the bushes, crushing them flat. She is getting closer. I run downhill to the river for I know she cannot swim. As I reach the riverbank she bursts out of the forest behind me. I leap to the water but she catches my ankle while I am still in the air. Her giant hands pull me back. I scream as her teeth cut into my leg!

I wake from my dream with a start. I sit up so quickly I hit my head hard on the underside of the log. I cry out in pain and lie back, breathing hard. Warm blood trickles from my forehead down the side of my face. My head hurts terribly. I lie without moving until morning. I dare not sleep again when Sonoqua is hunting me in my dreams.

The daylight returns. It is not as bright as yesterday. My forehead has stopped bleeding but it is very sore. I must clean the wound. The forest now seems cold and evil and I am frightened. I pray to Great Spirit but I do not feel His presence.

I move cautiously, watching for Sonoqua as I struggle through the forest. I find the nearest stream, take a deep drink and wash my face. My wound is too sore to touch. I splash it gently with cold water. In the stream I find a smooth white stone. I clean it and place it under my tongue to give me strength. I return to my log and pray to Great Spirit to protect me.

I pray to Great Spirit all day, but He does not answer. He does not save me from misfortune. The rain falls hard all morning. I stay under my log with my blanket wrapped around me. Later the rain is light so I look for more mosses and roots to eat. While I gather them a terrible thing happens. A great horned owl flies to a branch high above me to watch me work. What a black omen of Death this is! I shout at him to leave but he does not listen.

I hope this is not the Spirit you have sent to visit me, Great One, for I am throwing sticks at him. I do not hit him but one stick comes very close. He flaps his great wings and shakes out the dust and feathers of Death above me. I run as fast as I can so none of it will touch me.

I have stopped gathering plants now for I have lost my appetite. I cannot stop worrying that I have angered you, Great Spirit. Please send a sign that you have forgiven me. Say you did not send Owl to tell me I will die!

It is late afternoon. I have returned to wash my wound in the stream. Raven has come to visit me while my mind is heavy with fear and worry. He calls out a warning from a tree above. I look around in fear but I see no danger. I ask him what is wrong. He hops along the branch closer to me and he calls out louder.

I grab a sharp stick to defend myself against an attacker. I scramble up the bank. In my haste I crush a large slug under my foot. Its insides flow between my toes. I feel sick for this too is a bad omen. I climb to the top of a high rock but I see nothing. I clean my foot on the moss and put my moccasins on.

I watch around me carefully as I return to my log. Still I see nothing. I climb my log and look in all directions, but the forest is as still as Death. There is no Sonoqua, no Sasquatch and no mountain lion, not even Owl. But Raven follows me, calling out his warning from the trees above.

"What is it?" I cry up to him.

Again he hops closer and calls out louder. He is trying to warn me of danger. My stomach is nervous, but I see nothing. He calls out over and over as the afternoon light fades. As night arrives, he becomes frightened and flies away.

Suddenly I understand. Only Raven sees the invisible danger that comes with the night. He was warning me that the Ghosts of the Dead are near. Wasn't it Raven who released the Sun to drive them into the dark side of the world? Doesn't he still cry out at sunrise because he hates them so much? Did Owl tell the Ghosts I am alone in the forest without a fire to drive away their shadows? Is this the Death that Owl has dropped upon me?

Please hear me, Great Spirit! I have called to you all day. Why do you not answer me? I have been in the forest three days and two nights. I will return to my village tomorrow if you protect me tonight. I need your strength now for I am in great danger. The sun has gone and I am afraid that I will not see it again.

The night is black. I cannot see the stars or the shapes of the trees against the sky, but I cannot hide in the darkness. The Ghosts of the Dead are here. They have found me at last. I feel the chill of their breath on my arms and neck. They are jealous of my youth and beauty. They wait for me to close my eyes. When I sleep they will enter my dreams. They will pull me down into their dark, cold world and drain the blood from my body and I will become a shadow like them.

Save me, Great Spirit! I feel them touching me. They are drinking my tears. There is nowhere I can run. My wolf fur cannot disguise me. The stone under my tongue will not drive them away. Wrap me in your arms and keep me awake until morning. Without this I will die.

TWO

This much you must know. Great Spirit is wise and kind. He has loved Man since the time of Hagbegwatu, the first man. Our existence pleases Him. He listens to our prayers and is delighted by our offerings, especially those we burn for Him in our fires. The smell of the smoke that rises to Heaven honours Him. He protects us and guides our destiny. He is the source of all Goodness and Light, but it is in the Darkness that His love for Man shines the brightest.

In the beginning, there was only Darkness. Great Spirit lived alone in Heaven with His son Tsamsem. There was nothing to see or hear. This was long before the Great Flood that covered the valleys and mountains. It was before the time of Animal Spirits and birth of Man. It was before Creation, before time itself.

Great Spirit grew tired of Darkness. He longed for beauty and wonder so He designed a great plan and He called it Creation. He created the sky and filled it with the moon and stars. He made the earth and covered it with mountains and valleys. He made the waters that filled the oceans and the sacred rivers that fed them.

He clothed valleys in forests and crowned the high mountains with ice and snow. He filled the magical green forests with animals. The rivers and oceans he filled with salmon, oolichon, sea lions, blackfish and other creatures of the waters. He sent the Spirits to protect all the places he had created. For six days and nights he laboured hard until the world was finished. On the seventh day he rested.

Great Spirit saw the world He created was beautiful and he was pleased. Now He had a beautiful home but still He was lonely. There was no one to worship Him and no one for Him to watch over. He thought about this for a long time and then He knew what He must do. He sent His only son, Tsamsem, to give birth to Man and populate the world.

When Tsamsem arrived he looked for a partner to help him father Man. First he met Stone. She tempted him with her strength and permanence. She told him that if she was his wife, his son would be immortal. He would have a hard shell for protection. No spears or claws would pierce his skin. He would be free from sadness and pain and he would never need to eat or drink. Tsamsem thought these qualities would be practical but they did not satisfy him.

Then he met Elderberry. She tempted Him with her soft skin and sweetness. She told Tsamsem that if she was his wife, Man would be soft and beautiful to touch. He would feel the wind and be free to move with it. His heart would glow with love and joy. Her beautiful words seduced Tsamsem and she brought him to her bed. There they made love and together they created Man.

This is how Hagbegwatu came to be born. He was created in the image of the Great Spirit and Tsamsem. He did not have the hard skin of Stone. His skin was soft and warm and he was pleasant to touch like his mother Elderberry, but he was vulnerable like his mother too. Tsamsem taught him to hold a stone in his mouth when he was in danger so his skin might be tough to protect him from his enemies.

But stones cannot protect him from Death and suffering, for he is mortal. His life has seasons. He blossoms and grows strong, then spreads his seed and dies. He sees beauty and feels love, but he also sees ugliness and feels sadness and pain. These are his weaknesses.

His life is a dance between light and dark. The days sparkle with warmth and promise and beckon him to reach for the brilliance of his dreams, like the sun that rises to the top of the sky. But each day he falls back in defeat, like the sun which declines and is swallowed by the coldness of the night. And so his life continues until the burden of his tears becomes so heavy that he cannot rise again.

That is when Great Spirit cradles him in His arms and lifts him up to Heaven. He comforts him with His love and tells him that the loneliness will come no more. There will only be peace and light and the warm breath of the South Wind. The Darkness and suffering is soon forgotten and all that matters is Great Spirit's love.

Tsamsem fathered more men and women to follow Hagbegwatu and be his tribe. When Hagbegwatu was grown, he traveled with his people up the sacred river K'san, which we now call the Skeena, and built a village at Gilutsau. He tried hard to be a good Chief but life was difficult and dangerous for men. Darkness still filled the Heavens for there was no sun. The moon was dark and there was only the light of the stars. The Ghosts of the Dead roamed freely for the night is their realm. Hagbegwatu's people kept great fires burning to frighten away them away but the Ghosts killed his people when they left the fires to hunt or fish. His people were always hungry.

They lived this way for many generations. They did not multiply and spread across the earth as Great Spirit had planned. Then one year, the Animal Spirits taught them magic that changed their lives forever.

At this time the Chief of Gilutsau had a son who liked to play by the river with his best friend. They were close like brothers and they were skilled at throwing rocks. One day they killed a duck and they brought it to the Chief. He was proud of them and told them they would be great hunters someday. He skinned the duck and gave them the feathers. They were very pleased.

The Animal Spirits spoke to the Chief's son through his dreams and gave him the idea to make a disguise of duck feathers when they hunted. The next day he returned to the river with his friend and they killed more ducks. Soon they had enough feathers to make a cloak.

They took their disguise to the river and they soon discovered it had magic powers. After wearing it for a while, the Chief's son changed into a duck and he could fly short distances. He let his friend use the cloak and he learned to fly too. They hunted more ducks and made a second cloak so they could practice flying together. Each day they practiced flying, but they kept their magic a secret from the other villagers. Soon they were stronger and could fly great distances.

The boys also liked to listen to the stories around their fires told by the brave men who hunted in the night. There was much talk about how to solve the problem of the Ghosts of the Dead. One night they heard a story about the Chief of the Sky who lived a great distance away to the north. His village was built inside a great mountain and it was filled with a light so bright that no Ghost could come near, but the village was too far away to reach safely. The boys made a secret plan to use their magic cloaks to steal the light from the Chief of the Sky and save their people from the Ghosts.

They flew north to the Nass River and followed it inland for several days. They came to a great mountain that was so large that they could not fly around it. They noticed a hole in the mountain that opened and closed like a mouth. Each time it opened a bright light shone from inside and they knew they had found the village of the Chief of the Sky. They waited for the right moment when the hole began to open and they flew in. They reached the inside safely before it closed again.

Everything was bright and clear inside the mountain, so bright that it hurt their eyes. When their eyes grew accustomed to the light they saw a village in the distance on the far side of a small lake. As they flew towards it they saw two beautiful girls playing in the water. They landed on the lake and swam up to them. The girls were delighted to see such friendly ducks. They brought the ducks home and asked their father if they could keep the ducks as pets.

It so happened that their father was the Chief of the Sky and so the boys came to live in his house. The light that filled the mountain came from a burning globe that hung at the centre of the village outside his house. They tried many times to fly up to it, but the light blinded them and it was too hot to get close to. It would not be possible to bring it back to their village. The boys decided to live the rest of their lives as ducks under their magic cloaks, being fed and petted by the lovely Princesses who loved them very much.

The boys learned to love the Princesses too, as young men do. Each night when the Princesses were asleep they slipped out of their disguises and made love to them. The Princesses woke up but they did not dare to tell their father. They had longed for love but their father would not let young men approach them. He ordered servant women to follow them during the day and to sleep outside their chambers at night so they would remain virgins. The Princesses were grateful for their secret lovers. Their love was sacred and faithful, as first love always is.

The Chief of the Sky noticed changes in his daughters and he became suspicious. Then one day he saw that one of his daughters was pregnant and he was furious. He knew the ducks must have supernatural powers so he killed them. His pregnant daughter was distraught and begged him to let her child live. The Chief feared she would harm herself. He was also old and secretly wanted a grandchild, so he granted her wish. When the child was born he was loved and accepted. No one knew who the father was.

Great Spirit had watched the boys fly to the village of the Chief of the Sky. He was delighted by their bravery when they flew through the hole in the mountain. He liked the boldness of their plan and He saw that it was good. He decided to deliver the Sun to Hagbegwatu's people another way. It was Great Spirit who had made the princess pregnant, and her son was actually Tsamsem, the son of Great Spirit himself.

When Tsamsem was born he grew much faster than other children. Soon his mother took him outside to sit on the ground to play. Tsamsem saw the light that hung at the top of the Chief's house. He screamed and cried and pointed to it until the old Chief grew tired of his crying. He agreed to let him play with it. He wrapped it in a large sack so it could not burn or blind him and told two of his guards to watch the child when his daughter was busy with her duties.

The child was quiet and good when he had the ball so they allowed him to play with it each day. The guards learned to trust him and did not watch him so closely. One day when the guards were distracted Tsamsem, who had magic powers, changed into Raven and flew away with the bag in his beak. He escaped through the hole in the mountain and flew south towards the sacred river K'san and the village at Gilutsau.

The trip was long and the bag grew heavy. Tsamsem was tired and hungry after many days of flying. He saw people eating and drinking below and he stopped to ask them for food and water. Then he saw they were not real people. They were Ghosts of the Dead.

The Ghosts laughed at him and told him to leave them alone. Tsamsem grew impatient for his hunger was great. He told the Ghosts he had a bright light in his bag and if they did not feed him he would release it to punish them. The Ghosts did not believe him, but they offered him food. When he came closer they tried to catch him so they could eat him too, but Tsamsem was too fast.

He flew high above them and shook the ball free from its bag. It filled the air with a burning light. The Ghosts screamed and fled in panic to the other side of the world. Tsamsem flew back and landed on the ground. He changed into the shape of a man and ate the food the Ghosts had left behind.

Tsamsem never delivered the burning ball to Gilutsau. It flew away into the sky, becoming lighter as it grew. It floated higher and higher and grew hotter as it rose until it became the sun we see today.

That is how the sun came to be in the sky. The Ghosts of the Dead still flee its brilliance as it circles the earth. They build their villages in the Underworld for protection and they visit our world at night when the sun is sleeping. We hunt and trade in daylight and build fires at night to protect ourselves from the Ghosts. We honour our ancestors and follow the sacred rules we have been taught. If we do not, their Ghosts return when the sun disappears and they steal our souls in the night.

◇◇◇◇◇◇◇◇◇◇◇◇◇◇◇

People do not listen now when I tell our sacred stories, though they have been our truth for countless generations. The children who return to our village each summer do not respect the wisdom of their Elders. They tell me our stories are lies. Their minds are filled with doubts and suspicions they have learned in White schools. They do not believe in Great Spirit, Tsamsem or the powers of magic.

They laugh at the story of Stone and Elderberry, for they believe in the White God now. The Whites say God made Man out of clay. Clay is not sweet or immortal. It has no seasons. I ask the children if we were clay, wouldn't we wash away in the rain or turn hard and break apart when we were dry? They believe this story is true because the Bible says it is so, though it makes no sense.

The White schools also teach them our story about Raven and the sun is not true. I know because I was taught by White men too. I was surprised to learn that the sun does not circle around the earth. The ball Tsamsem set free flew much farther and grew much bigger than we suspected. It stays still while the earth spins in a circle around it. Still the children believe only what the White men tell them.

How do you know what is truth, I ask them. Perhaps both stories are true. How can that be, they ask, because the Whites teach them there is only one truth. They have not been taught that truth wears many masks. I light a match and hold it in front of my face. I ask them to tell me on which side of my face am I holding the match. The child on my right says it is to the right of my face. The child on my left says it is to my left. The child in front says it is in the middle. I tell them that each answer is correct. Each of us sees the world from a different place and we each see different truths.

But these stories cannot be true for they are not in the White history books, the older children say. What is history, I ask them. They have no answer for they have not been taught this either. I blow out the match. See, I explain, the flame is now history. History only tells us what used to be, what we have lost. It leaves our hands empty. Our stories are not history. They teach us who we are and how we should live. They walk with us and guide us towards the truth.

We call White people Driftwood because they drifted to our shores in their great boats like Ghosts from the other side of the world. They are not like us. They are bound to the sea, not the land. Our people know we belong to the land, but the Whites think the land belongs to them. They know many things that we do not, but much of their knowledge is illusion. It vanishes when you hold it in your hand. Does it really matter which one is moving, the sun or the earth? Our lives are spent half in light and half in darkness. That truth does not change.

Whites say they know much more than we do, but they do not. They know about science but nothing about Ghosts or Spirits. They do not live in harmony with the

Spirits. They tell us a Spirit can be broken. Their science only masks their fears and leaves them blind. It does not explain the Spirits or protect us from their wrath. This much I know for certain.

THREE

Though Great Spirit has always loved and watched over us, men have not always appreciated His wisdom and kindness. Sometimes men forget that it is Great Spirit who protects us, for we can be proud and arrogant. We forget the lessons we have been taught and must learn them again and again

After Tsamsem, in the shape of Raven, banished the Ghosts of the Dead to the Underworld, it was safe for Man to hunt and trade. People multiplied and traveled to distant lands. They built new villages, spoke new languages and learned new skills and customs. They prospered from the wealth of the forests and the waters, and traded their wealth with their neighbours.

A hundred generations ago our people, the Tsimshian, lived far from the sea, many days travel from here, over the mountains near the source of the sacred Skeena River. They built a great city and named it Damelahamid. Their city grew rich from their hard work and trade. Over time it became larger and more powerful than any city before it. It had many gates and walls that were strong and tall. At night it glowed from the light of ten thousand torches that filled the air like daylight.

People of other nations traveled great distances to see Damelahamid and do trade with our ancestors. Our city was respected and feared even by those who had never seen it. The people of Damelahamid had no enemies. No nation dared to challenge them for they could not equal its great wealth or strength.

Our ancestors believed Damelahamid would last forever. Their arrogance made them disrespectful and lazy. They no longer paid homage to Great Spirit, for they thought they did not need His protection. They stopped following the teachings of the Animal Spirits. Hunters injured animals for fun and food was wasted. Wives and husbands were no longer faithful. Children did not listen to their parents. Traders became dishonest and greedy and people stopped sharing their wealth with their friends and neighbours. Soon they began to steal and destroy each other's property. Then they began to kill each other.

Great Spirit was saddened by what He saw. He realized men had to change their ways or they would destroy themselves. He told them they must share their wealth and observe the teachings of the Animal Spirits, but they laughed at Him. They continued to fight and kill. Great Spirit became restless and angry. He warned them again to change their ways or He would punish them, but again they did not listen. They did not believe He could harm their great city.

Great Spirit knew then He must teach men a lesson. He commanded the sky to rain harder than ever before, so hard that the people could not leave their homes. It rained for forty days and forty nights and the Great Flood was created. There were great landslides. Ice and snow crashed down from the mountains. The waters of the river rose high and flooded the land. They broke through the great walls and washed the city away until nothing remained.

People tried to escape but the heavy rain filled their canoes. Most of them drowned in the angry waters or were buried by the landslides. But some were swept down the Skeena through the great canyon in the west that crosses the mountain to the sea. The ones who survived built homes along the great river or on the islands near its mouth. These people are the Tsimshian that we know today.

Others climbed into the valleys east of the high mountains and built new villages when the land was dry again. They became the Giksan. Others fled over the mountains to the north and settled along the other sacred river, the Nass. These people became the Nishga.

Great Spirit spoke to our Ancestors after the Great Flood. He told them we must hold potlatches to share our wealth. We must follow the teachings of the Animal Spirits and not be wasteful or conceited. He promised He would never send another Great Flood, but He would punish us in other ways if we forgot the lessons we had learned.

The Tsimshian, Nishga and Giksan lived separately after the Great Flood but we did not forget Damelahamid. For two thousand years we paid homage to Great Spirit and the other Spirits and we honoured our Ancestors. We traded in peace and shared our wealth in great feasts with our neighbours. Every winter we gathered to celebrate our history with sacred stories and dances. We told the stories of Damelahamid and the lessons Great Spirit taught us that must never be forgotten.

We built many new villages after the Great Flood but never another city as great as Damelahamid. We had learned that building great cities also builds great arrogance, so we kept our villages small. That is, until we built Metlakatla.

◇◇◇◇◇◇◇◇◇◇◇◇◇◇◇◇

This is the story of my people, the people of my village called Gitka'ata. It is also my story and the story of Metlakatla. Not the same Metlakatla where the Tsimshians of the Skeena gathered every year for two thousand years to hold our sacred winter ceremonies. That one we abandoned so carelessly after White men drifted to our shores in their great boats and set up the trading fort at Lax Kw'alaams, the Place of Wild Roses, the place the Whites named Fort Simpson. That Metlakatla was not a city but nine different villages built near each other. It was abandoned before I first saw it. By then it was known as Old Metlakatla.

This is the story of the Metlakatla we built later with the help of Duncan, the White missionary. It was our greatest city since Damelahamid and it became famous around the world. The Whites called it a miracle, but White miracles do not last. It too has been abandoned and is now no more than a small village. Now it is known again as Old Metlakatla, but not the same Old Metlakatla as before.

But first I must introduce myself and tell the story of my village.

My name is Gugweelaks, which means the sun that sparkles on the waves, the southern sun that brings good luck and promise. It is the name I inherited from my mother's brother before I was fully a man. It was the property of his mother's brother before him. My name has been the property of my mother's people, the Eagle Clan, for a hundred generations, since the Great Flood when my ancestors came through the mountains and saw the good omen of the sun shining on the sea.

When I was a child my people called me Ts'uwaas, which means Little Salmon. It was my child's name, not a Clan name. I was happy to leave it behind when I inherited my uncle's name. My village was poor but I wore my uncle's name with pride, for it is a name that carries great honour.

Names were very important when I was young. Every mountain and shore had its own name which called to the Spirit that guarded it. Even houses and canoes had names and each of these had a guardian Spirit too. Elders of each Clan had names they had inherited, names that no other Clan could use. They were men of high status. Their Clans had to find them worthy before they could inherit a name of honour, before they could become an Elder.

Our names were our history. Clans never gave out their names without careful thought. To give a lazy or dishonest man such a name would insult and anger our ancestors, and that would bring their curse upon us. Every name had many stories about our ancestors who once owned it. We knew each story in our hearts and we honoured our ancestors with our good actions. We understood that we spoke and lived for their honour as well as our own.

But much has changed since then. Many of my people have died and the Spirits of their ancestors are now lost without them. With no children to honour their names, they wander as Ghosts of the Dead with no ties to the living. Most who still live have forgotten their Tsimshian names, or they will not use them. They use White names now.

One day soon I will be a wandering Ghost too. My sister is gone and I have no nephew to inherit my name. In my heart I am still Gugweelaks, but my old name has no use now. The sun no longer sparkles on our waters. I am known only by my White name, Jack Campbell.

Whites have changed the names of the mountains and the waters too. They have given them names of unknown White people, as they have done with the Tsimshian people. They do not honour our long history or the Spirits that live here. The Spirits do not recognize the White names and they do not answer to them.

The people of my village were known as the People of the Cane. Other Tsimshians settled in the east, the north and the west after the Great Flood, but my ancestors escaped to the south. They crossed the mountains through the valley that leads down to Kitamaat, the Place of Deep Snows. Kitamaat was where they saw the sun shining on the long canyon of salt water that leads to the open sea.

When they reached Kitamaat, the Shamans told their Chief that they must not stay. The omens from the Spirits were not good. The Chief then told his people they must find a better place. Even though they were very tired and hungry they trusted the Chief. They built canoes and continued down the canyon towards the sea.

After a day's travel they found a small bay on the west side of the canyon. Two rivers flowed into the bay and it had a good beach for their canoes. The Chief told his people to build a fire and prepare a great feast. His people were hungry and anxious to eat, but he told them to burn the food and the serving bowls as an offering to the

Spirits. Some complained, but they knew he was wise so they obeyed him.

Suddenly a great abundance of fish appeared in the rivers and deer came out from the forests. The Chief was delighted for the Spirits had welcomed them. He planted his cane on the beach between the rivers and told his people to build the new village there. It was named Gitka'ata, the Place of the Cane.

Our village had a special location. It was on the sea but it was also several hours by canoe up the great canyon and hidden in our little bay where the mountains rose steep and high on two sides. The mountains protected us like a mother grouse's wings guard her chicks. And these were wings of great beauty. The tall firs were the feathers. They wore the morning mists and the winter snows with great dignity. The mountains were our parents and our village was their only child. They sheltered us from the great winter storms from the west but they also kept us in shadow most of the time.

The sun touched our village only for a few hours each day, and only on those rare days when the skies were clear. Those were my favourite days, the ones when my spirit flew the highest. It was the midday sun we felt, the sun that gave me my name. It brought me great energy. I welcomed it like the eagles that floated high above our village. They shone golden in the last rays before the sun hid behind the canyon walls.

Gitka'ata was not large but it was beautiful. It was far from the other Tsimshian villages on the Skeena River. We had grown apart because of this distance. We were still Tsimshian but we felt like strangers too. When we visited the northern villages, they did not always understand our words and they laughed at the way we spoke. But we still fished beside them for oolichon on the Nass and for salmon on the Skeena during the great migrations.

But the trip north was long and dangerous. Our canoes first traveled many hours south along the canyon to reach Tsamsem's Trench, the passage that leads northwest to the sacred fishing grounds. From there it would take two days to reach Metlakatla and two more days to reach the Nass. In some places the route was open to the winds from the sea with no islands to protect us. The angry northern wind brought great storms and sometimes we had to take shelter for several days. Many men have died because they could not find shelter in time.

The sacred winter ceremonies at Metlakatla were the most famous anywhere. The nine villages of the Skeena celebrated there, competing against each other to hold the biggest feasts and the best dances. Those who won gained great prestige and the favour of the Spirits.

Most of our people had never seen the ceremonies at Metlakatla, but there were always travelers with stories to share and ears that wanted to listen. Every ear listened, but never better than my two ears when I was still a young boy named Ts'uwaas. The stories they heard filled my mind with wonderful pictures and a craving to see new places.

My people were not jealous of the other Tsimshians. We did not need to worry as much about status and pride. The winter storms made the long journey north from Gitka'ata too dangerous so we celebrated alone. We danced and sang a thousand songs, such as the one about the Great Flood and how we came to live so far away from the other Tsimshian villages that we could not celebrate with them.

For a hundred generations we lived this way. The Spirits were content for we showed them our respect. Our Ancestors were satisfied for we honoured them with our stories. We lived in peace and order and we were grateful for our good fortune.

But maybe there was too much peace and good fortune. Perhaps we forgot how to recognize evil. The big changes came so quickly they confused us. We did not know what to do or how to stop them. Now everything is different. The villages of the Skeena no longer meet every winter at Metlakatla. And the glory of what Metlakatla became later, what the Tsimshians and the White missionaries built together, is also gone. The great ruins it left behind are fading away like footprints in the sand.

I remain here in Metlakatla, abandoned by my people long ago. I cannot return to Gitka'ata. My people deserted our village many years before that. If you visit the place where it once was you will see only the rotting house posts and totems we left to guard our home until we return.

But we will never return. Those who tried after many years in Metlakatla learned that the River Spirits became angry with us after we deserted them. They have built sandbars so our canoes could never use their beach again. Our people had to look for a new place to build their village.

The old totems still stand at Gitka'ata. They are the only ones who remain. Their paint has been worn away by the sun and the rain. Some stand tall and noble, while others are leaning, slowly beginning their return to the Earth. Their faces are grey and cracked like old men left to die. They are lonely for the company of men.

Their big eyes watch patiently for our canoes to appear around the mountainside at the end of the bay, but they never appear. Their big ears listen for our paddles and the sound of our boats scraping on the pebbles as they pull ashore, but they hear only the river and the waves. They stare across the water, to the canyon that leads to the sea. They cannot see that behind them the forest has taken back the places where our houses once stood. They do not see it creeping up slowly, preparing to crush them in its jaws.

FOUR

My childhood in Gitka'ata was a very happy one. Others have told me that ours was a poor village but that is not how I remember it. I was the son of the Head Chief and our house had more food than the other houses. We were never hungry.

My father's name was Neeshlak. He was a man of great pride and honour, and he was well respected in the village. He made his decisions carefully and he was always fair. He never showed his temper and he was generous as a Head Chief should be. He was also Chief of the Blackfish Clan, a position he inherited from his mother's family before I was born. At the time I was born, our family lived in the main Blackfish house with my father, his brothers and their families. I had never known a different life.

My mother, Memlaka, was the niece of Silgitook, the Head of the Eagle Clan. She was a hard-working woman. She worked to honour my father's name and position. She was very loving, but she was also strict about our behaviour, for we were the children of the Head Chief. We had to behave properly so not to dishonour him. My parents' marriage was arranged by their Clans when they were young to make a bond between our Clans. The arrangement was a good one. They loved each other dearly and their marriage was always a happy one.

My mother gave Neeshlak four children. Like our mother, we belonged to the Eagle Clan. My oldest brother, Amapaas, was the first born. My second brother, Gwasha-sip, came two years later and I arrived two years after him. My only sister, Miyana, the last one born, was a year younger than myself.

Miyana was the most important child. Without a daughter and a sister there would be no one to bear children who would inherit our names. I was once told that before I was born my parents prayed that I would be a girl, but I disappointed them. They loved me like their other sons, but they were greatly relieved when Miyana was born next year.

Our village was built in a long row along the shore of the bay. This was the way all villages were when I was young. Each house faced the water and the canoes rested on the beach in front of the door. Between the canoes and the house there were totems or men carved in wood to welcome visitors. The houses of the smaller Clans, Wolf and Raven, were on east and west ends of the village. Between them were the houses of the bigger Clans, my mother's Eagle Clan and my father's Blackfish Clan. My father's house was in the centre of the row, where the Head Chief's house belonged.

We were proud of our house. It was longer, wider and taller than the other hous-es. The corner posts had the most carvings and the front wall had beautiful paintings of the Blackfish Clan. They were bright and bold. Visitors who arrived at the entrance of our bay could see them easily in the distance. We also had more totems and taller totems than the other houses. The centre post of the front wall was made from a great old red cedar. It was carved from top to bottom and there was a large hole cut through its centre at the ground for our doorway. A deerskin painted with a Blackfish pattern covered the hole and kept out the wind and the rain.

I was lucky to enjoy the wealth and privileges of a noble family, but our village was small. Those who belonged to noble families worked side by side with commoners and slaves to make a good life for everyone. We could not marry commoners or slaves, but sometimes they were our closest friends.

One of our slaves, Hoshieka, became a second mother to us when we were too old to be carried and not old enough to help with the work. Memlaka left us with her whenever she had other duties. Hoshieka was a Tlingit woman from the north. My father purchased her from a Haida Chief for twenty deerskins after Amapaas was born. The Haida had taken Hoshieka from her village when she was a small girl. She was already skilled in cleaning fish and sewing when she came to live with us.

Hoshieka was happy to care for us. She loved to watch us play. We were eager to show her things or to perform for her. We felt her love and returned it with enthu-siasm. I was her favourite, for I always tried to please her the most. I picked handfuls of flowers for her and told her she was the most beautiful woman in the village. I was too young to know this was improper and she liked my flattery too much to tell me.

She was not as strict as my mother. She warned us to behave, but only because she was afraid our parents would punish her or us if they caught us misbehaving. When my mother told me to do something I would first look at Hoshieka for her approval. This frustrated my mother, but she appreciated Hoshieka's influence over us. I often heard her say, "Hoshieka, you must tell the children to stop doing that!" My father respected her too. He would never speak to her in public except to give an instruction. In private he often asked her for certain words in Haida or Tlingit he had forgotten for she knew these languages better than any others in our village.

When we were small, Miyana was my closest companion. I accepted her importance to my family without question. I saw my role as her guardian. Amapaas and Gwashasip were her older brothers, but she regarded me as her personal servant.

Miyana was clever and headstrong. She would not obey Hoshieka's warnings. She liked to scold her brothers as if she was Hoshieka herself, wagging her finger and making angry faces at us that were no more sincere than Hoshieka's. She always decided which games we would play. She made plenty of trouble for both of us, digging through my father's chest of family treasures or taking our carved serving bowls down to the river to use as toy boats. I stayed at her side to protect her no matter how much trouble she caused.

Life in our village changed with each season. In early spring when the birds flew north, the adults and youths made the trip north to our fishing camp on the sacred Nass River to harvest the oolichon. The oldest and the youngest were left behind, because the trip was too dangerous for them. Hoshieka and the other slave women cared for us for several weeks until they returned. I remember how quiet our village was then. At first we were sad and restless, but the Elders told stories and gave us treats to keep us happy. Soon we were rejoicing in our freedom, running in and out of the houses and making games with the children of other Clans.

Later in spring, during the days of long light and again in late summer, the adults left for our camp on the Skeena River to fish for salmon. It was a shorter journey but they stayed longer to clean and smoke the fish before they returned. Between the fishing camps and later in the autumn, small groups of men left on hunting trips or to trade with other villages. Some went to the White trading post at Lax Kw'alaams to sell furs. They told the stories of their journeys every night around my father's fire and I would always listen with great interest.

In the dark days, all hunting or fishing stopped. Everyone returned home to Gitka'ata for the winter ceremonies. The women began preparations for the great feasts. The Shamans moved to private huts to purify themselves with the juices of sacred roots and leaves. Dancers prepared their costumes and rehearsed their performances. My father and the Elders watched the preparations to be sure they were done well. At times they left to attend feasts in other villages and sometimes Chiefs and Elders from other villages came to share ours.

I was given simple tasks or told to stay out of the way. It was also my job to watch over Miyana and keep her out of trouble. We never wanted to go very far, for there was always much happening and great excitement at this time of year.

Each night we feasted on the foods we had collected and preserved throughout the year. We ate until our stomachs hurt. I lay down in my chamber when I could no longer stay awake and slept with the sound of many voices still talking around the fire. In the early mornings it was quiet, except for the sound of the winter winds and rain. Then I heard the soft sounds of the women gathering the serving bowls to begin preparations for the next feast.

Once the ceremonies began, we wanted to watch the songs and dances the most. Men sang the songs and women clapped their hands. The dancers twirled and swayed around our fire with graceful movements and cast great shadows on the walls around us. Their carved masks and bright costumes fascinated me. Each dance told a story. I tried to remember them so I could perform them for Hoshieka later.

The dances lasted for hours each night. Shamans chased away evil Spirits and made sacrifices to the good Spirits who protected us. Elders told us about our glorious victories or stories about the Animal Spirits. But the best dances were performed by the secret societies. They practiced their dances in secret places in the forest for several moons before the ceremonies. The Dancer Society told sad or funny stories using colourful masks and costumes. The Society of Dog Eaters had dances that were silly or disgusting, but every dance was fun.

The dance we waited for most eagerly was performed at the end of the winter. It was the dance of the Hamatsas, the Man-Eater Society, which lasted four days. It was only done when someone new joined the Hamatsas. It told the story of a young man who is kidnapped by Cannibal Spirits and taken to the far north where he is given supernatural powers. When he returns to the village three days later, he is wild and crazed with a hunger for human flesh. He runs through the village chasing everyone, biting those he catches until the Hamatsas calm him and help him to control his powers.

I saw the Cannibal Dance for the first time when I was three. How it terrified me to see the dancer bite into a man's arm! The adults laughed and tried to comfort me. I did not understand why they thought this was funny. When I was older I learned that the blood I saw was animal blood the dancer had hidden in pouches in his clothing to make his bite seem worse.

I also learned that the men he bit made arrangements beforehand to be his victims. He paid five blankets to each man who let him bite them. The men he bit wore their scars proudly like prized tattoos. When my brother Amapaas was fifteen he arranged for a Cannibal Dancer to bite his upper arm where girls would see his scar.

Knowing the dancer was an actor did not spoil my enjoyment. His painted face and wild moves were very convincing. We were never sure if he was truly mad or which way he would turn as he ran through the village. Everyone joined in the drama. We screamed and waved our arms as he chased us. The men he bit, who always bore real pain in silence, would cry out in agony and fall to the ground. When the dance was finally over the dancer who had done well was honoured like a hero. A great feast was held in his honour and he was courted for his favour for many weeks afterwards.

Miyana hated the Cannibal Dance. Even after she knew the Dancer was only acting she hated it. She refused to run. She covered her eyes with her hands and screamed whenever he came towards her, a scream so loud that even the Cannibal Dancer was frightened.

But I loved it more than anything. When I was six I decided I would be a Cannibal Dancer and a Hamatsa when I was grown. Only Chiefs, Elders and the husbands and sons of their oldest nieces were invited to join the Hamatsas, but this did not worry me. I never doubted that the Hamatsas would want the son of the Head Chief and my mother was the oldest niece of my great uncle Silgitook who was Chief of our Clan and the Head of the Hamatsas.

Miyana covered her ears when I spoke of it but I knew she would not be frightened of me. For a year I thought of nothing else. I even pretended to be possessed by Cannibal Spirits until my father warned me that if I angered them I would never be allowed to join. I did not speak of the Hamatsas again, but I never forgot my dream of being one.

That is why I was so excited when I was summoned to a meeting of the Eagle Clan the next year. I thought there could be no other reason for their summons except to announce that soon my training for the Hamatsas would begin. My mother dressed me in my finest clothes and led me by my hand to my great uncle's house where the Elders of our Clan waited for me.

My eyes took a while to adjust from the bright sunshine to the darkness of the house. Soon I could see the Elders looking at me. I felt the heaviness of the room. They watched me closely as my mother led me down the steps to the fire and beyond to the back of the room where Silgitook sat in his chair. I wondered if I looked foolish as their eyes followed me, but some of them nodded their approval as I passed.

When I stopped in front of my great uncle, I stood tall and still, the way I thought a Hamatsa should stand. My mother let go of my hand and walked back to the door. Silgitook waited until she was outside. He leaned towards me, placed his hands on my shoulders and looked directly into my eyes. He spoke to me in the solemn voice that Elders use when they wish to be heard. His first words raced to my heart and told me my wish would come true.

"Young Ts'uwaas, you are third son of my eldest niece Memlaka and you will be a name bearer of the Eagle Clan. It is the decision of your Elders that you should inherit the name and privileges of your uncle Gugweelaks when he passes to the next world if you prove yourself to be worthy of his name before that happens. From this day on you must behave in ways that honour his name and the people of your Clan. Do you understand me?"

I nodded silently, glancing briefly at my uncle Gugweelaks. I knew family names must be passed on but I had not thought much about it. I looked back at my great uncle as he continued.

"There are many things you must not do. You must never bring shame to your family by stealing or cheating. You must be generous and kind to others. Work hard to honour our traditions by learning our sacred dances and songs. Then you will be worthy of being an Elder of the Eagle Clan."

He sat up as straight as a totem and looked down at me as he waited for my reply. I was waiting too, waiting for him to announce that I would soon be a Cannibal Dancer. I must have looked as confused as he did.

"Do you understand what I have said?" He sounded concerned. I glanced at Uncle Gugweelaks, and back to him. I nodded my head slowly but said nothing. "I am sure you will have plenty of time to think about it," he smiled.

He invited me to sit with the Elders for the rest of the meeting. I sat on the ground beside the fire. I was hoping he had more to tell me and I was still trying to understand what he had already said. I wondered if I had done something wrong, if I needed to change my behaviour. I gazed up at Uncle Gugweelaks who now looked different to me. He saw me looking and smiled.

"Would you like to sit beside me, Ts'uwaas?" he asked.

I shook my head slowly. I saw a look of disappointment in his face and he turned away.

"It is all right, nephew," Silgitook reassured him. "Ts'uwaas can see you better when he faces you. Give him time to get used to his future." My uncle nodded humbly and smiled at me.

Uncle Silgitook was right. I had a long time to get ready for my future. For the next five years nothing seemed to change much. I busied myself playing children's games and watching the men do work I could not do. When Miyana and I were old enough, we went with the women of the Eagle Clan to pick berries on the good weather days of late summer. We left early for it took half the morning to reach the berry bushes that belonged to the Eagle Clan.

As we pulled our canoes onto the shore, we sang and clapped sticks together. We sang prayers of thanks, but we also sang to frighten bears out of the bushes, for there is nothing a bear likes better than feasting on sweet berries on a warm summer day. These days were the happiest times for Miyana and me. We ate berries until our stomachs ached and we sang until we sounded like frogs.

When I was ten I was told that berry picking was women's work. The older boys teased me, "Are you berry picking with the women tomorrow? Perhaps my sister has an extra shawl that you could wear!" I fell silent with anger and embarrassment. Then they laughed and put their arms around my shoulders and invited me to join them in hunting frogs along the riverbanks or spearing fish in the river.

I stopped berry picking and played with the older boys so they would not tease me. It bothered me not to be with Miyana. She was angry and refused to speak to me for several days, but the women seemed to understand. "Ah, you are a young man now!" they congratulated me. They did not seem disappointed that I would not be coming with them anymore. I felt hurt but I said nothing.

I was given light chores suitable for a boy who was too young to hunt. I was proud of my new responsibilities, for that meant I would soon be a man. One of my chores was to gather cedar bark and other kindling for our fires. I also collected the wood shavings I got from Tsangook, the wood carver, from his work place behind our house. I saved this chore for last so I could spend the rest of the afternoon with him. He taught me how to make bows and ax handles, but I mostly I preferred to sit quietly and watch him work. Sometimes I watched him all afternoon.

Tsangook did not come from a noble family. His people were commoners who did not belong to any Clan, but he was well respected and very popular. He was wealthier than other commoners too, for he was the best carver in Gitka'ata. His carvings won him fame in other villages too, for my father often presented them as gifts to visiting Chiefs.

I saw his work everywhere. He had carved several new totems and some of the house posts inside and outside of our house. He also carved our serving bowls and ceremonial chests but I preferred his masks best of all. His ghost and bear masks were very frightening. His Raven mask had a long beak that opened and closed by pulling ropes from inside. At first I helped him polish his masks and later he let me paint them. He taught me how to use abalone shells to make the eyes of his moon mask and how to make cedar bark hair for the mask of the Wild Man.

Tsangook was nine years older than me. He had learned to carve when he was a young boy, when he still lived with his family as guests in the house of the Wolf Clan. Even his first carvings revealed his talent. When he was sixteen, my father invited him to live in our house and to be his main carver. His parents were pleased, for it was a great honour for a commoner to be chosen to live in the Head Chief's house.

My father also wanted him to live with us because he was a Mahanna. That meant he had both the spirit of a man and a woman. At that time it was known that a Mahanna brought good luck to the household he lived in. Mahannas brought with them strong connections to the world of the Spirits. They made the work of the Shamans much easier even if they were not Shamans themselves.

Tsangook was also a member of the secret Dancer Society. Commoners were not allowed to join secret societies, but a Mahanna deserved special consideration. He was welcomed for the beautiful masks he carved for their dances and, most of all, because he was their best dancer. He loved dancing as much as carving. "Every Mahanna is a good dancer," he told me. "Only Mahannas can move like a woman." He spoke the truth for I have never seen a more graceful dancer.

Tsangook liked to have me watch him as he worked and we soon became close friends. My father never scolded me for ignoring my chores when I spent all afternoon with him. He encouraged our friendship. Perhaps he thought Tsangook's company would bless me with good luck, but I suspect he wanted Tsangook to encourage the Spirit of Mahanna within me. A Chief who fathered a Mahanna was certainly favoured by the Spirits. No other village would attack his village for fear of turning the wrath of the Spirits against them.

My father had no clear reason to believe I would become a Mahanna. My older brothers liked girls, but he was not sure about me. I had played with Miyana's toys when I was small but only because she insisted. Now we played apart and I was free to decide my own path. If there was a chance that I could become a Mahanna then Tsangook would be the one to wake the Spirit of Woman within me.

But the Spirits did not want me to be a Mahanna at that time. I was fond of

Tsangook for other reasons. He was funny and clever and he loved to tell stories. We discussed many subjects and I trusted him with my fears and problems. I told him how we chased the bears out of the bushes and why I stopped going with the women to pick berries. I explained that I still wanted to go but how the older boys would tease me.

"That is terrible! I would have accepted his sister's shawl and joined the other women!" He always spoke of himself as a woman. It fascinated me that he talked and moved like a woman when he said things like this, but when he was working alone he mostly looked and moved like any other man.

"Do you like berry picking?" I asked him, for he had the privilege of doing either the work of a woman or a man.

"No Little Salmon, I much prefer carving or dancing, but I would never refuse a good shawl if it was offered to me!" Then we both laughed so hard that our tears flowed.

Tsangook always knew how to make me laugh when I was troubled. I have had many teachers in my life. Some have made me wiser and some have not. I did not think of him as my teacher at that time, but now as I am old I see that he has taught me more wisdom than anyone else.

FIVE

When I was twelve, I moved from my father's house to live with my Uncle Gugweelaks in my Uncle Silgitook's house. It was my Uncle Gugweelaks' responsibility to teach me how to hunt and fish and the ways of our Elders. The move brought with it many changes. My great uncle's house was smaller than what I had known but I was respectful and did not to mention this. I slept in a small chamber next to the one my uncle shared with his wife Pashaleps.

My new life was filled with adult pains I had not known in my father's happy house. Uncle Gugweelaks was a quiet man of deep thoughts. He only spoke when it was necessary. He never complained but it was rare to see him laugh. Pashaleps was quite the opposite. She had moods that changed with each passing cloud. One moment she was noisier than a bossy crow. The next moment she was angry and in a silent pout that burned like fire. She was a jealous woman by nature, though I saw no reason for her jealousy. Gugweelaks was an honest and faithful man.

Pashaleps was from the Raven Clan, which amused me when she was squawking like a crow. She was unhappy with my uncle's status. He was third in line to inherit Silgitook's position so his chambers were not as large as those of his older brothers. She was also envious of her sister who enjoyed a wealthier life in my father's house. Her other sister had an arranged marriage to my father's brother, a member of the

Blackfish Clan. Pashaleps was not happy with my presence either. It was more work for her to look after two men, but she was not clever enough to keep her mouth shut.

"He is eating all our food!" I heard her complain loudly from their chamber beside mine.

Uncle Gugweelaks usually ignored her complaints but this one angered him. "Be quiet, woman, or I will bring you to Silgitook and you can make your complaint to him!"

This was a serious threat. If Silgitook thought she was interfering with the training of a future Elder he could end their marriage. Pashaleps would be sent back to the Raven Clan in disgrace. She was too old to be married again. Gugweelaks would lose prestige too, but my training was his best excuse to end their marriage with honour. Pashaleps realized this. She never complained about me again, but she was always cold to me.

Gugweelaks and Pashaleps were not able to produce children. This was the true source of their unhappiness. The Elders of the Eagle Clan accused Pashaleps of being barren, while the Elders of the Raven Clan blamed Gugweelaks for having a limp tsootz that left them with no heirs. Marriages were arranged to build ties between Clans, but a failed marriage could build walls instead. Resentments between Clans could last for many years. For this reason they could not divorce, so they remained together in misery.

Their tensions made me miserable too. I was very unhappy in my new home. I dared not speak to my father or my great Uncle Silgitook about it. If they spoke to my Uncle Gugweelaks I feared the tensions in the house would become much worse.

My oldest brother Amapaas now lived in Silgitook's house too. He was being trained by my Uncle Shoget, Gugweelaks' oldest brother and Silgitook's heir. I wanted to confide in him but he was more interested in flirting with girls. He did not like to hear about my troubles because Shoget's marriage was a good one and he was happy in their house. My life seemed more miserable when I saw his happiness.

My other brother Gwashasip had moved to another Eagle house to be trained by another uncle whose name and position he would inherit one day. He still did not know much about the ways of adults, so I sought advice from Tsangook while he carved.

"Little Salmon, this is a bad situation," he shook his head. "It worries me to see you wearing your sadness like a mask but I am not sure what can be done. The Spirits bring many problems to those who cannot bear children, and even more for those who can. But I think the Elders of the Raven Clan are right. Your uncle is the reason they cannot bear children."

"He is?" I was shocked.

"Yes, I am certain of it."

"That is not true! How would you know?" I wanted to defend my uncle.

"Trust me, Little Salmon. Any man who had that woman for a wife would have a limp tsootz for the rest of his life!" My anger quickly turned to laughter. "Yes, even young Amapaas, that horny brother of yours who grows a spear between his legs every time a girl walks by, even he could not keep it hard for that woman. It would soon be hanging its little head like a bird that has lost its mother!"

Now he had me laughing so hard my tears flowed down my face again. I was glad I had come to see him for I felt much better already. When I stopped laughing, I watched him work for a while in silence.

"Ts'uwaas?" He said, still looking down at his work. "Has your Clan arranged a marriage for you yet?" He paused and looked right at me.

"No. Uncle Gugweelaks told me the Elders are negotiating an arrangement."

"Are you worried?"

"The Elders will choose what is best," I said.

It was the only proper answer, but his question upset me. My feelings did not matter. If the Elders arranged a marriage with another Clan I must accept their decision. It was my duty as the son of a Chief and the grandnephew of another. Alliances between our Clans make the village strong and help to heal old wounds. A question like that only made sense to commoners like Tsangook. They were fortunate not to have arranged marriages. I thought it was wrong of him to ask my feelings about this and wrong of me to let my feelings show.

Of course, a good friend like Tsangook could see my worry. A cold fear had been growing inside me. The Elders had made arrangements for Amapaas and Gwashasip but I was not ready to think of marriage. I felt no desire for girls yet. How could I satisfy a wife without a desire for her? Perhaps I would acquire my uncle's problems along with his name and position. How could I live like that? I had said nothing about this to anyone, not even Tsangook, though these worries troubled me greatly.

"Maybe you will inherit Pashaleps with your uncle's title," he smiled. I was surprised that he had guessed my thoughts. "By then she will be an old woman with wrinkled lips, no teeth and breasts that sag to her waist." He bent over and made a face like a hag. Again he made me laugh, in spite of this fearful thought.

"Did you ever want to marry, Tsangook?"

"What? Would you prefer to watch me washing serving bowls instead of carving them? No, Little Salmon, I was not meant to marry. A wife keeps only one man happy, but a Mahanna keeps all the men in the village happy. I spend my days in the village carving and dancing, but my true talent is only seen on hunting trips.

"I didn't know you hunted."

"No!" he laughed. "Other men go hunting, my young friend! I carry their supplies through the forests and over the mountains. I set up the camp, chop the wood, tend the fire and prepare the food. It is work that is too heavy for an ordinary woman. And when the day is over and the men are fed and washed, I keep them happy and warm in my tent, one after the other. I reward the good hunters and cheer up the bad ones." He smiled proudly. "I don't need to hunt. My game comes to me."

"That is very noble of you," I grinned.

"That is true. The best hunter visits me first, and they all try to prove they are the best. They catch more game just to be first in my tent each evening. I think our people might starve without me." He wiggled his backside and smiled again.

"You are a crazy one, Tsangook!" I blushed as I laughed.

"Is there someone special you would prefer to marry, Ts'uwaas?"

"No, I am only twelve!"

"Of course. I have no doubt that any wife would like you. But will you like them? You should be careful to honour all the Spirits, Little Salmon. Perhaps you should speak to your uncle. He may have some influence with the Elders."

I had no chance to speak to my uncle. The Elders met two days later to discuss my future marriage. I was invited to the Council to listen to their discussion. Many arrangements were reviewed. Amapaas was promised to his Blackfish cousin Teshlah, daughter of our father's brother, our uncle Shoget. Shoget was Silgitook's heir and Amapaas was Shoget's heir. In time Amapaas would become Chief of the Eagle Clan and his oldest son, Neeshlak's grandson, would be heir to the Blackfish Clan and Head Chief of Gitka'ata.

Gwashasip had a fine arrangement too. He was promised to the sister of Doolyaks. Doolyaks was heir to the Chief of the Wolf Clan. Gwashasip's oldest son would be heir to Doolyaks. In future years his son would be Chief of the Wolf Clan.

Miyana was already promised to one of Doolyaks' brothers. Their children would belong to the Eagle Clan, like Miyana. Their oldest son would be Amapaas's heir and eventually Chief of the Eagle Clan.

The Elders had arranged for strong allegiances with the Blackfish and Wolf Clans. They still needed a new allegiance with the Raven Clan to ease the bad feelings caused by Gugweelaks' marriage to Pashaleps. The Raven Elders did not care to discuss another allegiance with the Eagle Clan until they learned I would be the groom. I interested them because my father, Neeshlak, was Chief of the Blackfish and the Head Chief of Gitka'ata.

My marriage arrangement was completed. The Elders decided I would marry Laguksa, sister of Jaleek. This was another good arrangement. Jaleek was nephew and heir to the Chief of the Raven Clan. Hard feelings caused by Gugweelaks' marriage would soon be forgotten. My first son would be Jaleek's heir and the future Chief of the Raven Clan. The Elders of our Clan were very pleased.

It was a good arrangement for the Raven Clan, too. Laguksa had been promised once before. Her husband-to-be had died of a fever a year before her marriage. The Raven Elders knew it would be difficult to find a new arrangement. The young men of nobility her age were already promised and there was a rumour that the Spirits had placed a curse on her. Jaleek needed her to have a good marriage or he would have no heirs. The benefits of this arrangement were clear to everyone.

But for me this was a terrible fate. Laguksa was a short, heavy woman with plain features. She was six years older than me and we had nothing in common. If we failed to produce children the tension between our Clans would be much worse. If she was truly cursed my life might also be endangered. But I had no choice. The agreement had been made and it must be honoured. Tsangook was correct. Only the Spirits could protect me from this fate, but I doubted that even they could help me.

I spoke to my Uncle Gugweelaks about my concerns later that evening. He listened to me but he agreed there was no honourable way to change the arrangement. He reminded me that if we did have a son, he would be the future Chief of the Raven Clan. My status and prestige would be secure until the end of my days.

"But I am not sure I can have children with Laguksa. She is six years older than me and she is very plain. I have no interest in her."

"It is true for men that marriage arrangements are meant to create heirs for other Clans. Alliances between the Clans are very important. You must do your duty to our Clan and our village. Perhaps, like your parents, you will find love in your marriage. Perhaps, like me, you will not. Laguksa is a hard-working woman with a pleasant nature. You could do much worse. Honour the Spirits and they will guide you to love."

"But what if they do not? How can I produce children when I am unhappy?" For a moment I saw pain on his face.

"Ts'uwaas, my heir, my marriage is not the best example. Someday you will inherit my name but not my problems. No two marriages are the same. Most are much happier than mine. But even if there is no love, you must remember that your purpose is much greater than your marriage or your status. You will be an Elder, a leader of our people. You must care for them above all else. You must be the best husband and hunter that you can be, and inspire others with your wisdom and your generosity as your father has always done. Ask the Spirits to open your heart and show you the path that leads to the source of your love. If you follow that path it will lead you to happiness."

He watched my face as I thought about this. His words seemed wise though I did not know what I should do. He smiled at my confusion. "Besides, you will not marry until you are fully a man. You still have a few years to find the love in your heart."

My uncle's words reassured me for the moment. My concerns did not vanish, but they no longer filled my thoughts each day. My uncle and I were much closer after that evening. We understood each other better. For the next two years we spent much of our time together. He taught me the sacred songs and stories of our Clan. He taught me the skills of hunting and fishing. We went on short hunting trips together and we joined others on fishing trips in the canyon.

As my body grew stronger I became more useful. When I was fourteen, I was invited with my uncle to hunt for blackfish with Elders from all of the Clans. We paddled all morning to the end of the canyon. I sat behind Doolyaks. I was fascinated with his beauty. He was only six years older than me, but he already had the broad chest and strong arms of man. The year before he had joined the Hamatsas and I had watched his Cannibal Dance with great pleasure. This day I watched his powerful shoulders only an arms length away as I matched my paddle strokes to his.

We reached the open sea by afternoon. A family of blackfish found us and swam past our canoes. I was thrilled. I had heard stories of the Elders chasing them since I was a small child. I had eaten their meat and gazed at their images painted on the front of my father's house, but this was the first time I had seen them. I had never imagined being this close. Their huge bodies moved with such speed and grace that we were like children next to them in our toy canoes.

I understood then what my uncle had taught me, that animals are blessed with much greater powers. They guide us and teach us how to hunt, and surrender their bodies only when we have learned our lessons. The Elders say the blackfish are the greatest of our teachers for they swim too fast to catch. They come close to our canoes to tease and humble us, but they rarely surrender to our hunters.

Their tall, black fins cut the surface of the water as they rushed past the first canoes. Several Elders threw their spears but they missed their targets. As a large male blackfish approached our canoe my uncle stood and threw his spear. It grazed the beast's back. Doolyaks was so eager that he stood before my uncle sat down and he heaved his spear so hard that he almost lost his balance. I reached up and held his thigh to steady him. I felt the muscles of his leg moving beneath my hands and I had a second rush of excitement, stronger than the sight of the blackfish, a rush I had never felt before.

Doolyaks seemed not to notice my hands. His spear caught the side of the blackfish and it held. The blackfish dove beneath the waves. The rope that tied the spear to the canoe strained and then broke. The great fish escaped. Doolyaks was disappointed, but he did not let it bother him for long. He told me the blackfish was not ready to surrender to him yet.

That night we camped on a sheltered beach near the end of the canyon. Doolyaks sat beside me by the fire after dinner. He placed his arm around my shoulders and thanked me for steadying him in the canoe. Two Elders warned him not to stand so quickly next time. They said the canoe might have tipped over, but they did not scold him harshly for his spear had done better than theirs. He spent the rest of the evening beside me but I cannot recall what we spoke about. I only remember the warmth of his voice and the sweet memory of his muscles straining beneath my fingers as I held his thigh.

I could think of little else but Doolyaks the next day. I was not disappointed that we returned to Gitka'ata without a blackfish for my heart had tasted love for the first time. The joy on my face pleased my uncle. He thought it was the sight of the blackfish that had made my face glow. He said he would ask the Elders to invite me to the fishing camps on the Nass and the Skeena next spring. This was one of the happiest days of my life. I believed I would never be left behind with the children of the village again.

But that winter the Spirits were angry. Large storms came up the canyon from the sea. They battered our village with high winds and heavy rain during the winter ceremonies. We tried to calm the Spirits with offerings. The Elders sang sacred songs while the women hummed and clapped their hands. Our Shamans, Tooklan and Wumgooks, blessed our finest cooking and burnt it as offerings in the fire to appease them. For several days the sharp smells of burnt food lingered in my father's house. Still the winds and rain continued.

At the end of the ceremonies the village Elders met to decide who would join them at the fishing camp on the Nass to harvest the oolichon. Gugweelaks asked them to invite me to come but the Elders said the omens were bad. There was too much risk for the smaller boys like me. My older brothers Amapaas and Gwashasip were invited but I had to stay behind again. The shame I felt was a heavy burden, but I said nothing. Only boys and men who are unworthy complain.

On the morning they left for the fishing grounds I watched Doolyaks load his supplies into his canoe. I hated being left behind but I was even more upset that I would not see him again for many weeks. I wanted to offer to help him but a tightness in my throat choked my words. He saw me watching and came to the rock where I was sitting. The pain in my heart grew stronger.

"It looks like the winds will be in our favour today," he said.

I could only nod my response. He looked at me with concern and I turned away. He sat down beside me. I was thankful that he did not put his arm around me for surely I would have cried like a child.

"I wish you could come along. Without you there will be no one to protect me." I looked to see if he was making fun of me, but his face had the sweetest smile. The shadow in my heart left me and I smiled back at him.

"Just don't throw any spears at the oolichon," I teased him.

"I promise to use nets like everyone else this year." We laughed together, and I was happy again.

I helped pack the last of the canoes and I watched them leave from the beach in front of Silgitook's house. They reached the end of the bay and disappeared behind the mountain walls of the canyon.

That year the village felt emptier than ever before. The heaviness in my heart returned and would not leave me in peace. Doolyaks was not the only one I longed for. My parents, my brothers, my uncle Gugweelaks, Tsangook and most of my friends had also gone. I could not stop thinking about what they were doing. I tried to busy myself by chopping firewood and doing small chores. I prayed to the Spirits to bless their trip and to show me the path to happiness again. I did not talk much, not even to Hoshieka and Miyana. They tried to cheer me up but they could not.

One morning my great uncle Silgitook found me sitting on an unfinished totem Tsangook had started. We traded greetings and talked about how the weather had improved since the others had left.

"It is difficult to be left behind, isn't it?" He said this with sadness in his voice.

His words surprised me. It is undignified for a Chief to show weakness, but only I had heard his words. I nodded out of respect for his honesty, but I did not know what to say.

"I have been to many fishing camps. It is hard work, but it is exciting, too. I wish I could go again but I am too old and feeble now. My time in this world will soon be over. You are very fortunate. You have a life full of such adventures waiting for you. I am envious of your good fortune," he added with a smile. He patted my head and strolled away.

Silgitook's words gave me strength. Still, I was lonely. One day I delivered firewood to the Raven House where Laguksa lived. She was old enough to join the fishing party but she had stayed behind to tend her grandmother who was ill. I found her washing clothing in the morning sun. We had seldom spoken since our marriage was announced two years before. We greeted each other as I laid the firewood outside the entrance but I said nothing more. I did not want my discomfort to show.

"Thank you for the wood," she said.

I nodded. I felt I should answer but I didn't know what to say.

"Why didn't you go to the fishing camp with the others this year?" My breath caught in my throat. My face burned with shame and anger. She knew the answer! How could she humiliate me this way? I wished I had not brought her firewood.

"My father said that you have been left behind to protect us." She giggled in amusement. She still saw me as a child.

"I think you need someone older to protect you, but I am glad to help where I can." Now it was her turn to blush. My feelings about our engagement were clear in my voice. I wished I had said nothing. She needed our marriage more than I did. "I think the fishing party needs protection more than we do," I added. "We should pray to the Spirits for their safe return."

She nodded in agreement. I turned to leave.

"Ts'uwaas, I did not mean to insult you. I think you are going to be a fine man. You are very handsome too."

My pain was sharper for a moment, but I did not let this show on my face. I nodded with dignity and walked away.

The days passed slowly as the time for the fishing party's return grew closer. Each day I climbed to the roof of my father's house to watch for their canoes. One afternoon, as the sun sparkled across the water, I finally saw them approaching in the distance. I climbed down and ran from house to house shouting, "They are coming! They are coming!" Soon everyone in the village was on the shore waving and shouting. Some of the others paddled small canoes out to meet them but I waited at the shore.

But something was terribly wrong. Few hands answered our greetings and there was no happiness on their faces. A great dread shut our mouths and lowered our arms as they drew nearer. The first canoes scraped onto the beach. The women from the canoes ran to their relatives and began to wail loudly. The men greeted each other in hushed and serious tones. Many whispers were exchanged but I could not hear what was said. I moved closer.

"What is it? What is wrong?"

They looked at me strangely and then at each other. No one said anything.

For a moment, I felt as though I had died and they were looking at my ghost. A body wrapped in a blanket was lifted from one of the canoes. Silgitook stood like a stone, staring at the blanket but saying nothing. I felt a panic rising inside of me. Doolyaks was standing beside me.

"Who is it?" I begged.

He opened his mouth to speak, but then turned to my father. Neeshlak hushed me with a wave of his hand. He put his arm around my shoulders and gently turned me away from the body. As we walked up to his house he spoke to me softly.

"Your Uncle Gugweelaks has died."

With those words my life changed completely.

The next day, Amapaas told me what had happened. On the trip home from the fishing camp our canoes were caught in a sudden storm. They hurried to the nearest shore but they did not have time to find a safe harbour. The canoes filled with chests of oolichon oil were quickly pulled onto the shore and unloaded. The work was almost done when a large wave caught my uncle and threw him onto the rocks. His head split open and his body was pulled back to the sea. Amapaas and Doolyaks swam out to rescue him but his Spirit left his body before they brought him to the shore. They wrapped his body in a blanket and placed it under a canoe for the night. The next day his skin was cold and grey and the sand was red with his blood. His brother Shoget put stones on his eyes and covered his face so his ghost could not follow our canoes home.

The village was in great distress while we made preparations for his cremation. We kept a safe distance from his body which lay covered outside Silgitook's house for two days. We dared not bring it inside. If his ghost followed the body into our house then we all might die. We took the side planks off the house to remove my uncle's belongings so his ghost could not follow their scent to our door. They were placed beside his body so his ghost would not hunt for them.

Our Shamans, Tooklan and Wumgooks, tied his body with cedar strings and placed it in a burial box. They hung the ends of the strings outside the box to show the Ghosts of the Dead we had severed our ties to his body. The box was set high on stilts behind Silgitook's house. Tooklan and Wumgooks blessed it and set it on fire so his Spirit might follow the ashes up to Heaven.

Silgitook ordered a totem to be carved to honour Uncle Gugweelaks and a feast was prepared the following week to honour his memory. At the feast, I sat in a special place of honour near Silgitook, for I was my uncle's heir. The Elders told stories of my uncle's life and the good things he had done. Offerings were made for his Spirit's well-being. Then Silgitook called me to stand before the Elders of the Clan. He announced that I would be given my uncle's name the following spring. Tooklan smeared my face and chest with charcoal and ashes so I would look like my uncle's cremated body. Then my belongings were moved from Silgitook's house to a small cabin at the edge of the forest. I lived apart from the others of the village for one year so that uncle's ghost would not return.

◇◇◇◇◇◇◇◇◇◇◇◇◇◇◇◇◇

At first my life in the small hut was difficult. It felt like a punishment. I missed my family and my friends. The Spirits had cursed me by taking my uncle away before he had finished my teaching. I was filled with fear and sadness.

It was hard to sleep, too. There were no soft voices in other sleeping chambers, no one moving, no coughing or snoring. When I did sleep, I was woken by the sounds of the forest. I heard squirrels on the roof, the croaking of frogs and calls of crows and owls. I had not known how noisy a forest could be. Even the rain and the wind sounded louder.

After a moon passed I grew accustomed to living alone. Hoshieka brought me my meals every morning and evening. She knocked on my door but she was gone by the time I opened it. Tsangook left his unfinished masks outside my door with pieces of sandstone, brushes and paints to keep me occupied during the days.

The villagers gradually grew bolder as the seasons changed. Doolyaks, Tsangook, Miyana and my brothers stayed to talk when they brought me work or food. I heard all the news of the village. Pashaleps returned to live with the Raven Clan. At first she wept and fasted like a proper widow, and she enjoyed the attentions and sympathy given to a woman in mourning. But then life returned to normal. Her loud complaints were heard coming from the Raven House every day.

Tsangook finished Gugweelaks' memorial totem. I heard the ceremony in front of Silgitook's house as it was raised. I could only listen from my hut. I waited to the first light of day the following morning to visit it. It was shorter than others that honoured past Chiefs, but it was beautiful. It had a beaver at the base to honour his hard work, a bear above to show his strength and an eagle on the top to honour our Clan. I was proud of Tsangook and I knew my uncle's Spirit would be pleased.

After two more moons I was allowed to help others with their chores during the day but every night I returned to my hut to eat and sleep alone. I could not go hunting or fishing, not even on the short overnight trips I once did with my uncle. Once again, I could not join the others at the fishing camp on the Skeena during the great salmon runs during the late spring and summer. I worried that I would forget the skills my uncle had taught me.

Uncle Silgitook came to visit me during the first salmon camp on the Skeena when the village was empty again. We traded the usual greetings and then he spoke.

"Nephew, in nine full moons you will inherit your Uncle Gugweelaks' name and his position as an Elder in the Eagle Clan. Are you happy with that arrangement?"

"Yes, great Uncle."

"There are many responsibilities that come with this position, Ts'uwaas. An Elder is not just any man. He must be a good man. He must be a leader and an inspiration to his Clan. When other Clans are present he must carry himself with great dignity. He must know the sacred songs and stories perfectly. He must help his Clan make important decisions. His decisions must be wise and fair. Do you think you can do all these things?"

"Yes, Great Uncle, I will do my best. I will learn fast."

"You will be the youngest Elder of the Eagle Clan, but I am sure the Spirits will guide you with some help from the other Elders. You will be an Elder before either of your older brothers. There may be some hard feelings between you. What will you say to Amapaas if he is jealous?"

"I will tell him that he is the oldest nephew. His name and honour will be greater than mine when he receives his inheritance, for he will be Chief of the Eagle Clan after Uncle Shoget, not just an Elder. He will need more time to prepare for his greater duties. And I will tell him he has a brother on the Council who loves him."

Silgitook looked surprised. "Excellent! I see you will excel in both wisdom and diplomacy." He smiled. "Perhaps you would also like some extra responsibilities as an Elder. Your Uncle Gugweelaks told me that you wanted to join the Hamatsas. Are you still interested?"

I stared at him with disbelief and an open mouth.

"Say yes if that is your answer," he laughed.

"Yes, yes, Great Uncle, yes! Oh, thank you! Thank you!!" I forgot my proper form. I jumped up and down and then I hugged him hard. I think I frightened him.

"Ts'uwaas! An Elder does not bounce around!" He paused for a breath and then continued with a serious voice. "An Elder is always heavy. You must learn to hold your joy and excitement within you. You must feel its richness quietly. This strengthens your Spirit and fills your soul with grace. Besides, you might fall on your head or step on something sharp bouncing around like that." He smiled again. "The Hamatsas have already discussed your situation. You will be admitted to the Society the week before you become an Elder, if you will prepare to do the Cannibal Dance at the end of the coming winter ceremonies."

"Yes, Great Uncle, yes! That is what I have always wanted!"

He smiled broadly. "That is good! No doubt you will be an enthusiastic Cannibal. I will make the announcement to the village that you will perform the Dance this winter. Remember to hold your joy inside." He nodded a goodbye and walked with grace and dignity back to his house.

I practiced holding my joy inside, but I suspect it was written on my face all summer. Silgitook made the announcement as he promised when the villagers returned from the Skeena. Their catch had been bountiful and the announcement added to their excitement.

The news made me very popular. Many villagers came to congratulate me and to wish me success. Gwashasip and Amapaas discussed with me what it would be like to be a member of the secret society of Man-Eaters. Miyana said this might be the first Cannibal Dance she would enjoy. She asked if I was scared and who I might choose to bite. I still lived apart from the others but now I felt honoured, not alone. I still mourned the past, but now I also prepared for my future.

In the autumn Silgitook and the other Hamatsas showed me their secret meeting places in the forest. I hoped Doolyaks would be my teacher, but I was taught mostly by the older men who had been Hamatsas for many years, such as my father's cousin Hahkwah and my Uncle Shoget. They taught me the skills I would need to learn to be a Cannibal Dancer. They showed me ways to move like a wild man and how hard to bite to break a man's skin, then to pull back to tear it with my teeth. That would cause scarring without hurting the muscle. I learned each stage of the dance perfectly and practiced my movements over and over.

There were many tricks to learn that other villagers did not see. They showed me how to hide fish bladders filled with animal blood in their clothing and how to break them at the right moment to make their bites seem much worse than they were. They also taught me that knowing the movements and techniques was not enough. I needed to prepare my mind and heart to let the Cannibal Spirits possess my body. They would not possess me until the fourth day of the Dance, but first I must be prepared to accept them.

The days grew shorter and hunting season ended. The villagers gathered to start preparations for the winter ceremonies. Silgitook announced the Cannibal Spirits would arrive on the tenth week of the ceremonies and the Cannibal Dance would happen three days later. I continued to practice in the forest during the days but I was allowed to watch the songs and stories in the evenings. I did not enjoy them as much as in other years for I thought only about the Cannibal Dance. I felt the Spirits coming closer. For the last eight days before their arrival I stayed in my hut and prepared to receive them.

A great storm hit our village a day before the Cannibal Spirits were to arrive. The rain fell hard. Strong winds broke off branches and caused trees to fall. It was unsafe in the forest. Silgitook announced to the village that the Cannibal Spirits were delayed. I was sure my fortunes were cursed. The Spirits would leave and the Dance would not happen. Tooklan burned offerings to the Weather Spirits to stop the storm. I prayed to the Great Spirit and waited for the storm to stop. In my hut I bathed and meditated. Time passed very slowly.

Three days later the storm ended. Silgitook announced the Cannibal Spirits were approaching. They would arrive the next morning. That night I slept in my father's house so my family would witness my abduction. I said a prayer, folded my clothing and climbed into my bed. I lay on my back and waited for morning.

SIX

The little ones ask me: why are there Cannibal Spirits and why do we celebrate them? They might just as well ask me why there is a Heaven and an Underworld. Why do some animals eat meat and others eat plants? Why do they have powers that we do not? Why are there wonders that we cannot understand? The answers are too big for our small minds, so I tell them to listen with their hearts instead. I tell them the story of how the Cannibal Spirits revealed themselves and why there are Hamatsas who honour them.

It began long ago in a village that is now lost and forgotten. A young Prince, the son of the village Chief, had come of age to start his own household. He was digging holes for his new house posts when he disturbed the ancient bones of Ancestors who had died there many generations before. He showed his father, the Chief, who then called a meeting of the village Elders. There was great concern, for these Ancestors were from a time long before, when men had been cannibals. They feared that their Spirits would return to punish them for disturbing their bones and they would all suffer horrible deaths.

The villagers asked their Shaman what they must do. He told them they must bundle the bones tightly in a sacred cloth so the Spirits would not see what was happening. Then the young Prince who had found them must carry the cloth high into the mountains and throw it into a lake where the Spirits could rest in peace and not be disturbed again.

The Prince did as he was advised. He traveled alone, high into the mountains until he found a lake and swam to the middle. He dropped the bundle of bones in the deepest part. Then he returned to the shore and rested.

He sang a prayer of thanks to Great Spirit for helping him to finish his task safely. He washed his skin with the juices of the wooms plant to purify himself before his journey home. But he was not alone, or as safe as he thought. One of the bones had fallen out of the bundle as he struggled up the mountainside and a Cannibal Spirit had followed him to the lake.

As he bathed by the water's edge, his happy song was interrupted by a terrible cry. Its sound was both human and not human, and it filled him with a great fear. A strange voice said, "I saw what you have done!" Then the Spirit appeared before him, walking out of a wall of rock like a Ghost. He was naked except for a headdress of cedar boughs and a small skirt of ferns. His face and chest were painted white and red. The skin that wasn't painted was grey like dead flesh but it glowed with magical powers. His eyes were fixed on the Prince as he walked towards him.

The Prince wanted to run but he could not. The glowing eyes of the Spirit made him powerless as he approached. The Spirit held the body of a dead child in his arms. The Prince saw that it belonged to a boy from his village who had recently drowned.

The Spirit stretched his arms out towards the Prince. His mouth did not move but the Prince heard him say "You must eat the body of this child."

The Prince, who was a brave hunter and warrior, trembled like a child himself and begged the Spirit not to make him do this.

The Spirit said, "Choose for yourself, but if you do not eat it I will drag you to the bottom of the lake where my people will eat you instead. Then you will lead us back to your village where we will eat your people."

The Prince realized that he had no choice. He accepted the body the Spirit offered him. The boy's body was almost weightless in his arms. It was not as cold as he expected. Although the body of the child had been dead for many days, the skin smelled fragrant and appealing. A powerful hunger grew within him. Perhaps this is a trick and not a real body, he thought. He bit into the arm slowly. He was amazed at how good the flesh tasted and how easy it was to swallow.

As soon as he finished eating, the Spirit commanded him to follow. Again, he could not refuse. They walked to the north for several days, but he did not tire or grow hungry. The Prince did not know what the Spirit wanted of him but he knew he would not allow him to die.

Finally they arrived at a great house in the middle of a wide meadow. There was a totem at the entrance carved with the heads of four figures. On top was a man's head with teeth and an open mouth. Beneath him were Raven and then another man. On the bottom was Sonoqua, the great cannibal woman with her black skin and outstretched arms.

"This is the home of Man-Eater," the Spirit's voice echoed in his head. The Spirit climbed between Sonoqua's arms and through her pursed lips, which was the door into the house. The Prince followed him, with his heart full of curiosity.

Man-Eater sat at the end of the great house, facing the great fire in the centre of the room. He was a giant man, even larger than Sonoqua who was his daughter. He had been waiting for the Prince's arrival. The Prince did not know what to say to him, but Man-Eater did not wait for him to speak.

His voice rang out with great power and the Prince saw that he had no fear of men. "Do you know what you have done? You dishonour me by throwing the bones of your ancestors to the bottom of a lake. Do you not know that all men were once cannibals?"

He stood to his full height and paced back and forth in front of his fire. He wore a necklace of human skulls and a belt decorated with the skeletons of severed hands. The Prince was too frightened to answer as he watched the bones rattle back and forth.

"Ha! Why do you stare? Do you wonder what your bones will look like when your meat has been eaten away? Are you afraid of your fate, or do you believe you can escape Death? Ha! The worms will eat you if we do not!" Man-Eater thought this was funny. He threw back his head to let out a great roar. The Prince saw his pointed, blood-stained teeth and a cold fear ran up his spine.

"Your people think they are no longer cannibals because they are too civilized. Ha! You still kill each other like animals but you pretend you are not like them. The Animal Spirits breathed life into man but now he thinks he is better than they are. At least animals do not kill for greed or jealousy. Ha! Man needs to be taught how easily the thin paint of civilization washes off. He needs to feel the hunger that created him!" Man-Eater stretched his arms towards the roof of his great house and laughed again. He laughed so hard the walls shook and the Prince had to cover his ears.

Man-Eater kept the Prince in his home for three days. The Cannibal Spirits who lived there taught him new songs and dances full of savage energy and passion. A great hunger grew inside him as he danced. The Spirits brought him vegetables from the earth and honey and fruit from the trees but these did nothing to ease his hunger. What he hungered for was flesh but the Spirits brought him no meat. The hunger grew until he could not control it. The Spirits taunted him with their limbs and fingers. He jumped at them but his teeth passed through them like air. After three days he was so crazed with hunger that he forgot who he was. Then the Spirits led him back to his village.

Three days in the world of Supernatural Beings is the same as three years in the world of men. The villagers had searched for the Prince for weeks until they were certain he was dead. They held a great feast to mourn his death for he was loved and respected, and they called it the Black Feast. They did not know he had gone to the house of Man-Eater and that one day he would return to haunt them.

One morning at daybreak, long after they had stopped mourning, the people of the village were woken by a strange call that sounded like "Eat! Eat!" It was heard behind each house in the village, but when the villagers ran to look they found no one. All that day they talked about what they had heard. Perhaps it was a strange bird or animal, or perhaps a dream, but how could everyone have the same dream?

The next day they heard the call again. This time rocks hit the backs and roofs of their houses and they knew it was not a dream. This continued for several days until everyone was afraid. A council of Elders was called and the Shamans were consulted. Hunters were sent out to find the strange animal but they found nothing.

At last one morning the calls and the rocks stopped. This excited the villagers even more, for they didn't know if the strange animal was gone or if it would now do something new. While they were discussing what they should do a Spirit walked out of the forest towards them. He was dirty and wild. They saw he was naked except for his skirt of ferns and a headdress of cedar boughs. He pulled a young man by a cedar rope.

The youth did not look much like a man. He was naked and filthy like an animal, not even clothed in ferns and leaves like the Spirit. His hair and beard were long and tangled. His muscles rippled and strained against the cedar straps that bound his wrists. His eyes darted back and forth. They had no focus. When he became too excited by the people around him, the Spirit shook a rattle of human bones and this seemed to calm him.

The crowd drew closer and they recognized in this youth their handsome Prince. They followed him through the village, staring in wonder at what he had become. When they tried to approach him he jumped at them and tried to bite their arms, shouting "Eat! Eat!" They knew at once this was the same cry they had heard for several mornings.

The Spirit led the Prince to his father's house. He explained to the Chief and all those who had gathered how Man-Eater had given the Prince supernatural powers but those powers were too strong for him. Cannibal Spirits now possessed his mind and loins and he hungered savagely for the flesh of other men. He told them the Prince would gradually recover if they bathed him for several days in the juices of the wooms plant. He needed to be watched at all times and never allowed to see the dead or the dying or hear others speaking about them.

In spite of these strange instructions the villagers rejoiced to hear that he would recover. The Chief chose several young men to attend him and keep him from attacking others. They made rattles to calm him and washed him in wooms juice every day. Slowly after several weeks he settled down. They cut his hair and dressed him in his best clothes and once again he looked like the son a Chief.

The villagers believed the Prince had fully recovered and the attendants were not needed anymore, but one day a messenger came from another village to announce that the Chief of his village was dead. At the mention of death the Prince became crazed with hunger and leapt at the messenger, biting him several times. When others tried to pull him off he bit them too. Several men tried to hold him down but his power grew stronger the more he panicked. He threw them off and fled into the woods.

Once again the villagers began to hear his cries of "Eat! Eat!" and the sound of rocks hitting their houses each morning. The attendants searched the forests for days until they found him. Their rattles were not enough to soothe him so they built a trap, a pit they covered with branches and grass, and laid the body of a dead child on the far side. The Prince ran towards it and fell into the hole. The attendants poured wooms juice over him from above until he fell quiet, then tied his hands behind his back and led him back to his house.

It took a year for the Prince to know the Spirits within him and how to control them. At times his desire for human flesh was so painful an attendant would take pity and offer his arm for him to bite. The Chief saw this and gave five blankets to the ones the Prince bit, for their kindness and their bravery. This is how young men came to offer their arms to the Cannibal Dancers and why the Dancers pay them five blankets each.

The Chief obeyed the instructions of the Spirit who had brought the Prince back from Man-Eater. He began a secret society for the Prince's attendants and he called them the Hamatsas. Only the most noble men, the Chief, the Elders and the sons and husbands of their first nieces were allowed to belong.

The Hamatsas never stopped attending to the Prince. He became their leader. They prepared wooms juice for him each day and he taught them the songs and dances he had learned in Man-Eater's house. His Spirit healed completely and he no longer lost control. He was now wiser, stronger and more disciplined than other men, like a great warrior. He taught the other Hamatsas how to summon the Cannibal Spirits into their bodies and then how to control their power so that they would become great warriors too. By learning what it meant to be a savage they learned better what it meant to be civilized.

Every man who was invited to join the Hamatsas was sent on a journey into the forest for three days to prepare to receive the Cannibal Spirits. The three days would feel like three years when it was over, three days the new Hamatsa would never forget.

Since I was a boy of six I had dreamed of being a Hamatsa, a dream I could not forget, a dream that was only four days away that night before my abduction.

SEVEN

The Cannibal Spirits abducted me from my father's house the next morning at daybreak. They carried me to their secret gathering place in the forest. They took away my boy's clothes and gave me a woolen vest and blanket of cedar and wolf fur. Then they sent me deeper into the forest with only enough food for a day.

I found a bed of cedar boughs they had made for me under a fallen log and I spent the next three nights there. The days passed slowly and the nights were terrifying. Sonoqua chased after me in my dreams, causing me to sit up quickly. My head hit the underside of the log, giving my forehead a painful gash. Then Owl visited me and shook out the feathers and dust of Death above me. I ran so they would not touch me but my troubles were not over. Raven came to warn but he could not tell me what the danger was. When darkness came the Ghosts of the Dead found me. They tried to make me fall asleep so they could drag me into their shadow world, but I held on through the night, praying to Great Spirit to hold me in His arms.

I was still alive when the Sun returned to chase away the Ghosts. My heart was full of joy and gratitude to Great Spirit. I had not slept or eaten much in the past two days, but I was filled with energy. I washed and drank in the first stream and then I walked as fast as I could downstream towards Gitka'ata. I did not have time to waste. The longest night of my life would be followed by the longest day.

By mid-morning I reached the secret clearing where the Hamatsas had left me three days earlier. I heard a rustle of bushes nearby and then silence. A Hamatsa had waited for me and now he would alert the village of my return. They would gather in my father's house and wait for me to appear.

I saw a bowl of wooms juice in the centre of the clearing. I drank it to cleanse myself so not to offend the Cannibal Spirits. Beside the bowl there were paints and brushes to colour my face and body and fish bladders filled with animal blood. I found the ceremonial blanket under the log where Jaksukjalee had placed it. I took off my woolen vest and my cloak of cedar and wolf fur and folded them carefully. When I opened the ceremonial blanket to wrap them up and I found a dancing robe, a skirt of ferns, a necklace of small animal skulls, a belt of rattles made from the skeletons of human hands and a headdress of cedar boughs with hair made from hanging moss.

I dressed and stood silently in the centre of the clearing with my eyes closed. My empty stomach growled and the Cannibal Spirits smelled my hunger. Slowly I began to dance, making steps of a Wild Man to attract them closer. I danced faster, shaking my head and leaping like an animal around the clearing. Then I felt them enter my body with the power of an angry river. I raised my face to the sky and made a great roar that echoed off the mountainside.

I reached the edge of the forest behind Gitka'ata. The Hamatsas had been waiting for me in their ceremonial robes behind my father's house. They pointed to a ladder they had placed that led up to the roof. Then they scattered in two directions. One half went to the front entrance and the others to a corner at the back of the house where there was a secret door for special occasions such as this. I climbed silently onto the roof to a hole that had been prepared for me.

All of Gitka'ata was waiting for my return around my father's fire. The Hamatsas entered the house from both ends at the same time. They ran behind the villagers making terrible faces, howling loudly and crying "Eat! Eat! Eat!" in high voices. As the village turned to watch them I leapt through the hole in the roof and landed heavily beside the fire. They gasped in surprise. My painted face was distorted with hunger and the craving for human flesh. My body shook with excitement. I gnashed my teeth, made strange moans and shook my rattles as I moved towards them.

Their shock was too real. Something warm dripped from my nose. The sharp boughs of my headdress had scratched open the wound on my forehead in my fall from the roof. Blood was flowing down over my face but it did not stop me. The stabbing pain only added to my agony and made me act more savagely.

The Hamatsas continued to cry "Eat! Eat! Eat!" at the back of the room. The salt of my sweat entered my wound and the pain became sharper. I cried out and put my hands on my face. Then I lunged at the nearest villagers with my bloody hands and they screamed. I saw two young friends who had arranged for me to bite them and I jumped on them. I bit one on his forearm and the other on his leg. They cried out for help, for I had truly frightened them. The Hamatsas ran down the steps to the fire to chase me away. I fled to the back of the house and escaped through the secret door leaving my skirt of ferns behind. The Hamatsas burned my skirt in front of the assembly to break the spell of the Cannibal Spirits.

I smeared my naked body with mud and waited in the forest for the morning to pass. The Hamatsas had told the village that I had fled down the beach. They left my father's house and waited by the shore, hoping to see me before I saw them. I stole up to my father's house and climbed the ladder to the roof again. I crept slowly and silently to the front of the house. Children were peeking around the sides of the house, hoping to warn the adults of my return. They had not seen me.

I leapt off the roof with a scream and ran towards the shore. Everyone scattered in a panic. I chased them screaming "Eat! Eat! Eat!" I ignored the oldest and youngest. I found three more young men who had asked to be bitten and they let me catch them. I used the pouches of blood I hid in my cheeks to make the wounds look terrible.

The Hamatsas circled me again to protect the villagers. They shook their skull rattles to calm me and to stop me from biting. A naked woman guide appeared. She was painted white like a Ghost from her head to her feet. She beckoned to me to follow her as she danced backwards towards my father's house. I followed, pretending to be captured by her beauty until we were close to the entrance. Then I leapt at her with a loud snarl and she fled screaming. It was difficult not to smile, so I chased after the villagers until the Hamatsas circled me once more.

This time Doolyaks appeared before me, naked and white. I did not need to pretend that I was fascinated. I followed as he walked backwards away from me, shaking his rattle and luring me in through the entrance. He led me to the fire. The villagers entered behind us and took their places around the fire.

The Hamatsas had built a totem at the far end of the lowest level that looked like the front of Man-Eater's house. It was supposed to remind me of where I been the past three days. The pole had four heads with open mouths and teeth, just like the one in the story of Man-Eater. I pretended to be excited at the sight of it. I ran to the back of the pole and climbed up the footholds to the top. I climbed it quickly for I had practiced on the pole in the forest during the autumn.

When I reached the top I gave a loud, sharp cry, "Eat! Eat!" I climbed into the mouth of the man at the top to show that my flesh was food for the Cannibal Spirits. Then I climbed down to the head of Raven and out of his mouth, for Tsamsem, who often took the form of Raven, had given life to Man.

I gave the Cannibal's cry again, "Eat! Eat!" I climbed down to the next man and into his mouth to show that Man's life is cycle of birth and death. We must be consumed by Death to be born again. Finally I climbed out of Sonoqua's mouth, for the Spirit of Man was born out of the Spirit of the Man-Eater. We remember our savage past to better respect the civilized men we have become. This was the Cannibal Dancer's message.

Again I gave the Cannibal's cry, though my voice was soft and weak. The Hamatsas circled me and sat me down. They lulled me to sleep by singing songs and stroking my hair. My headdress was lifted from my head and thrown into the fire. Then they bathed me in wooms juice until the Cannibal Spirits left my body. Their gentle hands and wet cloths felt wonderful on my tired skin as I pretended to sleep. After they had dried me I woke as a man like the others around me. I was brought men's clothing and the villagers cheered. The dance was over.

Everyone gathered around to congratulate me. The children came to stare at my skeleton rattles and my skull necklace. They dared not touch them for fear that the Cannibal Spirits would return. My friends asked if my bleeding was a trick. I told them it was a real injury caused by Sonoqua when I was in the forest and they were impressed. I felt like a hero.

But my glory was short-lived. My mother, Memlaka, and Miyana were concerned that my wound might become infected. They spoke to me as though I was a young child who could not take care of himself. They brought me goat's milk to give me energy. I grew impatient and irritable and I wanted to be alone.

I realized I needed to sleep. The Hamatsas led me back to my hut where I could rest but they too wanted to talk to me. They were as delighted as the others about my performance. Hahkwah said it was the best Cannibal Dance he had ever seen. Doolyaks agreed and he gave me a hug. He was so beautiful and had so much joy on his face. They left me to sleep but Doolyaks' sweet smile filled my thoughts and kept me awake.

That evening the Elders gathered to witness my acceptance into the Hamatsas. Silgitook sat in my father's usual seat as the Chief of the Man-Eater Society. The other Hamatsas sat beside him and then my father and the other village Elders. The Hamatsas honoured me and welcomed me into the Society with an official ceremony. They asked me to tell the story of my encounters with the Spirits in the forest. I described

Sonoqua's visit on my first night and how she chased me in my dream the second night. I told them about Raven's warning and the Ghosts of the Dead. These were good omens for they proved that I had attracted Cannibal Spirits and had befriended Raven. But I did not tell them about Owl, the Messenger of Death. They might think I was cursed.

After my story there was a feast in my honour. I was popular that night. Miyana and my brothers were very proud of me. There was so much food and laughter. Everyone joked about my appetite. Doolyaks smiled at me from across the room. The bare muscles of his arms and legs distracted me and I could not concentrate on the voices of my friends. After I had eaten my head and eyelids grew heavy. I did my best to stay awake but soon my head was dropping.

Doolyaks came to my table. The voices around me stopped as he lifted me into his arms. He carried me to my chamber and laid me on my bed. He covered me with a blanket and stoked my head before he left.

That night I dreamed that the Hamatsas came to me for help. Cannibal Spirits had possessed Doolyaks. He was naked and crazed like a wild man and bit them whenever they came close. They could not hold him for he was far too strong. Their rattles and the wooms juice did nothing to quiet him. They thought perhaps he would listen to me.

They brought me to their secret meeting place in the forest where Doolyaks sat. His eyes darted back and forth and his breath was strong, but otherwise he was still. I approached him slowly and touched his shoulder. His muscles tightened with animal strength under the softness of his skin, like the muscles of his thigh when I held him in the canoe. He turned to bite me but I jumped back. I approached him again several times and each time I was able to touch more of him before he tried to bite. Finally I tamed his mouth with a kiss. We joined our tongues as I stroked his body. The Spirits left his body and he lay weak and trembling. I embraced him. His smooth skin was warm and damp with sweat. The Hamatsas covered us with blankets and he slept in my arms.

◇◇◇◇◇◇◇◇◇◇◇◇◇◇◇◇◇

My Cannibal Dance was near the end of our winter ceremonies. The last event was the potlatch where I would be given my uncle's name. When I was young our potlatches were our most important ceremonies. They were how we honoured deaths and celebrated new names, marriages or inheritances. No change was accepted without a potlatch to honour it. Elders of the Clans came to witness what happened and listen to our sacred stories that explained why it was good. There was always a feast and the host gave gifts to all the guests. Those who witnessed the stories gave the change their blessing by accepting the host's food and gifts.

A potlatch for the son of the Head Chief was very important. I was the first of Neeshlak's sons to become an Elder so my potlatch was the biggest in Gitka'ata in many years. Elders from all the Clans were invited as well as Chiefs and Elders of the villages of Kitkatla and Klemtu. Even the Elders of the Heiltsuk village of Kitamaat were invited. My potlatch lasted four days.

It had taken much effort and time to plan. The preparations began as soon as Silgitook announced it the spring before. Each Clan helped to make gifts for my father to give to the visitors from other villages to impress them with the wealth of Gitka'ata. The Wolf Clan made mats and blankets of red cedar and carved our serving bowls. The Raven Clan carved horn spoons and boxes. The Eagle Clan collected eagle feathers, shells and hunted mountain goats for their special wool and meat. My father's Clan, the Blackfish, provided the most. They prepared most of the food and made special clothing, blankets and masks.

They had all worked hard for many moons to get ready for my feast. Extra salmon and oolichon were traded to the Kwakiutl for abalone and copper. The Giksan and Carrier traded beaver belts and moose meat for our shellfish and seal meat. The Haida gave us blackfish for berries and moose meat. The Tlingit traded dried salmon and ceremonial masks for their woven blankets and caribou skins.

The women were busy too, gathering seaweed and sea grass and drying it on the beach. Some of it they used for food and the rest they shaped and dried into flasks and cups. They cleaned and dried the fish and collected eggs and shellfish from the beaches. They picked berries and crab apples and stored them for winter.

In the evenings each house gathered around their fire. I was not with them but I knew what they said. They talked about the day's work and told jokes while they ate. After dinner, the children slept or played while the adults did quiet work by the light of the fire. Some spun goat wool, wove mats and baskets or worked on their carvings if there was enough light. Their hearts and thoughts were filled with a proud excitement, for a great potlatch with important visitors from other villages did not happen every year. No one spoke of my ceremony itself but they talked about the preparations. Men discussed the size of the harvests and possible trades with other tribes. Women talked about food and traded patterns for their weavings. Everyone was tired but happy.

As the seasons changed, I watched them from a distance. I could not help with preparations for my own potlatch or sit with them around their fires, but I felt their happiness. These were all the people that I had ever known and they worked so hard with love in their hearts for the success my potlatch. This thought humbled me greatly.

Then the winter ceremonies began. As the day of my abduction grew nearer I was too anxious to watch the other dancers. I stayed in my hut or sat on the beach alone. I could not relax until my dance was finished. But now my longest day was finally over. I had only two days to rest in my hut before my potlatch began.

The village was filled with commotion. There was less time to prepare because the storm had delayed my Cannibal Dance. Chiefs and Elders from the other villages arrived on the third day after the dance. The first guests were from Kitkatla led by their Chief, Ts'ibasaa. Natawalps, the Chief of Klemtu, and his Elders arrived next, followed by Shimcheeoost, the Heiltsuk Chief and his Elders from Kitamaat village. For the first time, I was part of the greeting party as they came to witness my new status as an Elder.

The arrival of the visitors changed everything. Everyone acted with the most proper behaviour. Children were hushed and kept out of sight. Nothing was left lying where someone could trip and injure himself. We did our best to attend to our visitors' comforts. We slept on mats on the floors so that they could sleep in our beds in the main houses. The food was prepared in the houses where no guests stayed so they would not see the hurry and confusion of our work.

The visitors were also on their best behaviour. There were proper exchanges of pleasantries, many compliments and discussions about hunting, fishing and the weather. The most important subjects were never talked about. There was a great competition amongst them for the best image, especially amongst the Chiefs. Each tried to show he had the qualities of a great Chief. Their status and prestige depended on how they carried themselves. The most imposing Chief was Ts'ibasaa of Kitkatla, who was also the most powerful. He was haughty and proud and he carried himself with grace and dignity. He did not smile and never showed weakness or clumsiness. He paid his respects to other Chiefs while demonstrating in his manner that he was also the strongest and wisest amongst them.

I had never dealt with people of power. I watched with interest how my father managed them. He told me he was most concerned about Ts'ibasaa who controlled the waterways to the north, but he did not show his concern on his face or in his actions. He did not act haughty or pretend to be as strong as Ts'ibasaa, like Natawalps and Shimcheeoost did. Instead he was kind and generous, for these too are traits of a great Chief. I believed Ts'ibasaa would be pleased by the way my father treated him, perhaps because they were both from the Blackfish Clan.

The feasts held for the four nights of my potlatch were the finest that winter. The best foods had been saved to impress the visitors. Every night there were new dishes. We were served roasted meats of deer, moose, elk, bear, rabbit and seal. There were bird meats too, like duck, goose and grouse. We had plenty of dried salmon, halibut and many types of shellfish. We ate these with sea grass squares, dried seaweed and preserved sea bird eggs. For sweets, we ate cakes of dried berries that we dissolved in hot water and ate with oolichon oil. One night there was even a special treat of mountain goat tallow mixed with fresh snow that some of the young men had collected in the afternoon by climbing half way up a nearby mountain.

After dinner the serving dishes were cleared away. The Elders and Chiefs washed and returned in their ceremonial clothes. They took their proper places around the centre of the room. My father, the host, sat in the centre at the back with his brothers and nephews of the Blackfish Clan beside him. I sat at a place of honour next to them. On one side sat the Elders of the other three Clans from our village and across from them the Chiefs and Elders of the other villages. Ts'ibasaa and his Elders sat closest to Neeshlak, and next to him Natawlps' tribe. Shimcheeoost and the Kitamaat Elders were farthest away for they were Heiltsuk, not Tsimshian.

Our Shaman, Tooklan, began the ceremony by circling the fire and spreading eagle down over the heads of the hosts and visitors. This was a pledge of peace between all the witnesses. The first night we listened to songs and stories of the Blackfish Clan. The Elders told of the founding of the Blackfish Clan and their claims that their Clan had been blessed over other Clans. They told the story of how our ancestors founded the village of Gitka'ata and how the Spirits had blessed us with a fine location so we could prosper from both the land and sea.

On the second night, it was my honour to tell the story of the name Gugweelaks and the stories of my many ancestors who had shared my name. In this way I showed the others that I was worthy of being an Elder. The praise I had received after the Cannibal Dance had excited my taste for performing. I did the songs and dances of my ancestors without shyness. Their Spirits guided me. I saw surprise and delight on the faces of the Elders who listened to my story telling and I felt proud. At the end of the evening Uncle Silgitook, Chief of the Eagle Clan, announced that I had inherited my uncle's name and from this time onward I would no longer be known as Ts'uwaas. There was much cheering and applause.

My father spoke on the third night and he was an excellent speaker. This is one of the finest qualities of a good Chief and he made us feel proud. He thanked our visitors for coming and he welcomed them to celebrate the richness and generosity of Gitka'ata. He told them our village had prospered while he had been Head Chief. He shared the stories of his victories and accomplishments. He joked that he had done more than Natawlps and Shimcheeoost though they were older. He was made Chief at a young age and the Spirits had told him he would live a long life. He sang songs of praise to the Spirits and invited the guests back the next night, the final night of the potlatch, where he would distribute gifts to show them his wealth and generosity.

White men say it is not polite to boast, though their leaders boast as much as ours. A Chief who boasts shows his neighbours that he is ready to defend his honour and the honour of his people. This day was my father's day of glory, for he was the host. If his gifts were generous on the last night his boasting would be justified. If they were not, he would be shamed and his failures exaggerated at the next potlatches in other villages.

On the day before the final feast the village was filled with excitement and anticipation for the gifts this evening would bring. There was warm sunshine and the first sweet smells of spring were in the air. In a few days we would be busy with a new season of fishing and hunting, but this afternoon was ours to enjoy. The elderly relaxed in the sun and watched the children play games by the shore. The adults shared stories about things that had happened in the past year. Everyone was in the finest of moods.

One guest from Kitkatla caught everyone's attention with a new knife he had bought with furs from the White trading post at Fort Simpson. The blade was as long as a man's foot and it shone brightly in the sun. He told us it was made of a metal the Whites called steel. It had a cutting edge shaped like waves. He showed us how it cut through leather as easily as our copper knives could cut through meat. He dropped it into the sand to prove that it would not scratch like copper.

We were all anxious to examine it. It was so wonderful to hold it in my hands! The blade had markings cut into it. We wondered what hand could carve such perfect markings into a blade so hard. Some said the Whites must know magic to make such a knife. The handle was made of hard wood. It was shaped to fit a hand and it too had strange markings on it. The visitor explained that the markings were sounds of the White language. We laughed at him for we heard nothing when we held them close to our ears. It also had a leather case with black letters and the small drawing of a deer's head. We scratched the drawing with our fingernails but it did not come off.

The visitor wore a leather belt around his waist under his cloak that he had bought in the White trading post. He showed us the metal buckle that held it in place. There was a loop of leather on the knife's case that he passed the leather belt through. He fastened the belt to show us how the knife rested on his hip so he did not have to carry it in a bag or in his hand.

The cleverness of it excited us. We had never seen anything like it. He told us the White fort had many things made of metal and leather, as well as fine woven cloths and wools. The Whites traded these treasures for simple animal furs. We talked of nothing else for the rest of that afternoon. I wondered if anything my father would give away that evening could be so wonderful.

As the light in the sky faded we gathered for the last great feast of the season. My father's house was very full, for everyone in the village was present. When the meal was finished and the serving dishes taken away, we waited around the fire in our proper places for the gift giving. My father welcomed us. He said this was the biggest potlatch in Gitka'ata in many years and he asked us to remember his generosity. Then he praised the visitors as good neighbours and trading partners. He complimented the Chiefs for their fine qualities of leadership and presented them with their gifts.

He gave Ts'ibasaa his gifts first. Ts'ibasaa got the finest furs of mink, sea otter, marten, beaver, wolf, bear and mountain goat. He also got carved masks, bowls, spoons and chests. My father gave similar gifts to the other Chiefs, only not quite as many. He gave furs, blankets, cloaks and woven baskets and cedar mats to the visiting Elders. Then he distributed gifts to the Clan Chiefs of Gitka'ata and their Elders. He gave a bearskin, bear claws and teeth and eagle feathers to each of our Shamans, Tooklan and Wumgooks, to use in their work. He had enough gifts to give to the commoners too. Most received only a few small furs or blankets and some food supplies. Tsangook also received new carving tools, and abalone and copper for decorating his masks.

He gave me new ceremonial clothing, carved spoons and serving dishes. He also gave me a beautiful, woven ceremonial blanket and a carved trunk to keep my prized belongings in. I saw that Tsangook had carved wooden gifts and this made me cherish them even more. Then Neeshlak announced that I would also receive my own canoe, now that I was a man. There was much cheering and clapping with this announcement.

The gift giving was finished. My father thanked everyone for their friendship and loyalty, and Tooklan offered prayers and sacrifices to the Great Spirit for the safe return of the visitors to their villages, and for peace and a prosperous new year of fishing and hunting. The meeting hall was cleared and the guests and villagers took their gifts away.

Before I went to bed my father showed me my new canoe which our servants had brought to the beach in front of our house. It was painted red with an eagle's head carved on either side of the bow. I thanked him many times as I ran my hands along its smooth sides.

Afterwards I moved my belongings from my hut into my new sleeping chamber in his house. It was the same sleeping chamber I had when I was younger but the bed was new. Two servants brought my chest filled with my other gifts to my new chamber. I studied each one to know them better. I said a prayer of thanks to Great Spirit and went to sleep. I was a man now, though my mind was filled with the bold dreams of youth. My sleep was filled with sweet dreams, but not dreams about my gifts I had received. I dreamt instead about the coming fishing season and about the beautiful steel knife and the many other treasures I might find in the White trading post, for a youthful heart always dreams about the unknown.

EIGHT

Our house was empty the next morning. My father had given away everything he owned except his most treasured family possessions. We did not feel poor, for we were now rich with honour. The villagers each came by to pay their respects to Neeshlak. They each brought small gifts of appreciation for his fine potlatch and the honour he had brought to our village. He thanked them for their kindness and loyalty. Soon our house was filling with new blankets and serving bowls again.

The visitors also stopped to pay their respects to my father before they left. They gave him gifts from their villages and thanked him for his hospitality. Ts'ibasaa presented my father with a rifle from Fort Simpson. It was made of wood and steel like the knife we had seen, but he did not know how it worked. My father accepted it politely but Ts'ibasaa could tell he did not know what it was. He asked Neeshlak if he knew how to use it, to humiliate him in front of the other visitors. We were horrified. It was shameful for a visitor to humiliate a host when he was supposed to be thanking him.

Ts'ibasaa showed my father a leather pouch filled with bullets. He offered to show him how to load the rifle. My father said that it was not necessary, that he did not want to delay his long journey home, but Ts'ibasaa insisted. He said it would not take long. The rifle seemed to break in half when he opened it. Two of our Elders groaned with disappointment but Ts'ibasaa only smiled. He was amused by the surprise on their faces when he closed the rifle and it looked as it had before. My father's face showed no surprise but Ts'ibasaa was not fooled.

"Let me show you how powerful it is," Ts'ibasaa said. He walked to the shore by the river and pushed his walking cane into the sand. He placed it in the exact spot that our first Chief had planted his cane when he had founded Gitka'ata fifty generations ago. He walked back to my father's side.

"This is not necessary, Ts'ibasaa." My father looked concerned.

"Watch this carefully," Ts'ibasaa replied. He placed the end of the rifle against his shoulder and aimed at the cane. The loud blast startled us as the top of the cane flew away. He loaded the rifle again and shot again. The cane broke again lower down and fell onto the sand. My father's face was very serious.

"You should learn how to use a rifle, Neeshlak, if you want to live as long as the other Chiefs. Your arrows and prayers cannot defend you from bullets. Of course, it is a long journey to Fort Simpson to buy them. We have plenty at Kitkatla and you can buy them from us."

Ts'ibasaa handed the rifle and the leather pouch of bullets to him. "Be careful, he cautioned my father with a smile, "The barrel is hot." He pointed to the barrel so my father would know which part that was. Ts'ibasaa said no more, not even goodbye. He walked to where his men were waiting and climbed into his canoe. They pushed their canoe in the water and began their journey home. We watched them until they were gone. Father's face was strained with anger and worry. Without saying a word, he turned and walked into our house.

The Elders of the four Clans met that evening to discuss our trip to the oolichon fishing grounds on the Nass River. We would leave in three days if the weather was favourable. The women had already begun mending the fishing nets and cleaning the storage boxes. I could not be more excited about my first fishing trip to the Nass. I would see many places I had heard about from my family and friends and I would share the work at the fishing camp as an equal.

This was also my first planning meeting as an Elder, but the other Elders did not discuss the preparations for our trip. They were angered by Ts'ibasaa's outrageous behaviour that morning. Many felt he had taken the best gifts but showed no gratitude or respect. They wanted to know how my father would respond.

Jaleek, the heir to the Raven Clan, complained the loudest. "You must demand an apology, Neeshlak. He has insulted your honour and spit on your hospitality."

"What should I ask him to apologize for, Jaleek? For giving me a White men's gun, for not saying goodbye or for blasting his own walking cane into pieces? He is a clever fox. His insults may seem obvious to you and me but he will deny them. If I ask for an apology he will claim that I have insulted his honour and his gift instead."

"He humiliated you in front of your village and the other visitors. You have lost honour by his actions. You must demand respect."

"Did I not earn honour for the fine potlatch I have just hosted, Jaleek? Perhaps you have forgotten the value of your gifts, or perhaps you feel I was not generous enough."

Jaleek hesitated, and then spoke more softly to my father. "I am sorry, Neeshlak. I did not mean to insult your generosity, but it angers me that he accepted so many gifts and then behaves so disrespectfully."

"He will lose honour for his behaviour. Sometimes you must let these things rest."

But Jaleek's frustration would not rest. "He has ridiculed our sacred heritage by placing his cane in the place our first Chief did and then destroying it. His words and actions were meant as a threat! If we do not retaliate we will look like cowards!"

"What would you have me do? Attack him? His village is twice our size. He has White guns and we do not. Do you think he cannot match our strength? Would you have our men slaughtered and have me look like a fool instead?"

Jaleek stared angrily at the floor. It was Neeshlak's cousin Hahkwah who spoke next. "Then what should we do, Neeshlak? If Ts'ibasaa is prepared to threaten us, we will need White guns to defend ourselves. If we buy them from him as he demands we will pay much more than he does. He will profit richly and he will buy many more guns. If we buy them from the White fort he will be angry and block our routes to the fishing grounds to punish us. If he does this, we will starve."

Neeshlak thought quietly for a while before he answered, allowing us to calm our feelings. "We must act carefully and without anger. We must pretend that we do not feel insulted or humiliated. He will not refer to his actions as an insult if we do not. It was more a warning than an insult, and warnings are sometimes no more than that. He needs our alliance against the Heiltsuk and other Kwakiutl tribes to the south. Meanwhile we will build alliances with the Heiltsuk and with Clans in Kitkatla through marriages. In time this problem will pass and be forgotten."

This time it was Doolyaks who spoke. "Neeshlak, our alliance will not be needed by either the Heiltsuk or Kitkatla if we are not armed as they are. We will be defenseless. This problem will grow worse long before we can build allegiances through marriages. I think there is another way." His handsome eyes sparkled while he waited for my father's permission to continue.

"What do you suggest, Doolyaks?"

"We could move to the White trading post at Fort Simpson! Already eight villages from the Skeena and Nass valleys are living there. We would not need to pass through Tsamsem's Trench to reach the fishing grounds so Ts'ibasaa would not be able to bar our way. We could buy whatever we want directly from the Whites and we would never need to deal with Ts'ibasaa's people!"

"That is ridiculous! Would you have us abandon our sacred past? These are our hunting grounds, our berry patches and our beaches where we gather our food. Our people have lived on this land for fifty-two generations! Do you think there will be unclaimed forests and berry patches waiting for our use if we move to Fort Simpson? How would we live? What would we eat?"

"We could live as traders. We could trade the goods of the White men with other tribes up the Nass and the Skeena or with the Tlingit and the Haida. We could even sell to Ts'ibasaa's people!" The other Elders sounded their agreement, which made Doolyaks smile. He continued with more enthusiasm. "When we have made enough money we could buy rights to new berry patches and hunting grounds. We could make new alliances with marriages to the northern tribes and then we would have access to their hunting grounds. When we have new alliances and as many guns as Ts'ibasaa we can return to Gitka'ata and claim our lands again!"

"Doolyaks, this would all take a great amount of time. Our lands will not wait for us if we abandon them. Other villages will lay claim to them. We may never be able to return. Life at Fort Simpson is not for our people. It is crowded and there is much competition between the villages living there. It will not be as easy to prosper as you think."

The voices of many Elders rose in protest at the same time as they tried to defend Doolyaks' plan. They begged my father to reconsider, but Neeshlak sat silently without responding. He let their voices fall silent. Then he spoke with great sternness.

"If you are willing to forsake the sacred past of Gitka'ata, perhaps you will remember that the White trading post also has a past and it is not so sacred. The Spirits have cursed it. Whites built the trading post there twenty-five years ago when we were still boys. Hundreds of Tsimshian listened to their greed instead of honouring their ancestors. They forgot their traditions and moved to the fort to get White men's goods. Four years later a great plague came and punished them with a horrible death. No one could save them and those who tried also died.

"We avoided the White fort for a generation. Now the young, who have no memory of the plague, outnumber the old and the villages have started returning to Fort

Simpson. Their greed for White goods blinds them from Great Spirit's warning. He will be angry that they have ignored His lesson. The curse remains and next time His punishment will be much worse than any harm Ts'ibasaa can inflict on us."

No one answered Neeshlak now. Their eyes were downcast. We had heard stories of the great plague but it brought bad luck to talk about it. My father's words would anger the Spirits of the Dead by mentioning it. A move to Fort Simpson would now be more dangerous. "I will hear nothing more about leaving Gitka'ata. We will plan our trip to the Nass, not the destruction of our history." With those words he dismissed the Elders and the meeting was over.

It was not like Neeshlak to silence the Elders with a heavy hand. If they doubted his strategy in dealing with Ts'ibasaa, they knew better than to start another discussion about moving to Fort Simpson before the trip to the Nass. But the women and commoners heard that the move was discussed and soon everyone had an opinion about it. My father was not deaf. He knew everyone was discussing it, but he pretended not to hear as long as they were preparing for our trip.

I thought about Fort Simpson too. I wanted to be wherever Doolyaks was, but I had to stay with my family. I prayed that fate would not separate us. For now we were all going to the Nass and I was excited about my first trip north. I helped with the preparations as I had for several years, but I loaded my own canoe the morning we departed.

Our boats could carry ten people, but we needed so many supplies for the fishing camp that there was only room in each for seven. Most Elders had canoes and they shared them with their wives, families, commoners and slaves. Since I had no wife or children I shared mine with Gwashasip, Miyana, Tsangook and three others. Amapaas traveled in my father's canoe with my mother and Hoshieka.

Finally the canoes set off according to our rank, led by my father. The canoes of the other Clan Chiefs and their heirs were close behind, followed by the other Elders. I followed them.

Our journey could not have started on a finer day. I was so excited that it made the others laugh. Some days it is impossible to hold the joy inside. It was also Miyana's first trip to the fishing grounds and she was as excited as I was. Uncle Shoget started a song that spread from canoe to canoe. We paddled in rhythm with our singing. What a joyous sound we made that echoed off the mountain walls. The sun rose higher as we glided down the canyon to the sea. Our singing stopped but our paddles chanted with a steady rhythm of their own. My heart was happy and at peace with the world.

At first the scenery was familiar to me. It was the same route the women of the

Eagle Clan followed when they took Miyana and I berry picking. We passed the beach where we used to pull up our canoes. I saw Miyana looking at it too, so I softly sang one of the songs we used to chase the bears away. She sang with me until we forgot the words and started laughing.

We continued south along the west side of the canyon. The steep mountains became shorter and their slopes more gentle as we approached the open sea. The green water was calm and deep. I tried to imagine how our canoes must appear to the Water Spirits who lived beneath us. I said a prayer to them as a grateful guest passing through their home. If they were watching me I knew they would feel my joy.

At midday we stopped in a small bay to eat a meal and rest our tired muscles. It was the same place we had spent the night two summers before after we had hunted for blackfish. That was my last fishing trip with Uncle Gugweelaks and now his name was mine. His Spirit surely knew I was thinking about him. Then the memory of holding Doolyaks' thigh returned and stirred my senses. I looked around for him and found him looking at me.

"Do you remember this place?" he smiled.

"Of course," I nodded, and then I blushed.

We could not afford to rest for long. We had almost reached the sea but our day was only half over. At the south end of our canyon there were several large islands and passages between them leading in all directions. From this point every place I saw was new to me. I regarded each mountain and shore with great interest.

We rounded the end of the canyon and turned sharply towards the northwest. The wind that had been our friend all morning was now in our faces and the waves were much rougher. We paddled hard across an open bay until we reached a passage-way so narrow that I thought it might be the mouth of a river. Gwashasip shouted to me that this was Tsamsem's Trench, the way to the sacred Skeena and the Nass Rivers.

I had heard mention of Tsamsem's Trench in many stories told around my father's fire. I had often dreamed of canoeing through it to see places in the north. In my dreams it was always sunny and the winds were favourable, but this day it was nothing like that. The headwind felt like a bad omen and I felt a nervousness in my stomach. I was aware that we were many hours from our village and I no longer felt safe. The Water Spirits seemed not so friendly. Perhaps these were the same Spirits that had killed Uncle Gugweelaks but I dared not think of that. I said a prayer instead and focused on the land on either side of us.

Tsamsem's Trench was so narrow that we could have lined up our canoes to make a bridge from side to side. We stayed close to the east side which gave us some protection from the wind. Our village was somewhere over the mountains to our right, Gwashasip told me. If there had been a passage from Gitka'ata to the west it would have saved us hours of paddling. The row of mountains on the west side were part of a long island that never seemed to end. Ts'ibasaa's village, Kitkatla, was on a small island the far side of this island, near the north end of the Trench. The beaches and berry patches we passed belonged to his people. Fortunately there would be no berries for several moons.

The Trench was as straight as a moonbeam and it seemed to continue forever. It narrowed even further before the day was over. We stopped in a small bay that opened on the east side of the passage and set up our tents for the night. I had never paddled so long in one day and my muscles ached. Tsangook massaged my shoulders and told me stories about the many times he passed through the Trench. We were only half way along it but he assured me that the next day would be easier. The wind had already stopped.

I slept hard that night in spite of my strange surroundings. Gwashasip woke me before it was light. The women were already preparing the morning meal. The men were taking down their tents and loading the canoes. They stretched and slapped their muscles to ready them for a good day's work. They talked about the weather and the good omens for the day ahead. The rain fell steadily but the wind was gentle and the water was calm.

We continued through the Trench most of the day. The rain fell without a break but it was not unpleasant. My cedar cape and wide rain hat kept me mostly dry and the paddling kept me warm. The sky was low and heavy. There was little I could see except the shores on either side. The clouds hid the tops of the mountains and made them look taller. The rain disturbed the surface of the water and it was difficult to see anything below us. Finally we reached the north end of the Trench. The passage widened and was divided by new islands. We set up camp in a sheltered bay on one of those islands and there we spent our second night.

On the third day there was a light wind and broken sunshine. A westerly wind made the seas rougher than the day before. We saw the tops of the islands and mountains clearly, and the Trench was soon out of view behind us. We followed the coast north to the sacred Skeena and reached its mouth by midday. There we stopped to rest while we ate our lunch by the great berry patches on the south side.

Everyone was happy that we had reached the Skeena. This meant we were half-way to the Nass. The Skeena was wider than any river I had ever seen. It flowed fast and brown, carrying branches and chunks of ice from further upstream. The Elders discussed the best strategy to cross it and then we set off again. Pieces of ice scraped along the sides of our canoes as we pointed our bows against the current. We paddled hard so that it would not take us too far off course, but it was strong and carried us out to sea like feathers on the wind. This was tiring and it added a great distance to our route.

We reached the far shore and headed for the shelter of a narrow passage behind a large island. It was clogged with ice, so we returned to the open water beyond the island. There we met a strong sea wind from the northwest and much bigger waves. I was not used to the violence of the open sea. I was afraid, but I was an Elder now and could not show my fear. Amapaas gave a cry as if he was charging into battle and pulled hard on his paddle. The others followed his lead.

We paddled hard in the open sea for three hours before Neeshlak lead us into a sheltered inlet. We were all thankful to be out of the wind and we slowed our strokes to give our arms a rest. I thought maybe we would stop there but we continued on until the inlet became a large bay. It was calm and beautiful. The others who had been here before were excited and began to shout. I saw the totems of a large village coming into view on the east shore. "Gitwilgiots!" Gwashasip shouted to me.

I was excited, for I had heard travelers mention its name many times. It was the first village I had seen other than Gitka'ata. We moved past the long row of painted houses along the beach. Smoke rose from only a couple of the houses and there were few canoes on the shore. Some young children and old men came to the water's edge to wave to us. The rest of Gitwilgiots had already left for the Nass. We waved back but did not stop, for the day was getting late. The sun already shone gold on the mountains behind the village.

We continued deeper into the bay. When we reached the north side we entered a narrow passage that twisted around rocky points and islands. On the beaches around us I saw house posts and totems of many abandoned settlements. I thought how strange it was that so many villages would be built so close together. Suddenly I realized where we were. I shouted for joy and the others in the canoes around me laughed. This was Metlakatla!

Tsangook had been here several times. He described to me what I saw. "Every village on the Skeena has a winter camp here," he shouted. He pointed to the camps on the island to our left as we passed them. "Ginaksangits, Gitlans, Gitsacatl." He pointed to another camp on a small island in the bay. "Gitsees!" He pointed to the camps of Gitpakslawts and Gitando on the north shore of the bay.

We set up our tents on the north shore at the Gitando camp near the centre of Metlakatla. From here we could see most of the other camps. They looked like they had not been used for several years. Still, the Spirits of the ancestors of all Tsimshian people surrounded us. They had celebrated here for more than fifty generations. Countless dances and stories had been performed here. I tried to imagine how it would look to have all the camps full and celebrations happening all around. How exciting it would be to be able to visit different villages and watch their dances!

Miyana and I wanted to visit other camps where we had seen the smoke from other fires, but this had been our hardest day and the others wanted only to rest. "Save your strength. Tomorrow will be even longer," Amapaas told us.

After our dinner was over and the light was gone from the sky, an old man came to visit our fire. He brought with him two of his grandchildren who were too young to fish on the Nass. They had come from the Gitlan camp not far away. Our Elders came forward to greet him and listen to his news.

He had brought his grandchildren to see the sacred lands. The rest of their village had continued to their fishing camp on the Nass and they would wait here one moon for their return. He told us many fishing parties from other villages had passed through Metlakatla in recent days. Tsi-basaa's people from Kitkatla had camped nearby the night before but he had not yet seen the Natawalps and the others from Klemtu.

The old man's eyes sparkled as he spoke. I could tell by the way he spoke that he enjoyed our company. I was eager to hear about the ceremonies.

"Were you here to see the winter ceremonies this year?" I asked him.

He shook his head. "No, there have been no ceremonies here for a few years. The villages of the Skeena met here many years ago so our people could all be together, but people of many villages have moved to Fort Simpson. They are together there, and they don't want to come to Metlakatla anymore."

"Do all the villages meet in Fort Simpson to celebrate? Are the ceremonies there as great as they were in Metlakatla?"

"No," he shook his head again. The sparkle left his eyes. "There is no place where all our people meet anymore. The people who do not live in Fort Simpson do not like to celebrate with those who do. They have changed too much. Their feasts and dances are not sacred anymore."

I did not understand. "Why don't the villages of the Skeena come to Metlakatla?"

"For a few years we tried to come together as we had before but some men who had moved from our own villages were angry that we did not celebrate with them at Fort Simpson. They came to threaten us and disrupt our ceremonies. Even those from Fort Simpson who were not angry with us brought with them White men's poisons in their hearts and minds. The joy and respect we once shared was ruined by fear and heartbreak so we stopped returning. Now the villages celebrate their winter ceremonies alone."

I wanted to know how this could be, how something so sacred and important could be abandoned so easily. I asked how White men had poisoned their hearts and minds. But the old man's face had grown tired. He begged me not to listen to the mutterings of an unhappy old man. He excused himself and returned to his camp with his grandchildren.

His words troubled me long after he had gone. Were these terrible things true for everyone, or were they just his fears and resentments? He did not seem either fearful or bitter to me. There must be some truth in his words, for the camps around us looked as though they had not been used for a long time.

The next morning, before the sky was fully light, we readied ourselves for our last day of travel to the Nass. The bay was more calm and beautiful than the night before. I felt sad that we too were abandoning it. I decided that it was the most beautiful place I had ever seen and I longed to remain behind. I made a secret promise to myself to return, not knowing that someday I would be a homeless prisoner here, wishing I had somewhere else to go.

The narrow passage where we had camped led back to the open sea. We turned north again. Distant islands in the west that basked in the morning sun offered us little protection from the wind. Large waves still battered our canoes and broke on the rocks along the shore, but the westerly crosswind was easier to manage than the headwind the day before.

We reached Fort Simpson before midday. It was much larger than I had imagined. Gitka'ata had fourteen longhouses and I had been told that Kitkatla had more than twenty, but here there were more than we could count. It was not a collection of scattered camps like Metlakatla. The houses were crowded close together with no trees around them. I saw nothing separating different villages. The houses covered a long point of land that stuck out into the bay. The end of the point was rocky and had few houses. At that moment it was severed from the rest of the villages by the high tide. As we followed the beach we saw few canoes. Most of the people here too had already left for the Nass.

The White fort sat on the highest point of land in the centre of the town. There were several men in strange clothing walking outside the fort. These were the White men I had heard about but had never seen before. We waved to them but they did not respond. I wondered why they were still here, why they had not left for the Nass too. Perhaps they did not know where our people had gone, but it was strange that no one had told them.

The White men had built a long wooden platform out over the water at the shore in front of the fort. There was a strange looking boat tied to the platform. It was too short to carry much and too wide to be fast. I wondered why they had built the platform. Surely they must know the posts that held it up would rot in the water. Why didn't they pull their boat onto the sand above the high tide? There it would be secure and easier to clean and the waves could not throw it against the posts and damage it.

A path led from the platform up to the White fort. The fort was the widest and tallest house in Fort Simpson, and much larger than my father's house in Gitka'ata. A great many people must live inside, I thought. A house this large could have enough sleeping chambers for half a village.

But it was a very strange looking house. The walls were the height of four men and they were made of logs that had pointed tops. They had no paintings on the outside like a Tsimshian house, but there was a large gate painted red with a white trim. There were small rooms on top of the walls at either corner facing the water. In each room there were metal logs that pointed out to the water. Gwashasip told me these were weapons the Whites used to defend the fort. They could shoot like Tsi-basaa's rifle, only much farther. I thought he must be wrong, for no man could lift such a heavy rifle.

We glided slowly past the fort and beyond the town. There was no time to visit if we hoped to reach the Nass by nightfall. My father's canoe paddled harder and soon it was far ahead of us. He wanted us to stop looking at the fort and move faster. He led us around a point of land to a beach out of view of Fort Simpson. Here we rested and had a small meal. He forbade us to talk about the White fort while we ate. He knew some men were disappointed that we had not stopped but he ignored them.

Our rest was short and it was the last one we had that day. Neeshlak told us it would take all afternoon to reach the mouth of the Nass and until nightfall to find our camp. To make us work harder he promised that we would visit the trading post on the way home if we reached our camp while there was still light in the sky.

We reached another point of land and turned into a wide canyon that led northeast. It was even wider than the great canyon by Gitka'ata and it stretched deeper into the mountains than we could see. The strong westerly winds were now at our backs, making our journey easier. We followed the canyon deeper and deeper into the mountains until the valley narrowed and seemed to break into two. One valley continued in the same direction, but it was much narrower. I wondered where it would lead. Later Hahkwah told me it would take another full day to reach the end of that canyon, but that was not our route.

The other valley led south and east. The bay at its entrance was the mouth of the sacred Nass River. What a thrill it was to see it! Its mouth seemed even wider than the Skeena's and its valley much more beautiful, for it was set in the heart of the mountains. We were still far from our camp. We paddled through the bay for a long time, passing the fishing camps of other Tsimshian, Nishga, Tlingit, Haida and Kwakiutl villages who had arrived before us. Their many fires shone brightly like evening stars as the light faded.

The bay narrowed as we approached our camp and I saw where the Nass entered the bay. It was still a big river, but not as large as the Skeena after all. Chunks of ice bumped along our canoes as we felt its current for the first time.

Our camp was on the south shore at the end of the bay. Like the other villages, we returned to the same camp every year, but it was new to me. I was filled with excitement, for I had waited my whole life to see it. I was also pleased that we had reached our camp before dark.

We hurried to set up the camp. The men built the fires and set up our tents while the women prepared the evening meal. There were still racks and fire pits to build and cauldrons to set up and fill with water, but that work had to wait until daylight. We rested around the fire while we ate. We listened to stories of past trips and discussed what this trip would bring. The omens said that this would be the best catch in many years.

The others retired early to their tents, but I was too excited to sleep. I sat quietly watching the fire with Klashwaht, the young slave who tended it. The night sky was almost clear. The moon and stars lit up the snowfields on the distant mountain peaks. Klashwaht poked at the embers with a long stick. The flames made loud cracking sounds and sparks floated up towards Heaven, some as high as the tops of the trees. Klashwaht stared at the fire as if it was his private lover. His beautiful face never glanced up at me.

We said nothing as we listened to the distant voices from other camps around us. The foreign sounds of Tlingit words came from the camp to the west of us. On the other side was a Nishga camp. I heard the laughing voices of youths playing around their fire. I understood some words of their strange Tsimshian dialect.

My feelings of peace changed to loneliness as I listened to their laughter. I wanted to join them, for it was clear that Klashwaht preferred to be left alone. But I thought perhaps that was not a good idea. I might not understand their words and I was afraid they might laugh at mine. I could not defend my honour against so many, so I sat and listened to them from a distance. Gradually, clouds filled the night sky. The fire hissed angrily at the first drops of rain. Klashwaht put on his rain hat and cape and crouched closer to the fire. I retired to my tent.

Our camp was awake by daybreak. The women prepared breakfast while the men assembled their fishing poles and nets. Other men dug a shallow pit to store the fish. Women gathered firewood and the slaves gathered large stones. They would stay on shore to work in the camp while men who belonged to Clans fished from the canoes. When the fishing equipment was ready the Clans waited on the shore for the arrival of the oolichon.

In those years, before White men brought their fishing boats and built their canneries, the seas were thick with fish. The arrival of the oolichon was the greatest miracle of Heaven and a wonderful sight to behold. As we waited beside our canoes, the first sign of their approach appeared. It was a thick cloud floating low above the water. I watched in amazement as it slowly drifted against the wind, up the canyon and into the mouth of the bay. Cries echoed up the valley from camp to camp to announce that the oolichon had arrived. Gwashasip patted my shoulder. We jumped into my canoe and paddled to a position he had chosen where the water was not too shallow and there was not much current. There we stood waiting with our nets in our hands. I could see men standing in many hundreds of canoes scattered across the bay to the farthest distance, a sight that I would never forget.

The cloud drew nearer and nearer. The screams of a million sea birds grew slowly, then louder and louder until we could not hear our own words. My heart pounded as they came towards us like a winter blizzard. Their wings darkened the sky as they surrounded us. Suddenly the waters around us churned with movement. The oolichon brushed against the canoe in such numbers that it began to move. I was laughing like a child, delighted and frightened at the same time.

Some men lifted nets full of fish out of the water before their canoes stopped rocking. I was slow and clumsy, for this was my first time using a fishing pole. I watched Gwashasip. He had only fished here for the past two years so he was not much better. Amapaas and Doolyaks were next to us. They filled their canoe much faster than we could. I was embarrassed. Most of the canoes around us left with full catches before ours was half full.

A canoe from the Nishga camp returned for its second load. Two youths our age smiled at us and nodded. We smiled back but I was ashamed. They would not want to meet me after seeing our small catch. I felt more like a child than an Elder. I made up my mind to fill our boat before they completed their second load. I worked harder and faster but Gwashasip complained that I was rocking the boat. That only made us look more awkward. The two youths smiled when they heard his complaint and I wished that I had stayed on the shore.

Finally we filled our canoe and returned to the camp. Tsangook and others met us and helped us carry our fish to the fire pit. The racks were ready for drying the fish. Oolichon had so much oil they would serve as candles once they were dried. We took the rest to the storage pit beside the big kettles where they would be boiled for their oil. The old women and slaves guarded the pits with branches and poles to keep the hungry sea birds away. It was hard to tell which of them made more noise and they gave us much to laugh about.

After our midday meal we returned for a second load. Already the thin blue smoke of many campfires floated over the bay. We steered our canoe carefully between the other boats until we reached the place we had been before.

The two Nishga youths had also returned to their same position. I looked at them closely and saw that they were brothers. They must have fished together before because they moved so smoothly without rocking their canoe. They lifted their nets with ease and emptied them skillfully into the boat. Each time they emptied their nets they repeated the same words but I could not hear what they were saying.

"Gwashasip, what are they doing?" I whispered loudly.

"They are showing their respect to the oolichon. They are thanking them for surrendering their lives to us so that we may live."

"Why aren't you thanking them?"

"I am. I say my prayers quietly. I thought you were saying your thanks, too. You are always so quiet when you pray." He smiled at me.

From that moment I thanked the oolichon each time I lifted my net. I said my thanks out loud so that the Nishga brothers could hear me. The younger brother smiled at me and nodded. He had such a beautiful smile that I had to smile back. I began to watch him closely as we fished. He was little taller than me and perhaps a bit heavier. He concentrated deeply as he moved his fishing pole with skill and grace. I copied his movements as best as I could, but his thanks still came more often than mine.

The midday sun broke through the clouds and warmed the air. The younger Nishga removed his rain cloak and continued fishing with his upper body naked. I paused to watch him. His long black hair was shining with sweat and it clung to the wetness of his skin. He stopped to wipe his face and shake his hair free from his back and shoulders. He pushed his fingers through his hair and stretched his strong arms up to the sky like an offering.

He looked around and caught me staring at him. He looked surprised, and then another beautiful smile flashed across his face. I looked away quickly and resumed my fishing. Gwashasip had seen me staring at him too. He wore a big smile and I felt my own face grow hot with embarrassment. I dared not look at the Nishga boy again until our canoe was almost full. He stopped to watch us as we left and he smiled when he caught my eye.

I was both confused and excited. I wanted to meet him, to be his friend, but I did not know how to meet him or what to say. I did not want to look like a fool. At least Gwashasip said nothing to embarrass me further that day. For that I secretly thanked him.

There was still time to make another trip after we emptied the canoe but there was much help needed around the camp. I was pleased to do something else. I had felt enough embarrassment for one day. I chopped wood for the fires and helped Klash-waht build a new pit for the drying racks. Then we carried hot embers from the fires to fill the pit.

We were all hungry and tired that first evening. We ate around the fire and then sang songs and told stories after the food and dishes were gone. Six youths from the Nishga camp came to visit with us. I recognized the handsome Nishga youth and his brother and my shyness returned. We exchanged greetings and we offered them some food. They had eaten already but they accepted small amounts to honour our kindness. Then they squatted around our fire smiling at us nervously. We smiled back. For a couple minutes no one said a word.

"You are Nishga?" Amapaas was the first to speak.

"Yes," they nodded eagerly. They were pleased a conversation had started.

"From Skeena?" the older brother asked of us. I heard his thick Nishga accent.

"No, we are from Gitka'ata." They nodded and looked at each other to see if anyone knew where that was. "It is two days south of the Skeena," Amapaas explained. They nodded and grunted their approval that we had made such a long journey.

"Is your village on the Nass?" Doolyaks asked. They nodded and grunted again. "How far?" he pointed to the mouth of the river.

"Half day," answered another youth. Everyone nodded. They were pleased with the conversation so far.

"You want to see our camp?" Amapaas asked. They stood in anticipation. Doolyaks and Amapaas led them to where the oolichon were drying on the racks. Klash-waht was tending the fire again. He rose when he saw us coming. He was not happy to have his privacy invaded, but he could not complain, for he was a slave. Amapaas showed them the pit by the kettles that held our first day's catch. They nodded their approval, though we suspected their pit was no different and their catch was no smaller.

I walked behind the others, listening to their conversation but not saying anything. I saw the younger Nishga brother looking at me. He flashed a welcoming smile and nodded. I smiled back. He came over and stood beside me though he said nothing. He was as shy as I was. The others began to talk in small groups. One of the Nishga was showing others a knife he had purchased at Fort Simpson. The younger Nishga brother and I followed the others back to the fire and he sat beside me.

"What is your name?" I asked him first.

"Tamlahk," he answered. His handsome face was beaming proudly. "Your name?"

"Gugweelaks."

"Gugweelaks," he repeated carefully. I nodded.

We talked freely, asking many questions back and forth. It took a while to understand some of his Nishga words but we were both eager to know each other better. I told him it was my first year fishing for oolichon. He said I was very good for my first year. He was a year older than me, but he had helped at the fishing camp for six years. He had been fishing with his brothers for four years. He was the youngest of three brothers, just as I was. The brother he was fishing with was Selwehk. His father was an Elder of the Wolf Clan in his village. Like his mother he was a member of the Frog Clan, a Clan that I had not heard of. He was in training with his uncle to be an Elder. He was impressed that I was already an Elder at such a young age so I told him I was a Cannibal Dancer too.

"You're a Cannibal Dancer? Really?" His eyes sparkled with interest. He started to ask me more questions.

"Tamlahk!" Selwehk called to him. The other Nishga youths were ready to leave. "We should go. It is late. You can talk more tomorrow."

"Can I come tomorrow, Gugweelaks?" he asked me.

"Yes! I will see you tomorrow, Tamlahk. Good night!" He followed the others to the trail at the edge of our camp. He turned to smile at me before disappearing into the bushes.

I smiled to myself as I stared at the fire. I was already thinking about my next meeting with Tamlahk. I saw Gwashasip grinning at me from the other side of the fire. "What?" I asked him. He just laughed and shook his head. I laughed too, even though he had read my thoughts. The world was too wonderful to be angry about that. I wished him a good night and went to my tent. I was not tired, but I wanted to dream about Tamlahk alone.

When I closed my eyes I saw Tamlahk's smile and he visited my dreams all of that night. He smiled at me as I watched him fish and as we sat beside a fire talking. He was standing very close and he reached out for my hand. I woke in the morning with his smile still glowing in my heart. I ate my morning meal quickly so that we could get out on the bay early. Gwashasip suggested that we try a different location. He laughed when he saw my worried face and then I knew he was joking. "Don't worry," he teased me, "we will find him.".

Tamlahk and Selwehk arrived shortly after we did. Tamlahk called to me as they approached. They stopped their canoe close to mine and we prepared our fishing poles. We watched each other as we worked. He slowed his pace to match mine instead of his brother's. I copied his movements as closely as I could. Selwehk and Gwashasip shook their heads and laughed at us. But Tamlahk was teaching me so they matched their pace to ours. Tamlahk and Selwehk still filled their canoe before we did but we were not far behind them. We each caught three loads that day and I was proud of my improvement.

Tamlahk came to visit me after dinner. He invited several of us to visit his camp. It was much the same as ours. Our camps were so close that I stayed behind when the others returned to our camp. Tamlahk wanted to know what it was like to be a Cannibal Dancer. The people of the Nass did not have secret Hamatsa societies but they had heard about ours. I told him how the Cannibal Spirits had abducted me and carried into the woods. I told him about Sonoqua and about my performance when I returned from the forest. His eyes were wide with admiration.

I started to tell him about my potlatch when a man called his name. The voice came from one of the tents. He placed his fingertips on my lips to silence me. He looked behind him, but he did not answer. The voice called again. It sounded like the voice of a sick man. "It is my father," he whispered. "I cannot talk now. You must go. I will see you tomorrow." With those words he disappeared into his tent.

I returned to my camp, wondering why he had left so quickly. Our camp was quiet for it was late. Klashwaht was tending the fire. I tried to make conversation but he did not have much to say. He looked at me suspiciously. When he saw I would stay he left to tend the embers in the drying pit. I wondered it Tamlahk would sneak away to talk to me some more. It started to rain again. I listened to the fire hiss for a while, and then I went into my tent.

For the next two weeks, Tamlahk and I spent as much time together as we could. Each day his canoe was next to mine. We even convinced our brothers to trade places so we could fish together in the same canoe. Our people thought this was strange but they did not stop us. Our friendship amused them.

One evening I met Tamlahk's father. He seemed like a friendly man and he certainly did not look ill. Still, something was wrong for Tamlahk was nervous around him. A few days later Tamlahk came to my camp for his usual visit but told me he could not stay. He said his father did not want him to have any more visitors.

"Did I do something wrong?" I asked. "Did I give him a bad impression?"

"No," he said in a low voice. He looked so unhappy.

"Is your father sick?"

"No," he shook his head, "but my father likes whisky." He looked impatient. "I must go now," were his last words before he disappeared into the hole in the bushes.

His answer made no sense to me. I knew only that whisky was a White man's drink. Did Tamlahk need to drink it with him? Perhaps there was a Nishga tradition I did not understand. But surely the drinking would not take long. I did not have the chance to ask him more about it.

I soon forgot this incident, for bigger news took its place. Tamlahk told me his village would be moving to Fort Simpson before the next spring salmon runs. I was excited for him. I told him our camp would visit Fort Simpson on our way home and that it would be my first visit there. I worried that I would not see him again, but now at least I knew where he would be living. From that moment onward the mention of Fort Simpson brought thoughts of Tamlahk to my mind. The more I thought about Tamlahk, the more I wanted to move to Fort Simpson.

NINE

The Nishga camp left two days before ours. Tamlahk and I said our goodbyes. We were sad, but like brave men we tried not to show it. We agreed we would meet again somewhere. I would ask for him in Fort Simpson when we visited the trading post next year. I might not find him there, but we knew we would meet again next year at the oolichon camp for certain.

The sadness of our parting was softened by the excitement of our coming visit to the trading post at Fort Simpson. The last two days after he left passed quickly, for so much work was needed to close the camp and prepare for our journey home. We stored the dried oolichon in large cedar baskets and the oolichon oil in wooden chests. Our catch was large as the omens had predicted, and our load was heavy. The trip home would take one day longer.

With our cargo it took us a full day's journey to reach Fort Simpson. When we left the bay and entered the canyon the wind was in our faces. It slowed our progress. We stayed close to the south shore where the waves were smaller. We found a sheltered passage behind a large island for part of the route but we were still exhausted by end of the day. We made camp on an island north of Fort Simpson. From there we could see the lights of their fires in the distance and that filled my tired body with excitement.

The next morning we left the slaves to guard our camp and we went to visit the trading post at Fort Simpson. Neeshlak let Miyana come with me. We were both excited, but she was especially happy to escape Hoshieka's watchful eyes. It was Hoshieka's duty to protect her from the advances of young men, which was not easy since Miyana was becoming a beautiful young woman. She hated losing her freedom so she made Hoshieka's job as difficult as possible. She tried to sneak away to flirt with handsome youths whenever she could. Hoshieka grew wise to Miyana's tricks and never let her out of her sight. She even shared Miyana's tent at the fishing camp. But that morning they were both happy to have a rest from each other.

We arrived at the gates of the fort while the morning was still young. The trading post was not open yet. Those of us who had brought furs to trade for White goods sat by the gates and waited. Miyana and I walked around the outside. A White man stood guard in one of the corner lookouts. I did not know then that it was a guard room. I thought perhaps he lived there. I saw him looking down at me so I waved. He turned away without smiling or waving back. I could make no sense of these White men.

Miyana led me between the houses around the fort to look at their painted fronts. There were many houses in all directions. She wanted to count them. We ran to the far end of the town near the forest and then walked back past the fort to the end of the point. There were more than a hundred houses. Several more were still being built.

Smoke was rising from most of the houses and people were entering and leaving. Children played outside and dogs ran by in small groups. Women washed clothes and prepared food outdoors for it was a sunny day. Many people greeted us and asked us where we were from. Most were from the Skeena or the Nass, though there were even some Tlingit and Haida. We were excited to see so many different people living together.

"Think how many languages we could learn if we lived here!" I said.

"Did you learn much Nishga from Tamlahk?" Miyana asked.

"A little. He speaks better Tsimshian than I speak Nishga. They're not that different really, when you get used to it. He knows some Chinook, too."

"I think it's more important to learn Chinook. Everyone speaks Chinook to do trading," she said. "Will you miss Tamlahk?" She studied my face for my reaction.

"A little," I lied. "His village is moving here after the next full moon."

"He's very handsome, isn't he?"

I nodded but didn't say anything. I did not want to think about that too much.

"I wonder where they will build their houses. Maybe they'll have to build them near the point," she pointed to the empty beaches at the end of the point. I tried to imagine his life here. He would make many new friends at Fort Simpson. Perhaps he would like them more than me. I began to feel sad.

"Come on, smile!" She kissed me on my cheek.

"What are you doing?" I blushed and wiped my cheek.

"I am just trying to cheer you up. Besides, you are the only boy I am allowed to kiss. I have to get some practice before Hoshieka is too old to catch me," she teased me with a smile.

"You are already old enough to outrun Hoshieka."

"I'm old enough to outrun you, too!" With that she pushed me away and raced down the beach in the direction of the fort. I chased after her and caught her just before we reached the gates. We were laughing and panting. Several adults from our camp were waiting outside the gates of the fort and they laughed with us.

"Where have you been?" Tsangook asked. "I have been waiting here for you half the morning. We don't have much more time!"

"We were looking at all the houses. Is the fort open yet?" I asked.

"Yes, it has been open for a while but the Whites only let five people in at a time."

"But it's huge! They could let all of us inside and still have lots of room!" Miyana complained.

"They want to watch us so that we don't steal anything. There is only one group in front of us. It will soon be our turn."

Tsangook was right. We did not wait long. I expected the big gates to open and reveal the inside of a great house, but instead a small door in the gate opened that was only wide enough for one person. Five men from our village walked out through the gate with their purchases which they were eager to show us. Jaleek had a new knife and Hahkwah was wearing a new pair of gloves. Our Shaman, Tooklan, had a small book with coloured pictures in it. We examined them until it was our turn to go inside.

Miyana and I followed Tsangook through the door. It did not look at all like I thought it would. The first thing I saw was the sky. There were walls but no roof. It was not one large house but an open courtyard with several houses around it. There were no paintings on the walls, but the houses were painted white with a red trim. Tsangook had been here before. He pointed to the largest house where he said the Whites lived. Then he showed us the trading post and a building where they stored the furs. There was also a room where the Whites made things out of metal. I saw stairs that led up to the guard house and a walkway that followed the top of the walls.

A White man with a rifle watched us from the guard house as we crossed the court-yard to the store.

The trading post was magical. There was a small glass window that let us see into the store. I had never seen glass before. I saw a White man behind a counter inside the store. He watched us as we climbed the steps to the door. The door was made of wood with a metal latch. Tsangook pushed down on the latch to open it. It swung open on hinges. Why didn't we make doors like these, I was thinking. I wanted to study it to see how it worked but Tsangook said the Whites would get angry if we kept it open.

The inside of the store was even more fascinating than the door. White light shone from the outside through the window and I could see the courtyard beyond. I examined it with delight. The glass felt cool to touch but no air came through with the light.

There was so much to look at inside. Oil lanterns hung from the ceiling and light-ed the rest of the store. They were so different from our lamps. Shelves covered the walls from the floor to high above my head. They were filled with countless treasures. Some had bottles and tins of different foods. They had coloured packages with draw-ings and White men's letterings on the outside. I was careful not to break them when I picked them up. I could not see what was inside or how to open them.

My eyes followed the shelves up to the ceiling. Above my head there was more glass. At first I thought it was a window into another room above us but everything was tilted on a slant. When I moved my head to see more I realized that it was not another room but a window that magically looked back at me. This magic astounded me. I wanted to climb up and touch it but in the glass I saw the White man at the back of the store watching me closely. He did not look happy so I moved away.

The next shelves were filled with folded blankets and clothing. They were made of fabrics that were new to me. Some had parts made of metal or bone that I had never seen before. I wondered how these were worn. I touched them to feel the material but I didn't open them up.

The White man who had been watching walked over to me. He looked at me sus-piciously. I smiled at him and nodded. He nodded back. I had never seen a White man this close. He was as fascinating as the products on the shelves. His eyes were blue. His skin was pale as a ghost's and it was covered with many small brown spots. He was as hairy as a Sasquatch. His thick beard was a strange orange colour. A thick bunch of chest hair stuck out above his shirt like orange moss. I wanted to reach out and touch it, but I was not sure if that would upset him.

He wore strange clothing that I saw stacked on the shelves. I looked at the folded cloth and then at the shirt he was wearing. I pointed to one of the flat, round pieces of bone on a folded shirt and then to one on his undershirt.

"Button," he named it for me, smiling a big grin at my ignorance. He opened it to show me how it worked. Orange moss flowed out from beneath it. I reached up slowly to touch the button and saw how it fit through a hole on the opposite side. He smiled and held still for my inspection. I unbuttoned a second button and more orange moss sprang out. It brushed my fingers as I pushed the button into the hole. It was soft and fine and it made my tsootz swell.

I wanted to keep going, to see how much orange hair there was and to feel it pass through my fingers, but I knew I should not. I fastened the button closed again. "Button", I repeated, to hide my embarrassment. That was the first English word I learned.

He found my curiosity amusing. He said something to the other White men in his foreign tongue and they laughed. I knew they were laughing at me. I felt offended but I pretended not to mind. Tsangook and Miyana had not noticed. They were inspecting rolls of coloured fabric and marveling over its texture. I moved along to look at other wonders.

Beyond the clothing, there were shelves of different footwear made of animal hides. They had hard bottoms and were laced together with strange cording. There were other shelves of black metal pans, pots and kettles for cooking. They had no carvings but they were shiny and smooth. How useful they looked! Other shelves and racks were filled with metal tools and knives. The White man, who still followed me, picked up a pair of scissors and showed me how they cut through a piece of cloth. I was delighted. Then he showed me a small coloured stick. When he struck it, it burst into flame. He laughed at my worried expression.

Then he lit a larger stick that had a string through its centre. It burned slowly with a flame smaller than my thumb. I called to Tsangook to look at it and he smiled back at me. He and Miyana were now looking at books and writing tools. Another man who was working there came over to watch. In Tsimshian, he told me that this was a "candle". His face was both Tsimshian and White. He asked where we were from and I told him. I introduced myself but he did not seem interested. He did not tell me his name.

I asked him about the rifles hanging at the back of the store. He told me the longer ones were better. He explained I needed a stack of mink furs as high as the length of the rifle to purchase one. That price was high but I still wanted one. I asked if I could hold one but he told me I must have the skins to buy it first.

Then I asked about the piles of sacks on the floor in the centre of the room. He told me they were full of rice, beans and other foods that were dried, like we dried our salmon or seaweed. I had many other questions but he grew impatient. He knew we had no furs to trade so he told us to leave so others would have time to buy things.

We met Doolyaks on our way back from Fort Simpson. He had been sent to tell us to return to the camp. We had to leave immediately if we wanted to reach Metlakatla before dark. Those who had stayed behind were already packing the canoes when we arrived. I could not stop talking about the White store. It was hard to hold the joy inside.

◇◇◇◇◇◇◇◇◇◇◇◇◇◇◇◇

The trip to Metlakatla was difficult. The wind blew hard and the waves grew higher as we headed south. We paddled with all our strength to cross the open water, but we reached the sheltered waters of Metlakatla before nightfall. Our village was not alone now. Several camps from the Skeena were resting there. Their fires flickered on the beaches around us. They did not seem so interesting now that I had seen so many houses and the trading post at Fort Simpson. The memory of things I saw inside of the store still filled my thoughts.

A storm passed by us to the north during the night. The wind was still high when we left the harbour. By this time the ice was gone from the passage behind the island north of the Skeena so we used it to escape the wind. Beyond the passage we entered the current of the great river. This time we let it carry us far from the shore as we traveled south. It pushed us towards the islands north of Tsamsem's Trench. There we camped at the same site where we had rested on the way north. On the fourth day the waters were calm and we made good progress. We made it most of the way though the Trench.

On the last day a large storm approached us from the north. The Elders decided that we could not wait two days for the storm to pass as our food supplies were low. We paddled hard to go as far as we could. A strong wind pushed us from behind until we reached the end of the Trench and the entrance to the great canyon that led north to Gitka'ata. But when we turned into the canyon the north wind turned against us.

We stayed close to the steep walls on the east side of the canyon where we found some shelter from the wind. We did not rest for lunch for the storm was growing worse. We made steady progress until late afternoon when we could see the entrance to our bay on the west side of the canyon.

But here our situation was dangerous. The wind had grown worse as the afternoon passed and it was raining hard. We would have found a place to camp for the night on the west side but the steep cliffs of the eastern side offered us no shelter. We had to cross the rough waters of the canyon to make it to the safety of our village.

The wind and rain hit hard in our faces as we pulled away from the protection of the cliffs. It was frightening, for the rain made it hard to see the other canoes. The waves climbed high and broke over the sides of our boats. Our heavy cargo helped to steady us but our feet were underwater in the bottom of the canoe.

We all reached our bay safely, though we were tired and shaken. The wind was still high but the waves were not breaking over the sides anymore. Gitka'ata was very close. Some of those who waited for us in the village had seen us coming. They stood on the beach in the rain, waving to us as we approached.

We felt safer so close to our homes, but we did not see the hidden danger. The large swells lifted us high and dropped us low again. Waves broke over the sandbars exposed by the low tide. As we neared the shore the bottom of my canoe caught the sandbar and it tipped over, throwing us and our cargo into the cold water. My feet found the sandbar but the waves pushed me away again. I struggled to the canoe. Soon the others came to help me push it to the beach. Our storage chests had broken open and much of the oolichon oil was lost.

Ten canoes spilled their cargo in the waters of our bay that night. No one had drowned or was badly hurt, but the lost oolichon weighed heavy in our thoughts. It was a bad omen for the coming year. The rain and wind pounded the roofs of our houses for three days as we listened to our thoughts in silence. The warmth of our fires did little to chase away our worries.

No one was more troubled than my father. He said little but he was restless. I knew he blamed himself for the accident, though he did not admit that to anyone. He was thinking he should have known that it would be too rough to land safely. He should have had us find shelter near the entrance of the canyon. We could have lived on oolichon for two days if the other food supplies ran out. It would have been uncomfortable in such a storm but at least we would still have our oolichon.

Our future problems bothered him more than the lost oil. The next year would be difficult without enough oolichon and much of our fishing gear was lost at the start of the fishing season. He was disheartened like the rest of the village, but he knew if he could not inspire them with hope somehow, many would be angry with his leadership. He let the fishing party rest for a day while the storm blew.

The next evening Neeshlak called a meeting of the Elders of the four Clans. The growl of the storm had not let up and it made everyone uneasy. It would be a difficult meeting, but he knew he could not wait another day. He could not let himself appear cowardly or discouraged.

Tooklan sprinkled eagle down over our heads to bring us peace. Neeshlak spoke first before a discussion started. He told us he knew the anger and disappointment in our hearts. He had surveyed each house. We had lost one third of the oil and half of our dried oolichon. He said the Spirits were also angry and needed to be soothed. Perhaps our spilled catch would help to pacify them. If this is what they wanted, we would share our wealth with them. He ordered our slaves to bring him six carved serving bowls filled with dried oolichon. Then he commanded Tooklan to bless them and throw the bowls into the fire.

We watched with dismay as more of our precious oolichon was destroyed. Neeshlak told us that that the Spirits would protect us from starvation if we appeased them first. He reminded us of the story of our first Chief who found Gitka'ata, who the Spirits blessed with abundance after he sacrificed his last food for them.

But he warned us we must not wait like beggars for their help. We must work hard to make more fishing nets before the first salmon run. We must hunt and fish more than other years so that we would have enough to trade with other villages for oolichon oil. It would be a difficult year but we would survive. His words reassured some of the Elders but others were restless to speak.

Jaleek spoke first. "Neeshlak, you mean well and you have tried your best. We have made several offerings to the Spirits this winter but still they have turned against us. What if these offerings do not satisfy them? Last spring we lost Gugweelaks and some of us almost lost our lives two nights ago. This could happen again and we cannot afford this. The route north has been cursed. We suffer in famine and loss while those at Fort Simpson prosper. Perhaps it is time for us to move."

"Must we speak of this every time something bad happens? We have endured these troubles before without abandoning our traditional lands," Neeshlak answered.

"There is much good in living in Fort Simpson," Hahkwah added. "We would have many foods and tools that we see Tsimshians using there. They are learning new things that we cannot learn here. If we lived there we could buy cloths and dried foods that would save us labour. We could buy guns to make our hunting much easier. The tribes there are growing wealthy while we have only poverty and famine."

This brought a response from Silgitook. "I am too old to move to a new home. My soul wishes to spend the last of my days here. I do not think it would be a good move for the rest of you either. Tsi-basaa will claim our lands. We will not be able to return, not even to die. And life will not be easy at Fort Simpson. There is not much good land left to build on. We will need many weeks to build our houses before the cold weather returns. We will need a potlatch for each new house. And there will not be enough time for our hunting. We will not have enough meat or the furs we need to buy White goods. How can we afford all this and still have enough for our winter ceremonies?"

The Elders were agitated and many arguments started. Neeshlak called for quiet. He reminded them that Tooklan had spread eagle down. He called for each Elder to speak his mind if he wanted to stay or move to Fort Simpson. There were more who wanted to stay than leave. Neeshlak said that those who wanted to leave could do so, but they would forfeit their share of what remained of the oolichon. Some were not pleased but most of the Elders felt this was fair. No one chose to move to Fort Simpson.

The Elders agreed to Neeshlak's plan. We would conserve our supplies and trade for more oolichon as soon as we could. The next day the storm had passed. The villagers searched the beaches for fishing equipment that had washed ashore. We repaired what we found and made new nets and poles too.

The move was not discussed again that spring. We kept busy fishing and hunting so we would have enough to trade. The Spirits seemed to be pleased with us. The leaves and flowers returned with the sunshine and we were blessed with good success. Our fears of famine faded and our joy returned.

The spring breezes also brought love. Three marriages were announced for the next winter ceremonies. One couple was Doolyaks and his promised wife Yuwahksa, the daughter of a Raven Elder. Their marriage had been arranged many years before but still the announcement excited the village. Doolyaks was the heir of the Chief of the Wolf Clan which required a large potlatch, and both he and Yuwahksa had beauty enough to make our hearts want to sing.

Their marriage was no surprise but the love for Yuwahksa I saw in Doolyaks' eyes shocked me. He had hidden his affections for her before, but after the announcement his joy shone for everyone to see. If I had loved him better I would have been pleased to see his happiness, but the love in his eyes did not shine for me. I felt only the strange, sad pain as treacherous jealousy chewed at my heart.

It was difficult to sit beside him at the meetings of the Man-Eater Society. I tried to joke and play with him but he talked only about his plans with Yuwahksa. I prayed the pain in my heart was not as visible as the love was in his. I distracted myself with thoughts of Tamlahk and the fun we had fishing together on the Nass. That made it possible to face Doolyaks with a smile, but it made me long for Tamlahk too. I set my hopes on seeing him at the salmon camps on the Skeena.

The Society had three secret meetings that spring to plan new performances in the coming year. We wanted to distract the village from its worries but we would not be ready for a new performance until after the summer salmon runs. We practiced our dances, shared new skills and tricks and discussed what supplies needed to be made or purchased. There was much more to being a Hamatsa than just painting our bodies and biting people.

During the fifth moon the Elders met to discuss possible trades. We preferred not to trade with Kitkatla but we had little choice. They had extra oolichon to trade for our furs and halibut. We sent a trading party and they returned with six chests of oolichon oil and six baskets of dried oolichon. We were much relieved for those supplies could last to the next spring if we were careful. Tsi-basaa was kind to take only a few of our best furs. He said he would wait until after the first salmon run on the Skeena for the rest of our payment. Our Elders agreed to his terms for we needed their oolichon.

I celebrated my sixteenth year at the end of the spring when the days were at their longest. Our village left for our camp on the Skeena on the same day. It was a beautiful day and I was filled with laughter and energy. We left early while the eastern mountains still threw shadows across the canyon. How beautiful the canyon was in the morning sun! We felt its heat as it touched us, but the breeze off the water kept us cool. The streams that flowed from the mountains were swollen with the melting snows. The canyon walls sparkled with many waterfalls.

By midday, we were paddling directly at the sun. The glare on the water stung our eyes, but we soon reached the end of the canyon and turned northwest towards the shadows of Tsamsem's Trench. The sun warmed our backs until it disappeared behind the western mountains. Dogwood trees and berry bushes flowered on both sides of the Trench and the smells of spring were strong on the breeze. Eagles circled on the winds high above us. How different the Trench looked when the weather was fine!

The good weather continued the next day. We passed through the Trench and set up camp in a small bay less than half a day from our camp on the Skeena. I was setting up my tent when I heard the excited voices of others shouting for me to look at something. I saw a white shape floating above the rocky point near the mouth of the bay. It was moving slowly and steadily towards the entrance. I realized it must be behind the rocks but what could it be? It was the height of several men. We dropped our work and ran to the shore.

A few moments later a great wooden sailing ship came into view. It was the first I had ever seen, and what a strange sight it was. There were no oarsmen, no one paddling to make it move. Amapaas explained that it was being pushed by the wind which was caught by its sails—those beautiful white sails! White men walked on the deck. It was so large they did not need to sit down. It glided by the mouth of the bay and disappeared on the far side of the entrance. The tops of the sails floated like a ghost over the rocks and trees for a few moments and then they were gone.

I was so excited that I could not sleep. My mind was filled with many questions. How could men steer such a big ship when the wind only blew in one direction? How fast could it go? How many men could ride in it? What did it look like inside? How did they get the sails up so high? How deep under the water did it go? I asked Tsangook my questions but he did not know the answers. He only knew that they had come a long way, from the other side of the world.

The next morning we packed up our camp and continued on our way. I watched for sailing ships but saw none. At mid-morning we reached the Skeena and by midday we arrived at the site of our salmon camp.

We spent the rest of the day setting up our tents, putting together the drying racks and laying out our nets. Before dinner my father and I canoed to the middle of the river to inspect thousands of spring salmon swimming past us. The omens were good. My father caught the first salmon in a net and brought it back to the camp, where we prepared it carefully. Tooklan performed a special dance to honour the Salmon Spirits, and then announced that the Spirits had told him we would have a big catch this year. He blessed the salmon and my father divided it into small pieces to share with everyone in our camp.

The Spirits kept their promise. The next day the waters of the Skeena were crowded with salmon. The large nets we stretched between our canoes were filled quickly. The men worked together to lift the heavy nets. In a short time our boats were full. We brought our catch to the camp where our slaves gutted the fish and prepared them for drying. The sky was clear and hot. It was perfect weather for drying fish.

I was happy to be at our salmon camp but I was more excited by the thought of seeing Tamlahk. How much fun it would be if we could fish together again! Every day I watched for him but I did not know where to look. The fishing camps on the Skeena were spread much further apart than on the Nass. From our camp we could see other camps on the other side of the river but they were not Nishga. Later I learned that there was a salmon run on the Nass and that the Nishga did not need to travel to the Skeena. My young heart felt the pain of loneliness sharply and I could not hide my disappointment. I even worried that he might not be at the oolichon fishing camp next spring and I would never see him again.

Our work at the salmon camp lasted one moon. The good weather held for most of that time, which allowed our catch to dry fully. We dined on fresh salmon every night and washed it down with fresh water from the mountain stream that fed our camp. We always gathered the bones after each meal and burned them in the fire so the salmon could be reborn. We honoured this tradition the Spirits had taught us so our next harvest would be a good one.

When our fishing was done and all the fish were dried and stored, we took down the camp and loaded our boats. The first night on our way home we camped at a peaceful site near the north end of Tsamsem's Trench. We were all happy for our large catch and the good weather that had blessed our trip. The next two days would not be difficult so we stayed around the campfire until late in the evening singing songs and telling stories.

The second day was calm and mild as we continued down the Trench. We were thinking how much easier and more pleasant this trip was than our return from the oolichon camp on the Nass three months before. But our good fortune was an illusion. As we approached the narrowest section of the Trench at midday, several canoes came out of a small bay where they had been hiding and they blocked our way. As we came nearer we saw they were from Kitkatla. Ts'ibasaa and several of his men stood in their canoes to greet us. Each of them held a rifle. We slowed to a stop, two canoe lengths away. A terrible dread gripped my stomach.

"What are you doing, Ts'ibasaa? Do you mean to prevent us from returning to Gitka'ata?" my father shouted.

"Not at all, Neeshlak. I have come to collect my debts. You have yet to finish paying me for my oolichon." Ts'ibasaa's smile was mean and taunting.

"This is not an honourable way to do business, Ts'ibasaa. This is an outrage! We can leave our men here and I will negotiate with you on the shore if you wish, but I cannot do business like this. We have traded in peace for many generations. We will honour that tradition."

"You will honour me and do as I say," Tsi'ibasaa ordered. "The rules have changed. We have guns and you do not. You are in no position to tell me how we should negotiate. We will take our share of your catch and then you can return to your village unharmed. In the future you will pay me each time your fishing parties use this passage."

Many disbelieving and angry grumbles came from our canoes. Neeshlak waited for silence and then he replied. "Ts'ibasaa, we will honour our debt to you but this is robbery, not trade. We are unarmed and we do not want to battle."

"Neither do I, Neeshlak, but I am prepared for battle and you are not. I have grown tired of your ingratitude. If you do not want to pay your debts willingly, I will take my share by force. Give my men one third of your catch right now or you will return with dead bodies instead of salmon."

"Thief!" screamed Amapaas, as he threw a dried salmon at Ts'ibasaa angrily.

"Son, NO!" Neeshlak shouted, but it was too late. One of Ts'ibasaa's men raised his rifle. A shot exploded loudly and echoed off the mountains on either side of us. We froze in fear, remembering how Ts'ibasaa's rifle had destroyed his walking stick on the beach in front of Gitka'ata. But my brother was still standing. The bullet had blasted though the side of my father's canoe near Amapaas's feet. Water poured in and Amapaas stared at the hole in disbelief.

"The next shot will be through your head if you move again," Ts'ibasaa laughed calmly. "But perhaps your head is harder than wood and the bullet will not hurt you. Would you like to find out?" He chuckled at his own cleverness. No one from our canoes replied. "We will be kind enough to take the salmon from your canoe first, Neeshlak, so it won't sink so quickly."

Ts'ibasaa waved for one of his canoes to move forward along side of my father's. Ts'ibasaa's men aimed their rifles at our boats while two others loaded the fish from my father's canoe into theirs. Then other Kitkatla canoes were loaded in the same way until Ts'ibasaa was satisfied. He had taken more than one-third.

"I will see you after the next fishing camp, Neeshlak. In the meantime, you'd be wise not to anger me." Tsi'ibasaa signaled to his canoes and they left us, heading north up the Trench towards Kitkatla.

Neeshlak ordered our canoes to shore. We emptied his canoe and patched the bullet hole in the side with twigs and sap the best we could before setting out for Gitka'ata. Our shock was soon replaced with anger but no one spoke. This was not the time to discuss what we should do. We respected the anger and humiliation Neeshlak must be feeling. We had to give him time to think.

It took another day and a half to reach Gitka'ata. Neeshlak scarcely said a word. We unloaded the remainder of our catch in silence when we arrived. My father called a meeting of the Elders that evening. Our hearts were filled with many dark thoughts. The Elders were ready for a long and angry discussion but they waited to hear what he would say first. He asked Tooklan to scatter eagle down over our heads as always, then he asked him to prepare an offering to Great Spirit to thank him for our safe arrival home. When this was done he looked at each of our faces carefully before he spoke.

"When we make offerings to the Spirits, they are grateful and they protect us. When we make offerings to Ts'ibasaa, it only feeds his arrogance and his greed. For generations our villages have benefited from peaceful trade. Now this has changed. He does not need our fair trade. He can take what he wants by force. He might rob us whenever he knows we will use Tsamsem's Trench and we cannot defend ourselves. There is nothing I can do to protect my people." He looked at our faces again to see our reactions. These were humiliating words for a Chief to say. We wanted to defend him, but we knew his words were true. Feelings of helplessness filled our hearts.

"Many of you will say we should buy White guns and bullets to protect ourselves. We cannot afford to buy enough. I have seen how many furs the Whites are asking for each rifle. Ts'ibasaa demands that we buy guns from him at a higher price. This will make him rich and keep us poor. We will not be able to buy enough at his prices even for hunting. If we buy guns we still cannot protect ourselves while we are paddling our canoes. Ts'ibasaa can ambush us from the shores of Tsamsem's Trench by hiding where we cannot see them.

"There is now a Grand Chief of all the villages of the Skeena. His name is Legiac and he lives at Fort Simpson. I see now that Ts'ibasaa wants to become Grand Chief over the southern Tsimshian, over Gitka'ata and Klemtu as well as Kitkatla. If we remain in Gitka'ata we must serve Ts'ibasaa. This was his message when he robbed us in Tsamsem's Trench. I can see no way to prevent this." He looked at us again. There was fear and confusion on some faces and anger on others.

He continued. "I know some of you would like to move to Fort Simpson and some would like to stay. I think it is time we discuss a move again. If we move, we will be free of Ts'ibasaa's control but we must serve Legiac instead. I do not know what kind of man he is, but it is likely that he is no worse than Ts'ibasaa. Those who wish to stay would protect our claim to our traditional lands. Those who leave would be free to return to Gitka'ata if the situation on Fort Simpson is not good. The Elders must choose to leave or to stay. I want you to think carefully before you decide. We will meet again in three days, after you have discussed the move with your Clans. I will not vote, but I will lead the group with the greatest number."

Neeshlak had spoken very wisely and his words caught us by surprise. The meeting ended without a discussion. The Elders had no reason to hold bad feelings towards my father, for each of them would have the right to choose his path. Women and children would follow their husbands and fathers. Slaves would follow their owners and commoners could do as they please.

The Elders returned to their houses and families to discuss what to do. Many knew what they would like but still their decision would not be easy. Clans would be divided and many allegiances would be broken. New chiefs would need to be chosen for each divided Clan and a new Head Chief for the smaller group to replace my father, but these decisions would wait until we knew who would leave. No one spread rumours or gossip. The questions before us were too important for that.

I felt the heaviness of the silence around me as the meetings continued. I prayed that we would move to Fort Simpson so I would be with Tamlahk, but that thought was too selfish to mention to anyone, even to Tsangook. Besides, it did not matter what I wanted. Our fate would be decided by the others.

My father was withdrawn. He said nothing and scarcely looked as his family for the three days. He called a meeting on the fourth day. It was clear that most of our village wanted to move and that my family would go with them. All the Elders of the Blackfish and Wolf Clans would move. Uncle Silgitook would remain behind and his heir, my Uncle Shoget, would be Chief of the Eagle Clan at Fort Simpson. Doolyaks and Yuwahksa would come with us but most of the Raven Clan chose to stay to have greater power in the village. Jaleek would become their Chief. Most of the commoners would move with us, including Tsangook. Tooklan would join us and Wumgooks would stay behind to become the Head Shaman in Gitka'ata.

Their choices were my salvation and I could not be happier. Soon I would be living with Tsimshians from many villages. I would be able to visit the White trading post and watch the great sailing ships that brought supplies to Fort Simpson. My family and most of friends would be moving with me while Laguksa and her family would remain at Gitka'ata. My marriage arrangement would be broken. But most of all I was excited to be living in the same place where Tamlahk's people would be. I would find him and we would become good friends again. Tsangook and Uncle Gugweelaks were both right. I had honoured the Spirits and now they blessed me.

TEN

often wonder how different our lives would have been if Tsamsem's Trench did not exist. There would be no sheltered passage to the north. Our canoes would need to use the open sea. We could not visit Metlakatla safely or trade with the Tsimshian villages on the Skeena. How would we have fished for oolichon or salmon each year? Our people would have been very isolated. We probably would have lived under Ts'ibasaa's control and never moved to Fort Simpson.

And yet the Trench could only exist by magic. Other canyons run from the mountains in the east to the sea in the west, while the Trench cuts across the mountains from north to south. It is very narrow while most other canyons are wide. They bend and twist but the Trench is two days long and it does not bend once.

Many have told stories of how it was created. Some say Great Spirit dropped his great stone ax and it sliced through the mountains. When he retrieved it, it left a sharp cut, straight and deep that filled with sea water. Others say He saw that the southern villages suffered from isolation and famine so He cut the Trench to help them so they would not starve.

However, there is another story that gave the Trench its name, a story I have always liked better. It is said that the Trench was cut by Tsamsem, the Son of God, as he chased a giant clam. This makes good sense of course, because most great things that Tsamsem did were done by accident. He released the Sun into the sky in a fit of anger to punish the Ghosts of the Dead and since then our lives have been much better. He copulated with Elderberry to make the first man because she was sweet and tender, and because of this men are also soft and beautiful. Some think that this was a mistake, that we would be better to have skin like Stone that stops spears and bullets, and to never die or feel the need for food or water, but men who think like this never make good lovers.

Many stories are told of Tsamsem's bad qualities. They tell that he was often greedy, gluttonous and deceitful. This is not how Tsamsem began when Great Spirit sent him to Earth to help men. He came as a Shining Youth from Heaven with skin that glowed blue. He had a gentle nature and a loving heart when he first appeared. The Haida boast that the Great Spirit sent him to help them, but they should be ashamed instead of proud for they corrupted him and gave him a bad nature.

It happened in a small village on the outer islands of Haida Gwaii, the land of the Haida. A kind Chief and his wife were mourning. Their only son had died in a tragic accident. They once had great hopes for him for he was a Prince of great beauty and intelligence. He was also a great hunter and leader. He was well loved by the village and everyone mourned with the Chief and his wife. Every morning and evening the women of the village gathered around his burial box. They wailed so loudly to ease the pain in their hearts that their voices carried up to Heaven.

Their wailing woke Great Spirit from His sleep. The noise was so terrible that it made Him angry. It was worse than a village full of noisy children playing. He left His house to find where this noise was coming from. He searched until He found the women crying in the village. He heard them talk about the death of their beloved Prince and He forgot His anger.

His kind soul understood their grief for He was a father too. His heart grew heavier each day as He listened to them wailing. After one moon they were still crying, and His heart was too pained to listen to their grief anymore. He decided to send His own son, Tsamsem, to ease their pain. He loved them so much that He gave His only begotten son.

And this is how Tsamsem appeared to the people of the Haida village. One day the Chief's wife and the other women came to cry at the burial box. They were shocked to see a beautiful naked boy sitting on the box. He looked just like the dead Prince except that his skin shone as brightly as blue flames. He smiled at them, but the women were terrified. They screamed and ran to the Chief's house. A short while later they returned with the men of the village.

The boy was still sitting there. He smiled at them with loving eyes. "Great Spirit in Heaven has sent me here to replace your son," he explained. "My Father understands your pain and wishes to help. I am His only son. My name is Tsamsem. I bring you His love."

The villagers understood that Tsamsem, who could transform into any shape, had taken the appearance of their dead Prince. Their grief was soothed when they saw his loving face. They were deeply honoured to have this holy visitor and they were astonished and grateful that Great Spirit loved them so much.

The Chief was delighted and he welcomed Tsamsem into his house. He gave Tsamsem his dead son's clothes and his son's sleeping chamber next to his own. He announced a great feast in Tsamsem's honour, a feast was so large that it took many days to prepare.

The feast day arrived but the Chief was disappointed that Tsamsem was not hungry. He was a Supernatural Being and took his nourishment from the light of Heaven. He did not need food but the villagers did not understand this. Some thought he was ill. Others thought he was not satisfied with the food they had prepared. They encouraged him to eat but he would not. Finally he realized that he might embarrass his new parents and insult the villagers' feelings so he agreed to eat a small plate of food. The Chief was relieved. He asked a serving slave to prepare a platter of the best morsels for him.

Now this slave had a mean spirit. He had once been a Prince of another Haida village before he was taken in battle and made to serve the Chief as a slave. He was jealous of the attention Tsamsem was receiving and he decided to have his revenge. He prepared a plate of the finest morsels as the Chief had instructed, but he secretly picked a scab from a scar on his leg and buried it in the food.

Everyone was pleased that Tsamsem was eating. They watched him closely to see if he was enjoying it. He ate all he was given and he pretended to like it. He even ate the slave's scab without knowing it.

The scab would not have hurt a man but it was poison to a Supernatural Being. Tsamsem did not become ill but a great hunger grew inside of him. He asked for more food. At first his new parents were delighted but he could not stop eating. His hunger grew larger the more he ate. He ate and ate until all the food at the feast was gone and he still wanted more. His parents were alarmed but they did not dare to refuse a Supernatural Being. The Chief ordered all the food in the village to be brought to him and he ate that too. As he ate he grew taller and broader. He ate for three days until all the food they had stored for winter was gone. Then he went outside to look for more to eat.

The people of the village were frightened and upset. The Chief realized he must lead them away from Tsamsem or they would starve. They packed all their property in their canoes and they left quietly. Tsamsem was so busy foraging for food that he did not see them leave. Later, he realized he had been abandoned and he did not know where to look for them.

Though he had lost his new parents the hunger still burned within him and he could think only of food. There was nothing left in the village so he walked to the shore to look for shellfish and bird eggs. By this time he had grown taller than Sonoqua. Excrement flowed from his bottom until it covered the shores around the village. No one has ever been able to live there again.

The mean-spirited slave was pleased that the villagers were upset with Tsamsem. When the Chief overheard him boasting about what he had done, the Chief became so angry that he had the slave executed. That is how men learned what had happened to Tsamsem and why he is often called 'Scab Eater'. Tsamsem wandered for the rest of his days looking for food to satisfy his hunger. At times he transformed himself into Raven to steal food or he used other disguises to trick Chiefs into preparing feasts for him.

One day Tsamsem changed into a fish to look for food in the sea. He was eating bait off fishing lines when he spotted a great clam resting on the floor of the sea. It was the Spirit Chief of Clams. Tsamsem transformed back into a giant and he chased after it. The great clam used its supernatural powers to dig deep into the mountains to outrun him. Tsamsem followed it, digging as fast as he could.

Eventually Tsamsem had to stop for he had cramps from doing so much exercise on a full stomach. The great clam escaped. Tsamsem left behind him a great trench that cut through many mountains and canyons and made many new islands.

That is how Tsamsem's Trench came to be. It was born of Tsamsem's greed and some of it remains in the Trench. His hunger has touched us each time we have used it for a safe passage. It filled us with the anticipation of wealth when we passed through it to our fishing camps. When we went north to trade our furs we dreamed of White goods or other riches that would soon be ours. Many years later, it became our trading route south to the cities of the White men and the promises of what we might find there.

It was also his greed that turned Ts'ibasaa into a thief. The day we left Gitka'ata for the last time we were fleeing the same greed, the greed that was now Tsi'ibasaa's. We fled to Fort Simpson to escape his tyranny and starvation, but as we passed through the Trench our hearts filled with dreams of White riches that we would find there.

FORT SIMPSON

ELEVEN

We needed six days to reach Metlakatla as our canoes were heavily loaded with all our belongings. We rested on windy days and followed the narrow channels behind the islands north of the Skeena so the waves from the open water would not swamp our boats. In Metlakatla, we rested for a day while my father and the Chiefs of the other Clans visited Fort Simpson to negotiate a site for our houses. They returned in the evening and announced that they had found a site.

We waited two more days for calm weather before using the open water to Fort Simpson. How difficult it was to wait! The beauty of Metlakatla and the mountains close around us did nothing to help us relax. There were many things to consider when moving a village. We talked about our plans and our concerns but we would have preferred to begin to work. We needed to build our new houses and start our new lives. My thoughts were mostly about Tamlahk. I wondered if I would see him as soon as we arrived. I wondered if he would be glad to see me and if our house would be close to his. I let the others worry about the rest.

After the third night at Metlakatla, the air was calm. We rose with the first light and set out for Fort Simpson before the afternoon breezes became strong. My heart pounded with excitement when I saw the first houses. Neeshlak led us to the outer headland where we would build our new homes. The tide was low. We pulled our canoes onto the sand and carried our food and belongings to the ground above the high tide mark.

Before we were finished, a man came towards us, shouting something and waving his arms. There was something terribly wrong with him. His forehead was bleeding and he walked with great difficulty. We thought perhaps he had fallen or had been attacked. We ran to help him but he waved us away. His expression was angry and mean. His hands and face were dirty and he smelled of something foul.

We could not make out his words. At first we thought he spoke a strange language. Then we realized that he spoke Tsimshian but his words were not clear. He was telling us to leave, that there were already too many people here. We looked at each other in confusion. Why would he worry about such a thing when he was injured? Surely it had nothing to do with his injury. Perhaps he had hit his head when he fell. It was strange too that no one had come from the houses nearby to help him with all the noise he was making.

He was drinking something from a strange container, like ones I had seen on the shelves in the White trading post. But he was not drinking properly. Smelly water dribbled down his face and clothes. We moved closer to comfort him, but he swung the container to keep us away. It slipped from his hands and shattered on the rocks at his feet. The strange water soaked into the dust and turned it brown.

He rocked unsteadily as he stared at it. He bent over to pick it up the broken top and almost lost his balance. Shoget and Hahkwah reached out to support him but he swung the broken container at them. He struck Hahkwah's belly and tore his shirt. Hahkwah shouted in surprise and fell backwards. The container had scratched his stomach and a few drops of blood escaped.

We backed away from the stranger, for we knew he was dangerous and we could not help him. Neeshlak called for Tooklan. Tooklan brought his medicine bag and took from it some powder which he sprinkled in a circle around the man. He told us evil Spirits that came from the broken container had possessed the stranger. He told us not to touch the broken pieces and not to come close to the stranger, for the Spirits may leap from him into our bodies.

The noise and commotion brought others out from their houses nearby. We thought they might know what to do but they were more concerned about the cut on Hahkwah's stomach than the possessed man. The cut had already stopped bleeding. They had no fear of the possessed man or his container. We watched in disbelief as two women collected the broken pieces and scolded him. He complained to them that we had caused him to break his "bottle". They told him he had drunk too much anyway. They apologized for his terrible behaviour and led him away.

As soon as he was gone, a small crowd of people from the nearby houses surrounded us. They were eager to introduce themselves and ask about us. We were still distracted and concerned about the possessed man, though we could no longer see him. We were told that he was a good man, but that he often got this way when he had a bottle. They said he would be all right by evening. We were left with many questions unanswered but they did not want to talk more about him. They helped us carry our belongings to where our tents would be set up.

We could not forget the incident on the beach as easily as our new neighbours did, but there was much work to be done. We spent the rest of the day setting up our tents and preparing the evening meal. As the tide rose we pulled our canoes closer to our campsite so we could unload the heavy house planks and roof beams.

We relaxed around our fire after our meal. The summer sky darkened slowly on this pleasant evening. As the tide rose the outer headland was cut off from the rest of the town. From our island we watched the beach fires and the smoke from the houses across the channel of water. I wondered to myself if this would be our home. Fort Simpson seemed even larger than when Miyana and I had explored it in the spring. How would I find Tamlahk in such a big place? The houses stretched along the shores on either side of the headland to the White fort in the distance and far beyond. We sat silently listening to the distant conversations and sounds of children playing. We heard many sounds from different places at the same time. For the moment I felt very small, and that the people of our village would scarcely be noticed here.

We went to bed early, for there was much work to be done the next day. Late in the night we were woken from our sleep by two gunshots. We rushed from our tents. I could only think that Ts'ibasaa had found us. We heard the shouts of angry men in the distance but we saw nothing in the darkness. Then there was silence again. Soon the voices of conversations across the water continued as if nothing had happened. Perhaps someone was shooting into the night air just for fun, Shoget suggested. We returned to our tents but now it was hard to sleep. I felt uneasy again, like I had that afternoon.

The next day we woke early to the sound of crows calling. The Elders gathered after the morning meal to discuss the placement of the houses. This site was not as good as in Gitka'ata. It was low so there would be danger of flooding in the storms. My father's house needed to be built first. It would be built on the highest ground for it needed to be dug the deepest inside to make enough benches for all our villagers to sit on during our most important ceremonies. We would use the planks and roof beams from our house in Gitka'ata which we had brought with us.

My father and the Clan Chiefs had negotiated the purchase of logs from other villages at Fort Simpson while we were still waiting to leave Metlakatla. They bought enough to make house posts for three houses. We would buy more as we needed them. Doolyaks, Amapaas, Gwashasip and ten others left with Shoget after breakfast and they returned with the logs in tow at the height of the morning tide. They were big red cedar logs suitable for carving and long enough to build up the ground around them. The men who had stayed behind helped them roll the logs out of the water and up the beach. While they were gone we had laid out the planks to measure where to dig the holes for the posts.

When the logs and planks were in place we rested. It was necessary for my father to honour the Spirits before we began. My mother, the other women of the Clans and the servants had begun preparing a feast as soon as Uncle Shoget took the men to collect the logs. We were careful to stay out of their way while we worked.

My father's feast was held at the end of the third day. He gave everyone a small gift whether they were helping with the construction or not. Then he and the Blackfish Elders told the stories of their crest and their famous ancestors. All of the stories were from Gitka'ata. Perhaps there would soon be stories to tell of our history in Fort Simpson.

The next day the construction began on his house. By tradition, all Clans worked together on the Head Chief's house to show their allegiance. Raising the posts, roof and the outer walls of a Blackfish house were the duties of the Eagle, Wolf and Raven Clans. The Blackfish Clan had to build and carve the inside of the house. Since my brothers and I were of the Eagle Clan we worked on the outside. We helped dig the deep holes for the house posts while others prepared the bottoms of the logs.

By the afternoon of the second day we had finished raising and securing two house posts. We were taking a brief rest when my father received a visit from Legiac, the Grand Chief of all Tsimshian villages in Fort Simpson. He came with several of the Elders from his tribe and Ginzadaak, Head Chief of the Gitlaan tribe. He wore the ceremonial clothes and face paint used for special occasions, which helped him look like Chief of great importance. He was a younger Chief, a bit younger than my father. He was not as tall but he carried himself with great dignity.

Neeshlak was embarrassed for he was not prepared for such an important visit. He had been working with the other Blackfish men to design the placement of the sleeping chambers and steps. His hands and clothes were dirty. Beside Legiac in his beautiful clothes, my father looked like a commoner. Legiac did not seem to mind.

From his headdress I could see that he also belonged to the Blackfish Clan. He apologized for interrupting our work. He said he would soon leave on a long hunting trip, but he wanted to welcome us first. He seemed in no hurry to begin preparations for his trip.

He inspected the work we had done and he nodded his approval. He said Neeshlak's plan of building up the site before cutting out the benches was clever. "Of course, it will be a small house compared to mine," he boasted. "My house is seven benches deep. I can entertain a gathering of more than three hundred people." He smiled at this fact with satisfaction. "Of course, your village is small and you would not need so much room," he added.

"Of course," my father agreed. Then I understood why Legiac had come. He wanted reassurance that my father's house would not challenge his prestige. He came when Neeshlak was working to embarrass him, to make him appear common next to himself. My father was humble but not ashamed. He called to Hoshieka to bring out a small ceremonial box that was with our family treasures. It was a small personal chest with a beautiful carving of a blackfish on the lid and shining abalone shells inset around the sides. He turned to Legiac and gave a humble bow as a commoner would give a Chief. "This has been in my family for three generations. I would like you to have it."

Legiac was surprised and puzzled, for this was not the proper time to give such a gift. He did not recognize that my father was playing the same game as he was. The beauty of the box clearly impressed him and he reached out to take it with the enthusiasm of a boy. Then he realized his mistake and with a sudden air of indifference instructed one of his Elders to accept it instead.

"Of course, I will have something much nicer for you at the proper potlatch when my house is done. This is a small token to thank you for letting us live with you at Fort Simpson." Neeshlak gave another small bow of respect.

Legiac's smile returned. "You and your people are most welcome at Fort Simpson, Neeshlak! This is a fine gift from one Blackfish to another!" He took the box from the hands of the Elder and inspected it carefully. "What fine work this is! I did not know that the southern villages made art as fine as the villages on the Skeena. I will show you my appreciation. My men will deliver to you ropes and tools made by White men to help you with your building. They are stronger and faster. You will not need your stone axes and cedar ropes anymore. I am certain we will become strong allies and friends, Neeshlak." He gave a small nod of respect, then turned and led his party back to the main part of town holding my father's box tightly.

"Father, was it necessary to give him one of your finest boxes without a proper ceremony?" I asked when Legiac was gone.

"No, it wasn't, but that makes my gift more effective." He turned and smiled at me. "Legiac is arrogant and proud, but not as cunning as Ts'ibasaa. It will be easy to convince him that I am his ally and his allegiance will be valuable to us. He can keep us safe and give us privileges. That will give us status in this place of many villages. A beautiful box is a small price to pay for all that."

Two of Legiac's men returned in a short time with long White ropes, axes and digging tools, each with a metal blade on one end. They showed us how to use the digging tools by pushing down on the metal blades with our feet. They made our work go much faster. The White ropes made the work of lifting our posts much easier too. White tools are so much better than our own, I was thinking, and that thought made me laugh with delight. By the next morning the house posts were done and we began raising the roof beams into place.

In two weeks the outside of the house was complete. We carried sand and soil to build up the ground around it and used sea water to pack it down so that nothing would grow on it. Men painted the front of the house white while Tsangook made designs on the house posts in preparation for carving them. Two weeks later the sleeping chambers were ready for my family to move in. My father held his potlatch to bless the new house and invited Legiac and the other village Chiefs to attend. The Blackfish Elders sang songs and told stories of our village and the Blackfish Clan. Then Neeshlak distributed gifts to the Chiefs and Elders from the other villages, saving the best of them for Legiac to secure his allegiance.

The other Clans began work on their own houses. Their houses would take longer for they worked on them by themselves and their work was interrupted for hunting trips and the late summer run of the Coho salmon. My brothers and I helped to build the Shoget's house for the Eagle Clan after my father's house was completed. Before the winter ceremonies began our village had finished three houses and started two others.

We saw many strange things in Fort Simpson that we had never seen before, but we came to know them quickly. Many people drank Spirits from bottles, especially in the evenings when the work was finished. Some drank all day and were never able to work. At times we could not recognize our neighbours when the Spirits filled their bodies. They reminded us of the old man who attacked us on the beach the day we arrived, but the next day they would act like themselves again. Even the old man who attacked us was pleasant and ready to welcome us when he did not have a bottle, but he became mean again whenever he drank. We no longer feared them but instead we learned to watch where we walked so we would not step where they had been sick.

The Bottle Spirits were always ready to possess people but there seemed to be no purpose for people to invite them inside. A man did not need to belong to a secret society, or to meditate or cleanse himself in preparation to receive them. It required no special skills but the people who were possessed did not seem to learn anything from the Bottle Spirits either. Neeshlak said the one thing they should learn is not to invite them in. He took Tooklan's advice and forbade any of us to drink from a bottle.

We still heard gunshots in the evenings too, but we no longer rushed from our beds. We convinced ourselves that people were having fun or perhaps just shooting at wolves or bears. After a couple moons we did not hear them in our sleep.

Not all the strange things we saw upset us. That summer to my delight I saw three White sailing ships in the harbour in front of the fort. I also saw a ship made of metal that moved without sails. Smoke came from the top of the ship and it made a loud whistle. White ships fascinated me. I used to be proud of our beautiful long canoes, but they were so small next to White ships. And the White ships had come from very great distances. Amapaas heard that these ships could go to the far side of the world. Indeed, they came from there. How I wanted to visit one, to explore the insides and climb to the top of its high masts!

But each time they came they also brought bad news. They brought more bottles with evil Spirits and that was followed by more gunfire and more killings. One man possessed by Bottle Spirits would insult another or accuse him of cheating at gambling. The other would kill him with a White gun. Later the dead man's Clan would seek revenge and kill the killer. Then others would be killed in revenge. The Bottle Spirits made them do these terrible things.

My mother, Memlaka, did not think the bottles were such bad things after the Spirits were gone. She said they were the best things made by the Whites and she was determined to have many of them. My father did not like the idea and warned her that the Spirits might follow the bottles into our house. She argued that women in all the other houses used them and they did not get possessed by Bottle Spirits, but before she brought them inside she boiled them to drive the Spirits out.

Memlaka was very proud of her collection and wanted Neeshlak to see how clever she was. She liked to tell us that the bottles were free, while other White goods that our men liked all cost many furs. Each day after a ship came in she would lead a party of Eagle women to gather empty bottles off the beaches. She especially liked bottles of different colours and shapes that she found in the garbage that the White men dumped at the edge of town. She was able to trade some of her finer bottles for White cloth and jewelry. That silenced my father's objections.

Those who lived in Fort Simpson used many different White goods instead of traditional tools and clothing. They had knives, axes, kettles, cooking pots and pans made of White metal and oil lamps and drinking cups made of glass, just like bottles. They used candles and matches if they could afford them and glass mirrors like the one I saw and thought was magic in the trading post. White men's blankets and cloths were popular too. Women collected buttons and sewed them onto the blankets for decoration. Some men now wore White boots and long pants that wrapped around their legs.

White goods brought status and prestige, and that made us more anxious to buy them. Other villages and even visitors could see we had just moved to Fort Simpson, for we had very few White treasures. Some people teased us and we felt ashamed.

It was not easy for my father to buy these things in the first summer when we were still building our houses, for we did not have much to trade with. He first bought us White clothes so that we would look like the others in the town, but many things we bought did not seem practical. Cotton shirts soaked up the rain and they were cold when they were wet. Wool pants shrank when we washed them and they would itch terribly. Other goods disappointed us too. Matches would not work if they were damp and pictures books warped and faded when they got wet. But we treasured the first things we purchased, even when they became ruined or broken.

Many things we saw in the store were beautiful and people bought them for decoration without knowing if they were meant to be useful. Sometimes we knew how to use them, but we bought them just for decoration. Miyana begged my father to buy her copper wire to make a bracelet like the other girls were wearing. My father told her she was silly and wasteful, but he bought it for her anyway.

Our men thought the best White inventions were guns. They were very expensive, but a good hunter would soon make the purchase worth his while. The men of Fort Simpson never used arrows or spears. Guns brought many more furs and it was no longer necessary to hunt late into the autumn. But we found many bodies of dead animals in the woods that hunters had skinned but left the meat to rot, and this made us uneasy. The hunters wanted extra furs to buy White goods, but we knew the Animal Spirits would be angered by this disrespect and wastefulness.

I visited the White trading post often. I loved all of the things I saw there. They filled me with delight and wonder, but I did not want to own them for status or prestige. I wanted to understand them. Their magic was the power of knowledge and possibility. I hungered to learn how they worked and how they were made. I believed everything the Whites made was better than anything we could make. I longed to ride the White sailing ships to the other side of the world, to visit the villages where these things were made. I was sure they must be more wonderful than their many goods they sent to us.

To me, the most magical invention of the White men was not made of metal, glass or fine cloth. It was their writing. I had seen it on the bottles and boxes and in their coloured picture books. It fascinated me, but I did not know what it was for or how it worked.

One afternoon an Elder from the Gitsees village who wanted to impress Tooklan showed us the magic of White writing. He asked Tooklan to whisper a word in his ear. He scratched the word on a piece of wood with a copper wire. Tooklan took the wood to another man who could read the White writing and he told Tooklan the word the Elder had whispered in his ear.

Tooklan thought this was a trick so the Elder told Tooklan to whisper a sentence instead. He scratched the writing onto the wood and again the other fellow told Tooklan the sentence he had whispered. Tooklan was upset that others who were not Shamans knew magic that he did not. He told us that White writing was the work of evil Spirits and he refused to look at it again.

But I begged the Elder show me how to read the writing. He explained that each shape had a sound and he taught me the letters 'T', 'P' and 'O'. I was proud and excited and I could not wait to show these letters to my family. This was not the magic of Shamans or evil Spirits but a skill that everyone could learn.

In the warm days of late summer I kept busy helping with my brothers build our Clan house. There was much to do, but I worried constantly why I had not seen Tamlahk. I explored the town from end to end after my work was finished. I talked to many others but no one had heard of him. By this time I was sure that his village had decided not to move to Fort Simpson. My heart was heavy with disappointment and loneliness. I prayed that I would see him again at the oolichon camp the next spring but that would be a long time to wait.

Then one day I saw his older brothers, Selwehk and Kemdahluk, who I had met on the Nass. They were walking on the beach near my father's house. I stopped my work and ran fast to catch them, surprising them with my urgency. Selwehk recognized me. He greeted me warmly and said I had grown in the past half year. His village had moved to Fort Simpson in the spring. They had built their new houses near ours but they had returned to their village for the past two moons to hunt, trap and fish.

They had only been back for two days.

They invited me back to their house. I had not finished working but I could not return without seeking Tamlahk. I followed them and saw him working with other men of his Clan in front of their new house. He was cleaning his rifle. How beautiful he was! For a moment a shadow crossed my heart for I feared he would not remember me, but then he looked up and stared at me in disbelief.

"Gugweelaks!" His dropped his work and ran to my side, throwing his arms around me and kissing my cheek. The other men laughed as we wrestled each other to the ground. He gripped my shoulders tightly and would not let me go. "What are you doing here? Are you visiting Fort Simpson? How did you find me?" He asked me many questions without waiting for my answers. I was so happy I could only watch his face and laugh.

Finally he ran out of breath. I told him my village had moved to Fort Simpson and we were building new houses nearby. He was delighted and hugged me again. He brought me into his father's house that his Clan had built in the spring. He introduced me to everyone, including those I had not met at the oolichon camp. His father, Pahsoousk, remembered me. He welcomed me pleasantly, but he reminded Tamlahk he had more work to do. That reminded me that my brothers would wonder where I was. We agreed to meet again after dinner when our work was done.

We met that night and as often as we could after that. Soon we became the closest of friends. We sat around the beach fires telling jokes and stories. Sometimes we wandered together by ourselves or sat on the beach late at night after our families had gone to bed watching the fire die. When only embers remained, we sat close with our arms and legs touching to keep warm. We shared our thoughts or sat quietly and watched the rest of Fort Simpson across the waters of the high tide.

We were always together, except for short periods when we left on hunting trips with our Clans. Tamlahk purchased a small canoe from the White store that summer with furs he had collected over the past spring. On good weather days when there was not much work to do we explored the bays and islands near Fort Simpson. He brought his rifle and we hunted small animals. He was skilled as using a rifle and he taught me how to shoot.

Tamlahk shared my fascination for White goods. We visited the White trading post to look for new treasures when we had furs to trade. Tamlahk was not interested in picture books or pretty things. He liked tools and things that had moving parts. Like me, he wanted to know how they worked but he was better at understanding these things than I was. The White men answered his questions for they knew he had furs. He had traded there many times before.

He did not know how to speak in sentences in the White language but he taught me the names of many things we saw in the store, such as "bullet", "rifle", "matches" and "knife". He also taught me "whisky" and "ship", and other words like "hello", "good", "please" and "thank you". We collected new words with other White treasures and we practiced them together until we knew them well. We could not have a conversation or ask questions, but this did not matter to us then.

We were also very curious about the White men themselves. We spent time around the fort, watching what they were doing. Only twenty men lived in such a big fort and there were only two women. Other men came to trade but they only stayed a few days each time. We learned to recognize the men who lived there and we gave them special names. Each man did mostly the same work each day. They did not share their work as our people did. The Chief of the Whites was a man named McNeill. He was a tall man with a serious face who did not leave the fort often. When he did, he never answered our greetings when he passed us.

Tamlahk told me the story about our own Grand Chief, Legiac, too. He heard that Legiac's uncle died four years before. Legiac was his heir but his uncle died sooner than expected. His uncle's younger brother Tumcoosh believed Legiac was not yet worthy to be Grand Chief. They fought for the title and Legiac won. Since then there had been bad feelings between them.

The next year a Haida man killed Legiac's younger brother after losing a gambling game. There were several revenge killings by both families after that. Legiac summoned the Head Chiefs of all the Tsimshian villages and he promised that he would end the feud once and for all and restore his family's honour. His own honour rested on this promise.

Legiac invited the all Elders of the Haida Clan he wanted to punish to a large potlatch. He pretended that he wanted to end the killings and restore the peace. He offered to make formal arrangements for two of his daughters to marry Elders of the Haida Clan at the feast and he would give them generous gifts if they accepted his offer. The Haidas accepted his invitation but they did not know Legiac planned to kill them. He secretly built a trick roof for his house that would collapse on the place where the Haida would sit. Then he invited the Head Chiefs of the Tsimshian villages to the potlatch to witness his ruthlessness, but he kept his plan a secret.

The day of the big feast arrived and everything was ready. Legiac instructed his Shamans not to sprinkle eagle down over their heads, the usual oath of peace. He apologized to the assembly that his Shamans had no eagle down, but a loyal Tsimshian Chief eager to please Legiac sprinkled eagle down over their heads as a gift. Legiac was horrified. Now the Spirits would be angered and they would curse him if he harmed his guests. He had no choice but to continue with the ceremony to avoid humiliation. Instead of punishing the Haida for killing his brother, he promised his two oldest daughters in marriage and made a pledge of peace between the two Clans. Then he had to give them generous gifts as he had promised. The people he hated the most were now his future relatives and he had to pretend to like them.

Somehow rumours of Legiac's failed plan spread through Fort Simpson. Legiac was deeply humiliated. He denied the rumours but Tumcoosh accused him of being a coward for not seeking revenge on the Haidas. Legiac tried to explain his choice to make peace, but a Chief who makes excuses or needs to explain his actions loses respect.

Tumcoosh was right that Legiac did not have the good qualities of a Grand Chief. He was selfish, arrogant and at times he acted like a spoiled child. He carried himself like a Grand Chief to show others that he was worthy of his position, but he had not gained the respect of the other Tsimshian Chiefs. He had a hot temper and had killed two men who made fun of him. Recently, after he had taken the Bottle Spirits, he shot and killed a young Haida man who belonged to the Clan that killed his brother, the Clan that was now his in-laws. They must have suspected their arranged marriages would not be good ones. I understood now why he was happy to have my father's allegiance. Perhaps Legiac was not such a good ally to have at Fort Simpson, but it was not my place to advise my father.

Tamlahk and I had no interest in politics. We were more interested in talking about traveling to the other side of the world in the White sailing ships. We were not sure how far that was. We wanted to go at least as far as Haida Gwaii and maybe farther. Whenever a ship was in the harbour we would take Tamlahk's canoe and paddle out to see it. The larger ships were our favourites, for they brought new goods to the trading post. White men loaded wooden chests into smaller boats that brought them to the wooden dock in front of the fort. Some Whites carried the chests up the path and into the fort while others pointed rifles at us to keep us away. They would not let us help them, so we decided that it would be better to watch from the canoe instead.

Sometimes these ships brought visitors too. We knew which ones were important, for Chief McNeill would come out of the fort to greet them. Then other White men would carry their bags inside. They held their heads high like little Chiefs and they pretended not to notice us. Sometimes they would glance at us but they would look away as soon as they saw us looking. Never had our men acted so strangely!

The smaller ships often brought whisky. Tamlahk did not like these ships and he became angry with me when I wanted to visit them. There were tears in his eyes and it frightened me. He did not explain why he was so upset, but I soon learned the answer.

One day a whisky ship arrived in the harbour. Pahsoousk ordered him to trade some furs for whisky. I went with him. I had never seen him so unhappy. We waited with a crowd that had gathered around a small boat which the White traders had pulled onto the shore. The Tsimshian men were restless and noisy, except Tamlahk. He waited until the others had finished trading before he brought forward his father's furs. He set them down and made no effort to negotiate. They gave him less whisky than they had given others. I was puzzled why he said nothing, but I also said nothing.

We brought the Spirit Bottles back to his father's house and gave them to him. Pahsoousk was angry. He said the good furs he had given Tamlahk were worth more bottles than he brought home. He asked him if Tamlahk was hiding any bottles for himself. Tamlahk said no, that he hated whisky. His father looked at him suspiciously. Tamlahk would not look at his father's eyes for they held no love for him.

He asked if he could leave but Pahsoousk ordered him to stay and drink with the other men. Pahsoousk opened a bottle and passed it around. Tamlahk refused to take the bottle when it was passed to him. His father commanded him to take a drink but Tamlahk did not reply. His face was red with anger as he stared at the ground. His father threatened to beat him but the other men of his house persuaded him not to. These things he did without shame in front of me, a visitor from another village.

"I'd be a fool to share good whisky with my cursed son who steals from me," he snarled at Tamlahk. "If you come home with my stolen Whisky Spirits on your breath I will beat you until you cannot walk!" Pahsoousk threw a serving bowl at him and ordered both of us to leave.

We went back to my village and built a fire on the beach. Tamlahk was so upset he could not talk and he would not look at me. I tried to put my arm around his shoulder but he shrugged it off. After a while he looked at me and apologized.

"Perhaps you should have negotiated for more whisky," I suggested.

"I don't want him to have more whisky! The Bottle Spirits just stay with him longer. When he drinks whisky he beats me! He wakes me from my sleep to beat with his cane."

"But he is your father. Why does he beat you?"

"The Whisky Spirits make him beat me. He has never liked me. He says I killed my mother. She died three days after I was born and he blames me. I don't know. How does a baby kill his mother? Maybe I am cursed, but he did not beat me until he drank whisky. When the Spirits are in him he says terrible things to me. Maybe the Spirits help him say the true feelings that are in his heart."

He turned away from me. I knew he was crying. I felt helpless. I put my arm around his shoulders and this time he welcomed it. When he stopped crying he turned to me. "Can I sleep in your father's house tonight?"

"Of course." Tears were blurring my eyes too.

I asked my father if Tamlahk could to stay for the night. He saw Tamlahk's red eyes and the trouble in his heart and told Hoshieka to make a bed for him on the floor of my chamber. Tamlahk was too worried to sleep and my concern for him kept me awake. That night the sounds of shouting and gunfire seemed much louder and closer. It was almost morning before it was quiet again.

Tamlahk returned to his father's house at daylight before the servants started working. I wanted him to stay longer but he was afraid that would make his father angry. Later, my mother and the Eagle Clan women were collecting bottles. I followed them past his father's house but it was quiet. I walked along the beach without stopping, leaving my mother's party behind. It was not a peaceful walk for there were many bottles that morning. I saw men sitting on the ground alone, unable to get up but still drinking. I saw another sleeping on his side with his pants half off. He had fallen over when he was relieving himself and his clothing stank of urine. Further along, a large patch of sand was red with blood but there was no sign of the victim.

All these sights filled my heart with fear. Tamlahk did not come to see me that night and I was sick with worry. I passed by his house several times but I heard nothing. On the second night he came to me while I sat alone by the beach fire. He called my name softly. I was excited to hear his voice, but he was not smiling. One side of his face was badly beaten, his mouth was swollen and his eye was blackened. I made a small cry of pain. I reached for his hand but he pulled it back. One of his fingers had been sprained when he raised his hand to stop a blow.

I tried to bring him to my chamber but he didn't want others to see him. I called to Klashwaht to bring my father. Neeshlak came and he summoned Tooklan. Together they led him inside to my sleeping chamber and removed his bloodied shirt. My heart was sickened. His father's cane had left several large bruises on his back and shoulders. Some of the blows had broken his skin. Tooklan applied a salve made of wooms juice to his wounds and placed a small bag of hot ashes on his bruises to ease his pain. Our attentions made him uncomfortable. He wanted to leave but Neeshlak insisted he stay the night. We made another bed on my chamber floor. This time I gave him my bed and I slept on the floor.

Pahsoousk came to our house the next morning looking for Tamlahk. He made loud and angry demands to see him immediately. My father came out to meet him wearing his ceremonial Chief's cape and headdress. Pahsoousk was humbled into silence when he saw him. Neeshlak led him away from the house to talk to him in private. When he returned he announced that Tamlahk would stay with us until he was healed and the evil Spirits were gone from his father's body. He told us Pahsoousk would not bother us until then. Tamlahk and I were both very pleased and grateful. We knew the evil Spirits would never leave his father's body.

Tamlahk healed quickly. We hunted alone for the next few days until the bruises on his face disappeared. He was ashamed of his situation but happy for my company. Our friendship grew stronger each day. We never discussed his family or his Clan, but for the next two moons he returned to the protection of my chamber whenever his father was drinking. He was welcomed in my father's house like one of our family.

His playful nature returned with his good health. Soon we were back to the fort trading in the store or watching the White men. We made a game of trying to talk to the Whites. We watched them when we were in the store, always smiling broadly whenever they looked at us. Outside the fort, Tamlahk would do funny dances to get the attention of the guards above us. Some guards liked this, but others were nervous and distrustful. After a while they ignored us.

One day as we left the store we saw there was no guard on the walkway above us. Tamlahk checked to see that no one was watching. Then he climbed the ladder to the top of the walls quickly. I objected, but he signaled me to follow him and I obeyed. From the top of the walls we saw above the rooftops of the houses around us. We saw our village on the outer headland and the beaches on both sides of the town. I followed Tamlahk to the guard post at the corner of the fort to look at the cannon.

The guard saw us as he returned to his post. He shouted something and pointed his rifle at us, preparing to shoot. We froze. Tamlahk put up his hands and shook his head. He pointed to the waters and pretended he was searching. The guard lowered his gun and signaled for us to climb down to the courtyard, but Tamlahk was in a playful mood. He pointed to the cannon and begged to the guard to fire it once. "No," the guard shook his head. He stepped towards us to guide us back to the ladder.

We had seen this guard before. We had named him 'Dark Beard'. As he came closer we saw he was a handsome man with dark eyes and not much older than ourselves. His beard was short and even, not like the bushy orange beard on the man in the store. Tamlahk gave him a broad smile and looked him over from side to side, nodding at me his approval. The guard was amused and he smiled back. Tamlahk reached up to touch his beard but he caught Tamlahk's wrist and shook his head. He looked around to see if anyone had seen Tamlahk do this. No one was watching. Tamlahk pointed to himself and said his name. He pointed to the guard with a questioning look.

"Peter," the guard introduced himself.

"Good!" said Tamlahk, and he shook the guard's hand tightly like White men do. Peter smiled broadly. Tamlahk reached up with his left hand and stroked Peter's beard before he could free his hand.

"No!" Peter whispered loudly as he jumped back. He looked around again. Tamlahk gave him a sweet smile and winked at him. Peter's face turned very red. He glanced around again, but he was still smiling. He signaled again for us to go.

"Thank you!" Tamlahk whispered as we climbed down the ladder. When were outside the fort he shouted Peter's name up to the walls. Peter looked down. Tamlahk waved at him and did a little dance. Peter laughed and waved back. We were very excited about our new friend and we talked about him often. We laughed about how his face turned so red. We added 'Peter' to our list of White words to practice and we called to him whenever we saw him again.

That autumn we met another White man. We did not know then that he would change our lives forever. He arrived long after nightfall in a large iron ship that brought visitors instead of supplies or whisky traders. We heard its loud whistle and we paddled out with many other canoes to greet it. Someone important was on the ship, for Chief McNeill was waiting on the dock. We gathered below the sides of the ship to watch. The Whites on the ship shouted at us and waved their arms to tell us to move away. They lowered a small boat to the water. Five men climbed down the ladder to the boat.

The last one to climb down was a man dressed in fine clothes. He was young, like the men who were working, but he did not help to row the boat. He acted differently. He seemed nervous as if he did not know what to do. He smiled and nodded at us as if he wanted to be our friend. No White visitor had done this before. We answered, "Clah-how-yaws!" a Chinook greeting that White traders use. He smiled at us again without saying anything. We were fascinated by him.

He waited quietly while the workers lowered two wooden chests of his belongings to the boat. He was definitely planning to stay for a long while. We followed the small boat as McNeill's men rowed him to the dock. We pushed our canoes onto the beach and walked beside him as he climbed the path to the fort. We were showing him our respect for greeting us. McNeill did not understand why we were following him. He shouted angrily at us to back away and make room for the young visitor and his luggage. He guided him through the door in the gate and I heard it lock behind him.

For the next few days we had many discussions about the new visitor, but no one knew why he had come. He did not wear the clothes of a worker or the ceremonial clothes of a White Elder either. He was much younger than most important visitors, but McNeill had given him a special welcome. Was he the son of an important Chief? White chiefs were never friendly to us but he had greeted us like a friend. Why then, we wondered, did he not leave the fort to receive our hospitality? But we were patient. We knew he would come out of the fort someday.

Most people soon forgot about him but Tamlahk and I did not. One day we saw him looking out over our villages from the walls of the fort. He was not carrying a rifle like a guard. "Hello!" Tamlahk shouted to him and waved. He smiled back and waved, then he shouted "Hello!" back to us. Now we were more fascinated than before. He was the first White man to say hello to us. We named him the Special Visitor. We waited by the walls for him, but we did not see him again for many days.

The next time I saw him I was visiting the trading post alone. He came in with a young Tsimshian man who I had seen before. I watched him as they talked. He was solid man, my height and a bit older than myself. His face was hairless and his cheeks were very pink. His clothes were clean and neat. His hair was black. It was thick and wavy and cut short like other White men. His eyes were blue and they sparkled like the summer sky.

He walked towards me and I pretended to look at hats on the shelf. He recognized me. He said hello and gave me a warm smile. I was pleased. He had come to look at the hats. He tried on several, turning to the other Tsimshian man and myself each time to see if we approved. Every hat looked silly on him so we always shook our heads. Soon the three of us were laughing.

Then he put different hats on my head and the two of them shook their heads in disapproval. I looked at the White men who worked in the store. They never let me try the clothing before when I had no furs to trade, but this time they merely watched us and did nothing, for I was with the Special Visitor. He finally chose a hat and took it to the counter. He offered to pay for the hat with pieces of metal but the man at the counter refused to take anything for the hat. I had seen Chief McNeill pay for things in the store, but they gave this Special Visitor a hat for free. I wondered why he received such special treatment. I followed him out of the store. He crossed the courtyard to the big house where most of the Whites lived. The Tsimshian man opened the door for him and followed him inside.

I told my story to Tamlahk that evening. He asked me what I said to the Special Visitor. I felt foolish. I was so nervous that I had not used any of the White words we had practiced, only 'hello'. I did not even ask his name. But Tamlahk liked the story about the hats. We agreed he must be an important prince if he was allowed to play with the hats and then leave with one without trading anything.

I told also Tamlahk about the young Tsimshian man who was with him. We had not seen him in the fort before. We did not know that a Tsimshian man could live with the Whites. We thought perhaps we would become his friend and he would invite us inside. No Tsimshian we knew had seen the inside of a White home.

We only saw the Special Visitor once more that year. It was in the following moon soon after the start of the winter ceremonies. Tamlahk and I had waited for our first winter ceremonies at Fort Simpson with great anticipation. There would be ceremonies in each village and visitors would come to ceremonies at my father's house too. Our people stopped building houses and we stopped watching the White men at the fort. We needed to help with the preparations that would make our villages proud.

But once the ceremonies began we were disappointed. Much whisky was served at the feasts and many people were drunk before the performances began. The meetings were loud and disorganized. Sometimes bottles were thrown and fights broke out. Those who fought were told to leave, but the fights would continue outside and many would leave to watch them or join in. There were many more fights than dances. Many times men were shot or stabbed. If anyone died there would be more killings for revenge in the following days. I understood finally why people of the Skeena did not want to join the winter ceremonies here.

Tamlahk hated the drinking. After a few days we no longer wandered to other houses to look for interesting dances or story telling. We watched the performances in my village for my father did not allow drinking in his house.

One terrible night, less than a moon after the ceremonies started, there was much fighting. We retreated to the dark shadows below walls of the fort where we could be alone. We sat with our arms around each other's shoulders and talked about the dances and story telling we had seen already. The shouting around the corner of the wall grew closer and louder but we tried to ignore it. No one could see us in the shadows.

"Gugweelaks, you must make me a promise."

"Yes, of course." I was so pleased to be his friend I would to promise him anything.

"Promise me that you will never drink whisky again."

"Yes, I promise." Tamlahk never drank. I had only tried it twice. I had tasted enough to feel the Spirits a few days before. They had made me playful and affectionate. I had laughed and talked like a silly child until I saw the fear in Tamlahk's eyes. His expression filled me with pain.

"In truth!" he insisted.

"In truth. I give you my word as your best friend."

"You won't forget?"

"No Tamlahk. I am sorry I had whisky the other night. When I saw your eyes I was ashamed. I could never be like your father. I could never hurt you even if I was drunk, but I promise I will never taste whisky again."

"I know. The Spirits bring out the feelings men hide inside. You are joyful and good. They only made you silly and playful now, but later they will destroy you anyway. It scared me to see you change, even though you were still pleasant. I don't want the Spirits to take you from me."

His words touched my heart. "I promise," I repeated and I hugged his neck.

Suddenly we were startled by a loud gunshot nearby. Then a second one. It was coming from the front side of the fort. I jumped up and ran to the corner.

"Gugweelaks, come back! Stay away!"

"I'm just going to look."

The lanterns that hung by the door at the front of the fort made a dim light on the path outside the gate. Three men were standing over a body lying on the ground. One held a gun in his hand. He was drunk and staggering. He swayed unsteadily and pointed his pistol at the body as he walked around it. He turned towards the light and I saw it was Legiac. He fired two more shots into the dying man. The body shook some more, and then it was still. "You will never cheat me again, dog!" he shouted down at the dead man.

I waited until Legiac and his men were gone. Then I ran to the dead man to see who it was. I turned him over and a terrible shock hit me. "Great Spirit!" I cried as I fell to my knees. It was Pahsoousk!

Tamlahk ran to my side to retrieve me but he froze when he saw his father. His father's chest was torn apart and his shirt was wet with blood. Tamlahk knelt slowly beside me and placed his hand on his father's head. His Spirit had left him. He gathered his father's body in his arms and lifted him off the ground. Then he turned and started back to his father's house. As we left I glanced up at the walls of the fort. The Special Visitor was watching us. His face was filled with shock and concern. I held his eyes for a moment. Then I turned to follow Tamlahk.

Tamlahk said nothing as he carried his father's body back to his house. The tide had come in. We waded through the water to get to our island. Not many of his family were home. He explained what had happened to those who were there. Two members of his father's Clan wrapped the body in a blanket and placed it in a tent outside the house for the night. There was much wailing and commotion but Tamlahk stayed silent.

I brought him some dry clothes, for his were soaked red. I sponged his arms and chest with clean water to remove his father's blood. I led him back to my house and to my chamber. I put him into my bed and pulled a blanket over him. He began to cry. I lay down beside him to comfort him and he hugged me. I held him tightly and stoked his hair to soothe him. He cried hard and long. How my heart ached for him! I kissed his face and wiped away his tears, though I was crying too.

"You are not alone, sweet Tamlahk! You will always have me. I will be the stone in your mouth that keeps you strong!" I kissed his cheek again though my tears.

He stopped crying and looked at me for a moment. There was gratitude in his eyes. He slid his hand behind my neck and kissed my lips gently. It felt so wonderful! He kissed me again. Our tongues met and danced together so sweetly. He rolled on top of me. We kissed again and again as his hands moved over my chest and shoulders. My hands slid down his back and around the smooth muscles of his bottom. I felt his tsootz grow large and mine swelled to match it. We hugged each other tightly as we rubbed together like two fire sticks. How beautiful our first taste of love was! How my heart sang with joy! When we were finished he kissed my wet skin and laid his face on my chest.

"Thank you," he whispered. He pressed his face into my neck and squeezed me gently. "Thank you!" his words echoed in my head. I remembered the first day I saw him. He was scooping oolichon out of the river and saying "Thank you". I had loved him ever since that day and that night I knew I would live the rest of my days with him, listening for his thank you's.

TWELVE

The next few days were the sweetest days of my life. We spent most of them lying together in my sleeping chamber, talking, kissing and sleeping in each other's arms. We needed to be touching all of the time. We ignored the calls for us to join the feasts and ceremonies in the father's house. We wanted to be alone. Finally, when our hunger grew strong, we ran to Hoshieka, begging her to find us some dried salmon. We devoured our food like mountain lions, and then retreated to my chamber refreshed. She must have thought we were mad.

There, in my sleeping chamber, our hearts blossomed like spring flowers. I never knew such strong feelings lived within me. They led me to a place within where I was frightened and wanting, but I could not choose another path. And there was so much passion in my flesh! My body ached with joy to be near him. His skin was magical to my touch. Every part of him was beautiful. And he felt as strongly as I did. He stroked my face and kissed me often. He talked about my beauty and how he had been in love with me since we met. He asked me to be loyal to him always, to never leave him even when I was old. I gave him my promise.

(I kept my promise, Tamlahk. I swear! We have parted but I could never leave you!)

Those days of such sweetness were also painful. Tamlahk was grieving his father's death. He felt guilt for hating his father and for wishing that he was dead. He was worried about his future too. A father, even a bad one, was responsible for his son's position. Without his father, Tamlahk would have no status and privilege in his village. Some in his Clan already believed he was cursed because of his mother's death. He believed they would blame his father's misfortune on him too. It was certainly a bad omen to lose both parents. We were both worried, for we did not know what his fate would be.

Tamlahk dreaded the return to his Clan's house. He was determined to stay with me. We spoke to my father to ask his permission for Tamlahk to live with us. Neeshlak said there was no spare room in the house as many from our village were still living outside in tents. I told him Tamlahk could sleep in my chamber.

"Gugweelaks, Tamlahk cannot sleep on the floor every night like a slave!"

"Father, he can share my bed," I answered. I slid my hand down Tamlahk's arm and we locked our fingers together.

"Oh, I see." My father glanced at our hands and he nodded his approval. Of course, he must have known we were in love by this time. Our hearts glowed as brightly as fires when we looked at each other. He must have questioned Hoshieka why we didn't join the others of the household for meals. Everyone must have heard the laughter and tears that came from my chamber and our lovemaking while they ate. We felt so much passion those first days that we forgot to be discreet.

"That solves one problem, but I cannot force your people to agree to this, Tamlahk. Your Clan must decide your fate." This was true, of course, and Tamlahk knew it. He was tormented for he was sure they would not grant his wish to stay with us. He would not approach them for fear that they would tell him to return to his village immediately. He chose to stay until they came for him.

Pahsoousk's body was placed in his burial box two days later. The following week Pahsoousk's nephew was given a Black Feast, like the one I had been given after my Uncle Gugweelaks' death. Tamlahk had to attend and he insisted on my presence. The Nishga ceremony was quite different from my ceremony in Gitka'ata. I wanted to ask Tamlahk the meaning of some of the rituals but I dared not. His heart was very troubled that day. I stayed at his side quietly, to give him my strength.

Drashwuk, the Chief of the Nishga village and his father's people, the Beaver Clan, led the ceremony. Drashwuk was Pahsoousk's cousin. Tamlahk believed he was an evil man and disliked him intensely. Drashwuk drank as much whisky as Pahsoousk and he often beat Tamlahk like Pahsoousk when he was drunk. Once, three years before when Tamlahk was still a boy, he had tried to force his sex upon him. Fortunately he was too drunk and Tamlahk had escaped. He never trusted his father's cousin again. He said if Drashwuk ever tried the same thing him again he would kill him.

Two days after the Black Feast, Drashwuk came to my father's house. He demanded that Tamlahk return to sleep in his house where he belonged. We came out with my father to speak to him. Tamlahk smelled the whisky on Drashwuk's breath and refused to look at him. Neeshlak said Tamlahk was his guest and he was welcome to stay if Drashwuk would allow him to. He told Drashwuk that Tamlahk was now my lover and he'd like us to live together. Drashwuk refused. Neeshlak offered to compensate Tamlahk's Clan if they would allow him to adopt Tamlahk. This only made Drashwuk angrier.

"He cannot have a partner without his Clan's approval. And he will not have my approval. I will not let a Nishga live under a Tsimshian's roof!"

Neeshlak's face became tense. "I have seen the bruises and cuts from Pahsoousk's beatings on Tamlahk's back! If you are his family, how could you let this happen and do nothing to stop it?"

Drashwuk pulled Tamlahk away. "That is not your business. You are not Nishga!" Tamlahk fought to free his arm but Drashwuk lifted his cane and struck him hard across his back. He pushed him towards his house and looked back defiantly at Neeshlak.

I could not keep silent after he had left, for my heart was panicking. "Father, we must do something!"

He thought for a minute. "Let's go see Legiac. Perhaps he can help." We set off to Legiac's house in the centre of town.

Legiac did not want to intervene. "Why should I intervene? I killed his father and he will want revenge. Why should you give shelter to my future killer?"

Neeshlak shook his head with confidence. "Tamlahk is no killer. He never liked his father much. He has often slept in my house to avoid his father's beatings. Drashwuk treats him no better. I am very concerned for his welfare now."

"It does not matter if he disliked his father. He still must kill me to regain his family's honour. I should kill him myself before I give him my protection."

"He is my son's lover now and I want them to live together under my roof."

"Is this true?" Legiac looked at me thoughtfully. "I thought it might be so. You are always together." Then turning back to my father he said, "This does change things, but what right do I have as Grand Chief of the Tsimshian to interfere with Nishga business? Why would they listen to me anyway?"

"You could tell them that you wish to make amends for killing Pahsoousk and that you will compensate them and provide a home for his son."

"You want me to apologize?" Legiac looked astonished.

"You have denied Tamlahk a future by killing his father. If you allow me to be a replacement for his father I will be responsible for his position. He will be happier in my home. He will be grateful to you and he will not seek revenge. Gugweelaks will be happy and I will be grateful for that. If you compensate Pahsoousk's Clan generously, on the condition that they allow Tamlahk to live in my house, you will be forgiven when they accept your gifts. You will have protected yourself from Tamlahk and his father's people. You will show that your mercy is great, even when your punishment is swift."

Legiac studied my father's face carefully. Then he smiled. "I suppose you are right. I have too many enemies already." He chuckled softly. "You are very clever, Neeshlak. You are a good friend indeed! I will see to this early tomorrow, before Drashwuk has had too much whisky." He laughed and patted my father's back.

And so Tamlahk came to live with us. I admired my father more than ever. He achieved his purpose and it did not cost him one fur. Pahsoousk's Clan forgave Legiac, for a handsome price in gifts, and the tension between us was forgotten.

We had almost forgotten the winter ceremonies happening around us. Now that Tamlahk's place in our family was decided, Miyana, my brothers, Doolyaks and Yu-wahksa begged us to come with them to visit the story telling and dances in other houses. We liked to see the different ceremonial robes and masks. Some of the tribes now used White blankets decorated with crests and many buttons sewn on in patterns. But we always left early when the drinking and gambling began, before the Whisky Spirits possessed the players and changed their behaviour for the worse.

After the darkest days had passed, the Whites began to behave strangely too. McNeill had given his men whisky bottles for gifts. Until then I had not known that Whisky Spirits liked White men too. We heard their noise and shouting inside the fort. Frequently they would fire their guns into the air. Tsimshian men around the town copied them like a game. The White men sang songs. We chanted and sang our own. They did not need to understand each other to have fun.

Tamlahk could not come with me when I met with the Hamatsas. He understood. He was pleased that I was still a Cannibal Dancer. Jaksukjalee was planning a surprise performance. Few people of the north had ever seen Hamatsas dance but there were many rumours about them. Jaksukjalee wanted to bring attention and prestige to our village but he had other reasons to introduce our dances to Fort Simpson. He believed the Hamatsas could show the other villages how the Whisky Spirits brought out the horror and savagery within them and why the Spirits must controlled.

"Cannibal Spirits possess us, yet we manage them," he explained. "We do this with discipline. When Whisky Spirits possess men's bodies and they lose control and they are blind to reason. They cannot see what is happening to them. We must show them what they become. We must teach them that it is possible to master the Spirits so that they will not be doomed to live as savages forever."

We agreed that our performance must be a surprise. With so many villages around us, we could attract a large crowd to any beach. Jaksukjalee gave Doolyaks and I the honour of being the lead dancers. We practiced our movements and waited for the right opportunity. Tamlahk was anxious to see me perform but I could not share any of our secrets plans. I could only alert him when I knew it would happen.

Finally the opportunity arrived. A Chief named Quthray, who was a slave to the Whisky Spirits, had a daughter who was ill and not recovering. He believed the Spirits had cursed his family but he did not stop drinking. He decided instead to sacrifice one of his slave women as a gift to the Spirits so they would let his daughter live. He announced this to the other villages so the Spirits would know his intentions. Many were horrified by his cruel decision. They thought the Spirits had damaged his mind, but a Chief had the right to do what he wished with his slaves and they could not stop him.

Quthray had chosen to kill the slave woman on the beach in front of the fort in full daylight so that everyone could witness it. He stood with his Elders by the shore and his daughter lay on a cot on the ground before him. A large crowd gathered to watch. He brought the slave woman to the beach. Her hands were tied behind her back and she wailed loudly for mercy. His Shamans prayed to the Spirits to leave the Princess's body and offered her slave woman as a blessing. Then Quthray shot the slave woman in her head with his pistol and she fell dead. His servants chopped off her limbs with an ax and threw her body into the sea. Many people were horrified but the men who had been drinking cheered loudly.

We were dressed and ready and hiding in Uncle Shoget's house. When we heard the shots, we ran across the channel and between the houses towards the fort. We divided into two groups. I led one group along the beach from the south and Doolyaks circled the fort to lead the other from the north. When we reached either side of the crowd on the beach we stopped.

Everyone turned to look. They were shocked, for they had never seen anything as frightful as Cannibal Dancers. We walked in a strange manner, stooped over with our arms spread wide and raising our knees high as we stepped towards them. Our eyes were wild and unfocused. We made deep moans as though we were in pain. Our skin was painted black and red with the white of our bones painted on our faces and bodies like skeletons. We jerked our heads, tossing our hair from side to side. We shoved our arms out to one side and then the other, demanding offerings from the crowd. We screamed "Eat! Eat!" in high-pitched voices, as we begged to be fed.

The other Hamatsas followed close behind, shaking their rattles to soothe us. They were clothed but their faces were painted. They shouted and waved the crowd back, "Stand back! Make way! The Cannibal Spirits have arrived! They smell dead flesh and they must feed!"

The old Chief and his Shamans were shocked into silence. They backed away in fear. They watched as we threw our heads back and sniffed the air. We whined as we searched the bloodied sands for the body. Then we saw it and screamed loudly as we ran into the water to retrieve it. The slave woman's blood was still flowing as we dragged her body back onto the sand. We crouched down and pretended to bite her flesh. The other Hamatsas closed in around us shaking their rattles. They secretly handed us fish bladders filled with blood they had hidden in their clothes. When they parted to let the crowd see, we appeared to be feasting wildly on raw meat torn from the slave woman's body with blood running from our mouths. Several women in the crowd screamed and two fainted, making our dance seem even more horrible.

The dance was a great success. Quthray realized that others saw him as a savage. He was shamed and humiliated. He gave the slave woman a proper burial and banned Whisky Spirits from his house. The story of our performance was told from the Skeena to the Nass in the years that followed. The Hamatsas were cheered and toasted at each house. Tamlahk was so proud of me.

But on that day, as the other Hamatsas tied my hands to lead me naked, with bloodied hands and face, back to Shoget's house, I looked up and saw the White men standing on the walls of the fort. They were most upset. They held their guns tightly, ready to protect themselves. The Special Visitor was there too. His face had a look of horror and disbelief. For a moment I forgot that I was a Hamatsa dancer. I felt I had done something terribly wrong that could not be corrected, something the Special Visitor could never understand. That uncomfortable feeling stayed with me even while my people continued to praise me and pay me honours.

It was not long before we saw the Special Visitor again. At the end of the winter ceremonies he left the White fort to visit each of our houses. This caused much talk and curiosity for no White man had done this before. This was proof that he wanted to be our friend. He came with the young Tsimshian man I had seen with him in the

White trading post. The young Tsimshian man spoke the White language and delivered the Special Visitor's words to us. He said the White man's name was 'Duncan'.

But Duncan's visits were very strange. He always came near meal times when all the members of the house were present. He paid his respects to the head of each house but he never accepted their invitations to stay for dinner. The Chiefs tried to impress him but he always refused their gifts. He did not know he was insulting them. White men were unfamiliar with our ways so they forgave him.

His assistant told us he wanted to count all the Tsimshian in Fort Simpson. This was certainly a strange task. What would he learn from this, we asked ourselves. The numbers changed each day as travelers and hunting parties came and left. Some Elders thought he planned to distribute gifts but White men had never given us gifts before. And he was not only counting Elders. He counted women, children, commoners and slaves too. He did not care about our ranks.

The counting was difficult for his visits caused much commotion. He asked the people who lived in each house to line up along a wall on one side, even the ones who were preparing the meal. He asked us to cross to the opposite side once he had counted us. The children thought this was a game. Some hid behind our legs while others crossed back and forth to be counted more than once. He laughed with them when he caught them, but I saw the frustration on his face when he started the counting over again.

Duncan's visits lasted several days until he had visited each house in Fort Simpson. Many meals were ruined in the process. Each day we discussed his visits and joked about his silliness. The young children followed him around from house to house asking for gifts and trying to get counted again and again. Then suddenly his visits ended and we did not see him again for four moons. We soon found better things to talk about, but we did not forget him. We still did not know his purpose at Fort Simpson.

The first winds of spring appeared after the counting. Our relatives from Gitka-ata arrived for a visit and we left for the oolichon camp on the Nass together. How different the journey was this year! It took less than one day to reach our camp. It was a very special time for Tamlahk and me, for it was the anniversary of our meeting. Each day we fished together in my canoe, saying our thanks in rhythm and smiling at each other. Each night we slept in our embrace like other couples. My family liked Tamlahk. He was a hard worker and a good fisherman and he made us laugh.

The time at the camp passed quickly. A hundred canoes heavy with fish headed back to Fort Simpson the day we left.

As soon as we returned, many men prepared for a long trip south to Fort Victoria. They talked of seeing the White trading post and the beautiful White women who lived there. They also wanted to trade with the Salish and Nootkas. The men of our village still had two houses to finish so we stayed in Fort Simpson. Tsangook worked on the carvings inside my father's house while we finished the roofs of the new houses. I stopped to inspect his work.

"You don't visit me much anymore," he said to me.

"I know. I am sorry."

"No, don't be sorry. You have a good reason. You and Tamlahk are very happy together. You are such a handsome couple."

"We are happy," I smiled. "I have never been so happy. He is so wonderful! How have you been, Tsangook? Are you happy too?"

Tsangook looked at me and smiled. I thought I could see some sadness in his eyes. "Don't worry about me. I am fine. Sometimes when I watch you two I wish I had just one man to satisfy. It would be easier than trying to please all the men in the village. But that is the duty of a Mahanna! Anyway, your father has given me too much carving and I have no time to think about men now. Be good to Tamlahk. He has had a difficult year. You must always treat him well."

"I will. I love him."

"Don't try to run his life like a woman. Never dishonour or embarrass him. Be ready to forgive him when he knows he has made a mistake." He looked at me and I nodded. "Remember, a man is a proud hunter. You are swift and strong but do not always outrun him if you want him to be loyal. Never tell him you are better than he is. Let him win too!" He paused. "I am sorry. I should not lecture you. I am not your uncle."

"It is fine, Tsangook. Thank you. You are wise and kind. I will remember these things. And I will visit you more often." I kissed his cheek and returned to the roof I was helping my brothers build. We finished the last houses that spring. The other Gitka'atans no longer needed to sleep in their tents every night.

The men returned from Fort Victoria after two moons. They told us it was very different from Fort Simpson. They told many stories of White women with soft white skin in beautiful clothes. They were most amazed about their huge bottoms which stuck out behind them under their dresses like the back end of a moose. Some argued that it was their dresses, not their bottoms, that made this shape, but they could not think of a good reason why White women would want to wear dresses like that.

They also reported that the Whites at Fort Victoria were now building small houses outside the fort. Some were growing crops for food and raising large, fat animals for their milk. Two Nootkas had shot one of these animals for food and that had upset the Whites so badly they had whipped the Nootkas in front of the fort for everyone to see.

They had heard stories of other strange events too. Some White men had discovered a yellow metal called gold in a place far beyond the mountains. It caused much excitement and chaos amongst the Whites. Hundreds of men were arriving every day from the south to hunt for this metal. They stayed only long enough to buy supplies for their journey over the mountains. White men who owned the stores were getting rich.

No one could tell me what gold was and why White men liked it so much. They said it was soft and shiny but not strong enough to make tools or containers. They said the Whites wanted it because it was pretty, but they were fools. They could not show others their gold for someone might kill them to steal it. What good was it to have something pretty if you could not show it?

We left for our salmon camp on the Skeena shortly after the men returned from Fort Victoria. It was Tamlahk's first visit to the Skeena. Now it was my turn to show him around as he had shown me the Nass. The Spirits blessed us with a large catch again this year. Our relatives and friends who had remained in Gitka'ata were happy too for Ts'ibasaa no longer bothered them. Gitka'ata was too small to interest him now. We gave them guns to help their hunting.

When we returned we received news that Duncan would soon visit us again. We had heard little of him since the counting of the houses last winter. After those silly games, we did not know what to expect. While we were gone he had visited some houses to help the sick we had left behind, but his visits upset more people than he helped. He sent messages to the Chiefs that all the sick should wear deerskin moccasins to keep their feet warm instead of being barefoot, but moccasins were only worn by nobility. He criticized the medicines of the Shamans and he taught the women how to clean wounds with a magic White bar called "soap" instead. Fortunately for Duncan, the sick recovered after his visits. The Chiefs were impressed but the Shamans were upset.

More and more the villages demanded to know why Duncan had come to Fort Simpson. They sought out Clah, the young Tsimshian man who helped him. Clah could not answer their questions, but he promised to tell Duncan what they wanted to know. So after the salmon camp, Duncan sent messages to each of the Head Chiefs of the nine villages that he would visit them to explain his purpose. We waited in great anticipation.

Instead of honouring our Grand Chief Legiac first, Duncan started at the outer headland and worked his way from house to house across Fort Simpson. Neeshlak received notice that he would visit our house first. We were told that he would come in two days at 'ten in the morning'. There was much discussion amongst the Elders as to what this meant. It was decided it must be at the end of morning just before meal-time. That was when he had come before.

The men gathered around the fire in my father's house at that time. We found Duncan pacing nervously like a restless mountain lion. Clah sat on one of the benches watching him. We learned that Duncan had waited anxiously for us for much of the morning. When the Elders were present they began to discuss the meaning of 'ten in the morning' again, but Duncan called for their attention.

We waited in silence while Duncan explained something to Clah. Clah seemed confused about his instructions. Finally Clah asked if everyone here was in the room. Everyone in the room grunted in agreement. Duncan began to count the people.

"He's counting us again," Uncle Shoget whispered to Neeshlak. "Obviously he has come to Fort Simpson to count us, but for what purpose?"

"Wait!" Neeshlak signaled Duncan to stop. He turned to Clah. "Does he want all the people of my village in the room? He cannot get an accurate count without the women, the children and the slaves. I will summon them if you wish."

Clah thought for a while before translating Neeshlak's words into the White language. "No, no, no!" Duncan flapped his arms like broken wings and shook his head. He explained something patiently to Clah for some time. Clah still looked confused. He turned to Neeshlak and said, "No."

"So why is he counting us?" Shoget whispered.

"I can make no sense of it," my father responded. "He will think there are fewer of us if he doesn't count the women and the children."

The counting was done quickly. We did not need to line up against one wall and cross the floor this time. When it was done Duncan greeted us in Tsimshian nervously. He looked around to see our response. Mumbles of surprise crossed the room. Some White traders spoke simple Chinook, the language of trade in the south, but Whites never spoke a word of Tsimshian, not even Chief McNeill. Duncan was encouraged by our smiles. He continued his message. His Tsimshian was simple and spoken poorly. We leaned forward and listened carefully to understand what he was saying.

"Tsimshian good people. I come from far away to help Tsimshian. I teach you good knowledge. I bring you message from Heaven. I bring you sacred teachings about Holy Father, who sent his Son save us. I teach you about Holy Ghost...."

The villagers gasped and turned to each other. He said the Tsimshian word for Ghost, a very bad omen indeed. Just saying the word would summon the Ghosts of the Dead. Was he trying to bring Death to our door? If a Tsimshian man said this word, a Hamatsa might jump up and bite him. We did not want to bite the Special Visitor.

Duncan saw the shock and concern on our faces. He knew he had said something terribly wrong. He whispered many questions to Clah in a soft voice. Clah tried to explain to Duncan what he had said. Then Clah spoke to us. "He meant Holy Spirit, not Holy Ghost."

The villagers nodded and laughed. There was a sigh of relief around the room. Duncan started again, less sure of himself. He said he could teach us how to speak the White language and read White writing. He would teach us about the White world. He would also show us new ways to give praise to Great Spirit. He asked Clah to kneel on the ground and placed his hands together. He closed his eyes and bowed his head. He said a short prayer in White language and then stood again.

"He behaves like a trained dog. What purpose does this serve?" Shoget asked. "Would you kneel like a slave, Neeshlak?"

"Perhaps, if this brings me special powers or grants me favours from Great Spirit." My father made a playful grin. "I believe Spirits still prefer offerings to empty words."

"He tries to impress us. He is learning our language and he already knows about Great Spirit in Heaven and his son Tsamsem. Does he want to become a Tsimshian too?"

"It would be the first time a White man became a Tsimshian, Shoget. They can do many things, but I do not think they are capable of that."

Duncan asked if we understood his message. There were many nods of approval. He thanked Neeshlak and the audience for listening. Then he left to visit the next house without accepting our food.

A few days later Duncan sent a message saying there would soon be classes for the children of the Chiefs in Legiac's house. Legiac had offered his house so that Duncan would not ask the other Chiefs. Tamlahk and I were anxious to join. We wanted to learn about the White world and how to read and write the White language. Neeshlak agreed. He thought it was a good idea for young men to learn new ways of thinking.

The next afternoon I met Duncan leaving our house with Clah as I was returning home. He had come to tell Neeshlak that classes would begin in three days. I beamed with joy to see him again.

"Hello Duncan!" I said proudly, for I had never spoken those foreign words to a

White man before

"Hello." He was surprised by my White greeting just as he had surprised our house with his Tsimshian greeting earlier. His blue eyes twinkled like pools of water on a sunny day. He still wore the heavy clothes and shoes he wore in winter and he had grown a beard since then. I wanted to touch it, but I was not as bold as Tamlahk.

He over looked at my naked chest. I wore less for it was a hot summer day. My appearance made him smile. He searched my face. Then his expression became less certain. Perhaps he remembered my Cannibal Dance. I felt uneasy until he smiled again.

"Gugweelaks", I pointed at my chest. I offered him my hand as Tamlahk had done with Peter, the guard at the fort.

"Duncan," he pointed at himself and he shook my hand firmly. I could see that he was impressed and this excited me.

"Look!" I pulled out my knife to show him. "Good knife, yes?"

He was delighted with my White words. "Yes, it's a very good knife!"

I pointed to White letters I knew on the handle and I said them aloud, "P! T! O!"

He laughed with delight. "You want learn?" he asked in simple Tsimshian, pointing to the other letters. He showed me 'A' and 'N' and taught me to read them. We both laughed with delight.

"Yes, I want to learn White words!" I said in Tsimshian. Clah translated for me. He invited me to come to the classes in Legiac's house in three days after my morning meal. I promised I would. We smiled at each other like good friends and shook hands. His blue eyes were so beautiful. His beard was thick and brown. I reached up and touched it. He jumped back in surprise.

"Forgive me," I said in Tsimshian, though I was still smiling. He smiled nervously and glanced around as Peter had done. How red Whites faces become when they are embarrassed! He shook my hand again and said goodbye.

I was as excited as a child for the next three days. I told Tamlahk everything. I said Duncan's eyes were blue like the sky and that he had looked at me like a friend. I told him the words we had spoken and that he had shaken my hand and I had touched his beard. He had also invited me to attend classes to learn the White language. Suddenly Tamlahk was upset and he would not look at me. I was confused but then I understood he was jealous.

"Tamlahk, of course you must come with me. I will not learn the White language without you! You must meet Duncan. He would want me to bring my lover." I held him in my arms and I kissed his neck. He looked much relieved.

"Are you sure I am welcome? He did not invite me."

"He told father that everyone who wants to learn is welcome, not just the children of Chiefs. He invited them first out of respect. He said he needs many students. Soon we will both know the White language and we will be able to speak it like White men. Others will come to us to ask the meaning of White words." We both laughed at this idea.

Five from our village attended the first class in Legiac's house. Tamlahk, Miyana and I brought Shoget's two children. There were only five students from other villages but more would come in the afternoon.

The first lesson was easy. Duncan taught us how to say "Hello" and "My name is…" Each time we said it correctly he said "Good!" He tried to remember our names by saying hello to each of us. He remembered Tamlahk's name but he had great problems remembering mine. We all laughed together each time he made a mistake, but he was not discouraged. We learned that he had two names. His first name was Mister.

He taught us how to count to ten. Then he tried to count us in Tsimshian which made us laugh. Clah had taught him how to count using sticks. Duncan did not know that we use words to count people. He taught us how to say "Goodbye" and then the lesson was finished. He asked us to come again the next day.

After Miyana took our cousins home I brought Tamlahk to meet Duncan. I put my arm around him to show Duncan that we were together. I told him that Tamlahk was my husband. Duncan laughed at my English. "No, no! You are "friends!" he said in the White language. He smiled with delight. He repeated the word in Tsimshian. "Husband is man. Wife is woman. Two men not husbands!" He said in broken Tsimshian and laughed again. He looked at us like we were children.

"He is my husband. I love Tamlahk," I explained in Tsimshian.

"Yes, yes. You are good friends. Best friends!" he said in White language. I was uncertain about White words so I did not argue. I was not sure if he understood me. Perhaps husbands were called 'best friends' in the White language.

Tamlahk and I practiced new White words every evening in our chamber. I was determined to speak the White language correctly. I wanted to learn sentences to speak in conversations but Tamlahk found this too difficult. He only liked to learn words and phrases. When I insisted on practicing conversations he grew tired. He would say, "All right, best friend!" and kiss my mouth to stop my lesson. Then we would hug tightly and make love. We did not learn much White language this way so I tried to practice sentences on my own. Soon I spoke it much better than he did.

Duncan taught us that the White language was called English. He was excited that I learned English so quickly. He encouraged me more than others and often asked me to say a word to show others how to say it properly. I was embarrassed by his praise and his attentions, especially when it made Tamlahk jealous. But jealousy did not make Tamlahk try harder, but we made love more often. I realize now that he was trying to hide his frustration and I tried to reassure him with my love.

One day after class Duncan asked to speak to me alone. Tamlahk promised to wait for me outside. Duncan asked me how I was enjoying the classes and I replied that I liked them very much. He told me that he thought so, for I was his best student. He said I was a fast learner and a good teacher too. Then he offered me extra English classes in trade if I helped Clah teach him Tsimshian. I would be paid in White money that I could spend in the trading post. He waited for my reply.

If I was alone I would not have hesitated to say yes, but I knew Tamlahk would not like this. I asked if Tamlahk could come with me but Duncan said no. There was only enough room for one extra visitor in his room. I said I would like that but I would think about it first. I did not want to tell him Tamlahk would be jealous.

I explained Duncan's offer on our way home. Tamlahk had nothing to say. He just stared at the ground as we walked. When we arrived at our chamber he held me tightly. I saw he was crying. I asked him why and he said he was frightened. I asked him to explain, but he only shook his head and held me tighter.

We lay on the bed until he was ready to talk. He said I was much better at learning English than he was. I told him he was much better at fixing things with his hands and better at carving and using tools. He was also a better hunter and fisherman. I said I admired him and that I would never leave him. I held him and combed his long hair until he stopped crying. He kissed me many times and thanked me and then told me I should accept Duncan's offer. I was careful not to show too much relief or joy. I promised to teach him the English that I learned and to share the money I was paid. That seemed to please him.

The next day I went to the fort with Duncan and Clah. I followed them in through the door in the gate and across the courtyard to the big house where the Whites lived. I looked up at the walls which I had a habit of doing. I saw Peter watching me with a puzzled look. It was not often that a Tsimshian was invited to visit the house of the White men. I waved to him and smiled but this time I did not call his name.

Their house was nothing like ours on the inside. I thought this could not be a place where men lived. There was only a narrow, dark passage with a low ceiling and wooden doors on each side. Everything was made of wood planks, even the floors. I followed them down the passage, expecting Chief McNeill to appear at any moment and tell me to leave.

Duncan opened a door along the passage and invited me into his sleeping chamber. It was much larger than mine with one space for his bed and his trunks and a smaller one for his desk and books. Clah and I sat on his two chairs and he sat on his bed.

He explained how he and Clah played games with words to make sentences, first in English, then in Tsimshian. Duncan was patient and he made the learning fun. He thought he knew how to make sentences in Tsimshian, though Clah did not correct him when he made mistakes. He realized this when I began to correct him just as he corrected me. I saw that he was happy to have me there. Clah was not much of a teacher. He seemed to be relieved that I accepted the job of correcting Duncan.

McNeill interrupted our first lesson to speak with Duncan. He said nothing when he saw me sitting on Duncan's chair. Duncan excused himself left me alone with Clah. Clah was a big man, strong and tall but very quiet. We sat without saying anything until the silence became uncomfortable for both of us. I knew he would not be the first to speak so I started asking him questions about himself. He was happy to have something to say.

I was nine years younger than Clah. He was from the lower Skeena and his village traded with many tribes along the coast. He learned Chinook, the trading language of the coast peoples, and even some English when he was a boy. When he was my age the White Chief before McNeill paid him to translate messages from Chinook to Tsimshian. Later, he did the same work for McNeill. When Duncan told McNeill that he needed someone to teach him Tsimshian he suggested Clah since he was living in the fort anyway.

I asked him why he did not live with his village. He said he was hiding. An evil woman had placed a curse on his family, causing a large piece of wood to fall on his uncle and kill him. Clah killed her in revenge. Later he was sorry and offered to pay thirty blankets in compensation to her family, but her son vowed to kill him anyway. He fled to Fort Simpson and begged the White Chief give him work and protect him. He had lived in fear inside the fort for five years. He would leave the fort now, but only in Duncan's company. Even then he watched others carefully.

As I became friends with Clah, Duncan became friendlier with me too. One day I was alone with him while Clah did errands. He asked me to sit beside him on his bed during my English lesson. He put his arm around my shoulders and hugged me. I asked him why. He said I was a good friend and he enjoyed my company. He looked at me like a needy child and he stroked my hair. I felt uncomfortable with his attentions. He saw my concern and he looked uneasy and confused. He tried to hold my hand. I pulled away from him and I told him I preferred to sit on the chair.

He looked troubled. He stood and paced around the room. Suddenly he turned and spoke to me in an angry voice. He told me he had seen me do the Cannibal Dance last winter. He asked why I ate human flesh. I was so surprised. I told him I never ate human flesh, that I only pretended to. I told him about the pouches of blood and salted deer meat. I tried to explain why we did the dance but he would not listen. He said the Whites would be angry if I did the Cannibal Dance again. He would not teach me again if I was still a Cannibal Dancer. I begged him not to stop my lessons and I promised to quit the Hamatsas. I felt hurt and frightened. How could he desire my friendship one moment and threaten to end it the next?

The next day he was relaxed and happy, as though nothing had happened. I was pleased that he was no longer angry with me. Once again he was my teacher and I was his special student. He did not try to hug me or hold my hand again. I quickly forgot about the day before, but I kept my promise and quit the Secret Society of Man-Eaters.

My English improved quickly with the extra lessons and Duncan paid me White money for teaching him Tsimshian as he had promised. I bought Tamlahk gifts from the trading post with the money. We still took lessons together in Legiac's house but these classes taught me nothing new. Soon I was helping Duncan with the teaching. Clah did not like teaching. Many of the students disliked him anyway. They called him a coward for hiding in the fort.

But Duncan was frustrated that his students did not come every day. Many of his students were adults and they had many other duties, such as house building and hunting, but he thought they should still come. He did not understand why other Tsimshians did not share my passion for English.

"What is so important about learning English?" Amapaas challenged me. "We speak Chinook for trading. For everything else we use our own tongue. English will not help us kill deer or make canoes. How would Duncan know? He does not work like other men. Who feeds him? Have you ever seen him hunt deer?"

I argued that Duncan's job was a teacher but Amapaas was not satisfied. "We each have many jobs. How can he feed himself if he only teaches and does nothing else? He teaches Miyana too. What good is it for a woman to learn new tongues? She will not become an Elder. She will not have a use for it.

I asked him why he did not want to learn English since he would be an Elder one day. He said it was boring to sit and listen to someone talk and play silly games. "I prefer to learn by doing things, not just listening and talking," he told me. This new language was not boring to me. It was a door into a new world that excited me. I could not convince him to love English or to share my dreams, so we never discussed the classes again.

Duncan had problems with his classes in Legiac's house. There were many distractions and he could not have classes during the winter ceremonies or when Legiac needed to meet with his Elders. Also, some Chiefs did not like Legiac and they would only allow their people to attend if the classes were held somewhere else.

For those reasons Duncan made plans to build a new school for his classes. He wanted it to be close to the town but away from the noise and distractions of people working. He found a site a short walk along the beach past the last houses. Legiac gave him permission to build there and he sent men to help him prepare the land.

Duncan asked me to come with him on the first day of work to translate his instructions to Legiac's men. I brought Tamlahk with me and he helped us to organize them. I told the men what work Duncan wanted them to do, but first they wanted to know what he would pay them. He was angry that they would not work for free but he had no choice. He had to promise them potatoes and tobacco and cotton cloth for their women before they would work.

Once that was agreed upon, the work began. The men cut ditches to drain the water. Then they chopped down the trees and cleared the bushes. By the end of the first day the land was cleared and leveled.

The next morning Tamlahk led the men to collect logs and bring them to the beach below the site. We had just started the hard work of rolling the logs up from the beach to the site when one of Legiac's men fell dead. Everyone was upset and frightened. Duncan pushed on the man's chest to wake his heart but nothing happened. Then he knelt beside him and asked the White God to bless his Spirit. We carried his body to the house where he had lived.

We did not work on the school again for several days after his body was cremated. The workers said Duncan had offended the Spirits that guarded the site. They believed that if they returned others might die. Duncan visited each Chief to ask them to tell the workers to return but this did not help. Legiac offered to send his Shamans to chase the evil Spirits away but Duncan did not want to use them. He said the presence of Shamans insulted his English God, but the workers would not return without them. After a few days Duncan had no choice but to return to Legiac and ask him to send his Shamans.

When the Shamans finished their work Duncan visited each house to ask the workers to return the next morning. The workers came but they waited. They were still uncertain if the offerings had not been enough to please the Spirits. They feared the first man to start the work would be struck dead.

Duncan was frustrated that we would do nothing. He walked to the first log and rocked it loose from the sand. He struggled to roll it up the beach by himself but he slipped in a patch of mud and almost hurt himself. Tamlahk and I ran to help him. We steadied the log and began to move it up the bank. Before we reached the top several other men joined us. Soon everyone was working hard. We were encouraged by our success and did not want to stop for our midday meal. By the afternoon we had moved all the logs up to the site where the school would be. Duncan was pleased with us and insisted we have a rest.

We began building the school a few days later, when Duncan finished the plans. There were many things we had never made before, such as windows and doors that swung open on hinges. It was so exciting to work with these new ideas. Soon several of us were discussing plans for the floor and roof. Duncan liked our enthusiasm and agreed with some of our suggestions. We wanted cedar planks for the floor like the trading post. That would keep it warm since there would be no fire in the school, only an iron box that burned wood. We set up the stove and helped to make a metal pipe to the roof to take the smoke away.

Tamlahk was not a good English student but he was an excellent builder. He learned the White ways of building quickly and he was soon skilled at using White tools. He discussed the plans with Duncan, and Duncan was impressed with his ideas. I watched the respect between them grow each day. There was no jealousy in Tamlahk's heart now. He was happy and filled with energy. His affection for me was strong. Our lovemaking was more passionate than when he was jealous!

We stopped building the school in the autumn. Many men had gone in the twenty canoes that left for Fort Victoria. Duncan warned them not to go. He said greedy men came to Fort Victoria making ready to search for gold. Those who had found gold returned to drink whisky and to buy women for sex. He said Fort Victoria was filled with sin and corruption. His warnings made our men more curious.

Tamlahk and I decided not to go with them, for this was also the best season for hunting deer and other animals. We went hunting with Doolyaks, Amapaas, Gwashasip and Shoget. We brought Tsangook with us, of course, to set up the camp and to cook.

We found a quiet bay on the north side of the passage to the Nass, only half a day from Fort Simpson. We set up our tents and built a strong fire. The weather was pleasant for autumn. The cold rains had not yet chilled the waters so we swam naked in the shallow bay. We played like children, splashing and wrestling until we grew tired. We rinsed the salt off our bodies in a cold stream that flowed from the hills behind. Then we sat by the fire wrapped in our blankets. We talked about the omens we had seen that day which promised a good hunt.

Tamlahk and I shared the same blanket. He sat behind with his arms wrapped around me and his cheek pressed against my neck. This was the time when our feelings for each other were the strongest. The others men affectionately called us 'the young lovers' and spoke of us as one. Their hearts were lightened by our tenderness for each other. That night the weather changed. We woke to the sound of heavy rain on our tent. We snuggled close to keep warm, and our passion soon grew hot. The noise of the heavy rain disguised the sweet sounds of our love making.

It was still raining lightly in the morning. We ate our meal by the fire, wrapped in our blankets. We sipped hot tea Tsangook had made from the wooms plant to purify us before the hunt. We discussed what animals we might see in these new hunting grounds. We joked about which of us would catch the most, for he would be first to visit Tsangook's tent that night. I suggested that Doolyaks would be the most successful hunter.

"I don't know. I am quite tired this morning. I didn't sleep much last night. I heard strange sounds that kept me awake most of the night," he complained.

"Maybe it was an owl," Shoget suggested. He wore a playful smile.

"No, it was too close. It sounded like strange animal moans."

"Was it coming from Tsangook's tent?" Amapaas joked, as he raised his arms to protect himself from Tsangook's wrath.

"Hah! Be careful or you will play by yourself this evening!" Tsangook pretended to be offended.

"No, no," Doolyaks shook his head. "The sound came from the other direction." They all turned to look at Tamlahk and me. I felt the blood rush to my face.

"We were very quiet!" I protested.

"I heard it too!" Gwashasip added. "I thought it was the rain on the bushes but I wondered how it fell with such a rhythm." The others laughed.

"You are all just jealous old men who have forgotten what a hard tsootz feels like," Tamlahk teased back.

"Oh no. Mine was hard most of the night!" Doolyaks grinned. The others laughed.

"You should have told me," Shoget teased him, for they shared the same tent.

When the teasing was over, we bathed in the stream again to cleanse ourselves. It is well known that animals are disgusted by uncleanliness. They would never surrender their bodies to even the best hunter if he smelled bad or was dirty.

The rain continued but we hunted every day. Tamlahk and I both had good success. We caught eight deer and many smaller animals. Amapaas shot a moose in a marshy clearing by the river. We worked together to drag its huge body out of the water. We skinned it on the spot and carved it into smaller pieces to carry it back to our camp.

We cleaned the skins at our campsite in the evenings, saying prayers of thanks to the Animal Spirits as we did our work. We rested around the campfire once we were done, drinking Tsangook's hot wooms tea to stay warm. The others took their turns in Tsangook's tent each night while Tamlahk and I made love in our own tent. These were happy times.

It rained the heaviest on the last day of the hunt. Tamlahk and I decided we had already caught enough. We stayed in our tent, making love instead of hunting in the rain. The others teased us that they would have to kill more to make up for our lovemaking, but that was not necessary.

A bear wandered into our camp that morning, following the scent of the meat we had skinned. We heard its claws tearing at the furs that covered it. Tamlahk leapt off of me, grabbed his rifle and ran from our tent. Before I could follow him, I heard the shot. As I stuck my head out I saw Tsangook come running from the forest where he had been looking for firewood. He stood at the edge of the camp staring at Tamlahk with his mouth open wide. Tamlahk was standing naked over the dead bear, his tsootz still hard and pointing to the sky like a spear.

He turned to Tsangook and smiled proudly. "He fell dead when he saw the size of my tsootz. I just shot him to be certain."

How that made us laugh around campfire that evening! How many times have I heard the story of how Tamlahk killed that bear in the years since then? Too many to count. He gave the bear's claws to Tooklan as a gift. Tooklan was delighted. He always told Tamlahk's story each time he used the claws in his Shaman rituals.

It was everyone's favourite story about Tamlahk. It is still my favourite too. It brings back the memory of when we were young and strong, when our hearts were in the full bloom of love. It was a time of our sweetest joy, the last time we would be together with my brothers and friends like this before Tamlahk changed. Before everything changed. The great White wave from the other side of the world would soon hit us, sweeping away our homes, our beliefs, our names and our joy in its undertow.

THIRTEEN

White men ask me how can I be happy living here, in a land such as this. They say this is an unfriendly land filled with steep mountains, dark skies, cold rains and high winds. Of course they are right. This is not a friendly land. It does not open its heart to strangers, and White men have always been strangers here.

The land does its best to keep them away. It confuses them with countless passages that lead in all directions. They might follow a wide one that leads them nowhere. Other times a narrow one might lead them to safety. They cannot tell which shores are islands and which are not. The clouds and rain hide the stars and mountain tops that they need to guide them. Their ships struggle against the currents of the changing tides. Their deep hulls break against jagged rocks under the surface or become grounded on sandbars. The steep canyon walls offer them no welcome. Where they find places to land, their way is blocked by the dense forest and fast running rivers.

The Whites do not want to live here. They think this is a poor land. It is too wet for them. It is not suited for growing food. There are no plains to build their cities on. There is no gold or silver in these mountains. They have no reason to come here but to buy our furs and sell us whisky. Still, it is important to them to think they own it. They call it their land now, though it never will be. They do not belong here.

These forests and canyons were our home long before their distant White nations were born. We know the countless valleys and lakes and the many Spirits that guard them. This land has learned to trust us. It has revealed to us its many secrets. We have seen the bashful mountains lift their cloaks of mist to celebrate the sun. We have been shown the safe routes and the best hunting grounds. It provides us with food from the forest, the rivers and the sea. Its bounty is so plentiful we can rest from our labours during the darkest months of winter. For us it is a land of great wealth.

But this wealth must not be taken for granted. It is offered to us because we have followed the teachings of the Animal Spirits. They have taught us right from wrong, the laws of nature. They protect us like older brothers. There were many times of famine before we learned the proper ways to show them our respect. We remember their teachings in the stories we tell. This is why our stories must not be forgotten, why I tell them now. Of all the lessons they have taught us, my favourite has always been the story of the Salmon Prince.

◇◇◇◇◇◇◇◇◇◇◇◇◇◇◇◇

There was once a time when famine troubled the villages along the Skeena River. The people stored fish for the long winters but it was never enough. They were starving before spring arrived. They went to the forest to gather the inner bark of trees. This was all they had to eat before the ice melted and the fish returned.

In one village the Chief and his wife had a handsome son. They loved him very much for he was their only son. He worked hard and he had a kind heart. They brought the young Prince many gifts. They gave him a slave boy to look after him, and the slave boy cared for him faithfully.

His parents could not bear to see him go hungry. One spring, they saw that the last their food was gone. The young Prince and his slave were mending nets in preparation for the fishing season so the Chief and his wife went to the forest to gather bark.

While they mended the nets the slave boy began to cry for he was very hungry. The kind Prince felt ashamed. His parents had given the last food to him and now he had none to share with his slave boy. The Prince searched through his mother's boxes to find food for him. At last he found a dried spring salmon that his mother had hidden in a secret place. He broke off part of the salmon and gave it to his slave boy.

His parents returned with bark for their dinner. His mother announced proudly that she had saved a special treat to eat with the bark. She went to her secret hiding place to find the salmon she saved. When she saw that it had been eaten she shrieked with anger. The Prince explained that he had given some to the slave boy for he was starving. This only made his mother angrier for her special treat had been wasted on a slave. She scolded her son loudly and she beat the slave boy.

The Prince was so angry that he decided to run away. He waited until after dark when his parents were sleeping. He apologized to the boy for his mother's beating and told him not to tell her where he had gone. Then he disappeared into the forest.

The slave boy was very upset. His kind master was gone and the Prince's parents would be angry with him again. He began to cry, and his crying woke the Chief. The Chief came to see why he was crying and he saw that the young Prince had left. The Chief quickly organized a search party. They looked for him all night but they could not find him. They did not know which way he had gone.

The young Prince ran deep into the forest until he was lost. He did not know which way to go. He struggled through the forest until he found a trail. It led him back to the river but far away from his village. He sat down at the base of a large tree and fell asleep.

He woke in the morning and he was hungry and cold. He didn't know where he was or how to get back to his village. His parents would be worried. He felt ashamed for his anger and the trouble he had caused. He did not feel worthy to be their son.

A canoe came towards him up the river. He had never seen a canoe like this before. It had a bow on each end and its colour was silver. It seemed to bend from left to right as it moved. It glided though the currents without making waves. He knew it must be a magic canoe. He watched with wonder as it approached.

The stranger gave him a warm smile as if he knew the Prince well. He held out his hand and said, "Please come with me, my friend. My father needs your help. In return, I will save your village from starvation."

The canoe stopped at the shore near him. Three men climbed out of the canoe. They helped the last man out. He wore the clothing of a noble. He walked straight to where the young Prince was sitting. The Prince stood to greet him. The stranger was a young man of great beauty, the same height and age as himself. His eyes were warm and kind and his skin seemed to glow. Even his clothing seemed to shine. The young Prince thought perhaps he was still dreaming, but he locked fingers with the young man and was guided to the magic canoe. The stranger seemed familiar. The Prince could not understand how he knew his village was starving, but he saw the kindness in his eyes and he did not resist his instructions. The stranger led him to his canoe and he helped him to climb inside. Then he climbed in behind the Prince.

"Where are we going?" asked the Prince.

"To my village," he answered. "Don't be alarmed."

The Prince wondered why he said this. Then the canoe pulled away from the shore by itself as though it was alive. The men paddled a few strokes and then pulled their oars out of the water. The boat went faster and faster without paddling. The young Prince was frightened.

"It is all right," said the stranger. "You will be safe if I hold you." He wrapped his arms around the Prince and pulled him back to rest against his chest. Suddenly the canoe sank under the waves and it continued to move at great speed. The water was not cold and he could still breathe when the stranger held him. The Prince felt his warmth and love and he trusted him completely. They traveled for a long time underwater until the Prince fell asleep.

He woke just as they arrived in a large village. All the houses were painted with drawings of salmon. The stranger helped him out of the canoe. He said to the Prince, "I want you to meet my father." He led him to the largest house in the centre of the village. "This is where my father lives. He is Chief of our village. He was very ill until recently but now he feels much better." He led the Prince to the back of his father's house, to the bed where his father was lying. His father sat up and smiled.

"Is this the young man who saved my life?" the old Chief asked as they approached him.

"Yes, father. He is the one."

The young Prince had no idea what they were talking about. "What do you mean? How could I save your life? I have never met you. I have never been here before." He looked at the stranger for an explanation.

"My father has been ill for two years, ever since your mother stored his former body in her secret hiding place. When you finally opened the box and gave some of his flesh to your slave boy, my father's health improved."

The young Prince was confused. "What do you mean my mother stored his former body?"

"My father is Chief of the Spring Salmon, and I am his son, the Salmon Prince. I have brought you to our underwater village to thank you for what you have done and to teach you the proper ways of treating the salmon people."

The Prince had heard stories of how Animal Spirits could take human form, but this was the first time he had witnessed it. "How did I save your life by eating your flesh, Salmon Chief?" he asked.

The Chief explained. "My soul longs to be young and healthy once more. But first, all of my flesh must be consumed and my bones must be burned in a fire. Only then can I be reborn and to swim in the rivers and oceans again."

"People of your village have been hiding their salmon instead of eating it," the Salmon Prince continued. "Every year their catches of salmon grow smaller because fewer of us are reborn. To save your village from starvation you must learn the proper ways of treating salmon. You must teach these ways to your people."

The Salmon Prince took his hand and he showed him around his village. Then he asked the young Prince if he was hungry. He said he was, for he had not eaten for a long time. "You must go behind the house where you will find the children playing. Select a plump one and club him on the head. He will be your meal. You must cook him over the fire and eat him. Take a drink of fresh water to help him be reborn. Then you must gather up every bone and throw it into the fire. His parents will thank you for his Spirit will be reborn."

The Prince looked for the children and he found them playing behind the house. He chose a plump one as he was told. At first he was afraid to strike it, but he knew he must never disobey an Animal Spirit. He reminded himself that he was very hungry and that these were not human children. He clubbed the child and it turned into a salmon. He cleaned it and cooked it. When he was finished he placed all the bones in the fire and he returned to the house.

Inside there was a new child in place of the one he had eaten, but this child was holding his eye and screaming in pain. The Prince hurried back to the fire and there he found the eye of the fish he had dropped by mistake. He threw it into the fire and returned to the house. The child was now playing quietly and his eye was healed.

He sought out the Salmon Prince and told him of his success. The Salmon Prince was pleased. "You are learning the proper way to treat the salmon people," he said, and the young Prince was proud. He saw the love in the Salmon Prince's eyes and his heart was moved. The Salmon Prince brought him to his chamber and there they made love.

The young Prince stayed in the village of the salmon people one year. It was the happiest year of his life. He walked everywhere with Salmon Prince, holding hands as lovers do. The salmon people were happy for them. They treated the young Prince like a hero. The Salmon Prince told him that he must return to his village before the next spring so he could teach his people what he had learned. But the young Prince wanted to stay. As the time grew near the thought of leaving the Salmon Prince troubled his heart greatly.

That spring the salmon people sent their scouts to the Skeena River disguised as cottonwood leaves. They waited for several weeks for news that the ice on the river was breaking. Finally the scouts returned and the Salmon Chief announced the date for their departure for the Skeena. The Salmon Prince came for his lover.

"Now I must take you back to your village. You must teach your people the proper ways that we have taught you. You must tell your parents to eat the salmon they have hidden. They must burn the bones in the fire so that my father can be reborn and lead my people up the river." The Prince packed his belongings with a heavy heart. He met the Salmon Prince and his men waiting by the shore in the magic canoe.

Again the Salmon Prince held him in his arms as the canoe went under the water. On the way back to his village, the canoe passed by the villages of the other salmon. They passed the village of the Coho. The fish on their houses were painted with crooked snouts. They said they would wait until the autumn to visit the Skeena. Then they passed the village of the Dog Salmon with rainbows painted on their houses. They said they would wait for the Humpback Salmon to pass before they left. The Humpbacks told them they would wait for the Spring Salmon. Finally they reached the village of the Trout Salmon with stars painted on their houses. They were waiting to lead the Spring Salmon into the Skeena.

"You see that everything has an order," the Salmon Prince told him. "The other salmon will not go to the Skeena unless the Spring Salmon arrive. If my father's flesh is not eaten and his bones are not burned, he cannot lead the Spring Salmon. No salmon will return to the river and your people will starve. I must leave you here and return to my village to help them prepare for their journey."

The young Prince's heart was filled with sadness. He thought he would have more time with his lover before they parted. The Salmon Prince felt his sadness and he held him in his arms.

"This is not the last time you will see me, my love. Help your people prepare the nets and poles for their fishing weirs. When the first salmon is caught, bless it with prayers and offerings and have your father share it with your people as you have been taught. I will come near the end of the run. Be waiting in the water near the shore of your village. I will find you. You must kill me. Do not dry my flesh but eat it freshly cooked and place my bones in the fire."

With these words the Salmon Prince kissed him tenderly. While they were kissing he passed a magic stone from his mouth into the mouth of the young Prince. "Hold this stone in your mouth and dream of me. It will protect you for the rest of your journey." Then the Salmon Prince changed into a salmon and swam away in the direction of his village. The magic canoe continued on and the young Prince fell into a deep sleep.

When he woke, he was lying on the beach in front of his village. He thought he was dreaming but the villagers gathered around him and they helped him to his feet. They led him to his father's house. His parents were thrilled to see him alive. They had mourned his loss since he left the village. They told him he had been gone for only a week.

He told his family the story of what had happened. He went to the box where the dried salmon was hidden and he explained what they must do to end the famine. At first they thought he had strange ideas because he was sick with a fever, but they did as he asked for they had saved the fish for his return anyway. They ate the last of the fish and they burned the bones as he instructed. The Prince knew the Chief of the Spring Salmon would be reborn.

Then he helped the other villagers prepare their weirs. He taught his father how to make offerings to the Salmon Spirits. He showed the villagers how to prepare and eat the first salmon. Then he helped them bring in the catch. It was the greatest catch in many years. The village celebrated for there would be no famine that year. They understood that what the young Prince had taught them was true.

Everyone was pleased except the young Prince. He grew sadder each day waiting for his lover to appear. He could not bear to eat any of the fish they caught. His parents and his slave boy worried for his health but there was nothing they could do.

On the last day of the catch when the nets were almost empty, he waited in the shallow water by the shore. A beautiful spring salmon swam directly to him and waited without fear by his feet. He knew this was the Salmon Prince and his heart was filled with joy. He killed him with a club and carried him in his arms to his fire. There he cleaned and cooked the meat. He was careful not to lose any part of his body.

When he lifted the first piece of flesh to his lips he felt his lover's kiss again. He held him in his mouth so he could remember the taste. When he swallowed he felt his lover's Spirit spread throughout his body like a warm glow. Each piece he ate repeated the sensations until his body ached with love. He ate slowly without saying a word until all the fish was gone. His lover's Spirit filled his body like a vessel. He gathered every bone and scrap left behind and he burned them in the fire. From that day onward he was never sad or lonely. Each year he fished for salmon with great joy, waiting for his lover to return. His people followed his lessons and they never suffered from famine again.

FOURTEEN

When our hunting trip was over we returned to building the school. We were eager and energetic. The men returned from Fort Victoria and they joined us. We finished the outside of the school just before the start of the winter ceremonies. Duncan surprised us with new desks and supplies from Fort Victoria. We were proud of our new building and anxious to start our learning again.

That autumn was a hopeful time for me and my village. We had left Gitka'ata only a year and a half before and already so much had changed for the better. We had six new houses that we had carved and painted with pride. The fishing camps were closer and we had rifles, so hunting was easier. We had escaped Ts'ibasaa's guns and I had escaped my marriage arrangement. The best friend I had ever known was now my lover and partner. Heaven had smiled upon us.

The future promised even more good fortune. The world of the Whites had opened to us and it was much larger than we could imagine. There were new tools, cloths and medicines, new ways of speaking and traveling, and so many new ideas. And most important of all, we had a new White Shaman who wanted to show us this world. His teachings were already changing me. The new world sparkled for us like sunlight on the sea, and it beckoned us towards the future. I felt certain that all our people would see the same light and they would follow it as I did.

But our Shamans did not want to follow the light. They did not like Duncan or his teachings. In the past year he had criticized their rituals and their methods of healing the sick. He had insulted them by telling our people that they no Spiritual powers.

Duncan held his classes all winter, even during the most sacred winter ceremonies, and the Shamans were outraged. He angered them further by saying they must end the ceremonies forever. They began to speak against him. What guest would come to another's home and behave so disrespectfully, they asked us. His teachings dishonoured our sacred traditions. They told us they were evil filth that would corrupt and destroy us. They cautioned the parents not to send their children to his school or Great Spirit would be vexed.

In my heart I understood their anger. They were the protectors of our traditions and Duncan threatened their status and the respect others had for them. But I was also sure that Duncan wanted a better life for us and that the changes he wanted were necessary. I believed that someday they would see that others had learned new skills and they would wish they had started learning from the Whites much sooner.

When the school was finished, Duncan announced he would start classes the next day. Tamlahk, Miyana and I arrived early in the morning, but few others dared to ignore the Shamans' warning. Duncan asked Tamlahk to climb the ladder and strike the steel bar that hung above the door to summon the other students. The loud ringing sound echoed off the distant houses. People came out to see where the noise was coming from. The Shamans appeared too, dressed in their ceremonial capes and headdresses. They stood on the path by the beach to remind us of their warning.

Keep ringing the bell until they come, Duncan told us. When Tamlahk's arm grew tired I took his place. Soon another student took a turn striking the bar. The people were delighted by our boldness and the crowd on the beach began to swell. They realized that the Shamans could do nothing to stop us and they began to walk past them to the school. By midday there were more than sixty students. By afternoon we had one hundred. We had won the first battle.

The Shamans did not give up easily. They stood on the path every morning, shaking their rattles at us. Some students mocked them as they passed by and the tensions worsened each day. Finally the Shamans went to Legiac and demanded that he close the school. At first Legiac refused, for he had supported the school from its start. They complained that many people had stopped attending the winter ceremonies. They accused Legiac of letting Duncan violate our traditions and causing the Spirits to be angry. Legiac's enemies, including Tumcoosh, agreed with the Shamans. They called him a cowardly leader and the school became an embarrassment and a threat to his leadership.

One morning Legiac came to the school himself. He told Duncan that the children made too much noise running past his house going to and from the school. He said they were disrupting the sacred ceremonies. He asked Duncan to suspend the classes for one month during the main ceremonies. His accusation was ridiculous, so Duncan refused. He explained in a soft voice that his lessons would better the Tsimshian people and that Legiac should support them. Legiac's face struggled with anger and frustration. He had no stomach for negotiation and he was not accustomed to such open disregard for his authority. He turned to the students and told us that Duncan was teaching us evil and not to come to his classes anymore. He left quickly, slamming the door behind him.

A few days later, during the darkest days of the year, Legiac held a special potlatch for his son. He made a public declaration there must be no school that day. Duncan was determined to hold classes anyway. Legiac's wife came to the school that morning and pleaded with him to stop even for a few hours. She was frightened of his temper. The Chiefs were mocking Legiac because he could not stop the school on the day of his son's feast. She heard the Shamans talk about killing Duncan. None of us would ring the bell and tempt Legiac's wrath. But Duncan was as stubborn as Legiac. He climbed the ladder himself to ring the bell. Soon there were eighty students and Duncan started to teach.

Everyone in the classroom was tense that day, for we expected a showdown. We were not disappointed. That afternoon Legiac marched to the school with seven Shamans dressed in their full ceremonial robes and headdresses. A young girl saw them coming towards the school and she screamed. Our hearts pounded wildly. We were not sure if we should sit still or gather the children and run out the back door into the forest.

Duncan signaled us to stay quiet and he moved to block the doorway. Legiac was shouting loudly, telling us to leave the schoolhouse. He had been drinking and his voice was shaky. Duncan cautioned us not to move. Duncan let the Shamans push past him, but he used his arm to bar Legiac from entering. He announced that people who had been drinking could not enter the school. Legiac was embarrassed, for only he was drunk.

The two men stood face to face. Legiac demanded the school close immediately for the remainder of the winter ceremonies. Duncan refused. He spoke his wisdom softly and carefully in his best Tsimshian. Legiac did not know what to do. He pleaded with Duncan to close it for only two weeks instead but Duncan would not negotiate. Legiac's temper flared again but Duncan continued to reason with him softly.

While they argued the Shamans watched them closely. I quietly guided several of the smallest children out the back door so they would not see the violence that was coming. I asked one boy to run to the fort to find Clah. The men locked in battle at the front of the room scarcely noticed the crunch of his footsteps on the stones as he ran towards town.

Time passed slowly. Duncan managed to stall Legiac for a long time. His voice gained confidence the longer he talked and Legiac became more uncertain as the whisky lost its effect. For a while we thought Duncan would win the argument. But Shamans had cleverly spread the word that Legiac would confront Duncan that morning and a large crowd had gathered on the beach to watch. The Shamans shouted to them, saying that Legiac was not a coward and that he would shut down the school as he had promised the Chiefs. They knew he could not bear another humiliation.

The Shamans' words excited Legiac's temper. In a loud voice, he demanded that Duncan clear the school immediately. Duncan refused again, calmly, keeping his fearless eyes locked on Legiac's. Legiac pulled out his knife and came at Duncan.

At the final second he looked over Duncan's shoulder and he froze. Clah, the coward of the fort, had entered through the back door. He was pointing a rifle at Legiac's head. Legiac stared at him in disbelief. Clah glared back at him and gently cocked the hammer of the rifle. Legiac's face turned whiter than Duncan's. He slowly lowered his knife and turned to the Shamans in confusion. He muttered something about no killing in front of the children. Then he led the Shamans out the door through the crowd and back to the town. Clah uncocked the rifle and set it down.

We woke from the nightmare and looked around at each other in shock. The children I had guided out the back door were huddled against the back wall and crying. I went to comfort them and bring them back in while Tamlahk and the other adults looked after the children inside. Duncan's body seemed to wither. He returned to his desk and collapsed into his chair. He held his face in his hands and he cried. After a while he dried his eyes and asked the children to return to their desks. Then he astonished me by beginning the lesson again as though nothing had happened.

The news spread quickly that Legiac and the Shamans had failed to stop Duncan from teaching. There was talk that Duncan had powers greater than theirs. But Legiac did not forget his humiliation easily. He made a public announcement to all villages that the school was closed. He vowed to shoot anyone who passed his house to go to the school the next day.

My father knew how much Miyana, Tamlahk and I liked Duncan and our classes. He believed Duncan was a good man, and that the school was the best gift the Whites had given the Tsimshian. He knew it was important for our future. That evening he asked me to take him to Duncan's room in the fort so he could warn him of Legiac's announcement.

Duncan was discouraged. If the school closed at this point Legiac might never let it open again, but he could not risk the lives of the students. My father offered him a solution. He said Duncan could use his house for classes until the end of the winter ceremonies. Duncan was delighted and he accepted his offer.

It was a bold risk for my father to take. Legiac was furious, of course, but there was nothing he could do. A Chief was master over his own house. Besides, Legiac knew the Chiefs wanted to humiliate him more than they wanted to close the school.

Neeshlak sent a message to Legiac reassuring him of his allegiance. He explained that the school was important and that he was only trying to keep the peace. Legiac accepted my father's explanation and forgave him, for my father treated him with more respect than the other Chiefs. Legiac had won a small victory. He had not stopped Duncan but at least he had closed the school until the end of the winter ceremonies.

There were many power struggles between the Chiefs at Fort Simpson. A small act of defiance could start a trail of murders and retaliations. A Chief like my father, who had a small village and who arrived after the others, had little influence at the Council of Chiefs. Many of the Chiefs distrusted him at first, thinking he was no more than Legiac's pet. His action to save the school could have turned them against him, but it did the opposite. The Chiefs saw he was strong enough to oppose Legiac and clever enough to keep his allegiance at the same time. He won their respect and admiration. Now he had prestige and they sought his allegiance.

Duncan's classes survived the winter ceremonies only to stop the next week when we left for the oolichon camps on the Nass. By the time we returned two moons had passed and the tensions between Legiac and Duncan were half forgotten. Respect for Duncan had grown, and without the winter ceremonies his classes were more popular than before. There were only enough desks for half the students. The others brought blankets to sit on the floor.

Duncan had the same routine every morning. He inspected the hands and faces of the adults for cleanliness as soon as we arrived. Then we helped him inspect the children. He counted us as he called our names. We answered "Yes!" loudly and he marked us in his ledger each time. The children loved this routine and he encouraged this by giving treats for good attendance.

Then we prayed to God, the Great Spirit of the Whites. Duncan asked Tamlahk and me to show the children the proper way to pray, just as Clah had shown us a year before when Duncan first spoke to us. We knelt on the floor and put our hands together as we bowed our heads. This made the young children laugh and they knelt by their desks to copy us. Duncan told them to close their eyes and repeat his words of prayer, but the children always peeked to see what he was doing.

At first the prayers were simple. Then he taught us longer ones. Sometimes the prayers were songs that we sang together while Duncan played a White instrument called a concertina. They were everyone's favourite prayers. Duncan had a beautiful voice too, the most beautiful voice we had ever heard. Sometimes he would sing alone while we listened. We all wanted to sing like him.

He taught us the White stories of how God created the world. He told us about the first man, Adam, and his wife Eve in the Garden of Eden. The children laughed at the story of how Eve was created. We learned how God destroyed great cities and sent the Great Flood to punish man for not obeying His rules. We all knew the story of Damelahamid so we knew he was telling the truth.

He also taught us about His Son Jesus and the Mother Mary and how we would burn in Hell if Jesus did not save us. He said we had to copy the ways of the Whites if we wanted to be saved. We did not question his teachings.

Duncan also taught us to read English words so we could read the hymn books and sing more songs. I had already learned to print many words in his chambers. I could read sentences too, so I helped the other students. He had loaned me the holy book of God's wisdom, the Bible, but I could not understand much of it yet. Clah and I helped him to write the words of our language in English letters so he could write prayers in Tsimshian.

English was more difficult than I expected. I could not understand why English letters make different sounds in different words or why sometimes they do not make any sound at all. It was so frustrating. Why would the English make so many silly spellings, I asked Duncan. He laughed and agreed they were silly. Why not fix the spellings, I asked him. To know this problem and not change it seemed foolish. This made him laugh very hard indeed, but he did not explain why. He only said it was not his decision to make. The English language is as strange and frustrating as the English.

When my reading improved Duncan gave me his dictionary. What a wonderful book it was! I could not believe there were so many words. How exciting it was to look for new ones! I showed Tamlahk. He liked it too, but he did not enjoy reading it as much as I did. I read it by the fire each night until my eyes were sore. My brothers teased me that the book had cast a spell upon me. They were right. It is still my favourite of all the English books I have read. I have read it many times.

The first days of learning English were magical. A new world of knowledge opened to me. I spent more time in the trading post reading the packages on the shelves to learn what was inside. Some had pictures. There were sacks with a drawing of a simple plant on the front and the word 'RICE'. A tin with the words "APPLE SAUCE" had a picture of an apple on it. There were drawings of beans on a bag of dried beans. Other packages confused me. There was a woman's face smiling on a tin of cookies. A terrible thought frightened me. Was this woman's body used to make these cookies? Could Whites be such savages? I felt ill. I did not dare ask Duncan. I thought he might laugh at me, or worse, he might confirm that my fear was true. I put the cookie tin back on the shelf and promised myself never to eat one if I was offered.

I also learned that Whites measure everything. It is not enough to have days, weeks and years. Each day was divided into hours, the hours into minutes and minutes into seconds. Duncan put a clock on the wall that we wound every morning with a large key. He taught us how to read it and plan our day with it. We played games of speed where seconds were important. We learned the meaning of the words 'late' and 'early'. Usually, late was bad and early was good.

He taught us about weeks, and the names of the days of the week so that we would know which day was Sunday, God's day of rest and prayer. He told us that working on Sundays was wrong so we asked why he worked on Sundays. He told us he did God's work and that was permitted. The children asked why God did not do his own work. He said he was God's servant and that he was following the teachings in God's book, the Bible. They wanted to know if God paid him. He became impatient and told us we would never learn anything if we didn't stop asking questions and listen. He reminded us that we must learn to read so we could understand the stories in the Bible.

How did he know a certain day was Sunday and not another, we asked. He said White men had counted the days from the beginning of time. We nodded our agreement, since we knew White men liked to count everything. If every day is different we wondered why they were called by the same names each week. How would you know which day was Sunday if the names didn't repeat, he explained. Why is it not better to work on a sun day than a rain day? Didn't God send good weather to help us do our work? Surely God would be pleased with prayers on any day. Our questions exhausted him. The answers to your questions were in the Bible, he sighed. For now we should concentrate on learning English so we could understand it better.

Duncan hung a calendar on the wall. Moons also became months, though there were only twelve in a year instead of thirteen. Each morning he would ask one of us to tell the class which day it was. We learned that ten years made a decade and a hundred years made a century. Whites had counted the years since the beginning of time, though they had to count backwards before Jesus was born. Each year had a number and each month had a name. Duncan's calendar told us that year was 1859 and that month he first hung the calendar was called April.

He taught us to measure many other things too. He had rulers and tapes to measure lengths and distances in inches, feet and yards. We learned to weigh things in ounces and pounds on a small scale he bought in the trading post. Duncan had also taught us to read a thermometer so we could record the temperature each day.

He even taught us the English system of money. But what strange ways of counting the English have! They had ten fingers like us, but they counted twelve inches in a foot, sixty seconds in a minute, sixteen ounces in a pound of weight and twenty shillings in a pound of money. We wondered how they could enjoy measuring so many things with such crazy ways of counting.

Those who did not attend his classes thought all this counting was foolish. They said they could tell if a fish was big enough to feed a family without weighing it. They could feel if the air was cold enough to need extra clothing without a thermometer. But Duncan said we would use these skills later for many reasons, such as buying things or building houses.

Tamlahk and I began to dress like White men too. Duncan took delight in teaching us about the proper clothes an Englishman wears. We bought leather boots, belts and hats first. The other clothes would come later.

The item that fascinated me the most was a little clock he kept in his pocket, fastened to his pants with a small chain. He showed me how to wind it and how to change the time when I was in his chamber. He called it a pocket watch. I saw one like it in the trading post. It was so beautiful. The silver cover had a scene of a White hunter and his dog. I visited the store often to look at it. It was kept in a glass case on the counter. I was too shy to ask the clerk with the orange beard if I could hold it. I only pointed at it and said, "Very good." He only grunted and shook his head. He patted his hand to show that it was worth much money.

I saw the price and did not worry that it was expensive. I saved the money that Duncan paid me until I had enough to buy it. When that day came I waited patiently at the counter for the clerk as he helped another trade furs for a rifle. I visited the store so often they hardly noticed me now. While I waited I opened the glass case and held it in my hand. I felt the metal carvings on the cover and I opened it. I wound it and it made a beautiful ticking sound! I held it to my ear.

"No! Bad!" The clerk with the orange hair snatched the pocket watch from my hand. He glared at me angrily and he inspected it for damage.

"Please, I want to buy the pocket watch. I know how to wind it." I spoke in my best English, trying to sound exactly like Duncan. I had practiced these words for several days. I pulled the money Duncan had paid me out of my pouch and placed it on the counter.

"You speak English?" He stared at me in surprise while he set the pocket watch down on the counter slowly. He had seen me many times but had never spoken with me. His English sounded different than Duncan's but I could understand it.

"Yes, a little. It is two dollars and fifty-nine cents, isn't it?" I counted the money in front of him.

"Yes, of course, you speak English. I mean, you must know how to use it." He stared at the money on the counter without picking it up. I had counted it correctly. "You have money?" he asked me.

"Mr. Duncan pays me. I help him learn Tsimshian. The money is good, right?"

"Oh yes, of course. Well I'll be damned!" He was smiling now.

"Please, what is the correct time?"

"Just a second." He pulled out his pocket watch to check the time. "It's 3:35. Here, let me set it for you."

"No, thank you. I must practice." He stared at me in amazement as I set the hands to 3:35. "How often should I wind it?"

"Every morning when you get up. Would you like to buy a chain for your watch?" he asked with enthusiasm.

"No, thank you. I have no pocket for my pocket watch. I must buy some pants first." This must have sounded funny for he laughed loudly.

"That's terrific!" he chuckled, extending his hand. "My name is Bill."

"My name is Gugweelaks," I said with great dignity, taking his hand.

"Good to meet you, Googeelots! Come and see me again, whenever you need those pants!" He laughed again. He smiled at me as I left the store. He waved to me through the window as I crossed the courtyard of the fort.

After that, Bill was always happy to see me whenever I visited the store. I liked his big smile, though he never remembered my name. He always asked how my watch was working and I would show him that it was fine. If there were other White men in the store, he would ask me to speak English for them.

"Listen to this young lad, will ya! He speaks English better than a parrot! I swear he's going to be a right proper Englishman one day! Show them what you can say."

I introduced myself to them. Most of them just laughed or made comments about me to Bill. Others would say it was good to meet me, but they never told me their names.

Their rudeness made me uncomfortable, but I did not complain to Bill. He did not notice my discomfort and he was not trying to upset me. Besides, he had once given me a small wooden cross to wear on a string around my neck. He had taught me how to make a cross on my body to praise God by touching my forehead, then my chest and shoulders. I was eager to show Duncan what I had learned.

"Who showed you that?" he snapped at me loudly. I told him about Bill and how we met. "That Romanist dog! You must not listen to him. He is a Catholic! Catholics know nothing about God!" He ordered me to take the wooden cross off my neck. Then he changed his mind. "I suppose you can wear it and cross yourself if you wish, but it won't help you any if you do!" he added sternly.

"Mr. Duncan, what is a parrot?"

He looked puzzled. "Parrots are big colourful birds that makes lots of noise. They live in the hot jungles, in places like Africa."

"Do they live in India too?"

"Yes, some come from India."

"Can they speak English?"

"Some can be trained to make sounds like words but they do not understand what they are saying. Why do you ask?"

"Bill said I speak English better than a parrot."

"The nerve! I am sure you do. I dare say you speak better English than he does! Don't listen to his insults. A man who says that to you is not your friend."

I did not know before this that White men worshipped different Gods. This was troubling news. I asked Tamlahk how we know if we learned the right truths from the Whites if they believed different truths? He was not very concerned. He said Duncan was a Shaman and Bill was not. He said we should listen to Duncan and follow his words. I thought it was unkind of Bill to compare me to a bird that did not understand English. I decided not to visit the store so often. I took off the wooden cross and stored it away in my room.

That summer Duncan asked Clah and I to help him with a special project. He wanted us to translate the Bible into Tsimshian. Duncan was excited by the project, but he was also concerned that we understood each passage carefully first. It was important to get God's words correct, he said. He asked us to repeat the stories in Tsimshian so that he knew we understood the meaning. We were inspired by Duncan's enthusiasm. I was happy to finally understand the stories. I had tried to read them before but there were many strange words that I had never heard anyone use.

It was a very large project and it was hard to satisfy Duncan. Clah was soon bored. He found reasons to go to the store or to do errands in other parts of the fort. After three weeks he found things to do outside of the fort. For the first time in years he left the fort by himself. He risked his life to avoid translating the Bible.

I found pictures in Duncan's Bible that I was curious about. They showed Jesus with long hair, dressed in robes. I wondered why Duncan told us we should dress like Englishmen to show that we are Christians when Christ himself did not dress this way. Duncan explained that those times were long ago. He said Christians did not dress that way now, but he did not say why.

The houses and the trees were strange too. There was a lot of sand and no forests. I asked him where these places were. He told me they were on the other side of the world. He had once shown me pictures of England and told me it was other side of the world too, but this was not England. I wanted him to explain. He said I asked him too many questions, but promised to teach me about the world later if I concentrated on translating the Bible.

I never let him forget his promise. He ordered a book of maps from Fort Victoria and he invited me to study it with him. He even let Tamlahk come with me. These were the first maps we had ever seen. They were colourful and interesting, but they did not tell us much about where these lands were or what they looked like. Duncan told us the world is round but the maps were flat. Many things Whites taught us required great faith.

There were many lands with strange names. Beside each map were drawings of the people who lived there, dressed in the clothing they wore. Their skins were different colours and so were the houses and the trees. Tamlahk and I had so many questions that it was hard to wait for the answers. Duncan showed us a map of our lands too. He showed us where Fort Victoria was and Fort Simpson. Gitka'ata and Metlakatla were missing from the map but he showed us where the Nass and the Skeena were. It was all the world we knew, and we thought it was very large, but the map was so small I could hold it in my hand. Beside our lands was a drawing of a man, not one of our men but perhaps a Haida or Kwakiutl. Beneath the picture was the word 'Indian'. "Who is this Indian? I have never heard of a people called Indians."

"The English call all the different peoples from here 'Indians', the Haida, the Kwakiutl, the Nootka and your people too. When we found your lands a long time ago we thought we had found India. The Indians of India have darker skin, and we knew they lived on the other side of the world too."

"The Indians must live close to us if they are on this side of the world too."

"No, they are also on the other side of the world from you too, just a different side. They are as far from you as they are from England." He showed us another map.

We thought about this for a few seconds. "How many sides is the world?" Tamlahk asked. Duncan laughed, "You mean how many sides does it have? Many sides I suppose, but then it also has no sides because it is round." He laughed again. "I will buy a round map of the world for all the students the next time I am in Fort Victoria. I will get more picture books of other lands too."

The thought that Indians looked like us but they lived on the other side of the world impressed me deeply. Duncan told us that he had traveled more than half of a year from England to reach Fort Simpson. English ships could travel much faster than our canoes, so that must be very far. If the Indians lived as far away as England, how did they come from India to our lands? Did they sail here on big sailing ships too? If so, what happened to the sailing ships? Perhaps our ancestors had traveled to India instead, but how did they go so far in our small canoes?

Tamlahk was as excited as I was about the maps, but he was as puzzled as I was about the Indians. We lay together on our bed talking about the places we would like to visit. He said we should travel to India one day to see these people for ourselves. We would dress in their strange clothes and see if we looked just like them. We also wanted to visit the Holy Lands of the Bible and England. Maybe we would find Duncan's village too. Tamlahk had not seen Gitka'ata and I had not seen his village, but we dreamed of seeing the other side of the world first.

Our imaginations gave wings to our bold dreams. They helped us to forget the whisky and the killings in Fort Simpson. They bound us closer together and fed the love in our hearts. Now we shared both the present and the future, but our dreams made us impatient too. We were bored with our lives in Fort Simpson.

We escaped on hunting trips during the beautiful days of summer to be alone by ourselves. We found a sheltered bay on a small island and it became our favourite place. We swam naked in the warm waters after the tide crept in over the hot sand. We played like porpoises in the shallow water. Then we raced back to the beach, grabbing and holding each other back trying to be the first to reach the shore. We lay on our backs at the edge of the water. We let the waves wash over us while we watched the clouds crossing the blue sky.

"Gugweelaks, what would you do if I died?"

"What a terrible thought! What makes you say this? You will summon the Spirits of the Dead by asking such a question."

"I was just wondering. Would you forget me? Would you find another lover?"

"I would place you in a burial box beside my house. I would mourn you for all of my days and I would never take another lover."

"But what if I drowned at sea and my body was not found. I would become a lost soul, an evil bogwas. I would roam the hills looking for people to kill."

"Then I would search for you in the hills. I'd find you and let you to blow in my face so that I would die. Then I would spend eternity with you. Now stop this talk. It bothers me deeply."

He was so foolish with his words. I turned away from him to pout. He snuggled next to me and begged my forgiveness. He stroked my cheek tenderly. How gentle he could be! His lips found mine and we kissed again and again. At first we rocked with the rhythm of the waves but as our passion grew he crashed into me like a storm pounding against the rocks. How rough he could be! When we were finished we laughed for we found ourselves on the dry sand above the water line. He held me to his chest and we talked once more about traveling together.

It seems like the world was in love that summer. Doolyaks and Yuwahksa had married the past autumn and Uncle Shoget had announced that Amapaas would marry Teshlah in the coming autumn. The four had become strong friends since our move to Fort Simpson. Doolyaks and Yuwahksa took great delight in helping Amapaas and Teshlah prepare for their marriage. The women of Teshlah's Blackfish Clan, Miyana and my mother Memlaka helped with the marriage preparations.

In the peak of summer, Doolyaks, Amapaas and Gwashasip left with two hundred others in twenty canoes to visit Fort Victoria. They returned in mid-September after being away two months. They had many stories about Fort Victoria, about the many roads outside the fort where the Whites built their houses. Some of their houses were larger than our longhouses while others were small. People rode tall animals called horses that Tamlahk and I had seen in the picture books. The trading post was bigger and had many more things than ours. There were other stores outside the fort that sold mostly one thing, such as meat, clothing or furniture. The Whites who had come to look for gold were gone now and many new buildings were empty.

They also told stories about the camps they shared with the other peoples of the coast, the Haida, Kwakiutl, Salish and Nootka. There they saw much drunkenness, fighting and some killings too. Gwashasip told me many Indian women sold their bodies to White men for money and liquor. These were the vices Duncan had warned us about.

But these vices were in Fort Simpson too. More ships arrived to sell us whisky and rum that fall than ever before and the ugliness that followed them drove the warmth and joy of our summer away. We heard fighting and gunfire every night. The Haida raided our neighbouring villages for revenge killings three times and Legiac's men killed two of them. And so the pattern repeated.

We tried our best to ignore the cold rains and ugliness around us as we proceeded with Amapaas and Teshlah's marriage. It was a time to remember our traditions and to celebrate our future. We had much to be happy for. Their parents and the Elders of the Blackfish and Eagle Clans had arranged their marriage when they were still children. We knew the Spirits had also blessed their union for they were in love. Teshlah would bear Blackfish children who would be heirs to my father's name and position.

Before their wedding day, relatives of the Blackfish and the Eagle Clans met to throw rocks and mud at each other. It was our custom to drive away all resentments from our hearts, and it was good fun. Eight men of the Blackfish Clan carried Teshlah to Amapaas on a marriage robe. They placed the marriage robe in front of him and he sat on the robe beside her to her right. They stayed beside each other for three days without food or drink. Our families visited, sang and celebrated around them. The children teased them to make them make them laugh and they struggled not to smile. On the fourth day Tooklan sprinkled eagle down over their heads and the marriage feast was declared. After the food was cleared away, my father gave gifts to all the guests.

First he asked Amapaas and Teshlah to bless the marriage with a kiss. Just as they kissed, a bullet struck the wall of our house. Everyone was startled. For a moment there was silence. Then we heard shouting and more gunfire outside our door. A Haida war party was attacking the Nishga camp next to us. We heard Drashwuk's drunken curses and threats. My father asked everyone to remain seated and he continued with the ceremony. If the gift giving stopped the marriage would not be completed.

Twice more bullets struck our house. We were all nervous. It was a bad omen, but Neeshlak spoke to honour this marriage. "This marriage will keep our houses strong, and a strong house will keep the bullets out." The guests cheered at his wisdom and toasted Amapaas and Teshlah. The gift giving was completed and the families were united. The two moved into Amapaas's new chamber in Shoget's house, next to our chamber.

The celebration was over but the violence remained. In the mornings bodies were scattered the beaches and passages between the houses. Some were sick from the whisky. Others were injured or dead. The young children were afraid to walk to school. Often they arrived crying and terrified that the Ghosts of Dead had followed them to school. Duncan asked the adults to gather the children each morning. Tamlahk and I led them to the school holding hands and singing hymns as we walked.

But the hymns were not enough to protect us. One morning we found a five-year-old girl unconscious on the beach. She drank a bottle of rum the night before. Her parents were too drunk to notice she was missing. Another day, a girl who was neglected by her drunken parents fell from her seat in school. We ran to help her and found she was dead.

Shamans brought more trouble once the winter ceremonies began. They asked Legiac to close the school but my father promised to hold classes in his house again if he did. The Shamans stood on the path to the school each morning and cursed the students as they passed. The younger students were frightened. The older ones were tired of their threats and bullying and grew angry. One day a student saw a Shaman dancing in circles to put curses on Duncan's hat. The student mocked him and the Shaman took after him with a knife. The boy pulled out a gun and shot him dead.

That winter, drunken fighting happened throughout the day. We tried to keep our school routine, but violence surrounded us. Sometimes rocks struck the outside of the school and the children would start to cry. One day two drunks were fighting over a woman on the beach beside the school. One shot the woman dead and a gunfight began. A bullet broke a window and hit the ceiling. We led the children out the back door and hid in the woods until the fighting stopped.

Duncan showed no pity to the men who drank and fought. One night I was translating scripture with him in his chambers when Nakeeda, Drashwuk's wife, came to see him to ask for White medicine. Drashwuk had been stabbed in a fight over gambling. Duncan saw cuts and bruises from Drashwuk's fists on her face and he was furious. He said he would not give her medicine until he cleaned and dressed her wounds first.

When he was finished he told her that if Drashwuk wanted medicine he must come to him to apologize for his sins and he must promise to change his behaviour. Nakeeda panicked. Her eyes filled with tears and she shrieked, "No, no, please!" She told him Drashwuk would beat her when he saw her dressings if she returned with nothing for him. She fell to the floor, begging for Duncan's mercy. Duncan refused her and told her to pray for her husband instead. She began to wail loudly and refused to leave. After a few minutes the White guards from the fort came and dragged her to the gate.

Drashwuk was angry with Duncan. The next night he attacked the school. He chopped through the door with his axe and smashed all the windows. We found the floor and the desks covered with broken glass. A thin layer of fresh snow had blown through the windows and covered everything. Duncan was upset but he told the students that we must be brave and continue on. We swept up the broken glass and wiped off the desks. We covered the windows with blankets and wood to keep out the wind. We hung gaslights to keep away the darkness.

One event lifted our Spirits in the darkness of that winter. That was Amapaas's naming ceremony, where he took the name of his Uncle H'sahkool and became an Elder of the Eagle Clan. It was a proud moment for my family and the Eagle Clan. Teshlah was already pregnant with his child. If it would be a son he would be the future heir to the Blackfish Clan and Head Chief of the Gitka'atans after my father died. If it would be a girl she would pass on the titles of the Blackfish Clan through her children. It was a proper time for my brother to become an Elder.

My father held a great potlatch for Amapaas, a ceremony fitting for a son responsible for the future of his Clan. All the Tsimshian Chiefs were invited as well as a Haida Chief and Drashwuk, the Nishga Chief. He gave Duncan a seat of honour at the ceremony too. For a brief time there was great interest in this potlatch and the violence around us stopped. For three days we feasted and told stories. Amapaas was an eloquent speaker. Everyone said he was much like Neeshlak, a natural leader.

On the final night my father spoke of the need for the Tsimshian Chiefs to work together as a Council and not to fight each other. He spoke well of Legiac's leadership and presented the greatest gifts to him. Then he distributed gifts to the other Chiefs. By tradition, Drashwuk and the Haida Chief had fewer gifts for they were not Tsimshian.

Drashwuk was drunk again. He felt slighted by the smaller number of gifts and he became unpleasant. He stood and shouted insults at Neeshlak, saying he did not treat him fairly like other Chiefs. Neeshlak was upset. He told him that he had given him what he deserved for he did not have the manners or dignity of other Chiefs. His words brought a large cheer from the others. Drashwuk was humiliated and he left.

My father continued the gift giving to the Elders. Before he finished Drashwuk returned. He stood quietly at the back near the door. My father saw him enter. The room fell silent. They waited for Neeshlak to speak.

"Have you returned to join us, Drashwuk? I apologize, for I should not have spoken to you when I was angry. I have no hard feelings now. It was the whisky that made you speak against me. You are welcome to take your rightful place with the other Chiefs."

Drashwuk looked around slowly. He met our stares. He took three steps towards the centre of the room. We thought he was returning to his seat, but suddenly he pulled out a pistol. He pointed it at my father and shot twice. Then he turned and fled out the door.

Beside me my father cried out and fell to his knees. The crowd rose to their feet and rushed towards us. My fathers' arm was bleeding. It was not a fatal wound and I felt relief, but then I saw Amapaas and horror gripped my heart. The second bullet had hit his face. He fell to the floor beside my father. His body shook for a couple moments and then he was still. Duncan struggled through the Elders to my father's side to help but it was already too late. Amapaas was dead.

The sight of my brother's shattered face was so horrible a wave of panic overcame me. I fell to the ground. The rush of people around us made me dizzy and I emptied my stomach. As my strength returned I saw Neeshlak hugging Amapaas's body and crying. Tooklan and Shoget were trying to stop the bleeding of Neeshlak's wound. Tamlahk found me and he helped me up to one of the benches. I panicked and struggled against him. I wanted to go to my brother's side but there were too many people and nothing I could do. Tamlahk held me tightly while I cried.

Teshlah and Memlaka fought their way through the crowd of men to my brother's body. Miyana was there too. I remember her shrieks and wailing. Even Memlaka could not calm her. She vowed to kill Drashwuk herself. Legiac was upset too. He sent his men after Drashwuk but they returned saying he had fled from Fort Simpson in his canoe.

My father's face was blank. He did not look at the others as they bound his wound. He did not react to the news that Drashwuk had fled. Legiac offered to bring Drashwuk's family to Neeshlak before they escaped too so he could kill them in revenge. Neeshlak stared at my brother's body, which was now covered by a blanket.

"No, Neeshlak, please. This will only lead to more killings later," Duncan pleaded. "These killings must stop. It is wrong to kill. That is God's teaching."

"Neeshlak, you must keep your honour. You cannot allow Drashwuk to escape unpunished," Legiac argued.

My father looked at Legiac and then at Duncan. He spoke slowly. "I would kill Drashwuk myself if I could find him. A man like that does not deserve to live. He is a danger and a shame to all of us." He turned to Legiac again. "But I will not kill more innocent people in revenge. There has been too much of this, Legiac. It is not good for our people and it must stop.

"As for you and your God, Mr. Duncan, I know you mean well. You say your God has mercy, but He does nothing to stop the killing. Perhaps this is His punishment for us because we have not stopped the drinking and the murders. Now it has gone too far and we cannot stop it. Our children see death every day. They learn to drink and to kill. This is what we teach them. Many of them will die even before they are grown. Maybe it is too late to save the adults, Mr. Duncan, but you can still save our children. Take them away from us, away from the alcohol, the guns and the killing. Keep them safe and teach them about goodness again. We do not deserve to be their parents."

My father's words fell like sharp stones. Their truth stabbed our hearts and choked our voices. Legiac and the other Chiefs stared in shame at the floor, at Amapaas's lifeless body. There was only the sound of the women sobbing. But Duncan looked deeply into my father's eyes. He said nothing but I could see he had accepted my father's challenge. His eyes were filled with promise and determination.

FIFTEEN

My brother's death changed my family forever. The light was never as bright in my father's eyes. His arm healed but the wound to his Spirit remained. He stayed quiet and withdrawn. He was no longer concerned about the vanities and power struggles of the other Chiefs. Gwashasip was no longer carefree and happy. He became angry and rebellious. He wanted to avenge Amapaas's murder but my father strongly forbade it. So he broke my father's rules against drinking. He came home drunk many nights or he did not come home at all.

Teshlah went into her mourning period. When the necessary time was over, she returned to help the other women with their duties. She worked hard but there was no light in her eyes either. Her only joy was Amapaas's child growing in her belly. It became her reason for living.

Miyana was no comfort to her. She had worshipped her oldest brother. The sadness of our family and the promise of an unhappy marriage to Gadonai only made her grieving worse. She often escaped Hoshieka's watchful eyes to wander as she pleased. Hoshieka complained to my father about her behaviour, but neither of them would speak to her harshly for she would scream in anger and run away. Neeshlak did not have the heart to punish her, for she was suffering as much as he was.

Only my mother remained strong for the rest of us. If my father was the roof and walls of our house, my mother was the framework that held them together. She did her best to manage the household crises and perform the duties of a Head Chief's wife, but she never spoke of my brother's death or the framework would have collapsed.

It was the darkest and most miserable of our winters. The wind and sky felt our pain and spread our suffering to all of Fort Simpson. The cold came early and stayed long. The snows grew deeper and did not melt. Death stalked us that winter. Many in the town fell ill with fevers and congestion and several died.

When the Shamans could not stop the fevers, the Chiefs turned to Duncan for help. Soon he had too many patients to continue with his teachings. He closed the school until the broken door and windows were replaced. He spent his mornings and evenings tending the sick and teaching their families to pray to the White God. He convinced the Chiefs to provide shoes and boots for the commoners and slaves, to prevent the spread of the fevers.

But Duncan fell ill too. He complained of pains in his chest and he had frequent coughing bouts that worried me. I begged him to rest to build his strength but he ignored my warnings. He said he must do God's work and help the sick. He wanted me to continue my studies in his chambers too. He liked to have me near when he was sick. I read quietly or talked to him while he rested in his bed. Often he would fall asleep. I would close the curtains and gently pull the blankets over him. I guarded him and prayed to the White God for his recovery as he slept.

Duncan's mood darkened like the winter skies when the sick he tended did not recover. One day a young girl who suffered from a foot infection died. She was one of his favourite students. When I arrived in his chambers that afternoon I saw that his eyes were red from crying. I sat beside him on the bed and put my arm around his shoulders. He rose quickly and turned away so I could not see his tears. He dried his eyes and looked out his window at the falling snow.

"I don't belong here, Gugweelaks. There is nothing I can do to help your people. I am not a doctor. I am only trained to heal men's Spirits, not their bodies."

His words alarmed me. "But we need you. Our Spirits are also important. You give us hope!"

"False hope I'm afraid." He turned back to me. "I have lost my little friend, Gugweelaks. There was nothing I could do to save her." Tears rose in his eyes and he turned away again. He began to cough hard, covering his mouth with his handkerchief.

"I cannot even save myself," he added, looking at his hand. There was blood on his handkerchief. "I live amongst the dying and I am dying too."

How that blood frightened me! I told him he would get better, and I prayed to God to make my words come true, but he refused to admit to me that he was ill. We had both seen many people die to feel comfortable talking about it.

When he was resting between his visits to the sick, I tried to distract him from his worries. I asked him to tell me about the people who lived in other parts of the world, about the people in the Holy Lands where Jesus lived or about the Indians on the other side of the world. The subjects did not interest him. Then I asked him about his home in England and his Spirit brightened.

He told me the story of his life in northern England when he was a boy. His father died before he was born. He lived in a small house with his grandparents in a town larger than Fort Simpson, but smaller than many other English towns. His family had lived there for many generations. His grandfather taught him how to make things out of animal skins and he helped his grandfather run a business. He wanted Duncan to run it on his own when he got too old, but Duncan wanted to do God's work instead.

In his town there was a great building called the House of God where people came to pray to God. It was the largest building in the town, even larger than the Head Chief's house, for God is more important than a Head Chief. It was as tall as the highest trees and many centuries old. It had windows of coloured glass that filled the space inside with magical light. He spent much of his time there. That was where he learned to sing God's songs. His teachers, who lived in this building, asked him to come to Fort Simpson to do God's work.

I asked if God really lived in his house and what he might look like. He thought that was funny. He explained that every town in England has a House of God and some had many. God lived in them all for He could be many places at the same time. He needed so many houses to be close to the people. They could not see Him but they could feel His presence.

He told me about the beauty of his town, how it looked in the sunshine, about the bridges over the winding river and the trees and flowers that would soon blossom there. He talked for a long time, using English words I did not know. He spoke more to himself than to me. His eyes were far away, staring beyond the falling snow outside. Then he grew quiet. I saw that he missed his home greatly and wanted to see its beauty again. I was afraid that someday he would return to England and never come back to Fort Simpson. I decided not to speak about England again.

Duncan opened the schoolhouse as soon as the door and windows were repaired. I hoped his teachings would help him forget his thoughts of England, but it seemed to tire him more instead. He was still sick, and feelings of homesickness and despair still clouded his heart. I saw his temper for the first time when he shouted at a boy who was teasing another student while he was trying to teach. He ordered the boy to stand outside as a punishment. When the boy refused, Duncan pulled him by his ear to the front of the class and beat him hard with his leather belt in front of the other students. The boy was brave and did not cry, but many of the younger children began to cry. The older students tried to comfort them, though they were upset and frightened too.

Finally the winter storms began to weaken. Most of the sick had either died or recovered. Duncan's health returned slowly too. We began our preparations for the oolichon camps on the Nass. Now that spring was coming and the days were growing longer, the smiles returned to our faces.

We worried about leaving Duncan. Perhaps he would feel lonely while we were gone and return home to England. I invited him to come with us to the Nass to watch us fish for oolichon. At first he said he had too much work to do, but Tamlahk and I begged him. We told him many stories about how wonderful it was until he finally agreed. He said he would come for a few days near the end of the camp.

After three weeks Tamlahk and I returned with four others to Fort Simpson to bring Duncan up to the Nass. It was his first trip in a canoe. We set up a small box with a cushion in the centre of the canoe for him to sit on. He watched nervously as we pulled away from shore. When the first big waves rocked the canoe he hung on tightly to the sides. The winds died down when we turned east into the great, wide canyon that leads to the Nass. There he was finally able to relax.

We sang Tsimshian traveling songs for him as we paddled in rhythm. Then he sang Christian hymns for us with his voice like a bird. By afternoon he was quiet, but his Spirit glowed like sunlight. His blue eyes sparkled as he stared at the new scenery. He laughed like a child when a family of blackfish raced past our canoes only a short distance away. He had never such great fish before.

We had set out too late to make the journey in one day. We set up a camp on a beach half way to the Nass. After dinner Duncan taught us hymns as we sat around the fire. The clouds parted and for a short while the moon lit the tall mountains to the north.

Duncan was impressed. "This is certainly a magnificent country. The mountains are much higher here. Did you know this is my first trip away from Fort Simpson since I arrived two and a half years ago?" We nodded in agreement. "I could never forget this beauty, even if I never see it again."

We looked at each other with concern. "You leaving us?" Tamlahk asked.

"Oh no! I don't think so. Not anytime soon. There is no one to replace me." He smiled at us but it did not reassure us. We wondered silently if he was hoping for someone to replace him.

We reached the wide mouth of the Nass near noon on the second day. The air was blue with smoke and filled with the sounds of countless screaming sea birds. Duncan was astonished by the thousands of people working in the camps along the shore. We navigated past hundreds of canoes fishing on the bay. He kept repeating, "I had no idea!"

When our canoe reached the camp the others stopped their work and crowded along the beach to receive him. Doolyaks waded out to the canoe and carried Duncan to the shore on his back. We pushed the canoe onto the beach and unloaded Duncan's bags. My father came greet him and lead him back to the tent that we had set up for him. That evening he ate a dinner of salmon and rice with the Elders. We sang songs and beat a rhythm with sticks while he played his concertina. He surprised us with gifts of tobacco for our hospitality and everyone was happy.

The next day we followed my father as he led Duncan around our camp. He showed him the racks where we dried the oolichon over the embers and great pots where we boiled the oolichon for their oil. He showed him how we lift them out of the hot water with paddles and leave them to cool. But when Duncan saw the women pressing the oil out of the oolichon with their bare breasts he was horrified.

"How else can it be done?" asked Neeshlak. "It is forbidden by the Spirits to touch the oolichon with our hands. Women's breasts are perfectly suited for this work."

"But surely the oil must burn them. And they get that oil all over themselves. That must be awful for them." The women looked at each other and giggled with amusement. Duncan was using his hand to hide the sight of their shining breasts. His face was red with embarrassment.

"They do not press the fish until they are cool enough. If they are too eager they soon learn. And their men enjoy helping them clean off the oil when they are finished." Neeshlak winked at the women and they giggled again.

"But I'm sure I can make you a press out of wood that would be faster, cleaner and less wasteful." Duncan was struggling to regain his composure. "Please let me try to make one. I'm sure you will agree that it will be more useful."

"All right. We could try your wooden press next year. If the Oolichon Spirits are not offended and it works better, I am sure we will appreciate it. The men can still apply oolichon oil to their wives' breasts in their private chambers if they wish." Everyone laughed but Duncan, whose face turned red again.

The news of Duncan's visit spread quickly. The Nishga Chief from a camp up the Nass came to meet the White holy man he had heard much about. He invited Duncan, Tamlahk and me to visit his village, the village where Tamlahk was born. His brothers, Selwehk and Kemdahluk, came with us. Along the way, they pointed to the mountains and the landmarks. They told us the stories of the battles and Spirits that were part of their history. I was very happy to see the land and the village where Tamlahk was raised. It is indeed a beautiful land. Duncan was excited by the tall mountains and his first sight of the great rivers of ice.

It took us a day to reach Tamlahk's village for there was still much ice in the river. The sight of his village made Tamlahk anxious at first. I did not know why until he asked the Chief if Drashwuk was hiding there. The Chief had news that Drashwuk had fled to Fort Victoria where he could hide. The mention of his name brought back the painful memories of my brother's death. I was glad he was far away, for I could not have stayed if he was there. But it also made me sad that he had escaped punishment for his terrible crime.

The people of the village were waiting on the banks to receive their Chief and his guests when we arrived. Their scouts had seen us approaching from down the river. The Chief led him to his house with great ceremony and then they left him to wash and rest before the evening's feast.

The Chief invited him to stay to watch the dances and ceremonies afterwards, which he had arranged specially for his visit. Duncan refused, saying he came to deliver the words of God, not to watch the unholy practices of people who had not accepted Christianity. The Chief was taken aback. Our faces burned with shame to hear Duncan's ungrateful words, but the Chief responded with the grace of a great leader.

"You must come. If you won't then you may enjoy my food and rest the night, but tomorrow you will leave without delivering the words of your God. If you won't come to listen to us, we will not come to listen to you. I leave you to make your choice." With those words he turned and left us.

Duncan watched the dances and ceremonies so not to waste the purpose of his trip. The Chief arranged for us to sit in a place of honour. After several short dances telling the stories of Tamlahk's people, the Chief himself performed a peacemaker dance. The villagers clapped hands and banged drums. The Chief leapt out from behind a curtain in full costume wearing a mask decorated with abalone shells and crowned with porcupine quills. The quills held a mound of eagle down which came loose and floated like spring snows as the Chief shook his head to the rhythm.

Duncan looked alarmed by his singing and violent movements. Near the end of the dance, the village Shaman surprised Duncan by blowing eagle down in his face. We explained that this was a pledge for peace and good will between Duncan and the Chief's people. The Chief then said a prayer to the Great Spirit, staring through the hole in the ceiling so that his message would rise with the smoke to Heaven. He asked the Great Spirit to bless Duncan. He told Him that Duncan had come with a message from Heaven and he asked that his words would help his tribe become better people.

Then it was Duncan's turn to speak. He thanked the Chief and his people for their hospitality. He told them he was sent from the other side of the world to bring them the word of God. He told them about God's love and how he sent His only son to deliver them from evil. The Nishga muttered their agreement and approval. Then he read the Ten Commandments and asked Tamlahk and me to kneel in prayer as he read the Lord's Prayer in Tsimshian. The Chief was impressed and thanked him for coming. The villagers brought us dried salmon and rice for our journey home.

Duncan was filled with zeal after this visit. He said he must make more trips to visit other villages to spread the word of God. He was so happy that he insisted on helping to paddle the canoe back down the river, though he had no idea how to steer a canoe. He copied our movements as the strong current carried us downstream without effort. On the way he spoke at great length about how the lives of the Nishga and Tsimshian will be so much better when they accept the teachings of Christ. Perhaps he hoped to impress Selwehk and Kemdahluk, who had not yet attended his classes.

He insisted that we stop in a small Nishga village downstream to announce his visit to the Nass. The Chief invited us to lunch with ten of his Elders. After the meal Duncan gave a small amount of gunpowder to the each of them. As we were climbing into our canoe, Duncan presented the Chief with a bar of soap for his wife. The Chief reminded him that he had two wives. They were both standing beside him and they had each brought us a basket of potatoes for our journey. Duncan told the Chief that God does not approve of two wives, that God created one man and one woman and that each man must have only one wife.

The first wife shouted at the Chief that the Duncan's words were true. She said the second wife should be put to death. The second wife screamed back that the first wife was fat and ugly and could not produce children. She said the Chief preferred her and that the first wife should be killed instead. The Chief looked confused and displeased. We quickly said our final goodbyes, climbed into our canoe and pulled away from the shore. The Chief's wives were still screaming and hitting each other as the current carried us around the bend and out of view.

It was late April when we arrived back at Fort Simpson. An iron ship was anchored in the harbour. It had brought supplies for the trading post and a message to 'William Duncan, Missionary' from 'James Douglas, Governor of British Columbia'. The White Chief McNeill brought the letter to Duncan as soon as we returned. He opened the letter with great excitement as soon as Tamlahk and I carried his bags into his chambers.

"Who is this man, James Douglas?" I asked him.

"He is the Head Chief of all White people from Fort Simpson to Fort Victoria and for a great distance inland beyond the mountains too. He is very important."

"Why he send you a message?" asked Tamlahk in his simple English.

"He is answering a letter I sent to him in February. He is also inviting me to come to Fort Victoria for the summer to help him with the Indians there."

Tamlahk and I looked at each other. There was alarm in our voices as we spoke at the same time. "Are you leaving? Why do the Indians at Fort Victoria need help? We need you here."

"Many Indians from different tribes are drinking whisky and fighting. He has no White Shaman there to help him. He says it should only be for a short time. Another White Shaman should be coming soon."

"We not want you go. We need you at Fort Simpson. If you go you not come back. Must you obey Great White Chief's instructions?"

"No Tamlahk, it is only a request, not an order. But I would be a fool not to accept his invitation. He is very powerful and I need his help. If I do not help him he will not help me. In February I asked for his permission to move my teachings to a new place. It is an idea your father gave me, Gugweelaks, the night Amapaas was killed. He asked me to take the young people away from guns and whisky so that I can teach you a new way of life using God's laws. I have asked Governor Douglas for money to build a new village."

"Where will you build this new village?" I asked.

"I don't know. Governor Douglas has asked me the same question. First I must ask the Council of Chiefs for advice. It will not be easy to find the perfect place. I want a peaceful location with a good harbour near the sea where there is plenty of land to build a large village. It must be away from Fort Simpson so the drinking and fighting do not disturb us. But I also want it to be close enough so that we can come to buy supplies and return again the same day. I want it to be beautiful too, a place that will inspire the love of Heaven."

The answer seemed to shout inside my head. "Metlakatla!" I exclaimed. Duncan and Tamlahk looked puzzled.

"Metlakatla is where our people met for more than fifty generations to celebrate our sacred winter ceremonies together! It is very beautiful! We stopped returning each year when many tribes moved to Fort Simpson. It is only four hours from here by canoe."

Duncan was not interested. "I don't think I want the new village to share the memories of your evil winter ceremonies, Gugweelaks. I want them to be forgotten and replaced with a better way of life."

"The ceremonies were not evil then, Mr. Duncan. There were no guns or alcohol. It was a place of goodness where we forgot our differences and celebrated together. It is a Spiritual place sacred to all Tsimshian people. Much of the land has been cleared of trees already. It has a large harbour and it is the most beautiful place I have ever seen."

Duncan was inspired by my enthusiasm. He asked my father and he agreed it was a good idea. Father brought the suggestion to Legiac and the Council of Chiefs, who quickly gave it their blessings. They knew Duncan would be less of a problem for them if he moved away from Fort Simpson.

Duncan wanted to visit the site before he left for Fort Victoria. He chose eight men from our village to take him there, including Doolyaks, Gwashasip, Tamlahk and myself. We left early in the morning so we could return the same day. The day was cloudy but the winds were light. Duncan insisted on helping us paddle the canoe. His paddling skills were improving. He sat like the others now without a cushion. He followed our rhythm, though often he grew tired and had to rest his arms. He was only nervous when we were far from the nearest land.

The sun came out as we entered the harbour. Great Spirit wanted him to see our sacred home in its greatest beauty. We paddled gently as we glided through the narrow channel. Duncan watched the scenery unfold with great awe. I too had forgotten the greatness of its beauty and was thankful for this chance to visit it again. Small trees had taken root closer to the shore and young bushes filled the spaces up to the edge of the waterline. Many of the house posts from before were gone. Perhaps they were chopped down and used for firewood by passing travelers. We reached the end of the passage and the water opened to the great bay beyond, sprinkled with islands. The channel beyond the bay stretched deep into the mountains that were covered in a fur of dense forests.

"This is magnificent! I had no idea there was a place as beautiful as this so close to Fort Simpson. Metlakatla, eh? What does the name mean, Gugweelaks?"

"It means a passageway between two great waters."

"Yes, and it could be a passageway between two great peoples too, the Tsimshian and the English! It could become the passageway between your old way of life and your future. It is wonderful! We must keep the name. But the channel is narrow and shallow. It is fine for your canoes but bigger ships might be broken on the rocks."

Doolyaks pointed to the south side of the bay to the other channel that led back to the sea. "There is another way out where larger ships could enter."

"Then the south side of the passage is an island that protects the harbour. This site is perfect! Yes, this is definitely where we should build. I don't need to see more for the moment. Let's get back to Fort Simpson. I need to pack my belongings for Fort Victoria."

Visiting Metlakatla gave Duncan energy but his departure for Fort Victoria still filled us with concern. Many bad things could happen to him and he could still change his mind.

"Will you come back to Fort Simpson?" Clah asked two days later as he helped us carry Duncan's bags to the ship. He was close to tears for Duncan was taking most of his belongings with him.

"I hope to be back by the end of summer, but I cannot promise. I am not sure when my work will be done. It wouldn't be fair to promise if I don't know, right? Don't worry. If I cannot return another Christian teacher will come to help you. Meanwhile, be good and practice what I have taught you."

We did not want another Christian teacher. Duncan had become our guide to a new world and it was hard to see him leave. Some of us followed his ship to the open sea in our canoes, rowing hard to keep up with it, but its steam engines were too powerful. Eventually we tired and returned to Fort Simpson. We wanted to believe he would return but after he was gone we did nothing but worry. What if the Great White Chief James Douglas did not want him to return? What if he refuses to give Duncan the money to build a new village at Metlakatla? Would he stay in Fort Victoria if his life was easier there? Would he get homesick again and return to England without telling us? We wanted to be with him to know what he was doing and to remind him of his promise to return.

"We must follow Duncan to Fort Victoria," Clah insisted. "We must convince him that we need him." Many people had the same idea. Three days later fifteen canoes were preparing for the long journey south.

Gwashasip and Doolyaks were both in the lead canoe as they had been to Fort

Victoria the year before. Hahkwah brought his family and five other Blackfish in his canoe. Tamlahk, Miyana, Yuwahksa, Clah, Tsangook and Klashwaht shared my canoe. Even Tooklan joined us, though he was not fond of Duncan. Our worries about losing Duncan were replaced by the excitement of a visit to Fort Victoria. We had heard many stories about it. They said it was now much larger than Fort Simpson and much different. We heard our furs would bring a greater price there and there was much more to buy. Duncan had often told us it was a place of sin and evil, but he could not deny us a visit now that he had gone there himself.

The trip south to Fort Victoria took only two days in an English steam ship but by canoe it took more than two weeks. We reached the mouth of the Skeena on the first day. On the second day we reached the narrowest point of Tsamsem's Trench, where Ts'ibasaa's men had robbed my people of their salmon. Late in the third day we crossed the mouth of the great canyon that led north to Gitka'ata. How our hearts ached to visit our village again, but it would take a full day to go up the canyon and return. The other canoes would not wait for us and we did not dare do the rest of the journey alone.

We continued south on the route past lands I had never visited before. The channel was not straight like Tsamsem's Trench. It bent and twisted east and south as we followed its steep canyon walls. Two days later we reached Klemtu, the last Tsimshian village. We reached Bella Bella the next day, where Tooklan and other Shamans had trained when they were young. The next day we arrived at the open sea.

These were the lands of the Kwakiutl, though we did not see many of their villages. We passed the mouths of many great canyons that led deep into the mountains. Hahkwah told us that there are no passages over these mountains for they were much too high and covered with ice.

We followed the coast for two more days until we saw the mountains of the Great Island, which the Whites call Vancouver Island. It is so large that three nations share its length, the Kwakiutl on the north, the Salish on the south and the Nootka on the western side that faces the endless waters of the Great Ocean. Fort Victoria was on the south end of the island. Hahkwah told us it would take us six more days to reach it.

We stopped to rest for a day at Fort Rupert, a Kwakiutl village with a White trading post much like Fort Simpson. It was on a small island between the Great Island and the coast. We learned that all travelers and White ships stop here as they go north and south along the trading route.

There was not much interest in our arrival. Only a few men came to greet us. Clah knew some Kwakiutl words but he spoke to them mostly in Chinook. They showed us a place where we could set up our tents on the beach. I was disappointed that we were not treated like guests, as we would be at other villages. They told us they received too many visitors to entertain everyone.

There was not much to do the next day but to rest. Tsangook wandered through the village in hopes of meeting some handsome Kwakiutl men. Doolyaks and Gwashasip brought Tamlahk and me to the White fort to see the trading post. Miyana was angry for Gwashasip had told her to stay with Yuwahksa in our camp. He said Kwakiutl men would only make trouble for a young, beautiful Tsimshian princess. There was not much to see at the trading post anyway. The Whites were not much interested in visitors either. The trading prices for our furs were better than in Fort Simpson but Doolyaks said they would be better still in Fort Victoria.

We left early the next morning, eager to reach our destination. For two more days we followed a narrow channel beside the steep walls of the Great Island. We reached our first Salish village just past the narrowest part. The mountains were now smaller and the land was more inviting. The weather was always sunny and pleasant in the south, Gwashasip told me. The summers were warm and cloudless. He told me the Salish live here because they are not strong enough to endure the harsh winters of the north coast.

We needed three more days to reach Fort Victoria. How exciting it was to be approaching the end of our trip! Our bodies were tired and sore but our Spirits soared like eagles. We watched the shores carefully for the first signs of the settlement. We saw a few large White houses on the slopes above the shore. They filled our hearts with delight. We could not hold our joy as we rounded the point and turned into the harbour.

Our first view of Fort Victoria unfolded as we glided closer. Our joy caught in our throats and our hopes slowly changed to apprehension. I had expected something like Fort Simpson, only much larger and more beautiful. I imagined painted Salish houses along the beach outside a large trading post with the houses and streets of the White town around them. But this was very different.

On one side of the harbour different coast peoples lived in camps that covered a great space of land as large as all of Fort Simpson. Most of them were living in tents. Some had built smaller wooden houses. The air was blue with the smoke from many campfires. It was as crowded as the oolichon camps on the Nass, but the people here were not fishing or working. We heard the angry voices of drunken men shouting threats at each other. An unpleasant smell of filth and waste drifted from the camps.

"It smells disgusting!" Miyana turned to me. "We are not going to make camp there, are we? Why are they all camping so close together? There is much more room on the other side." We turned our canoes towards the other side. We passed two sailing ships anchored in the harbour. They seemed deserted except for a couple of White men on their decks. They watched us as we paddled by. They looked at us unpleasantly and did not return our greetings.

The White town was on the other side. It did not look like I had imagined either. The walled fort looked larger but not as well kept as Fort Simpson's. Part of it was hidden behind other buildings. There were many wooden buildings, mostly smaller than our longhouses. Many were not painted or tidy. The buildings along the water had docks where small White boats were tied. A large steam ship was tied to the largest dock. Through the spaces between the White buildings I saw White people riding large animals, which I knew must be the horses that I had seen in Duncan's picture books. My first desire was to get closer to see them better.

The White town was not as beautiful as our villages, but we could not understand why no coast people wanted to camp beside it. There was plenty of room away from the docks, and the trading post and stores were all on that side. We pulled our canoes onto the beach and began preparing the ground for our tents.

Suddenly we were startled by a gunshot. A bullet hit the sand a few feet away. Two White guards with rifles were running down the banks. They shouted at us to leave. I spoke to them in English. I asked them why we could not use this land as no one else was using it. They told me this was White men's land. They said that Red men stay on the other side, pointing to the crowded camp.

I was puzzled. "We are not red men. We are brown," I tried to reason with them.

"Leave or we'll shoot holes in your canoes!" they shouted angrily and raised their guns. We had no choice but to leave. We were upset. This was no way to treat visitors who had traveled for so many days. The Whites at Fort Simpson were not friendly, but they were not angry or mean to us like this.

We did not want to settle in the crowded camp so we continued further into the harbour. We passed under a low wooden walkway that stretched from one side of the harbour to the other. We had never seen a bridge like this before. Several coastal people walking along it stopped to wave and shout greetings to us. We were happy to see some friendly faces at last.

We saw longhouses of the Songhee village, the Salish people of the area. They were not painted or carved as beautifully as Tsimshian houses but they looked much nicer than the crowded camp or the White town. We stopped on their beach and asked if we could make camp on their land. They said too many people were camping on their land already. They told us they were still building their village. It was once on the other side of the harbour, but the White men had forced them to move away two months before.

We wanted to be close to Fort Victoria so we set up our tents on the far end of the crowded camp. We were not pleased with our site but we were tired and there was no other choice. We used our canoes to look for firewood along the shores, for there was no wood near the crowded camp anymore. There was only one stream near the camp. The water was dirty with so many people using it to drink and wash. Often there were fights when someone muddied the water above where others took their drinking water. There were many mosquitoes too.

Tamlahk and I begged Gwashasip to show us to Fort Victoria early the next day. Tsangook and Hahkwah came with us. We hated the noise of the camp but we could not avoid it. We had to walk through the full length of it to reach the footbridge that crossed the harbour. The smells of rotting food, urine and human waste were strong in the morning sun. Swarms of flies surrounded us and landed on our arms and faces.

The huge camp was already busy with activity. The people were different from Fort Simpson. They wore clothing from many different nations along the coast and spoke in different tongues. Many nodded greetings but they did not try to talk to us. The flies and mosquitoes did not seem to bother them as they did us.

The trip seemed worth it when we reached the wooden footbridge. What a thrill it was to stand above the water and watch the ships in the harbour! We did not stand for long, for we were eager to visit the trading post and explore the White town.

The White town was peaceful after walking through the big camp. I was excited to see more people riding horses in the streets. We saw other horses pulling wagons full of supplies while the drivers steered them with leather ropes. They were such beautiful animals, like small, lean moose. I wondered if their meat was as tasty as a moose.

Some stores were beginning to open. We walked along the street, looking at the windows and reading the painted signs. The Whites paint their signs in bright colours like we painted our houses. Some had coloured drawings like picture books. Many had large windows to show what was for sale inside. It was just as others had told us. Some stores sold only clothes or books. Others sold furniture or meat. I was anxious to trade my furs for many of these new treasures.

The fort was at the end of the main street. The gates were not open so we walked around the outside walls. They were in poor repair. Some of the logs had rotted and had been removed. We looked through the holes. There were several buildings at the far end but most of the space inside the walls was an empty yard. In was strange that it was not in the centre of the town. The town had grown away from it. It did not look important at the end of the street.

Later that day we returned to the White town to trade our furs for White goods. We brought them to a clothing store where we had seen a fine coat made of furs.

"What are you doing in here!" the White owner shouted at us. "Get out of here! I don't want your stinking furs. Go trade them for money at the fort. But don't come back here afterwards. I don't need your money!" He ushered us out the door and closed it behind us.

For a moment we stood outside and looked at each other. We did not know what we had done wrong. Gwashasip's face was red with anger. I felt ashamed but I did not know why.

We took our furs up the street to the trading post which was open now. They gave a better price than the trading post at Fort Simpson, just as Doolyaks had told us. We bought shirts there but they were not as beautiful as the shirts in the clothing store. We tried to shop in other stores in the White town but they would not let us in or accept our money either.

It was a disappointing day. I was very discouraged. I wanted to return home but we had traveled such a long way and we had not found Duncan yet. We searched for him around the town for several days, but the Whites would not help us. It was clear that they did not like us in the town. After the first week we stayed mostly in the camp except when we needed to buy something at the trading post.

We did not feel safe in our camp either. Many of our belongings were stolen when we were not watching. In the evenings the drinking and arguing would begin. Later there was fighting and sometimes killings too. Many Haida canoes arrived in July and the crowding became worse. I am sure there were more people in the camps than in the White town. There were many fights and killings with the Haida for they had a long history of attacking other people.

Whites ignored the gunfire and killings in our camp. They only punished men who committed crimes against the Whites, and then their punishment was swift and cruel. We saw two Nootkas being whipped in public for killing a cow on a White man's farm. A Salish man shot a guard who was trying to capture him. The Whites killed him in the most horrible way, by breaking his neck with a rope. They left his body to hang for a day to remind us of his punishment.

As soon as they killed him an old woman walked slowly to where he was hanging. She stayed there all day kissing and hugging his feet while she sobbed. Finally the White guards cut the rope and let his body fall. She pleaded with them to give her the rope to remember her son. The guards were ashamed and they granted her wish. She kissed it and placed it around her neck. Her tears flowed like rivers down her cheeks. Tears flowed hot down my cheeks too.

One afternoon in late July, someone in the Haida camp shot at a White ship that was passing in the harbour. Soon more than a hundred guards with red jackets from the fort came over the bridge and began to search each tent in the area. A large crowd of people from the camp gathered to watch. The Red Jackets told us to go back to our tents until the search was finished. We backed away but we did not return to our tents. We were too upset. We needed to see what would happen.

The Red Jackets were nervous. They did not want us behind them. They said they would shoot us if we did not obey. Some of the crowd became angry and others started to panic. Just then another White man appeared and he tried to calm the soldiers. Then he turned to reassure to the crowd. My heart rejoiced, for I saw it was Duncan. I pushed through the crowd to reach his side.

"Mr. Duncan!" I cried, embracing him in my arms.

"Gugweelaks! What are you doing here!" he stared at me in delight.

"We have come from Fort Simpson to find you! Tamlahk is here. So are Miyana, Gwashasip, Tsangook, Doolyaks and many others. We have been here for a month but we could not find you!"

Duncan asked me to wait while he comforted the people who were being searched. While he was busy I ran to find Tamlahk. He returned with me and we watched until the guilty man who had fired the shot was captured. He was not a Haida after all. It was Drashwuk!

Duncan stayed with Drashwuk as the Red Jackets led him away. He translated for him at his trial the next day. The White Elder, Judge Begbie, ordered Drashwuk to be whipped in public and then to stay two months in a White jail.

Tamlahk asked Duncan how he could help Drashwuk when he knew he was an evil man. Duncan told him even evil men need help and forgiveness. That was God's wish. Tamlahk was humbled. Duncan did not want to see the public whipping but Tamlahk did. I stayed with him and watched too. Tamlahk's hatred changed to pity when he saw the bleeding cuts on Drashwuk's back. When it was over he told me that he had forgiven Drashwuk. Later, the Red Jackets led him to the jail. Drashwuk pulled out a knife he had hidden and tried to attack them. They shot him dead.

Our time in Fort Victoria was easier once we found Duncan. He had started to build a school for Indians there. Duncan asked Tamlahk and me to help him. We were happy to help for there was little to do at our camp. He paid us English money too, for Governor Douglas had given him some to build the school. He had promised Governor Douglas that he would teach the first students until another teacher came to replace him.

We told Duncan of our problems spending money in the White stores. He decided to come shopping with us. He told us that the Whites would respect us better if we cut our hair like a proper White gentleman. He led us to a barber's shop and we waited outside while he spoke with the barber. Then he brought us inside and the barber cut off our long hair for the first time. At first we looked so strange in the mirror. We laughed and teased each other but we both liked it. We did not let our hair grow long again for many years!

Then Duncan took us back to the White clothing store that had refused our money and insulted us when we first arrived. We tried to tell him that the man did not want us in his store, but Duncan would not listen. He led us inside and introduced himself. When he explained that he wanted to have us suited in English clothes the man complained. Duncan's temper flared.

"My dear man, I came to this land to teach these people the way of the Lord. Do you wish to stand in the way of God's work? Do you want them to stay savages for the rest of their lives? If you don't cooperate I'll have a word with Governor Douglas myself."

The man in the store blushed and apologized. He set about finding new clothes that would fit us. We dressed in new shirts, trousers and jackets. We looked in the long mirror and we laughed in delight, for we looked so different.

"Now you finally have a pocket for that pocket watch of yours, Gugweelaks," Duncan laughed. "My boys will be welcome to shop here in the future, won't they, sir, provided that they are dressed appropriately?" He winked at us.

"Of course, Mr. Duncan," the storekeeper nodded politely. He smiled at us. We were amazed at Duncan's power to tame the hatred in men's hearts.

We walked proudly by his side through the town. We greeted the surprised White faces we passed with smiles and elegant nods. Some returned our greetings. Others only stared with their mouths open. Duncan's face was full of pride for us when we left him in the White town. Our hearts were filled with joy as we walked back to our tent through the crowded camp. Many eyes followed us in our strange English suits. Some made remarks in tongues we could not understand. We began to greet them as we had greeted the Whites, with smiles and elegant nods and that made them laugh with us.

When we reached our camp our friends gave us lots of attention. Tsangook shouted, "Look everyone, here come two handsome English gentlemen! But something is wrong. They must have been left in the sun too long. Their skin is all brown!" Yuwahk-sa giggled with delight. She said we looked cute. Miyana said our mother would be so upset that I had cut my long, beautiful hair. We shrugged our shoulders and smiled. She was right but there was no way to stop what had already happened.

In our tent we removed our new clothes and stored them in our bags so that they would not get dirty. I gazed at Tamlahk's naked body. How different he looked with short hair, but the difference was beautiful! We lay on the bed and stroked each other's heads as we kissed passionately. Our love felt new again.

The weeks passed and summer ended. We asked Duncan many questions about his plans and how long he would stay in Fort Victoria. He was not sure. He said there was much work to do to help Governor Douglas with the Indian problem. We wanted to know what problem the Indians were having.

"Actually, it is a White problem, not an Indian problem. The town's people are angry and annoyed with all the drunkenness and fighting in the Indian camp. They say there has been too much theft and killing. They say the road west to the naval base at Esquimalt is no longer safe. Indian women are selling their bodies to the White sailors along the road and the people of the town are disgusted. They say it is spreading disease and ruining the morals of the sailors and other young men. I am more concerned about it ruining the morals the Indians than the vulgar sailors."

"But if they are disgusted then why do they buy our women?" I asked.

"That is a good question, Gugweelaks. Obviously if they had good morals in the first place they wouldn't. But the pistol duels between rival suitors are making the road unsafe, not the Indians."

"What would you do for this White problem?" Tamlahk asked.

"I have told Governor Douglas that there should be a separate camp along the waterfront for every Indian nation, the Haida, the Tsimshian, the Kwakiutl and so forth. There should be a guard and a jail in each camp to help keep the peace. Each person who arrives to a camp must register their name and turn over their weapons for safekeeping. Each person should also pay a fee to help pay the guard and the improvement of the camp. There should be a school and a place of worship in each camp and everyone who stays there should be required to work."

"What if some people refuse?" I asked.

"Then they should be sent back to their villages," he said firmly.

I had to think about this for a minute. His plan could bring many improvements but it had so many rules. It would be difficult to convince all the nations to cooperate.

"Does Governor Douglas like your idea?"

"He thinks that most of the Indians will resist. He says it will be too difficult to control. I hope to convince him that it would be worth trying. I think he will listen to me in the end," he smiled proudly. "I would like both of you to meet Governor Douglas," he continued. "Perhaps he will invite us to dinner. I want him to see what fine progress you have made."

"What do you mean?" Tamlahk asked.

"I mean, when he sees that you look like fine English gentlemen and he hears how well you speak English he will see that I am doing good work. You see, at first he did not want me to go to Fort Simpson. He told me that it would not be possible to help the Tsimshian. He said it was too dangerous. When he sees how civilized you have become he may give us the money we need to build a new town at Metlakatla. But you should let Gugweelaks do most of the talking, Tamlahk. His English is much better than yours."

Tamlahk frowned.

"Does Governor Douglas want to help the Indians?" I asked.

"Oh yes, I am certain of it. He is married to an Indian woman, you know."

"Is this true, Mr. Duncan? Which nation is she from?"

"I don't know, Tamlahk. It isn't polite to ask such a thing."

Governor Douglas proved to be a very busy man. He did not have time to meet us. Instead Duncan decided to introduce us to Bishop Hills. He was the Chief Spiritual Shaman for all the Englishmen along the coast from Fort Victoria to Fort Simpson, Duncan explained. He had recently arrived in Victoria and he did not know any Indians. Duncan wanted to interest him in helping the Tsimshian and he hoped he would give us money to build Metlakatla.

Duncan arranged a visit to Bishop Hill's house one evening in mid-August. He suggested we meet first at Reverend Cridge's house, the house where Duncan was staying. He asked us to bring our gentlemen's clothes to the house before we put them on so that they would stay clean.

Reverend Cridge was a White Shaman like Duncan. We liked him instantly. He greeted us warmly and welcomed us into his home, which did not happen with most White men. We changed into our White clothing and joined the others in the sitting room. His wife Mary had prepared a generous dinner for us. We sat on chairs around a table with his children like White people do. It was our first meal with forks and knives. We watched the others carefully and concentrated on eating like they did while Duncan and Reverend Cridge talked. We could tell they were close friends.

"You're wasting your time with Hills, William." Reverend Cridge used Duncan's other name. "You know how he stood on the Black issue. He wants a separate section in my church for coloured people, as is done in all respectable churches in the world you know," he added in a funny voice. "I've had to walk a fine line with that one!"

"Surely he appreciates your judgment, Edward. You've been here almost six years. You've been Superintendent of Schools since you've arrived and you've run the hospital for a year. Surely he sees that you are doing the Lord's work."

"I dare say he cares far more about his fine clothes and impressing the upper classes than doing the Lord's work. He was just a vicar at Yarmouth, you know, the spoiled son of an admiral. I have heard he flirted shamelessly with Lady Burdett-Coutts to get this position. She financed the establishment of the diocese, you know, and she insisted he be made Bishop because she fancied him. I pleaded with England for support and this is the help I am sent! Trust me. He cares nothing for those in need of Spiritual guidance, White or Indian. All he appreciates is pomp and ceremony, you'll see. With all the drunkenness and violence in this town that last thing we need is further excess."

"Perhaps I can convince him to fund Metlakatla as a credit to his diocese. Maybe he could convince some of the wealthier Victorians or his contacts in England to donate towards the civilization of the Indians to the betterment of his image."

"The settlers around here don't care about the betterment of the Indians. They only want them to stay away. They have no interest whatsoever in helping them integrate into our society. They abhor the idea. I might as well be preaching to a bunch of paving stones."

"But if Metlakatla is successful there could be fewer Tsimshian making trips to Victoria. That could be a selling point."

"I suppose it's worth a try, but don't get your hopes up. If he was interested in your ideas don't you think he would have invited you to dinner at least once in the ten weeks you have been here? As far as he is concerned, we are not the right class to be hobnobbing with, William. Just be thankful that he is not your direct superior. He likes to be referred to as 'Your Holiness' you know. What a joke!"

"Yes, I've heard that," Duncan smiled.

"Do me a favour, won't you? Ask him which hole he is referring to."

"Edward, really!" Duncan blushed and glanced quickly at the two of us. Mary laughed and covered her mouth with her hand.

The evening sky was fading as we walked up the road to Bishop Hill's house. It was no different than the other houses around it. Duncan knocked lightly on the door. It was opened by a tall, handsome White man wrapped in a beautiful robe and smoking a pipe.

"Good evening, Your Holiness. I have come as we agreed." Duncan bowed slightly.

"Hmmm. As you asked, don't you mean, Mr. Duncan? Well come in then. Let's get this over with. I see you have brought your savages with you. Close the door behind you." Bishop Hills crossed the room to a tall chair by the fireplace. "Have a seat, won't you, or would they prefer to sit on the floor?"

"The chairs will be fine, Your Holiness," I said, bowing slightly like Duncan.

"Bravo, Duncan! You've trained them well, I see. I think I can even hear the rustic twang of your northern accent. Have you taught them to perform any other tricks?"

Duncan's eyes sparkled like dark fires. "They are learning the teachings of the Lord and helping me to translate the Bible into Tsimshian, the language of their people. I am sure Your Holiness can appreciate the value of this work to our Church."

"Don't get sarcastic with me, Duncan! I have no intention of interfering with the pet projects of my missionaries. Would you care for some tea? My housekeeper, Mrs. Trites, kindly made us some before she had to return home to put her children to bed, leaving me to pour my own tea like a commoner."

"In all due respect, Your Holiness, I am not your missionary. I was hired by the Christian Missionary Society and I answer directly to them, not to you."

"I'm well aware of that, Duncan. Do you wish to stay for tea, or not?" I saw he disliked Duncan and he wanted us to leave.

"Yes, please," Duncan spoke quietly.

"Very well," Bishop Hills smiled, "You can pour." He lit the tobacco in his pipe again and sat back in his chair. "Now, since I am not your employer, what is it that you have come to waste my time over?"

Duncan spoke his words carefully. "I have come to ask Your Holiness's support in financing a new Christian community in the north near Fort Simpson. The Tsimshian are dying from the cruel ravages of alcohol and guns. Some have pleaded with me to save their children from their heathen lifestyle. They are ready for change. I want to lead them away from the suffering and chaos to a new way of life following the teachings of our Lord."

"What! You must be kidding. Are you mad? Can't you see I am living like a peasant in a house smaller than the cottage occupied by that moron, Reverend Cridge? I have no regular servants. I have to answer my own door. There isn't even a hall or a passageway where I can receive my guests! How can people of this unruly town be expected to respect the dignity of the Anglican Church when their own Bishop must live in a shack barely suitable for a gardener? You want me to build new housing for savages in the middle of nowhere before I have a decent house to live in or a decent church to preach in? You should be more concerned in serving the good Anglicans of this town before you go squandering the Church's limited resources on primitives who cannot appreciate what you are trying to do. You cannot even get them to stop killing each other!" Bishop Hills took a deep breath to calm himself and he straightened his robe.

"I could get them to stop killing each other if you gave me a chance."

"Christ, you are a stubborn man! Why don't you ask your precious Missionary Society to finance you, since they favour the spiritual well-being of the heathen over our own pious countrymen?" He banged his pipe hard on the table to loosen the ashes. "Very well then, if you really want to impress me with the servitude of your new followers, have them make five hundred hassocks for our congregation to kneel on. Cridge thinks his parishioners should be taught to kneel on the hard floor like Quakers! I will instruct him to have the material ready in time for your return to Fort Simpson. That will be all for now."

Duncan was too upset to answer our questions on our way back through the darkness to Reverend Cridge's house. We hurried to keep up with his angry footsteps. He instructed us to leave our English clothes with Mary so that she could clean them and press out the wrinkles. We changed into our Tsimshian clothes and said our goodbyes.

We walked slowly down along the street towards the centre of town. We were confused about this night's events. There were so many harsh words and bad feelings. We did not know what they meant or why they were said. But it was over now. We were alone in the quiet of the night and we were happy to be together. Tamlahk put his arm around my shoulder and he smiled at me as we walked.

Suddenly, there was a gunshot and a bullet hit the fence beside us.

"Get outta here, you stinking, Red bastards!" A drunken White man waved a pistol at us from outside of the house where White men drank whisky. He shot again and the bullet hit the road and made a spray of dirt. We ran like deer between the houses to the water. We climbed along the docks to the footbridge and ran as fast as we could until we reached the Indian camp on the other side. We passed between the crowded tents, past the drinking and fighting to the safety of our camp and the quiet of our tent.

My thoughts kept me awake. I wondered why the Whites call us Red Men. We were not red. Whites were much redder when they are embarrassed or angry. Duncan had told us that if someone sees red it means he is angry. Perhaps they call us Red because we make them angry. Tsangook said they are blind to the truth that all men are red on the inside.

◇◇◇◇◇◇◇◇◇◇◇◇◇◇◇◇

Twenty more Haida canoes arrived in the harbour that week and the Whites saw red again. They did not listen to Duncan's suggestions. Governor Douglas sent a gunboat to block the entrance of the harbour so that no more canoes could enter. He sent another up the coast to stop canoes coming from the north. Duncan saw red too, when he read the White newspapers to me. Their words were filled with hatred for Indians. They called us dangerous thieves and killers and they said we spread diseases.

One day the Red Jackets came again. They did not come to search our tents this time. They came to tell us that the Great White Chief, Governor Douglas, had come to speak to us. We gathered at the edge of the camp near the footbridge to hear his message. He told us that that a great disease called measles was spreading up from the south and we should leave immediately if we did not want to catch it. Panic and confusion spread across the crowd. Then a Salish Chief asked how could that be. His men had just returned from the south and there was no such disease. Governor Douglas became impatient. He said we could stay if we wanted, but if the disease came many would die a horrible death. With those words he turned and walked back over the footbridge.

The crowd began to return to their camps. I heard concerned voices speaking in many different languages and they pushed towards us. I grabbed Tamlahk's hand and pulled him through the crowd. We ran across the footbridge and caught up with Governor Douglas on the other side.

"Governor Douglas, please wait!" The Red Jackets turned to protect him. They raised their rifles and blocked our way. "Please Governor Douglas, can we speak with you?" He turned to look at us. He waved his hand and the Red Jackets lowered their rifles and backed away. He took three steps towards us and stopped. He looked at our faces and English haircuts carefully. He was a solid man with brown skin and the steady eyes of a Great Chief.

"You are Duncan's boys, aren't you? I've seen you walking with him in town."

"Yes Sir, my name is Gugweelaks and this is my best friend, Tamlahk." Douglas glanced down. I was still holding Tamlahk's hand. He looked back at our faces and we smiled at him.

"I see." He turned to the Red Jackets. "You can leave us. I will be all right." They saluted, turned and marched towards the fort.

"If you'd like, you can talk with me as I walk to the hospital. Reverend Cridge wants to ask me for more money for supplies. I'm afraid I have a very busy day ahead."

"Thank you, sir. Mr. Duncan has told us you are a very busy man. He told us you are too busy to meet with us."

Douglas stopped and looked at us suspiciously. "What is it that you want to talk about?"

"Were you telling us the truth, sir, about the disease coming up from the south?"

He looked at us while he thought about what he would say. I could see in his face that his story wasn't true. "The Indian camps are severely over-crowded, Gugweelaks. There is a shortage of good drinking water and too much sewage. The living conditions are terrible. Perhaps no disease is coming from the south at this time, but this is a port. Several ships arrive every week. Sooner or later one will bring a White disease. It will find the camps and it will spread death like a fire in a dry forest. Do you understand?"

"Yes sir." I looked at Tamlahk. He looked worried but he let me do the talking. "Why don't you try Mr. Duncan's plan?"

He looked surprised. "About the separate camps along the waterfront? He told you about that, did he? I suppose he would. It would take a lot of time to make new camps. Mr. Duncan forgets that I have many people to satisfy, not just the Church. The people of Fort Victoria don't want any Indian camps nearby, let alone several camps. Do you believe Mr. Duncan's idea would work?" He watched my face carefully again.

"I am not sure," I hesitated. "I think it could be better, but it would not be easy. Our people would not like so many rules. We have always traveled without rules. Most men would not like to give their names when they come and go and they would not want to pay each time."

"Exactly! If only I could convince Mr. Duncan of this." Douglas smiled broadly. "Maybe I can with your help."

"But it is not right to send the gun ships to stop our people. They come in peace to trade furs. They know White men want furs. They will not understand why there are ships with guns." I remembered Ts'ibasaa's guns in Tsamsem's Trench when I said this.

"I'm sorry. I didn't want it to come to this. If your people traded their furs and left it would be fine, but they stay here all summer. The town is already upset. They hate the smell, the drinking and the fighting. And the newspaper is stirring up trouble. The damned editor hates me as much as he hates your people. I must do something to keep him quiet, you understand. Maybe someday your people and mine can live together but we are not ready yet. Right now, I just need to buy some time."

The idea of buying time confused me. Did Whites have the magic to buy time? I wondered if they sold it too. "What furs do you use to buy time?" I asked him.

He stopped walking and looked at me with surprise. "That's a very good point, young man! The price might be too costly. You are wise beyond your years. I have worried about this since I dispatched the ships. Driving your people away without explanation could do permanent damage between our people. I wish there was some other way. Your people need something to busy themselves so they are not so tempted to come down to Fort Victoria every summer. Is Mr. Duncan doing good work up in Fort Simpson?"

"Yes, sir!" Tamlahk and I spoke together.

"He is very important to our people!" I continued. "Many of us have come to Fort Victoria to find him. We want him to return to Fort Simpson. But he told us that he must stay as long as you need him."

"Is that so? That is good to hear. It seems he gets along with your people better than he does with ours. For that matter, so do I most of the time. My wife is part Indian, you know. Maybe I will ask Mr. Duncan to bring you over for dinner this week so we can talk further. I would like you to meet my family. I have five lovely daughters, though I doubt you boys will be interested in them." He smiled at this thought.

"Yes sir, but if you are too busy...."

"I'm not too busy when the company is good. Mr. Duncan can be tedious at times. He spends most of the evening telling me what I should be doing without a clue of how to do it himself. To be honest, I was afraid to send him up to Fort Simpson. I thought he'd cause more trouble than good. Don't mention this to him, of course. Meeting you has opened my mind."

He stopped in front of a small house. "I must say goodbye here. This is where Reverend Cridge has his hospital. Mr. Duncan will tell you which evening to come for dinner. Don't tell him I invited you first or he will be upset. Let him tell you, right?" We promised not to mention our talk.

Governor Douglas turned to go but then he stopped. "Does Mr. Duncan know that you boys are special friends? I doubt he understands. He is blind to these things, you know. I don't think you should tell him. He is uncomfortable with the idea of love between a man and a woman. I am sure love between two men is more than he could handle. That's what missionaries are like, you know." With those words he wished us a good day and disappeared into the house.

Two days later, while we were working on the schoolhouse, Duncan came to us with great excitement. He told us Governor Douglas had invited us to dinner the next evening. He made plans for us to dress in our English clothes at Bishop Cridge's home before dinner. He asked me to practice what he wanted me to say. He reminded Tamlahk to let me do the talking.

Duncan's instruction upset him. "Of course, he always talk and talk!" Tamlahk said in English. He glared at me and then he winked.

But Tamlahk did not stay quiet at the dinner. Governor Douglas preferred to talk to us instead of Duncan. He asked us what we did while we visited Fort Victoria. Tamlahk told him in his poor English how we were building the schoolhouse. When he forgot the words he showed him with his hands how he did things. Douglas laughed with delight but Duncan was anxious. He tried to stop Tamlahk from speaking so that I could explain it more clearly. Douglas delighted in ignoring him and asked Tamlahk more questions instead. Tamlahk winked at me and talked on proudly.

Duncan grew more uneasy. Finally he interrupted again. He asked Governor Douglas if he had thought about his plan for the Indian camps in the harbour. Douglas said he was still thinking about it. He would need to discuss it with the Town Council. Then he asked Duncan about his ideas for Metlakatla. Duncan had mentioned it in a letter before he came to Victoria. Duncan described his dream of building a special village with no whisky or guns. There the Tsimshian would learn the ways of White men and the teachings of the Bible. He said we could become good people again.

Governor Douglas asked me what I thought about Duncan's plan. I spoke with much enthusiasm. I told him about the beauty of Metlakatla and how it was sacred to our people for many generations. He asked Tamlahk what he thought about it. "Me love to build!" he smiled, and he showed us in the air how he hammered nails into boards.

Douglas laughed with delight. He told us he had good news for us. A new teacher would arrive on the next ship from England and Duncan would soon be free to return to Fort Simpson. He promised us money build Metlakatla when we were ready. We were all excited by the news.

As soon as our dinner was finished we raced back to our camp to tell the news. There was much excitement and gossip. We made ready for our journey home. Two days later fifteen of our canoes left Fort Victoria for Fort Simpson. Our hearts were full of joy and our heads full of dreams. We were anxious for our future to begin.

SIXTEEN

Duncan's ship arrived at Fort Simpson a few days after we did. He brought with him two Whites to help us build our future, a young White Shaman named Reverend Tugwell and his wife. Duncan had asked his missionary society in England last winter to send us help and they sent the Tugwells to answer his prayers. They arrived in Fort Victoria after our canoes had left and just in time to join Duncan's ship on its trip north.

The Tugwells were a happy couple, filled with a new love for each other. Duncan explained that they had just married before they left England. Their company delighted him and he spoke only praises for them. For the first two days he was always with them, talking about England and telling them about his plans for Metlakatla until they lost interest. When he was silent, they held hands and kissed as though he did not exist. He watched them as they stared into each other's eyes. I saw his pain and jealousy when Mrs. Tugwell stroked her husband's handsome face.

On the first Sunday back from Victoria, Duncan welcomed the Tugwells and gave a sermon full of joy and promise. He told us the story from the Bible that I am most fond of. It is the story about a man who sowed seeds of grain. Some of the seeds fell on sand or stones and they did not grow. Some grew but they were choked and killed by weeds. But other seeds fell on good soil and they grew strong. Duncan said our people were good soil where the seed of God's word could grow. He told us his Christian teachings were also good soil where our souls would prosper.

Our people were good soil for Duncan too, for his joy and passion grew stronger each year. But where some men find soil, others find only sand and stones. Most Whites cannot grow roots on our rocky shores. I think of the Tugwells when I hear this story, for I quickly saw that their seeds would not survive. They had no interest in us and they were so pale and slender I thought they might not survive their first winter.

Duncan brought them to meet my father the day after they arrived. He greeted them in his ceremonial clothes in front of our house, nodding to them and offered his hand as White people do. They shook hands but afterwards Mrs. Tugwell wiped her hands on her handkerchief. My father ignored this insult and invited them inside. At first they refused for they said they did not want to bother us. Duncan was embarrassed. He told them it was better to bother us than to insult us, and he insisted they go inside. Klashwaht lifted the deer skin over the door and my father led them in.

Tugwell asked his wife to go in first, for the English do things backwards. She made an unpleasant face and bent low so she would not touch the deer skin. When she was inside she brushed her dress hard, though there was no dirt on it. Tugwell stood close to comfort her but she could not relax in our house. She refused to sit on the guest blankets that our servants brought and she jumped whenever someone came near. My mother offered them fresh salmon but they would not touch it. They explained that their stomachs were upset. She told the servants to bring them plants to help their digestion but they refused them too. My mother was frustrated. She told us later that people who refuse good medicine should not complain about their stomachs.

The Tugwells did not impress the other Tsimshians either. They made no effort to learn our language or our names. We tried to be friends with them and teach them our ways, but they only liked their own company. They smiled pleasantly and answered us when we spoke but they preferred to say nothing. At first they followed Duncan closely, but Mrs. Tugwell soon decided she did not like Fort Simpson. As the weeks passed she refused to leave the fort. They stayed inside together where we could not see them.

Duncan was concerned. He was sure Mrs. Tugwell was too frail to survive so far from home. She began to complain about the cold even before the summer ended. He tried to speak to Tugwell alone about his plans for Metlakatla, but Tugwell worried about her constantly when they were apart and could not listen to his words.

Duncan's joy changed to disappointment and his jealousy to anger. He wrote to the missionary society and told them they should have chosen our help more carefully. After that he left them alone and went about his plans as though they had left.

A week after he returned from Victoria, an iron gun ship arrived. White Chief McNeill told Legiac that the Chief of the ship, Captain Pearce, wished to speak to the Council of Tsimshian Chiefs. The Council assembled the next day to listen to Pearce's message. Duncan joined them to interpret for the Chiefs. My father returned from the Council with news that we must now obey White laws. Killing others in revenge was no longer allowed and all slaves must be set free. He summoned Hoshieka and Klash-waht and told them they were no longer his slaves. Klashwaht was very happy, but Hoshieka cried and cried. She begged my father not to send her away. He explained that nothing would change unless she or Klashwaht wanted to leave. They both chose to stay.

The same afternoon Duncan summoned the adult students to the schoolhouse. He spoke strongly about the evils of whisky and selling our bodies to White men for money or alcohol. He said he returned to Fort Simpson to stop these things but he would leave for good unless we promised never to do them again. We gave him our promises and we begged him not to go. I wrote my promise not to drink alcohol on a sheet of paper. Tamlahk and forty other students printed their names below to make their promises too.

Duncan told us that if we were speaking the truth we must speak to Captain Pearce and ask him to stop the whisky traders. The next day we went to the fort and showed him our promise paper. I spoke for the others for I had the best English. I asked him to stop the whisky traders. I told him they caused the killings and other troubles at Fort Simpson. He was very pleased with my speech. I wanted to give him our paper but he told us we should keep it to remind ourselves of our promise.

Duncan decided we should show Captain Pearce and the Tugwells that we were now good Christians. We sang the songs of God to them in the courtyard of the fort while he played his concertina, and then we read words from our notebooks. When we finished there were tears in Captain Pearce's eyes. He told us that before this day he did not believe there was any good in Indians.

It was a proud time for Duncan and his students. Captain Pearce's tears made us eager to be good Christians and show Whites that we were good people. Legiac want-ed to win the favour of Captain Pearce too. The next day, he came to Duncan's Sunday service with his hair cut short like a White man's. This was how he showed Captain Pearce that he would honour his instructions. We were too surprised to speak, for we had never seen a Chief with short hair, but Duncan was quick to tell to tell him how good he looked and that made him proud.

We were eager to start building Metlakatla as soon as Captain Pearce left. We wanted to start before the winter storms came but Duncan first wanted the approval of the Council of Tsimshian Chiefs. At the end of September he brought two Chiefs and seven Elders from different villages in Fort Simpson to Metlakatla to help him decide the best place to build a new village.

Tugwell came too. We could not stop ourselves from laughing as he climbed into the canoe. He was so nervous he almost fell into the water. Duncan sat in front of him to show him how to use a paddle, but Tugwell was too frightened to paddle. He held the sides of the canoe tightly as the others climbed in and paddled away.

They returned to Fort Simpson the next day. Duncan and the others were very pleased for they had chosen a good site, but Tugwell fell ill from the cold rain. He stayed in his room for the next month. Duncan said nothing, as though this did not matter, but I knew he was unhappy.

Just before the start of the winter ceremonies he made a second visit to Metlakatla. This time he asked Tamlahk, Doolyaks, Klashwaht and I to come with him. We brought two canoes filled with tools and our tents. Tugwell agreed to come too, and he brought Mrs. Tugwell, though she was more frightened of canoes than he was. She said she wanted to be sure Mr. Tugwell dressed properly and stayed warm. How strange it was that this White man did not know how to dress himself to keep warm! They wrapped themselves together in a blanket and held onto the sides while the others paddled. The motion of the waves made Mrs. Tugwell sick before we reached Metlakatla.

The weather was difficult this time. The autumn rains fell hard every day. The Tugwells stayed in their tent while Duncan and the rest of us worked hard for four days preparing the land to build the first buildings. We cut down trees and dug ditches to drain the marshes. When we were not working on the land we hunted geese and deer for our food. Tamlahk taught Duncan how to shoot a rifle. Another canoe of workers arrived after four days and helped us finish the work. Legiac visited too, to bring us cranberries and a fresh cooked goose.

After eight days we returned. The weather was too dark and wet to do more that winter. Duncan opened the school again. This year the winter ceremonies were much quieter. Our classes were not interrupted by the Shamans or by drunken violence, but Duncan needed to close the school for three weeks after Christmas to care for the sick.

Duncan left Reverend Tugwell to lead the prayer services on Sundays while he attended the sick. Tugwell's services were boring. He could not play the concertina and did not know the Tsimshian words to the hymns we knew how to sing. He did not explain his lessons like Duncan. He was nervous when we asked questions and he never answered them clearly.

One day he told us a story we did not know, the story of the Last Supper. He told us it was one of the most important stories for it was the last night before Jesus was captured. In the story Jesus told the Disciples that the bread they ate was his body and the wine they drank was his blood. We said that was horrible, but Tugwell explained that the story taught us to give thanks for everything we ate. He taught us a new way to give thanks to Jesus, like the Whites do in the churches of England. He told us to kneel and open our mouths. He gave each of us with us a piece of a cracker. Each time he said "body of Christ" as he placed it on our tongues. Some of us did not like this but he said we must eat the cracker to show that we accepted Christ.

This interested me, but it confused me too. I had many questions for Duncan that evening. I asked him why Jesus wanted the Disciples to eat him. Did Christ want them to be Cannibals? Did his blood make them drunk like wine, and was this a good thing? Is it wrong to drink wine if Jesus did? Was it right to think about eating the body of Christ when I had my dinner? The Hamatsas tame the Cannibal Dancer so he will not eat human flesh. Did Christ mean that this is wrong? How could Cannibals be good Christians?

My questions made Duncan angry. He told me not to ask such stupid questions and that Tugwell should not have taught us this story. He tried to explain that Christ only wanted us to respect how important our food was, and that he loved us so much he would die for us. He insisted that no one had eaten Christ and I should not let the story upset me, but I was not upset. I told him my favourite story had the same message, the story of the Salmon Prince. He asked me to tell him the story. When I finished his face was red but he said nothing.

I thought he did not understand me. I tried to explain why the story reminded me of Jesus Christ. "I think Christ is like the Salmon Prince. The people had to learn how to pray and respect the Salmon People before they could be saved. The Salmon Prince saved them from starvation, but he had to die to be reborn. He came again, just like Christ will come again to save us and we must embrace him again. Maybe we are supposed to eat him when He returns." I was proud of my idea but Duncan stared at me in disbelief.

"Don't try to interpret the lessons of the Bible. If you want to know what they mean, ask me and I will explain them to you. Don't think up your own ridiculous ideas. They have nothing to do with your heathen stories!"

"But the Disciples loved Christ the same way as the human prince loved the Salmon Prince, didn't they?" I asked him.

"For God's sake, NO! How could you think that Christ is such a person? That is FILTHY! DISGUSTING!!" I had never seen his face so red. He leapt to his feet and flapped his arms up and down, like he was shaking seaweed off his arms after a swim. He turned to me and shouted, "I never want you to repeat that story again! It is horrible! You obviously know nothing about Christ's message. I want you to forget the story of the Last Supper and especially the story of the Salmon Prince." Then he turned away from me and told me to leave.

I was so upset I could not stop my tears. I did not understand what I had done wrong. I had gotten the message of the story very wrong, but I still could not know how it was wrong. I could not eat my dinner or speak to others that evening. Tamlahk was worried but I could not explain what had happened.

The next morning Duncan scolded Tugwell in front of the schoolhouse for telling us the story of the Last Supper. Tugwell argued that it was necessary for us to learn the message of the story, but Duncan said we were not ready. He told him we were cannibals before he came to Fort Simpson and that Tugwell had given me bad ideas about the story. What he said about us being cannibals was not true. I felt so awful I had to leave and Tamlahk followed me.

Tamlahk stayed near me all that day to comfort me. We did not return until the next morning. I thought Duncan would be angry with us for leaving, but instead he apologized for speaking angrily to me. He asked me if I was feeling better and he asked us to forgive him. We forgave him and stayed, but we were never offered crackers after our prayers again.

I was so pleased that Duncan had forgiven me that I thought no more about it. The story of the Salmon Prince was forgotten and we were friends again. It was the Christmas holiday season and Duncan did his best to make it fun. We had a celebration at the schoolhouse on New Year's Day. Duncan taught us English games with blindfolds and we raced each other by hopping with sacks around our legs. Then he taught us how to stand on our heads and we tried to copy him. We had so much fun that day that our stomachs hurt from laughing.

He invited some of his best students to a celebration in the fort that evening, including Tamlahk and I. All the Whites were there, including the Tugwells. Reverend Tugwell read a prayer and Chief McNeill read messages of good wishes for the New Year from Governor Douglas and the English Queen.

Tamlahk and I stood at the back of the room behind the others, where we could see everyone in the room. Peter the guard was standing at the back with a friend too. They were not much interested in the speeches. I saw Peter's friend reach behind him and squeeze his backside playfully. Peter pushed his hand away and looked around nervously. They saw Tamlahk and I watching. They looked at each other, wondering what to do. Tamlahk winked at them. He put his arm behind me and squeezed my backside. Then he folded his fingers with mine to show them we were lovers. They smiled and beckoned us to stand beside them.

At that moment McNeill invited Duncan to speak. We dared not move because Duncan was watching us from the front of the room. He thanked Chief McNeill for his invitation and said his mission at Fort Simpson was more successful than the year before. He promised the next year would be even better. He said it would be best if one of his students could tell them about our future plans. Then he summoned me to come to the front of the room to speak to everyone.

I was so surprised at first I did not move. He beckoned to a second time. I felt my shyness growing as I made my way to the front. All the White faces were smiling and staring at me, waiting for me to say something. I did not know what to say. Duncan asked me to tell about my visit to Fort Victoria. I told them about our trip south in canoes, about building the schoolhouse and about meeting Reverend Cridge, Bishop Hills and Governor Douglas. Duncan suggested I tell them about our plans for Metlakatla. I told them how we would build a town with no guns or alcohol. We would be good Christians and learn White men's ways. I also told them that Tamlahk and I loved ships and we wanted to see other parts of the world someday. I hoped that when we were older the Whites and the Tsimshian would live together in the same villages as friends.

The Whites shouted "Bravo!" and clapped their hands. They were impressed that I could speak English. Chief McNeill patted my back and shook my hand. Others congratulated Duncan for teaching me so well. I disliked the attention and returned to Tamlahk's side as soon as I could.

Peter and his friend came to talk to us when another man began to speak. He introduced his friend Jacques, who whispered that Tamlahk and I were a handsome couple. I had to ask him to repeat his words. I did not understand his strange accent. Some men looked at us when they heard us whisper so we stopped talking.

Chief McNeill began to speak again. He offered a drink of wine to each of us to welcome the New Year. Duncan gave him a stern look and shook his head but McNeill ignored him. Duncan announced it was time for the Tsimshian men to leave and he ordered us to follow him. We nodded goodbye to Peter and Jacques. I turned to go and I felt Jacques' hand on my bottom. I looked at him with surprise and disbelief. His eyes were lustful and greedy. I left in a hurry, feeling hurt. I said nothing of this to Tamlahk.

The remainder of that winter was difficult for our house. My father decided not to hold winter ceremonies. The death of Amapaas the year before weighed heavy on our hearts and no one wanted to celebrate. Tooklan was upset. He told my father our Ancestors would punish him if he did not honour them with the ceremonies, but Neeshlak answered that they had punished him already. He had no interest in discussions anymore. He made firm rules and then expected us to leave him alone. My mother worried for his Spirit for she could no longer console him.

Then Tsangook fell ill with a fever and we all worried for his health. We moved his bed beside the fire to keep him warm. Teshlah and Miyana made him hot broths and nursed him like a child. Duncan paid him visits too. Tsangook loved their attention and sought it long after he no longer needed their care. Great Spirit is most kind to those who look after the sick, he told them, and he did not want to deprive them of His kindness. As he grew stronger, he repaid us with simple dances and his favourite stories while we sat around him, though he had coughing spells when he laughed or sang. He almost healed when it was time for oolichon fishing on the Nass, but we left him home to rest.

As soon as we returned from the Nass we wanted to start building at Metlakatla but Duncan was distracted by many other projects. He wanted to move the schoolhouse further down the beach so we would not be disturbed. He also wanted to build a house for himself beside the schoolhouse. None of this pleased us. We thought he should be building a new schoolhouse and homes at Metlakatla instead.

He also talked about visiting the villages of the Nass again and starting a new mission in Fort Rupert with the Kwakiutl. We asked him how he could build Metlakatla while he was doing so many other things. He told us we would build it very slowly, perhaps over many years. The Tugwells had survived the winter so he thought we should build a house for them at Metlakatla first so that they could supervise the building of other houses. We were discouraged. The Tugwells knew nothing about work and could not supervise anything. We argued with Duncan but it did no good.

But we did not build a house for the Tugwells that year either. Duncan planned a simple house for them but they wanted a much larger one. They wanted to care for many children who had lost their parents. This was not necessary, for other families who shared the same houses cared for them, and they did not want to give their children to the Tugwells. They suggested that Duncan give the Tugwells dogs instead.

The Tugwells were determined and they told Duncan they would only stay if Duncan let them adopt. Duncan did not really care if they stayed since they did little to help with his work. He refused to discuss finding children with them for the rest of the summer. Everyone felt the bad feelings between them and it made us uncomfortable. Finally two sisters who were almost young women offered to let the Tugwells adopt them to end their feud with Duncan. This satisfied the Tugwells, but Duncan was no longer in any hurry to build a house for them. We did not start to build at Metlakatla until the later in the fall.

Duncan was exhausted by his many plans and his struggles with the Tugwells. In September he went to Victoria to visit Reverend Cridge for a short rest. He promised he would only stay two weeks so we did not follow him. He kept his promise but he was not rested when he returned. Bishops Hills had scolded him for not making the five hundred hassocks for his congregation to kneel on, and Duncan was angry with Governor Douglas for he had done nothing to organize camps for Indians around the harbour. Perhaps Douglas was right that he enjoyed the company of our people best.

Duncan also did not know how to rest. He spent his time in Victoria buying new furniture and supplies for the school. He also bought a round map of the world that turned on a pole. Its beauty fascinated me. The seas were coloured blue and the different lands had other colours. Duncan stuck pins where Fort Simpson and Fort Victoria were and he showed us the route his ship took from England. Our two-week journey to Fort Victoria looked very short indeed. He showed us England, the Holy Lands of the Bible and the land of India too. Finally I understood how the world has many sides. I showed them to Tamlahk and we dreamed again of traveling to far away places. We were anxious to see if the lands were really those colours.

Our other dream was to be baptized as Christians. Duncan had spoken about this for several months. He said it was a very important ceremony and that we would be given Christian names that we would keep all our lives. Then we would be true Christians, just as good as the White Christians in Fort Victoria.

Duncan could not do the baptism ceremony himself. He said he needed a White Shaman who was ordained, someone who had been trained in a special way. They had the special title "Reverend", like Reverend Tugwell, though it surprised us that he had any skills at all. Now that Tugwell had two new daughters and he was friends with Duncan again, they took pleasure in planning the special ceremony together for the next summer. Duncan told us this would be one of the most important days of lives. Our anticipation grew as it approached.

I thought the baptism would be a great potlatch, like the one my father held when I took my uncle's name and became an Elder of the Eagle Clan. I was most excited for Tamlahk, for he had lost the chance to become an Elder when he left his Clan to live with me. I told him about the stories and the dancing and the great feasts that went on for days.

It was a great disappointment to learn that there would be no Chiefs or Elders watching, except Chief McNeill, Reverend Tugwell and Duncan. It was disheartening too that there would be no dancing, story telling or even a feast. Duncan would only allow us to sing hymns. For years I regretted that there was no food at English ceremonies. Years later I tasted English food and I understood why they did not care to have feasts.

On the morning of our baptism we dressed in our best White clothes and we walked to courtyard inside the fort with Duncan. Peter, Jacques, Clah and all the White traders at the fort watched us from the walls or the back of the courtyard. Reverend Tugwell read passages from the Bible and we prayed together. He called me to come forward and stand before him. He asked me if I had accepted Jesus Christ as our Lord and I said yes. Then placed his hand on my head read more from the Bible. He told me that baptism was like a marriage with the Holy Spirit. Then he sprinkled water on my head and gave me the Christian name that Duncan chose for me, Jack Campbell. I prayed with him and when we were finished Chief McNeill and the other Whites applauded me.

In this way he baptized six other students, including Tamlahk and the two girls he had adopted. I waited quietly beside Duncan while they took their turns. Tugwell gave his girls the Christian names Catherine and Elizabeth Tugwell. Then he summoned Tamlahk as it began to sprinkle rain. I whispered to Duncan that God was baptizing him from above. He hushed me with a finger to his lips.

He gave Tamlahk the Christian name Tom Smith. Tom asked Duncan if he could have the same last name as me, but Tugwell told him that only sisters and brothers could have the same last name. Tom started to say that Catherine and Elizabeth were not sisters, but Duncan hushed him. Tugwell told him that Duncan knew what was best. So Tamlahk and I came to have different family names, but I was honoured that he asked to share my name. When he returned to my side I held his hand, but Duncan saw this and told us not to.

When it was done Duncan gave each of us a picture of Jesus Christ with a bright glow around his head, like the Shining Youth from Heaven. Tamlahk and I left the English fort and walked home together through the longhouses of the different Clans, just as we usually did after school each day. But that day we had new English names, like magic invisible powers that made us just like the Whites. I looked into Tamlahk's eyes and said "Tom". He looked into mine and called my new name, Jack, and we laughed and danced about. When we reached our chamber we kissed passionately for several minutes. Then we knelt and prayed so the English God would see our joy.

Duncan only used our Christian names after that day. He treated us with a special honour in front of the other school children who were not baptized. He told them they must be good Christians if they wanted to be baptized like us. The other students looked at us with envy and respect. Duncan told us we must show our best behaviour at school in front of the others. We understood that we must behave as Elders, for we thought of ourselves as Elders of a new Clan, the Anglican Church.

We told everyone who knew us our new Christian names as soon as we were baptized, but reactions were sometimes displeasing. Some thought our new names were funny. Others asked me what my name meant but I did not know. No one had told me its stories. They asked me how my Christian name could be as important as my Tsimshian name if I did not know its stories. That bothered me but I pretended not to care. I explained I had two names now, so it did not matter.

My new name amused my mother. She used my Tsimshian and Christian name together. She called me Gugweelaks Jack Campbell, which sounded ridiculous. But my father's reaction was not so kind. He refused to use it for I had forsaken my sacred, traditional name for a Christian one. He said it would anger our ancestors and bring bad luck, for I was Tsimshian, not English. He told me that he was disappointed in me, for I cared more for Christianity than my own family. His words hurt me deeply.

We were naïve to think our friends and families would like our new names. I thought they were being disrespectful. I tried to show Christian forgiveness as Duncan had taught us but I was still angry. I told myself those who did not accept our new names were old fashioned and superstitious, even my father. I did not understand that the arrogance of my youth had married the arrogance of Christianity, and I was the one who was disrespectful.

My father was right to be angry with me. I was so interested in being a good Christian and a student of English that I was ignoring my family and my duties as an Elder of the Eagle Clan. One day he came to me with the shocking news that Miyana would not be marrying Legiac's cousin Gadonai as our Clan had arranged, for she and Klashwaht had fled to Fort Victoria. I could not believe it. I felt ashamed too. Before Tamlahk and I were lovers and before I began studying with Duncan, Miyana and I were so close that we shared every passion in our hearts.

With my father's permission, our Eagle Clan had promised Miyana to Gadonai to build a tie between our village and Legiac's Clan, the most powerful in Fort Simpson. They were to be married the next winter. But Gadonai was much older than Miyana and he liked to gamble and drink. Miyana had let her hatred for him grow instead of accepting her fate and his weaknesses. I knew of this for she had begged Uncle Shoget, Chief of our Eagle Clan, to stop their marriage. But he told her that she must honour her duty to our Clan and as a daughter of our Head Chief and marry Gadonai. When she swore she would not my father confined her to her chamber for a week. Then she apologized and relented to marry Gadonai and I thought the problem was forgotten.

I had not noticed her feelings for Klashwaht. Neeshlak had known though. He had seen him looking at Miyana for the past two years.

Miyana ignored Klashwaht's attentions until the winter before when he fell ill. Miyana helped care for him when our other servants were ill too, and that is when my father saw the changes in her. He said nothing but he knew he must do something. A love between a former slave and the daughter of a Chief was unthinkable. He quickly hired other commoners to care for Klashwaht and gave Miyana other work to do.

At first Neeshlak believed Miyana would never dishonour her Clan and that Klashwaht would respect that he had freed him from slavery and had given him shelter in his house since he was a young boy. But as he watched the feelings between them grow he began to doubt this. He spoke to Miyana and she admitted she was deeply in love with Klashwaht and wanted to marry him. My father was furious and forbade her to see him anymore.

Their love was still a secret to most others so he said nothing to Shoget or the Eagle Clan. Instead, he banished Klashwaht from his house. He thought it would be easier for Miyana if did not see him every day. Klashwaht moved to live in the Gitsees village across the channel from ours. Miyana was distraught and did not eat for three days. Neeshlak told our household that she was feeling ill and he had Hoshieka prepare special foods and bring them to her chamber. On the third day she came out to eat with the others and we thought she was feeling better. The next day she disappeared.

Tamlahk and I had not come home for dinner that evening, for we were practicing Christian hymns with Duncan's choir. When my father learned that Miyana was missing he looked for Klashwaht at the Gitsees camp and learned that he was gone too. He spent all evening going from village to village looking for them. He heard the rumour that Klashwaht and Miyana had fled to Fort Victoria. Klashwaht had stolen his only daughter and brought ruin to our family and our Clan.

My father was not angry when he approached me. He was filled with shame and remorse. If he had not been a Chief he might have begged for my help, for if I could find her she might listen to my advice and follow me home. I had no time to waste for the news would spread quickly.

I spoke to Shoget and he called a meeting of the Elders that evening. The Elders were angry with me. I was expected to know the troubles of the Clan, especially those of my own sister. They were upset that she was in love with Klashwaht. They would never let her marry a commoner who was raised as a slave. She was expected to give birth to the heirs of the Eagle Clan. They ordered Gwashasip and I to find her and bring her back to face their justice.

Uncle Shoget agreed to come with Gwashasip, Tom and I. So did Hahkwah, Doolyaks and Tsangook. Yuwahksa insisted on coming to be with Doolyaks and to comfort Miyana when we found her. Before we left I spoke with friends in the Gitsees village. They told me Klashwaht left others two days before Miyana disappeared because he did not want to witness Miyana's marriage to Gadonai. She had come asking for him the day she left her chamber. When she learned he had left she began to look for other canoes leaving for Fort Victoria. They had heard that a party of Nishga canoes had left the next day. Tom spoke to the Nishga camp and learned that Miyana had gone with them.

We packed quickly, for the Nishga canoes were only two days ahead of us. We kept the canoe light so it would be faster. The Nishga canoes were heavy with furs so there was a small chance we could catch them before they reached Victoria.

My father came to speak to me before we left. I saw he wanted to be brave but his eyes were soft with worry. He told me he no longer cared what happened to himself but he could not bear to lose both Amapaas and Miyana. He told me to find her as soon as I could and to promise her his love and forgiveness if she came home. The sadness in his eyes followed me until I returned.

We paddled hard and steady each day as long as there was light. Each night at our camp Tom and I prayed to Jesus for her safety. Each morning I was anxious to start early. We looked for signs of their passing as we traveled south. We thought perhaps we found their camp in Tsamsem's Trench, but many canoes traveled this route at this time of year. We spoke to several canoes coming from the south but they had seen many canoes going south in the past two days.

My worries increased with each day. I wondered where Miyana would stay in Fort Victoria or how she would buy food without money. She must know we would follow her to the Nishga camp so she would not stay with them. If she did not find Klashwaht she would have no one to protect her. I had heard stories of many terrible things that happened to our women at Fort Victoria. I tried not to think about them but I could not stop my thoughts.

The closer we came to Fort Victoria the more I questioned what we needed to do. I wondered, if she was already with Klashwaht, if he would let us take her back to Fort Simpson without a fight. Would he die fighting for her and who else would be injured or killed? And would Miyana come willingly or would we need to tie her up like a slave to keep her from running away. I knew that would make her my enemy forever and that would break my heart.

I wondered too what life waited for her back at Fort Simpson. Soon all of Fort Simpson would know she had run away. Legiac's Clan would be most upset. There could be no greater insult than a bride running away with a slave boy. What punishment would they demand for her? Surely something that would dishonour her in front of all the villages. Who would marry her then? She would live a life of shame and misery and Gwashasip and I would never have heirs. Would it not be better to leave her in Fort Victoria with Klashwaht where at least they would have each other's love?

That thought gave me no peace either for it would break my father's heart. I had promised him to do my best to bring her back. And if I did not bring her back Legiac's Clan would seek revenge on ours. Legiac had killed for much less. Then Captain Pearce and the White gun ships would return to punish us and more would die.

These were the thoughts that tormented me in the days and nights on the way to Fort Victoria. My silence worried Tamlahk terribly. He sat beside me always when we were out the canoe, holding my hand and keeping his arm around my shoulders. At night he hugged me tightly from behind and I felt his tears on my neck, but they gave me no comfort. I needed him near me yet I could not be comforted.

In Fort Rupert we learned the Nishga canoes had camped there the night before and we were encouraged. Two Kwakiutl men joined us for rest of our journey south. We were grateful to have their strength for the winds were strong against us. We reached the narrowest passage two days beyond Fort Rupert but a White gun ship blocked our way and told us to return home. We begged them to let us pass but they refused to listen. When I tried to ask about the Nishga canoes they began to shoot at us. We turned around and paddled back towards Fort Rupert.

At first we were discouraged, but the Kwakiutls knew of another passage behind the island to the east. By the time we found the passage it was time to make camp for the night. We had not seen Miyana in the canoes going north so we knew the Nishga must have passed the narrows before the gun ship arrived. The next day we continued our journey south. We had only lost one day.

The sight of the harbour at Fort Victoria did not bring us joy. Duncan was right that Governor Douglas had done nothing improve the Indian camp on the west side of the harbour. The great camp was now twice as large as Fort Simpson and more crowded than the year before. It was filled with noise and smoke and the smell was terrible. We looked for hours to find a place large enough to set up our tents together.

I was exhausted from our long journey with little sleep, but I could not rest. The noise and confusion of the camp made me more anxious. I did not know where to begin the search for Miyana or the Nishgas. But that first day it was too late. It was dark before we had set up our camp. After we finished our dinner and we were too sore and tired from paddling against the wind. Hahkwah convinced us to stay in the camp until daylight.

Somehow I slept that night. I woke to the smell of Tsangook cooking meat for breakfast. Even Tamlahk was awake and dressed. He had been careful not to wake me. His smiling face was as joyful as the sunlight on the tent.

After breakfast we split up to search the Indian camp to find the Nishgas. The search was not easy, for most of the people spoke other languages that we did not know. Many times we were invited into a Chief's tent to receive his hospitality while we waited patiently for his people to find an interpreter. We did not find the Nishga camp. By the end of the day we learned only that many people came and went each week and most were searching for their relatives. We were told many stories of terrible rapes and murders that had happened that year and they upset us greatly.

We were unsuccessful and quite discouraged by evening. Hahkwah found the Gitsees camp where Klashwaht had slept but he had disappeared without taking his belongings. The Gitsees knew nothing about Miyana. Hahkwah went back to their camp with Gwashasip that evening but Klashwaht had still not returned. Shoget was suspicious. He was sure the Gitsees were hiding him to protect him from us.

The next day our luck was better. Tom found the Tlingit camp and they knew the Nishga camp. The Nishgas told him Miyana had come with them but she had only stayed one night with them. They could not afford to keep her so she left to find work. They thought she had gone to the road to Esquimalt, where women earned money by selling their bodies to the White men. They said we might find her there in the early evening when sailors from the White ships came to buy sex.

This news made me sick and angry. I could not believe she would sell her body to the English sailors. I did not want to look for her there but Shoget said we must.

There were not many other ways an Indian woman could earn White money. I could not eat my dinner. After the others were finished, we left Tsangook and Yuwahksa to guard our tents and we walked to the road that led to Esquimalt.

The light in the sky was almost gone. At first we saw nothing, but as we walked further we saw several Indian women walking alone beside the road. There were young women and old ones. I felt sick with shame when I looked at them. Some were drunk and most of their clothes looked dirty.

White soldiers and sailors walked along the road too. Some spoke to the women. They showed the sailors their arms and legs. Some men tempted them with alcohol, then grabbed their bottoms and breasts while they drank. Some women let the soldiers touch them before they led them into the bushes by the road. I was horrified. Others pulled away from the soldiers, who struggled harder to hold them close. One drunk tried to force his sex on a girl who cried and struggled against him. I started to go to her but Doolyaks stopped me.

"The Red Jackets will shoot you dead before you get near," he whispered in my ear. "They will tell others you tried to rob them. If you hurt one of them and escape they will hunt you down like a deer. Remember, we are here to find Miyana."

Of course he was right, but both hatred and helplessness burned in my chest. It did not last long though. Several women ran to help the girl. They kicked and scratched the soldier. They pulled his hair and bit him until he let go of her. He tried to strike back but there were too many of them. He ran along the road until he was free of them, and he paused the rub his wounds. The other soldiers did not pull their guns. They laughed at him instead and encouraged the women to chase him. He swore at them, then walked towards Esquimalt where his ship was harboured.

As soon as he had left it was as though nothing had happened. We walked among the women looking for Miyana. I prayed softly to Jesus that we would not find her there. Many women disappeared when they saw we were Indians. They feared we were their relatives and we had come to punish them. Others walked past without looking at us. We spoke to them but few answered us. Finally, we found a Tsimshian woman who had worked on the road all summer. We described Miyana to her but she was sure she had not seen a Tsimshian girl like her.

There was no reason to stay any longer. We returned to our camp to tell Tsangook and Yuwahksa what we had seen. Doolyaks and Gwashasip went to the Gitsees camp to ask for Klashwaht again but they did not find him. Tamlahk said that we should go to Governor Douglas to ask him for help us find Miyana. This was a good idea but the Red Jacket guard on the bridge would not let us cross. Indians were not allowed in the

White town after dark because a White woman had been raped last year.

We returned to our camp feeling angry. Miyana could be in danger. The Red Jackets protected White women while they raped our women. I thought it was probably a Red Jacket who raped the White woman anyway. I was so upset I could not speak. Tamlahk tried to reassure me as he lay beside me. He said we would try again in the morning. He held me in his arms while I cried until I could not stay awake any longer.

The next morning we learned that Gwashasip had not returned to our camp. Doolyaks had left him drinking with other men at the Gitsees camp. We returned to their camp and found him lying on the ground. A Gitsees woman was tending him. She told us he had been in a fight with another man. She was feeding him hot tea, for he was still drunk. He had many cuts and bruises and a deep knife wound on his arm. He had lost much blood. He tried to stand up and say something to me but I could not understand his words. The smell of whisky was strong on him.

"We must find a doctor but I don't think he can walk," Doolyaks said. I looked towards the town. A Red Jacket was still guarding the bridge.

"They might not let us cross the bridge. Stay with him for a few minutes, Doolyaks. I have an idea." I took Tamlahk back to our camp. We changed into our English clothes and returned. Doolyaks lifted Gwashasip into his arms and followed us to the bridge. I walked briskly up to the guard.

"We must take this man to Reverend Cridge's hospital," I said.

"I am sorry. I can't let anyone cross who has been drinking," he answered, "and they cannot take Indians at the hospital."

"Please! We are Christians and friends of Reverend Cridge. My brother has lost much blood. He needs a doctor," I insisted.

He looked at Gwashasip and then at Doolyaks. Doolyaks made a sad face, as if he was holding a wounded puppy. The Red Jacket looked at our English clothes and he nodded. "All right, sir. It is up the main street on your left."

"I know, thank you." We hurried across the bridge to the main street.

"All right, sir!" Tamlahk teased me, nodding his head like the Red Jacket. I tried to give him an angry look but Doolyaks was already laughing.

We turned onto Government Street, walking as fast as we could. Whites on the sidewalks stared at our Tsimshian faces and English clothes in confusion. When they saw my drunken brother and his bleeding arm and their expressions changed to disgust. I did my best to ignore them. We led Doolyaks to the cottage where Reverend Cridge had his hospital, where Governor Douglas had said goodbye to us the summer before. We knocked on the door and Reverend Cridge opened it.

"You don't need to knock. Just come right in… Gugweelaks! What a surprise! What are you doing here?"

"Good day, Reverend Cridge. My name is Jack Campbell now. Do you remember Tamlahk? His name is Tom Smith now. We are baptized Christians. This is our friend Doolyaks and this is my brother Gwashasip. He was stabbed in a fight. We need your help."

"My goodness! That's wonderful… I mean that's terrible! Please excuse me. You have caught me by surprise. Bring your brother over to the table. This is Mrs. Ross. She is my assistant here. She will clean and dress his wounds."

We helped Doolyaks lay him on the table and remove his shirt. Mrs. Ross prepared a washing bowl while Reverend Cridge looked at his wounds.

"He's quite a mess, isn't he? Most of his wounds are not deep though, except this one on his arm. I believe he has lost quite a bit of blood but it's not bleeding much now. When did this happen?"

"I am not sure," I replied. "He did not come back to his tent last night. We found him this morning. Will he be all right?"

"Oh, I'm sure he will be fine. We'll need to sew up that cut on his arm first. We'll do it while he is still drunk. He should stay here a few days on a good bed while he builds up his strength. Then we can change his dressings daily. Why don't I show you around the hospital while Mrs. Ross finishes the cleaning?"

He led us down a hallway to a small room with four beds. "We will put your brother in here. We have just received two extra beds, but that's barely enough. We don't usually have enough room to help people from the Indian camps. There are enough fights in town on the weekends to keep us full. You are lucky that this happened at the start of the week when most of the beds are empty."

He showed us a second room where there were five more beds. "So, are you happy to be baptized? Mr. Duncan told me in his last letter that Reverend Tugwell would be baptizing some of your people. Do you like your new names? They must feel strange to you, eh?" He looked at both of us.

"Yes, we like Christian names," Tamlahk answered. "Easy! Tom Lahk Smith," he smiled. Reverend Cridge laughed loudly.

"We are proud to be Anglicans like the Whites in Fort Victoria," I said.

"Well, I am very pleased for you both. You are most welcome to worship in my church any day. Maybe next year your friend and your brother will be baptized too." Doolyaks just smiled. Cridge signaled for us to speak softly. He whispered, "So why have you come to Fort Victoria, Jack? Mr. Duncan is not here." He led us into another room along the hallway. He crossed the room to open the window.

"We have come to find my sister who has run away. She followed a man she loves because she does not want to marry the man our Clan has chosen for her. We have searched for her everywhere but we cannot find….. Klashwaht!"

Klashwaht was lying in a bed in the third room. His head and his arm were in bandages. He was asleep. We looked at Reverend Cridge for an explanation.

"You know this man?" Reverend Cridge asked. He looked surprised.

"We have been looking for him too. He is the man my sister followed. How did he come here? You said you do not take Indians?"

"Mrs. Ross's husband found him unconscious two nights ago and he brought him here. I am afraid he was beaten by some drunken soldiers on the edge of town. The soldiers are the real savages. They like to pick fights with Indians for fun. They always claim the Indians start the fights, but there are always many of them and only one Indian. It appears they beat your friend with a large stick. They broke his arm and his collarbone and gave him a serious blow on his head. He's lucky Mr. Ross found him. He is recovering but he still needs his sleep. I gave him some medicine to help him sleep."

"Has my sister come to see him here?" I was hopeful.

"I don't know your sister, but he has had no visitors. What does she look like?"

"She is eighteen and very beautiful. She is a bit shorter than me with long hair. She speaks English."

"A woman who attends my services, Mrs. Trites, told me this morning that Bishop Hills has just found a new housekeeper, a very pretty young Indian girl as you have described. You may want to pay a visit to his house. She probably would be doing the cleaning at this time of day."

Tamlahk and I thanked him for this news and ran immediately to Bishop Hill's house. We knocked on the door. While we waited I wondered what I would say to Bishop Hills. But he was not at home. Miyana opened the door. She was wearing a White dress I had not seen before. I was excited to see her, but she was not pleased to see us. She backed away from the door and then tried to push it shut. I stopped it with my foot.

"Miyana, what are you doing?"

"Why are you here? I don't want to speak to you. Go away! Leave me alone. Don't tell anyone you have seen me here!" She turned and ran deeper into the house.

I shouted into the house, "We have found Klashwaht!" My voice found her and pulled her back to us. She approached us slowly.

"Where is he?" she asked softly.

"He is in the hospital. He has been beaten by the Red Jackets."

She made a small noise and covered her mouth. Tears rose in her eyes. "Is he hurt badly?"

"I think so. He will not die but some bones are broken. You should come with us to see him. It is not far."

"No. I will not return to Fort Simpson. I cannot marry Gadonai."

I could not tell her then what I had promised our father or what our Clan had told me to do. I thought of the terrible fate that waited for her and I only wanted to protect her. "I cannot force you to return. I just need to know you are safe. Father is so worried. His heart is heavy with sadness. He told me he could not bear to lose you now that Amapaas is gone."

She wept loudly when she heard my words. I embraced her and stroked her hair. "Dear sister, what is wrong? Are you not happy that we found Klashwaht?"

She told us about her trip south and what had happened since she left the Nishga's camp. She knew she could never sell her body so she visited the White store in town to buy a nice dress with the little money she had saved. Then she asked several stores if they had work for her. She told them she was a Christian and she could also do cooking and cleaning and care for children.

Most women would not talk to her but one woman had told her that Bishop Hills needed help. She brought her to his house. He offered her food and a place to stay if she cleaned his home. He told her she could start the next day. He found a place for her to stay in a good Christian house nearby.

She thought she was lucky to find work so quickly. She did not mind doing the work of a servant or that she would not be paid money. Klashwaht would take her away when he found her. Until then she had a good place to stay and food in her stomach. She hoped the Bishop would marry them in his church when they were settled.

But her situation was not as good as it seemed. The next day Bishop Hills led her through his house to show her what to clean. He began to touch her. First it was her shoulder and then her waist. Then he began to speak about her beauty and he passed his fingers through her hair. She did not like it but she was afraid to tell him to stop.

The second day he followed her around the house as she cleaned. He held her hand as he showed her how to polish his table and he pressed his face against hers. She pulled away but he grabbed her and pulled her back. He tried to touch her breasts but she cried out and pushed him away. He became angry and warned her not to refuse him. He threatened to tell the Red Jackets that she was stealing from him. No one would believe her if she denied it. He told her many worse things would happen to her in their jail after they took her away. A panic seized her and she began to cry loudly. He shouted at her to stop but she could not. Her fears had tormented her since Klashwaht disappeared and this was the first time she had cried. Hills told her to consider what he had said and he left.

That had happened the day before. Hills was attending a funeral when we found her but she was terrified that he would return at any moment. I was also afraid he might return before we left. I felt such a rage in my chest I knew I might kill him.

"You cannot stay here. We must leave before he returns. You are a princess, the daughter of a Chief, not a White man's servant or whore. I will protect you."

"Where will we go?"

"We will decide that later. You should come to see Klashwaht now."

"Oh no! I do not him to see me like this. I am ashamed."

"Why should you be ashamed? You did nothing wrong. I will not tell him about Bishop Hills. He will not know you were here. He needs you now and he will be so happy to see you. He will like your beautiful new dress too." My words made her smile.

Reverend Cridge had finished sewing Gwashasip's wound by the time we returned to the hospital. Klashwaht was awake and talking to Doolyaks. Miyana moaned when she saw his bandages. He struggled to sit up when he saw her, but a pain gripped his chest and he fell back again. She hurried to his side but she did not know what to do.

"Please tell him not to try to sit up by himself, Doolyaks. His collar bone is broken." Reverend Cridge had entered the room behind us. He walked over to the bed. Doolyaks translated his words, and then helped Klashwaht sit up. Cridge put pillows behind his back so he would be comfortable.

I introduced Miyana to Reverend Cridge and she thanked him for helping Klashwaht. We stayed to talk with Klashwaht while Mrs. Ross made tea for Gwashasip. Finally she told us we should go so they could sleep. We took Miyana back to our camp.

We returned to visit Klashwaht and Gwashasip many times over the next three days. On the third day my brother was strong enough to leave the hospital. Klashwaht was growing stronger too. He soon found a way to sit up on his own. He was always happy to see us and we treated him like our brother.

Miyana never wanted to leave Klashwaht. She offered to help at the hospital during the day so she could be near him. It filled me with joy to watch her tend him. I remembered my father's story about how they had fallen in love while she cared for him last winter. I was grateful that I witnessed their love, for that helped to guide me through the difficult days that followed.

She never returned to Bishop Hills' house, not even to explain why she had left. At first she was happy to be with us in the camp, for she felt safe and loved. But we saw that she would not leave Klashwaht and Shoget grew impatient. He reminded her of her duty and warned her what might happen to her brothers or her Clan if she did not return. This only upset her and made it impossible to talk about a solution. She promised she would kill herself if they forced her to marry Gadonai.

I tried to explain how much our parents missed her, but that did not help either.

"It's not fair for you to lecture me," she complained. "The Clan would have married you to Laguksa if we had not moved to Fort Simpson. Would you leave Tamlahk now if they said you must?"

She was right. I could never leave Tamlahk, but we could not leave her in Fort Victoria without protection either. I knew she must return with us. Neither our Clan or our father would let her marry Klashwaht, a man with no status, but I knew I must not let them force her to marry Gadonai. I spoke my mind with Shoget, until he promised not to force her to marry if she returned to Fort Simpson right away.

But Miyana did not want to leave Klashwaht and he would not be fit to travel for several weeks. He still needed care but he could not stay at the hospital. Reverend Cridge explained that the Whites would be angry if he was still there on the weekend when they needed his bed. He offered Klashwaht a bed in his home until he was ready to make the trip to Fort Simpson.

But Miyana would have no place to stay. Bishop Hills would cause trouble if he learned she was living with someone from his church. Klashwaht told her it would be wise to return with us. He promised he would return to Fort Simpson as soon as he could.

We thought we had convinced Miyana, but she was also afraid that Klashwaht might be attacked when he returned. We knew he had done nothing wrong, that he had not known that she had followed him from Fort Simpson, but she was afraid Gadonai and his Clan would not believe us. Reverend Cridge offered to write a letter for Duncan to read to Neeshlak and Legiac. The letter would explain that Klashwaht and Miyana had not met in Victoria until he was in hospital and that nothing improper had happened between them. Finally she agreed to return with us.

I worried for her on our way home for she was much too quiet. She was sad to be apart from Klashwaht and afraid to face our parents. As we drew closer to Fort Simpson we feared she might change her mind and try to escape. We distracted her with funny stories and songs around the evening fires and Yuwahksa stayed near her to give her courage. I prayed with her and told her to have faith in God. He would guide her and bring her together with Klashwaht if it was meant to happen. By the time we arrived in Fort Simpson she was as brave as a Chief's daughter should be.

She had no need to worry about my parents. They were delighted to see her and they prepared a small feast to celebrate her return. The letter from Reverend Cridge helped them feel better too. They were not happy that she refused to marry Gadonai but they knew her stubborn heart and agreed it was best not to try to force her. Father spoke against the marriage to Shoget and the Elders of the Eagle Clan. What good would an unhappy marriage be to either Clan if it did not produce heirs?

Our worst fears were avoided. Our crisis was settled without a feud or revenge killings. Neeshlak lost the respect of other Chiefs for raising a daughter who refused her duty, but most of them just shook their heads and sighed. They understood that daughters her age were the most difficult to manage and they were grateful this had not happened to them. Gadonai's drinking and gambling had become an embarrassment to Legiac, so he convinced his Blackfish Clan to accept the generous compensation we offered, but he was no longer a close friend to my father or our Clan.

Klashwaht returned to Fort Simpson in late October, before the winter storms came. He stayed again in the Gitsees village across the channel from our village. My father forbade him to visit us or Miyana to visit him either. He made an arrangement with the Chief of the Gitsees that Klashwaht would be banished from Fort Simpson if Miyana came to visit and he announced this to Legiac and the Tsimshian Council.

My father did this to show them that Miyana's insult to the Blackfish Clan would be punished. He pretended not to see that I made trips between our villages each day to read Miyana's love notes and to return with Klashwaht's answers. He also knew that Klashwaht began attended Duncan's classes to see Miyana during the day, but he said nothing. He waited patiently for their passion to fade, just as they waited patiently for God to bring them together.

In October, the Tugwells abandoned their plans to raise our orphans and returned to England. We were not disappointed to see them leave and neither was Duncan. He convinced them to leave Catherine and Elizabeth behind in his care for they would be homesick for our people in England. Once they left Elizabeth and Catherine adopted the family name Ryan.

We hoped Duncan would now begin to build our new homes at Metlakatla and forget his other plans, but first he wanted to finish the new school and mission house at Fort Simpson. We built them at a new site further down the beach. The autumn rains were hard and the mud was deep. It was difficult to roll the heavy logs up the hill. Many times we wanted to give up but Duncan did not let us. We finished in early December. By then the days were too short and the weather was too wet to build at Metlakatla. Tom and I prayed that Duncan would begin the building in the spring, but spring seemed a lifetime away.

When I was a child, our winter ceremonies filled me with joy and wonder. The dancing, feasting and storytelling seemed to last forever. They were such happy times. My mother once told me that children have magic in their eyes, for what they see becomes magic in their minds. But now at Fort Simpson I was no longer a child and the magic was lost forever. I only remember dark days of bad weather, sickness, drunkenness, violence and death. They, too, seemed to last forever.

The darkness of this winter brought only dread and despair. We did not know then that this would be our last winter in Fort Simpson. If we had known only this, maybe hope would have come easily, but if we had been able to see the future, our hearts would have been filled with fear beyond our worst nightmares. For most of our people at Fort Simpson, this was their last winter ever.

Perhaps the Spirits knew this. Perhaps they encouraged the Shamans to make these last winter ceremonies as great as they once were, for this winter the Shamans tried harder than ever to make themselves popular again. Months before the ceremonies began, they visited every village in Fort Simpson to dance and invite the Spirits of the Ancestors to make these coming ceremonies special. Soon all of Fort Simpson felt the Shamans' passion. Only our village did not hold the winter ceremonies. My father and Duncan's students kept their promise not to drink or to attend the ceremonies, but everyone else joined in the feasting and the dancing.

Again the ceremonies brought with them more drinking, fighting, shooting and killing, but this year it was much worse, for the Tsimshian villages fought each other. Each Chief tried to have greater potlatches than the others to increase his prestige. When they could not afford to, there were many jealous insults and accusations. Some Chiefs, fearing humiliation, sent their men to richer villages to destroy the gifts that other Chiefs hoped to give away. Clans and villages attacked each other for revenge. Property was burned or smashed and some servants were killed. We stayed on the outer headland to guard our homes, listening to the gunfire and smelling the fires of their battles. The sins of Damelahamid had returned.

Everyone was grateful to see the last of the ceremonies, but the wounds left behind were deep, and not the kind to be soon forgotten. The villages were tired and bitter when it was time to go to their fishing camps on the Nass. Our Clan from Git-ka-ata arrived with more bad news that saddened our hearts. My great uncle Silgitook died during the first of the dark days in November. He was the oldest man in Gitka'ata and he had been ill for several months, but his death was a bad omen to our Clan. It promised a season of more loss and sadness. Already part of my childhood had died with him.

A White ship brought some hope for the new year in February. It had a cargo of new maps and books for the school and our first printing press. Duncan had spoken about the printing press many times. He planned to print hymn books and school books in Tsimshian language. I could write and spell better than the other students so he wanted to teach me how to use it. He promised to start my training after I returned from the Nass, but that was not meant to be.

Chief McNeill came to Duncan one afternoon while we looked at the printing press. He took him aside and spoke to him quietly for a couple of minutes. When Duncan returned his face was as white as a Ghost. For a minute he said nothing. He looked confused and worried. He stared hard at me, as if something in my face would tell him what to do. I became frightened.

"What is wrong?" I asked him.

"Jack, something very terrible has happened. I need you to find Legiac and bring him to my office immediately. Then see if you can find the other Chiefs. Please hurry. This is an emergency."

I ran as fast as I could. I found Legiac, my father and three other Chiefs. Duncan waited until all of us were seated. He paused before he spoke.

"A canoe arrived less than an hour ago. It brought very bad news. A terrible sickness is spreading quickly in the Indian camp at Fort Victoria. Thirty people have died in the first week and many more are falling ill. Indians are fleeing the camp to return to their villages. They may be bringing the sickness with them. If it is the disease we suspect, it could kill many, many people. It is called Smallpox."

Smallpox! That word blows a cold wind around my heart and stops my breathing. It drains the blood from my veins. No English word has ever frightened me more or made me feel so helpless.

But on that day in May of 1862, it did not mean much to me. That was the first time I heard its name. I wondered how something small could kill so many people. We should be thankful it was not Bigpox. We worried more for the safety of our friends and families visiting Fort Victoria than our own safety. Some said we should go to Fort Victoria to help them, but others said the Council of Chiefs must decide what to do.

The news spread across the villages of Fort Simpson like the shadow of an approaching storm. We searched for the ones who had brought the news to ask them questions. They told us there was no purpose in going to help. The Whites in Fort Victoria had ordered all Indians to leave. The great camp would already be empty. Stories of horrible deaths spread like fire. They told us the sick had many red spots and high fevers. Then great sores spread over their bodies and their skin turned black. No one was able to help them. Those who tried soon fell ill and died too. Surely these stories must be exaggerations, we told each other. Without disbelief there would be panic.

Some Elders had heard the name Smallpox before. It was the curse my father had spoken of in Gitka-ata, the sickness that had killed so many at Fort Simpson when he was not yet a man. His words returned to me with a great force. Was it true that the curse was sent to punish us? Would it kill more of us than before as he had suggested?

As a great dread grew, Legiac summoned the Council of Chiefs to discuss what to do. Some said we should prevent canoes from returning to Fort Simpson, but others said that was nonsense. How could we turn our families and friends away? Instead, they asked the Shamans to bless our houses and make sacrifices to the Great Spirit to spare our lives. Surely this would do little to stop a plague but what else could we do?

We went to Duncan to ask if he had White medicine that could protect us. He said there was medicine but he did not have any. He had already sent a message to Reverend Cridge to ask him to send some medicine. He was not sure it would arrive soon enough, but he had made a plan while he waited. We would move immediately to Metlakatla to build a new village. We had no time to waste.

He sent his students to each village to invite their families to move with us. He organized work teams to tear apart the school and the Mission House. They made rafts from the timbers to float them to Metlakatla. He sent Tom and I with another team of men to prepare the ground at Metlakatla where the buildings would be built again. We loaded our canoe as fast as we could and set out with the others.

Our prayers had been answered. We were finally moving to Metlakatla! But it was not happening as we had dreamed. It was too fast and for the wrong reason. How could we be grateful? How could we thank the Lord for sending the plague? And what would happen to our families we left behind? We did not have time to convince them to move with us. I thought my father would move our village, but he had promised nothing when I asked how soon he would come.

A small group of twenty men including Tom and I worked hard to cut the trees and clear the land at Metlakatla. We were alone without news of the others who said they would follow. We put the panic in our hearts to good use during the days, but in the evenings it was unwanted company. Time passed slowly and stubbornly. It brought no news of our families or friends. The red glow in the morning sky seemed like a great fire, as though the breezes themselves carried the plague to us from the south. Each day that we heard no news our worries grew, but we dared not speak them for fear that they would come true.

Finally after a week, another team arrived to bring us food and to help us build. Then another team arrived three days later. Tsangook was among them. After that more people arrived every day, but Duncan and the people of my village were still missing. Those who did come gave us hope. They told us many families were preparing to move. The school and the Mission House had been broken apart and the rafts would soon be ready to tow. Duncan would bring three hundred more people so we needed to clear as much ground as possible.

The plague had not reached Fort Simpson yet, but more canoes had arrived from the south. They brought news that the plague had spread north to Nanaimo and Fort Rupert. The Shamans had visited each house in Fort Simpson. They had danced in a group and burned offerings to Great Spirit. They announced that Great Spirit had told them He was pleased with their show of faith and Fort Simpson would be saved. I do not know if they believed this or if they hoped to give the people courage. The people who moved to Metlakatla did not want to wait to see.

The Shamans angered Duncan. He told the Chiefs they had been warned by the hand of the White God to change their ways. He said they must denounce the Shamans and their sins and follow him to Metlakatla if they wished to be saved. The Shamans said this was a ploy, that Duncan was using their fears to trick them. They told the Chiefs that they would be known as cowards and fools if they followed him.

Most listened to the Shamans but some did not. They came with Duncan the next week. What joy it brought to our hearts to see more than forty canoes approaching! We saw the rafts of logs they towed from our clearing on the banks above the channel. We stopped our work and ran to the shore to greet them.

I was happy to welcome so many faces that I knew, but nothing concerned us more than our families. I found Shoget, our Eagle Clan, Doolyaks, Hahkwah and many others. Miyana and Gwashasip came running to me. Miyana threw her arms around my neck and began to cry. Our parents had refused to come with them. Neeshlak told them he must stay to guard their house. Gwashasip had begged him to come but his mind was set. Memlaka would not leave without him and Hoshieka and Tooklan had stayed behind to serve them.

My joy was crushed by this news. I wanted to return to Fort Simpson that day but Duncan assured me it would be no use. He had spoken to my father himself. He told me Neeshlak believed his actions had brought the plague upon us and that it would follow him to Metlakatla if he came with us. Duncan had asked others still in Fort Simpson to try to change his mind. He asked me not to return, but to pray for them. The Lord would speak to them in time, but I was needed in Metlakatla to help the new arrivals.

There was much chaos and excitement in the next few days. Everywhere I looked there were people working. More land was cleared and tents were set up. Hunting teams were formed and great fires prepared. The rafts were broken apart and at the first high tide we rolled the logs up the steep banks to the clearing we had prepared. Then we began to build the foundations for the school and the Mission House.

The rain returned but it did not slow our work. We set trap lines and planted potatoes. We also built a simple meeting house where Duncan could speak to us. It kept out most of the rain but it was soon much too small. The next week thirty more canoes arrived from Fort Simpson with two Chiefs and three hundred more people. My parents were not among them.

A White ship on its way to Fort Simpson surprised us with a visit. The captain gave us an English flag to fly over our meeting house. That evening, we gathered with Duncan for to sing and pray. It no longer mattered which families, villages or Clans we belonged to. We prayed together as one at Metlakatla. Our dream had begun to grow.

The captain also brought a special package for Duncan from Reverend Cridge, which is why he had come to Metlakatla. Cridge had sent the White medicine Duncan had asked him for. There was a medical book and a letter in the package. We gathered at the meeting house to hear Cridge's letter. It told us there was enough medicine for seven hundred people. He sent it to us secretly from his hospital for there was no money for medicine for Indians. It had been purchased for the Whites of Fort Victoria. They had more than they needed, but he could not send more or they would know it was missing. Duncan said we must tell no one.

Duncan started the treatments at once. He told us the medicine would give us special powers to fight the Smallpox, but we were nervous. The medicine was a strange magic which we did not understand. He asked me to be the first, to show the others that the treatment was safe. He used a knife to break my skin and then he placed the medicine on the wound so it would enter my blood. In my chest my heart was pounding but I did my best not show fear on my face.

Then others were willing to take the treatment. Tamlahk and Clah helped Duncan by keeping them in a line. Yuwahksa and Teshlah washed their arms where Duncan would make his cut. I recorded their names on a sheet of paper as they were finished. At first Duncan was slow and careful, but he worked faster with more practice.

Duncan did his best to make the treatments easy. He smiled and joked with each person to relax them. He made it into a game for the children to help them be brave. Each time he pressed the medicine to a wound he asked God to save the life of his patient. His blessings reassured us. At the end of the day we knelt together and prayed to God to help the medicine work.

It took us two days to treat everyone in the camp. Each treatment had to be checked the next day. If there was no red sore a new treatment had to be done. The sores reassured us too, and quieted the tongues of those who doubted the powers of the medicine. But the special powers were too strong for some and they became sick with fevers and weakness. Duncan explained that sometimes our bodies fought with the medicine, but our bodies would win the fight and make the medicine serve us. Still, their fevers frightened us. We prayed to Lord God to make the medicine our ally.

Duncan required everyone in Metlakatla to take the medicine. In less than a week the red sores, fevers and weakness were gone. But the treatments did not free our minds of worry. We continued to work on the foundations of the Mission House and school house each day to distract our thoughts. More canoes still arrived from Fort Simpson and other villages. We became fearful that they would bring the Smallpox with them. Duncan only allowed them to stay if they agreed to take the treatment. This was the first of many rules that our new town became famous for.

We built a small hut along the beach away from our tents for the ill who might arrive. It was my duty to meet the new arrivals, to keep the records of their treatments and check for the red sores the next day. Every morning and evening, after we gathered to pray for God's protection, Duncan checked my records. So far no one had arrived with the sickness. The hut was still empty.

The day after we finished the foundation of the Mission House three canoes brought the news that Smallpox had arrived in Fort Simpson. Many more soon followed. Their faces put terror in our hearts. They told horrible stories about hundreds of people falling ill and dying. We asked about our friends and families but they could not tell us who had fallen sick. Those who were strong enough to travel were leaving as fast as they could. The sick were left without care and dead bodies lay on the ground unburied. Still there was no word of my parents. We could only wait and pray.

Legiac arrived with his wife and children too. They had first fled to the forest when the sickness broke out in his house. They came to Metlakatla without their food or belongings, but many offered them what they had for he was still our Grand Chief. They took the medicine like others before them, but Legiac did not trust it was enough. He asked Duncan to baptize his family to spare their lives, but Duncan refused. He had not forgotten the day Legiac wanted killed him to stop his teachings. He told Legiac he must first prove he was a good Christian before he would be baptized, but he asked us to pray to God with them to spare their lives.

The Smallpox arrived at Metlakatla in early July. Prayer and the medicine had not been enough to keep it away. A young girl who fled Fort Simpson with her family fell ill with a high fever and a rash on her face and arms. A young man named Qeesh, who was baptized with Tamlahk and I the summer before, also fell ill after he helped to carry her to the hut.

No one dared to approach the hut except the relatives who tended the sick. They left their dinners and firewood on the rocks a few yards away from the door. Duncan forbade us to do more. At first they were well enough to collect the food and firewood but after a couple days they sat there untouched and the fire died. The girl's grandmother went to the hut to light the fire again and bring in their food. She was not allowed to return to us.

We watched them from a distance, horrified and helpless. Both Qeesh and the girl died, and so did the girl's grandmother who had tended her. Two other attendants fell ill and died too. We prayed for their souls that God should receive them in Heaven, and that the disease would not spread beyond our hut. We burned their bodies and their clothes instead of burying them. We cleaned the hut with bleach and planted crosses so Jesus would remember them.

The week after they died, Chief McNeill sent an urgent message to Duncan, asking him to come to Fort Simpson. He wrote that he was sick with Smallpox too, and there was no White doctor. We begged Duncan not to go but we could not stop him any more than we could stop the tides. He promised that God's love and the medicine would protect him. He would leave the next morning.

His courage made some of us brave. Since he was going, we asked to go with him to find our relatives and belongings we had left behind. I asked to go too, to beg my parents to return with us. He agreed to let some of us come for he needed our help to paddle the canoe. He told us the medicine would protect us, but we must also follow his instructions. We must always keep a cloth tied around our heads to cover our noses and mouths and we must not touch the sick, the dead or the people who tended them. He gave each of us a piece of soap and told us to wash our hands each time we touched anything.

Gwashasip wanted to come with me, but I would not let him. Only one person was needed and I was the one who was baptized. I insisted that Tamlahk stay behind so he became angry with me. He had never known the love of his parents and could not understand why I would risk my life. But his anger was only a disguise for his fear. He did not come to the beach the next morning with my other friends and family to wish me well. That filled my heart with pain and sadness and made my trip more difficult.

As we paddled north in silence a terrible dread grew within me and replaced my hurt. We entered a thick fog as we approached Fort Simpson. The chill surrounded us and closed in against our skin. We stayed close to the shore, paddling slowly and carefully until we saw the outer headland.

The canoes were gone and the beaches deserted. We glided by the outlines of houses, vague and quiet like the houses of the Dead. I thought I saw shadows floating between the houses but each time they disappeared as we approached. I was too afraid to call out, for many things that are evil are invisible to the eye. Then a horrible smell reached our noses. Duncan handed us the cotton cloths and we tied them around our faces. We pulled our canoe onto the beach beside the dock. We stepped onto the shore, and into the strange blue light of Hell.

SEVENTEEN

I am standing outside the entrance to my father's house. My feet are wet for I have waded across to the outer headland through the shallow waters of the incoming tide. I am trembling. It is more from shock and fear than from the cold. I have just seen the body of a dead man lying near my path at the water's edge. He was rocking in the waves as if he was alive and in pain, as if he was trying to summon me. I hurried to his side before I understood that he was already dead.

I do not know why, but terror struck me with such force when I saw his open eyes staring at me. Was it his tortured Spirit passing through me? I had never imagined a death so terrible. I froze in my step, unable to come closer or to retreat. His naked arms and face were covered in sores and pitted with holes, as if the teeth of the Cannibal Spirits had chewed them raw. His flesh was bruised and bloated. Was this from the water or from the disease? How did he get here? Did he fall here in his struggle to escape the talons of Death or did someone throw his corpse into the waves? He seemed to look at me. His face rocked gently from side to side as if he was shaking his head. Was he warning me not to approach or was he telling me that I had done something wrong by coming here?

I slowly crept closer to see if I could recognize his face. A vile smell rose from his body, stronger than the stench I smelled from the canoe and as I walked along the beach from the fort. This must be the smell of Death. I held my breath and leaned over him. A black crab crawled out of his mouth and I backed away in horror. I pulled the cloth I had been wearing away from my mouth and collapsed to my hands and knees. There I vomited the contents of my stomach on the sand.

I am at the doorway of my father's house. The taste of my vomit is still strong in my mouth. The smell from of the dead man is still in my nostrils, or is it coming from inside the house? The child inside me wants to run away, far away, through time and memory to the warmth of the fire of my childhood home in Gitka'ata. He needs the arms of his loving parents to protect him. He wants to hide under the fallen tree where I once hid from Sonoqua, where I last felt such a terror in my heart. He wants this story to end happily, as it did then.

But my parents are not far away in Gitka'ata. They are on the other side of this doorway, inside this house that greets me with the smell of Death. I tell the child inside me not to cry. There is no place I can hide. I tie the cloth over my mouth and nose again. I lift the deerskin cover and enter the house.

It is dark and cool inside, for the fire has burned low. I wait for my eyes to adjust. Slowly, the shadows become shapes. The room is almost empty. My mother, Memla-ka, is alone. She sits on a box outside of my sister's bedroom with a blanket wrapped around her. She is not moving. For a moment a panic grips me and chokes my voice. Is this my mother's Ghost? She senses my presence and wakes from her trance. She turns to look at me but says nothing.

"Mother? Why are you sitting here alone in the dark?" I pray that she will speak and prove that she is not a Ghost, but I am terrified of what she will say. Instead she utters a small squeal and covers her mouth in fear. She looks at me as if I am the Ghost. I remember the cloth over my mouth and nose but I am afraid to remove it.

"Mother, it is me, your son Gugweelaks. What has happened here?"

"Gugweelaks?" she asks softly. She stares at me in disbelief. "Why are you here? You cannot stay. You must go now. Leave Fort Simpson or you will die!" Her voice rises in strength as her panic grows.

"Mother, what is wrong?" I move towards her. "Where is Father?"

"No! Go away! You must not touch me! You must not touch anything here. Go back to Metlakatla where you are safe." A thought comes to her. She clutches her dress and opens her mouth in fear. "Has the plague come to Metlakatla too? Are Miyana and Gwashasip sick?"

"No, they are fine. Duncan has given us a special medicine that stops the sickness. We are all safe. You must return to Metlakatla with me where you will be safe too."

"Why do you have that cloth over your mouth? Do you have sores too?"

"No! Duncan says this will help stop the sickness. Why are you sitting outside Miyana's room? She is not there."

"Hoshieka is sleeping in her bed. She is very sick. I am tending her. She tended your father until... until she fell sick too."

"Where is father? Is he still sick?"

She lets out another small sound and covers her mouth. She points to my parents' chamber. I walk towards the doorway. "No, no! You must not go in! Come away, please. Do not touch him." Her voice fades away until it is a soft squeak. She is standing now, holding her dress at her neck. The glow from the fire reflects off her tears.

I pushed the deerskin aside and looked inside the chamber. It was too dark. I see nothing. The smell of Death is too strong and I cannot enter. I close the deerskin again.

"How long has he been... like this?" I cannot speak the words that he is dead any easier than she can.

"A few days. I don't know. It is hard to remember. I wrapped him in his favourite blanket." She begins to cry harder.

"Mother, we cannot leave him lying there, not like this. We must do something."

"You must not touch him or you will die." She shakes her head and sinks down onto the box slowly. She pulls her knees up to her breasts and sobs like a child. I go to her side to comfort her but she panics and won't let me near.

I hurry outside into the fog. I cannot escape the smell. I am trembling again. I want to scream but I cannot. I must not panic. I do not want to go back inside but I cannot leave my mother alone. I must stay until I can convince her to come to Metlakatla. Perhaps Hoshieka is not too sick to travel.

I walk to Shoget's house, where Tom and I once stayed, to find firewood. The smell of death is strong inside there too, though everyone in his house moved to Metlakatla. Perhaps some of the sick were kept here. It is too dark to see far inside for the fire has gone out. The firewood is stacked inside the door. I bring some to my father's house to build up the fire. Soon it glows brightly and the chill is gone. Memlaka is calmer now. She thanks me for bringing the wood. I bring fresh water and prepare a simple meal. We are not hungry but we eat to keep up our strength.

One of the men who came from Metlakatla this morning has come to tell me it is time for our canoe to leave. I tell him I must stay in Fort Simpson to help my mother. He is upset and says I must not stay. He leaves and returns with Duncan, who also tries to convince me to return with them. Duncan is concerned but he understands.

He says he will pray for us. He says he will come back for me in a week. He gives me some dried salmon and another bar of soap. Then they are gone.

My mother seems relieved that I have stayed. I see how tired and frightened she is. She is not able to take proper care of herself. I pray to God in front of her for strength and guidance. I ask him to heal Hoshieka and to convince my mother to come with me to Metlakatla. She looks at me with confusion. Christian prayer means nothing to her. She asks me if that makes me stronger against the sickness. I tell her I think so.

I ask her what happened after we left. She says the Shamans' offerings were worthless. Neeshlak and Tooklan fell ill soon after the sickness arrived. The others moved into Shoget's house to keep away from the sickness, but then some of them fell ill too. There was a great panic and many left for their villages of their Ancestors on the Nass or the Skeena. Some of our village returned to Gitka-ata. She fears they have taken the sickness with them. I ask how they could leave her. She shakes her head and says they could do nothing to help her.

She smiles bravely and asks me about our camp at Metlakatla. I speak about it with enthusiasm. I tell her she will like it. Her smile disappears. She looks at the floor and says she cannot leave. Does she believe she is cursed?

I ask if Hoshieka is too sick to be moved. She nods her head. She tells me that Hoshieka would not let her help to care for Neeshlak. Hoshieka said it is a servant's work, but she knew Hoshieka was trying to protect her. Then Hoshieka fell sick. She tells me Hoshieka has risked her life to serve Neeshlak and now she must serve Hoshieka.

She starts to cry again, but then there is a noise from my sister's chamber and she stops. She listens at the doorway. Hoshieka is stirring. She disappears inside the room and comes out again. She makes her some tea and puts molasses from the White trading post in it to give her some energy. She says Hoshieka has too much pain to eat food and the tea must not be too hot for she has sores in her mouth. I pull a burning stick from the fire to make a torch. I follow my mother into my sister's chamber so that Hoshieka can see to drink the tea.

The room has a heavy, thick smell. It is not as strong as the smell of Death but it is unpleasant. Hoshieka is lying on her side with her back to us. Her hair is tangled and matted with sweat. Memlaka gently touches her shoulder and tells her she has brought tea. Hoshieka slowly rolls onto her back and looks at us. My breath catches in my throat. Her face is raw with sores. Her skin is moist from sweat and pus. I scarcely know her. I find the courage to greet her. She looks at me but says nothing.

Memlaka speaks softly to soothe her. She asks her to open her mouth so she can look. She asks me to bring the torch closer. Hoshieka's mouth is filled with pus. I cannot bear to watch so I look away. Memlaka asks her to spit it into the cloth she holds to her mouth. She tells her it is looking better today. My mother must surely be lying to her. She holds the cup of tea to her mouth for Hoshieka is too weak to hold it herself. Suddenly I feel sick. I stand the torch in a large pot on the floor and leave the chamber.

I wash my hands, though I touched nothing in the chamber. Memlaka follows me after a few minutes. She washes her hands too. I put more wood on the fire, to drive away the shadows. It is hot but I am still trembling. She looks at me but says nothing.

"Is she really getting better?" I whisper. "Will she be all right?"

Mother just shakes her head and looks at the ground. "She is very weak but she drank the tea. Your father refused the tea when he was sick. He wanted to die. He blamed himself for causing the plague."

"I will build a burial box for him tomorrow. I will take off the side boards and remove his body through the wall so his Spirit cannot come back."

She shakes her head again and looks at me. "His body must be burned. It is the only way to kill the sickness. You do not need to worry about his Spirit. There have been many deaths here. The house is already filled with Spirits."

When she says this I hear a small sound behind me. I turn around. A dead man is standing above me! His bony frame throws a giant shadow on the wall behind him. His rotted flesh hangs loosely from his bones. It is grey and yellow in the light of the fire. His face is scarred with deep holes and twisted in pain. His mouth is open. One eye is half eaten.

A small cry of fear escapes my throat. I fall back, almost into the flames. I scramble to my feet and hurry backwards in a panic to the other side of the fire. He is staring at me, watching as I move away. He does not chase me. He sways slightly as if he could fall at any second.

"Tooklan! What are you doing out of bed? You must rest to get strong!" Memlaka climbs up beside him. "Do you see, this is Gugweelaks. He is wearing a cloth around his mouth. He has returned home to help us."

Tooklan? How can this withered Ghost be Tooklan? Is he alive? He doesn't answer my mother. He just stares at me as my heart pounds.

"I didn't see you come out of your chamber. You must be feeling stronger. You have not walked in three weeks." She gets up and wraps a blanket around his shoulders. "Are you thirsty," she asks him.

"I am hungry," he answers weakly.

"Good! Your stomach must be feeling better. I will make you some potatoes. They are easy to digest."

"Why is he frightened of me?" Tooklan is still staring at me. "Am I dead?"

"No, no, you are alive. You surprised Gugweelaks, that is all. I did not tell him you are still here. Come now. You must rest. I will bring you some potatoes in a few minutes." She guides him back towards his chamber. He looks over his shoulder at me again before he disappears behind the deerskin.

Mother asks me to help her with the potatoes. She is very quiet. I think she is angry with me. I feel ashamed to have reacted to Tooklan with so much fear. I am still shaking with fear, but I am not sure why. I offer to take the potatoes to Tooklan when they are ready. I stay with him while he eats.

He does not eat much. I clean his bowl with soap after he is done. My mother looks so tired. I am worried for her. How terrible it must have been for her to be here tending the sick alone. I ask if she is feeling well. She nods her head, though I know it is not true. She says she has a bad headache. I tell her to rest while I tend the fire. I expect her to refuse but she retires to her room without another word.

◇◇◇◇◇◇◇◇◇◇◇◇◇◇◇◇

The night passes slowly. I have only the crackle of the fire to keep me company. This room was always filled with the sounds and voices of many people. The quiet feels unnatural and it bothers me. I feel a sadness for this house. It has known so much pride, so much happiness, but now it only knows Death. Spirits of the Dead fill every corner. No one can ever live here again.

Sometimes I hear Hoshieka's faint moans from my sister's chamber. I can hear Tooklan's soft uneven breathing too. There is no sound coming from my mother's room, but I feel her presence. But it is my father's room that has my attention. His Spirit does not rest. I feel him near to me, watching me. I fear him for the first time in my life. I fear the part of my heart that wants to be with him, the part that has lost the fear of Death. Why does he watch me? Does he want me to follow him?

The night wind is blowing the flap over the door. It speaks to me and puts fear in my heart. I place stones against it to stop the noise. I add more wood to the fire to make it brighter and sit closer to keep the chill away. I try to stay awake to listen for sounds from the chambers, but the emotions of the day have drained me. I am afraid to sleep. The Spirits will be waiting for me in my dreams. I kneel and pray to God and Jesus to spare the lives of my family, the ones who are still living. I ask Him to guide my father to Heaven and to protect me from the Spirits of the Dead who surround me.

The prayer and the fire comfort me. I cannot stop myself from falling asleep. I find myself walking along the banks of a stream. The forest beside me is dark and hard to see into. The waters of the stream flow by swiftly. Suddenly a large white bear walks out of the forest and stands on the path before me. He looks into my eyes as though he knows me. I can see that he is a supernatural Spirit. Then other animal Spirits appear out of the forest from all directions in the shapes Raven, Deer and Beaver.

The Spirits watch me, never looking away. I see anger and judgment in their eyes. They do not attack, but they move slowly towards me. I back away from them into the stream, up to my chest as they reach the water's edge. There is no way to stop what I have started. I cannot go back to the trail and I cannot fight the strength of the current. It lifts me off my feet and carries me backwards faster and faster. I hear a great roar approaching. I grab a passing branch that hangs from the bank and hold on. I look over my shoulder and I see I am at the top of a high waterfall. The current is pulling me hard towards the edge and my arms are weakening. I wake.

◇◇◇◇◇◇◇◇◇◇◇◇◇◇◇◇◇◇◇

The morning air is cold and heavy. The fog still surrounds the house but I can see other houses across the channel now. The tide is high and our headland is an island again. What horrors are breeding on the other side in that crowd of many houses? I see others moving slowly between them in the distance. They walk strangely, like Ghosts of the Dead, so I do not call out. Fires are burning somewhere. A sharp smoke hangs in the clouds around me and stings my nose. I feel protected from the Death on the other side, but also like an animal trapped on this island.

I bring back firewood and fresh water. I feel safer inside now, near the glow of our fire. Memlaka has still not risen. I make tea for the four of us and bring it to Hoshieka and Tooklan. Then I prepare more potatoes. There is not much food in the house. My mother is still not up. I bring her some tea.

She is lying in her bed. Her arm is across her eyes. She wakens as I near her.

"No! No! You must not come here," she tells me.

"Why?" I ask, though I know the answer.

"I am sick. Put the cloth on your face. Do not touch me."

"Perhaps you are just exhausted. You have been working so hard."

"No. I have a great pain in my head and I have a fever. This is how it starts. You must leave or you will die."

I wrap the cloth over my mouth and nose and I move closer to look at her. She covers her face with her hands. There are small red spots on her hands and arms. When she takes her hands away I see they are on her face too. For a minute I cannot say anything. My heart is pounding hard. I want to scream, "Please, Great Spirit. Please Jesus! Not my mother!"

I ask her how she is feeling. She tells me her back is sore and there are waves of pain in her stomach. She accepts my offer to make her some tea. I touch her forehead to check her fever. She is very hot. The heat from my torch bothers her. The tea does not agree with her either and she turns away. I go for fresh water to wipe her forehead. I am crying silently.

I cool her forehead and neck with the wet cloth. She is moaning with pain. I can do nothing to help her. She rolls towards me and vomits on the floor. She lays back and rests. Her pains have eased. I watch her for a while until she seems to be asleep. I clean the floor and wash my hands with the soap.

Hoshieka is crying now. I go to see her. How terrible she looks! Her skin is growing darker with the spreading bruises. She is too weak to move. She cannot focus her eyes and her smell is worse. She will not drink any tea or answer me. She closes her eyes and I listen to her breathing. After an hour I leave to check my mother's condition. When I return, Hoshieka's eyes are open. She is dead. I cover her with my sister's blanket.

My mother's fever grows worse through the night and the following day, but the spots disappear. She waves her hands and arms as she fights the demons inside her body. She is speaking but not to me. I cannot understand what she is saying. I pray to Jesus for mercy as I kneel beside her bed. I pretend she is praying with me. I stay beside her throughout the day, except to feed Tooklan. He now has more appetite than I do. I help him walk from his bed to sit by the fire.

The next day, my mother's stomach is not as painful. Her fever is lower but the spots have returned. They cover much of her face and arms. As the day passes they grow bigger and rise up into blisters. They are on her lips and inside her mouth too. After three days they are white with pus. I watch with horror as her condition worsens. The blisters spread to the rest of her body. She is in great pain, but I am helpless. I cannot comfort her and God does not hear my prayers.

Time passes without night or day inside the darkness of my father's house. I have grown numb to my mother's suffering. I can no longer smell the Death around me. I no longer cover my nose and mouth and I forget to wash my hands. I cannot care about these things now. Only Tooklan keeps me moving from my chair outside my mother's chamber, for I have to prepare his meals. Strange Spirits from my life before the plague visit me in my dreams. I dreamt that Duncan came with Tom and Doolyaks to visit me. They asked if I was well and left us a basket filled with food. But perhaps it was not a dream, for today Tooklan and I am eating fresh salmon and salted seal meat.

The salted meat makes Tooklan thirsty. I go outside to get more water. A fresh breeze from the north has carried away the fog and the smell of Death and burning corpses. I remember briefly the beauty of life, the way it once was. I feel a sudden fear that I will never know it again, but the fear passes. It is replaced by a sadness too deep to measure. I realize I might die and no one will take care of my father's body. I decide to take his body to one of the fires and burn it while I still have my strength.

I stare at his tortured face and body. How long has he been lying here? Maggots are feasting on his flesh. I will not dishonour him with my fears or remorse. I do my best to feel nothing. I do not let myself remember his strong and proud stature or his kind heart. I do not let the smell of Death weaken me. I say a prayer for him and wrap his corpse tightly in his favourite blanket. I drag his body to the entrance.

Tooklan stops me. He says it is wrong to bring his body through the entrance for his Spirit will return to haunt us. I have no fear of this, I tell him. I say it does not matter anymore. If we survive we will move to Metlakatla and leave this house to the Ghosts. He cannot be consoled. He says I will surely die if I do this. He is afraid of being left alone more than anything else. In his eyes I see the horror he has survived. I agree to do remove his body the traditional way for I cannot bear to see him so upset.

I remove planks from the side of the house and pull the blanket with my father's corpse through the opening. I drag him across the channel to the nearest fire. There are others there who stop what they are doing as I approach. They greet me with silent nods, grateful to see another living being but cautious not to get too close. I wonder how many of them will soon be ghosts too? They come to me without asking and help me to throw my father's body into the fire.

I return to his chamber and remove his belongings. I throw them in the fire too, so that he can have them with him in his next life. Then I remove Hoshieka's body in the same way and bring it to the fire too. I replace the planks and return to my chair. I have no strength. I try to pray but I cannot.

My mother is dying. Her sores have broken and some are bleeding. Her face is wet with pus and sweat, as Hoshieka's once was. Her breath is feeble. She is too weak to drink. I cannot help her. It hurts her even to be touched.

I feel her pain. It is pressing down on my chest like a great weight, preventing me from leaving my chair. I am too weak to cry. I want to stop my breath so I can die, but I cannot do that either. Now Tooklan is bringing me food, though I cannot eat it. I see him standing before me, holding it in his hands. Just dried salmon and water. He is still too weak to prepare tea. I see his concern for me in his one good eye and realize how beautiful he is. I beg God to keep him alive until someone finds him. That thought sharpens my pain. It rises to my throat and chokes my breath.

◇◇◇◇◇◇◇◇◇◇◇◇◇◇◇◇

I hear voices from another world. Their images float by in the shadows around me. Their faces are white. They have no noses or mouths but they are calling to me. They beckon to me to follow but my muscles are stiff and sore. It hurts to move.

I see them wrapping up Memlaka's body in a blanket. They take it away to the Underworld, to the Land of the Dead. Then they bring a blanket for me too. They wrap it around my body but they do not cover my head. Then I am lifted off the ground and taken beyond the walls of my father's house. I know I am dead for the brightness burns my eyes. I am floating above the ground, nestled in the strong arms of a man. I pretend that the Cannibal Spirits are abducting me. I tremble like a small animal in need of their love and protection.

The Spirits place me carefully into their canoe, to transport me to their distant village. They are speaking to me. I recognize my name but I do not understand their strange language. They are offering me food and water. I am suspicious of their offerings but my hunger is too great. I accept my fate with their offerings.

They have brought Tooklan with them too. He is wrapped in a blanket like I am and he is sitting in front of me. The Spirits are paddling hard. They have removed their masks. They seem familiar though they are from another world. I now realize they are my friends, Doolyaks, Tamlahk, Shoget, Clah and Duncan. They have returned to bring me back to Metlakatla. I see this but I feel no joy. I understand that they are alive and I am the one who is dead. They have come to reclaim my Spirit but I can feel nothing.

The smell of the sea brings back memories and it helps me to wake. I realize that they have been talking to me, asking me how I feel, but I have said nothing. Doolyaks asks if I would like some water. I nod but I still cannot speak. Tamlahk is looking over his shoulder at me. His face is wet with tears. They plead with me to speak. I can do nothing but look away.

We enter the bay and then the narrow channel that is Metlakatla. It feels like many months have passed since I left, though not much has changed. It is summer. Could it still be the same summer? There are more tents set up than before. The walls of the Mission House are almost finished and they are starting to build the roof.

Familiar faces of friends and family gather near us at the shore. They do not cheer our arrival. They are filled with fear and concern. Duncan orders them to stay back as our canoe scrapes the beach. My rescuers in the canoe put on their masks and lift me onto the shore. Everyone stares at me. They can see that I am dead. My sister Miyana is calling to me, asking me if I am all right. I tell her I am, but the look on her face tells me that I am not.

Doolyaks carries Tooklan to shore and sets him on his feet beside me. Some of the women scream when they see his scarred face and his half-eaten eye. The crowd pulls back in fear. Their voices gasp and their fingers point at him. They are talking about him as though he was dead. Tooklan stares at them, then he bows his head in shame. His eye fills with tears. My Spirit returns to my body, raging like a fire through a dry forest. I am awake and alive. I turn to the crowd and scream as loud as I can, "Shut up! Shut up!" Tamlahk and Duncan try to calm me. They lead me away to the hut but I continue to scream until my voice fails me.

THE RISE OF METLAKATLA

EIGHTEEN

For two weeks I stayed in the small hut the village had built for those who were sick. Five people had died in the hut before me. The room had been disinfected with bleach and their bodies had been burned, but I still felt their tortured Spirits around me.

In my solitude, my anger for what I had suffered was replaced with sadness and self-pity. I heard distant voices talking around the campfires in the evenings. At first my isolation felt like a punishment, but their singing and laughter reminded me that I was alive, that I had returned from the Land of the Dead. I started to feel grateful and soon the joy of being alive returned to me. I was able to pray again.

Duncan came to visit me each day. He examined my mouth, my arms and face. He asked me many questions about how I was feeling. I told him I felt fine. He seemed relieved that I had no fever or rashes. He told me it might take many days for the sickness to grow inside me. I needed to stay in the hut until he was sure I was healthy.

At first, he worried about me greatly. He sat beside me for long periods, holding my hand and telling me how frightened he was for me when I stayed with my mother in Fort Simpson. He told me I was his closest friend and that he loved me very much. He said his heart would break if anything happened to me. I remembered the needy child I saw in his eyes four years before, when I'd sat on his bed beside him in his chambers. His words caused fear and sadness to rise in my heart and I cried. He stroked my cheek and wiped away my tears. He told me to have faith in God and we prayed together.

The days passed and my strength improved. He was happy and the needy child inside him was gone. I looked forward to his visits each day. He brought me news of the others and told me who had arrived from Fort Simpson. I learned that the White Chief McNeill did not have Smallpox. He had panicked when he got sore joints. That made me laugh. Duncan also shared his plans for Metlakatla. He wanted to build a great village with stores and roads like Fort Victoria. There would be a saw mill and workshops and someday we would all be baptized with Christian names. His dreams excited me and I was restless to help with the building.

In the evenings, after the day's work was done, everyone gathered by the Mission House to sing hymns with Duncan. This pleased me the most and I sang along as I lay on my bed in the hut. On the second week I stood outside my hut to sing along. Someone heard me and everyone cheered. The next evening Duncan brought the villagers closer to the hut and they sang hymns for me. I did not feel so alone after that.

Only Duncan was allowed to enter the hut and he always wore a cloth over his nose and mouth. Every morning and evening Miyana placed my meals on a rock a few yards from the door. Each time she called out to me and I came to the door. She asked me how I was feeling and I told her what I had told Duncan. I could not feel any sickness within me.

Late one evening, after the laughter around the campfires had stopped, I heard footsteps on the stones outside my door. I lit my lantern. "Mr. Duncan?" I called out, but there was no answer. "Who is there?" I shouted. I wanted to scare away any animals or Spirits that had come to kill me.

"Sssssssh!" It was Tamlahk. "Jack, it is Tom. Turn off the light and open the door." I did as he said. He was standing right at the door. "Why are you here? You should stay back. Duncan will be angry."

He threw his arms around my neck and hugged me tightly. How good he felt! I pulled him inside quickly and closed the door. He kissed my neck and cheek as we embraced. When I tried to speak he kissed my mouth to silence me. We kissed for several minutes and then he pressed his face into my neck. He was crying. I stroked the back of his head until he calmed down.

"You should not be here. Duncan will be upset." He hugged me more tightly. "Aren't you afraid of Smallpox?" He said nothing, but his hair brushed back and forth against my neck as he shook his head. "If you die I will die too," he mumbled weakly.

"I am not going to die," I said to comfort him.

"I know. Duncan said you will leave the hut tomorrow."

"So, that is why you are so brave! You could have come to visit me before if you wanted to speak to me. We could have talked from a distance."

"I wanted to hold you," he said. He began to sob hard. I held him tightly. His body shook in my arms. My heart filled with his pain and soon I was crying too.

"I am sorry I did not wish you well before you left for Fort Simpson. I felt terrible after you left." I tried to tell him that I had forgiven him but he placed his fingertips on my lips so I could not interrupt him.

"I got news that both my brothers died at Fort Simpson. I was so afraid I would lose you too. When we came to see you in Fort Simpson I smelled Death in the air and I was afraid. You looked so lost. You did not see me or answer our questions. I thought the Ghosts had taken your soul. I begged Duncan not to leave you there. He said you must stay there to care for your mother. I wanted to stay too but he would not let me. I was afraid you would die and we would never speak again. I was sick with worry and shame! I thought you would never forgive me!"

He was almost shouting in his excitement and crying as he spoke. I kissed him to silence him. I forgave him and reassured him that I was no longer upset. For a while we were silent as we embraced and kissed again. I never loved him more than that moment. We pledged to love each other forever and then he asked if he could sleep with me. I could not refuse him.

We were making love the next morning when we heard Duncan's voice. He was speaking with Miyana. We heard their footsteps crunch on the stones as they crossed the beach to the hut. I remembered Governor Douglas's advice and I pushed Tom off of me.

"Hurry! Get dressed!" I whispered. "He must not see that we are lovers!"

Tom dressed quickly. He was putting on his shoes when I heard Duncan tell Miyana to wait outside while he brought my breakfast bowl to me. Duncan called for me to open the door, but it was Tom who opened it.

"Tom! What are you doing in there?" Duncan looked us with anger and alarm on his face.

"I came to visit Jack," he answered honestly.

"I gave strict orders not to come within twenty feet of the hut! You know how many people died at Fort Simpson. You saw what Smallpox has done. We can't afford to take chances. Couldn't you wait another day?"

Duncan set my breakfast bowl beside my bed. "And why are you still in bed, young man? Are you not feeling well? You are usually up by now."

"No, I am feeling fine! Tamlahk... I mean Tom, told me that I might be working tomorrow so I thought I should rest longer today."

"Oh! So that is why you came to visit, eh?" he turned to Tom. "You couldn't wait to break the news! Well, you should have asked my permission first. I suppose it is no harm as long as you didn't touch anything." Then he turned back to me. "He's telling the truth. I've decided that you can leave the hut tomorrow if you are still feeling fine. You haven't developed any spots have you?"

Before I could answer he pulled back my covers to look at my body. I covered myself with my hands for my tsootz was still hard. Duncan quickly looked away. He said, "I'm sorry" as his face grew red. Tom covered his smile with his hand and that made me smile too.

"I see that you are feeling very well indeed, as healthy as any young man," Duncan said, clearing his throat. "I should have a look at your arms and face, and a look inside your mouth. I hope you don't have any surprises for me in there." This time Tom and I laughed.

"I can't see anything wrong. I suppose you have an appetite like an ox too."

"What is an ox?"

"It's a large animal bigger than a cow. It has an appetite like a bear!"

"I am very hungry," I agreed, and I picked up my breakfast bowl.

The next day Duncan kept his promise and let me leave the hut. The villagers cheered my return. I was happy to help them finish the roof of the Mission House and school. I shared the tent with Tom again, though we were careful to be quiet when we made love. We set up Tooklan's tent beside ours so we could watch over him. We cooked our dinners together and kept him company.

Miyana and Gwashasip had many questions about the death of our parents. It was hard to talk about what happened, but they needed to know. I told them they struggled bravely and that they died in their sleep, though I did not know if this was true. I told them their bodies were burned with their possessions so they would have them in the afterlife. I said I prayed for their souls and that Jesus told me in a dream that they were safe and happy now. I don't know if they believed me but I saw that they wanted to.

Only five people had died of Smallpox in Metlakatla, but everyone felt a huge weight of sadness and loss. We all lost many of our families and friends in other villages. My father's prediction had come true. The plague killed many more this time than it did when he was young. This time it spread to all the villages on the Nass and the

Skeena and even to Gitka'ata and the other southern villages. For months afterwards we received news of more people who had died. Some we were never sure of, but they were never seen again. When the Whites counted our numbers after the plague they discovered that more than half of all Tsimshian people had died.

Perhaps we should have remembered my father's wisdom then and returned to our traditions that honoured the Spirits. Instead, we were fascinated by the miracle that had spared our lives at Metlakatla when other villages had suffered so horribly. Some said we were spared because of Duncan's treatments. Others said we survived because we prayed to the Christian God. Many believed that God had punished those who did not follow Duncan to Metlakatla, for he had told the Chiefs at Fort Simpson this is what would happen if they stayed.

Our people needed to feel safe from the plague. We asked Duncan which had saved us, the prayers or the medicine. He answered that the medicine is powerful but that God only saves those who believe in his teachings. We did not understand the science of White medicine, but we knew how to pray. Those who stayed at Metlakatla accepted Duncan as our Christian Shaman and we embraced Jesus and the Christian God with all our love and gratitude.

Many people came from smaller villages to receive Duncan's protection. Their faces and bodies were often scarred like Tooklan's. We welcomed them to our village. They saw in our healthy faces that the plague had not touched us, and they wept. We told them that God had forgiven them for not following Duncan's advice. He had given them a second chance to obey his teachings and we helped them become good Christians.

Everyone lost faith in the Shamans, even those who stayed in Fort Simpson. No one listened to them anymore. It no longer mattered which had saved us, the medicine or our prayers. The Shamans had not stopped the plague. Only White men's ways were strong enough to protect us now.

Tooklan never practiced the ways of a Shaman again. He could not heal others if he could not heal himself. He was half blind and still as weak as a child. Some were angry with him for having been a Shaman who had opposed Duncan's teachings. We reminded them that God had spared his life for a reason and that good Christians must learn to forgive. Our family became his and he stayed close to us whenever he could. For the first few months after the Smallpox we found him crying if we left him alone for long. He was never baptized. He never took a Christian name but he attended church to be with us, and because it was required.

It took a long time to cleanse our hearts of anger and grief, but Duncan kept our hands busy and our thoughts focused the new town we were building. He received money from Governor Douglas to pay for building supplies and he was anxious to share his ideas with us. He showed us his plan for the town before the Mission House was finished.

It was a strange plan. It showed where we would build the first twenty-five houses. The houses looked like simple English houses in Fort Victoria with glass windows and wooden doors. Each one was the same size and shape and they were in a perfect row. They each had fifty feet of beach front for our canoes, but they were set back far from the water. Duncan wanted a road along the shore between the houses and the sea.

Only Duncan liked the plan. We all asked him to change it. Why did the houses need to be so far from the water, we asked. We would have to walk much further to get to our canoes. Many complained they would not be able to hear the sound of waves that we loved. Why not put the road behind the houses where it would not be in the way of our canoes? And why were all the houses exactly the same? Did they need to be in such a perfect row? We all agreed that looked very strange indeed.

He said it would look nice and we would have a nice surface to walk on. We disagreed. We preferred to walk on the beach. He wanted us to build a small lavatory for each house for cleanliness, and he wanted them behind the houses so they could not be seen from the harbour. He did not want them to be beside the road, so the road could not be behind the houses.

He said the houses must be the same for we were all equal now. There would be no more slaves, no servants, no privileged families or nobles. There would be no Chief with a larger house in the centre of the village. Instead we would build a large meeting hall in a separate building. It would be larger than the houses and it would belong to everyone.

Each house would have two floors with a stairway inside. The upstairs would be broken into four sleeping chambers, like the fort in Fort Simpson. Each room would have a window. On the lower floor there would be rooms to prepare and eat our food and a small common room.

No one was happy with the new design. The windows and the doors would be good but the rooms were too small, the walls between them too solid and no one liked the stairs. There was not enough room for our families to live together and the common room was much too small. Worst of all, they would only have small iron stoves like the schoolhouse. There would be no fire to gather around to share our stories at the end of the day. No smoke would rise to Heaven through a hole in the roof.

Duncan was frustrated with our complaints. He said we must learn new ways of thinking and living and change how we have done things in the past. We must learn to live like English people if we were to be good Christians. We must not paint designs on our walls, raise totems in front of our houses or live with our uncles and cousins. Men must live with their wives and children in separate houses as English people did in English towns.

We did not understand his reasons. They did not make sense. We asked why we must change if the changes did not make our lives better? Perhaps the Whites should change so that we can accept them instead. And why would the Whites be upset if we lived with our uncles and cousins if the Whites were not living with us?

I felt as strongly as the others. I had learned many things from Duncan's picture books that the others had not. Jesus did not wear English clothes and he did not live in an English house, and certainly he was the best Christian. But I was baptized now and it was my duty to show others how to be a good Christian. It would not be right to disagreed with Duncan in front of the others.

Duncan had changed. At Fort Simpson he taught school and offered his help and advice. He asked for our help when he needed it but he never threatened to leave if we did not do what he wanted. But at Metlakatla he made rules and gave orders. At times he was as loving and comforting as a father, but if we did not follow his instructions he was angry and impatient.

My people were frightened and confused at that time. We had lost our Chiefs and our Shamans. Duncan did not run away or panic like Chief McNeill when the plague came. He had behaved like a leader and he had protected us. Even Legiac came to beg for his protection. So when he told us he would not discuss the plans anymore and threatened to return to England if we did not accept them, we fell silent. He had become our Chief and our Shaman and we did not want to lose him.

News of the miracle that Metlakatla had escaped the plague spread to the villages up the Skeena and the Nass, and much farther to the Tlingit in the north and the Haida to the west. Many survivors arrived over the next few months. They brought with them their old ways of drinking and gambling. Duncan was furious and ordered them to leave even before the Whisky Spirits had left their bodies. Shoget, Hahkwah and I spoke to calm him down. No one had explained to them that drinking and gambling were not allowed at Metlakatla, and they had nowhere to go in the middle of the night. We told him it was unfair to force them to leave.

Duncan finally agreed and let them stay. Two days later he called a meeting and insisted that everyone must attend. There were now seven hundred people at Metlakatla. We all gathered to hear him speak about good and evil and changing how we had lived at Fort Simpson. He said he could make our people strong again and stop the plague from returning, but we must accept his new rules or he would not be able to help us. Those who refused would not be allowed to stay in Metlakatla.

Our people did not like the idea of living with rules. The hall was loud with complaints, but he called for our attention again. He said Metlakatla would not follow the path of sin like Fort Simpson. We must know what is allowed and what is not. The rules would protect us from those who made our lives miserable and things that angered God. He said his rules were simple and most people already knew them. The room fell silent again. He pulled down a blanket that was pinned to the wall. Behind it was wooden sign with English words painted on it. It listed six things we must and must not do. It read:

I agree to follow the rules of Metlakatla.

> 1. *I will not participate in winter ceremonies.*
> 2. *I will not call in Shamans when I am sick.*
> 3. *I will not gamble.*
> 4. *I will not hold potlatches.*
> 5. *I will not paint my face.*
> 6. *I will not drink liquor.*

He explained each of these rules for those who could not read English. Then he uncovered a second sign. It listed eight rules of what we must do at Metlakatla:

> 1. *I will rest on Sundays.*
> 2. *I will attend religious instruction.*
> 3. *I will send my children to school.*
> 4. *I will keep myself clean.*
> 5. *I will be industrious.*
> 6. *I will be honest in trade.*
> 7. *I will build and keep a neat house.*
> 8. *I will pay my village taxes.*

He asked if the rules were clear. Some heads nodded but others looked confused. The noise of their voices began to grow. How would we know if we were clean enough?

How much work would prove we were industrious? How would he know who was honest? Duncan called for silence again. He explained that we came to Metlakatla to create a new life and to find God again. Everyone agreed. He asked us to stand if we accepted his rules. The people looked at each other, for many questions were still unanswered. Tom and I stood with the rest of Duncan's students. We were proud to be first. The others had no choice. Slowly they rose until everyone was standing.

Duncan hung his signs by the door of the Mission House. Every day at prayer time he reminded us of the rules. We had to repeat them without reading to show we knew them in our hearts. Whenever someone broke a rule Duncan brought them to the front of the assembly to discuss their behaviour with the village. Everyone feared this humiliation.

We had much more than rules to worry about. Many buildings still needed to be built. Our first concern was the roof of the Mission House where we met each day after work to hear Duncan's announcements and to pray. Then we needed to put together the school that we had floated from Fort Simpson and to build the foundation of our new church.

With all his other duties there was too much building for Duncan to supervise. Tom was good at organizing the men, so Duncan asked him to supervise the building of our first row of houses. We worked hard and fast from daybreak to sunset. If we did not finish before the winter storms came we would have no dry place to live. We wanted to work on Sundays too, before the snows came, but Duncan would not hear of it.

We worked hard but Duncan worked harder. He ordered our building materials, prepared his school lessons and tended the sick. He would not rest when he was tired. His own sickness returned and he was coughing blood again. Workers needed advice or instructions, or wanted him to settle arguments. White tools were still new to some of us and we needed his instruction. He became irritable and unhappy with us. His mood was darker than the autumn skies. On bad days we heard him shouting orders or calling someone lazy. It was a difficult time for everyone.

The winter storms came early. It was difficult to work in the cold wind and rain but our hard work brought us success. The first house was finished before November. Two weeks of good weather at the start of December helped us to finish the windows of the Mission House and the school. The new schoolhouse was large enough for a hundred and fifty students. Duncan began classes the week before Christmas. We finished the outside of the new church that week too, just in time for Duncan to hold his Christmas service. It had eight equal sides and was sixty feet across. It had no furniture but seven hundred people could fit inside of it.

We finished thirty houses before winter. Each house was built for eight people. That was only enough beds for a third of the town, so many had to sleep on the floors of the houses or in the main hall. Still, this was not enough room for the many people who continued to arrive from other places. Duncan would not allow anyone to sleep in the church, for it was the house of God, so some build simple huts of bark and tree boughs that did little to keep out the wind or the cold.

All the buildings were crowded. At nights they were filled with sounds of babies crying and people coughing. The old and the sick were given places closest to the iron stoves, but there were never enough of these places for those who needed them.

It was a difficult winter. Besides the cold weather, it was our first year without our winter ceremonies and we still grieved the deaths of our friends and families. It was too cold and dark to work outside so everyone stayed in the houses during the days. There was barely enough room to step. The kitchens were too small to cook for so many people and we did not have much food. We had harvested our first crop of potatoes but there had been no time for fishing and hunting. Even those in Fort Simpson had also been prevented from hunting or fishing so everyone was hungry. The snow was deep and many animals wandered into our town looking for food. One day one of Legiac's servant girls fled to the forest to escape a beating for stealing food. We found her body the next day, half-eaten by the wolves.

Snow and rain beat against our new windows that showed only blackness outside. We opened the doors of the iron stoves so we could watch the flames of their fires. They reminded us of the big fires we had enjoyed in our earlier homes. There was no room for dancing, but we sang hymns. I told stories from the Bible, but they were not as interesting or as much fun as the old stories done with dancing and masks. My audience was unhappy but they listened. There was not much else to do. Christianity had made everything smaller—our houses, our rooms, our fires and our stories.

Tsangook hated his life at Metlakatla more than most of us. Duncan did not allow him to carve or dance. He expected Tsangook to do the same work as other men. When Tsangook asked Duncan for other work, Duncan thought he was lazy. Bad feelings between them grew. Duncan scolded him for talking like a woman. This upset Tsangook greatly, but he worked hard and did not speak when Duncan was around for he feared he would be asked to leave Metlakatla. He hated our new houses too. They were so plain without paintings or carvings, and he felt it was wrong that Duncan would not let us put up totems. He said none of these changes made our lives better. He would have left Metlakatla but we were his family since his own family had died in the plague.

Duncan knew we were tired and unhappy that first winter. He wanted to give us something to celebrate. After our Christmas service, he taught us to sing happy English songs while he played his concertina. He organized a Christmas feast with food from Fort Victoria, which he paid for with some of the money Governor Douglas had given him.

In the weeks before Christmas he taught us how to build bread ovens, though we had never eaten English bread. Then he asked for ten men to be bakers. Tsangook liked preparing food so he was the first to volunteer. In spite of their differences, Duncan was pleased with his work. Tsangook's bread was popular at the Christmas dinner so Duncan made him the head baker. For once Tsangook was happy.

On New Year's Day, Duncan held a ceremony for those who wanted to stay in Metlakatla. We wondered why it was necessary, if everyone was obeying the rules, but Duncan insisted that it would be fun. He asked me to go first to show the others what to do. We had to stand in turn in the front of the assembly to tell why we wanted to live at Metlakatla. Most of the others repeated what I said. We each promised to obey the rules of the town and the assembly gave them permission to stay.

After a few times, it became more fun. We shouted "yes" and cheered loudly each time we gave permission. When we were done, Duncan gave each of us a badge with the words 'faith, love and loyalty' in the middle and the words 'United Brethren of Metlakatla' written in a circle around the edge. We cheered each time he pinned a badge on someone's chest. But the ceremony continued all day. Before it was over, we were exhausted and the fun was gone.

Duncan divided the town into ten groups, which he called 'companies'. Each one was named after a colour. These were not Clans, he insisted. There would be no Chief or nobles and men and women could marry within the same company. Each one would choose two men to be Church Elders and three to join the Town Council. Twenty others take turns at being Constables to keep the peace. Later, he assigned other jobs for the fire brigade or construction work. Couples and their children would stay together and every company would have separate houses once all the houses were built.   Duncan put Tom and I into different companies. I was in the Purple company and Tom's company was Red. This meant I could not be with him. I begged Duncan to keep us together but he would not change his mind. He wanted a baptized student in each of the companies. He only allowed us to share a room with others for a few months until more houses were completed.

Uncle Shoget, Tsangook and Tooklan were in my company. Doolyaks and Legiac were in the Red company with Tom. My company chose me to be one of the Church

Elders, for I was baptized and I had survived the plague at Fort Simpson. It was my duty to watch for those who were not attending prayer meetings or resting on Sunday. I thought it was an honour to be chosen but I soon disliked this job. When I reported someone to Duncan he humiliated them in front of the assembly. If they did not improve he asked them to leave Metlakatla. I tried to warn or encourage others to follow the rules. If some, like Tooklan, could not change I pretended not to see.

Tom was chosen to be a Constable. He served one week out of every ten. When he was on duty he blew the curfew bugle at 9:30 every evening and watched over the town to make sure no one was outside when they should not be. It was his duty to arrest people who were fighting and to guard them until morning. There was no jail so they slept in the schoolhouse. Duncan bought beautiful belts and blue uniforms for the Constables. I loved see Tom in his uniform. He knew I watched him and it made him feel proud. When Duncan was busy and could not see us, I would sneak out to give Tom a kiss. The Town Council replaced our Council of Chiefs, since there were no longer any Chiefs. It was fun, but we mostly elected the men who were once our Chiefs. It seemed like the only proper thing to do. Each company voted separately. The men who wanted to serve on the Council gave their names to Duncan. Each company stood in a line with their fists behind their backs. Duncan stood behind them and he called out each name on the list in turn. To vote for someone whose name was called we opened our fists. Duncan counted the votes. Only he knew how we voted.

When the election was over, Duncan put us to work again. The English work even in the darkest days when the snows are deep, and Duncan never wanted to see us idle. He trained the Constables and the Church Elders on their new duties and met with the Town Council to discuss his many plans. We usually followed his advice. He told the Council to create taxes so we could afford new projects. He wanted racks for our canoes and tracks to launch them at low tide. He also wanted to build a hundred garden plots near the town.

These changes gave us much to discuss around our stoves in the evenings while it was cold outside. Not everyone agreed what should be done first. There was so much to build and not much money. Duncan never forced his ideas on the Council, but he would not give up. He would raise his ideas again and again, explaining why his ideas were needed in different ways until most of the Council supported him. He always got his way in the early years. Only he understood his vision for Metlakatla and how to build an English town. He reminded the Council of this again and again and they were afraid to question his wisdom.

By February, we started the road between the houses and the canoes as he had shown us in his plans in the fall. The work was muddy and difficult. We did not get far before it was time to leave to fish for oolichan on the Nass. It was a great relief to be away from all the new rules and his constant watchful eye. Being free to dance and tell stories around a large fire again filled us with delight, but our trip to the Nass reminded us of the plague. When we entered the mouth of the Nass, we saw for the first time how many people had died. We looked at the empty camps in disbelief, but we could not speak the terrible thoughts that filled our minds and weighed heavily in our hearts.

It no longer mattered which village we belonged to. There were not enough survivors from Gitka'ata to open our camp so we shared the Gitsees camp, which had a better location closer to the mouth of bay. When our work at the camp was nearly finished, Tom and I canoed to the far end of the bay to visit the camps where we had met. Both were empty and it brought tears to our eyes. We learned that Tom's village now shared the camp of another Nishga village. They were thrilled to see Tamlahk. They did not know that he had survived. They told us sad stories about how his brothers and uncles had fallen ill and died. We stayed to eat a quiet meal with them around their fire. Afterwards, we shared the good news about Duncan and Metlakatla. They were happy for us but they did not want to leave their lives on the Nass to join us.

An English gunboat was anchored in the bay when we returned to the Gitsees camp. We joined the many canoes that came out to greet it. We were very surprised when Duncan came to the side of the boat to greet us. He summoned us to come aboard.

I was surprised to see Bishop Hills standing on the deck talking to the English captain. Duncan introduced me to Captain Pike, who had come to the Nass to look for whisky traders. Bishop Hills had come with him to baptize new Christians.

Duncan asked us to collect the people who wanted to be baptized and have them return to Metlakatla immediately. Fortunately, our camp was ready to leave. We set off without delay and arrived back before Captain Pike. Duncan had asked us to wait at the shore when we saw his ship, instead of surrounding the ship with our canoes like savages. We watched quietly as the crew lowered Duncan and Hills into a small boat and rowed them to the beach.

The boat scraped onto the sand. The crew jumped into the water and began to carry bags to the shore. Hills came to the bow of the boat and looked for a safe way to step out without getting his feet wet. Captain Pike jumped easily onto the sand.

"Would you like me to carry you, Your Excellency?" he asked.

"No, I can manage, thank you Captain Pike." Hills tried to leap but the boat rocked. His left foot landed in the water and he made an ugly face.

Duncan followed him, jumping lightly onto the sand. Next came the man we did not know. He was a tall, attractive man about Duncan's age. He had big white teeth, which caught my attention, for two of them were missing. He made a powerful leap and landed in front of the others, which made us laugh with delight. He bowed to us and smiled.

"Hello! I am Robert Cunningham," he said, not waiting for Duncan or Hills to introduce him. He offered his hand to me.

"I am pleased to meet you!" I shook his hand. "My name is Jack Campbell."

"We-e-ll, that's a good Scottish name if I ever heard one! Did Duncan give you that one?" He showed him missing teeth again. He spoke with a strange accent.

"No, Reverend Tugwell baptized me."

"Tugwell, eh? I heard he didn't last here very long. Well, I think you'll find me a might bit heartier! And who is this lovely lady?"

"This is my sister, Miyana."

"Pleased to meet you." She curtsied like a lady as Duncan had taught her. She greeted his attention with a big smile.

"I hope to see more of you!" He winked at Miyana. She gasped and glanced at Klashwaht. He did not know much English, but he saw the wink and he was ready to fight.

Cunningham ignored him. Duncan called to Cunningham and he excused himself. He followed the others up the hill to the Mission House. We looked at each other. We did not know what to make of him. Englishmen do not usually introduce themselves in such a manner. Miyana gave Klashwaht a look of apology. She stroked his pouting face and he smiled broadly. She took his hand and he glanced at me bashfully.

The rest of us followed the visitors to the Mission House. Duncan was telling Cunningham and Captain Pike the story of how we had built the Mission House and how it was used. Then he led them to the new church. We stood by the doorway and listened as he described how it was built. Bishop Hills entered through the back of church while Duncan was talking. He had changed his shoes.

"My accommodations will be adequate for the short time I am here, Mr. Duncan. I hope I am not inconveniencing you by taking over your quarters."

"Not at all, Your Holiness. It's my pleasure. I'll be using an empty room in one of the houses nearby. Some of our people who are not yet ready to be baptized are still fishing on the Nass."

"I must say, I have a better appreciation of the hardships you endure here."

"These are not hardships for me. My chambers are quite suitable for my needs."

"I'm certain they are," he said with a smirk, "but surely you're not going to leave the church in this state, are you?"

The smile left Duncan's face. "Is there something wrong with our church, Your Holiness?"

"You told me it is finished but it's just a hollow shell. A simple table with a white cloth at the front and three basins of water with which to minister your blessings? How can you expect your converts to be inspired by that? There are no external aids to appeal to the senses and create an atmosphere of solemn prayer. Where is the colour, the ornamentation, the decorations, the music?" Bishop Hills enjoyed the sound of his voice as it grew to fill the empty space of the hall.

"My converts are inspired by the Lord's words and my teachings, not by colours and decorations. This is how Our Lord first brought His words to the Jews. As for music, we make our own. We sing together as I play."

"Not a fiddle, I hope!" Hills gasped.

"I have a concertina," Duncan answered softly. Hills made an unpleasant face. "I know our church is plain but the Tsimshian are still learning the basics of Christianity. They cannot yet grasp the complexities of symbolism. I do not wish to distract them from the simplicity of the Lord's message. They are a superstitious race. They attach undue importance and powers to those who perform rituals and ceremonies in God's name." Duncan glanced at us to see if we were listening. We were.

"But it's so empty. It doesn't even have paint. It is only unfinished logs and spars. Jesus was born in a manger but that doesn't mean we have to worship in the stables, does it? This space seems more suitable for livestock. You are going to teach them about civilization, aren't you?"

Duncan's voice strained with anger. "Pardon me, Your Holiness, but where will we find the money for such frivolity? If I had the money I would spend it on other things first. We have a whole town to build. Most people here don't have a house to live in yet. We need to build roads, a dock and wells. We need more medical and school supplies. We were short of food this past winter. This church was one of the first buildings constructed so we would have a safe, dry place to meet and worship. Perhaps when other needs have been met we can look at some simple decorations."

"Easy, Mr. Duncan, easy! Rome wasn't built in a day. From all your accounts it sounds like Metlakatla will soon outgrow its new church anyway. Perhaps you are right not to put too much investment into a temporary structure. We can talk more about this later when you are planning its replacement. Now if you'll excuse me,

Gentlemen, I think I will catch some rest before dinner." Bishop Hills returned to Duncan's chambers.

Cunningham turned to Duncan and chuckled as soon as the Bishop left the room. "Whew! I thought wolves and bears would be the greatest threat I'd face out here."

Duncan's face was still red with anger. He did not answer Cunningham. After a pause, he spoke to Captain Pike instead. "Are you sure you wouldn't prefer to stay onshore, Captain Pike?"

"No thank you, Mr. Duncan. I will enjoy the beauty of this harbour from the peaceful solitude of my ship. After three weeks of His Excellency's company I could use a rest." He smiled at Duncan and bid him a good evening.

Duncan showed Robert Cunningham to the visitor's house. He returned with his arms full of papers and books. "Could you help me carry these to Legiac's house, Jack?" he asked me. "He has leant me a temporary room to stay in while the Bishop is here. I'd like to make one trip if possible."

I carried his books as we walked. "Will Bishop Hills be here for long?" I asked.

"Just long enough to make himself useful by baptizing those who have been waiting. He'll leave as soon as he can. He doesn't much like it here and I have no intention of making it too comfortable for him. I still have lessons to plan and the baptism ceremony to organize. I plan to busy myself as much as possible. If I can make it through the next few days without fighting with him I'll be grateful."

"Who is Cunningham? Will he be staying?"

"Yes, I'm afraid he will. The missionary society in England sent him here to help me. I'm not sure he'll be much help. I asked for an ordained English minister who could baptize new Christians. Instead they sent me an uneducated, non-ordained Irishman."

"Is it bad to be an Irishman?"

"Hopefully not in his case, Jack. Most Irish like whisky and women too much. We certainly have no place for that here! At least he's not Catholic and he looks stronger than Reverend Tugwell. He was a prize fighter before he turned to God, you know."

"What's a prize fighter?"

"He was paid to fight men for the entertainment of others. That's how he lost his front teeth. After a few losses he thought it was time to stop fighting. I suspect he chose a life with the church because he wanted to travel overseas at the church's expense. I wish he was ordained like Reverend Tugwell. Then I'd know he was more serious about his beliefs."

I wanted to ask why the Irish paid men to attack other men for entertainment and how much it costs to travel overseas, but there were too many questions on my mind at once. "You are serious. Why are you not ordained?"

That's just what Bishop Hills wants! He spent half a day on board Captain Pike's ship trying to convince me to be ordained so that my opinion would not matter anymore. Then I'd be working directly under him and he could order me to do whatever he wishes. I might as well forget my mission here if that happens. He has no respect for my work with your people. We scarcely agree on a single point."

Bishop Hills stayed three days. Duncan kept busy and spent little time with him. Hills did not help Duncan prepare for the baptism. There was great excitement in the town. Many people had been waiting for months to receive a Christian name. The ceremony began on the second day. Each person was brought before Bishop Hills. He questioned them carefully about God, Jesus and the Bible and why they wanted to be Christians. Everyone was prepared, for Duncan rehearsed the questions with them over the winter.

Bishop Hills baptized seventy people. Duncan, Cunningham, Captain Pike and his crew stood to witness the ceremony. It continued for two days. Each person chose a Christian name and Duncan assigned the family names. It was much the same as the first ceremony when Tom and I had been given our names. We were not told the meaning of the new names. We were not told the stories of the Ancestors who owned them before.

Miyana chose the name Mary, for that was the name of Reverend Cridge's wife whom she liked very much. Gwashasip chose the name George. Duncan gave them the family name Campbell, the same as mine. Doolyaks took the name Daniel Carter and Yuwahksa became Jennifer Carter. Uncle Shoget chose the name James and Duncan let him keep his name as a family name. His wife became Anna Shoget. Amapaas's wife Teshlah, his daughter, became Ruth Shoget. She chose the name Caroline for Amapaas's daughter. Hahkwah became Henry Richardson and his wife chose the name Louise.

Bishop Hills wanted to stay longer to baptize more of us. He was concerned that the Roman Catholics and Methodists had baptized more people than the Anglicans had. Duncan, of course, did not agree with him. He believed new Christians must study with him for a long time before they could be baptized or they would not understand the teachings. He told Bishop Hills that baptism was like a label on a can of salmon. It was a guarantee that the contents were good.

He did make some exceptions. He allowed Hills to baptize Chief McNeill's wife Neshaki, a Nishga princess he had not taught, so that he would keep a strong allegiance with the trading post at Fort Simpson. She chose the name Martha McNeill. He knew Neshaki was not a good woman. She had tried sell us whisky on the Nass only three weeks earlier. Duncan agreed to baptize her only after he had given her a serious scolding, but the baptism did nothing to change her.

Legiac was another exception. He had studied with Duncan less than a year, but he begged once again to be baptized. Duncan agreed, for he hoped Legiac's baptism would inspire others to be baptized. He chose Paul for his Christian name and kept Legiac as his family name. He was never a good Christian and he inspired no one. Duncan told me a year later that he regretted his decision.

The other person Duncan allowed to be baptized early was Klashwaht, for he and Miyana wanted a Christian wedding as soon as possible. They were eager to raise a family and Duncan was afraid they would not wait. Klashwaht was a faithful Christian. He believed the Christian God had intervened to bring him and my sister together. He was so happy when Duncan agreed. He accepted the name Joseph Talbot.

Bishop Hills also performed three marriages before he left. Duncan first taught the couples the Christian traditions of marriage. He taught us the vows that must be said and that a Christian woman must change her family name to the name of her husband. Their children would follow their father's name, not their mothers. Like many English customs, it seemed strange to us.

The last of the three marriages was Klashwaht and Miyana's. They could not be more happy. My sister was proud to share the name Talbot with him. She was no longer a princess and he was not a slave. Their marriage was impossible under our old ways, but now they were equal and free to marry without fear of reprisals or consequences. They believed this proved that the Christian God could perform miracles.

NINETEEN

The gloom of the first winter was replaced by a busy and happier spring. We started many more houses, continued building the road, digging wells and planting new gardens. That satisfied us, but Duncan's dreams were bigger. He started planning for more baptisms the following year and many more exciting changes. What surprised us the most was his plan to buy a sailing ship for Metlakatla.

It was a crazy idea. Why would we buy a sailing ship when there were so many other things we needed? But Duncan had thought about it for a while. He said if we had our own ship we could bring our furs to Fort Victoria where they could be sold for higher prices. We would be the first Indians anywhere to own a sailing ship and the people of Metlakatla would be remembered in history for this.

Tom and I loved the idea and soon Duncan's enthusiasm convinced the others. He collected donations from the town and I recorded them for him. The Town Council gave him some tax money and others donated furs to sell too. In the first week we collected more than four hundred dollars and a hundred marten and mink skins. He said that would be enough to purchase a small schooner.

Tom and I had dreamed of traveling on a sailing ship for years, so we begged Duncan to bring us to Fort Victoria with him. He was pleased with our enthusiasm. He said we could come if we helped him to sail it back to Metlakatla. That was even better! We assumed he knew how to sail a ship for he had traveled on them for months. In fact, he knew less about sailing a schooner than he knew about canoes when he first came to Fort Simpson.

He arranged our transport to Fort Victoria in May on a steamship. He brought another young man, a friend of ours named Samuel Pritchard, who had been baptized with us at Fort Simpson. Samuel was as excited about sailing ships as we were. On the way south we talked about the things we could do with a sailing ship. The crew of the steamship were so impressed by our enthusiasm that they donated another $25 for our purchase. When we stopped at Fort Rupert and Nanaimo, Duncan spoke at missionary meetings and raised a few more dollars. We arrived in Fort Victoria ready to sell our furs with our heads filled with dreams too large for our purse.

The harbour had changed greatly since our last visit. There were more ships and more docks. The Indian camps were mostly gone and the White town was larger. It was now called Victoria instead of Fort Victoria. Our ship docked. We said goodbye to the crew and carried our bags into town.

Duncan had arranged to stay with Reverend Cridge but he first wanted to find rooms in a White hotel for the three of us. As we walked through the town, he told us we must never stay in the Indian camp again. He said we must use our Christian names in Victoria, for we were equal to Whites now. He stopped a well-dressed gentleman and asked him where he could find a good hotel. He told us directions to the Metropolitan Lodging House on Yates Street.

We were impressed by the many changes in the past two years. The streets and sidewalks had been improved. There were new lamps and name signs for the streets. There were no more empty houses or stores. Houses made of wood had been replaced by ones made of bricks and stone. New buildings had two or three floors. There were more gardens and iron fences. Duncan told us that some day Metlakatla would look like this. Now we understood his dreams more clearly.

The Metropolitan Lodging House was a large building. The sign said it had comfortable rooms for one hundred people. We looked around at the fine woodwork in the reception room while we waited to pay for our rooms. There were signs and doors for a "Ladies Salon" and a "Men's Salon" on opposite sides of the room. We asked Duncan why there were separate rooms for women and men. He only replied that these were evil places for drinking and we must not go in there.

The man at the desk told Duncan there were no rooms available. Duncan argued that the sign outside said there were several rooms available. The man looked at us and then back to Duncan. He said the hotel had a policy that no Indians were allowed to stay there. Duncan's face grew red and he demanded to speak to the manager.

The man at the desk nodded and disappeared. He returned with another man who introduced himself as Mr. Lush. He looked at Tom, Samuel and myself and then asked Duncan if there was a problem. Duncan composed himself and spoke calmly with great dignity. He explained who we were and that he was only looking for a simple room for the three of us for a week or so. Mr. Lush said he could not help us. The hotel had strict rules against Indians staying there. Duncan's face grew red again. He said we were all good baptized Christians and we expected to be treated as equals by other Christians.

Mr. Lush was not impressed. He told Duncan the hotel was the most respectable in Victoria and it had a reputation to maintain. "You can dress up a cow and change its name but that doesn't make it a horse, does it? Do you realize how this town has suffered with all the diseases these filthy heathens have spread in the past year?"

Duncan was choking on his anger as his voice rose louder. He said the Whites brought the disease and that the Indians had suffered far greater than the people of Victoria. He told him each of us had lost our families in the plague. He asked how anyone could not treat us with respect and sympathy after all we had been through, especially since we had accepted God and the ways of the English. He challenged Mr. Lush, saying if he turned us away he was not a good Christian. "What type of reputation do you think you are maintaining in the eyes of God?" Duncan asked him.

Mr. Lush looked ready for a fight. He replied that he was a good Irish Catholic, not a simple-minded English Protestant. He told us to take our business elsewhere and not to come back again.

"Fine! I'll certainly tell others what I think of your sinful hotel!" Duncan guided us towards the door. As we left the building he turned back and shouted, "I should've guessed you were Irish with a name like Lush!"

We were all quite shaken by then. "I'm sorry about that," Duncan said to us softly. We were not sure if he was sorry for losing his temper, for what Mr. Lush had said to us or because his usual influence had not worked, but we knew not to answer him while he was so upset.

We carried our bags down the street, following behind him until he found a shop that served food. We sat at a table and he ordered a pot of hot tea for the four of us. We watched people and horses passing by the window as we sipped the tea in silence. After a few minutes the sun came out and Duncan's mood brightened. He checked his pocket watch.

"Well, we can't let a simple setback like that spoil our whole day, can we?"

He asked our woman server if she knew of a simple hotel for good Christians in Victoria. She told him the management rented rooms above the store for only one dollar per week or five dollars with food. He explained he was looking for a room for the three of us for a couple weeks. He explained that we were clean, baptized and civilized Christians who would cause no trouble. He told her he was a personal friend of Reverend Cridge and could be easily reached there if any problem arose.

We felt uncomfortable as she looked at us nervously. She started to explain the hotel policy that did not allow Indians, but she stopped when she saw the anger rising in Duncan's eyes. She excused herself to talk to the manager. She returned with a smile on her face. She said we would be welcome to stay as long as Duncan stayed with us.

Duncan was not happy with this arrangement, but he was too tired to make another fight or to look for another hotel. We took two rooms on the second floor. He spoke as if he was pleased, though our rooms were very plain and the beds were old.

"This is perfect, isn't it? We have a good view of the street, and it's less than half the price of the Metropolitan. There's no point spending our money on rooms when we could use it to pay for the ship, right? You see, God guides us to the right places if we have faith in Him." He wiped a line of dust off the window sill with his fingertip. He walked to one of the iron beds and sat down. It made a loud creak as it sagged terribly in the middle. "Oh dear! We'll have to put the mattresses on the floor if we don't want sore backs."

He decided that I should share his room and that Tom and Samuel would share the other. Tom and I looked at each other and then at Samuel. We could not explain to Duncan that we wanted to sleep together.

"Excuse me, Mr. Duncan. Could I please share your room?" Samuel spoke out. He knew we were lovers and he wanted to help us.

"Why?"

"I want to practice English with you. I can help with your papers too."

"Well, Jack usually helps me with my papers, and I'll be too busy to help you practice your English." Duncan looked at me. I smiled sweetly and shrugged my shoulders as if it did not matter to me. He looked confused and disappointed. "Very well then. You can have the other bed." He glanced back at me to see if I would change my mind. Tom nodded at Samuel and we took our bags to our room. Duncan excused himself to pay a visit to Reverend Cridge while we rested.

Tom was delighted to be alone with me in our room. He went to the window to look at the street while I combed my hair in the mirror. He came up behind me and placed his arms around me. He kissed my neck and smiled at our image in the glass. Then he crossed the room and pulled our mattresses onto the floor between our beds.

"Why are you doing this now?" I asked him. "I want to change my clothes and the mattresses will be in the way."

He lay on the mattresses and pulled me down beside him. "I help you change clothes," he said in bad English, and he began to undress me. "First, we make love on English mattress on English floor in English hotel." He paused to kiss me, and then added "with no English clothes!"

It was wonderful to make love in a strange hotel. The excitement of being in Victoria and the pleasant outcome of our long day filled us with joy and passion. When we finished making love we rested in each other's arms. The afternoon sun shone down on us through the window. I stared up at the blue sky and the lace curtains that moved in the breeze. I stoked Tom's hair as he slept on my chest and listened to the sound of horses' hooves on the street below.

"What a great afternoon it has turned out to be!" I heard Duncan's voice say to Sam in the next room. I shook Tom awake and we got up quickly. We scrambled to get dressed. Duncan's fist knocked on our door and then it opened. We were still pulling our pants on.

"What have you two been doing?" Duncan stared in surprise at our mattresses lying together on the floor. I wondered if the smell of our sex was still in the air.

"We were resting, but now we are changing our clothes," I answered softly. I was afraid to look at his face.

"Good. You should clean up too. Reverend Cridge has invited us to his house for dinner. Put on your best clothes. We are expected in an hour." He closed the door and returned to his room. I smiled with relief. Tom winked at me and kissed my lips.

◇◇◇◇◇◇◇◇◇◇◇◇◇◇◇◇

Buying a sailing ship took much longer than we expected. Duncan took Reverend Cridge's advice and placed an announcement in the newspaper. He also took us with him to the docks to ask if anyone knew of a sailing ships for sale. We were discouraged by the high prices they quoted. We did not have enough money even with our furs to buy the size of ship we had hoped for. Even ships that were too small asked for more money than what we had.

Duncan asked Governor Douglas for more money but he was not in favour of us owning a ship. He said we would hurt business at the trading post at Fort Simpson, but he gave us five hundred dollars in spite of this. Bishop Hills did not allow us to raise money in Reverend Cridge's church during his Sunday service, but Reverend Cridge let Duncan use the church hall one evening to hold his own public meeting. Cridge convinced many wealthy Christians at his church to come. Duncan spoke with enthusiasm and they gave him almost three hundred dollars more for our ship.

Still, it was a full month before Duncan found a ship we could afford. Duncan brought us to look at it. It was a small schooner with two masts. It was small, but we were excited to find a ship at last. It was named the Carolena. The captain wanted fifteen hundred dollars for it. Duncan asked him to lower the price because we were Christians, but this caused the captain to burst into laughter. He said it was only five years old. Others were interested in paying that price if Duncan was not, he told us. He was only selling it so cheaply because it had run aground near Victoria a few months before and he could not afford to repair it. He told Duncan to have faith in God and He will find the money. He laughed again at his own joke but Duncan was not amused.

It was true. It had a hole on the bottom and it could not sail until it was fixed. Duncan decided to buy it anyway. He used the monies from the furs and the public meeting to pay for part of it and he borrowed money from that his missionary society had given him for the rest. Then he used the money from Governor Douglas and the taxes the Council had given to him in Metlakatla to buy building supplies and food for Metlakatla.

He could not convince Captain Campbell to lower his price but he had better luck when he spoke to Admiral Kingcome in Esquimalt. The Admiral sent six men and two carpenters from the gun ships to repair the Carolena. They fixed the hole and spent a week scraping and painting the ship. They built extra berths for us to sleep in on our way home.

Then Duncan placed another announcement in the newspaper looking for a captain while the Carolena was being repaired. Many men answered the ad, but Duncan would not hire anyone who admitted to drinking alcohol. Samuel, Tom and I were eager to leave for home. Every day, while Duncan interviewed men who wanted to be our captain, we helped Admiral Kingcome's men sand and paint the Carolena.

Duncan finally found a captain who did not drink alcohol. His name was Patterson. He was a serious man who did not say much. He was not happy to learn that we had never been on a sailing ship before. When he learned that Duncan knew nothing about sailing a ship either he almost changed his mind. After Duncan told him of our noble cause and how Patterson could help to make our history he agreed to take us to

Metlakatla. He must have needed the money badly.

Before we left Victoria we bought lumber and other supplies for Metlakatla. Captain Patterson was upset when he saw how much we had purchased. He said there was no room for so much cargo on such a small boat. Duncan could not return them and he refused to leave them behind. They had an angry argument before Captain Patterson became silent. We knew they would never be good friends.

Governor Douglas met with Duncan the day before we sailed. He made Duncan a Magistrate with powers to arrest the whisky traders. Duncan was pleased. He told us he would put all the whisky traders in jail and they would never bother us again. We did not understand how he would catch them and take them to jail if they did not want to be there, but he believed he could do it.

Governor Douglas also invited all of us to lunch in a restaurant on Government Street the same day. He was pleased to see us again. Samuel was shy and did not say much but Douglas was friendly to him anyway. Douglas asked Tom and I if we were happy to be living at Metlakatla. He saw Tom smile at me before he spoke, as loving husbands do, and his question was answered. He asked us if we were excited about our trip back on the sailing ship. We said we were. Douglas said to Duncan, "I hope you appreciate what fine lads you have helping you, Mr. Duncan. Such loyalty and devotion are hard to find in these parts."

Duncan seemed surprised by his words, but he looked at us and smiled. "Yes, these men are good Christians. The Lord's words have brought faith and goodness to their hearts. The Tsimshian are a changed people." Duncan then asked the Governor about the land around Metlakatla. He asked him to reserve it for the use of our new Christian town. Douglas said he would think about it. Then they discussed Duncan's new duties as a Magistrate.

Two men approached our table while they were talking. The first one, a heavy, bald man with a beard, bowed slightly and begged our forgiveness for interrupting our meal. Governor Douglas introduced him as Thomas Harris, the Mayor of Victoria. We stood and shook his hand. He introduced the second man as Amor de Cosmos, the Editor of the newspaper, the Daily British Colonist.

"Please don't stand on my behalf, Governor. I'm just a humble tradesman, you know," Harris said. He laughed loudly as he patted his large stomach. "It is a pleasure to meet you again, Mr. Duncan. You gave a fine speech at your public meeting. The Mrs. and I were most impressed by the wonderful work you are doing in the north. I dare say it sounds like quite the adventure! Mr. de Cosmos tells me you have found yourself a ship and a captain. Bravo!"

"Thanks in part to your generosity, Mayor Harris. We are ready to set sail for Metlakatla tomorrow. Hopefully someday you will be able to see the fine work we are doing there."

"Oh, that does sound lovely, if me and the Mrs. can find a time when the Council doesn't need me. And how have you and your family been, Governor? We haven't seen much of you lately. The Council was hoping you would attend the last meeting. We were discussing the budget for road improvements in town."

"My family and I are quite fine, thank you, Mr. Harris," Douglas answered him. "Unfortunately, I've had to make another trip over to New Westminster this month. I used to be able to govern both colonies from here with only two trips a year to the mainland. But those days are over, I'm afraid."

"You seem to have a talent for wearing two hats, Governor." Amor de Cosmos stared hard at Douglas as if he was challenging him to a fight. "First it was Chief Factor for the Hudson's Bay Company and Governor of Vancouver Island. Now it's Governor for Vancouver Island and Governor of British Columbia. How ever do you manage these feats without a conflict of interest?"

"I am well aware of your opinions, Mr. de Cosmos. I read your paper. You think I've spent my life swapping baubles and blankets for furs at two thousand per cent profit, if I remember correctly. It isn't as easy or as profitable as you think. You will be pleased to know that I won't be wearing any hats in a year from now. This running back and forth has made me eager for retirement. I am certain by then there will be a separate governor for each of the colonies, now that the mainland colony has been established. You will have twice as much to write about. You can quote me on that."

"And speaking of conflicts of interest, I understand you have just been made a Magistrate, Mr. Duncan. Until now I have been impressed with your efforts to keep the Indians up north where they belong. Your speech at the public meeting and your new ship has everyone talking. I have also heard you have found yourself a teetotaling captain. It seems your requirements and expectations go well beyond those of the law. So which laws will you be administering when you are Magistrate, Mr. Duncan, those of the courts or those of God?"

Duncan's face turned red. "I like to think that in a good Christian society those laws are much the same, Mr. de Cosmos. God is fair and forgiving."

"Perhaps, Mr. Duncan, but human beings are often not. That's why we pass laws that apply equally to people of all faiths and convictions."

Mayor Harris was uncomfortable. "Amor, please! Mr. Duncan has done nothing wrong. We should let these gentlemen eat their lunch in peace."

"Thank you, Mr. Harris," Governor Douglas replied. "Our stomachs appreciate your concern. I will do my best to attend the next Council meeting and we will talk more then."

When they had left he turned to Duncan. "You see, Mr. Duncan, what I must deal with on a daily basis. I began this position as an administrator but now it demands the skills an acrobat. I advise you to avoid attracting the attention of journalists and editors. They are the main source of ill health for all those in the public eye."

◇◇◇◇◇◇◇◇◇◇◇◇◇◇◇◇◇

On July 29th, 1863, we set sail on the Carolena for Metlakatla, exactly two months to the day after we arrived in Victoria. We left at the first light of dawn for we hoped to travel a great distance that day. The sunrise was colourful and full of promise. Samuel, Tom and I were ready for Captain Patterson's instructions. It was a proud and exciting time for all of us. It was too early for most people to be up but Reverend Cridge and his wife Mary came to the dock to wish us a safe trip. Their kindness was a good omen.

Even Captain Patterson was in good spirits. He and Duncan had had a heated argument the day before, after our lunch with Governor Douglas. He did not like how we had stored the goods we were bringing back to Metlakatla. Not everything fit in the hold. He insisted we take many things out and pack them again. Even after we packed it better he was displeased, for the boat was too low in the water. But this morning they had forgotten their differences. He stood behind Duncan on the deck and he smiled at his speech. Reverend Cridge broke a bottle of holy water over the bow of the ship to bless the ship and to make it Christian.

We set the sails and untied the ship. We pushed it away from the dock with our poles and waited for the wind to move it. The morning breeze was very light. For a minute we stood helplessly looking at Reverend Cridge on the dock and then back at the sails. Captain Patterson called to us to change the position of the sails but we did not know what to do. He ordered Duncan to take the steering wheel while he showed us how to move the sails. We did everything wrong and soon Captain Patterson was angry again.

Patterson adjusted the sails himself one at a time. As they caught the wind better the ship began to move. He shouted instructions to Duncan to turn the wheel as we crossed the harbour, but he turned it too far and the sails lost the wind. We needed to set the sails again. A few minutes later the ship began to move again. We cheered as we crossed back across the harbour.

As we reached the far side we were near where we had started. Patterson told Duncan to steer to the starboard but he turned the wrong way. The ship started to turn back towards the dock. "No, no, NO!" he shouted to Duncan, who turned back the other way sharply. The ship leaned. I slipped, lost my footing and fell into the water. Tom shouted my name and dove into the harbour to help me.

"Jesus Christ, what are you doing?" Patterson screamed at us. "You don't jump in! You throw him a rope!" He threw a coil of rope into the water and we swam to it. We pulled ourselves up the rope to get back on the deck. Duncan had let go of the steering wheel to scold Patterson for using the Lord's name in vain and he screamed at Duncan to get back to the wheel. Duncan refused until he apologized. Patterson's face was red and said nothing more. He went to the sails and took each one down.

"What are you doing!" shouted Duncan. "We have to leave right away!"

"We aren't going anywhere until this crew understands the laws of sailing. If you think you can sail this thing without me go ahead and try!" Patterson scolded us harshly for several minutes.

He told us the importance of obeying his instructions promptly and correctly. He warned us about the dangers in the open waters and about tides and rocks between the islands that could destroy the Carolena and kill us all. He taught us again how to set the sail and how to walk safely on the deck. He made us practice like school children 'port' and 'starboard' and other words that sailors use. Duncan was frustrated. He hated being spoken to like a child and being told what to do. He thought Patterson should respect him, for he had hired him, but he could not sail the ship without him.

A crowd had gathered at the shore of the Indian camp, attracted by the shouting and the sight of our little ship going back and forth across the harbour. Other Whites had joined the Cridges on the dock. Their laughter embarrassed Duncan. He agreed to obey Patterson's orders and Patterson agreed not to swear or use the Lord's name in vain anymore. We set the sails and the ship began to move again. We were able to get our ship out of the harbour an hour after we had started.

Captain Patterson had never sailed north of Victoria. He did not know the islands or the narrow channels between them. He did not know how best to navigate their currents of the changing tides. We preferred the narrow channels in the protection of the islands when we canoed but he preferred the open waters where the winds were stronger. He steered the ship around the southern tip of Vancouver Island and further east past smaller islands into the great strait between the two colonies.

It was exciting to learn the workings of the sailing ship. We loved to feel the wind catch the sails and the ship begin to lean. As we picked up speed even Duncan and Patterson relaxed and enjoyed the ride. It was fun to move without paddling. The ship did not suffer the waves as much as a canoe. The deck was higher above the water and we could see much more. How gently and smoothly we glided along!

We headed east towards the mainland of British Columbia and then back north-west towards Vancouver Island. Then we crossed again and again, each time moving us a bit further north. It took us five days to reach Nanaimo, though other sailing ships did it in a day and steamships in even less time.

The day we left Nanaimo, the Carolena struck a reef near Savary Island. That frightened us. The Salish say the island was once an evil sea serpent named Ayhus, with a head on both end of its body. Tsamsem turned Ayhus into an island when it tried to steal his food. Since then the serpent could only feed by causing boats to sink on its reefs, and we did not want to be its next meal.

Our ship did not sink. Instead Duncan and Patterson had another terrible fight. Duncan accused him of trying to kill us. Patterson said accused Duncan of overloading the ship. They shouted and called each other many bad names but still we were caught on the reef. Duncan suggested we pray to God to set us free. Patterson agreed, but only to silence him. A few minutes later, the rising tide that lifted us off the rocks. Duncan said it was an act of God but Patterson laughed and called him a fool. He said the tide would have lifted us without prayers. This started another fight and more name-calling.

After that, Patterson and Duncan only spoke to each other when they were fighting. Duncan asked why we were making so many crossings that each took so long. Patterson admitted he had never captained a sailing ship, that he had only worked on one for a year and that was years ago. Duncan had a fit and accused him of lying about being a qualified captain. Patterson was angry that Duncan had not told him his crew had never been on a sailing ship. Arguments like these happened at least twice each day, but we now feared more for our safety than the speed of our ship.

It took us another ten days to reach Fort Rupert. Somehow we made it through the narrow passages where the open waters end, where the English gunships had stopped us two years before when we were looking for Miyana. Many canoes and ships passed us going north and south. There were smiles on the sailors' faces for they could see that we did not know what we were doing.

Duncan was anxious and unhappy about our progress. Buying our ship and making preparations had taken much longer than we had expected. Our people would be worried about us. Steamships can sail from Victoria to Fort Simpson in less than a week. Sailing ships took ten days, or a bit more when the weather was bad. Canoes usually need two weeks, but if the canoes that passed us had gone all the way to the Nass and returned, they would have found us only half way to Metlakatla on their way back.

The wind was strong the last day before Fort Rupert. The boat rocked wildly and the motion made Samuel quite sick. He spent the night on the deck for he got sick again each time he went below. He stayed there through the wind and the rain and caught a bad head cold. He swore he would never travel on a sailing ship again.

We were all pleased to arrive safely at Fort Rupert. It was a joy to stand on dry land again. Duncan boasted to the Kwakiutl of the town that our ship was owned by the Tsimshian at Metlakatla. They were impressed. We invited them onto the deck and to see our berths below. Duncan told them they could do many great things too, just as White men do. He did not mention the problems we had experiemced because we knew nothing about sailing.

Duncan asked the White Chief of the fort for an experienced captain who could lead us north. He said we might die before reaching Metlakatla if Patterson was our captain, but no captain was free to come with us. He learned that two Catholic priests had arrived at Fort Rupert to begin a new mission. That did more to upset him that all his arguments with Captain Patterson.

Finally, a steamship offered to tow us north to the open water. It was the best offer we had. There were still many days of travel ahead and many more islands and narrow passageways. While we were being towed, we met another steamship going south. Duncan pleaded with the captain to give him an experienced man who knew the waters. He gave us a man named McKay to guide us the rest of the way back to Metlakatla. Captain Patterson had suffered enough humiliation. He returned to Victoria on the other steamship and we never saw him again.

McKay was a better captain and we made better time. Duncan was happy and grateful for his safe guidance until he saw him taking a drink of whisky one evening. He lectured him that the Carolena was a Christian ship. McKay did not care. He said that if Duncan wanted safe passage he must leave him alone, and Duncan was wise enough to say no more.

In less than a week from Fort Rupert, we reached the familiar waters near Gitka'ata. We passed another sailing ship heading south in the narrow waters of Tsamsem's Trench. It was a whisky ship. The two crew on the deck were clearly drunk. They recognized Duncan in his missionary clothes and waved to him. They saw the Carolena was low in the water and they shouted to us that we must have lots of whisky on board. Duncan was furious. He shouted back, saying all whisky traders would rot in Hell. They laughed and replied that Hell would be more fun than preaching the Bible.

Near the north end of Tsamsem's Trench we saw a canoe approaching. It was Doolyaks, who was now Daniel Carter, my brother George, Clah and five others coming to look for us. They had heard from others going north that we had sailed from Victoria a month before and they were worried for us. They tied their canoe to our ship and celebrated with us when we anchored. They slept on the deck of the Carolena that night and followed us back to Metlakatla the next day.

We arrived in Metlakatla on the first day of September. Robert Cunningham had organized a reception for us. The people of the town lined up along the beach to greet us. The men gave a gunshot salute and everyone cheered as the Carolena dropped anchor. We rowed Duncan ashore and followed him along the beach as he shook each person's hand.

That evening there was a great feast to celebrate our return. Duncan spoke to the assembly about our time in Victoria, about buying the ship and our troubles on our way home. He made our problems sound fun and amusing. He said Whites in the south wanted us to bring them furs, dried fish and berries, cedar lumber, mats and artwork for trade. We would sell our goods and use the money to build a saw mill, a store and other new buildings. He also announced he had new powers to arrest the whisky traders, so they would never bother us again.

He spoke about the wonderful new life we would soon know. He said it would be a time of peace and prosperity of all of us. It sounded so clear and simple. Still, none of us knew how to sail the ship. Our voyage to the future would be long and dangerous. It would be filled with storms, narrow passages, strong currents and reefs. If we were able to navigate these dangers safely, our passage to Victoria would still be blocked by the hatred of the Whites that threatened us like a gunship.

TWENTY

O ur first year at Metlakatla was behind us and the coming year promised peace and happiness. We had new homes and we were free of alcohol and guns. We had White medicine to protect us from disease and Duncan's new powers to protect us from the whisky traders. Our sailing ship would bring us better prices for our furs and more goods from Victoria. We had all agreed to the new rules and worked together to build all that we would need. We believed we had found peace at last.

However, Duncan needed war. He fought with anyone who opposed him, with the Chiefs and Shamans who practiced the traditional winter ceremonies, with Bishop Hills and other Whites who did not share his vision of Metlakatla, and with the Catholics and the Methodists who set up missions on our coast. He fought with his own missionary society for more funding. He even struggled against time for there was always too much to do. But most of all, he fought the whisky traders.

The whisky traders were busy that summer. In July, Duncan asked Governor Douglas to send a gun ship to arrest them. A ship named the Grappler arrived in our harbour in mid-October. It brought a young Anglican minister from England named Reverend Dundas, who had begged the captain of the Grappler to take him up the coast.

The captain's name was Verney. He enjoyed our harbour as much as the other

captains who had visited before him. He was not in a hurry to catch the whisky traders. He told Duncan they were hard to catch. They hid their whisky in secret places in
Tlingit lands in Alaska except when they were trading the whisky for furs. The English
gun ships could not go there because these lands were controlled by other White men
called Russians. The crew of the Grappler rested in our harbour for two weeks and
watched us work from their ship.

Their idleness bothered Duncan greatly. He grumbled his discontent, saying he
did not invite them to Metlakatla for a vacation and he did not like Reverend Dundas,
who was also was acting like a tourist. He refused Captain Verney's invitation to share
drinks and conversation on the deck of the ship in the evenings. He said he had too
much work to do and his place was with our people, not his.

But he was careful not to speak too angrily to them, for he needed their services.
He put their visit to good use by asking Reverend Dundas to baptize and marry more
people. Tsangook was one of those to be baptized. I was excited for him. I combed his
long, beautiful hair and helped him dress for the ceremony, but when Duncan came
by to inspect him he insisted that Tsangook hide his hair down the back of his shirt.
Tsangook did not argue. He was happy to finally be a Christian like Tom and I. Perhaps Duncan had forgiven his womanly behaviour, but if not, at least he would have
equal status with other Christians.

His baptism did not go smoothly. He had great difficulty choosing a name that
pleased Duncan. At first he wanted a name that honoured his talent. He asked for the
name 'Carver' but Duncan said this was too close to 'Carter', which was Doolyaks' new
name. Duncan suggested 'Baker' but Tsangook considered baking a lesser talent. He
asked instead for the name 'Dancer' but Duncan said that was not a good Christian
name. He did not explain why.

Duncan suggested that he take a colour for his name, such as 'White'. This excited
Tsangook but he wanted 'Red', for our people were 'red', not white. Duncan said 'Red'
was unacceptable. He suggested 'Grey', 'Black' or 'Brown' would be better, but Tsangook said these colours were boring. He wanted a brighter colour, such as 'Yellow',
'Blue' or 'Purple'.

"Definitely not," Duncan shook his head. White people are never used those
names, but he did not explain why.

By this point both Duncan and Tsangook were frustrated. Reverend Dundas tried
to help, which only made Duncan angrier since he considered Dundas to be lazy. He
told Tsangook to accept the name 'White'. Tsangook refused to be baptized. Finally,
Dundas suggested the name 'Green' and this satisfied them both. The baptism contin-

ued and we cheered when it was finished.

While the Grappler rested in our harbour Duncan thought of a plan to catch whisky traders. Chief McNeill told him traders were selling whisky on the islands off the coast of Fort Simpson. He decided to trick them. He gave furs to one of his baptized students, John Tatham, and sent him to trade them for whisky. That way Duncan would have proof that they were selling whisky. John was uncomfortable for Duncan had taught him it was wrong to lie, but Duncan explained God did not mind if he was doing the Lord's work when he lied.

Duncan's plan worked. The Grappler arrested the traders after John bought their whisky. Captain Verney brought them back to Metlakatla. Duncan held a short trial on the deck of the Grappler the day they arrived. Duncan found them guilty. He fined the owner of the ship two hundred dollars and kept his boat. Captain Verney took them to Victoria to a White jail.

Duncan was thrilled with his success. He brought John before our assembly and told us he was a hero for tricking the whisky traders. He asked Governor Douglas to let him keep the fine to pay for more buildings at Metlakatla. He also wanted to burn the ship on the beach at Metlakatla to show whisky traders how he would punish them. Governor Douglas disappointed him. He told Duncan to return the ship to Victoria where it would be sold, and half of the fine went to the government in Victoria.

Duncan was disgusted with Douglas's decision, but he had other wars to fight. His biggest war was against our people. He had done much for us and we rewarded him with our love and our loyalty. He used our gift against us to change how we lived and thought. He claimed he was trying to save us, that he could see what we needed better than we could see ourselves. We needed to live with beds, tables, chairs, forks, knives and wallpaper that White people use, if we wanted to be Christians.

Many of us resisted the changes he wanted. They feared we would anger our Ancestors if we forgot our traditions. Duncan would not let us bless our new houses with potlatches or offerings. Some were afraid to sleep on raised beds, for evil Spirits could hide in the spaces beneath them. Church Elders like myself had to argue against our beliefs and reassure them that God and Jesus would protect them if they said their prayers before bed. Duncan required us to work the same hours every day like White people. Then he changed the rules so we had to complete more work to get the same pay. He made us work in the rain and snow in the darkest months, when we used to rest. If we refused we would not have enough money to buy food or clothing.

At times he denied us the things we needed. There were too many single men and not enough women. Our men asked Duncan if they could marry brides from other villages but Duncan would not let them, for the women would not be Christians. He required all women to be taught by him for two years before they were ready to marry. He told the young men if they suffered a bit longer God would reward them, but they felt only His punishment. Some of them chose to move to Fort Simpson instead of waiting.

Even if a man chose a woman from Metlakatla and the Town Council approved the marriage, he could not be sure Duncan would permit him to marry. Tom and I had become close friends with Samuel Pritchard. One day he told us in secret that he was deeply in love with Catherine Ryan, one of the orphans the Tugwells had adopted. He had loved her for two years but he had not found the courage to tell her. The love he saw between Tom and I gave him the courage to ask her. We were flattered by his confession and promised to help him in any way we could.

He spoke to Catherine and she was most pleased by his offer, but Duncan was her guardian and she needed to ask him first. Sam was one of Duncan's best students so he was sure Duncan would say yes, but Duncan forbade it. He told Sam she was too young for marriage. She was only eighteen and Samuel was twenty-six. Samuel promised Duncan he would work hard and be a good Christian, but Duncan refused to discuss it further. Sam was deeply in love with Catherine, so he tried again twice to convince Duncan. Duncan finally told him that Catherine had secretly said she did not want to marry him, but that she did not have the heart to tell him herself. He cautioned Sam not to speak to her again.

Sam was confident that Catherine truly wanted to marry him, so he came to see Tom and I the same night Duncan told him to stay away from her. He was so upset that he could not stop crying. He begged me to speak to Duncan and change his mind. I said I would, though it was hard to change Duncan's mind once it was set. The next day Duncan was teaching me how to use the printing press he had bought before we left Fort Simpson. I decided to speak to him when he finished his instruction.

"I hear that Samuel Pritchard wants to marry Catherine Ryan," I said as I worked on the press.

"Who told you that?" he asked suspiciously.

"I heard it several times. Catherine has told others that she is happy he proposed." He stared at me intently without speaking as I continued to work. "Is it true?" I asked.

"He has approached me," Duncan said quietly, "and we have spoken about it."

"Sam has a good heart and a strong faith. They are both good students. He would be a good husband for her. Don't you agree?"

"I think he is too old for her. I have told him so."

"A man can be too young, but can he be too old? He is two years younger than you." My words surprised him, and his reaction surprised me more. For a moment he said nothing. His face turned bright red and he moved the papers on his desk nervously. His hands were shaking.

"I do not believe he is too old, but that is what I told him." Duncan looked at me. His face was filled with shame. "Jack, I don't know what to do. I have not been honest with Sam, but I couldn't tell him the truth. You must not say any of this, promise me!" He crossed the room and sat in the chair beside the printing press where I was working. He looked up at me with the eyes of a child.

"I promise. But why would you lie to him? He is an honest man and he is loyal to you."

"That is why I cannot tell him. I don't want to hurt him. Ever since the Tugwells left and Catherine has lived in the Mission House I have thought she would make a perfect wife for me. I cannot tell him that." I stared at him in disbelief. He was hurting Samuel for his own selfish reasons. I felt the embarrassment one feels for a Chief who fails in front of others. My embarrassment seemed to bother him more.

"I mean…. she was always a good girl. The Tugwells adopted her when she was still young and they taught her well. She carries herself like a proper, civilized young White woman. She would not be an embarrassment to the Church if I married her. She is almost ready for White society. Why wouldn't she want to marry me? I would be the perfect husband for her. I could complete her education and she would be welcomed into White society as my wife. It makes perfect sense, doesn't it?"

His words and his childish expression bothered me. He had lied to Samuel and now he was insulting Tsimshian women. I had never acted so dishonourably. I looked back to the printing press before I answered. "Have you told her your thoughts? Have you asked for hers?"

"I asked her for her hand two weeks before Samuel came to me, but she said she was not ready to marry me. She seemed uncomfortable with the idea but she did not explain why. She is not a girl of many words. I decided that she was too young to make such a decision. I know she will see the wisdom of my plan in a couple of years. She needs more time to think about it. So you see I can't let Samuel ruin everything. I didn't really lie to him. She is too young for either of us for now."

"But if she had said yes to you then she would not be too young, right?"

The child in Duncan's eyes disappeared. "Perhaps you are also too young to understand this," he snapped. He pushed himself out of the chair and walked back to his desk. "Remember your promise not to mention a word of this to Samuel or anyone else."

I kept my word. I told Sam only that Duncan thought she was too young. I told him to court her from a distance but to wait for a year or so before asking her again. This thought depressed him. He knew he could not stay in Metlakatla and avoid Catherine too. He asked Duncan to make him one of the crew of the Carolena, even though he hated his first voyage so much. Duncan granted his request to keep him away from Catherine.

When Samuel was gone Duncan shifted his concern to Robert Cunningham. He learned that Cunningham drank and gambled when he visited Fort Simpson. Cunningham denied the reports but there was no doubt he was fond of Tsimshian women. He flirted openly with the orphan girls who boarded in the Mission House whenever he could. Duncan felt he should be kept as far away from them as possible, so he sent him to work with Sam on the Carolena.

Cunningham protested that he belonged in Metlakatla doing the Lord's work, but Duncan would not hear of it. He told him that he needed him to supervise the crew and that he could use the time to learn our language if he wanted to be useful to our people later. Cunningham was unhappy, but he had no choice since he did not want to return to England.

"The Lord's work, my word. More like the Devil's work!" Duncan exclaimed to me once Cunningham was out of earshot. After that, whenever a man criticized Duncan or did something that upset him, jokes spread that he would soon be working on the Carolena.

That autumn Duncan separated Tom and I too, though he did not know we were lovers. When the last new houses were completed we had to live with our companies. I stayed in the house of the Purple Company and Tom moved into a new house built for the Red Company. Tom shared a room with Samuel and I shared with Tsangook, who had taken the name Timothy Green. He joked that purple and green were good together.

Samuel let me sleep with Tom in the Red Company house when he was on the Carolena. When he was in town, Timothy changed places with Tom so we could be together. Others in our houses knew of our arrangements but they said nothing to Duncan. They knew he would not understand. There were many things it was best not to tell Duncan for fear that he would forbid them.

I saw little of Tom during the days that winter, except through the window of Duncan's office. Tom supervised the men who were building the new store and the jail house. He was jealous of me, working inside with Duncan while he worked in the rain and snow. He did not need to be. Duncan was a difficult boss. He was quick to lose his temper if I made a mistake with my spelling or my math. I often wished I was working outside with Tom.

I cleaned and organized Duncan's office. I sorted his letters and papers into files. Sometimes he asked me to count things or to look for something in his files. He encouraged me to practice my English by reading The British Colonist newspapers, which arrived on the ships from Victoria several days after they were printed. It took me a while to understand what I was reading. Duncan helped me to find new words in the dictionary and he explained the stories I read if I still did not understand. My English was improving. I read the papers for him and drew his attention to interesting stories I found. That was my favourite task. I developed a passion for newspapers that I have not lost to this day.

Duncan worked long hours, even during the darkest days of winter. Setting up the new store took much of his time. He taught me how to write purchase orders and how to keep the sales and purchase ledgers. He also taught me how to take inventory.

He decided Tsimshian men should be trained to manage the store, so he could do other work. He called a meeting of the Chiefs and Elders to interest them in the business of the store. He wanted them to learn how to trade with the Whites in Victoria. Paul Legiac was interested. He and his friends invested their money so they could share in the profits. Duncan was pleased that they wanted to help. He taught them the business of the store and he left them to manage it.

But Legiac and his partners had different ideas about running a business. As soon as they started managing the store, they gave away free goods to their friends and allies to show they were generous and powerful. This had been their privilege when they were Chiefs and Elders in Fort Simpson. Those with no money bought goods on credit but their debts were never collected.

This continued for two months. Legiac assured Duncan everything was fine, but it was not. Duncan saw many people leaving the store with new goods and he was pleased. I noticed this was happening but I did not know how bad it was until I did the inventory. When I finished I knew there would be big trouble. Legiac and the other investors had spent more on supplies than they earned in sales. I thought I had made an error with my math, but the totals added up the same again and again.

Duncan was furious when I showed him the record book. He scolded my math but I knew my counting was correct. He did the inventory with me and he checked the sales records again. He realized I was right and he apologized to me, but that was not reassuring. His anger grew worse.

He called a meeting with the investors and he asked them to explain. When he understood what they had been doing he yelled at them for two hours. He used my record book to accuse them of their wrongs. They glared at me in anger. They said I betrayed them and I began to hate my job. After that, Duncan never let the investors make decisions. He canceled their privileges to buy goods from the store at special prices and they no longer had free rides to Victoria on the Carolena. They complained he had broken his promises but he did not care. He said he would buy back their investments if they did not want to share the profits.

Duncan managed the store himself from that day onward. Only he gave permission for a trade or a refund and the sales clerks were not permitted to sell anything for credit. He inspected each case before it was shipped to Victoria and he checked my sales and inventory books each day. He also made my job worse by sending me to collect the debts that Legiac had created. I was not popular that year.

The business of the ship and the store became more important to Duncan than his teaching. Cunningham proved to be a lazy teacher, so he had no choice but to close the school. He only taught the eight girls who lived in the Mission House, including Catherine and Elizabeth Ryan. His other students were unhappy. He told them they had no school because our people could not run be trusted to run the store. He was punishing them unfairly and they became rebellious.

Chiefs and Elders at Fort Simpson also grew angry with him. Many of their people had left for Metlakatla, where they had to abandon their traditional beliefs. Their families and Chiefs in Fort Simpson turned against them or tried to convince them to leave Metlakatla. Duncan realized that he must do something or there would be trouble. He invited a hundred of the Chiefs and Elders of Fort Simpson to a feast at Metlakatla. Their meeting had an anxious start when Duncan refused to let their Shamans sprinkle eagle down over our heads at the dinner table.

But there was no showdown. He spoke like a Head Chief in his best Tsimshian. He had learned the art of boasting about his great deeds. He told them that only he had a sailing ship and his own store. Only he was training Constables and fighting the evil of the whisky traders. Only he had medicine against Smallpox. He was building roads and churches and schools, but they were not. He led them through our new town and told them his great plans for the future. Then he invited the Chiefs to invest in his trading business. He said that they could use their wealth this way to keep their traditional trading privileges. Some Chiefs were convinced and they invested, but Duncan still made all the important decisions himself.

Duncan did not know much about trading. Competition made him tense and irritable. He was rarely satisfied. He threatened to fire his agent in Victoria whenever the agent negotiated prices for our good that Duncan thought were too low. "That incompetent fool!!" he growled as he paced back and forth across the office. He would leave the room and slam the door. Later, when he was calmer, he returned to write a letter to the agent.

Duncan's letters were never as angry as his fits of temper. When his agent explained that the trading post would pay no more than the prices he got, then Duncan was angry with the trading post. He believed they wanted to punish us for having our own store and sailing ship. But there were many problems. Food often spoiled on the long trip to Metlakatla and sometimes tools he ordered were broken or did not work as they should.

He kept his profits a secret from the crew of the Carolena. His agent was not allowed to pay them their wages until the morning they were leaving Victoria. He did not want them to have money in their pockets to spend on sinful things. He was rarely pleased with the men of his crew. He fired every captain who worked for him, either because they drank on shore leave or missed church services. No captains wanted to work for his low wages and Duncan did not trust Cunningham. Finally, he hired Sam to be captain once he had enough experience. The captain he had just fired wished Sam "Good luck!" as he left the ship.

No White man caused Duncan more trouble than Robert Cunningham. When we returned to Metlakatla from our fishing camp on the Skeena in the summer of 1864, Duncan and Cunningham were not speaking to each other. The anger between them hung over the town like a great storm that was ready to break. Duncan had caught Cunningham kissing Elizabeth Ryan behind the Mission House when the Carolena was anchored in the harbour. Duncan exploded and Cunningham threatened to strike him. Duncan threatened to send him to the jail house if he did, and then send him back to England if he ever came near the Mission House or spoke to Elizabeth again.

This battle Cunningham could not win. He was no longer allowed to help Duncan with his church services on Sundays and no one dared to take messages to Elizabeth for him. He kept out of sight of Duncan, but he paced around as angry as a wounded bear.

Duncan was fearless against men but he was weak against women. They defeated him easily. Elizabeth was so upset with his treatment of Cunningham that she refused to eat or to leave her room. Duncan worried terribly. Elizabeth's suffering caused Catherine to overcome her shyness. She scolded Duncan for standing between people who loved each other. Her anger surprised and hurt him. He still would not let Cunningham visit Elizabeth, but when Catherine declared her love for Samuel Pritchard he allowed them to marry.

Sam was thrilled. He had prayed each day for six months for Duncan to change his mind and God had answered his prayers. Duncan consented to their marriage, for he knew they would need to wait seven months until Bishop Hills visited us again. He secretly hoped she would change her mind before then.

Sam continued to pray for an earlier marriage date and again God answered his prayers. The missionary society sent a new ordained assistant for Duncan. He arrived from Victoria on the Carolena in late July. His name was Arthur Doolan. He was a man of my age. He was tall, shy and handsome, with many brown freckles on his face. He showed his kind heart when he greeted us and everyone liked him instantly.

Doolan was ordained so he could marry Christian couples. He planned to work hard for Duncan for a few years so he could start his own mission. God was in the mood to answer Doolan's prayers more quickly too, even before he could start his work in Metlakatla. The week after he arrived, two Catholic missionaries landed in Fort Simpson on their way to start a new mission on the Nass. Duncan sent Doolan to the Nass to start an Anglican mission before they did. He sent Robert Cunningham with him to keep him far away from Elizabeth Ryan.

Doolan married Samuel and Catherine before he left. Sam was so delighted he forgave Duncan for making him wait. Duncan asked Sam to quit the Carolena to help at the school and the store so he could teach classes again. Sam said his offer was like a wedding gift and he accepted it happily. Duncan thought losing Catherine in exchange for losing Robert Cunningham was a fair trade.

Shortly after Cunningham and Doolan left, Chief Moffat of Fort Simpson caught whisky traders who were selling whisky. He arrested them and asked Duncan send our Constables to bring them to Metlakatla to be tried. Duncan sent five Constables to bring them back, including Tom and Daniel Carter. The Constables tried to bring the whisky traders back to Metlakatla on their own ship, but they pulled out hidden guns and started shooting. They shot Daniel in the leg, wounded two others and killed a Constable named Jimmy Peterson.

The Constables surrendered to the whisky traders, who stole their guns and badges and threw Jimmy's body into the sea. They left Tom, Daniel and the other two Constables on an island with a canoe. Tom used the canoe to search for Jimmy. Then the four of them took two days to paddle back to Metlakatla with Jimmy's body.

We knew that something terrible had gone wrong by the third day. I was sick with worry as I waited at the Mission House for news. Finally they arrived and we gathered around to help them on the shore. I was greatly relieved that Tom was unhurt, but we were all upset about the others, especially poor Jimmy. Duncan was as concerned about the Constables too, but he was more upset that the whisky traders got away. He stomped back and forth across his office, angry and frustrated and letting his hatred for them grow. He had more reason to be upset than anyone. They had made him look helpless as a Magistrate and they had shown other whisky traders how easy it was to beat him.

After a couple hours his frustration changed to a determined resolve. He decided to go to Victoria to speak directly to the Governor about the situation. He asked he Council to send a canoe to the Nass to bring Cunningham and Doolan back to watch over Metlakatla while he was gone. The next day he got passage on a boat headed for Victoria.

When Cunningham arrived, he strolled around the town like a proud child who had escaped punishment. He did not watch over us. Instead, he told us not to work hard while Duncan was away. He spent all day with Elizabeth while we were working. Then he announced to us that he and Elizabeth would marry. Doolan, who knew nothing about the fight between Cunningham and Duncan, agreed to perform the marriage. We knew Duncan would be upset but he had told us to obey Cunningham's instructions while he was gone. Catherine and Sam were so happy for Elizabeth that we did not want to interfere. After the ceremony, Elizabeth packed her belongings and returned to the Nass with Doolan.

I fretted every day how I would tell Duncan. I waited for his return for six weeks. When he arrived he first had to tell me the troubles he had on his trip. Governor Douglas had retired in the spring, so Duncan traveled to New Westminster, the capital of the new mainland colony British Columbia, to meet with the new Governor, Frederick Seymour. Seymour, he discovered, was fond of whisky and drank from a flask during their meeting. Why would Seymour punish whisky traders when he loved alcohol himself, Duncan asked me.

Duncan also had an unpleasant exchange with the newspapers. The Vancouver Times editor said Duncan was foolish to send untrained savages to arrest White men and they deserved to be shot. He claimed the Constables were disrespectful to Whites and that they had committed a crime, not the whisky traders. The editor who was angry and disrespectful and reading his words made me angry too.

After he finished his story, Duncan asked if there had been any trouble with Robert Cunningham while he was away. I hung my head and told him about his marriage to Elizabeth. His anger was worse than I had feared. He cursed Cunningham and Doolan and said he could not trust us for a minute out of his sight. He asked why we had not stopped Cunningham and I did not know what to say. My heart burned with shame. I decided it was no use telling him that Cunningham had brought whisky from the Nass to drink while Duncan was away.

Duncan wrote to Doolan after he calmed down. He blamed himself for not telling Doolan about his fight with Cunningham before he left for Victoria. He asked Doolan to never marry Tsimshians again without his permission, but there was nothing he could do to keep Robert and Elizabeth Cunningham apart now that they were married.

I felt sorry for Duncan for all the things that had gone wrong. In spite of our new houses, store, jail house and sailing ship, and many new people baptized and married, it was still a year of disappointments. Besides the marriages of the Ryan girls, he was still upset that we could not run the store ourselves, that he did not have time to teach and that the new Governor and the English newspapers would not help him catch and punish the whisky traders.

We suffered his dark moods that winter. He made Tom and his crew work outside on a new, larger church until the dark skies filled with snow to make up for his bitter disappointments. It was a bitter, cold winter and many people fell sick. He lost his temper at one Sunday service with so many people coughing and sneezing. The next week he was so sick himself that he could not give his service.

The roof of the new church was finished just before Christmas and the first service was held there in January. Tom installed a new bell Duncan had bought in Victoria. What a wonderful sound it made! The bell and the new church put Duncan in a good mood, but that only last a few days.

Paul Legiac had also had a bad year. He had lost control of the store and his privileges on the Carolena. Duncan's harsh words had insulted him and when Duncan invited the Chiefs from Fort Simpson share the profits of our trade, his profits shrank. He decided to oppose Duncan by organizing others who were unhappy with him and helping them get elected to the Town Council. For the first time, Duncan could not count on the Council to approve his plans.

That same month we shocked to hear from Doolan that Elizabeth had lost a child at birth. We did not know she was pregnant before she married Cunningham. She caught a fever and a strong cough in the harsh winter on the Nass. Her sickness caused their child to be born early and it only lived three days. The news was upsetting, especially for Catherine and Sam, but the next week another letter from Doolan arrived with worse news. Cunningham left the Nass a week after the baby died to visit the trading post in Fort Simpson. He left no one to care for Elizabeth while she was sick and depressed. She found some whisky he had hidden and she drank it. The Nishga found her wandering around the camp in her nightclothes, drunk and singing. Since then her illness had grown much worse.

Sam and Catherine begged Duncan to let her return to Metlakatla. He agreed. The next week Cunningham brought her down in his canoe. He wanted to stay with her. He was bold enough to ask Duncan to put him in charge of the Carolena. He foolishly thought Duncan had forgiven him in the four months that had passed, but Duncan's anger had grown like a forest fire. He exploded with rage at Cunningham, saying he should not have left her while she was sick. He told him to leave Metlakatla at once. He wrote a note to the missionary society the same day and six weeks later Cunningham was fired.

Elizabeth moved into the Mission House again. Cunningham moved to Fort Simpson and Chief Moffat hired him to run the store at the trading post. Still he was not free from Duncan's rage. The following summer Duncan accused him of finding Indian women prostitutes for visitors who stayed at the fort, though he had no proof. Cunningham was caught selling whisky at the trading post a short while later. Our Constables arrested him and Duncan made him pay a large fine. They remained hateful enemies for the rest of their lives.

A week later our hunters saw villagers from Kitimaat with canoes filled with whisky kegs. Duncan sent four Constables to arrest them. The Constables returned with whisky kegs and Kitamaat prisoners. Two Constables had tested the whisky several times and they were quite drunk. Duncan was furious. He ordered the Constables to pour the whisky into the sea. He locked the Kitamaat men in our jail house. He shamed the Constables who were drunk in front of the congregation the next Sunday and he took away their badges.

The Kitamaats were upset that we stole their whisky and jailed their men. Two months later five Kwakiutl men took revenge and killed a Tsimshian boy at our fishing camp on the Skeena. Duncan promised to catch the killers and bring them to justice. Captain Turnour returned to help him. They went up the great canyon past Gitka'ata to the Kitamaat village on the Clio. Turnour ordered the village to turn over the killers but no one surrendered. Duncan had Captain Turnour arrest five Kitamaat men from the village. He said he would let them go if the five guilty men surrendered. Again no one surrendered so the Clio left to take their hostages to Victoria to be punished.

The Clio arrived in Fort Rupert to rest for a day and to take on supplies. News of the Kitimaat hostages on board reached the town and the Kwakiutl wanted revenge. They rushed at the ship and tried to climb on board to set the hostages free. The soldiers fired their guns. The Kwakiutl backed away. Captain Turnour decided to teach them a lesson. He arrested their Chief and told the Kwakiutl to leave their houses. The ship fired its cannons and smashed the first row houses into many pieces. The Kwakiutl tried to surrender but Turnour told his men to keep firing. Once all the houses were destroyed the soldiers went ashore and set fire to them.

We were horrified. We wanted the killers of the boy to be punished, but we did not want innocent people to suffer. The five hostages were not killers. The Kwakiutl of Fort Rupert were right to be angry over the unfairness of taking innocent hostages. The government in New Westminster set the Kwakiutl hostages free, but many Kwakiutl at Fort Rupert died that winter with no homes or food supplies. We learned that Whites did not believe in justice or respect for our people. The British Colonist was pleased with the attack at Fort Rupert. Amor de Cosmos wrote that the Clio's guns taught the Indians "a wholesome dread of the law."

TWENTY
ONE

After the attack at Fort Rupert, Duncan was no longer as eager to fight the whisky traders. He was filled with guilt over his part in the attack and he was frustrated that the Whites in the south always set the whisky traders he arrested free. He did not worry much about losing the respect of the Whites in Victoria, but it bothered him greatly that he had also lost the respect of the many Tsimshians and Kwakiutls. His plans to start a mission at Fort Rupert now seemed impossible. He decided not to concern himself with whisky traders unless they tried to sell whisky in our town.

The attack at Fort Rupert frightened us too. The war on whisky traders brought trouble and bad stories about us in the White newspapers. It was clear that most Whites had no place for us in their hearts. It made no sense to try to please them. We worked hard on our own dreams and we asked our Lord to grant us our prayers. We wanted only to build Metlakatla and live our lives in peace there.

The White towns meant little to us, then. Our trips south became less frequent, except for the supplies the Carolena brought. Without the support of Governor Seymour or the White newspapers, Duncan also lost interest in visiting Victoria. We did not celebrate as other towns did when the two colonies of Vancouver Island and British Columbia joined together in the summer of 1866.

God listened to our prayers in the years that followed. There were no whiskey wars, no plagues and no more trouble with Whites. New magistrates were chosen for Fort Simpson and the Nass. Duncan no longer needed to worry about troubles beyond Metlakatla. He stayed home and worked beside us. It was a time of peace for the people of Metlakatla. We were happy and proud, but we were humble too. We prayed for the Lord's deliverance and we held the joy inside.

We prospered too. Our town made many crafts. Women wove mats and baskets and knitted woolen shirts. Duncan allowed Timothy to carve bowls and masks when he was not baking. We built the saw mill that Duncan had dreamed about a mile from the town and made many kinds of lumber. Legiac's trapping business on the Skeena grew. He sold his furs to Duncan, who shipped them with our lumber and crafts to Victoria on the Carolena to sell to the Whites.

Tom was a good carpenter and good at organizing other men, so Duncan gave him the job of supervising the saw mill. Tom taught Joseph and many others the skills of carpentry and he supervised the workers who built new houses, including a house just for visitors.

I continued to improve my English by reading and Duncan taught me more about using the printing press. We started a small newspaper for the people of Metlakatla. He sent copies of our newspapers back to the missionary society in England. I felt proud to know that our newspaper traveled to the other side of the world!

There was plenty of love too. Many babies were born in those years. The Spirits blessed my friends Daniel and Jennifer Carter with a baby girl. I secretly wished they would have a boy who would grow as handsome and strong as Doolyaks was when he was young. I never mentioned this to anyone, not even to Tom. Daniel was proud, for a girl meant there would be heirs for Jennifer's Raven Clan. He carried her through the town for everyone to see. I smiled for him too, even though at times I also felt a emptiness so strong I almost cried. I was grateful for Tom's love, even if we could not have children.

Arthur Doolan visited Metlakatla shortly after she was born. He gave her the Christian name Anne. Duncan held a small ceremony in the church after his Sunday service. The next month Daniel held a naming feast for his family and friends. Members of every Clan were invited, for he had once been an Elder and an heir to the Chief of the Wolf Clan in Gitka'ata. Daniel praised his marriage and the union of the Wolf and Raven's Clans, which he did because Duncan was out of town. Then he praised his friendship with Tom and I, naming us as her Christian godfathers. An Elder of Jennifer's Clan gave the baby a Tsimshian name, Le'hawah, a Raven name that was property of her Clan. Daniel gave each man some tobacco and all they witnessed was accepted.

One month later my sister Mary and her husband Joseph had a boy. They were proud too, and all the Eagle Clan shared in their joy, for he was the first child born to our family since my sister was born. My brother George was most pleased for the boy would be his heir. There were many suggestions for his name but we could not agree. George liked Jonathan and I wanted Peter. When we asked Mary what name she preferred she looked at Joseph. They told us they had not decided.

Our suggestions angered Joseph. He was raised a commoner and a slave and was never part of a Clan. In his heart the child was his, not ours, so he refused to have a Clan naming ceremony or listen to our suggestions. Clan names were not Christian, he told us. Christianity had rescued him from our Clans. Uncle Shoget and the others of our Clan were disgusted at his show of disrespect, but I understood his anger and defended him.

He and Mary held a Christening ceremony three weeks later, with Arthur Doolan and Duncan present. We were all invited but they kept the name they had chosen a secret. When it came time to tell Doolan they announced proudly that they wanted his name to be Jesus. Doolan looked shocked and turned to Duncan for guidance.

"Absolutely not!" Duncan shook his head. "Only the son of God can have that name. You'll have to choose something else."

Joseph argued with him but he could not change Duncan's mind. Doolan would not contradict Duncan's decisions. Joseph complained that everyone was against him. He marched out of the church in frustration. Tom and I ran after him. It took several minutes to calm him down and bring him back. Duncan tried to make peace. He suggested 'Christopher', which comes from 'Christ', but Joseph did not want his suggestions. Doolan offered 'Jesse' because it was close to Jesus. Mary liked the name so Joseph agreed to it, just to spite Duncan.

So my nephew's name was chosen from spite, not from love as they had planned. But his life did not seemed cursed for he was surrounded by so much love and attention. The name Jesse suited him. He was joyful child full of laughter and curiosity. I was delighted to help care for him and I loved him as if he was my own son. Mary appreciated my help, for Jesse was quiet when he was in my arms.

That year Doolan performed many marriages. The shortage of single women had passed. Newly arrived women must have thought they were in Heaven as they were besieged by lonely suitors when they came to our town. Most young men chose their wives long before Duncan finished their training. As soon as their classes in Christianity were finished they were married.

That year my brother George married too. He chose a woman of the Wolf Clan from the village of Gitsees on the Skeena. She took the Christian name Gertrude when she was baptized, though we called her Gertie. George and Gertie wasted no time having children. They had three girls in five years—Karen, Linda and Josephine. Gertie called them her little Wolf pups.

Mary and Joseph had two more boys in the years that followed, Earl and Lester. In only seven years I had three nephews, three nieces and a godchild. They regarded Tom as their uncle too. Sam and Catherine also had two children in these years and they played with our nieces and nephews every day. Our lives were suddenly filled with children. They made so much noise that they must have disturbed the Heavens themselves, but we never once complained. The children were our future and our future was full of promise.

Jesse and Anne had the closest friendship of all the children. They were not related but they seemed closer than brother and sister. They held hands when they walked and shared their food at meal times. They preferred to sing songs and play games by themselves instead of joining in the play of other children. They only argued or cried when they were separated.

Tom and I were their favourite uncles. Jesse would climb up on my knee whenever he saw me, claiming me as his own. Annie would climb on me too, or on Tom if he was sitting beside me, for she did whatever Jesse did and went wherever he went. The other adults and children understood that they had a special friendship.

When they were four we took them out in our canoe on summer evenings to watch the bears feasting on crabs along the shores. Nothing excited Jesse more than seeing a bear. He would stand in the canoe, clap his hands and make growling sounds. He could not to hold his joy inside. We tried to quiet him so we could get closer without scaring them away. Annie loved our canoe trips too, but she was delighted more by Jesse's reaction than by the bears. They were always too excited to sleep after we brought them home.

Jesse was as fascinated with bears as I had been with Hamatsas when I was a boy. Like me, he did not lose his fascination as he grew older. Joseph gave him a bear skin for his tenth birthday and when he was twelve Timothy made him a bear claw necklace. These were his favourite possessions. I often teased him that he must have been born to the Bear Clan, not the Eagle Clan. Tooklan said he would have become a Shaman if he had been born in our father's time.

The children brought our families closer together. Tom and I loved being uncles and it strengthened the love between us. These were the finest years. We had been together for ten years and our love was sturdy and comfortable. Everyone treated us as a couple, everyone but Duncan. Even our Elders respected us as equals, though Tom was Nishga. In those years we wanted for nothing and I believed that our happiness would last forever.

These were good years for others in my family too. My father's cousin Hahkwah, who was christened Henry Richardson, and Uncle Shoget were elected to the Town Council. Tom finished his time as a Constable and was elected as a Church Elder instead.

It was an easy time to serve on the Council or to be a Church Elder. Everyone in Metlakatla obeyed the town rules and did their best to be good Christians. Rarely did someone cause trouble by gambling or sneaking whisky into town. If Duncan learned that a rule had been broken, he would raise a black flag over the jail house to let us know a wrong had been done. Rumours and discussions would start. Most times the person who had broken the rule would pack his canoe and leave before Duncan summoned him before the assembly. No one wanted to be shamed that way.

Not everyone in Metlakatla was a baptized Christian, but most people wanted to be. It was an achievement and an honour to be baptized, just as it had once been an honour to be a member of a Clan and to earn a Clan name. Christians were given special privileges too. They could be chosen as Constables, Church Elders or elected to the Town Council. Only Christians could marry or leave a bad marriage. If a Christian woman's husband was mean or unfaithful Duncan would not allow him be a Christian, and he let Christian women leave their men if they refused to become Christians.

Paul Legiac became a Christian at the end of his life. He died in the spring of 1868 at the age of forty-five. He was the last Grand Chief of the Tsimshian. Duncan had given him many privileges to win his cooperation, such as a house that was larger than all others. When he died, special privileges for Chiefs died with him. His house was made into a guest house for visitors. His wife died the next year. Their three daughters and their son, Paul, kept their father's name, Legiac, as White people do, instead of taking names from their mother's Clan.

Legiac was given an honourable funeral and there was much sadness, but we did not feel we had lost our leader. He had surrendered his leadership and given his loyalty to Duncan long before he died. Duncan was our Chief now. He had a stronger Spirit, more wisdom and more vision than Legiac. He was a harder worker and a better speaker, and he protected us fiercely as a great Chief should do. We had forgiven his past mistakes and were pleased with his leadership now. It also seemed right to have a White leader. We had chosen a White way of life and we needed a White man to guide us.

Duncan never stopped trying to change us, to make us more like the English, even when we were having fun. He had us build a playing field like they have in England. He taught us to play English games like football, where one team would win and the other would lose. At first it did not feel like fun to make our friends lose. It felt unkind. He taught us many different games and races so we would have many chances to win. He gave money to the winners to make us try harder.

I was a fast runner, but I did not like to win. I did not want Duncan's money. I hated to see the disappointment on the faces of my friends when they lost. I wanted everyone to win. I did not want us to struggle against each other.

Duncan scolded me when I did not try my hardest. Once I won win just to please him but it angered him when I tried to share my prize money with the other runners. He told me they did not deserve it for they had not won. I said if it was my money I could give it away if I wanted to. I thought we should share the money if we had all tried our best. But the other runners refused my money. They thought I pitied them.

I hated racing against Tom most of all. We were happy until we raced against each other. If I let him win he would accuse me of treating him like a child, but he was always more upset when he lost. I hated to see his pain. He would not talk to me for days, or he would say things to hurt me. He said I beat him to impress Duncan, but Tom was the one who tried to impress Duncan. Duncan had given him respectable work supervising workers in the saw mill, but he was jealous that I worked in Duncan's office. He did not believe me that he had the easier job.

Duncan liked me and he knew I worked hard for him, but that did not make my job easy. He never trusted my work. He inspected everything I did as though I was a school child long after I knew it well. Often he made me do the same task many times until I did it exactly as he liked it.

He made me learn many skills that other men did not need to. Besides doing the bookkeeping, inventory and purchase orders, he taught me how to do the layout for our newspaper. Most of all, he made me practice my English by writing letters and stories for the newspaper. He taught me to write down the names of every White person I was introduced to, so I would never forget them. I did my best to please him but he always found things to criticize.

I was happy to learn these special skills. I felt proud when Duncan showed my stories to other Whites, but he praised my skills to Whites who could write English better than me. He told them my stories were my own words, but that was not true. He always checked them before others saw them and he changed my words if they did not say what he wanted me to say. Bill, the clerk at the trading post in Fort Simpson, had told others that I spoke English better than a parrot. Now Duncan praised my writing. I suppose that meant I wrote better than a parrot too.

Duncan also boasted about my skills to his students. He wanted them to work harder so they would be as good as me, but his boasting made me feel ashamed. The others remembered that I was the one who collected Duncan's debts. Some of them called me Duncan's dog, for he had taught me to do special tricks. I hated that he praised me in front of Tom. I told Tom how I felt about Duncan's praise, but he only mocked me with false sympathy. Sometimes he said nothing, but I knew he would remember Duncan's words the next time he was angry or jealous.

It was difficult to work for Duncan even when he did not boast about me. His temper came and left like the wind. One moment he was a patient teacher. full of praise and encouragement. Then he was irritable about something I forgot. He was impatient if I made a mistake or I could not find a file or a newspaper article quickly. Many times he interrupted my work to send me on errands. Then he would tell me I was careless or lazy if I forgot to finish my task when I returned.

He bought a typewriter for me and taught me how to type, but he wanted quiet when he wrote sermons and letters so I often could not use it. He only spoke to me when he needed something or when he wanted to read a letter to me that he had written. I like the quiet too, so I worked best when he was out of the office.

My favourite task was reading the newspapers from Victoria and New Westminster. He asked me to look for stories about missionaries or Indians. There were many things were happening in other places in the world and talk of war with the Americans south of Victoria. They wanted to take all the coast up to Fort Simpson away from the English. There were also stories suggesting that British Columbia should join other English colonies for defense, but the other colonies were a great distance away, half the way to England.

There were few stories about Indians on our coast. I was glad, for their stories always blamed us for drinking whisky or spreading their diseases. However, there were stories about the Indians on the other side of the world, stories about English colonies and victories there. Sometimes there were pictures of elephants and Indian princes with cloths on their heads wearing strange, beautiful clothes and jewelry. They did not look like any Indians I had seen, even in Victoria. The stories did not explain why they were fighting the English, but I prayed that they would find someone like Duncan to help them become English without fighting.

One year, a new missionary arrived in Metlakatla while we were at the salmon camps on the Skeena. His name was Robert Tomlinson. I expected he would not last long. Most Whites were either too weak, like the Tugwells, or too lazy and unreliable like Robert Cunningham. Even Arthur Doolan, who was neither weak nor lazy, left his mission on the Nass and returned to England after two years because he could not learn the Nishga language.

The omens were not good for Tomlinson either. He was Irish and not ordained, like Cunningham, and Duncan had shown us that neither of these traits were good. As soon as he arrived, he criticized Duncan and they had a serious argument. He left before we met him. Duncan sent him to the mission on the Nass where Doolan had worked before we returned from the Skeena, just as he had sent Cunningham away when he arrived three years before. But I was wrong about Tomlinson. He was nothing like Cunningham. His disagreement with Duncan was not about drinking or womanizing. Duncan was greatly troubled by their disagreement and chose to speak to me about it before I asked.

I had assumed Tomlinson had broken some rule that had angered Duncan, but it was quite the opposite. It was Tomlinson who accused Duncan of having bad judgment. He said it was wrong of Duncan to live in the Mission House with young, unmarried women. It did not matter that they slept in separate rooms or that Duncan wanted to protect them. He said his behaviour was improper and that he would embarrass the missionary society.

Duncan hated to be criticized or lectured, especially by a younger man who was supposed to follow his orders. He told Tomlinson either he too must stay at the Mission House or return to England. Tomlinson agreed to stay there until Duncan sent him to the Nass, but he also sent a letter to the missionary society to complain about Duncan's arrangement.

Duncan was troubled by Tomlinson's words and what others would think. He asked me if the Tsimshian thought he was wrong to live in a building with unmarried women. I told him the truth, that we trusted him, but he still worried what the missionary society would say when they read Tomlinson's letter. He did not move but Tomlinson's advice would seem wise many years later.

Later that summer Governor Seymour paid us a visit. He waited many months before accepting Duncan's invitation. Duncan hoped to impress him with our town so he would send more gunships to search for the whisky traders who had been bothering the Haidas. Duncan asked us to cancel our hunting trips so we would be in Metlakatla to receive him. We prepared a large feast and a practiced a concert of hymns for the night of his arrival.

Our choir greeted his ship with 'God Save The Queen' as the crew rowed him to shore. We cheered him as he stepped onto our new dock. He was a tall, serious man. He moved like a great Chief but his eyes were as dark and cold as Ts'ibasaa's'. They did not sparkle with warmth and intelligence like the eyes of Governor Douglas. He showed us no gratitude for our warm reception and he did not look at our faces. As soon as his bags were on the dock he followed Duncan to the Mission House.

Duncan introduced me to him in his office an hour later. He wanted to impress Seymour with my ability to write but the Governor was not interested. He looked tired and bored. He asked Duncan to start the tour of our town immediately so that it would be over sooner. I smelled whisky on his breath when he spoke. I looked at Duncan but he said nothing.

I did not accompany them but later Duncan told me that the tour was short. Seymour did not ask questions or make many comments. Then he retired to his room until dinner. After dinner, he spoke briefly to our assembly. We expected him to praise our good work as many had before him. We hoped he would promise to send more gun ships to arrest whisky traders, but instead he spoke against us. He said we must obey White laws if we wanted peace with the English government. He warned us that an English gun ship could destroy Metlakatla as the English had done to Fort Rupert. We were shocked. We had done nothing to deserve his threats. We did not applaud when he finished speaking and he did not stay to answer our questions. That night he slept on his ship. He left for Fort Simpson at dawn without saying goodbye to anyone. We were pleased he had left.

Seymour returned two years later in May of 1869. He stayed two days this time, but the first day he was too drunk to leave his ship. Duncan was told that he was sick with a cold, but we suspected otherwise. When he came ashore on the second day his face was grey and sunken. His breath was foul with the smell of whisky and he looked weak. He agreed to tour the town again but we did not get far before he was too tired to continue.

Duncan said nothing about his drinking, but he was clearly upset. He complained instead that the Governor had done nothing to arrest the whisky traders in the past two years. Seymour became irritable. He said he had many other things to do with his time and money than to chase whisky traders that would only be set free again. He refused to talk more with Duncan and he returned to his ship. He left the next morning and we never saw him again. He died before he returned to Victoria. The newspapers said his blood was poisoned from too much alcohol.

His death meant little to us. He was never our friend and he cared nothing for us. We had little interest in the White governments after Governor Douglas retired.

More than six years had passed since Tom and I last visited Victoria, the summer Duncan bought the Carolena. We were not as curious about the world of the Whites anymore. We had forgotten the misery of Fort Simpson and we had lost our passion to see foreign lands. We were content with the peace and the industry we had created in Metlakatla.

It was fitting that Duncan sold the Carolena that year. The delight of owning our own sailing ship had also faded. It was mostly Duncan's ship to those who did not work on board. Now it was old and needed too many repairs. The Hudson's Bay Company, which ran the trading post in Fort Simpson, offered to lower the prices in its stores and to pay more for our furs if we sold our ship and let them run our store. The new arrangement pleased everyone.

Our peaceful life ended with the suddenness of a storm that catches travelers unprepared on a warm summer's day. One evening shortly after New Year's, Duncan stood up at our assembly to make a special announcement. He seemed a bit nervous but pleased abut something he was about to announce. This was the time of year he made new plans for Metlakatla. We thought he would surprise us with a new purchase or with a plan to build a new building so we listened eagerly. Then he told us the shocking news. He had decided to return home to England.

He told us why he was going and how he had thought about this for a long time. He probably said that he would not stay long and that he would return to us in a few months. I am sure he mentioned different things he would do while he was there, but we heard none of this. We only heard that he was leaving us. That idea was so big there was no room in our minds for any other details.

We heard only words that frightened us, that he did not know when he would return, that Mr. Rutland, the Hudson's Bay man who had arrived recently to run the store, who did not know us well, who had shown his impatience to many customers, would look after Metlakatla while he was gone, and that Robert Tomlinson, who we barely knew, who Duncan did not always like, would come down from the Nass to visit us from time to time.

Duncan saw panic growing in our eyes, so he tried to soothe our fears. But the more he talked the more his departure felt certain. We realized he might never return. How could our leader abandon his people? We had been loyal to him. We did everything he had asked of us. We had worked so hard to build Metlakatla together. It had been his dream, not ours. He let us share it and he gave us back our pride. Rutland and Tomlinson knew nothing about his dream and we felt helpless. We did not know how to deal with the Whites who ran the government or the ones who bought and sold our goods. How could we manage without him? Who would protect us from the whisky traders or sicknesses now? We would be lost without him.

He had left us before, but this time it was different. This time he was going much farther and we could not follow him to England in our canoes to beg him to return. We pleaded with him not to go. We signed a petition asking him to stay but he would not change his mind. I remembered his stories about England, about the great church that stood high above all the other buildings where God had first called to him. I remember the sad look in his eyes when he talked about the flowers and the river. His heart needed to return. There was joy in his eyes that he could not hide from us when he spoke of his journey, even as he grew miserable as we listened to his words.

A gun ship arrived in our harbour to take him away. It stayed the night. He went from house to house speaking to each person to say goodbye. He asked each of us to pray for his safe journey, and to work hard and be good Christians while he was gone. He spoke longest to those who were old or sick, even to old Tooklan, who never liked him much and who had refused to become a Christian. There were many tears, even in the eyes of our men.

There was not enough time to say all that we wanted to. Tom, myself, and many others gathered at the Mission House to talk more with him before he left. He stayed with us though the night until it was time for his ship to leave. It was still dark as we carried his bags to the dock. We waited to shake his hand one last time and the Constables fired their guns in the air to salute him. Ten canoes followed his rowboat to the gun ship, just as we had followed his rowboat to the dock in Fort Simpson when he first arrived more than twelve years before. Then they followed the gun ship until it was out of sight.

The day had broken by the time the canoes returned. The women ran to meet them, to hear if Duncan said anything more from the deck of the ship. Of course he could not. The canoes could not keep up with the steam ship once it left the harbour.

Everything looked the same as the day before, but everything had changed. The town felt empty and frozen, as if a spell had been cast over us. No one wanted to work. We gathered together to talk about what Duncan had said on his last day, but we could not talk about the future without him. Some hoped that he would change his mind before he reached Victoria and that he would return on the next ship north. No one spoke the fear that was on everyone's mind, that if he went beyond Victoria he would never return.

TWENTY TWO

We heard no news about Duncan in the days that followed. We worried that something terrible had happened. We accepted that he was gone, but our hearts were empty and without hope. We did not work through the dark days of that winter, even though he would have wanted us to. We gathered around our iron stoves with their doors open so we could see the flames. We told stories about our times with Duncan. Tom missed Duncan greatly. He stayed close beside me and I held him as we talked about traveling again. We agreed that someday we would go to England to visit him.

For some, their despair changed to anger. Duncan had threatened to leave us many times unless we followed his plans. We always relented and obeyed his wishes, but he left us anyway. Some felt he had betrayed us and they broke the town rules. Someone brought whisky back from Fort Simpson and several men became drunk and started fighting. The Town Council held an assembly the next evening. and told us they would not forget the rules Duncan had taught us. They told us to gather again in the church every Sunday to pray for Duncan's return. The next day we raised the black flag over the jail house and those who brought the whisky packed their canoes and left in shame without another word.

Two months passed and spring arrived. We left for the fishing camps on the Nash and forgot some of our worries during the hard work. We sent a canoe up the Nass to Robert Tomlinson's mission in Kincolith and he returned to speak to us. He had just received a letter from Duncan. Duncan was safe and well. He had taken a boat south from Victoria to San Francisco and from there he rode on a great iron carriage that took him to another great city called New York. He was still in New York, waiting for a boat to take him across the sea to England. He said New York was very big and full of activity and excitement. He hoped we were fine and we were still following the rules.

We returned to Metlakatla in good spirits. Our oolichon catch was large and we had the good news about Duncan to share with those who had stayed behind. We were filled with encouragement and we tried harder to live as he had taught us. If God was our leader even though we could not see Him, then we decided Duncan was still our leader while he was gone. We wanted to make him proud of us, to show him that we still followed his rules and plans when he was gone. We repaired the road and houses and fixed the broken fences. We cleared more land to make new gardens. We practiced the hymns and gathered for prayers every evening after our work.

In early May, Tomlinson brought his new wife Alice to Metlakatla as we were preparing to leave for the salmon camps on the Skeena. He saw we had kept the town clean and repaired and he praised our work and our courage. He read a sermon and sang hymns with us on that Sunday. He also read us another letter from Duncan, who was now in England. Duncan had visited Arthur Doolan in London, the capital of the British Empire which, we believed, must be even greater than Damelahamid was. He had also visited the great church in his town in northern England. No one had recognized him for he had been gone for thirteen years and he had grown a beard since then. He had visited his mother and the Christian Missionary Society. He said he was learning how to make things that he could teach us to make when he returned.

The mention of his return excited us greatly. Tomlinson shared our delight. He gave us Duncan's address and told us we should write to him to tell him what had happened after he left. He stayed two more days to help us to write our letters and mail them through the store. After I helped Tom write his letter, I spent a long time writing mine. I wanted to show him that I had not forgotten the English he had taught me.

It was good to know Tomlinson better. He was younger and taller. He had a thick beard like Duncan's, but without any grey hairs. He was a good speaker, a good teacher and he listened to our concerns like Duncan. His eyes were dark instead of blue, but they were full of love for us and a passion for God. We asked him to stay in Metlakatla until Duncan came back, but he said he must return to his mission on the Nass. He promised to visit us more often and, if Duncan did not return, he promised to move to Metlakatla to take his place. His promise reassured us.

He kept his promise to visit us often that summer and he became our close friend. I taught Tom how to work the printing press and he helped me print the newspaper again. Many people brought us stories to print and we sent the newspaper to Duncan. Duncan was delighted. He had shown it to the Christian Missionary Society and they were pleased too. He reminded us that we needed to check more closely for spelling mistakes.

Duncan sent us coloured drawings of the Queen's palace in London and the great church in Beverley, his hometown. There were beautiful green fields and trees and many gardens filled with flowers. The Town Council decided to make Metlakatla look more like England. We ordered small trees and flower seeds through our store. When they arrived we planted them around the Mission House. We hoped that when he saw them he would never need to return to England again.

The women tended the gardens, but not many flowers appeared. Tomlinson explained it was too late in the year to plant flowers and that Metlakatla did not have the right soil for them. One morning a deer found the garden and it finished off the last of the flowers. The autumn frosts turned the leaves of our new trees red and they fell to the ground. Tomlinson told us this would happen every year, but no new leaves came the next spring. It was very discouraging.

But we received more letters from Duncan and they reassured us. He had raised more money for Metlakatla and he was buying many things for us. He had visited Ireland too, where the Irish come from. He had learned to work a weaving machine and he would teach us to make rugs. Best of all, he planned to return before the end of the year.

The autumn months passed slowly. We were anxious for news from him as he prepared for his return. He left for New York in November. He caught the train to San Francisco and he arrived in Victoria before Christmas. How happy we were that he was so close! His letters arrived quickly now, but he did not. He told us he must stay in Victoria for a few weeks for business reasons. We were impatient to see him and we did not understand his delay. We worried that he would stay with Reverend Cridge and never return. We wanted to canoe to Victoria to see him but the winter storms made us wait.

Finally, he sent word that he would arrive at the end of February. A steam ship brought him to the mouth of the Skeena. John Tatham, Samuel, Joseph and Daniel met him there and brought him back to Metlakatla. There was so much excitement the morning he arrived! We gathered on the beach with Tomlinson to welcome him. The Constables shot their muskets when he stepped onto the dock and we cheered and applauded. He was happy to be back. He shook hands with each of us and we carried his bags to the Mission House. That night, we sang hymns and shared a great feast. After the feast we talked with him about his travels and his plans until we were too tired to continue.

We were surprised by the many crates Duncan brought with him from England. He told us they were filled with new machines and supplies. When the welcoming ceremonies were over, we were anxious for him to show us what he had brought. We carried the crates to the Assembly Hall and we waited for the townspeople to fill the room.

We opened the first crates. The objects inside were beautiful. They had strange shapes and were made of shiny brass. We had never seen anything like them, not even in the trading posts in Fort Simpson and Victoria. We were as curious as children and asked him to explain what kind of tools these were. He laughed with delight and so we knew these were something special. He asked us to sit down so he could show everyone.

He pulled out the first one out. It was smaller than some of the others. He said it was a coronet. It was long and thin, but wide at one end. He placed the narrow end to his lips and blew into it. It made a loud noise that startled us. The hall filled with many voices asking what this thing was and how it made such a sound. Many men approached Duncan to look at it closely, but he waved his hand and asked us to sit again.

He brought it to his lips again, but then he paused. "You cannot make a good sound if you are smiling," he said, but saying that made him smile and we laughed. He took a deep breath and relaxed his face. He put his finger to his lips to quiet us and raised it to his lips again. He blew into it and moved his fingers. It played "God Save The Queen". We stared in awe, for this tool was surely filled with magic. When he finished we cheered and clapped and begged him to play more.

"Wait," he said as he pulled more instruments out of the crates. There were many different shapes and they made different sounds. None of them looked or sounded like his concertina. He showed us a trombone and then a saxophone. One, called a tuba, made a low sound like a moose's call. Then he showed us also different drums. One was so large that it filled a whole crate by itself.

Duncan invited us to stay after the assembly to make sounds with the instruments. He gave each of us an instrument and told us to go to the edge of the forest to practice. I took the tuba and Tom took the big drum. No one could wait until we reached the forest. We blew our horns and banged our drums as we walked through the town. It was a terrible noise! A crowd followed us to the edge of the forest to listen to us or to have a chance to play. We surely frightened away many animals and maybe as many Spirits too, but we had great fun.

The next week Duncan chose twenty men to make a band. Both Tom and I were chosen. I played the coronet but Tom liked the bass drum he had tried first. Duncan met with a few of us each day to teach us how to play and how to read music. He could not play much better than us, but he knew how each instrument should sound so we learned them together.

We practiced three times each week for the rest of that year. By winter we knew several songs and we played with the choir at the Christmas concert. Duncan had kept another surprise for us, which he unpacked before the concert. He gave each of us uniforms to wear when we played at special ceremonies. They had brass buttons which we kept polished and shiny like our horns.

Being a member of the band was as honourable as being a Constable or a Church Elder, but it was more fun. Two members were chosen from each company. We practiced often and played our best so that we could stay in the band. No other town had a brass band, so ours was soon well known. We visited Fort Simpson, Kitkatla and other towns to play songs for them.

Duncan brought other machines and supplies from England. Some machines were used for cutting and polishing wood. We built a new workshop and Duncan had books that showed how to make chairs, tables, cabinets, doors and window frames. Other machines were used to make rope, brushes and even leather shoes. We were delighted, for we would not need to buy these things anymore. There was also a weaving machine we wound to make rugs. The first things we made were not very good, but by the end of the year some were fine enough to sell in Victoria.

We were all busy working and learning that year. News spread to other villages that Duncan had returned and he was teaching us new skills. More people moved to Metlakatla and they needed new houses. The saw mill was kept busy cutting wood for boards and furniture. Tom supervised most of the new building while Duncan taught the band, the fire brigade and those who were learning to use the new machines. He taught school to the children in the evenings too, and if someone was sick or injured he was also our doctor.

I worked in Duncan's office again and I ran the printing press. He gave me more freedom now. He let me write stories by myself for he was only in the office when he wrote his sermons, letters or lessons for the children. He did not like me to disturb him at these times.

Duncan also brought back picture books of New York and London to give me, which I gave to Tom. The buildings were large and beautiful. The streets were wide and filled with horses and carriages. He showed me the picture of the places he had visited, including Queen Victoria's palace. He also had a book about steam trains, like the one he took from San Francisco to New York. But my favourite book was about India. It had pictures of strange animals, like peacocks, tigers and monkeys, and other pictures of great temples and incredible mountains that reached high into the sky.

Some evenings after we finished our dinner, Tom and I showed the pictures to Annie and Jesse. Annie loved the clothes and the carriages but Jesse was only interested in the animals, especially the ones that were large and dangerous.

After the children went to bed Tom would lie with me by the stove and look at the pictures. I read the words to him or shared stories Duncan had told me. Pictures are magic, for they put dreams in ours heads. Victoria no longer fascinated us. We dreamed about exploring lands farther away, with their mountains and cities to large to imagine.

The newspapers came again now that Duncan had returned. They also brought news of far away lands. That spring, British Columbia joined the five provinces of Canada in the east. The leaders promised to build a railway that would run five thousand miles from the Atlantic Ocean to New Westminster to join the country together. Soon it would be possible to visit the east without a ship.

Duncan was not excited about the union. The government of Canada was now responsible for our people and he thought this was a bad thing. They were too far away and they would not understand our needs. The capital was a city called Ottawa, which was much harder to visit than Victoria. It would take many years to build the railway and many weeks to cross the country without a train. But these concerns did not matter to Tom and I. We would someday travel as Duncan had, and we would not mind how long it took.

That summer, while we dreamed about our future, my past followed me too. The last of the villagers of Gitka'ata moved to Metlakatla, leaving behind only the house posts and the totems. I had not seen the old Hamatsa Jaksukjalee and Daniel's father Nakmoosht for several years. They were too old to work in the fishing camps by this time. Nakmoosht moved into the house where Daniel's family lived. He was as stubborn as before. He did not like his son's Christian name and would only call him Doolyaks.

Jaleek was still Head Chief of Gitka'ata. He brought his father's cousin Pashaleps,

Uncle Gugweelaks' wife, with his own family. Pashaleps was quieter now but only because she could not shout as loud. Her back was bent and her hair was grey. She still squawked like a sea bird when she was frustrated and she struck out at those who tried to help her. I remembered when I was twelve how Tsangook pretended to be Pashaleps as an old woman and I smiled.

Jaleek also brought his sister Laguksa, who I was meant to marry before my family moved to Fort Simpson. I had met her at the fishing camps many times over the years after we moved to Fort Simpson. She knew Tom and she was used to our Christian names now. She had married a man from Kitkatla the year after we moved away. They had four children. When Smallpox reached Kitkatla, she had sent her children and her mother to Kitamaat to keep them safe but the Smallpox followed them. They all died except her youngest daughter Charlotte. Laguksa fell ill too but she survived. The Smallpox left deep scars on her face and arms. Her husband lost interest in her. He fell under the spell of the Whisky Spirits the next year and he left her.

Laguksa was a brave woman. She talked about these things without fear or shame. She cried to think she was not with her children when they needed her. Her past was very sad, but it did not steal the brightness from her eyes. She was small and round, but strong and full of energy. She laughed and said I was lucky I did not marry her, for she was cursed just as people had feared when I lived in Gitka'ata. She liked Tom. She said I was lucky for he was more handsome than her husband and he would never leave me. I knew I was blessed, but I was also ashamed that I had not seen her beautiful Spirit when I was younger. We became close friends from this time onwards.

There was another surprise Duncan brought from England. It was a dream that had bloomed in his heart when he saw the great church in Beverley. He too had feared that he might want to stay there once he saw it again, but instead he decided to build a great church in Metlakatla when he returned.

He discussed the plans for a large church with Bishop Hills four years before. He even hired a man in Victoria to draw a design, but the plans were too difficult for him to understand so he refused to pay him. Hills told him the work was too difficult and there was not enough money for supplies to build it. He put the plans away and did not discuss them again.

But when he returned from England he was filled with passion and ready to try again. This dream excited him more than all his other plans. It made his eyes sparkle and made him laugh like a boy. Like many times before, his passion became ours. Soon everyone was as excited about building the church as he was.

Like a child, his dream had grown larger and more difficult over the years, but so had his passion. He wanted it to be bigger than any church in Victoria. It would stand tall above everything in Metlakatla, like the great church in Beverley stood above its town. It would be the height of fifteen men. Inside there would be seats for more than a thousand people.

We could not imagine such a large church, but Duncan said it was possible to build it and we believed him. He drew many designs and discussed them with the Council and Robert Tomlinson for more than a year. The Council chose a site for the great church near the centre of Metlakatla, on a high point of land that stretched out towards the water. Duncan named this land Mission Point.

Bishop Hills thought his plans were too grand. He would not give him the money he needed. Duncan was not upset. He told us he preferred to build it without his help so that it would be only ours. Tomlinson and the Council said we could not afford to buy all the supplies for such a large church without the Bishop's help but Duncan did not agree. He said we could make our own timbers and the windows and the seats too, but only if we first built a larger saw mill that could cut enough lumber.

So the plans for the great church were delayed until a larger saw mill was built. There was no stream strong enough to cut the timbers we would need but Duncan did not give up. He sent Tom and Joseph up the mountain to find other streams that had more water. They found a lake and a stream that flowed to another side of the mountain. Duncan ordered some explosives from Victoria and they blasted a channel from the lake so it drained down our side of the mountain instead. The stream then had enough water to turn a large waterwheel.

After the blasting was done and the new saw mill was finished, Duncan asked Tom to supervise the building for the church. Tom was so proud of his new duties that he spoke of nothing else with me. He worked with Duncan on the plans for many hours each day in Duncan's office. They discussed which type of wood they should use, how many timbers should be cut and what size they should be. Once the construction started I had little time alone with him. He worked long hours and came home tired each night. We did not make love as we did before. I was so happy for him that at first I did not mind. I was pleased to see him in Duncan's office, but after our first greeting he seemed to forget I was there. Once he and Duncan agreed on the measurement, he left in a hurry without saying goodbye. His indifference troubled me greatly.

Duncan was not in his office during the construction and there was less work to do there. I decided to help Timothy and the other bakers every morning. It was a comfort to see more of my old friend again. I watched him as he worked as I had done when I was a boy. He wore a woman's kerchief over his long hair, which was tied together at the back of his head. He was the last man in Metlakatla with long hair.

"Timothy, why does Duncan let you keep your long hair?"

"Oh, he tells me to cut it, Little Salmon, but I told him I like my long hair. I would be unhappy without it. And I would not look so good, would I?" He pulled his hair back behind his head with his hands to show me. "Do you see? I would look terrible!" He made an awful face to prove his point.

"But what did he say when you told him that?"

"He said I did not look very English. Of course, I told him, that is silly because I am not very English. That did not please him. He told me I must cut it if I want to be a baker. He said no respectable Englishman wears long hair. I told him that is not true. Many Englishmen in our history book have long hair and it is very beautiful. I told him I want to look like William Shakespeare. He was surprised that I knew about Shakespeare."

"Who is William Shakespeare?"

"He was a dancer and a story-teller like I am, but he wrote his stories on paper. I found a book about him on Duncan's shelf in the school."

"Did you read his stories?"

"Oh no! The reading is too difficult. I could not understand the words. They were written many generations ago, before the Whites learned speak English properly. But he is famous to the English. I saw a picture of him on the front of the book. He had long hair down to his shoulders and it curled in like this." He showed me with his hands. "Anyway, Duncan could not tell me Shakespeare was not respectable. I read the words inside the cover. It said the English have loved him for almost three hundred years!"

"So he let you keep your long hair! You are trickier than Raven. Why does he let you wear a woman's kerchief? Does Shakespeare wear a kerchief too?"

"No, but that was easy. Duncan told me I must wear something to keep my hair away from the fire and the bread. English men do not wear kerchiefs, but their women do. Duncan wants me to wear it so I will feel ashamed, but I like it. Long hair looks good with a kerchief. I like the apron he makes us wear too. You see, I wear one on both sides so it looks just like a woman's dress. Maybe I will tell him my pants make me sweat too much and he will let me wear only the aprons." He laughed at his crazy idea.

"Timothy, you are still the same crazy Tsangook," I laughed. Only he did things that Duncan did not allow others to do. "Do men like your kerchief and aprons? Are they still fond of you?"

"Sometimes. Most men are too Christian now. They tell me Christian men do not lie with other men. They know Whites do not understand and they worry that Duncan will find out. But some still visit me. They need my kind of love and they cannot find it in other beds."

He smiled, but his words made me uneasy. I was a faithful to God, but I was also faithful to Tom. I knew I would always want to lie with him. I wondered if I was a bad Christian. Maybe Tom had been ignoring me because he wanted to be a good Christian. Timothy noticed my silence and saw my my face deep in thought.

"How is Tom?" he asked.

"He is working very hard at the saw mill, making timbers for the new church. He works long hours but he is happy." My words did not sound happy. "Tsangook?" I used his Tsimshian name when I needed to discuss something important.

"Yes, my friend, what is it?"

"I think Tom has stopped loving me." He stopped his work and looked up at me with concern in his eyes. "He is always working. I do not see much of him during the day and when I do he does not like me to interrupt him. He comes to our bed late or he goes to bed before me. He is too tired to make love or to hold me like did before. I don't know what to do."

Timothy was curious. "Is he always too tired?"

"No, not always, but he only loves me from behind now. He does not kiss me when we make love and never with as much passion as before."

"I see." He studied my face for a few seconds. "Maybe he has another lover?"

"Yes, of course he does. It is the church." We both laughed.

"Well, I am happy it is not a woman. You must be patient with him. All my lovers have other lovers. Men are born to hunt, and love is their favourite prey. You must not be jealous of his other lovers, especially if it is only a church. It is important to keep your love warm for him and not to punish him. Only a good love is patient enough to forgive. Jesus wants us to be forgiving, right? The church makes him proud for now but it will not give him warm arms and tenderness when he needs them. Someday the church will be finished and he will be yours again."

"But then he will build something else. He loves making buildings more than he loves me. What can I do to make him care about me again?"

He thought for a moment. "You must capture his attention. Use the skills that you know best to please him. You still write stories for the newspaper, don't you?"

"Yes, but what do you mean?"

"Tom wants to be proud and you can help him feel proud. You can write a story about the new church and the saw mill. Perhaps Duncan knows someone in Fort Simpson who can make pictures. You can print pictures of Tom and talk about his work."

"Timothy, I do not know how to put pictures in the newspaper. We do not have the right machines."

"I am sure Duncan will be happy to buy the right machines. Then he can show his Chiefs in England the great things we are building and they will send more money. He will show you how to use the new machines. He likes to do that."

"But I would be embarrassed to write about Tom. Everyone will know I am writing the story because he is my lover."

"Everyone will know except Duncan. Tom will know too. He will see you still love him and so will the others. That is what you want. He will be interested in you again."

He watched my face as I thought about his words. I smiled, for he was so clever. No one knew more about pleasing men than he did.

It was easy to convince Duncan that we should have pictures in our newspaper. He had thought about it many times before but he had been too busy with his other projects. It pleased him too that I wanted our newspaper to look better and that I had ideas of my own for new stories. He told me we would have a big ceremony before we began the church and he would invite many important visitors. Pictures of the ceremony would look good in our paper. He ordered a camera and plates from Victoria the next morning and when they arrived we practiced using them together.

The ceremony to start the building of the church was held in the late summer. Joseph Trutch, the Queen's Representative, came from Victoria to lay the first stone. The Constables fired their guns and the brass band played "God Save the Queen" to welcome him. Afterwards we had a great feast for everyone in the town. We did not need to use our camera though. Trutch brought a photographer with him. He took pictures of the ceremony and the feast and gave the plates to Duncan.

I used two pictures about the ceremony for my story. In one picture Joseph Trutch was bending over with a shovel beside the first stone while Duncan and the Town Council watched. The other picture was of Tom and I playing with the band, but our faces were not clear.

The next day I took pictures of Tom and the other men at the saw mill. I wrote a second story about the hard work they were doing cutting boards for the new church. I took another picture of him standing beside Duncan and I wrote about their plans for the great church. The stories were in the next issue of the newspaper which I printed the following week. It was a big issue with more pages than usual. The entire town was excited about the pictures, but no one more than Tom. He told me many times how much he liked the stories. That night he made love to me more sweetly than he had in months and we were happy again.

Trutch came on the ship of an English Admiral named Cochrane. Cochrane did not believe our people could make such a large church on our own. He said this loudly to Duncan in front of us, as if we were children who could not understand his words. Duncan smiled and gave him a tour of our town. He showed him our carpentry workshop. When he saw many our people making furniture he was shocked. "These men cannot be Indians! They are White men!" he said to Duncan. Perhaps he did not have good eyes, but we did not object. He gave us ropes and pulleys to help us build the church.

Many Whites did not believe we could make the great church. The stories in the White newspapers scorned our plans and said Duncan was arrogant and foolish. Duncan said they wanted us to fail. He told us not to be discouraged by the meanness of their words. He said we should work harder to prove that they were wrong.

I joined men building the stone foundation of the church. It took several weeks, for it was many times larger than our houses. Others hauled the long timbers on wagons from the saw mill that we used to make the frame of the church. As it rose higher and higher, our pride and delight slowly changed to disbelief. We did not realize how high our church would be until we the frame was finished. Then we knew why the newspapers said we were foolish. We had never seen a building so tall. We asked Duncan if he had made a mistake, but he smiled and said it was perfect. Once again we understood that his dreams were so much larger than ours.

I took pictures of the great frame and Duncan sent them to the Whites newspapers. They were silent, for they could not believe it. No Indians had ever built anything like this before. We had already achieved more than they thought we could. After that they watched us quietly, waiting to see if we would make mistakes.

But we worked carefully and we did not make mistakes. The newspapers printed more of our pictures showing the tall walls and the buttresses that supported them. They saw the skill of our work and the joy in our hearts that guided our hands. They stopped saying bad things about us, for they became excited too, and they cheered for our success. Their cheers were finer than warm breezes on a summer afternoon.

The months passed slowly as the walls grew higher and higher. Our hearts filled with pride and our minds were filled with wonder. Surely this church was greater than any building within the walls of Damelahamid. Everyone wanted to help with the building. Some wanted to please God. Others wanted to have stories to tell their grandchildren when they were older. Duncan did not have enough money to pay everyone but they were willing to work just for food to be part of the excitement.

Finally we started the roof. I had dreaded this moment for many weeks for I had a great fear of falling. But Tom wanted me to work on the roof with him. He said it was the closest we could be to God. I said it was too close. I was not ready to meet God yet. He begged me, and promised he would stay close beside me all the time. We had worked apart for so many months that I thought this was a wonderful idea.

The English do not make simple roofs like the Tsimshian. They are tall and pointed and too steep to walk on. We started on the bottom edge, nailing on the boards and then the shingles. The ground was the height of eight men below me at the edge of the roof. I felt dizzy with fear but I tried not to show it. We tied ropes to the beams and around our waists in case we fell. Tom stayed close and watched over me as he promised. I saw his pride for me shining in his eyes and it gave me strength.

Each day we moved a step higher. My fear faded as I became accustomed to the height. Every afternoon after we finished working, I looked back at what we had done. The beauty of our work touched my heart and I was eager to start again the next day.

One day, when the roof was almost finished, Tom was sitting on the peak to have a rest. I was still nailing shingles onto the boards below him.

"I want to watch the sunset from here," he said. He looked out over the channel to the open sea.

"That would be nice, but I do not want to climb down in the dark," I answered.

"There is still enough light after it sets." He stretched his arms up over his head. "I feel like an eagle," he said as he held his arms out like a bird. A cool breeze rose from the water below. "I can feel God's breath up here! I feel His love on the breeze. It fills my heart with joy."

He smiled at me. His beautiful eyes sparkled with love. His chest was golden in the late afternoon sun.

"Jack, we never built like this before the Whites. We could not have these feelings or know the love of their God. The love of God helps us make miracles. I see God up here. I have no fear!" He stretched his arms wide and pushed his head back.

My love for Tom made me brave. "I have no fear either!" I cried, raising my hands to the sky. I balanced on the top edge of the shingles I had nailed. I untied the rope around my waist to show him. I meant to tie it again in a more comfortable way, but first I wanted to scare him.

"What are you doing, you fool? Tie on the rope. You might fall!" He did not look brave anymore.

"No, I won't. I never fall. I trust God too. This height does not scare me now." I smiled at him and I started to tie the rope around my waist again. He began to scold me, but the shingle below my right foot broke and gave way. I started to fall. I reached for Tom's leg but I did not get a good hold. He grabbed my arm and stopped my fall. All my fear returned and I almost fainted.

"Come here. Pull!"

He pulled my arm with all his strength until he lifted me up to the peak. I shook as I sat facing him. His face was pale. I saw the shadow of my death in his eyes. Only then did I realize that I had almost died. He pulled me tightly to his chest and kissed my neck. I felt his heart pounding through his skin.

I mumbled "I'm sorry," as he hugged me.

"Are you all right up there?" It was Duncan's voice from the ground below. He must have seen my hammer and the shingle fall. I looked around. The other carpenters on the roof had stopped working and were watching us. Duncan and others on the ground were watching us too. Tom did not care. He would not let go. He was sobbing like a child and his tears fell onto my neck.

Duncan arrived at the top of the ladder a few seconds later. "Are you all right? What happened? Why don't you have your rope on, Jack?" We said nothing.

Another carpenter told Duncan what he saw. The others climbed along the roof to help us climb down.

"Well, come along then, Tom," Duncan called up. Help him tie the rope on properly and you can lower him down to me. I'll take him from here."

Tom squeezed me tightly and kissed my neck again. I loosened his arms gently. I tied the rope around my waist myself and he helped lower me down to Duncan, who waited at the top of the ladder. Tom's face was wet with tears.

Duncan stared at Tom with a puzzled look. "Why are you so upset, Tom? Jack didn't fall. There's nothing to cry about. Be thankful instead." He guided me to the ladder. "You two must be more careful from now on," he added as he started down ahead of me.

That day, something had changed. I was uneasy when we returned to work on the church the next day. I had a new fear of falling. Tom refused to let me work on the roof again and I was happy to follow his orders. It did not matter, for the roof was almost finished and there was much left to done elsewhere. We worked inside, installing paneling on the walls.

I felt a presence of something new when I was in the church, something I had not felt before. It was invisible but large enough to fill the great hall. The sense that it was watching me sent chills up my spine and made my hands shake. It was just my imagination, I told myself, but the sense that I was being watched never left me. I thought it was best not to mention it to the others if they could not sense it. I did not want them to think I was sick or cowardly.

I could not ignore it so I decided it must be the Holy Spirit, come to watch us create the great church in its honour. A good Christian believes in no other Spirit. I did my best to open my heart to it although it frightened me. I welcomed it in my prayers and spoke to it in my head hoping that I could feel its love. When I polished the wooden pews I pretended I was Mary Magdalene rubbing oil into the feet of Jesus.

"Why are you crying, Jack?" Duncan once asked me from the foot of my ladder as I nailed a sheet of paneling to the wall. I told him I could feel Christ's pain as the nails entered his body. He shook his head and said I had too much imagination, but the Spirit had put this unwanted idea into my head. It wanted to frighten me, not share its love.

Many others worked inside the church near me. Some were putting the pews in and some fixed oil lamps to the paneling we had installed. Others worked in teams to raise the tall windows into place. High above us men worked on scaffolds to finish the ceiling. These were my friends and relatives but I sensed a danger with them working near me. Tom felt my uneasiness, or he was just concerned about me. He never left me to work alone.

As the days passed, my fears grew worse instead of better. I woke from terrible dreams of something or someone falling on me. When this happened I could not go back to sleep. The English say we fall asleep and this thought was enough to keep me awake.

I woke Tom, calling out and moving my arms in my sleep. He held me as I told him about my visions and he kissed me and stroked my hair to calm me down. As my dreams grew more frequent, he suggested they might stop after I spoke to Duncan. I followed his advice, but Duncan did not take my visions seriously. He said I was shaken up by almost falling and that I should pray to Jesus to protect me if I wanted the dreams to stop. I prayed to Him every night before bed, but they did not stop.

I remembered that my father had told me dreams are messages brought by the Spirits. If I listened without fear their messages would be clear. I practiced watching without fear what was happening in my dreams. I felt the Spirit's presence in the shadows of the church rafters. Its coldness sank down on me like a gust of wind and passed through my bones like silent thunder. At the same instant someone above me fell. I was not afraid for myself but for the others in my dream who did not see the danger.

I shared my dream with Tom. It made him uneasy. He said it was unwise for me, as an Elder in our Church, to speak with others of Spirits that are not in the Bible, but the thought also made him nervous. He kept a careful watch over the other men working with us. He did not let them walk below those working above in the scaffolding or under a window that was being installed.

His words were timely, for later that same week a man fell from the high scaffolding. A lower scaffolding broke his fall before he rolled off and fell to the floor below. In the fall he cut his head, broke a leg and two ribs. The next day a pulley broke that was holding a tall window. It fell to the floor below, and it shattered like a wave breaking on the rocks. Many people were cut by the flying glass. One man's arm was bleeding badly and a woman who got a piece of glass in her eye was screaming. Duncan stopped the work for the rest of that day for everyone was upset.

Those who had serious injuries were sent to the hospital in Victoria on a boat the next morning. Duncan sent with them an order for a new window and a note to Reverend Cridge explaining what had happened. The note asked him to keep the accident a secret from the White newspapers. After the boat left he called the workers into the Assembly Hall where we prayed for the swift recovery of the injured workers.

He caught some of the men talking about bad omens. He scolded them for believing false superstitions, and he did his best to strengthen our hearts with a sermon on Christian faith. He praised us for our good work, too, and reminded us that the great church was almost done. It would soon bring us fame and admiration, he told us.

Duncan reminded us to pray to Jesus for protection every morning and evening, but he also had us test all the ropes and pulleys before the work resumed. Those who worked on the high scaffolding were told to tie themselves to the frame as they worked so they would not be able to fall far.

The last few weeks of work passed without further incident. The blacksmiths finished the railings for the front stairs and a large cross fixed to the peak above the door. Duncan had ordered the great bell from New York the year before. It had arrived in the summer and we had kept it in the jail house where it was in no one's way. On a cold, grey morning in December, we used ropes and pulleys to lift it into the bell tower.

The next day Duncan rang the bell to call the people of Metlakatla together. They watched as we hoisted the tall, pointed steeple up to the church roof and fastened it onto the top of the bell tower. Some of them cheered but most were quiet with awe. Its beauty amazed us. It stood above the roof at the height of twenty men, and an iron spire on the top rose even higher as it pointed to Heaven above.

As soon as the workers had secured it, Duncan asked Henry Richardson, the Chief of the Town Council, to ring the great bell once again. The workers joined the others gathered in front of the church as the first snowflakes of winter began to fall. Duncan gave a brief service in front of the steps. The three great windows at the front of the church looked down at us coldly. On Duncan's command, we knelt to pray.

For a moment, the vestibule of the entrance at the top of the stairs were Sonoqua's pursed lips. The tall open doors were her mouth and the railings that reached down the steps towards us were her arms. We knelt before her, offering her our prayers. Then we followed Duncan up the stairs. We passed through the vestibule like communal offerings and made our way down the aisles. We passed through the waves of light cast down by the high windows on either side to kneel in silence before the altar.

How small I felt to be on my knees in the darkness of the church's great belly. I gazed up into the dim shadows of its great ceiling, too high and too perfect to be made by men alone. Duncan read a sermon about the greatness of God and how those who accept God's love will be reborn into Eternal Glory. I remembered the teachings of Man Eater and the Salmon Prince, that we must be consumed completely before we can be born again.

TWENTY
THREE

The church was the greatest building our people had ever built. No stories of Damelahamid ever spoke of anything so splendid. It was many times larger than the greatest of our longhouses. Everyone in Metlakatla was immensely proud of what we had created. We knew future generations of Tsimshians would speak highly of us for building it.

Duncan named it St. Paul's Church, though we knew it was ours. He said it would bring our town great fame and admiration, and he was correct. The first service was held on Christmas Day in 1874. Visitors came from Fort Simpson and from villages farther away, risking being caught in a winter storm just to see it. Even those who were not Christians came. The great hall, which could seat twelve hundred people, did not have enough seats for everyone.

O the morning of the service, there was great energy as the visitors arrived. Some wandered along the road to look at our English houses. They gathered in small groups outside the church, sharing news and getting reacquainted. It was a cold, clear morning. Small clouds from the warm conversations hung in the air as Tom and I wandered among them.

Duncan rang the great bell and asked us to move into the church. He stood by the doors to welcome everyone who passed through. The seats were soon filled and others stood along the sides of the hall against the walls. Still, we seemed small in the great hall that rose so high above us. Two reporters and a photographer from Victoria were also there. The photographer set up a camera at the front to take pictures of the service. The flashes made the children squeal with delight.

Duncan's eyes beamed with pride as he thanked everyone for coming. He told us that this was our church, even for the visitors, for God has no boundaries. He mentioned that St Paul's was the largest church west of Chicago and north of San Francisco. This meant nothing to most of us but it impressed the reporters. He said Whites in Victoria would now see that we were good Christians and skilled workers too. He said now they would respect us, for our church was the biggest.

After the service, the photographer asked everyone to gather in front of the church. It took a long time to get everyone into the right position but in the end it did not matter. He had to move the camera so far back to capture all of the height of the church that our faces were too small to recognize. That picture hung in Duncan's office for many years afterwards.

The same picture was printed in the White newspapers in Victoria. The story below it said Duncan had created a miracle in Metlakatla. They made no mention our people or how hard we had worked on making the church. They said nothing about us being good Christians or skilled workers. They spoke as if Duncan had built everything himself.

It was printed again in the Christian Missionary Society's newsletter with a story about the miracle of Metlakatla. Duncan's was the greatest Anglican mission in the world, they claimed. They wrote about the Mission House, the school, the saw mill, the blacksmith and carpentry shops, and they included pictures of our jail house, our road and a long row of our houses that Duncan had sent them. They said the missionary society had paid for everything.

Duncan read their story to us at his Sunday service. He laughed and cried and wiped his tears away with his handkerchief as he read it. It gave him more pleasure than the stories from Victoria. That did not surprise me. It was mostly about him and he had given them the information for the story. We were pleased that our church was now famous, but we wondered if there was not greater work done in God's name in other parts of the world? Did the missionary society not know about the larger churches in Chicago and San Francisco?

It bothered me that they said Duncan built the church himself, with no help from others. Duncan explained that they meant no White men had helped him. He assured us that they knew we had helped him. But why did they not say so? Why do they only mention White men working? And did they not know we raised most of the money ourselves?

But we could not change what was printed. They sent their newsletter to Anglican missions around the world and it brought fame to Metlakatla. Letters began to arrive. Duncan showed me where each letter came from on a map of the world. I was amazed that they came from so many places far away. Duncan gave me the postage stamps and taught me to collect them in a book. This became my hobby for the rest of my years.

I read their letters to practice my English. They praised Duncan's good work. Some wanted to know more about our town and some wanted to visit. Some sent money and promises of free supplies. We kept the letters in a box. Duncan wrote answers to each of them at first, thanking them and telling them his plans for the future.

More letters arrived each week. They soon filled several boxes. The fame and praise felt good at first, even if it was mostly for Duncan. We were tricked into thinking it was the best thing that ever happened to us. We thanked God for our good fortune. I soon forgot about the evil Spirit in the church.

But our fame became a curse. Like alcohol or sex, it deceived us. Duncan was deceived too, perhaps because the Bible does not warn us about fame. The long hours spent answering letters left him with little time for his other duties. He could not keep up with them as they continued to arrive. He grew tired and irritable. He learned to hate the mailbags and the ships that brought them. I learned to avoid him. The Spirit of the Church had begun to cast its long shadow over our lives.

I was the first to notice it. If others felt as I did, they said nothing. Everyone wanted to believe that we had been blessed. Like good Christians, they ignored what their senses told them. There was no point to mention the forebodings I felt in my heart. It was just my imagination, they would say. They would accuse me of being ungrateful for what God had given us.

They had forgotten what every Tsimshian once knew. Spirits are everywhere. They are on mountains and in lakes but they are also in houses, canoes and even in the spaces under our beds. Small Spirits lived in small spaces but bigger, more powerful Spirits needed larger spaces. The great hall of St. Paul's was the largest room we had ever made, and of course, the Spirit it attracted was huge.

A man might think a Spirit that lives in the house of God would be a good Spirit, but I knew better. I had felt its chill and I had seen how it tried to harm us. It did not lie quietly in the forests or the currents of the sea like other Spirits, waiting to punish those who trespass. Every morning and evening its great bell rang out across the town and echoed off the mountains. The people of Metlakatla came like obedient servants. They knelt in the hall of the great church to pray for God's mercy, but they felt uneasy. They trembled like children before an indifferent father.

Duncan felt its chill too, though his Christian faith gave him way to describe it. At first, he came to the great hall seeking inspiration and refuge from his duties. I often found him there alone, staring up into the darkness of the ceiling. I watched him light the lamps to chase away the cold shadows, but they were never enough. He could not find peace there, not on the quiet days of rain and fog or the hottest days of summer. After a while, he only came to the hall for his Sunday services.

I tried a few times to talk to Tom and others about my suspicions, but I could not convince anyone. After that I said nothing. Speaking about an evil Spirit can give it strength and draw it to you. I did not want to make the situation worse. I smiled with the others when they praised our good fortune, but mine was a nervous smile.

The power of the Spirit was much greater and more cunning than I imagined. It could lure others to Metlakatla from great distances and it could divide our hearts with fears and hatred that would tear us apart without remorse or pity. It cast its shadow over White men too. The first man it lured to our town was Reverent Cridge.

Cridge was Duncan's closest friend and ally. He loved our people so we celebrated his visit. There was no reason to see it as a bad omen. Duncan had invited him many times but Cridge was always too busy with his church and his hospital duties to come. The completion of the great church changed that. The Spirit beckoned him to see the church and it used his visit to start a war.

Duncan, the Town Council and our new brass band greeted him as he landed at our dock. We could not wait to show him our town. He was excited to see our saw mill and workshops. He shook hands with the workers and chatted with them. Duncan invited him to give a sermon in the great church. He praised our work and told us how Duncan and Christianity had improved our lives. He reminded us that God's teachings were simple messages of love and peace.

But Cridge had not come to spread love and peace. He had come to seek Duncan's help. Duncan had been his trusted friend for sixteen years and there were things he could only speak to Duncan about. He wanted to speak about Bishop Hills. I was working in Duncan's office when he spoke.

"It had to come to this eventually, William. There was no way to avoid it. I couldn't stand Hills from the moment he was appointed. Putting that spoiled aristocrat in charge of the new diocese was a pure insult to all the good work I had done. I established the Anglican Church in this colony. I should have been given his position.

You know that."

"Edward, you know he is aware of your feelings. He has tried to be pleasant to you in spite of your feelings. He did offer you a promotion to Archdeacon of Nanaimo six years ago." Duncan's words could not soothe him.

"You know what that was all about, don't you? He just wanted me out of Victoria so I would not interfere with his plans. He would have gladly ruined all I have done. We have nothing in common. He is consumed with pointless ritualism. He enjoys worldly amusements like card playing and dancing that distract men from God's teachings. How could I leave knowing what he was like? There was no one to run the hospital or Mary's school for girls. He cares nothing about these things."

"How are Mary and the children, Edward?"

"They are fine, thank you, William. We both struggled for some time after little Sarah died. You know that's the fourth child we've lost. The Lord has given us a hard road to walk but it has made us stronger. We thank Heaven we still have five healthy children to brighten our lives, but I am worried that I will cause them more grief than they deserve."

"That's ridiculous, Edward. I know they love you very much. They have faith in you and they will give you strength at this difficult time. I only wish it had not gone this far. Are you sure you cannot resolve your problems another way?"

"It's impossible, I'm afraid. My fate was sealed when I spoke against Archdeacon Reece of Vancouver at the opening ceremony for our new church the last year. That was my church, William. He had no right to preach about the glories of ritualism in my church. He knew that was against everything I stand for. I had no choice but to speak against him as soon as he left the pulpit. Hills has never forgiven me. He demanded an apology but I refused. I will not bow to such a man. We have not spoken since, though we exchanged angry letters every week for a year after that. Then Hills began to disrupt my Sunday sermons to challenge and embarrass me in front of my own congregation. I had no choice but to refuse him entry to the church."

"But he was your superior, Edward. You cannot bar your superior."

"He's not my superior anymore, William. He revoked my license to preach. I refused to stop so he went to Chief Justice Begbie to have me removed. Begbie first tried to get us to talk, since he is a friend to both of us, but I saw no point to that. Begbie had no choice but to ban me. I am never allowed to enter my church again, William. Hills is even trying to ban me from the hospital because it receives church funds."

"This is terrible, Edward. You can't let him do this! Surely your congregation sees that you are more valuable than he is."

"You're right, William. Most of Victoria sees that he is a snob. The newspapers were filled with angry letters when his decision was announced. Most of my congregation have stopped coming to his Sunday services in protest. He doesn't care. He says God will punish them. He forgets that he too will be judged."

"What are you going to do now?"

Cridge's voice lost its angry tone and his eyes lit up with excitement. "That is what I have come to speak to you about. I am going to set up a new church. I am going to call it the Reformed Episcopal Church. I will have to base it in San Francisco, of course, since Hills won't permit the government to let me base it here. Most of the congregation supports me. They have been most generous. James Douglas is behind me too. He has given me ten thousand dollars to begin building a new church!"

"This is amazing!" Duncan's excitement brought him to his feet. "Why haven't you told me this before?"

"It has all happened so fast in the weeks since we made plans for my visit. I can scarcely believe it myself. I wanted to tell you in person for I have something very important to ask of you that I could not ask in a letter. I need you support, my friend, if the new church is to be a success. The Anglican Church is very powerful. Douglas is old and retired. He has no influence in the government now. Already he is forgotten or disregarded outside of British Columbia and the support of people of Victoria mean nothing to England when the existing government supports Hills."

"How do you imagine my support will be more useful than his?"

"Don't you see, William? In a few months the fame of St. Paul's will reach every corner of the world! Nothing this great has been built in other Anglican missions. Your success will touch the hearts of every Anglican. You will soon be more respected and cherished than Hills. Your support will mean more than anyone else's!"

Duncan could not keep the smile from his face upon hearing this compliment. "Imagine," he told me later, "that Cridge thinks me more influential than Douglas!" In the coming days wrote to the missionary society. He gave his support to Reverend Cridge and he criticized Bishops Hills for causing the break in the church.

Hills and Duncan had lived in peace while they were far apart and had little to do with each other, but Duncan's letter changed that. He had used his new fame to make a stand against Hills and the Anglican Church. What had been broken could not be repaired. The fires of war had been ignited.

Our great church attracted the eyes of the world and they were watching us. Duncan told us we must always show that we are good Christians who are worthy of such a church. Many people wrote asking for permission to visit Metlakatla to see the work he had done. Duncan honoured their attention with invitations. He knew their visits would bring new donations. We used our first donations to build a second house for our visitors. It was usually full, except during the darkest months of winter.

Some asked to stay in Metlakatla to help Duncan. They wanted a share of his fame and success. He was wary of their intentions. He needed help, but he had bad memories of the Tugwells and Robert Cunningham. He would exchange several letters before accepting their offers. He needed help with the school most of all. Letter writing, planning new buildings and other duties prevented him from teaching. He tried training our students to be teachers, but they were not as good or as fun as he was.

But no teachers had asked to work with him so he wrote to the missionary society, begging them to send a qualified teacher. They sent an Irish couple, Henry and Marion Collison. I feared the worst for I knew Duncan's hatred of the Irish, but Henry Collison seemed comfortable in Metlakatla. He did not challenge Duncan or make trouble for him as Tomlinson and Cunningham had. He did not complain about the many rules Duncan gave him to follow.

He began teaching right away. Duncan helped him for the first month. After that he taught alone. He was firm with the students but he also enjoyed a good joke. The students became quite fond of him. He was impressed with Metlakatla and this pleased Duncan very much. Maybe Duncan was learning to like the Irish for Tomlinson had also become a good friend. Either way, the newspapers could not say he worked alone anymore.

Marion Collison also liked her new life in Metlakatla. She was a nurse who had known many hardships. She had tended injured warriors on English battlefields and tended the sick in Ireland when Smallpox came. I was impressed by her courage. She spoke to us firmly like a mother and we trusted her readily. By that summer, she had taken over most of Duncan's duties tending the sick.

Some of Duncan's troubles ended but others took their place. The Chiefs at Fort Simpson were angry with Duncan. He had stopped them from selling whisky and the new church convinced many of their people to move to Metlakatla. When they needed a new preacher, they chose a Methodist named Crosby to upset Duncan. That gave Bishop Hills a reason to attack Duncan. He accused Duncan of not paying enough attention to Fort Simpson, though Duncan was already too busy and Hills had done nothing himself. He said if Duncan had been ordained this could not have happened and he threatened Duncan that he would come to Metlakatla to ordain Robert Tomlinson or Henry Collison if Duncan still refused to be ordained.

His threat worried Duncan greatly. He asked several of us, including Sam Pritchard, John Tatham and myself, to write letters to Hills asking him not to come to Metlakatla until he had made peace with our friend Reverend Cridge. Hills thought of us Duncan's trained pets so I doubt our letters impressed him, but he did not reply or come to Metlakatla either. The war between Duncan and Hills remained quiet for a few months.

Duncan was not happy that the Anglicans lost Fort Simpson. He liked Methodists more than Catholics, but he wanted to set up more missions before other churches could. His first concern was for the Haidas, who had no Christian missions. He sent the Collisons to Masset on Haida Gwaii, leaving him without a teacher or nurse to help him.

That fall, a new schoolteacher came from England. His name was Henry Schutt. He was not as clever as Collison and his wife was not a nurse, but they did their best to teach school and tend the sick. Schutt was fun too. When Duncan organized our musical evenings he joined and played his harmonica.

When Schutt took over the teaching, Duncan made plans to start a mission in Fort Rupert. He wanted to make amends to the Kwakiutl. He was still ashamed about the Clio's attack on their village years before, and many at Fort Rupert still blamed him. He sent John Tatham to meet with their Chiefs and to offer his apology. Tatham returned with two Kwakiutl men who offered to teach Duncan their language. Duncan was thrilled.

That was in August of 1877, the same month that Reverend James Hall arrived in Metlakatla, a man we would never forget. There was nothing strange about Reverend Hall himself. He was a young man of plain features who arrived in our town with little knowledge of life, much like Arthur Doolan and Robert Tomlinson before him. He was good-hearted like Doolan, but not as nervous. He was pious like Tomlinson, but not so self-righteous. He had the face of a boy, but he was ordained and as passionate about God as the Apostle Simon. Unfortunately, his best features, his innocence and his passion, were no match for the Spirit of the Church, which took advantage of them to spread its evil.

Duncan once wanted the missionary society to send him someone ordained, but he had changed his mind by this time. An ordained assistant had to be loyal to Bishop Hills and not himself. He now needed allies who stood with him against Bishop Hills. The missionary society had trusted his wisdom for years, but other churches were now baptizing more new followers than the Anglicans. They pressed Duncan for more baptisms but Duncan argued that other churches were only interested in numbers, not the souls of the baptized. The missionary society disagreed. They sent Reverend Hall for he could baptize new converts at the missions in Kincolith, Haida Gwaii and Metlakatla, as well as the new one Duncan hoped to start in Fort Rupert. There was nothing Duncan could do to change their decision.

The week Hall arrived, Duncan had an emergency. Our Constables had arrested a whisky trader who was a friend of our local Indian Commissioner. The Commissioner took away Duncan's powers of a Magistrate, which he needed to fight the whisky traders. He left for Victoria immediately to speak to Dr. Powell, the Chief of the Indian Commissioners. He left Henry Schutt in charge of Metlakatla. He had no time to train Hall, the boy-faced Reverend who we had just met. He told Schutt to send for Tomlinson in Kincolith if there was a problem he could not handle himself.

Duncan left on a Tuesday morning. Hall had little to do for the next five days but walk around the town introducing himself to everyone he met. He was filled with great energy, like a puppy that was eager to run. When he greeted us, he bowed his head and raised it again slowly as if God Himself had filled him with Divine Grace. He invited each person he met to his first Sunday service, which he promised would be a most important sermon.

Some were amused by his introductions and others were confused. He seemed like a good man but no one understood why he acted so strangely. His manner started us talking and we became curious about what he would say on Sunday.

Duncan had told Hall to ask me for help with small tasks. He came to me on Friday to ask what he should use for a pulpit. I did not understand what he meant. He explained that ministers in most churches preach down to their congregations from above. I told him Duncan always spoke to us from behind a simple table at the front of the church, but Hall insisted he needed to be higher up. I introduced him to Joseph in the carpenters' shop, and Joseph made him a platform to stand on. Then he asked for something to rest his Bible on. I found a tall wooden crate and covered it with a white cloth. He was satisfied with that and thanked us for our assistance.

These requests made us more curious about his sermon. Everyone in town came to listen to him on Sunday when the bell rang. Tom and I arrived early to get a seat near the front. Mr. Schutt welcomed us in his best Sunday clothes, standing by the door of the church where Duncan usually stood. We asked if Reverend Hall was sick. Schutt told us he would arrive shortly.

The bell rang until the church was almost full. Still we did not see Reverend Hall. The ringing stopped and we fell silent. Reverend Hall entered from the back of the church. He wore a long white robe that went down to his feet. It was more beautiful than the one Jesus wore in the pictures in our Bible. Everyone was surprised, for Duncan had never worn anything like that before. Many voices filled the church as he climbed up onto the platform. He looked across our many faces as he waited for us to be quiet again. Then he spoke.

"Dear people of Metlakatla, thank you for coming this morning to hear the word of God! I am honoured to be giving this sermon to you today. For several months I have waited to see your famous church and to speak to the people who created this miracle!" He paused for a moment. He raised his hands and his eyes to the roof far above us. We followed his gaze but we saw nothing.

"I have longed to help you give thanks to our Lord Jesus! I am sure as you look up at me this morning you are thinking that I am too young to be offering wisdom to those who are much older than myself, but this is not my wisdom that I bring. It is the wisdom and message of our Lord Jesus that fills my heart. God doesn't care if you are young or old. He sends his message to people of all ages. He loves us equally. He reaches down from Heaven to open our hearts to His love."

God's love was all powerful, he continued. It had led him half way around the world to spread His message to new lands. He praised the simple beauty of our church. He spoke about its power and its size. He said he could feel the presence of the Holy Spirit within its walls. It was there above us, waiting to be accepted into our hearts. It would fill us with joy and lead us to God's green pastures of eternal salvation. He read messages of God's love from the Book of Psalms and passages from the Bible where Jesus helped the sick and the needy. Between each reading he asked us to kneel in silence while he read a prayer.

When the prayers were finished he asked us if we had accepted the Holy Spirit into our hearts. We looked around at each other. Some of us were brave enough to shake our heads. Duncan had never spoken to us about the Holy Spirit. He had told us that it was dangerous to invite Spirits into our hearts as the Hamatsas had done. We remembered how they had made us wild. Cannibal Dancers like Daniel and I had promised him that we would never let them enter us again. Surely the Holy Spirit was more powerful and dangerous than the Cannibal Spirits.

But when we shook our heads Reverend Hall looked sad. He shook his head too, and said that God was waiting for us to accept the Holy Spirit. He asked us why we disappointed Him. He pointed around us at the walls and ceiling of the great church and said the Holy Spirit had inspired us to build this great miracle. He told us he would give another sermon in the afternoon for those who wished to accept the Holy Spirit and then he left his pulpit.

Everyone was talking after we left the church. We had never heard a sermon like that or seen one delivered in that way. Duncan always stood on the ground at our level and he spoke to us in the calm voice of a patient teacher. He watched our eyes and asked us questions to see if we understood his message. He never tried to excite us with talk of the Holy Spirit. Reverend Hall was truly different. His passion stirred our hearts and confused our thoughts.

Some suggested he was different because he was ordained and Duncan was not. Perhaps only an ordained preacher could teach about the Holy Spirit. Others questioned this but we all wanted Reverend Hall to teach us more about the Holy Spirit. We returned to the church a few hours later for his afternoon sermon.

Reverend Hall's second sermon was about miracles. He spoke again about the miracle of our church and how we had made God happy by building it. He read stories from the Bible about how God parted the sea for Moses and how Jesus fed thousands with one loaf of bread. God made everything possible for those who had faith in His love. Those who believed in God would be given everlasting life. Duncan had told us the same stories, but Reverend Hall made them new to us. Their message filled our hearts as never before.

Hall was encouraged by the excitement he saw on our faces. He invited us to a third sermon after dinner. The church was full for that sermon too, when he spoke about God's forgiveness. He told us all men were sinners, but that God had sent Jesus, His only begotten son, to die for our sins so that we could be forgiven. He asked us to stand if we had ever done wrong to another person. Only a couple men stood. Hall said these men were brave, but the truth was that each of us had sinned and done wrong in God's eyes at some time.

He asked us to kneel, close our eyes and remember a time when we had disappointed God by lying or stealing. He asked us to pray for His forgiveness. Then he asked us to remember a time when we had been unkind or unfair to others. He asked us to pray for God's forgiveness again, but this time he asked us to speak our words. He did this two more times, until many voices were crying out loud for God to forgive them. He finished this sermon with a prayer of thanks for sins God had forgiven that evening.

Hall said we were very close to accepting the Holy Spirit into our hearts. He would give a fourth sermon at eleven o'clock to give us one more chance at Salvation. I had never sat through three sermons in one day and I did not look forward to another. I wondered why we all had to be saved on his first day. I suggested to Tom that we take a walk on the beach. It was a warm summer night and the skies were clearer than my head.

I hoped that Tom was as tired as I was, but Hall's sermon had filled him with energy. I wanted a quiet walk but he could not stop talking. No one had ever taught him to hold his joy inside.

Tom was most impressed by Hall's style of speaking. "His voice was so strong! Could you feel the Holy Spirit in him? He has such grace! He raises his arms up like this and he feels the power of God!" He was dancing beside me with his arms in the air. I smiled in spite of my tiredness.

"Be careful! You'll trip on the rocks." I sounded like my Uncle Silgitook.

"I won't trip. God is protecting me. Jack, aren't you excited by Reverend Hall's words?"

"Yes, I have had so much excitement I am ready to sleep. Aren't you tired yet?"

"No, no, you can't go to bed. The night has just begun. We must hear his last sermon. I want to accept the Holy Spirit into my heart. You will accept it too, and then you won't be tired. Please come with me."

I agreed to come with him, but mostly to keep him out of trouble. He stopped dancing and held my hand as we walked, but as eleven o'clock drew closer he became anxious to return to the church.

TWENTY
FOUR

The church was almost full even though we were half an hour early. We sat near the back where there was still room. The gas lamps along the walls had been lit now that it was dark. Another lamp sat on Reverend Hall's pulpit to light the Bible. Their glow created more shadows than they chased away. The crowd was noisy with anticipation. It was hard to hear ourselves speak. Once again, the great bell rang out, though the everyone was already seated. The congregation fell silent. Hall waited for the last voice to stop before he floated down the aisle slowly with his arms spread wide.

He climbed up onto the pulpit and stared into the darkness of the vaulted ceiling in silence. Then he looked out over our faces as though he could read our minds.

"The Lord God is pleased that you have returned to hear His message. The Holy Spirit awaits you," he began. His last sermon was about the power of God's love. He told us it had the power to change our lives forever, to bring us happiness, to heal the sick and to turn our enemies into friends. He spoke with great passion for several minutes about how the Holy Spirit carried God's message and His love into our hearts.

The lamp on the pulpit cast his shadow on the wall behind him. As he spoke it swayed back and forth. As he moved his arms it made great gestures that stretched up to the darkness above. From our place near the back of the church it seemed that the shadow itself was speaking.

"The Holy Spirit wants you to open your hearts to God. Drive away your fears and doubts so He can enter. Reach out for God's love and invite Him in!" he instructed us. The shadow's arms stretched right to the ceiling and a thousand arms in the congregation followed its lead.

He asked us to kneel in prayer and to beg God to help us receive His Spirit. He called out to the Holy Spirit, asking It to fill our great church so that we might embrace God's love. He asked us to repeat the words, "Please Lord, let your Spirit enter my heart." He asked us to repeat it louder as we raised our arms up to receive. He was shouting his words as the great arms of the shadow touched the rafters.

But it was not the Holy Spirit that answered. It was the Spirit of the Church, proud and arrogant, that lusted for power over us. It entered those around us and one by one they stood and shouted, "I feel the Spirit!" as it gripped their hearts. I felt it enter me too, as I had once felt the Cannibal Spirits when I was a boy. Then I heard Tom shouting beside me, "Yes, Lord, I feel you! Thank you! Thank you!" He startled me. Fear rushed back into my heart and the Spirit left me.

Something was terribly wrong. The church was filled with noise and confusion. People were jumping and shouting with excitement. Tom had left my side and was among them. They started to leave the church. Schutt tried to block their way but they carried him out with them. His face was filled with alarm, like Duncan's face the day I performed as a Cannibal Dancer on the beach in front of Fort Simpson.

Hall was not alarmed. He was smiling broadly. His face beamed with pride as I ran up to him.

"Reverend Hall, what is happening? Please tell them to come back," I begged him.

"They won't listen to me, Jack. They are listening to the Lord's voice now. If you were listening to His voice you would follow it too."

"But where are they going at this time of night? Aren't you concerned?"

"They have accepted the Holy Spirit. Can you see the change in them since this morning? Mr. Duncan will be very pleased with me. I only wish you had accepted the Holy Spirit too, Jack." Schutt forced his way back into the church against the flow. He looked worried when he heard Hall mention Duncan.

The church was almost empty now. I went out the door to look around. People were scattering into the darkness in every direction. I heard their voices calling to the Lord above. I shouted for Tom, but he did not answer. I ran down the stairs and towards the Mission House. As I turned a corner he grabbed me from behind and pulled me close.

"Jack, this is wonderful! I feel the Lord's Spirit inside of me! He has blessed me!" He kissed my neck and then left to hug other men who were under the Spirit's spell.

"Tom, wait!" He let me catch up to him. "We should go home now. It's late. I will make some tea and we can rest."

"I'm not ready to go home yet," he protested impatiently. He saw Joseph and Mary and called to them. They were as excited about Reverend Hall's sermons as he was. Indeed, I seemed to be the only one who was not.

Tom invited them to our house to share our tea, but Mary said we should come to their house instead. She wanted to put my nephew Jesse to bed, though it was obvious that he was also too excited to sleep. On our way there we met Catherine, Sam and Elizabeth. Joseph invited them to join us.

My sister-in-law Ruth Shoget and my niece Caroline showed up at Mary's house soon after we arrived. They stayed all night, just as we did. I struggled to stay awake as they talked about Reverend Hall's sermons and God's love until dawn. By then they were too tired to talk more.

Our rules were broken that night. The Constables did not perform their duties, the curfew was ignored and men and women met together. No one seemed to care, not even the Church Elders. People wandered through the town, singing hymns and talking in small groups until the sun came up.

I was grateful when Tom and I returned to our bed in the early morning. We slept most of the day, but my sleep was broken by strange dreams of the events that had just happened. Tom stirred but he did not wake. I tried to understand what had made him and so many others act so strangely. He was beside me, but his face was so distant I felt I was alone.

We did not rise until the light of the new day was fading. I hoped Tom would be his usual self when he woke but he seemed as distant as the night before. It was dark by the time we had finished our meal. I felt uneasy, as if day and night had been reversed. No one had worked that day. Tom did not seem to care. He announced that this was a religious holiday.

His sleep had refreshed him and he was eager to leave the house. I ran after him, asking where he was going, but he did not answer. I followed as he greeted each person he met with joy and enthusiasm. He needed to be with others who felt as he did. He shook their hands and asked if they could still feel the Spirit of the Lord. When they said yes, he commanded them to follow him to the church. When they arrived at the church he started to ring the great bell. It echoed off the mountains and the people of the town came out of the darkness to answer its call.

The church was soon full again. I stood at the side as Tom spoke in front of the pews. He asked others to tell stories of how the power of the Holy Spirit had touched them since the night before. One man spoke of a dream where he saw the light of Heaven, which he was sure was God. Others said they were filled with a strange energy and that pains and illnesses had disappeared.

Henry Schutt entered the church and asked Tom what he was doing. Tom ignored him. Schutt turned to the congregation and told us Duncan would be upset that we had not worked that day. Tom replied that he had not received the Holy Spirit and did not recognize the work of the Lord. Schutt tried to argue with him but Tom turned away. He started singing one of our favourite hymns. He moved his arms to the rhythm as Duncan did and soon the congregation was singing with him.

Reverend Hall rushed in. Schutt pulled him aside and spoke to him as the hymn continued. As soon as it finished, Hall walked quickly up the centre aisle to where Tom was standing. He thanked everyone for the beautiful singing and said he was happy that the Spirit of the Lord was still with them. Then he added that they must return to their duties the next morning, as the Lord would have it. He suggested that they go home now and make ready for a good night's sleep.

Tom glared at him impatiently. As soon as Hall paused to hear their response, Tom raised his arms and began to sing another hymn. The congregation sang with him more loudly than before. Hall tried to interrupt the singing, but they felt the Spirit within them and they did not need him anymore. Hall's look of confidence changed to alarm. He looked back at Schutt helplessly, hoping for guidance. Schutt gestured for him to do something.

As soon as the hymn was over, Hall climbed onto his pulpit and commanded the room to listen. He did not look as impressive without his white robes. He told everyone to leave the church, to return to their homes quietly and honour their commitment to God by doing their duties the next day. They stood to leave. Tom began another hymn and led them singing down the aisle to the door. Soon they scattered into the night, but they continued to sing.

I ran after them to catch up with Tom. I found him on the road to our house, speaking to John Tatham and Sam. They were talking excitedly about spreading the word of God. I saw there was no hope of getting them to return to their homes quietly.

Tom decided we should all go to my brother-in-law Joseph's house again. Joseph was at home with Mary, readying Jesse for bed. Joseph welcomed us back and Mary joined us when she was finished. Their conversation was all about the power of God's love and how they could teach others to feel the Spirit as they did. My sister asked if I felt the Spirit. I said yes but suggested, with a yawn, that Reverend Hall was right. The Lord wanted us to return to our duties the next morning. They looked at me blankly for a moment and then turned away. After that they ignored me.

Just before midnight Tom said we must return to the church to feel the presence of the Spirit again. He said the Holy Spirit was the Ghost of Jesus and as we knew ghosts came to our world in the darkness of night, just as the Spirit had visited us around midnight the night before. Mary stayed to watch over Jesse but the men were eager to follow Tom.

I did not want them to return to the church but I knew they would not listen to me. I followed them to watch over Tom in case something went wrong. My heart pounded with fear as we reached the door. Duncan had never forbidden us to go into the church alone at night, but I had felt the Spirit of the Church the night before and was afraid I might feel it again. I mumbled a prayer to Jesus as Sam fumbled with the latch.

The latch gave way and the door creaked open. We stepped in out of the wind and closed it behind us. The gas lights had been turned off. Joseph lit a candle. Its pale light faded away before it reached the rafters above us. The ceiling above us was darker than the sky outside. The first pews appeared as our eyes grew accustomed to the dark. The rest of the hall was swallowed by the blackness.

"Do you think the candle will frighten away the Holy Ghost, Tom?" Sam asked.

"No, It is too strong to be frightened by a candle. I can feel its power near us. We need the candle to see. We must get to the front to pray at the altar."

"Maybe we should not be here. I don't like the darkness. We should light the gas lamps instead of a candle," John Tatham suggested.

"No, then others will come to see what we are doing. The Holy Spirit won't speak to us unless we pray alone. You must trust the Spirit and it will guide you."

We stayed close behind Tom as we crept down the centre aisle towards the altar. More pews came into view as others faded into the darkness behind us. The light reflected off the glass covers of the gas lights along the sides. It shone back at us like a bear's eyes in the night. Finally we reached the altar. Joseph put the candle into one of the holders and we knelt to pray.

"What's that?" Tom cried. He jumped to his feet, startling all of us.

"It was just the wind moaning," I tried to reassure him.

"No, no! I heard a voice. It was not outside. It was very close. It came from there, the table where Duncan gives God's blessing!"

"Oh, Great Spirit, what should we do?" John was panicking.

"Light the lamps! Maybe someone is hiding behind it." Sam lit the closest lamps on either side of the table. There was no one there.

"Oh my God!" John gasped. He fainted and fell to the floor. I rushed to his side to try to revive him.

"The Holy Ghost has spoken! Come! Hurry! We must tell everyone!" Tom took the candle and led Joseph and Sam back to the door. I called for them to wait for us but they disappeared.

John woke and sat up slowly. "Where are the others?" There was panic in his voice again.

"They have gone to tell others that they heard a voice. They will return soon."

"We cannot stay here alone. We must leave!"

"Stand up. I will lead you out."

"Where is the candle?" he whined.

"They took it with them. Come on. We'll leave the gas lamp on so we can see our way to the door." I took his hand and led him into the darkness. Outside we heard shouting and running. Tom, Joseph and Sam were gone but many others were hurrying towards the church. I asked if they had seen Tom. Some had seen him running from house to house, spreading the news of the Spirit in the church. John and I resigned ourselves to waiting on the steps for his return.

Soon every house was awake again and people came towards us from all directions. They hurried past us to pray in the church, barely stopping to say hello. Tom returned with Sam, his wife Catherine and their two children. He asked us to come inside with them, but John was afraid to return and I chose to keep John company. Tom sneered at us and moved on.

Timothy arrived late when the church was almost full. He wore a woman's shawl around his shoulders to keep warm. "What is wrong with this town? Don't they know it is three in the morning? Has everyone gone mad?" We greeted him but did not answer his questions. He climbed the stairs to the door. "Are you two coming in? The night wind will make you sick if you stay out here."

John shrugged and we followed Timothy inside.

The great hall was still dark except for the lamps Sam had lit near the altar at the far end. The crowd pressed into the aisles and pews as close to the altar as they could. Tom was standing on Duncan's table telling a story about what had happened. His arms cast shadows that danced on the walls above him. John was frightened again so we stayed by the door.

To my surprise, Tom was saying that he heard God's voice telling him to spread the word of the Gospel. He claimed the Spirit had chosen him to preach God's message to others. Sam and Joseph then climbed onto the table beside him to give witness. They claimed to have heard the voice too. Joseph said God had told them to take His message to other villages. Their audience burst into noise, both wailing and cheering.

"What voice are they talking about?" John looked at me with a puzzled expression. "Did it speak after I fainted?"

"No, I think not," I told him. "I would have heard it."

"What is going on here?" Henry Schutt asked suddenly.

He and Reverend Hall had come up the stairs behind us. They looked concerned. I tried to explain, but I did not know what to say. They marched down the aisle and pushed their way through the crowd. Schutt ordered the men to get down from the table but Tom continued to speak to the crowd.

"God has spoken!" Tom shouted, and the crowd cheered.

Schutt shouted at everyone to leave the church at once. They fell silent in confusion. Tom answered Schutt, saying God had called them to the church to hear His word. He turned back to the crowd and told them to make preparations to spread God's word to other villages. The people cheered and moved towards the door.

John and I moved aside to let the crowd pass. Tom shouted at me to prepare for a trip to Fort Simpson at dawn. He ran down the steps and disappeared into the crowd before I could speak to him. Timothy joined us on the steps. After the crowd had passed, we walked together until we reached our own houses. We parted and said good night.

I hoped Tom would be home already. On the way I thought about what I could say to convince him not to go to Fort Simpson to spread the Word of God. I worried what Duncan would say if he did. The street around me was filled with people talking to God and singing hymns. All of Metlakatla had gone mad.

I saw Laguksa coming towards me. She was searching anxiously through the crowds in the darkness.

"What are you looking for, Laura?" I asked her.

"Have you seen my girl Charlotte, Jack? Ruth told me Caroline and Charlotte went off with some other young girls after they left the church."

"I am sure they will be all right. They will come back home when they are tired."

"No, Jack, I'm worried." She squeezed my arm and I saw panic on her eyes. "Some men saw them leading the other girls towards the woods. The girls told them they were looking for a sign from God. They were singing and carrying on like they were possessed by Spirits. This isn't right, Jack! They can't go into the woods at night. They could be attacked by a bear or a wolf or something. I am worried sick."

"I am sure if they are singing it will frightened away any animals. Besides, how far can they go into the woods when it is this dark? As soon as they step in mud they will realize it was a bad plan."

"No, Charlotte and the other girls have been talking crazy all day. They say the Holy Spirit will protect them if they have faith. Reverend Hall put all these weird ideas into their heads and they are not themselves. The younger girls think Charlotte and Caroline are some kind of Shamans. Henry Richardson told me Caroline took a lantern from the church. He tried to see where they were going but he lost them in the crowd. He is as worried as I am. How will they see if the lantern goes out when they are in the woods, Jack? How will they get home?"

The more Laguksa spoke the more excited she became. I had never seen her so anxious before, but I could understand why. Charlotte was the only one of her family who had survived the Smallpox. She wiped her eyes with her handkerchief and tried to steady herself. She was trembling, perhaps from fear or perhaps from the night wind.

"Go home and wait for them in case they return. You will hurt yourself or get lost wandering around alone in the dark without a light."

"Charlotte is all I have left, Jack. You must find her. No one else will help. I don't understand what is happening to her. She is not like this."

"I will look and I will find them. Don't worry. In an hour there will be some light in the sky again. I will find them and bring them back. I promise. Now go home and wait in case they return there before I find them." She nodded at me and turned away.

I had no idea where to look. Maybe they had gone down the road to the saw mill, so I set off in that direction. I thought it would be a relief to be away from the madness in the town, but the darkness and the silence were more frightening. The night was black. There were no clouds and no moon. I moved slowly, for the road was rough and full of muddy holes. I called out to Caroline and Charlotte, knowing if they did not hear me at least the bears and the wolves would.

I turned around. By the time I reached to the town again the streets were mostly empty. Several men were on the beach, filling canoes with supplies for their trip to Fort Simpson. I saw John Tatham, Daniel and my brother George amongst them. Tom and Joseph were waiting beside our canoe. Tom's eyes were filled with anger.

"Where have you been? We have waited for you. I told you to be ready! You have done nothing!"

"Charlotte, Caroline and some younger girls have gone into the woods. Ruth and

Laura are sick with worry. I promised I would look for them and bring them home safely. I cannot come with you until that is done."

"We cannot wait longer for you! Two canoes have already left for the Skeena and another has left for Kitkatla. Why did you make those stupid promises? God will protect them if they have faith. You heard Reverend Hall's words. I have been watching you. You have no faith. That is why you won't come with us!"

His words hit like stones. They filled me with pain and anger. "Why did you lie to the others? Why did you tell them you heard the voice of God? You heard nothing but the sound of the wind. I was there. I know!"

"What do you know? God spoke to me, not to you. He does not speak to those who have no faith. He will not speak to you and I do not want to speak to you either!" He turned away from me and told the others they must leave right away.

Daniel and my brother George hesitated, until Tom shouted at them again. They pushed their canoes into the water and climbed inside. I watched them leave as jealousy and betrayal tore my heart apart like two wolves fighting. Tom did not look back as they paddled away towards Fort Simpson.

I was angry and confused. I regretted having run into Laguksa and I wished I had not given her my promise. I was also angry with the girls for going into the forest. I was angry at Reverend Hall too, but I was also sad, for Tom was right. I had no faith in what was happening around me and I did not want them to leave for Fort Simpson to spread the word of God.

I made my way to Laguksa's house to see if the girls had returned. Laguksa was sitting at her kitchen table. She looked exhausted. I told her to get some sleep and I would look some more.

I searched the edge of the forest behind the town and I walked along the beach. The tide had washed away any footprints. I found a scarf that might have belonged to one of the girls. The town was quiet after a night filled with talking and singing. I was dead tired, so I sat on a log on the beach and rested. A faint light was growing in the eastern sky. It would soon be time for the town to rise and start their work, but I doubted any work would get done that day.

I waited there, hoping others would come by and help me search the forest. It was late morning when I heard the girls' voices. They had come out of the forest to the east and were marching along the shore towards the town singing hymns. I ran to meet them. My niece, Caroline Shoget, was marching beside Laura's daughter Charlotte. They seemed to be in a trance. Caroline carried a large branch upright in front of her. A dozen other girls followed in step behind them.

"Where have you been?" I scolded them, shouting loud enough to interrupt their singing. "Your mothers are sick with worry!"

They looked at me calmly and smiled. My words did not seem to concern them.

"Look!" Caroline said, thrusting the branch towards me. "We have found the cross of Jesus! The good Lord has given us a sign. It is a miracle!" The other girls mumbled their agreement. I looked it over. It did look somewhat like a cross, bleached white by sun and salt water.

"It is only a branch with an odd shape. Where did you find it?"

"It was on the beach at the edge of the forest back there." She pointed down the beach behind her. "We prayed for hours for a sign from God and He sent us this. He put it there so we would find it." The other girls started speaking all at once in excited voices.

"It is just a dead branch, not a cross. Leave it on the beach!" I was sick of talk about miracles and I wanted it to stop. The girls looked at me with distrust in their eyes, as though I was the one who was crazy. Caroline raised her chin in defiance. She lifted the branch higher and began to sing a hymn. The other girls joined in the singing and followed her as she marched past me towards the town. I had no choice but to follow behind them. At least they were moving in the right direction.

Once they reached the town they went from house to house to announce they had found the cross of Jesus. There was much commotion as people hurried out to see the miracle. A crowd swelled as the girls led them through the town. Henry Schutt came out of the Mission House. He looked alarmed and frustrated as he watched us pass.

The girls stopped at the end of the road at the west side of the town. Caroline climbed onto a log. She told the story of how the girls had prayed to God and how He led them to the branch that looked like a cross. The crowd loved the story and began to cheer. They decided that it must be brought to the church and fixed to the wall beside the altar. Caroline let them back to the church, holding the branch more proudly than before, while they sang another hymn.

Henry Schutt was discussing the situation in the town with Reverend Hall at the door of the church. When he saw the crowd approaching he stood at the top of the stairs with his hands on his hips. The girls stopped at the base of the steps. He asked them what they were doing. They told him that God had instructed them to hang the branch beside the altar. He told them that God had said no such thing and that he would not let them bring that dirty branch inside. Many angry voices shouted back that he had no right to stop them.

Schutt turned to Reverend Hall. "You started this mess, young Messiah. You had better put an end to it right now or Duncan will have your head displayed on top of that stick when he gets back."

Hall looked nothing like the man who stood on the pulpit two days before. He was a frightened boy waiting for his punishment. He glanced nervously at Schutt before moving to the top of the stairs.

"My dear people. I am flattered that you have taken my words to heart but we must not get carried away. We can't go hanging branches in the church just because they look like a cross. We must be certain of a miracle before we do anything rash."

More angry voices answered him. They said they listened to the words of God, not his words. They demanded that he let them hang the branch by the altar. Hall lost his voice. He looked at the crowd with panic in his eyes, like an animal trapped in a fire. The crowd began to climb the steps to force their way by him.

"Wait, wait!" I rushed up the stairs to move in front of them. "Reverend Hall is right! We cannot do this without Duncan's permission. If you act without listening to his wisdom you will anger him. This can wait until he returns."

The crowd was confused. They disagreed about what they should do. There were angry voices on both sides and I was worried that a fight might start. Finally they agreed to plant the branch in the ground in front of the dock to guard the town until Duncan returned. Some thought they should leave someone to guard it in case Schutt would try to remove it after they left, but he promised them he would not touch it as long as they kept it outside the church. So they planted the branch by the dock. They gathered around it and sang hymns to give it their blessing.

I returned home to sleep but my rest was uneasy. Our empty bed reminded me of Tom's angry words, and they filled me once again with sadness and worry. I was woken a few hours later by cheers and shouting. Daylight was already fading. The cheers were for Tom and the other men who had returned from Fort Simpson.

I ran to the beach to meet them, hoping that Tom had forgiven me. They were unloading their canoes onto the beach when I arrived. Tom saw me but he turned away. At least he did not look angry. Daniel and George greeted me with large smiles and I smiled back, relieved to see them.

"Jack, you should have come. It was amazing!" Daniel laughed. "We have seen miracles in the sky!" My smile faded.

"What kind of miracles?" I asked. I tried not to show my disappointment.

This time my brother George replied. "There were angels in the clouds over Fort Simpson! We saw them. They were so beautiful!"

"How do you know they were angels? You have ever seen one before."

"What else could it be that floats in the sky and sings to us?" Daniel asked me.

"They sang to you?" I could not believe that he was telling me this.

"Some of us heard them. They were very far away," he explained with hesitation. I was speechless. I wished they had not told me this.

Tom called to Daniel and George to follow him. I came too, along with the crowd that had gathered on the beach to greet them. He led them up the hill to the front of the church. There, from the steps of the church, he told them how the angels appeared in the sky on their way to Fort Simpson. As soon as they landed, they spread God's word and news of the miracles they had heard in the church and seen in the sky. The people they met spread their message to the rest of Fort Simpson and soon the whole town was full of excitement.

As he finished his story Tom stared up to the sky, just as Reverend Hall's eyes had gazed up to the ceiling of the church two days before. The crowd looked to see if there were angels there, but the sky was clear. Tom spoke with the voice of a Shaman as he told us that seeing God's angels had changed him forever. The others were impressed, but I was not. Why had he changed when Daniel and George had not? Suddenly, he fell to his knees and he began to pray aloud, "Thank you, Lord, for sending your angels to open my eyes! Thank you for telling me that I have been chosen to lead my people into salvation!"

I walked away in disgust. He did not look at me as I crossed in front of him. Anger choked my throat and tears burned in my eyes. I left quickly so he would not see me cry. I had not gone far when I saw Sam Pritchard rushing towards me with two other men. He was wearing the simple Church Elder robe he wore when he was helping Duncan and Schutt with the Sunday service. He stopped me and spoke to me with urgency.

"Jack, is it true that Tom is possessed?" His face was full of worry. Sam had not gone to Fort Simpson with the others.

I looked back at Tom. He was still praying loudly to the sky. "I do not know. He is acting very strange and he says he sees things that I cannot. He will not speak to me."

"I have brought Holy Water from the church to drive the demons from his body! Come with us. We might need you!" He hurried past me to where Tom was praying. "Everyone please stand back!" he shouted. "Demons have possessed Tom. I must drive them away with Holy Water or he will die!"

The crowd backed away in surprise. Sam poured the Holy Water over Tom's head. Tom looked at him angrily for a instant and then continued to pray aloud. "Forgive him Lord for he does not know what he is doing."

Sam splashed him with more Holy Water until it ran down his pants. He stood up and glared at Sam. He wiped his face to soothe his anger and then he spoke in a calm voice. "Thank you, Mr. Pritchard. The Lord's Holy Water feels good on my face. The Holy Spirit filled my heart with so much love I forgot where I am." He turned to the crowd around him. "Come! We must go to the church to offer thanks to our Heavenly Father. He can hear us better there." He glared at Sam again and pushed past him as he led the crowd up the stairs of the church.

The madness continued for two more weeks. The townspeople slowly returned to their daily routines and the nights became quieter, though the Constables were still not enforcing the curfew. For Tom and I, life was not the way it had been before Reverend Hall's sermons. The Spirit still possessed Tom and he had many followers. Each day he summoned them to prayer with the church bell and each day they came. I watched them from the back of the church hall.

Every night he chastised me for my lack of faith. We fought and argued or we sulked in silence. He would not touch or kiss me when we climbed into bed. He slept with his back to me. When I tried to hold him and ask him to forgive me, he pushed me away and separated our beds. I thought for certain I had lost him forever and I could not stop my tears.

Henry Schutt and Reverend Hall were still troubled by what they saw. Each day they spoke calmly to those who gathered in the church to pray with Tom. They asked us to follow the rules that Duncan had given us. Hall did not admit he had misled us, only that we had misunderstood his message. He wore his white robes the next Sunday and tried to speak with grace but his voice was timid and uncertain. The congregation did not listen.

Schutt and Hall's gentle manners were proof to Tom that they were afraid his powers. He became bolder and more defiant. He told his followers that their trips made to Fort Simpson, Kitkatla and the Skeena would bring boatloads of new converts to Metlakatla. He said if they prayed throughout the day the boats would come sooner. This angered Schutt. He told Tom that he had no right to hold services in church for he was not ordained. The next morning when Tom came to ring the church bell, he found Schutt had locked and chained the door.

Tom was not upset. He held prayers meetings on the steps of the church each evening, asking God to send ships of new converts. He invited the Spirit to fill his heart and he led his followers through the town as he blessed each house they passed. They prayed on the beach around the branch that looked like a cross. They asked

God to give them a sign of His love by bringing their sacred branch back to life. They decorated it with flowers and ribbons and sprinkled it with juices of the wooms plant.

One afternoon, two weeks after the Spirit touched them, a woman saw a ship entering the harbour. She told Tom, who sent his followers from house to house to alert the town that the first ship of new converts was arriving. Even I was anxious to see if his prediction had come true. I gathered with the rest of them on the beach.

The crowd cheered as the ship pulled along side the dock and the sailors secured the lines. Tom led us in a hymn to welcome the new converts as they lowered the gangplank. The sailors laughed and shook their heads with amusement as if we were fools. Tom's followers paid them no mind as they continued singing louder.

But only one man waited at the top to descend. He wore a black bowler and a long black coat too warm for summer weather. He had a thick bushy beard that was black and silver and he carried a small suitcase. He stood at the top of the ramp and glared at us as we sang. Our voices caught in our throats and faded away. It was Duncan!

He walked down the gangplank and stopped on the dock. His face showed no joy at seeing us. His blue eyes burned hot as he looked over the crowd. Seconds passed like minutes. Without saying a word, he bent his head down and walked along the dock towards us. Tom started to sing Duncan's favourite hymn and other voices joined in.

"Silence!" Duncan's voice shook like thunder. The singing stopped and we parted like the Red Sea to let him pass. He did not look at anyone as he marched briskly passed us. He stopped just beyond the crowd at the place where the twisted branch was planted in the sand. He slowly looked towards it and surveyed the flowers and ribbons that decorated its branches. His mouth tightened.

"What is this?" he barked. No one answered. I saw his face grow red and his eyes fill with fire. "What is THIS!" he yelled again, turning quickly to look at our faces.

We bowed our heads to spare ourselves from the power of his eyes. For a few seconds I heard only the sound on my heart pounding in my chest. I glanced at Tom. His face was red and full of fear as he stared at the ground.

Duncan threw his briefcase on the ground. He marched to the branch, like Jesus entering the temple, and tore it out of the ground. He struck it hard against a nearby rock. Its dry, rotten limbs splintered into many pieces. He struck the rock again and again, breaking off more and more until the piece that remained was smaller than his arm. Then he tossed it into the water.

He turned back to look us, his face red and sweaty, and we all looked down again. He picked up his briefcase and marched up the hill to the Mission House. He disappeared inside and slammed the door.

TWENTY FIVE

We stood in a confused silence, not knowing what to do next. I looked to Tom but he was still staring at the ground. He seemed flushed and worried. I pushed my way past the others and hurried up the hill as fast as I could. When I reached the Mission House I realized I had no idea what to say. Duncan would be too angry to listen to my explanation of what had happened. I needed to give him more time.

I walked to the end of Mission Point and sat down. The crowd on the dock was dispersing. They were probably as upset as I was. The great church loomed above me at my back. I felt its cold, cruel Spirit watching me through its dark windows. It must have been delighted by the trouble it had made. How could I explain to Duncan that the Spirit had caused the insanity, not Reverend Hall, Tom or the others who had acted so strangely?

My mind was filled with fears. How would Duncan punish Tom? Would he be angry with me too? I rehearsed what I would say to him. He would only accept the truth, but what was the truth? None of it made sense. At least I felt relief that the madness would now stop.

After an hour I decided it was time to go to Duncan's office. I brought his mail as I would have done on other days. When I reached his door I heard voices. I pressed my ear to the wood. He was speaking with Schutt and Hall. Schutt was trying to explain what had happened. He was telling him about Reverend Hall's sermons.

"They were innocent enough, Mr. Duncan. I think the people were not used to hearing his passion and him speaking to them from a raised pulpit in his white robes...."

"What pulpit? What white robes?" Duncan's voice was controlled but I could tell his rage was rising. He would not hold it back for long. I knocked on the door while it was still safe to enter.

"Yes?" He did not sound pleased with my interruption. I nodded humbly and showed him the mail I was holding. "Just set it down," he snapped. I placed the small pile on his desk and waited beside Schutt to offer my account of what happened. "You can leave now, Jack. Thank you."

I closed the door. Their discussion resumed after a few seconds. It was Duncan who spoke first. I bent over and held my ear to the keyhole to hear his words more clearly. "Let me begin by telling you what I heard while I was in Victoria," he began.

The Victoria newspapers had described the visit of our men to Fort Simpson. The Tsimshians in Fort Simpson said our men were telling stories of seeing angels following them and White money and feathers of peace falling from the sky. The papers said the Tsimshians of Fort Simpson were drunk on whisky while the Tsimshians from Metlakatla were drunk on religion.

The stories were printed beneath Duncan's picture and they accused him of causing the problem. They said it was proof that Indians could not handle Christianity in a civilized manner and that Duncan should tend his flock instead of visiting Victoria. As soon as he read the stories he bought passage on a boat heading north without waiting for an answer from Chief Commissioner Powell.

It was Schutt and Reverend Hall's turn to explain how they lost control of the town. Hall apologized so many times that Duncan barked at him to shut up and get on with it. Hall mentioned his sermons but said nothing about how he acted as though he himself was possessed. He told Duncan that we needed to appreciate the love of God more and he wanted to inspire us.

"You had barely met anyone here, Mr. Hall. How dare you take it upon yourself to decide what is needed here without any knowledge of these people and their culture, and without my permission!" Duncan paused a moment to catch his breath and calm himself before continuing.

"Well, now you see what happens when you inspire them, don't you? I hope you've learned your lesson well. Now I am the laughing stock of Victoria and no one there will ever take our accomplishments seriously. In one day you have destroyed twenty years of my work. How do you plan to explain that to the missionary society?" Reverend Hall stuttered as he tried to apologize again. I could barely hear him. There were a several seconds of silence. I imagined Duncan pacing back and forth across the room, staring at the floor or out the window wondering what he must do next.

When he resumed, his voice was calm. "I am sorry, Mr. Hall. This mess is my fault, not yours. You meant to do well. I should have left you explicit instructions of what to do and what not to do. Your training is my responsibility and I have let you down. Please continue with your story. We need to figure out how best to correct this mess."

Hall and Schutt continued with their stories of what happened over the next few days. They knew nothing of what had happened in Fort Simpson.

"What are you doing Jack?"

Robert Tomlinson had come up behind me. He startled me so badly that I banged my head on the office door. "Who is it? Come in!" Duncan shouted from inside the room.

"Mr. Duncan asked me to wait outside," I whispered.

Tomlinson's eyes twinkled with amusement for a moment. "It's just me, William," he answered, opening the door. "I came as soon as I heard." Then he turned back to me and whispered sternly, "I think you had best wait somewhere else." He winked at me and slipped into the room.

I wanted to stay close by in case Duncan wanted to speak to me, so I sat on the steps of the Mission House. The meeting in Duncan's office lasted another two hours. The others finally left but Duncan stayed. The orphan girls who lived in residence at the Mission House approached me. They had made Duncan's dinner but they were too afraid to bring it to him. They asked if I would take it to him instead.

I knocked on the door and he invited me in. He was deep in thought as I set down his dinner. He thanked me and gave me some letters to file. He watched me as I filed them. "What happened here, Jack? Did you go to Fort Simpson with the others?"

"No, Mr. Duncan. The others wanted me to go but I was looking for Charlotte and Caroline. They had gone into the woods with some other girls and we were worried for them. I promised Laura and Ruth that I would keep looking. The girls were the ones who found that branch that looked like a cross. They claimed it was a sign from God."

"I see," he nodded. "I'm glad you had enough sense to do what was right." He looked up at me. "What do you think happened here?" His eyes watched my face closely to see if I was telling the truth.

"I am not sure, Mr. Duncan. I think our people wanted to let the Holy Spirit inside their hearts. Reverend Hall told us…"

"Yes, yes, I know. He has explained all that to me. Do you really think they were feeling the Holy Spirit, Jack?"

"They were feeling something, sir, but I don't know what. I felt a Spirit, too, during Reverend Hall's last sermon, but it scared me. I think it was an evil Spirit and it wants power over us. I think that Spirit is still in the church, Mr. Duncan. It worries me."

"Thank you, Jack." He was not pleased with my answer. He believed anything that was not written in the Bible was superstition, and he hated superstition. "You can go now. I need to be alone with my thoughts. I will take my dishes to the kitchen when I am finished."

I hesitated. I wanted to him to know everything, how the madness had frightened me, how it had affected Tom and how that hurt me. I needed him to understand that we were in danger. The Spirit was not just silly thought, but I had disappointed him by mentioning it. He was no longer interested in what I had to say, so I left.

Over the next few days Duncan spoke nothing of the events that happened in Metlakatla while he was away. He visited the workshops and spoke to each worker to ask how they were. One day he visited the saw mill and interrupted Tom leading the workers in a midday prayer. He asked why they had stopped working. Tom said they were offering thanks to God for showing them the way to Salvation. Duncan told them they should pray for strength and guidance at the start of each day before work began, and again after they had completed their daily duties to thank God for what He had given them, but not during working hours before their duties were done. He stayed to watch them until they started working again.

On the first Sunday after Duncan's return the townspeople gathered in the church to hear his sermon. We were hushed and anxious, like children expecting a scolding, but he spoke gently. He said Christianity had improved our lives. He knew we were grateful and we all wanted to be good Christians. It was natural for good Christians to want to feel the Holy Spirit, he told us, but the Holy Spirit does not possess us and make us do foolish things or distract us from our daily duties. It does not tell us to disobey the Christian rules that we have promised to uphold. It does not trick us into telling lies about what we see and feel to impress others.

His tone was gentle but his words stung Tom and the other men who had visited Fort Simpson. They interrupted his sermon, shouting out that the Holy Spirit had not tricked them and that they had not lied to impress others. Duncan first tried to speak over them with a louder voice, but this did not work so he stopped and waited. When their voices fell silent he told them to listen with respect to his sermon or leave. Tom stood and left the church. Twenty men followed him.

The town was tense the following week. Most supported Duncan but Tom, Joseph and other men spoke angrily against him. They wanted more of us to walk out of church service the next Sunday if Duncan denied that they had felt the Holy Spirit. Not many were still willing to follow Tom now that Duncan had returned, even if they believed they had felt the Spirit. Duncan could not be intimidated like Hall or Schutt, and opposing him could only bring trouble and heartbreak for the rest of us. But Tom and his followers were stubborn and many angry words were spoken. The Spirit of the Church had succeeded in dividing us.

The greatest tension was between Tom and me. I asked him to speak with Duncan privately and to follow the guidance of the Town Council instead of walking out of Duncan's sermon. Instead, he threatened never to speak to me again if he left the church next Sunday and I stayed behind. My heart was pained. He would not let me hold him and show him my love, for he believed I only wanted to change his mind. I prayed to God for a solution, but no answer came.

But perhaps my prayers were answered. Duncan heard news of their plan and he canceled his service for the following Sunday. He called for a meeting of the town's men in the schoolhouse instead. It was a difficult meeting that lasted all afternoon. Duncan said he would not hold a service while men were plotting against him. The men who planned the protest promised not to walk out if he did not speak against them. Duncan said he had every right to speak against them for they had broken many rules that they had promised to keep. He said they had brought shame and ridicule to himself and all of Metlakatla. Many voices rose in anger. He waited a couple minutes until there was silence before he spoke again.

He reminded them that ours was a Christian community. Everyone had given an oath to follow our rules and no one should break them without permission of the Town Council. Some men were still defiant. They questioned his leadership and his authority and quoted the Scriptures to prove that their actions were just. Duncan kept a calm voice. He used reason against their passion. He asked them to repeat the words they had heard and he showed them that many of the words were not in the Scriptures. That proved that the Holy Spirit had not spoken to them, he said, but that the Devil had tricked them.

This created doubt in some minds, but the arguments continued another two hours. Slowly, most of the men began to question what they had heard and accept Duncan's logic. He let them go, but he asked Tom, Joseph, Sam and two other leaders to meet with him in his office the next day.

Tom could not sleep that night. He was so frightened and upset that he was crying. I asked him to tell me what was bothering him. He complained that Duncan had confused the other men about what they had seen and heard. He said Duncan had not heard the voice of the Holy Spirit and did not know what he was talking about. I tried to comfort him. I said I would always love him even if Duncan did not, but my words did not stop his tears. I suggested that he pray. We knelt in prayer beside his bed for an hour. Then I went to bed, but he stayed there praying all night.

The next morning, he was calm. He went to Duncan's office with courage and faith, determined that Duncan would not change his heart. He said he would not forget, as other men had, the words that the Holy Spirit had spoken to him. I tied our beds together once he left and waited restlessly on the steps outside the Mission House until the meeting as over.

The meeting in Duncan's office lasted a long time. I heard the door to the office open and I stood up in anticipation. All the men but Tom passed by me, their heads bowed in silent defeat. They did not look at me as they passed. If was clear Duncan had won again, but Tom was still in there. My heart panicked. Tom was no match for Duncan on his own.

An hour later, Tom came out. His face was filled with pain and wet with tears. He glanced at me and walked by. I followed him to our room. I hoped he would not get angry when he saw our beds tied together, but he was in no mood to fight. He sat on the edge of the bed in silence. I begged him to talk. At first he said nothing, but tears flowed down his cheeks. I stroked his neck and kissed his cheek. When his words started to come, they would not stop.

The men had argued for hours but Duncan would not listen. He insisted they had heard the words of the Devil, not the Holy Spirit, but Tom refused to accept this. The others finally accepted it so he let them go, but he commanded Tom to stay. When they were gone, Duncan told him he would not tolerate defiance in his church. Tom had to admit he was wrong or Duncan would summon him to the front at the next assembly, damn him to Hell in front of our people and banish him from Metlakatla forever. Tom wept like a child as those words left his mouth. I wept too at the thought of him leaving me and Metlakatla. I hugged him tightly and as our tears fell on each other's shoulders. When they stopped, he whispered "Thank you" in my ear. We lay down together and I held him all night.

The next day Tom apologized to Duncan and admitted that he was wrong, but it took the town months to forget the pain of what happened that August. Duncan was determined it must never happen again. He made us attend special Bible classes each evening for the next two months to correct our thinking about the Scriptures, but he did not scold or threaten us again. He knew his victory had come at a painful price and he treated us with great respect and patience. He was quick with kind words and warm smiles to help the painful bruises in our hearts to heal. Slowly we learned to trust each other again.

Most of the town was happy that things had returned to normal. We wanted Duncan to be our leader. The crazy nights of madness when he was gone had frightened us. When the rebellious men repented we knew again that he was our rightful Chief.

For a few others it was different. The memory of those events was not a nightmare. They had felt the presence of the Spirit and it had stained them. It had showed them a power they had never felt before, a power that told them they did not need the permission of Whites to follow their hearts. They knew now that such a power existed and its memory could not be erased. Duncan had driven it into the shadows for now, like a bear retreating to the forest, but it watched us with its cold eyes from a distance where it could not be seen. It waited for its chance to return and tear us apart.

The events of August were not forgotten in Victoria, either. Bishop Hills and Duncan began a war of words in the White newspapers. Hills said Duncan was a bad missionary. Christianity means nothing if Red men do not understand God's Scriptures, he wrote, and he accused Duncan of betraying the Anglican Church by supporting Reverend Cridge's new church. His actions have taught our people to break the rules too, he claimed. Duncan retaliated with accusations that Hills did not care for the well-being of Indians. He also accused Hills of collecting money from England for Metlakatla but using it for his own purposes instead.

That might have been true but it no longer mattered. Once Duncan attacked the Bishop's honour he started a war that would never end. Our people were dragged into the war and it was unlike any war we had known before. There were no arrows or guns and no blood or death. Its weapons were lies, treachery and deceit. Its battles could not be seen on the surface. They burned deep below the ground, like the fires of Hell, hidden from our eyes. Like a Spirit beast, we felt its breath but we could not see its claws.

The war was bad for both sides. Neither Hills and Duncan would forgive the other or look for a solution. Hills was jealous of our great church, which was so much larger than his own and provided fame and protection for Duncan. The Anglican Church backed Hills, but he could not defeat Duncan on his own. He invited another bishop, Bishop Bompas of Athabasca, to visit Metlakatla and decide on a solution to their war. He trusted Bishop Bompas would agree with him and force Duncan to follow his orders.

Duncan welcomed news of Bompas's visit enthusiastically. We had never heard of him, but Duncan said he had a reputation for being kind and fair. He led the Anglican Church in the lands far inland, beyond the Skeena and the Nass, beyond the great mountains where the rivers flowed to the north instead of the west. Duncan believed Bompas would see our great church and the beauty of our work at Metlakatla and he would protect us from Bishop Hills. He had faith that his visit would bring us peace again.

We were less certain. White men were usually unfair to our people. Bompas would likely want to protect Bishops Hills instead of our people. Fighting two Bishops would be worse than fighting one, but Duncan's confidence convinced us to do our best to impress Bompas and win his allegiance. The Town Council and Duncan's students signed a letter and mailed it to him welcoming him to Metlakatla.

A message from Bishop Hills said that Bompas would arrive in fall, most likely before the first snow. We began plans for a great reception for him that would rival our largest potlatches. We worked hard each day to be ready in time for it was already the end of September. Men hunted for deer and moose for the feasts. Women made preserves and sewed new linens for his bed. We carved cedar bowls and boxes to give him as gifts. The Constables polished their uniforms. Our brass band and choir practiced our hymns, like the secret societies that once practiced their performances for the winter ceremonies. We repaired every building and cleaned the beaches and the streets. We made a banner to welcome him and we hung it over our dock. By the end of October our preparations were complete.

We waited. A week passed and he still had not arrived. Then another week passed. The first autumn storm damaged our banner so we hurried to make a new one. The first snows came and melted. Then came the second snows. The town became impatient. Six weeks had passed since we had finished our preparations and still we heard nothing. We asked Duncan if he was sure about the invitation. He assured us Bompas was coming soon, but we saw worry on his face too.

Finally our concerns were answered. A White miner arrived on our shore two weeks before Christmas. Two women saw him pull his small river canoe onto the beach. His skin was brown with dirt, his shirt was torn, his beard was long and tangled and he smelled badly. He asked the women to bring him to the Magistrate, Mr. Duncan. They were suspicious of his unpleasant appearance, but they led him to Duncan's office as he had asked.

We stared at the ragged stranger as he passed by. We followed him to ask where he had come from. He had come down the Skeena River. We asked if he had heard news of Bishop Bompas. Yes, he had, but he told us he wanted to speak to Duncan before he said more.

A crowd gathered outside the Mission House to wait for more news, which we were certain must be bad news. An hour later Duncan walked out alone. He looked surprised and asked why we were waiting, but there was a playful smile on his face. We asked impatiently what news the miner had brought of the bishop. "Ah!" he grinned. "I see you have already met Bishop Bompas." He laughed aloud at the shock on our faces.

We were not introduced to Bishop Bompas properly until the next day. He looked so different that we thought at first he must be someone else. His beard was gone and his clothes were clean and pressed. In fact, he was wearing Duncan's clothes while the girls of the Mission House residence washed and repaired his own.

He was not the man we had expected. He was older than Duncan and Bishop Hills. His body was brown and hard from long days of canoeing. He had traveled alone for six weeks over the mountains and rivers to reach Metlakatla, something neither Hills nor Duncan could have done.

We did our best to impress him, but Bompas impressed us more. Even our own men would not make such a long, difficult journey alone. Bompas did not boast about his accomplishment. He told us he often had to make such long journeys, for his territory was so large. We were listened to him with so much fascination that we almost forgot to start the celebration to honour his arrival. I was thrilled when Duncan asked me to be Bompas's servant during his stay. Everything he did gave us reason to tell stories about him for years to come. He was not spoiled by comforts like Bishop Hills. In fact, he was not accustomed to the simple comforts we offered him. He refused the bed and the new linens we had made for him. He slept on the floor instead so he would not forget the hard life he knew in the land called Athabasca. He did not need or want a servant but he allowed me to stay because I asked to.

He was a humble man, unlike other powerful and famous Chiefs. His eyes sparkled with light and his voice was full of song. His words were kind as he praised the beauty and industry of Metlakatla. He asked us many questions about how we lived and our answers always delighted him. When he spoke he looked into our eyes with a steadiness that told us he was a man of great love and faith. Our hearts surrendered to his gentle strength like the treetops that bow to the summer breezes.

Duncan and Tomlinson were as impressed by him as we were. They followed him around like young sons eager to win their father's approval. They had given up many comforts of English life to suffer for their love of God, but they lived in luxury compared to Bompas. Still, he did not seem to suffer his hardships as much as other Englishmen did. Duncan and Tomlinson wanted to learn from his strength and wisdom, and how to find the peace and joy that glowed from inside of him.

Without knowing it, Bompas also helped heal the rift between Duncan and Tom. I thought Tom would never speak to Duncan again. He had refused to bow when Duncan threatened to shame him in front of the congregation, but he broke like a child when Duncan said he would banish him from Metlakatla forever if he did not admit he was wrong. If he had been banished I would have followed him, but that was not enough for Tom. He needed Duncan's forgiveness, but he was too proud and stubborn to ask for it.

For weeks he avoided Duncan. He sat at the back of the church on Sundays to be furthest from him. Duncan said nothing to him either, until the day he brought Bishop Bompas to the saw mill. Duncan was kind and respectful and he was full of compliments about Tom's work. He told Bompas that Tom had helped oversee the building of our church. Tom glowed with pride. The next week Duncan asked Tom to look over details on other building plans and all was forgiven. Tom was as happy as a child at Christmas to be working with him again. I was relieved too, to finally see him smile again.

Duncan was anxious to know if Bompas favoured us in our war against Bishop Hills, but Bompas would not be hurried. He listened to our stories and watched how we lived without telling us his allegiance. While he was with us, he baptized many adults and children and he performed many confirmations, but he said little else until he was ready to make his decision.

The people did our best to win his heart too. Our brass band and choir performed for him eagerly and we honoured him with feasts and speeches, for we admired him. The Town Council even invited him to stay with us in Metlakatla instead of returning to Athabasca.

Bompas accepted our tributes with warmth and grace but they seemed to make him uncomfortable too. He was not accustomed to such attention and often preferred to be alone. On mornings when there was no rain, he took his canoe out before the light of the sun touched our harbour and he stayed away until dinnertime unless the rain returned. At first we worried that we had offended him in some way but he was always happy to see us when he returned. When we asked why he had left us, he explained that he needed to speak with God alone.

Our Christmas celebrations were large and joyful that year. Everyone felt the love of God when he was with us. A crowd assembled outside the Mission House on Christmas Eve to sing Christmas carols and to pay our respects to Duncan and Bompas. Christmas morning, the Constables visited each house to make peace with the people they had punished over the past year. They raised the British flag over the jail house and helped Duncan hand out little flags at the Christmas service in the great church. We pinned the flags to our clothes and wore them with pride. When Bompas told us it was the best Christmas he had ever known, we were filled with pride and delight.

When the New Year's celebrations were over, Bompas began to discuss solutions with Duncan to the problems between Bishop Hills and himself. I heard them talking when I delivered Duncan's mail. Bompas's voice was always gentle. He spoke to Duncan as Duncan often spoke to us. He did not tell Duncan he was right or wrong, but he said there must be compromises. Duncan was not a man of compromise and he wanted Bompas to tell Hills that nothing must change at Metlakatla. He argued angrily and defensively against every suggestion Bompas offered. He became a defiant son instead of Bompas's faithful disciple.

Bompas told Duncan it would be best if he apologized to Bishop Hills. He also said an ordained minister under Hills command should manage our town. Duncan threatened to leave if Bompas placed someone in charge over him, because an ordained minister would interfere and make his work here impossible. Bompas did not accept his way of thinking. Other churches in the area had ordained ministers who could baptize new Christians. Bompas said Duncan must consider the needs of the church before his own vanity. His words troubled Duncan greatly for he had often accused Hills of the same selfish vanity.

Bompas was a reasonable man. He did not want to upset Duncan so he did not order him apologize to Bishop Hills. He decided to ordain a minister before he left but he would not ask him to govern Metlakatla. He first asked Tomlinson, for he was Duncan's friend, but Tomlinson refused to work directly for Bishop Hills. His second choice was Collison, and Collison accepted his invitation. He came from Haida Gwaii for a week so Bompas could question him on the Scriptures before he was ordained.

Bompas made many other changes before he left. He gave his blessing for Collison and Tomlinson to set up a new mission with the Giksans up the Skeena, far beyond the place where the ancient city of Damelahamid once stood. He said Collison could advise Duncan from there and baptize new Christians whenever he visited Metlakatla. He sent Reverend Hall to Fort Rupert to work with the Kwakiutl and he sent Schutt to Kincolith to manage Tomlinson's mission on the Nass.

I thought Bompas's decisions were fair, but Duncan was not pleased. He was still allowed to manage the religious affairs of Metlakatla but Bompas thought someone else should manage the business affairs. Bompas felt that Tsimshian men should be taught to run the store and they should do more of the teaching and missionary work.

Duncan did not like any of his suggestions. He remembered how we had behaved when he left us with Reverend Hall, how Legiac and the Chiefs had failed to manage the store and how none of the teaching assistants he had trained knew what to teach or how to write lesson plans. As soon as Bompas left with Tomlinson and Collison for the Skeena, he wrote a letter to the missionary society to tell them Bompas did not understand our needs as well as he did.

Bompas's decisions did little to end the war between Duncan and Bishop Hills. Hills was not pleased that Bompas left Duncan in charge of Metlakatla and that he had not required Duncan to apologize. Collison was ordained but he was too far away to manage Metlakatla or to take instructions from Hills. Duncan had won more of the battle than he had lost. He wanted more but he was wise enough to not boast about his victories. He stayed away from Victoria and he did not speak or write to Hills for a full year.

We left for the fishing camps on the Nass as soon as Bompas left. When we returned our lives continued as they had before. His visit brought few changes but most of the bad feelings from the madness of the previous August had been forgotten.

TWENTY
SIX

The year that followed was peaceful. There were no other important visitors and no angry words. We worked hard, our spirits stayed high and our jail house stayed empty. Our fish catches were better than the previous two years. There was more money and we were not hungry. We enjoyed peace with other towns too. The magistrates who had taken over Duncan's work in Fort Simpson and the Skeena now respected Duncan and came to him when they needed advice.

Many new people moved to Metlakatla to share our prosperity. Others came to escape their troubles. If wives or servants had been beaten, Duncan offered them shelter in our town. News of his kindness spread and others started to arrive. We helped them start new lives as we once had.

We taught them to work hard for their pay, and how to start and stop work at the same time each day like we did. We showed them our English furniture and wallpaper and how to eat with English cutlery. It occurred to me how English we had become. We built and lived in English buildings and belonged to the Church of England. We had become the people Duncan wanted us to be. We were proud of the changes we had made, and Duncan was proud of us too.

The town was growing quickly and there were always more buildings to finish. We improved the saw mill and built a new carpentry shop. We trained many new carpenters and they made the furniture for thirty new houses that we finished by the end of that year. We built a library and we added new rooms to the schoolhouse so it could hold two hundred students.

We also built an art gallery and filled it with pieces donated by past Chiefs and Elders, such as the chests and ceremonial clothes. Other pieces we made ourselves for the collection. Tsangook carved beautiful masks and boxes, and women wove blankets we once used before we had English wool and buttons.

Admiral Prevost, the Captain who brought Duncan to Fort Simpson twenty-two years before, visited Metlakatla the next spring. He brought us gas street lights and several fruit trees as gifts. They caused much excitement. A hundred men volunteered to build a new road by the shore that was half of a mile long. We planted the trees along the road and set up the gas lights. When the work was finished the town gathered to celebrate as the Constables lit the lamps. Everyone clapped and sang as our band marched back and forth along the street playing hymns and "God Save The Queen".

The summer of that year, in 1879, I accompanied my family and friends on a visit to Victoria. The women wanted to shop for clothes. The rest of us wanted to see it again for we had not been there in several years. It was the first visit in sixteen years for Tom and I, when we had traveled with Duncan to buy the Carolena.

Mary and Joseph brought their son Jesse, who was now a handsome youth of fourteen years. Daniel and Jennifer Carter brought their daughter Anne, Jesse's constant companion. Uncle Shoget came with my sister-in-law Ruth and my niece Caroline. Charlotte begged her mother Laura to join us and to take her too, so she could be there with Caroline. Timothy also joined us. He said he needed to watch over us, but he was more eager to shop than the women.

We decided to spend money on proper English hotel rooms and passage on a steam ship. Most of the group had never been on a ship. It would be cheaper to go by canoe, but the Indian camps had been removed and we would have no place to park them where they would be safe. The ship was faster and the hotel rooms more comfortable than camping. This vacation would be a luxury for us.

Others wanted to join us but they could not afford the passage and the hotel. My brother George and his wife Gertrude stayed behind to care for two of their girls who had the measles. Tom did not seem to care that I was leaving him behind. He was too busy at the saw mill supervising work for the new houses to come with us. I promised to bring back a special gift for him.

The trip caused much excitement, especially for the women. They had saved to go shopping for several months. Hour after hour, they discussed what things they wanted to buy, and of course those who could not come had shopping lists for us too. When they were not talking about shopping, they discussed what clothes they should bring to wear and how much space to leave in their luggage for what they would buy. The men wanted no part in such bothersome planning, except for Timothy.

The ship arrived in our harbour in late morning after leaving Fort Simpson. We were in the finest of moods. The men carried the women's trunks up the gangplank, and the women carried the smaller bags. I offered to carry Laura's trunk, but she would have nothing of it. "I am not such a White woman yet that I can't carry my own trunk," she laughed.

Jesse and the girls set about exploring the ship before it left the dock. We left our luggage in our cabins and returned to the deck to wave at those who had come to see us off. It was fun to look around from such a height above the water. The ship pulled away from the dock. We stayed on deck and watched our town grow smaller and disappear from view. The last thing we could see was the church steeple.

The ship stopped at Port Essington, a new White town at the mouth of the Skeena. It was large, but it was not a town like Victoria. There were few stores and no women or children, just a large salmon cannery and many residences for the men who worked there. Most of them only stayed for the spring and summer, for they had families in other places. Even some of our men had come here when there was no work at Metlakatla.

The steam ship waited there as many of the passengers disembarked to look for work. Uncle Shoget spit over the gunwale as he looked at the cannery.

"Do you remember that these lands used to be covered in berry bushes, Gugweelaks?" He had started to call us by our Tsimshian names again and he preferred us to call him Uncle Shoget instead of Uncle James. "They were the finest berry bushes on all the Skeena and now they are gone."

"Yes, I remember, Uncle Shoget. They were an hour from our fishing camp."

"That's right! They were the property of the Eagle Clan of Gitsacatl village. The Whites did not care who they belonged to. It was that scoundrel Robert Cunningham's idea to build the cannery. He got permission from the village to build a store here and before we could stop him he and his partners had ripped the bushes out to make room for the cannery. The people from Gitsacatl complained bitterly but the Whites threatened to bring in a gunship to flatten their village like they did at Fort Rupert. That's White justice!" He spit again in disgust.

The story was known to everyone at Metlakatla. White fishermen had built the cannery at Port Essington six years earlier. Duncan had no respect for it. He told us they were stealing our salmon. He was right too. Already our catches were much smaller, for the Whites did not honour the Salmon Spirits.

The people of Gitsacatl were still angry about the berry patches they had lost. They considered anyone who worked for the cannery to be an enemy and a traitor to his people, but work was scare and our people were poorer now that the salmon catches were smaller. Many men had to work there if they wanted to feed their families. There was nothing Duncan or our people could do about it.

The next morning our ship continued south through Tsamsem's Trench. We watched for familiar landmarks from the deck. Jesse and Anne were most excited, for they had heard stories of our village since they were young children. We showed the different places we had camped and where Ts'ibasaa's men had ambushed us on our way home with our salmon catch. Then we left the Trench and passed by the mouth of the great canyon that led to our former home, Gitka'ata.

"It is up there, half a day by canoe," Uncle Shoget pointed.

"Where is it? Can you see it from here?" Jesse asked impatiently. It was pleasing to see his interest in the village where his ancestors had lived.

"No, son. It is hidden in a bay to the west. Do you see where the channel bends in the distance? The bay is on the left side just before the bend."

Jesse groaned and slumped back into his chair. He had waited to see Gitka'ata all morning. We felt his disappointment, for we too longed to see our home again. I thought of the many places I had loved that Jesse would never know.

The ship stopped at Klemtu and Bella Bella before we reached the open water. Wind and rain drove us below deck. Some of us were sick. We were not used to the rolling sea in such a large ship where we could not see the horizon. I joined Ruth on the deck when she could not bear to stay below any longer.

"This is no way to travel, Jack. The children should learn how to travel by canoe like we did instead of being spoiled like lazy White visitors. They would see more from a canoe and it would make them stronger."

"Uncle Shoget is too old to make such a long journey by canoe, Ruth, and Laguksa has pain in her shoulder. The young ones can travel by canoe another time."

"Laguksa! Are you using Tsimshian names now like father does? Perhaps you are getting old, too!" She laughed for the first time that day, but her smile did not last. "Amapaas would want us to go by canoe. His family would not travel on a White ship."

It troubled me that she summoned my brother's ghost so carelessly. Our minds were already filled with too many memories and he had been dead for almost twenty years.

"How do you know what he would want? He would not be young anymore either."

"I know." She looked at me and I saw she was speaking the truth. "He speaks to me in my dreams, Jack. His Spirit follows me. He still calls me Teshlah. I understand why father uses our old names. They are our true names. I could never call Amapaas by a different name."

She paused to wipe the rain from her face. "He asks me to come with him, but I cannot leave. I tell him I need to stay here to look after Caroline. But Caroline will be nineteen this year. She will not need me much longer. What will I say to him then? I miss him, Jack. I want to be with him."

"Caroline will still need you and so will her children, just as we do. You must tell my brother to be patient. When your purpose is finished here you can spend Eternity together." I smiled at her. "You must be getting old too, if you spend your nights talking to Spirits."

She laughed again. "Some days I feel old. But you have made me feel better now. I am sure Amapaas will respect your wisdom. Come! We should warm up inside before we old folks catch a fever."

The ship harboured at Fort Rupert that evening. We went ashore with Uncle Shoget to visit with a Kwakiutl Chief he had known for many years. The old Chief invited us to stay for dinner. They traded news about our two towns. The old Chief told us that many of his people had moved to other villages after the White gun ship shattered their homes fourteen years before. They did not want to live near a White fort anymore. Those who stayed repaired their houses, but they would never trust the Whites again. Everything had healed except the wounds in their hearts.

We met Reverend Hall on our way back to the ship. He was happy to see us and spoke to us like lost friends. He told us his time in Metlakatla had been difficult but the past year in Fort Rupert had been much worse. The Catholic priests before him had left Fort Rupert in frustration and he felt he might soon do the same. He wanted to return to Metlakatla. I pitied him for his loneliness. He was a handsome young man, still not much more than a boy. It was not right that he lived alone so far from his home and family.

The weather was fine and the waters were calm on the final day of our voyage. Only one thing upset us. As we stood on the deck watching the shore, Daniel saw a dead tree that looked like a cross. He teased Caroline and Charlotte that he would ask the captain to stop so they could bring it back to Metlakatla. Charlotte started to weep and ran below deck. Jennifer, Ruth and Laura surrounded him like angry wolves and made him to apologize to the girls. Caroline still would not speak to him for several days. Later, Timothy and I teased him, saying that he should think before he speaks, or he might be sent to Fort Rupert to live with Reverend Hall.

Victoria had grown much larger since I had last seen it. The crowded Indian camp had been replaced by White houses. The Songhee village remained on the west side of the harbour. The harbour itself had more docks. There were four steamships tied up but only one sailing ship anchored in the middle of the harbour.

The dock where we disembarked was noisy with activity. Workers unloaded cargo around us and people waited to greet passengers who were leaving the ship. The children were excited and fascinated with everything around them. They had never seen a harbour like this. Anne bumped into a child of a White family waiting on the dock. They glared at her angrily and pulled their children closer. Anne apologized but they looked away instead of answering her.

We made our way through the crowds to Government Street. It looked nothing like the town I had seen years before. There was no building as large or high as the great church at Metlakatla but the street was impressive. The rows of stores, hotels and offices made walls of brick and stone on both sides of the street for several blocks. Many buildings now had two or three floors and each one was different. Some were wider or taller. Some had large windows or flower boxes. We stared up at them in wonder.

Horses and carriages made lots of noise as they rolled by us in both directions. There were more people walking along the wooden sidewalks too. It was difficult to look around without running into them. We rested with our bags at a street corner while we decided where to go next.

Caroline and Charlotte were excited by the dresses they saw in the shop windows. They pulled the older women over to show them the ones they liked. Timothy was drawn to the carved masks in a curio shop window next door. I remained with the other men at the corner while they waited. Jesse stood beside me and Anne was with him, as she usually was. They asked me what they could do in Victoria and if we could bring horses back to Metlakatla. They competed to see who could ask me the most questions but I never tired of their attention.

"Doolyaks, my good man!" Shoget complained. "You will need to carry me to the nearest toilet if we wait here much longer, and I won't be much fun to carry if I don't make it on time!" Daniel nodded and called to Jennifer. He told her we must go and she collected the others. She could organize women faster than a Chief's wife.

We continued up Government Street another block. Our progress was slow, for the women and children were distracted by every window display. Their cries of delight brought stares from Whites on the sidewalk as they pushed by us. They seemed confused by our brown skin and Indian faces when they heard our good English and saw our fine White clothes.

We needed to find a place to stay. Daniel led us away from Government Street, where the sidewalks were not so busy and there were fewer store windows. I saw the hotel where Tom and I had made love on the floor. I led our group there for it was not fancy and the rooms were not expensive.

Unlike the rest of the town, the lobby had not changed much. The desk clerk looked uncertain as we approached. I feared they still had a policy against Indians, so I mentioned that I had stayed there before with Reverend William Duncan of Metlakatla. She glanced at our faces and our English clothes and said,

"I am sure there will be no problem." She led us to our rooms.

"We are lucky to find five empty rooms in the same hotel," I said.

"Not really," she shrugged. "Most hotels in Victoria are half empty. The steamer from San Francisco goes directly to New Westminster now so we don't get as many visitors. Indians can get rooms in most hotels if they are dressed nicely." She thought about her words and her smile faded. "Please excuse me. I didn't mean to insult you. My name is Marie. I hope you enjoy your stay here." She offered her hand to me. "Perhaps it is easy to find hotels with empty rooms, but I am happy that you found our hotel. We have heard many wonderful things about Metlakatla. Bishop Cridge talks about it all the time. He has told us about your huge cathedral."

I was confused. "Reverend Cridge is a Bishop now?"

"Yes, he has started a new church, the Reformed Episcopal Church, and he is our first Bishop. He didn't get along with Bishop Hills. Not many do. Oh, you must come to our church on Sunday. All my family goes. Bishop Cridge will be so happy to see you. You will be our special guests!"

We agreed to go, but we had two days to pass before then. The next day was Friday and excellent weather for shopping. The men took our furs and Tsangook's carvings to the trading post and then we went with the others to Government Street to spend our money. I bought a beautiful shirt with fine brocades for Tom and a leather belt for myself. In an hour I was finished. I waited with the other men for three more hours until Timothy and the women had finished their shopping.

On Saturday the women were eager to go shopping again but the men complained that they did not want to wait around again. Timothy told us that we must be patient or find something else to do. "In the villages the women must wait for the men when they go hunting, but in the city the men must wait while the women do the hunting." Of course, he went too. I was disappointed that they took Jesse and Anne with them.

Joseph, Daniel and I walked through the streets at the edge of the town to look at the fine houses of the rich English leaders. How far the city had grown in such a short time! We walked several miles before we returned to the hotel. Our lunch with Uncle Shoget was interrupted when the others returned crying and in a panic. They told us that Jesse had been arrested for stealing. My heart sank.

"He didn't take anything. I was with him and I know," Anne moaned. They had been shopping apart from the others when he was arrested. "He was looking at flints. The store manager did not want him to touch anything so he told him to leave. Jesse argued with him and the store manager called the police. He told them Jesse tried to steal a compass but he didn't! He wasn't even looking at them!" She began to wail loudly. Jennifer held her to calm her.

Joseph wanted to go to the police immediately but Uncle Shoget and Daniel stopped him. They said the police would put him in jail too if he made a fuss about Jesse. I suggested that we find Bishop Cridge and ask him to help us. We sought out Marie and she gave us directions to his new church. Timothy stayed with the women. The other men went with me to look for Bishop Cridge.

We found his church easily. I recognized it from our morning walk. A wedding had just finished and the reception was about to begin. Small groups of people were chatting on the lawn in front of the church. I saw Bishop Cridge talking with the bride and groom near the entrance. His hair was white now but he still had the energy of a young man. He recognized me as we approached. He smiled and his eyes sparkled brightly. He came forward to greet us.

"Jack Campbell! Well, by the grace of God! I haven't seen you here for many years. How have you been?"

"I am fine, sir. It is good to see you in Bishop's robes. You look like a great Chief indeed. This is my Uncle Shoget, my mother's brother. Do you remember my friends Klashwaht and Doolyaks? They have Christian names now—Joseph and Daniel."

"Yes, of course I do. It is good to see you both again. It is wonderful that you have Christian names now. I am pleased for you. What brings all of you to Victoria and to our church on such a fine day?"

"We arrived two days ago. We came to see the town and do some shopping. We planned to come to your service tomorrow but we need your help today. We are sorry to trouble you. Can you come with us?"

"What's wrong, Jack?" Bishop Cridge searched our faces with great concern in his eyes. "Is there a problem?"

"Yes, I think so. Do you remember my sister Miyana who I brought to see Klash-waht at the hospital? Her name is Mary now."

"Yes…"

"She is now Joseph's wife and now he is my brother. They have a son named Jesse."

"Yes, yes. That is all wonderful, but is this what you have come to tell me?" Cridge nodded quickly to two guests who passed, then looked back at me.

"No, sir. Their son, my nephew Jesse, has been arrested. The manager of the store told the police he tried to steal something, but he did not. The police have taken him to the jail. We are very worried. He is just a boy of fourteen and he has never been in trouble. We are afraid if we ask them to set him free they will put us in jail too."

"Oh dear God! You are probably correct. I must go with you. Please excuse me for a minute. I must tell my Vicar and the guests that I while be gone for a while." He went inside and we waited. He appeared again before long, still in his Bishop's robes. "We must hurry. The less time he spends in that jail the better."

We followed his quick pace through the streets to the jail house. He went directly to the Sheriff's office next door. The men in the office stopped their work when they saw him approaching in his Bishop's outfit. He recognized the sheriff and asked to have a word with him.

"Sheriff Wilcox, I believe there has been a mistake. You are holding a young lad of fourteen years in your cells, the son of this good man here. They tell me you have charged him with theft although I am told he stole nothing. Is this true?" He looked sternly at the sheriff.

Sheriff Wilcox stood to greet us. "Mr. Huntley says he tried to steal a compass from his store, Bishop Cridge. Do you know the young man?"

"No, not exactly, but I know these fine men and they are good Christians."

"But they were not with him in the store, sir. It's the boy's word against Mr. Hunt-ley's. I'm afraid I cannot just let him go."

"Well you can just go and summon Mr. Huntley then, if you don't mind. I am not leaving here until this is resolved." The Sheriff frowned and signaled to his Deputy to fetch Mr. Huntley. The Sheriff waited with us nervously until the Deputy returned with Mr. Huntley. Huntley was a heavy man with curly blond hair and a red face. He was not happy to be summoned to the jail. He greeted Cridge meekly, bowing his head twice.

Bishop Cridge pointed to Joseph. "Mr. Huntley, you have charged this man's son with theft from your store. What exactly did he steal?"

"A compass, my Lordship."

"Which compass did he steal? What does it look like?"

"One of my best ones, your Lordship." Huntley's face grew redder.

"Did you see him take it with you own eyes? Did he try to leave the store with it? I remind you, Mr. Huntley, that the Lord above is listening." Bishop Cridge searched his face for the truth. Huntley's voice grew soft as he looked down at his feet.

"Not exactly, your Lordship. He put it back on the shelf before I reached him."

"Mr. Huntley, in that case every customer in your store would be a thief. Looking at something and then putting it back is not thievery! You have sent an innocent young boy to jail for looking at your merchandise. How can you explain this?"

Huntley summoned his courage and looked at Cridge. "It was just a matter of time, your Lordship. He would have stolen something. They all do. Pardon my language, sir, but I don't want those dirty bastards coming into my store."

"I will not pardon your language, Mr. Huntley! And I would think twice about harbouring such thoughts if I was you, or you will find St. Peter thinking the exact same thoughts about you when you arrive at Heaven's Gates! Now Sheriff Wilcox, I believe we have heard enough. Please release the boy to his father immediately."

The Sheriff nodded at Cridge and made an angry face at Huntley. He went through a door into the jail house and came back with Jesse a couple minutes later. Jesse looked down at the floor in shame. We were shocked. His beautiful face was bruised and his left eye was swollen. We asked him what happened but he looked away. He seemed ready to cry. Mary pulled him to his chest and hugged him tightly.

"Sheriff Wilcox, why is this boy's face bruised?" Cridge demanded.

The Sheriff looked anxious. "He fell when I was trying to put him in the cell."

"I did not!" Jesse cried. "He tried to make me say that I took something but I wouldn't, so he hit me!"

"Sshhh! Don't shout." Mary tried to comfort him, but Joseph looked as if he was ready to hit the sheriff. Cridge placed a hand on his shoulder and gently pulled him back.

"Mr. Wilcox, you ought to be ashamed of yourself for striking a child like this! Is there more crime in our jails now than on our streets?" Cridge turned to Jesse's parents. "You should take him back to your hotel and see that he is looked after. There is no reason for us to stay here any longer."

Cridge walked with us back to our hotel. We thanked him many times before he returned to his church. The women gathered around Jesse to tend to his bruises. He was glad to be with us again but he shied away from our attentions. We cleaned his cuts but we could not do much to mend his injured pride.

That evening he sat by the fire, watching the flames in silence. It reminded me of his father many years before when he tended our fire at our fishing camp on the Nass. Daniel sat down beside him. He placed his strong arm around Jesse's shoulders and hugged him gently. He stroked Jesse's head and shoulders. My heart raced as I remembered how he had comforted me this way when I was Jesse's age, after he had carried me from my home with the other Cannibal Spirits. How I missed his touch! He was older now and his name had changed but he was still the same Doolyaks I had always loved.

The next day we went to the service in Bishop Cridge's church. He greeted us warmly at the entrance as we arrived. We introduced him to ones in our group he had not already met. He inspected Jesse's eye and gave him encouragement. When the service began he asked his congregation to welcome us. He talked about our great church in Metlakatla and had many good things to say about our people and Mr. Duncan. He reminded them that we had supported him after Bishop Hills had forced him from the Anglican Church. The congregation applauded us and we were humbled.

Cridge invited us to come to his home the next day for tea. He had good news to tell us. Bishop Hills would no longer be our Bishop. The coast from Fort Rupert to Alaska would become the Diocese of Caledonia, and we would soon have our own Bishop.

Uncle Shoget and Daniel were as curious as I was about our new Bishop, for they too were members of the Town Council. Cridge told us that the new Bishop had already arrived in Victoria. He did not know where he was staying but he had learned a few things about him. His name was William Ridley. Cridge said Ridley and Duncan had some things in common besides their Christian names. Ridley had been chosen by the same missionary society that paid Duncan and that he was only a couple years younger. He was not from a rich family like Hills, but from a simple family like Duncan. His father was a stonemason and he had been a carpenter. He knew nothing of Ridley's beliefs but he had a good feeling that the new Bishop and Duncan would get along nicely.

A carpenter like Jesus, I thought. How exciting! Of course he would be better than Hills. I imagined he would work beside us as Duncan always had and that he would listen with his heart as Bishop Bompas had. He would have lots in common with our own carpenters like Tom and Joseph. I was certain he would be pleased by our great church and the other good things we had done, and that he would love us like a father.

How sweet the taste of hope can be, but how cruelly it betrays us! If the great church we built so carefully with all of our love and faith could become the home of an evil Spirit, then why should I expect a bishop who was once a carpenter be good? If I had known the evil Spirit of the Church had led him here, I would not have filled my heart with such fantasies.

Bishop Hills had abandoned his war with Duncan but the evil Spirit had not. Hills only wanted control of Duncan and Metlakatla, but the Spirit hungered for our destruction. It would have us fight each other until all we had built was destroyed. The new Bishop would arrive soon, as the fires of Hell were drawing closer to the ground beneath our feet.

THE FALL OF
METLAKATLA

TWENTY
SEVEN

We left for Metlakatla on a steam ship two days later. Our baggage should have been lighter, but it was not. The women bought an extra trunk so their new dresses would not be crushed in our bags. My bags were packed tightly too. I had bought several picture books of trains and ancient cities and the new shirt for Tom.

We were anxious to tell our friends and families about the new Bishop, but we were disappointed to learn they already knew. Before he had spoken to us, Cridge had sent a letter and Duncan had read it the congregation on the past Sunday. Everyone was excited to meet him and wondered what he would be like. Duncan had not mentioned that he had been a carpenter so I broke the news to Tom and the others in the shops.

Duncan thought I was too hopeful. He had feared an ordained minister might interfere with his work, but a powerful bishop definitely would. Not many bishops are like Bompas, he told me. Maybe Ridley would choose Fort Simpson for his home instead of Metlakatla, but that was unlikely. Reverend Crosby and the Methodists already had their church in Fort Simpson and they would not want him there. More importantly, he would want the great church to suit his great position.

Ridley was in no hurry to meet us. He and his wife stayed with Bishop Hills for three months before coming north. Duncan became anxious as the weeks passed. He was certain Hills would try to turn Ridley's heart against him. Finally, in the second week of October, a letter arrived asking him to come to Victoria to escort the Ridleys to their new home in Metlakatla.

Our congregation wanted to impress them as they had for other visitors. We hung our welcome banner hung over the dock. Our Constables and Church Elders stood proudly in their uniforms beside the Town Council as their ship entered the harbour. Our band and our choir waited on the shore to start playing as soon as the signal was given. Hundreds more stood behind them to welcome the Ridleys.

They stood beside Duncan on the deck as the ship docked. Ridley wore a wide purple hat, which he held on his head with one hand so it would not blow away. He seemed not to notice us. He stared at the steeple of the great church as if the Spirit had captured him and he could not look away. Duncan spoke to Mrs. Ridley as he waved to us. We cheered and waved but the Ridleys did not smile or wave back.

We played "God Save The Queen" as the Ridleys walked down the gangway. They wore expensive city clothes. Duncan followed them, wearing his plain black overcoat and bowler hat, the clothes of a lesser Chief. They stood at the end of the dock waiting for the music to end. Ridley looked around at our faces with a disinterested expression, as if we were trees or rocks instead of people.

The music finished and the Town Council stepped forward to welcome the bishop. A cold autumn wind crossed the dock and brought the first drops of rain. Mrs. Ridley gripped the collar of her overcoat tightly to keep in the warmth. The Bishop stepped forward to shake our hands. He was thinner than Bishop Hills. He had an unpleasant expression and he seemed impatient.

My father's cousin Hahkwah, Henry Richardson, was the first to greet him, for he was Chief of the Town Council. As they shook hands, a mischievous wind caught Ridley's hat and flipped it off his head. He made a small cry and grabbed for it, but it landed in the water beside the dock.

Several boys raced to retrieve it before it sank. The boy who reached it first tried to shake the sea water off. Ridley must have thought he meant to steal it for he shouted at boy, "Give it back!" The boy climbed onto the dock, trembling from the cold water. He bowed to the Bishop and handed him the hat. Ridley snatched it from him without a 'thank you' and shook it off with a show of disgust. He glared at the boy as though he had ruined its shape instead of the sea water.

The wind picked up. It tossed Ridley's hair back and forth. "For Heaven's sake, Mr. Duncan, must we stand like idiots in the cold wind on this Godforsaken dock? Don't you have a proper receiving hall?"

"My apologies, Bishop Ridley. We had hoped for better weather. Would you prefer that we put this off until this evening?"

"That should be obvious," Ridley snapped at him. Duncan turned to the crowd and told us the ceremony would be held that evening in the Assembly Hall instead. He thanked the Town Council, the Constables, the band and all the others for coming to greet them. He chose six youths to carry the Ridleys' luggage, which the ship's crew had stacked on the dock. Then he led the Ridleys through the crowd towards the Mission House along the wettest and muddiest path. The youths followed with their trunks, choosing a drier route instead.

The reception in the Assembly Hall that night went poorly. We had prepared a large feast but the Ridleys chose not to eat with us. They asked that their meals be brought to their room instead. Henry Richardson asked Duncan if they were ill. He said they had told him they did not wish to eat with Indians. Duncan's eyes glowed with satisfaction when Henry gasped in dismay. Duncan clearly did not like them and would not soften the sting of their insults. His loyalty was to us.

After they had eaten, the Ridleys came to the Assembly Hall so that we could welcome the Bishop properly. He stood in his ceremonial robes with his chin raised high as the band played "God Save The Queen" again. The assembly stood and sang along. Duncan introduced him to our Town Council once again. Henry, the Chief of the Council, offered his hand but Ridley looked away and offered the back of his hand instead. Henry hesitated and looked to Duncan with a puzzled expression.

"I see you have not taught them how to properly greet a Bishop, Mr. Duncan."

"I am sorry, sir. Neither Bishop Hills nor Bishop Bompas required them to kiss their hands. He wants you to kiss his ring, Mr. Richardson," he nodded to Henry.

Henry glanced again at Duncan to see if he was joking before he leaned forward to kiss the Bishop's ring.

"Don't touch your lips to my hand, you fool!" Ridley shouted at him and pulled his hand back. Henry's face burned red with embarrassment. "For Heaven's sake Mr. Duncan, can't you show them how to do it properly?"

He held out his hand for Duncan to kiss his ring, but Duncan ignored it. He raised Henry's hand instead and bowed to kiss it as if Henry was the bishop. His lips did not quite touch his finger where the ring should be. He straightened and winked at Hahkwah to ease his embarrassment. Ridley withdrew his hand and glared at Duncan, who did not seem to notice.

"Please continue, Mr. Richardson," Duncan said.

Ridley held out his arm and looked away in indignation. Henry copied Duncan's bow and kiss exactly, then winked at Duncan when he was done. The assembly laughed. Ridley glared at us accusingly, not knowing what he had missed. Once the hall was quiet again, he held his hand out and turned his eyes away as each of us bowed in turn to kiss his ring. After the Town Council was finished, Tom and the other Church Elders did the same.

Then it was Ridley's turn to speak. He did not apologize for rejecting our company at dinner. Instead, he spoke about the good reputation Metlakatla had back in England. He said we had waited many years for an ordained minister to guide us, a man who was properly trained in the Scriptures. Our good work and patience was now rewarded with something no other town on the north coast had, its own bishop. He would make many changes but we should not be concerned. We would thank him for the glory he would bring to Metlakatla and for showing us the proper way to Salvation.

Sparks in Duncan's eyes betrayed his anger as Ridley spoke, but he calmly thanked him for telling us what we could expect. He said that the bishop would soon learn that we were already good, law-abiding people. He pointed to a sign that listed the rules that everyone in Metlakatla had agreed to before the Council permitted them to live with us. He began to explain how the Council and the Church Elders were elected each year and how we made decisions about what was best for our town.

"True Christians would post the Lord's Commandments instead," Ridley interrupted him. He told us no rules were superior to the Lord's and that we would not need a Town Council anymore. He would make all decisions for us. Sounds of surprise and dismay rose through the room. Many voices called out questions but Ridley ignored them. He offered his arm to Mrs. Ridley and they retired to their room without thanking us for their reception.

For a few moments it was quiet but then the questions were asked out again. We needed answers. Who chose this man to be our bishop? Why do we need to obey him? Can we send him back to England? If we must have a bishop, can't we ask Bishop Bompas to be our bishop instead? But mostly, we were worried about our Town Council.

"What are we going to do, Mr. Duncan?" Henry asked. "We have always had Councils of Elders and Chiefs, even before we met White men. He cannot tell us that our concerns do not matter." Many voices called out in agreement.

Duncan's face was stern and determined. He spoke softly with the eyes of a warrior. "Unfortunately, we cannot send him back to England. He will stay here, at least for a while, and we must make a show of trying to please him, but we will do nothing differently if it can be avoided. We will not change how we run our town. He cannot take away what you have built with your own hands if you do not let him. For now, you must trust me and follow what I tell you. If he tries to force us to change we must resist him together as one. He has no power without your support."

◇◇◇◇◇◇◇◇◇◇◇◇◇◇◇◇◇

When Ridley first gazed up at the steeple from the deck of the ship, the Spirit of the Church saw that he had the weak mind of a spoiled child. It captured his thoughts and poisoned his heart from that moment onwards. How else could I explain the cruelty of his actions and the coldness of his heart in the months and years that followed? Our people knew nothing of whisky before White men came and so it was easy for it to enslave us. In the same way, Whites knew nothing about Spirits and they were helpless against the evil ones.

Ridley did not interfere with business of the town at first. He tried to look like a Chief but he did not behave like one. He visited the schoolhouse, the weaving looms and the carpenters shop but he had little interest in common workers. I could not believe he had once been a carpenter himself. He refused to walk the mile to see the saw mill when he saw the road was muddy and filled with puddles. Tom was not disappointed, for he did not want to see him or kiss his ring again.

Bishop Ridley's first demand was that we build a house for him and his wife. He wanted it to be much larger than our houses which many people shared. He wanted a big room on the main floor to welcome important visitors for he said the Assembly Hall was too plain and large. He demanded that it needed to be made of stones and wood from places far away with expensive furniture and lights from Europe. It would cost as much as fifty of our houses but it would only be for the two of them.

Our Council was angry. We had no choice but to reject his demands as we did not have the money to pay for such things. Duncan had worked hard as our leader for many years and he had never asked us to waste money on his glory. He was pleased with our anger. He asked us to show Ridley how little money we had as well as a list what projects we needed the money for.

The Council did not to tell him that we would not build his house. We offered to build the foundation that year, as Duncan suggested, and to provide any materials he needed from Metlakatla. We agreed to pave the paths between his house and other common buildings with stones as he requested, so he would not step in puddles where he walked.

He was not satisfied, but he could not complain loudly when we offered to help him in other ways. He also requested a large chair suitable for a bishop to be placed at the front of the church for him to sit on while Duncan gave his sermons. Duncan referred to it as "Ridley's throne". He suggested to Ridley that our best carver, Timothy, could carve the back and the legs to make it very special. Ridley liked this idea but he had to wait months until the carving was done. Timothy still had to work in the bakery every day.

Ridley sat in a common chair until his throne was finished. He complained that the chair was too hard. Duncan folded a woman's shawl to make a cushion. The congregation smiled for it is unmanly to sit on a woman's shawl, but Ridley was blind to this joke.

Christmas Day approached and the town worked hard to prepare a Christmas feast. The Ridleys ate with us for the first time. They invited Duncan and Mr. Rutland, the White storekeeper, to eat at their table. Duncan refused to sit with them when they insisted on drinking wine. Ridley also insisted on leading the Christmas Eve and morning ceremonies, which upset Duncan further. He performed many rituals we had never seen and he used a strange language we did not understand, so we did not enjoy his services.

Afterwards, Duncan visited each house to give us gifts of tobacco, potatoes and sugar. In past years he had invited us to the Mission House on Christmas Day to receive our gifts but he wanted us to see the gifts were from him and not from Ridley.

The next week Duncan summoned me to his office. He had a favour to ask of me. "Bishop Ridley has asked me to provide him with a servant. I wonder if you would be willing to help him." He watched my face for my reaction. I did not disappoint him.

"What does he want a servant for? If he needs help to make his dinners and do his laundry he should have a woman servant. These things are a woman's work," I complained bitterly. "Besides, I do not like him."

Duncan smiled. "No, I have already found women to help him with his cooking and his cleaning. He needs a man servant to help him dress and to carry his bags when he travels."

"He does not dress himself?" I gasped. "How could a Chief admit to such a weakness? Why will his wife not help him?"

"No, it is just that... well, bishops often have man servants. It is a sign of status."

I felt a deep disgust. "Bishop Cridge said he is the son of a stonemason. He is a commoner. He is not nobility. I am the son of a Chief. He should be my servant first." I blushed with shame for speaking such angry words, but Duncan smiled broadly.

"Of course, Jack. I know you are a finer man than him. But it is no dishonour to serve a bishop, even if his father was only a stonemason. I could ask another man. I could choose someone clumsy and stupid who does not speak English as well as you. That would be better than he deserves, but I need your help for a special reason." He gave me a mischievous smile. "I want you to win his trust, to write his letters and then tell me all of his plans and everything he says and does."

This did not seem like a good idea to me. "If he sees that you know what his plans are when he tries to hide them from you, he will soon know that I am your eyes."

"I promise to be careful. I need to plan strategies that will prevent him from causing a disaster in our town. He is a dangerous man, Jack. I need someone I can trust, someone who is clever and who knows English well."

I agreed to his plan reluctantly. I hated being around Ridley, but it was easier knowing I was secretly Duncan's servant and I was helping to protect our town. The work was easy. I laid out his clothes each day and I helped carry his bags and move heavy things in his home. Sometimes he or his wife sent me on an errand or to fetch or deliver something but most of the time there was nothing to do. That was hardest part of my job.

The Ridleys were like the Tugwells. They did not belong so far from England. They hated the long, dark days of rain that soon followed their arrival. They spent most their days behind their closed door in the Mission House. They ate their meals there too, away from the rest of us. A couple times each day they took short walks to get some air. They spoke to no one if they could avoid it. I held umbrellas over their heads whether it was raining or sunny.

Their two rooms in the Mission House were small and dark. They were unhappy living there. Mrs. Ridley complained that most things were "uncivilized". This time of year spiders would come indoors to find warm, dry places to live, and she hated them. She would scream at me each time she saw one, as if the spiders were my fault. I would chase them and she would scold me if I failed to catch them. When I caught them I carried them outside and let them go. Why should they suffer when they behaved more civilized than she did, I asked myself.

The spiders, the rain and her tedious life without friends kept her in a foul mood most of the time. She frequently complained and argued with Ridley, which would be followed by hours of silence between them. I tried to help them adjust to their new life, if only to make my life easier, but there is not much one can do to comfort those who create their own misery. They reminded me of Uncle Gugweelaks and his wife Pashaleps. Fortunately, the Ridleys were not my family and they wanted to remain strangers.

There was little to report to Duncan. Ridley rarely spoke to me except to give orders. He treated me like a child when he was in a good mood and like a dog when he was not. Sometimes he had me wait by the door while he finished a letter he wanted me to put in the mailbag. I felt pity for his loneliness at times and I tried to talk with him. Once I asked him about a letter he was writing. He was offended. He told it was none of my business and ordered me to wait outside in the rain. I sat quietly and said nothing, out of loyalty to Duncan, though my thoughts screamed loud inside my head.

When he wanted privacy, he sat me in the hallway outside his door with nothing to do. I learned to hate that hallway as much as I hated him. Duncan had taught me the Lord's blessing of hard work and I hated to be idle. I was a healthy man and I wanted to work with others who liked me and needed my help. I tried to think only of happier times when I had been on fishing and hunting trips, but that only made my frustration worse.

I prayed the Ridleys would become so unhappy they would leave Metlakatla. That hopeful thought gave me joy when they argued, but Duncan did not think Ridley would leave. Back in England he would be a commoner's son again, not a bishop, and his status was very important to him. As the winter months passed, their arguments stopped and they grew quiet. Ridley read books or wrote letters and Mrs. Ridley knitted or embroidered. She learned to kill spiders with a cloth without my help.

They had less need of me. I only had to wait on them for two hours every morning and three hours every afternoon. For this I thanked the Heavens. Duncan would not let me help in his office, for he did not want Ridley to become suspicious. Instead he suggested that I help in the bakery, so I would not be too far from the Mission House if the Ridley's needed me. This was a relief, for I could talk to Timothy about my frustrations.

"Is he nice to you?" Timothy asked me.

"No. I don't like him," I answered. "He treats me like a slave. He calls me 'boy' and he never talks to me unless he is giving me orders. His wife has many little things for me to do and all of them are useless. This is not a job for the son of a Chief."

"Maybe he needs a commoner like me," Timothy grinned. "Perhaps if I showed him my talents he would respect me. I am sure he would not call me boy for long." He smoothed out his apron like a beautiful woman who corrects her appearance.

"How could you think of being close with him?" I asked. "He knows nothing about love. His wife has born no children. He is probably a dead fish in bed. He would surely make you cut your hair. Then you would be sorry!"

Timothy laughed. "I am only teasing you. I know that he is not kind. I think you are very brave to accept Duncan's request, but it saddens me to see that awful man steal the smile from your face." He looked at me with such concern that I felt my cheeks blush red. I looked away.

"I know something that will make you smile." He took off his apron and beckoned me to follow. "Come with me. I want to show you something."

"What is it?"

"I must show you." He led me out of the bakery, through the rain to the carpenters' shop where he did his carving. The piece of cedar that he was carving was leaning against the wall. It was for the back of Ridley's "throne" which he would sit on as he listened to Duncan's sermons in the great church. It was finished except for the final polishing. I stared at it in amazement. It was carved as beautifully as a Grand Chief's personal chest.

I was so impressed I used his Tsimshian name. "Tsangook, this is magnificent! It is so beautiful, but how can I smile when I know it is for such an ungrateful man?"

"Watch closely, Little Salmon!" He lifted the back of the chair and turned it upside down. Suddenly the elegant carving looked much different. I saw the image of a large silly mouse with tall ears, big eyes and a wide smile so full of teeth that it stretched from side to side across the back of the chair. I could stop myself from laughing.

"Timothy, you crazy Mahanna, you will be in big trouble when he sees that you have made fun of him!"

"How will he see it? No one else has seen it except you, not even Duncan, and you could not see it until I showed you. When the chair is finished you will need to stand on your head to know that it is there. The Bishop will not do that, and if he did he would only see what he wants to and not what is there. This is our private secret."

Timothy had put a smile back on my face again. When he finished the chair a month later, Duncan presented it to Bishop Ridley in the great church and everyone praised Timothy's carving. No one recognized the joke. Ridley sat on the chair as if he was the most important man in the world. When he caught me smiling at him, he thought he must look good, but I was laughing like the Silly Mouse behind his back.

From that day onwards, Timothy and I called Bishop Ridley "Silly Mouse". I told Tom and Daniel the joke and they told Joseph and John Tatham. Soon half the town knew the joke and called him by that name. Ridley never found out that Silly Mouse was laughing at him. He understood nothing about the world around him. He did not respect us or our rules. He was important to himself but to no one else in the town.

One evening, shortly before the next Christmas, I held his umbrella over his head as we through the town looking for Duncan. We found him in the schoolhouse preparing his lessons. Ridley had come to complain about the supply ship's delivery.

"Mr. Duncan, the bloody quartermaster of our supply ship is totally incompetent. He has forgotten my order and it will take more than a month to receive another order from Victoria. This is intolerable. I want you to do something about it."

"Everything we ordered a month ago came in last week, your Holiness. Nothing was missing." Duncan continued to write his notes without looking up at Ridley.

"That is not true! I ordered a case of wine and it didn't arrive!"

"They didn't forget it. I removed it from the order."

"What are you saying?" Ridley gasped in surprise.

Duncan looked up at him fearlessly. "After you gave your order to Rutland, he brought it to me and I canceled it. There is a rule in Metlakatla that has existed since its beginning that no alcohol of any kind is allowed here. Everyone in Metlakatla must first agree to that rule before the Town Council will permit them to live here. It would not be right to show them that you have no respect for our rules, would it?"

"HOW DARE YOU! Who do you think you are?" Ridley flapped his arms and paced back and forth but seemed uncertain what to do. Duncan returned to writing his notes as though he was alone.

Ridley shook his finger at him. "I will not let you get away with this, Mr. Duncan! I won't stand for it! I am placing that order again and you are not to interfere with it or I'll…" Duncan glared at him. "…I'll have your salary cut in half! I am not here to be told what to do! I am the one who decides what the rules are. Don't you go treating me like one of your… converts!" Ridley glanced at me to see my reaction. I looked away.

"Very well, I will send in your order, your Excellency," Duncan said softly.

"You're damn right you will! And you'll never change my orders again!" Ridley grabbed the umbrella from my hands and he marched into the rain without waiting for me. I had to run to catch him.

Duncan brought Ridley's order for wine to the Town Council the next evening. The Council requested the bishop's presence without saying why. Henry told him that Duncan had brought his order to them to ask permission to bring wine to Metlakatla. The Council had discussed the proposal but they did not agree that he should have exception from the laws of Metlakatla. Henry asked him respectfully to cancel his order.

Ridley told them he would not be told what to do by people who should be taking instruction from him instead. He said that we had better not interfere or he would have the Constables arrest us. The members of the Council looked at each other with surprise.

"The Constables do not work for you, Bishop Ridley. They answer to the Town Council," Henry explained politely.

"Perhaps all of you have a drinking problem but I do not! It is not evil to have a drink of wine. Even Jesus did that! Duncan has put foolish ideas into your heads. His ideas have nothing to do with the Bible. You can't fool me with your silly Christian charade. The only reason the people of this town come to church on Sunday is because the Constables force them to. I have seen them standing guard to keep order at the entrances and sides of the church." Ridley glared at the Council proudly.

The Council was shocked. How could he think such a thing? "The Constables are our friends and family. They wear their uniforms because they are proud to serve Metlakatla. They wear their uniforms to honour God. Many in the congregation have served as Constables too at other times," Henry tried to explain.

"Don't you contradict me! If you interfere with my wine order I will have them arrest all of you. If they refuse to, I will summon Indian Commissioner Powell in Victoria and the Constables will be arrested too!" He turned and left the Council without another word.

The Council decided it was best not to fight Ridley. They could not punish a bishop. They allowed his order for the crate of wine. It arrived four weeks later but the youth who delivered the crate tripped on the doors sill and dropped it. Five bottles were broken. Ridley was furious. He summoned Duncan and accused him of instructing the youth to drop the crate. Duncan told him that was ridiculous for the Town Council had allowed his order and he had respected their wishes. "It was probably just an act of God," he grinned. Ridley was not amused. He called Duncan a liar, but Duncan refused to fight. He turned his attention to the youth who had cut himself on the broken glass.

The struggle over wine started again in the great church the following Sunday. Bishop Ridley interrupted Duncan's sermon. He instructed Duncan to read the story of the Last Supper of Jesus instead. Duncan explained that he had already prepared his sermon, but Ridley shouted at him to do as he was told. Duncan glared at him. Ridley asked him if he was ashamed to read the story of the Last Supper since he had lied to the congregation that it was wrong to drink wine. Duncan opened the Bible and found the story. He began to read it to us.

He reached the part when Jesus tells his Disciples that the bread they are eating is his body and the wine they are drinking is his blood. Bishop Ridley jumped out of his chair and shouted "There!" Duncan stopped reading.

"Jesus not only drank wine himself, but he instructed his Disciples to drink wine too. Mr. Duncan has been telling you that wine is evil and that those who drink it are immoral. Now you see Mr. Duncan thinks Jesus himself is immoral! He thinks he knows more than Jesus. Maybe he thinks he is God and he can rewrite the Bible. I tell you he cannot! Making good wine is an art. Christian monasteries have made wine in the name of God for thousands of years!"

Duncan tried to stop him. "Sir, I never told them drinking wine is a sin..."

"Furthermore, Jesus told the Disciples that the bread they were eating was his body!" Ridley continued. "All proper Anglican churches offer a piece of bread to their congregations after the sermon each Sunday. Those who are willing to be a Disciple of Christ come to accept a piece of bread and they are blessed. This is called Communion. Bishop Hills tells me that Mr. Duncan refuses to teach you this too. This must become a proper Anglican church. We will have a proper Communion after every Sunday sermon starting today. I have brought bread from our bakery for our first Communion. Anyone who wishes to be a true Disciple of Christ can come to the front now to accept the Communion and be blessed."

Duncan's face was red with anger. The congregation was not sure what to do. Some began to rise slowly and move towards the front. Duncan raised his hand and they sat down again.

"HOW DARE YOU!" Ridley screamed at Duncan. He shook his finger at him. "I am not going to forget this. I will teach these people how to be good Christians in spite of you!" He walked the length of the great church angrily. We watched him in silence until he reached the door and slammed it behind him.

Ridley and Duncan did not speak to each other for several days. When they did, they politely tried not to fight. Ridley did not insist on Communion the next Sunday. He did not interrupt Duncan's sermons to contradict him during his service again. They still had disagreements but they argued in Duncan's office instead. I heard every argument, for I still carried the Bishop's umbrella. Duncan always spoke calmly and with reason. Ridley answered him like a father scolding his disobedient son.

Ridley told Duncan he should give his sermons in Tsimshian. Other missionaries taught in the languages of the people they serve, he told him. But Duncan had given up his efforts to translate the Bible many years before. He said it would take too much time to translate it and he was sure his translation would not be accurate. It had been difficult enough to translate our hymns, for we had no written language. He told Ridley we preferred to hear sermons in English because it helped to improve our English. Speaking and hearing English would help us fit in with English society better, he reasoned.

"I think you are kidding yourself, Mr. Duncan. You can teach these people to mimic civilized behaviour but they will always be Indians. They will never fit in with proper English society and they would be unhappy if they tried. You should not fill their heads with false ideas and hopes. They should be encouraged to stay where they belong. They will never appreciate the full meaning of the Lord's teachings but we must help them to understand right and wrong as well as they are able. Surely hearing the gospel in their own language would be a comfort to them even if your translation is not perfect."

Duncan struggled to contain his anger. "How is it that you know so much about these people when you have never spoken with them? Did Bishop Hills tell you these things? He has never spoken with them either. He prefers to woo the upper classes instead, but you won't find any upper classes here, Bishop Ridley. These people are the only Christians who come to our church. I have taught and listened to them for twenty-two years. They were not Christians when I first met them but they are now. Perhaps you should learn how to speak to them before you tell me how I should speak to them."

Their arguments were always much the same. They started calmly and then the tensions between them grew. After several minutes they needed to be apart to let their tempers cool. They defended their opinions without compromising, for fear of losing ground that they would never win back. Still, they had no choice but to deal with each other. Ridley could not manage Metlakatla without Duncan and Duncan could not afford to anger the missionary society who had sent Ridley to us.

TWENTY EIGHT

One day in spring I followed Ridley to Duncan's office. He needed Duncan's help with a special task. The missionary society had asked him to visit to other parts of his Diocese, such as the villages on the Skeena and the Nass and the new mission near the Giksan village of Kispiox where Tomlinson and Collison worked. It was a great distance up the Skeena River, beyond the high mountains and the furthest Tsimshian villages. He wanted to know if Duncan used a boat to visit them.

"Yes, I do. It is called a canoe. Everyone here uses canoes. Ocean canoes are hollowed out logs. They are long and very heavy and seat ten men. You will need a lighter river canoe to visit the villages on the Skeena or the Nass. They are much shorter but big enough to carry you and your supplies."

Ridley stared at him in disbelief. "Surely you don't expect me to paddle up wild rivers like a fur trader!"

"No, I don't. Bishop Bompas does but I believe he is an exception. I am sure I could find men willing to do the paddling for you. I choose to help with the paddling when I travel with others but they won't expect that of you. I didn't paddle either for the first couple years I lived here."

"Good Heavens, you can't tell me there are no steam ships that go beyond Metlakatla! I have seen them pass our channel heading north."

"They go only as far as Fort Simpson. It is another eight to ten hours by canoe from there to the mouth of the Nass, depending on the wind. You might find a ship for hire to take you to the bay at the mouth of the Nass, but they cannot go further up the river. Some ships stop at the salmon cannery in Port Essington on their way south. It's up the Skeena about an hour, but you will need a canoe to continue further from there."

"Surely we could hire a boat, couldn't we?" Ridley whined.

"There are no steam ships for hire on either river. Everyone travels by canoe. There is no other choice. It can be quite pleasant actually, once you get used to it, provided that it isn't raining or windy."

"Impossible! You can't expect me to travel by canoe. It isn't dignified!" Bishop Ridley's voice was rising with his fear.

"I don't expect you to do anything. It is the missionary society that expects you to visit your Diocese. It is not impossible. Two years ago Bishop Bompas of Athabasca traveled in a canoe for six weeks over three mountain ranges and hundreds of miles of wild rivers to visit Metlakatla. He did the whole journey there and back alone. He camped and made his own meals along the way. The people here still tell stories about his bravery."

Duncan watched Ridley's face turn pale with fear. This was the first conversation with the bishop that he enjoyed. He pretended to be sympathetic. "I understand your concerns, Your Excellency. It's a big task. You have been given a very large and wild Diocese. Most of the villages you need to visit are great distances up fast-moving rivers that few White men have ever seen. I don't envy you. I know I could never do it!"

"What are you saying? Surely, you are not going to leave me to do this alone. You must be my guide! I don't speak the language and I would never find my way!" Ridley's voice squealed with panic.

"I'm afraid I wouldn't be much use to you. I have only visited a few villages near the mouths of each river. I don't know the territories beyond. I have no idea what dangers you will encounter further upstream. I am getting too old for such adventures anyway. And I can't translate for you. I can barely speak a sentence in Nishga and I don't know a word of Giksan. Besides, I can't leave Metlakatla unattended. I am sure you heard what happened the last time I did."

"I couldn't possibly make such a trip without a steam boat. I caught a fever doing missionary work in India ten years ago and I have had a serious breakdown from working beyond my strength since then. My doctor in England has warned me it could happen again." Ridley sounded like a child on the verge of crying.

"Then you'll need to write to the missionary society to ask what you must do." Duncan was tired of Ridley's complaining. He had always faced these problems himself without asking for help.

Ridley said no more about the boat, but he wanted Duncan to offer him help in other ways. "A missionary is one thing, but a bishop should not be expected to write his own letters like a common secretary. I need a scribe," he demanded.

"Jack can assist. His English is excellent. He has taken several letters for me."

Ridley looked at me with surprise. "You can write English?"

"Yes, Your Excellency. Mr. Duncan has taught me English for twenty years."

"That is more schooling than most English lads receive," Duncan added.

Ridley was suspicious of my abilities but when he saw how well I wrote, he was pleased. He dictated a letter to the missionary society, asking for more money to build a proper bishop's mansion. He lied to them, saying that Duncan and our people were not willing to spend any money on his needs. He complained that our primitive houses and furniture were not worthy of a bishop. He said nothing of the beautiful chair that Timothy had carved for him. His words angered me, but I wrote them down just as he spoke them and I said nothing.

He also asked them for extra money to pay for a steamship. He told them using a canoe would be savage and undignified and would cause too much strain on his nerves. Canoes were unsafe, he insisted, for they tipped easily and he feared he would drown in strong rapids or be washed ashore and eaten by wild bears.

He had never been in a canoe and his fears about bears were ridiculous. "Bears do not eat men," I told him. "They usually run away when we come near them."

"Well they don't know that at the missionary society, do they?" he snarled.

"And we are very skilled with canoes. We do not tip them in the rivers," I added.

"Don't contradict me! Just write what I tell you to or I will have you punished!" There was no point in correcting him. He was not concerned about telling the truth.

Ridley began to interfere more and more with Duncan's work and the business of the town over the following months. He wanted to force Duncan to follow his orders, but Duncan was clever. Bishop Hills had told Ridley that Duncan did not like decoration in the church, so Ridley ordered him to add more decorations. He wanted the ceiling and the upper walls painted, but Duncan told him that work was too high up and dangerous for us to do. He wanted the windows replaced with coloured glass but that was too expensive. Ridley then asked that the beams be carved. Duncan lied to him, saying Timothy was the only carver in Metlakatla and it would take years for him to do the carving by himself.

When Ridley persisted, Duncan pretended to like his ideas. If we could not afford coloured glass, he wanted us to hang tapestries on the walls instead. Duncan said that was a wonderful inspiration. During his sermon the next Sunday, he complimented Ridley for his idea and asked the congregation to accept it. Ridley glowed with self-importance. Then Duncan suggested that we could hang weavings made by the women of the town. The congregation was thrilled but Ridley was shocked and indignant. He wanted fine tapestries from Europe instead. Duncan asked the congregation which we would prefer. We cheered loudly for our own tapestries and Ridley stomped out of the church angrily before the cheering had stopped.

The winter changed to spring and the spring into summer, but the ice between Duncan and Ridley did not thaw. Duncan gained a new ally instead. The missionary society sent a carpenter named George Sneath to live with us. He came alone, but he made friends with us easily. He was a tall man with wide shoulders, strong arms and he always wore a handsome smile.

Sneath had worked with Black-skinned people at a mission in Africa for three years before he came to Metlakatla. He had heard many good stories about our town from such a great distance, but the stories did not tell of all the wonderful things we had created. He was impressed by the beauty of our harbour, by the great church, the saw mill and our large carpentry shop. He was delighted when he heard of our brass band and choir too, for I am sure they were the best in British Columbia.

Sneath admired Duncan greatly and praised his work many times in front of others. Ridley turned against him when he heard him praise Duncan. He asked Sneath to repair things and then he insulted and criticized his work in front of others. Sneath became upset and unhappy working with us in Metlakatla. The Collisons left Kispiox that summer to return to Haida Gwaii. They took George Sneath with them. We never saw him again. Two years later he left Haida Gwaii to work with a church in the United States, far south of Victoria.

Duncan was furious when Sneath left, but Ridley was neither frightened nor satisfied. He wanted Duncan to leave too. That summer the missionary society sent the money to pay for Ridley's expensive new house and they approved his suggestions for pay for the missionary staff. Ridley had the highest wage. Tomlinson and Collison had half his pay. Hall and Schutt had even less, but Duncan was given the pay of the lowest servants. Nothing could thaw his hatred for Ridley after that.

They also gave Ridley the money to buy a new steamship. He booked passage for himself, Mrs. Ridley and me to go to Victoria to receive it. Tom was upset that I was going. This would be my second visit to Victoria without him. I had no choice. I did not want to leave him either, especially as a servant to such unpleasant company.

I was miserable. I waited on the Ridleys from morning until night. I had no friends or family to keep me company. It was shorter that my other trips but the days passed so slowly. I missed Tom greatly but the Ridleys did not care about my needs or how much trouble they had caused for me.

Bishop Hills and his wife met us at the dock when we arrived in Victoria. They were the Ridleys' only friends outside of England and they enjoyed each other's company immensely. When they were together they chatted endlessly like children. Their favourite topic was their common hatred for Duncan and Bishop Cridge. They told lies to delight each other. Ridley told Hills that Duncan mistreated our people and that we liked him better. I stayed quiet and listened. They did not seem to notice me. Hills did not realize he had met me before and the Ridleys never thought to introduce me.

Three days later we returned to Metlakatla on Ridley's new steamship, the Evangeline. Bishop Hills had invited members of his church to gather on the dock to watch the ship be launched. Ridley spoke down to them from the deck of the ship, boasting that he would use this ship to set up new Anglican missions along the Skeena before other churches arrived. The crowd on the dock cheered. Mrs. Hills broke a bottle of champagne over the bow to christen it and they cheered again.

The Evangeline was larger than the Carolena and it had an engine. It only needed five workers as crew, for it was a steamship. It had sails for extra speed on the open sea but most of our trip followed passages between islands and through Tsamsem's Trench. The ship's engine was weaker than most steamships so it took six days to reach Metlakatla.

Ridley frequently mentioned his dislike for ships but he was proud of the Evangeline because it was his. He stood at the bow in his Bishop's robes for all to see as though he was its Holy captain. I stood beside him, holding his parasol to protect him from the sun. He watched the passing shores and waved at anyone who saw him. Sailors gathered along the gunwales of ships that passed us heading south. They waved and shouted greetings. When they were far enough behind us they began to talk. I could not hear their words but I heard the laughter that followed.

The crew of the Evangeline listened respectfully when Ridley spoke to them but most of the time they worked as if he was not there. I enjoyed watching them work whenever I could. The Captain was a quiet man named John Tavish. His curly black hair was sprinkled with silver. He nodded and greeted us but he never spoke more unless he had to. If he had to, he spoke softly and his answers and instructions were always short.

The others did not speak much either, except to each other. The three youngest chatted when they worked or rested together, but only when the Ridleys were not close enough to hear them. They had friendly smiles, but they talked mostly about women, drinking and fighting so I left them alone.

The First Mate was the only one who was friendly to me. He had orange hair that reminded me the clerk at the trading post in Fort Simpson who taught me my first English word, "button", but this man was younger and more handsome. His body was strong and swift and he was well-liked by the crew. The Captain gave his instructions to him and he instructed the other three. He joked with the crew and showed them how to do things, but he never stayed when they started talking about women. I liked him and wanted to meet him.

He twice caught me staring at him before I could look away. The second time he smiled at me. His beautiful smile sparkled like sunshine. I did not want to get in trouble so I only glanced at him after that. Once I caught him watching me. He did not look away and that made me more uneasy. I ached with loneliness and I wished that Tom was not so far away.

On the third morning, just after we had left Fort Rupert, I went up on deck to watch the morning sun on the mountaintops. The air was still and cool. A family of blackfish passed our ship heading north, swimming strongly and churning the water with their high dorsal fins.

The First Mate startled me. "They are beautiful, eh? It is amazing how fast they can move." He had come from behind and he was standing at the gunwale beside me. He smiled when he saw my surprise. His blue eyes sparkled in the light of the morning sky.

"Yes. Sometimes my people hunt them but they are too fast for our canoes. We can only catch them when their curiosity brings them back to us. They are very clever and they know that we are too."

"It's a pity then that we kill them, isn't it? The English call them 'killer whales' but the real killers are us men."

"Yes, I suppose." I had never considered this. He said "we". I wondered if he killed them too, or was it possible that he thought of Indians and Whites as equals? His unusual comment helped me to overcome my shyness.

"Do you hunt them too?" I asked him.

"No, but my people have killed thousands of the great whales. They are intelligent beasts too, though most of them are gone now."

"Your people must have great appetites to eat so many whales!"

"I'm afraid we didn't eat them," he sighed. "We killed them for their fat and left their meat to rot on the shores. We used their fat for the oils. Our appetite was for other goods we could purchase with the oils. Now that most of the whales are gone we are poor again. We travel to find other work."

"That is a shame. The Animal Spirits teach us not to waste the food we kill, or they will not be reborn. Are you working on this ship because the whales are gone?"

"To earn a living, yes, and to see the other side of the world. I was never a whaler, though my father and my grandfather were."

"Are you Irish?" I asked.

"Heavens, no, I'm Scottish!" He laughed again at hearing his own words. "I don't suppose it makes much difference to you though!" His eyes fixed on mine again and he smiled. He said nothing for a few seconds. My heart beat faster and the blood rushed to my face. I looked down at the darkness of the water that churned with invisible currents like the blood in my veins.

"I'm sorry! Please excuse me! My name is Stuart Sutherland." He held his hand out towards me and gave me another broad smile.

"Pleased to meet you. I am Jack Campbell," I smiled back at him, still blushing.

"Campbell! Now that's a good Scottish name!" Stuart laughed. I laughed too, though I felt foolish to be using a name that belonged his people.

"Of course it was not my Tsimshian name. I think Scottish names are beautiful. I am told that Scotland has mountains and canyons and weather much like our own."

"Yes, it's true, but it's not as great or as beautiful as this coast. What is your Tsimshian name? You are Tsimshian, aren't you?" I was surprised that he guessed this.

"Yes, I am. My name is Gugweelaks. It means the sun that sparkles on the water."

"Now that is a bonny name! As beautiful as this morning. As beautiful as the man who owns it." He smiled at me again, a fearless smile that shone with love and respect. His smile chased the loneliness from my heart and filled me with joy. I returned his smile, and I did not look away this time. I longed to hold him in my arms and kiss his mouth.

"Boy!" Bishop Ridley barked at me from the doorway. "Have you forgotten your duties again? The Mrs. and I are waiting for our breakfast. Are we expected to starve while you laze around on deck with the crew? Get a move on!"

With his first word, my beautiful feelings turned to rage.

"I am coming!" I shouted back, but I did not look at him. I did not want him to see the hatred in my eyes.

I wanted to apologize to Stuart for my anger. I expected to see pity in his eyes, but what I saw was his shock and anger. He was prepared to defend me like a brother or a lover. When I saw that he needed only a signal from me, my anger disappeared.

"Please excuse me, Stuart. His Excellency does not know how to feed himself." I winked at him and smiled. His anger faded too and he smiled back. His eyes followed me as I left the deck.

The rest of the trip passed quickly as the Evangeline approached Metlakatla. I met Stuart's eyes secretly many times as we passed through Tsamsem's Trench but we had no chance to speak alone. I wished I could sit by a campfire with him as I once had done with Tom, but I was afraid to be alone with him too. I had never been unfaithful to Tom. I prayed to reach the end of our trip without any further temptations.

It was late August when the Evangeline arrived in Metlakatla. Ridley wanted to leave for the upper Skeena the same week, before the first frosts turned the leaves of the bushes to red and gold and the North Wind brought the first winter snows. He told the crew to fill the hold with wood and supplies for Tomlinson's new mission at Kispiox, supplies that Tomlinson had asked for in his letters to Duncan. We also carried on chests full of Ridley's ceremonial clothes and Mrs. Ridley's dresses. He wanted to impress the Tsimshians in the villages on the Skeena with his fine clothes. He did not know the villages had heard many stories about him from their relatives in Metlakatla. They had not yet met him, but they knew he was a fool.

I had told Duncan how Ridley had lied to Bishop Hills, saying we liked Ridley more than him. Duncan told me my news was important to him. It proved that Ridley could not be trusted and that I needed to stay with him.

Tom was furious that I was leaving again so soon. He wanted me to tell Duncan that I would not go, but I told him Duncan needed me to go. That only made him jealous that Duncan needed me more than him. Tom said our trip was stupid anyway. He said anyone could see that the Evangeline was too weak to fight the currents of the Skeena. He said a steamship that was strong enough would have a hull that was too deep for such a shallow river. I prayed that he was right.

When we were ready to leave, Ridley told us to ring the church bell to call the town to a prayer meeting at the dock. He stood on the deck in his Bishop's robes and spoke to the people who gathered. He said he would spread the Lord's Gospel and the glory of Metlakatla to the villages on the Skeena and that we would become famous. He asked us to bow our heads and ask the Lord to help the people of the Skeena become good people like the Christians of Metlakatla. We looked at each other in disbelief. Did he not know that most people in Metlakatla had come from the villages on the Skeena?

Stuart Sutherland was delighted that I would be on another trip with him so soon after we landed. He sought out my company whenever he could and did not hide his interest in me from the others. He was even friendly to the Ridleys so that he might be near me when I was with them. The others seemed puzzled by his attentions at first but they did not seem to mind. I lost my fear of being with him. His company was much more pleasant than being alone, and much more welcoming than Tom's angry pouts.

We did not make it far the first day. The winds on the sea grew strong while the Ridleys fussed over their baggage and we listened to the bishop's lengthy and tiresome speech. An hour beyond the harbour Mrs. Ridley fell ill from the motion of the sea. We reached the Skeena and docked at the cannery in Port Essington in the afternoon. We stayed there for the remainder of the day.

The Manager of the cannery invited Ridley to speak to the workers that evening. I copied Duncan's habit of counting crowds. Fewer than a hundred men stayed after dinner to hear him speak. Mrs. Ridley sat at the front of the room facing him from the side. Stuart sat beside me near the front. Captain John Tavish sat near the back but I did not see the other three crew of the Evangeline.

Ridley did not seem to notice. He said the glory of God had brought him to Metlakatla and he congratulated the audience for finally having their own bishop. He said he had been sent to bless us, to correct Duncan's mistakes and to expand the Anglican faith up the Skeena River. He said God had provided him with his lovely new ship, the Evangeline, to help him achieve this purpose. He told us that the next morning he would begin his historic mission and that someday we would tell our grandchildren about his wonderful work. He led us in a prayer to bless his mission with success.

His speech did little to excite the cannery workers. They were polite but they did not applaud much when he was finished. Ridley was pleased with his speech but he commented that the men there were not good Christians. He refused the Manager's invitation to stay on shore longer. He announced with a tone of disgust that he and Mrs. Ridley would retire to the ship for the rest of the evening.

Stuart and I stayed on the dock long after the last light had left the mountaintops and faded from the western sky. We felt at peace. In the darkness our skins were the same colour and our friendship was no longer suspicious. I asked him many questions about his travels. He held my attention with his stories and the beauty of his Scottish accent. He had been to many different places in the world. I questioned him about India. He had been there, though he did not like it much. He said it was too hot and smelly.

"Do the Indians there look like us?" I asked, hoping he would say yes. "Duncan says the English call us Indians because we look the same."

"Hmmm, perhaps to ignorant Englishmen who didn't know any better. I can't say I see much of a resemblance."

I changed the subject to hide my disappointment. "Do you miss your home in Scotland?"

"Aye, I miss the heather on the mountains and the places I played when I was young. I miss my mother and my grandparents too. I don't miss the rest of my family though. My father hated me and we fought like dogs. I was the oldest. I left home when I was fifteen. My brothers were too young to remember me well. That was seventeen years ago. I haven't seen them since. They will be young men by now."

The heaviness of his words placed a silence between us. He was thinking about his family. I wanted to comfort him, to hold him close to me, but I dared not move. My concern was mixed with desire. I stayed very still with my eyes closed. I felt the heat of his arm so close to mine.

"Where is your family?" he asked, to break the silence.

"My brother and sister live in Metlakatla with their families. My oldest brother was murdered when I was eighteen. My parents died with the Smallpox three years later. They did not make it to Metlakatla in time." Now the sadness of my own words silenced us. I had not mentioned Amapaas or my parents for several years.

"Jack, I am so sorry... I didn't mean to upset you." He placed his hand on my shoulder and moved closer to me. I pulled away for I did not want to cry.

"Excuse me. I am all right," I said softly after a few seconds. "My people do not talk about the Smallpox often, for we have all lost many of our families and friends. We do not want to awaken their ghosts and renew their suffering."

"I'm so sorry. What I meant was... well, do you have a wife and children?"

The question surprised me. I saw it was the same question he had asked before. I hesitated, for I had never been asked this before. "I don't have a wife or children, only..." I stopped for I did not want to tell Stuart about Tom. "I only have my nephews and nieces. Do you have children?"

"No, I've never married. I don't think I want a wife or children. Just as well, I suppose. I wouldn't make much of a father the way I travel around." A silence fell between us again. I did not know if he would say more or if he wanted me to say that I did not want a family either, but we said nothing more. A wind came off the water and we trembled in its chill. We agreed it was time to go aboard the ship. We said good night and returned to our separate beds to dream alone.

The Evangeline left Port Essington early the next morning. Ridley announced his departure to the Manager. He had us wait several minutes for the workers to stop and gather on the dock, but no one came. Finally, in frustration, he told Captain Tavish to start the engines. He said they would regret missing his historic departure, but he could not wait all day.

The morning had brought us fine weather. Ridley was as excited as a child as the ship pulled away from the cannery. He told me to bring two chairs onto the deck so he and Mrs. Ridley could watch the journey up the Skeena. He had me stand behind them and hold his parasol to protect them from the sun. He pointed to things that excited him and made several comments to Mrs. Ridley. She nodded in agreement but said very little.

The Skeena is two miles wide at Port Essington. It looked very large that day for the tide was high. It hid the many sand bars that made the river look much smaller when the tide was out.

"Boy, what is that over there?" Ridley asked me.

"My name is Jack, your Excellency."

"Yes, of course, but what's that!" He shook his finger at a village on the far shore.

"That is the village of Gitsees. It is the first Tsimshian village on the Skeena."

"Tavish!" he shouted at the Captain who was at the wheel behind us. "Can we stop at that village over there? I need to present myself."

"I doubt it, sir. The waters are likely quite shallow near the shore. I have been advised by the Manager of the cannery to stay in the main current where the river is deepest. They do not have a proper dock anyway. We would need to use a canoe to go ashore."

"That's ridiculous! How can we visit villages along the route if none of them have proper docks? What good is this boat then? Will we be expected to swim ashore each time we stop?"

"I'm not sure, sir. We'll have to cross that bridge when we come to it."

Bishop Ridley looked back at the currents of the river. His face filled with alarm for a minute as he thought about this problem. Then he relaxed again and returned to looking at the passing scenery.

"Oh good Lord! Look, there's another village over there, on the other side!"

"That's the village of Gitsacatl," I told him.

"My goodness, we've just got started. There must be hundreds of villages along the river. Do you know all their names, Jack?"

"There are nine Tsimshian villages on the Skeena. I have only visited these two.

The others are many hours or days up the river. Beyond them there are the villages of the Giksan."

"This is marvelous! I feel like a great explorer! These are all new lands. Even Duncan has never seen them. Every mile we pass is adding to my territory!" He stood up, cupped his hands around his mouth and he shouted up the valley. "I claim these lands in the name of the Church of England!"

The river bent to the right. We passed salmon camps on either side. I had never seen them at this time of year when they were empty. The valley was so much more beautiful without the smoke of our fires. I watched our camp as we passed by but I did not draw attention to it. I was not able to go to the camp this year, for I had to serve Bishop Ridley. I felt sadness and anger rise in my breast. I was afraid that if he stood to claim our camp for the Church of England I would throw him into the river myself.

The river changed. It narrowed after we passed the first islands. It bent to the left around a tall mountain that stood in its path. I had never been beyond this point. Here the current was stronger and the mountains were close on both sides. They formed a high canyon that left us in shadow. The canyon walls opened again as we passed the mountain, but now a large island broke the river into two narrow channels. We entered the south channel but the current was too strong. Captain Tavish let it carry the Evangeline backwards out of the channel so we could cross to the north side.

The north channel was calmer but it was also shallow. The ship scraped the bottom twice as it struggled against the current. Stuart shouted orders to the crew as they tried to push the boat away from the rocks with long poles. The Ridleys stood in panic and demanded that Tavish do something. He told them to stay out of the way. They clung to the sides of the cabin as Ridley shouted a prayer to God to save them. Tavish lost his patience and threatened to send below if they were not quiet.

Finally we were past the island and the channel widened. The current was gentle again but the Ridleys and Captain Tavish were still upset with each other. Tavish warned them not to interfere again or he would turn the ship around and return to Port Essington. He had just won their cooperation when we saw another island blocking our path. This time the north channel had most of the water and the current was much stronger than before. The south channel was clearly too shallow for our ship.

"I'm afraid we can't go any further, sir," Captain Tavish told the Bishop.

Ridley stared at him in disbelief. "What are you saying? You cannot stop here! We have barely started. We've only been on the river three hours. I have told everyone that I am going all the way to Kispiox and I demand that you take me there."

"And how can I do that in this ship? It can't beat the current on the north side and it will likely get stuck in the south channel or hit rocks and sink. Is that what you want? There just isn't enough water on this side."

"So we must go next spring when the river is deeper!"

"Then the current will be stronger. This just isn't the right boat for this river, sir. It isn't strong enough."

Captain Tavish finally convinced Ridley. He turned the ship around and we rode the current back downstream. We reached Port Essington in afternoon. Workers began to gather on the dock to watch our approach. Ridley saw them smiling and laughing at us, so he ordered Tavish to take us directly to Metlakatla. He did not want to face the cannery workers after his speech the day before.

The Evangeline reached Metlakatla just before dinner. Word of our arrival spread quickly and a crowd had gathered on the dock before we stepped off the ship. Duncan was the first to greet us. He was delighted that Ridley had failed. He gave him false words of sympathy, while struggling to hide his smile. He asked with exaggerated concern what Ridley would say to the missionary society who had paid for his boat. He said they would probably want to know how Tomlinson made it all the way to Kispiox twice, and how Bishop Bompas could do it alone without any help.

"Shut up, you idiot!" Ridley screamed at him in front of all of us. "Just shut up!"

"But I am not the one who looks like an idiot now, am I?" Duncan laughed.

Tom was waiting on the dock too. He too was pleased the Evangeline had failed as he had predicted, and even happier I was back so soon. I gave him a strong hug. He helped me unload the supplies and we carried them to the stockroom. When we were safely inside I told him about Ridley's silly speech to the men at the cannery and about his panic on the boat when we were on the Skeena. We laughed about Ridley's fight with Duncan on the dock. Then he stopped and looked into my eyes.

"I missed you," he told me. "I want you to stay here with me."

"I will," I promised him. "It is too late in the season to travel again. Besides, I don't think the Bishop will use that boat again next year." We laughed again. Then he embraced me tightly with his strong arms and he kissed me with great passion.

The door of the stockroom opened with a creak. We pulled apart but it was too late. Stuart was standing inside the door. His arms were filled with supplies from the ship and his mouth was open in surprise. A look of pain crossed his face, and he looked down at the floor.

"Excuse me," he apologized. He set the supplies down quickly and left.

Tom was alarmed. He pushed me away. "What will we do now? He will tell

Duncan."

"No, he is my friend. He will keep our secret. Wait here. I will find him." I ran back to the ship. I found Stuart sitting on a crate in the hold. He looked up at me and I saw sadness and pain on his face. I felt helpless and ashamed. I could not speak. I stood silently for some time. I was afraid I would lose him, though he was not mine and I could never have him.

"Is he your lover?" he finally asked me.

"Yes," I nodded.

"Have you known him long?"

"Since I was sixteen. He has been my only lover." He nodded and stared at the floor. I sat on a crate across from him. "I am sorry, Stuart. Are you angry with me?"

"No, I'm not angry. Why shouldn't a wonderful man like you have a lover? I am disappointed, and envious, but I am not angry." He reached across to hold my hands. "I will be fine. I want to be your friend. It is not easy to find men who need a man's love. Perhaps it is easier for your people to understand such a love. I have searched for a long time. It is not an easy burden, especially when I meet someone as fine as you."

"Once it was easier, before the missionaries came." This made both of us laugh. Stuart's eyes sparkled as he smiled at me. Then we heard the footsteps of his crew on the deck above us. We stood up quickly. He grabbed a sack of rice and handed it to me as they climbed down into the hold.

"I think we should take the food back to the store first," he said as he winked at me. I left him to go to the store and then to find Tom. I never had another chance to speak with him alone. I spent the next few days with Tom. The following week, Bishop Ridley sold the Evangeline to a buyer in Fort Simpson for half of what it had cost to make. Stuart and the crew left with the ship before I could say goodbye.

I was relieved that Ridley's trip up the Skeena had failed. I needed to be near Tom. I had not betrayed him but my attraction to Stuart filled me with a secret guilt. I was sweeter to Tom because of it and he responded in kind. I felt reassured.

TWENTY NINE

The cannery at Port Essington was on everyone's mind that fall. After a poor salmon catch in June, many men in town worked there to feed their families. My brother George was one of them, although he was upset to leave Gertie and his three girls. The White fishing boats with their big nets brought in so many fish that he worked long hours every day that September. He had no time to visit his family. Tom and I helped Gertie whenever we could. The two oldest girls, Karen and Linda, were thirteen and eleven so they shared in the work, but the youngest, Josephine, was only eight and she kept us busy by getting into trouble.

There was an emptiness in our town we were not used to with most of the men gone. It lasted longer than the fishing camps and husbands were separated from their wives. The saw mill had few workers for Tom to supervise, and there were fewer carpenters in the workshops too. No new buildings were being built. Everyone said things would go back to normal once the men returned, but more salmon disappeared each year. I feared this emptiness would be our future.

Duncan saw our families were being torn apart and he was afraid that our town would suffer. His decided we should build our own cannery so our men could stay with their families. We agreed with his idea and began collecting money to pay for it. He asked Senator MacDougall, his business agent in Victoria, to borrow six thousand dollars to purchase a steam ship for a cannery. He promised to have the money for the cannery by the time the ship was built.

Ridley believed Duncan should teach us more about God's word if he wanted us to be happier instead of concerning himself about the business of the town. He thought the cannery would be a waste of money. He was blind to our suffering. He only cared about stopping Duncan's plan.

He dictated a letter to me to send to the missionary society in England, asking them not to pay for the cannery. He asked them to spend their money on new missions up the Skeena instead. Duncan should have started new missions earlier, he told them, but he also blamed them for not sending more missionaries. He did not blame himself for wasting their money on the Evangeline or for not visiting the villages along the Skeena as they had asked him to do. He blamed everyone else for his failure. He even accused them in his letter of not giving him enough money to buy a stronger boat, though they had given him all money he had asked for.

I told Duncan what Ridley put in his letter. Duncan did not want the missionary society to take away the money we had raised for the cannery, so he dictated a letter to me telling them that the town might starve or fall apart without the cannery. He asked the Town Council and the families of the men who were working in Port Essington to write letters to England too. And so the war of letters began and I was the scribe for both sides.

At the end of September, a trader from Kitsumgalum on the upper Skeena stayed two nights in Metlakatla on his way to Haida Gwaii. He told Ridley that he had four acres that would be a perfect place to build a mission. Ridley bought the land with the Church's money, without telling Duncan or waiting for an answer from England.

Ridley boasted of what he had done and Duncan was furious. He wrote another letter to the society, complaining that Ridley did not value their counsel enough to wait for their response. He said Ridley had paid a ridiculous sum for a piece of land without seeing it and there were no missionaries to start the new mission there. The land he had bought would lie empty.

A letter from the missionary society arrived in November. They were not happy with the price that Ridley had paid for the land, which pleased Duncan, but they were not sure if they should spend church money on a cannery instead of new missions. They said they would discuss it and send their answer before spring.

The delay frustrated both Duncan and Ridley. They proceeded with their plans without waiting for the decision from England. Duncan asked the congregation to write to Indian Commissioner Powell to support of a cannery, and he wrote a letter to Powell as well. Ridley sent letters to Bishop Hills in Victoria, Tomlinson in Kispiox and other church leaders pleading for them to send someone to help start the mission in Kitsumgalum.

As I expected, Tomlinson supported Duncan's plan instead of Ridley's. Ridley reacted with shock and anger. He strode back and forth across his office, slapping Tomlinson's letter against the furniture and accusing him of insubordination. He did not wait until he was calm before dictating his reply. He accused him of going too far up the Skeena to start a mission at Kispiox, allowing other churches to set up missions in Tsimshian villages further downstream. He ordered him to come to Kitsumgalum to start the new mission or he would cut off supplies to Kispiox.

Tomlinson was the only man I knew who had a temper worse than Duncan's. He did not answer Ridley. Instead, he left immediately for England to ask the missionary society to support his mission in Kispiox. The Collisons were upset that Tomlinson left without speaking with them first. Collison was ordained so he had no choice but to follow Ridley's orders. He abandoned the mission in Kispiox and left for Kitsumgalum.

It was snowing in late October when the Collisons arrived in Kitsumgalum. They wintered in a simple shelter with only a small fire to protect them from the bitter cold. They left Tomlinson's wife Alice and their newborn daughter in Kispiox without enough wood or food supplies. They were all lucky to survive. The Tomlinsons and Collisons never forgave each other for the terrible discomforts they endured that winter, but Ridley had caused their suffering, Ridley and the Spirit of the Church.

Duncan supported the mission in Kispiox and Ridley wanted to shut it down, but the missionary society wanted to meet with Tomlinson first. We waited through the winter rains and darkness for news of their decision. Their reply arrived with Tomlinson on a ship from Victoria in February. He beamed with pride as he stepped onto our dock. The missionary society told him to continue his mission at Kispiox and they would send someone else from England to set up the mission at Kitsumgalum. The Collisons could return to Kispiox as soon as the new missionary arrived.

They also decided in favour of our cannery, but we lost in another way. They decided that Metlakatla should be governed by committee made up of Tomlinson, Collison, Schutt, Duncan, Hall and Bishop Ridley. Ridley would be the Head of the committee but each man would have an equal vote. Duncan would handle finances and make the town's business decisions. Their letter expressed hope that this arrangement would allow everyone work together.

It did not work, of course. Ridley strutted through town full of self-importance now that he was head of the new committee. He felt he must interfere with the business of Metlakatla constantly. Collison always voted with him, since he was ordained. Tomlinson supported Duncan while Hall and Schutt were caught between them, unable negotiate a compromise. Every week the struggle to control our town grew louder and more bitter, but neither side could win.

Meanwhile, our Town Council had lost the most. It had no role in this new arrangement. Duncan and Tomlinson would speak for us as long as we agreed with them, but the voices of our people were silenced. The Council decided to continue meeting as it always had, like our ancestors had done before the Whites came. We tried to live as simply as before and avoid the war between the two sides of the White committee. We pretended it was their problem, not ours, but every decision became a battle. The only winner was the Spirit of the Church who played with all of us like toys.

Old Tooklan died that spring after we returned from the fishing camps on the Nass. He had lived a quiet life since we rescued him from Fort Simpson. He had kept his Tsimshian name and never became a Christian, but he had agreed not to practice the ways of Shamans so he could stay with us. He secretly visited the dying who were not baptized, and the graves of those who had not been cremated, to chant and comfort their Spirits, but he never danced in his ceremonial clothes again.

I felt his loss deeply, for he had lived in our house for many years. His death brought back memories the Smallpox and the deaths of my parents. I had watched over him as he grew weaker. I was the only one he allowed to tend him while he was ill, for I had saved his life by bringing him to Metlakatla. On his last day he begged me to give him a traditional cremation or his spirit would never rest. I promised not to deny him his dying wish.

I asked the Town Council for permission to cremate his body. They said a Christian burial was required by the rules of Metlakatla, but I argued angrily that this would offend his spirit. I recounted the story of his life and begged them to grant his last request. The Council discussed it and finally agreed to respect his wish. They sent news of their decision to the White committee and asked them to allow it.

Ridley refused their request without hesitation. He said the Town Council had no right to make suggestions and he would not allow heathen ceremonies on Christian land. He refused to allow the Council a chance to explain their decision. This angered them, even the ones who had wanted Tooklan to have a Christian burial. They presented their request to Duncan instead. He had never allowed a traditional burial before, but Ridley's treatment of the Council changed his mind.

When Ridley learned that Duncan supported a traditional ceremony, he forbade us to hold it in Metlakatla. The Council did not want to anger him further but Duncan explained that Ridley and the White committee only had power over Anglican lands. We had no idea what he meant. He showed us a plan of the town with lines that marked the church lands. We could to do whatever we wish outside those boundaries, he explained.

The idea of invisible lines confused us. We knew that Metlakatla belonged to our people. How could it be otherwise? We lived here and had taken care of the land with love and pride for countless generations. We had built every building on it with our own hands. No change in ownership had been announced or witnessed in a public ceremony. No goods or gifts had been offered in exchange. The idea that some of our land now belonged to people in England who had never seen it was ridiculous.

Duncan spoke about the lines without shame or apology, like a teacher explains the world to his young students. He meant to reassure us and give us hope but his explanation distressed us greatly. The invisible lines were on his map. Why had he kept them a secret from us?

News of the invisible lines spread across Metlakatla and it was greeted by shock and disbelief. The sadness of Tooklan's death was replaced by feelings of anger and betrayal. We cremated his burial box at the edge of the forest outside the invisible lines. Even those who did not know him attended the ceremony in protest. We said goodbye to his Spirit with both Tsimshian and Christian prayers.

Ridley was furious. He complained to England that Duncan had given his support for our heathen ceremony, though Duncan had not attended. Duncan wrote to them too. He explained that only Christians should be allowed Christian burials.

After the ceremony, I could not tolerate being Ridley's servant anymore. I thought Duncan would try to make me change my mind but he was happy to deny Ridley my services. I was relieved to work in Duncan's office again and he seemed happy to have my company. He never explained why he had not told us about the invisible lines, but he was pleased that we directed our anger towards Ridley instead of him. I did not care what Ridley thought of me after I returned to work for Duncan. I did not speak to him again for a long time.

The White Committee did not meet again for several months. Their fighting died down until the end of summer, but our had innocence died too. The thoughts of the invisible lines lived inside us like an invisible disease that eats away at a man's body. They could not be forgotten or dismissed. We no longer trusted what was ours and what was not. Invisible lines became invisible cracks. Invisible flames rose through the cracks. We could not see them, but I felt them burning in my heart.

The town still looked the same. The people continued with their lives like the sick who have faith in a cure. To prove we were healthy, we built new houses and gardens, a larger Assembly Hall, a blacksmith shop and a telephone line that ran from the Mission House to the saw mill. We agreed that we would never let Bishop Ridley take any part of our town, but we consulted Duncan's map and built outside the lines as a precaution.

The fighting between Ridley and Duncan never stopped. Ridley would storm into Duncan's office without knocking and begin screaming at him for something he or the Town Council had done. Sometimes he glared at me for a moment, but then he turned back to Duncan and soon forgot that I was in the room. Duncan usually ignored him or listened to him like a parent patiently enduring a child's pointless whining. Sometimes it became too much for him, but he never let on while Ridley was in the room. Once Ridley had gone he would stand up and stare out the window or pace the room. At times he stayed behind his desk, holding his head in his hands, but he never compromised to appease Ridley.

When the Committee met in late July, the war heated up again. It was worse than ever. Ridley struck first. He asked the others to fire Duncan and replace him with another missionary. Like a wise Chief, Duncan had built his allegiances carefully. When he left the room the Committee voted to keep him on. Duncan struck back at Ridley, asking that communion not be part of our church service. The committee agreed, in spite of Ridley's angry insistence that it must be included. Ridley refused to accept their decision. He sent his complaint to the missionary society, asking them to intervene. A letter arrived in September, telling the Committee to reverse their decision.

Duncan could not ignore this. He wrote an angry letter back to the missionary society, telling them that if they wanted the Committee to succeed they must not interfere with its decisions. He told them our town was healthier than ever before because he, not Ridley, knew best what our people needed. And then, to press his point, he told them that we did not need their money anymore.

The Committee met again in September. They were determined to end the fighting. They voted again to bar communion from the Sunday services. They also decided that they did not want the Church of England or Bishop Ridley to govern Metlakatla anymore. They hoped to frighten the missionary society into accepting their decision. If they did not accept it, Duncan told me he would send them a longer explanation to encourage them to negotiate.

As usual, Ridley did not wait for the church's answer. At the next Sunday service, in the presence of the Spirit of the Church, he interrupted Duncan's sermon to declare that the Committee would not meet again and that he would govern our town himself. A rumble of unhappy voices rose from the congregation. Before it grew too loud he added that he would offer communion after each Sunday service starting that morning.

Duncan waited for him to finish. He began again in the slow, careful voice he used to control his temper. "Obviously, Mr. Ridley is more concerned about communion than the word of God, since he feels it is necessary to stop our sermon. Your Town Council and the Committee that governs our town, including Robert Tomlinson, Mr. Schutt and the Collisons, do not want communion at our Sunday services, and we do not want Mr. Ridley interfering with the business of our town. We have written to England to tell them so."

"I am your Bishop! If Mr. Duncan had any respect for the Church of England he would address me by my title, not like a common servant, and he would respect the laws of the Church! Communion is an essential part of Sunday services everywhere else in the world and you deserve to have the same service as everyone else."

"Mr. Ridley wishes to offer you a wafer representing the body of Christ and a glass of wine representing his blood. You are not cannibals and you have each agreed not to drink alcohol in Metlakatla. Your Town Council no longer wants to be manipulated by people who do not respect our rules and agreements. Receiving communion is not necessary for you to understand the word of God. Of course, you are free to accept Mr. Ridley's offerings if you wish, but I advise you not to." Duncan's eyes burned like fires as he scanned our faces, waiting for our reaction.

Like the children watching their parents feud, who are asked to choose sides, the congregation was dragged into the war between Duncan and Ridley. I was used to their war from the first day I worked for Ridley, but my heart sank to see the anguish on the faces of my friends around me. They looked at each other, wondering what terrible thing had just happened and what they should do next.

Most of the hall remained seated, but some felt Duncan had been unfair to them in his business dealings. Others had been humiliated by him in the Assembly Hall for breaking the town rules. Slowly, after a long, uncomfortable pause, they stood in defiance and made their way up the aisles to accept Ridley's communion.

A hush fell over the great hall of St Paul's Church. At this moment, under the watchful eye of the evil Spirit, we became a divided town. The defiant ones cast their eyes down to avoid Duncan's angry glare as they made their way to the front. Only a few rose to challenge him but there were more than he had expected. Later in his office, he told me that each time someone accepted a communion it was an act of betrayal. He would never forgive them. There would be no turning back.

Ridley looked greatly relieved when the first people stood in defiance. For the first time he had followers, though I doubt any of them thought of him as their leader. As each person approached him, he smiled broadly, repeated a short prayer and placed a wafer of their tongue. Then, in a voice loud enough to be heard across the great hall, he thanked them for choosing to be a good Christian.

For the first time, the invisible lines that divided our town also divided our people. Those who supported Duncan were on one side and those who took communion from Ridley were on the other side. Tensions between them grew over the following weeks. Those who rose to take communion were scorned and heckled. They were forced to leave our houses and move to the other side of the lines. They felt as betrayed as we did and their hearts hardened against us. Our Sunday sermons were never sacred again. Like the winter ceremonies in Fort Simpson, they became angry and unholy.

Duncan had not yet received an answer to his letter to the missionary society, asking them not to interfere with the business of running our town, but he dictated another letter to them explaining what Ridley had done and how this was dividing our town. He said we needed the Gospel to be simple and clear, but Ridley was insisting on rituals that confused and misled us. He said my people used to celebrate cannibalism and we thought communion was a form of cannibalism. His words upset me and I stopped writing.

"Mr. Duncan, that is not true. We were never cannibals. Our Hamatsas were actors who taught us the importance of being civilized."

"I didn't say you were actual cannibals, Jack, but communion might seem like cannibalism to some Tsimshian. It is a difficult concept to understand."

"Do you think we cannot understand the truth?"

"Of course most of you can, Jack, but it takes time. There is no point starting with confusion."

I wanted to argue this was not the start, but fighting communion was a matter of pride to him. He had been teaching us the Christian Gospel for more than twenty years, but he still would not listen to me. He told me to continue writing the letter.

The rest of the letter made more sense. He said it was illegal in British Columbia for Indians to consume alcohol or for Whites to give it to them. He explained that we had moved to Metlakatla to get away from the drunkenness and violence in Fort

Simpson, and that everyone had agreed to our town's rules before they were allowed to live here. The strictest rule was that no alcohol was allowed in the town. No one who lived here was allowed to drink it even when they were away from the town. It would be contradictory and confusing to hand out wine at our holy services. It would teach us that the Church has no respect for the law and our own rules, established for our good, would mean nothing.

Ridley, he added, had no respect for either the law or the town's rules. He only wanted to destroy what we had created. He said was an enemy of the town who could not be trusted and that we wanted nothing more to do with him.

That fateful letter was sent. Winter mail was dreadfully slow in those years before the railway was finished. We knew it might be spring before an answer would come. Meanwhile Ridley handed out wafers and wine every Sunday and Duncan continued with his plans for the cannery. Early in the New Year, Duncan called a meeting in the new Assembly Hall to raise money. Fifty men, including Tom and I, pledged a hundred dollars each to buy the machinery.

Once the money was collected, he wasted no time booking passage on a ship to Victoria. He asked me to come with him. This time I was able to convince him that we needed Tom's skills to help with the machinery. We left for Victoria when most of the town was preparing to leave for the oolichon camps on the Nass.

It was not a romantic trip like the summer we purchased the Carolena. The winter rains followed us south and kept us focused on our work. There were only the two of us with Duncan and he was with us most of the time. We were careful not to show our affection for each other in front of him. We had separate bunks on the steamship and separate rooms in Bishop Cridge's home in Victoria. Still, Tom was happy that Duncan had invited him to join us. Duncan wanted him to learn how to take apart and put together the canning machines so he could teach others when we returned home. This made him feel important and put him in a wonderful mood.

The day we arrived, Duncan brought us to the government buildings to meet his business agent Senator MacDougall for the first time. His office was smaller than Duncan's but much neater. The walls were beautiful, made from a strange dark, shiny wood. There were many tall shelves filled with large books with leather bindings.

The Senator was a short man with a red face and long sideburns. He greeted us with cheery smiles and firm handshakes. He asked us a couple questions, perhaps to impress Duncan, for he did seem not to listen to our answers. Duncan had little in common with him, except they were both clever and very busy. MacDougall was more gentle and patient in manner. His words were softer and he thought carefully before he spoke. He only mentioned trade and profit when he spoke about Metlakatla with Duncan.

Duncan told us that the Senator had many important friends in both Victoria and Ottawa but he was frustrated by him too. He thought MacDougall was too busy to give proper attention to the affairs of Metlakatla. Duncan rarely thought others cared enough about our town, especially those who lived far away.

His next visited the post office to have his mail sent to Cridge's home instead of Metlakatla. The next day a letter arrived from the missionary society. It was a response to his first letter. They flatly refused the Committee's request for them to give up control of Metlakatla. They asked Duncan to return to England to discuss the situation. Duncan read it aloud to us and then gave it to Bishop Cridge to look over.

"You are going to go, aren't you William? They'll surely be upset if you don't."

"I can't possibly go, Edward. There's the cannery to set up or the entire spring fishing season will be wasted if I do. Besides, that's just what Ridley wants, to have me out of the way for months on end while he messes with all that I have done."

"The Missionary Society could be valuable as allies against Ridley. You'd be much more likely to convince them of your reasoning in person."

"They're not my allies, Edward. The Society has changed. They're not the same men who sent me to Fort Simpson. They all think like Ridley does now. They're only interested in pomp and ceremony. They don't appreciate what I have done for the Tsimshian or the Church. And they certainly don't want to let go of Metlakatla. They're only summoning me to keep me in line. I won't be humiliated that way!"

"But they still own most of the land and they paid for many of the buildings. You can't expect them to just let it all go without good reason."

"I spelled out my reasons in a second letter that I sent two weeks after the first. It's obvious they had not received it when they wrote this. They will understand my point of view when they do and the whole trip to England will be pointless anyway."

"But what if the second letter has gone astray? You can't risk all that you have done without that consideration."

"I'm not suggesting that I refuse to return outright. I'll tell them I won't be able to leave until late spring or summer at the earliest. What are they going to do? I have done more than any of their other missionaries. They can't fire me. Ridley can't manage the town himself. They need me if they want the mission to succeed."

Not even Duncan's best friend could change his mind. He wrote his answer to the missionary society and posted it the next day. We continued looking for the machinery we had come to buy. We completed our purchase three weeks later and returned to Metlakatla. The only thought on our minds at that point was setting up the cannery.

Ridley met us as we docked, standing proud and determined. He ordered Duncan to his office immediately. The contempt between them hung like fog in the air. Duncan turned away, saying we needed to unload the ship first before it rained. He kept Ridley waiting for more than two hours. He brought Tom and I with him to Ridley's office to witness what Ridley would say. We expected an angry confrontation.

To our surprise, Ridley was not upset that we had kept him waiting. We were greeted by his childish delight and arrogance as he paced back and forth in front of us. He sneered at us and enjoyed our impatience as we waited for him to speak. Duncan had no tolerance for his foolishness. He asked him to say what he had to say so we could leave. "Bishops might not need to work but missionaries do," he said.

"So! You have no respect for your superiors. You think you can get away with anything you want, is that it?"

"I have no respect for you, but I hardly consider you my superior. I doubt anyone, even your wife, considers you a superior." Duncan's blue eyes glared at him fiercely.

Ridley choked back his anger. "This! This is what I am talking about." He waved a letter in front of Duncan's face and jabbed at it with his finger. "You thought you would say nothing about it and I would never find out, but the missionary society isn't as stupid as you think! They wrote to me too! They did not invite you to visit England for a holiday! This was a summons! You cannot refuse!"

"It's none of your business what I do! I don't answer to you!" Duncan shouted back.

"I want to know if you are returning to England as you have been ordered." There was a strange smile on Ridley's face as though he knew a secret joke.

"I'm afraid I have to disappoint you. I'm not going. I have written to them with my response and I have no intention of changing my mind. That is all I will tell you."

"Fine!" This was clearly the answer Ridley was hoping for. "You are fired!"

"You can't fire me. I don't work for you," Duncan growled.

"I'm not firing you. They are. They asked me to give you this dismissal letter if you refused to return to England." Ridley shoved the letter at him. Duncan's face grew dark as he read it. Ridley watched him with cruel delight. When Duncan finished reading, Ridley said, "Pack your things and be ready to leave on the next ship."

Duncan said nothing. He turned and walked out the door without waiting for us to follow.

We ran to catch up with him as he marched to the Mission House. He swung his arms wildly as he made long strides. This was how he walked when he was too angry to speak. Perhaps it was not the best time to ask him, but I could not keep silent.

"Mr. Duncan, what does this mean? What will happen to you?"

"It means Ridley is an ass, Jack. And nothing will happen to me that wasn't bound to happen sooner or later." He did not look at me as he spoke. Tom and I glanced at each other and we saw the fear in our faces. Could Bishop Ridley remove our leader so easily? Captain Patterson and Robert Cunningham left when they were fired and we did not want this to happen to Duncan.

"Will you leave us?" Tom asked.

That stopped his stride. He turned to look at us before he spoke. "That will depend on the people of Metlakatla, won't it?" He walked through the doorway into the Mission House. We followed him down the hallway to his office.

"We want you to stay!" Tom and I said together. Duncan paused at his office door and thanked us with a smile. He asked us to give him a minute to think, and then he went inside, leaving the door open.

We waited near the door for several minutes, not knowing what to do or say. We feared if we turned our backs that he would disappear. He stood behind his desk and stared out window, but he was not quiet for long.

"Jack, I need you here to pack up my papers. Tom, I want you to find Henry Richardson and the others of the Town Council. Tell them what has happened. Tell Henry I must move out of the Mission House immediately. Ask if he can find me a place to stay tonight. Then see if you can find some men to help me move my belongings. Can you do that?"

"Yes, I go now." Tom squeezed my arm happily and winked at me. Then he turned to leave.

"Tom, wait! Tell them I will hold a meeting in Assembly Hall at seven o'clock tonight to discuss what we should do. Spread the news about the meeting." Tom nodded and ran out the door. Duncan smiled to himself and my heart filled with joy. I knew he would not leave us now. He was preparing for a good fight.

He asked me to sort the mailbag from our ship while he packed the papers on his desk. Among the several business letters for Duncan I found another letter from the Christian Missionary Society. I gave it to him and he opened it quickly.

"Imbeciles!" he cried as he read it. "They have read my second letter and now they want to work out a solution with me. Ha!" He folded up the letter and put it in his pocket. "Let's see if they sent a second letter for Bishop Ridley?" We sifted through the pile until we found it.

"Are you going to open it?" I asked him.

"I don't need to. I know what it says. They don't want him to fire me until they see if we can work things out. I want you to take it to Ridley right away, please. Don't tell him that I have received a letter, too. I want to see what he does."

I hated to speak to Ridley again, but I went to his house with the letter as Duncan asked. I knocked on the door. My stomach grumbled uneasily as I heard his footsteps approach. He opened the door and made an unpleasant face when he saw who it was.

"Well, if it isn't the little traitor! What do you want?" he snapped. I said nothing as I handed him the letter. I waited for him to open it. Instead, he gave me another sneer and shut the door in my face.

Ridley could not bring himself to apologize to Duncan or ask him to stay. I suppose he thought the missionary society would be angry with him for firing Duncan so quickly. He left for England immediately to explain his actions to them in person. That evening, he and his wife boarded a ship bound for Victoria without telling anyone except the Collisons. We did not see them again for several months.

We knew nothing of this as we packed up Duncan's office and private belongings. Our people were excited that he was coming to live in one of our homes. Several asked for the honour of having him live with them. He chose a room in the house of a Town Council member. Several men came to help him move. By early evening it was done.

We met in the Assembly Hall after dinner to hear what he would say. It reassured us to see that he was smiling and full of determination. He told us not to worry. He was still our leader and he would not leave if we wanted him to stay. Henry Richardson stood and asked the assembly to make noise if we wanted him to stay. We cheered loudly, chapped our hands and stomped on the floor until the room shook.

Once we were quiet, he warned us never let an evil man like Ridley destroy our town. He said the missionary society had a change of heart but he wanted us to leave them anyway. We will never be able to work with Ridley, he told us. He said we would create a separate mission in Metlakatla with our own cannery, and the Church of England would have no power over us. Ridley would eventually learn that he was not wanted and he would return to England. We answered his message with more cheering and applause.

When we heard the next day that the Ridleys had left for England. We felt our prayers had been answered. The town met at the dock to celebrate. Tom and I joined the other members of the band with our uniforms and instruments to lead them along the promenade. We played our favourite hymns while the choir and townspeople clapped and sang along. We finished the day by sharing food and kneeling in prayer in the Assembly Hall. We thanked the Lord and prayed that we would finally live in peace again.

THIRTY

Unfortunately, our problems had just begun. The next day, when we went to the church to hear Duncan's sermon, Henry Collison stopped us at the door. Ridley had placed him in charge while he was away. He had told him Duncan was no longer allowed inside. Collison told us our church was the property of the Church of England and it was not to be used by Duncan, for he no longer worked for them. He also said Ridley would come back after he met with the missionary society and Duncan would be forced to leave Metlakatla when he returned.

We were shocked. Collison had never stood against us before. We had considered him to be our friend, like Tomlinson, and surely he understood that we had built the church with our own hands long before he or the Ridleys had come to Metlakatla. We tried to reason with him but he would not listen. So this is how ordained men act, I thought to myself.

The crowd had grown large and angry by the time Duncan arrived. We stepped aside to let him speak to Collison. Duncan told him the church did not belong to the missionary society. It had been built outside of Church lands so they did not own it. Collison was trespassing on Tsimshian land and Duncan asked him to leave. Collison argued that the church was built with the missionary society's money so it belonged to them. He refused to leave and threatened to summon a gun boat from Victoria if we tried to push past him.

The Spirit of the Church must have been pleased to see us fighting on its doorstep. It fanned the hatred in our hearts. We would have forced our way past Collison if Duncan had not stopped us. He delivered his sermon in the Assembly Hall instead. The next day, I returned to the church with Tom and several others and found that Collison had locked the doors with a large chain. We broke the lock and removed the altar and bishop's chair that Timothy had carved, which our Town Council had paid for. The tapestries on the walls our women had woven were ours too, but they were too high to reach. We would return for them another time.

We nailed boards across the doors and the lower windows so Collison and Ridley's supporters could not use them. The next Sunday morning four of Collison's men came to remove the boards, but our men stood guard prevent them from entering church. They argued that they had a right to use the church and we argued that we did too. If they prevented us from using it then we would prevent them. They threatened us with the crowbars they had brought to loosen the boards. We fought back with rocks and drove them away.

They were bruised and bleeding as they ran. I was shocked at what we had done. I had never hurt another Tsimshian, not even when we were surrounded by violence in Fort Simpson twenty years before. I felt sick and ashamed. Our violence could not be blamed on whisky this time but somehow we had lost control of our anger and our Christian beliefs.

The Spirit of the Church had successfully driven our town from its home. We held our Sunday services in the Assembly Hall. Collison held services for his small group in the reception hall in Ridley's residence. Each side organized teams of men to guard the great church from dawn to midnight to make sure the other side was not using it.

Tensions between us grew uglier every day. Collison told we were not allowed to meet in the Assembly Hall for our services either, but Duncan argued that we had paid for it from the sale of Tsimshian goods, not with money from England. Collison had been in Kitsumgalum when it was built so he had no proof otherwise. He still tried to stop us but we had twenty men for each of his. He decided it was wise not to provoke us, but our side provoked them by calling them "wafer eaters" and "Christ's cannibals".

We were convinced that their side would steal as much as they could from us. We studied the lines on Duncan's map to know which buildings were on our land and which ones were on Church of England land. The saw mill, the workshops, the Assembly Hall, the library, the jail, the schoolhouse, the store and our homes were on our land. The Mission House, the guest house for visitors and the Bishop's residence were on Church lands. We marked the lines between our lands and theirs with wooden stakes and string. Our Constables guarded the lines in shifts to prevent Ridley's men from crossing them.

The lines between our lands were now visible. The lines in our hearts became clearer too. We forced Collison's people out of our houses like traitors. They moved to the guest house. There were forty of them, so some had to sleep in tents or on the floor of Ridley's residence while he was away. We posted a list of their names on every building throughout our side of the town. No one spoke to them, even their friends and families. They were allowed to visit the store but our Constables escorted them there and back to their side when they were done. Not even Collison himself could cross the line without permission.

I believed that we could use Christian kindness to bring our two sides together again, before the wounds between us hardened into scars. During our Sunday sermon I asked the others to turn the other cheek and forgive Collison's followers. Duncan said it was a noble idea but he doubted it would work. He left it up to the congregation to discuss.

Some argued that their side had to first agree to allow us to use the great church and promise not to try to steal our other buildings. Others wanted to wait. They felt certain the other side could not live without us and they would learn their lesson. They were too proud to trust the lessons of Christian gospel, and pride is the fuel of war. When I could hear the Spirit of the Church laughing when I failed to convince them to forgive.

Our hearts softened as the months went by. We might have forgiven each other with a little more time, but the Ridleys returned from England at the end of June. They brought with them a letter from the missionary society that supported Ridley's actions. He read it to us defiantly from his side of the string fence next to the great church. It did nothing to win us over. We only hated him more.

Duncan called a town meeting. He urged everyone to come. We packed into the Assembly Hall tightly. Duncan reassured us that it did not matter what the missionary society said or wanted. We had decided we did not want their money or guidance. We would we set up our own church, like Reverend Cridge did in Victoria. We would call it the Christian Church of Metlakatla. The room exploded with loud cheers and when we were quiet again we voted to make it so.

We were excited to start a new church! In the following weeks, we spread the news to Fort Simpson and other villages, inviting them to join. We began to collect

donations too, to repay the missionary society for the money it had given us for building the great church. It was obvious to us that Ridley would not need it for his small
group of followers. We believed they would eventually sell the it to us. Ridley was a
stubborn, spoiled child who would do anything to get his way. He was determined to
stay in Metlakatla for now, but it made no sense. Collison was his only ally. Tomlinson,
Schutt and Reverend Hall supported Duncan.

In the midst of our fighting, two new staff arrived. The new school teacher, Mr.
Chantrell, chose to stay with our side even though Ridley promised him more money.
Our new doctor, James Bluett, had read about Metlakatla and told the missionary
society he wanted to work with Duncan. They offered him the salary that Chantrell
had refused and paid for his fare, but they did not tell him they had fired Duncan. Our
Council had no money to pay him but he chose to work for Duncan anyway. Bluett
was from a wealthy family and he could afford to work without pay.

Ridley was furious, of course. He stormed over our fence with our Constables
following close behind. He found Bluett and accused him of tricking the missionary
society without any intention of working for them and he called him a thief. Bluett
explained, in his warm, gentle voice, that the missionary society had been dishonest
with him. He chose to work for Duncan, he said, because it is better to work for people who do not deceive you.

Duncan proceeded with plans for the cannery. He proposed that we build it near
the beach east of Mission Point. The Town Council accepted his plans and it was
finished by the end of May, before we left for the salmon camps. Duncan hired a
White manager who had run canneries before. When we returned from the Skeena,
he taught us how to can our salmon. It was a proud moment for our town, for our
men no longer needed to leave Metlakatla to feed their families. We blessed the first
can of salmon with our prayers and we shared it with each worker in the cannery, as
just as the story of the Salmon Prince taught us to share the first spring salmon at the
fishing camps on the Skeena.

Bishop Cridge and Senator MacDougall accepted Duncan's invitation to visit
Metlakatla in July to see our new cannery. We proudly gave them a tour the cannery
but we also showed them the stakes and strings we had set up to mark our divided
town. They were saddened when they learned of the tensions between us. Cridge had
brought good news to cheer us up though. He had heard that Collison had asked to
be assigned elsewhere because he was unhappy working for Ridley.

MacDougall had good news too. The new Indian Act of 1880 gave buildings on
reserve lands, like St. Paul's Church, to the English Crown. It was no longer the prop-

erty of the missionary society. Duncan thought this was hardly an improvement, But Cridge pointed out that it would be better to deal with the Queen of England than the Church of England.

When Ridley learned Senator MacDougall was in town he invited him to tea in his residence. MacDougall arrived at his door with Bishop Cridge. Ridley called Bishop Cridge a "heathen" and would not let him in. This angered the Senator and they both left. They returned to Victoria the next week without speaking to Ridley again.

Senator MacDougall was a popular man and was well-respected in Victoria. He was patient and reasonable and rarely made enemies, but the insult to Cridge turned him firmly against Ridley. In August, he spoke to the congregation in Cridge's church. He told them it was a mistake for the Anglican Church to send Ridley to Metlakatla. He was useless for missionary work and he was destroying all the good work Duncan had done. The Victoria newspapers quoted his words and the Senator was dragged into the war.

Ridley was upset. He told the papers that MacDougall said these things because Duncan was his business partner. Collison joined his attack, saying Duncan had borrowed thousands of dollars from the Senator. MacDougall admitted this was true. He told the papers he had loaned Duncan the money because he believed in the good work that Duncan was doing. He did not want to see Duncan's good work ruined by Bishop Ridley.

Ridley even lied to make Duncan and the Senator look bad. He told the newspapers that Tsimshian men with guns surrounded his home and followed him whenever he went. He claimed that we planned to slit his throat and burn down the Mission House soon. Duncan answered with his own letters, saying none of this was true. He said Dr. Bluett, Mr. Chantrell and other Whites who worked with him would testify that these were lies.

Ridley was a silly man. Everyone could see that he was a fool and a liar, but that year he showed he was without morals or scruples. He tried to destroy Duncan and MacDougall's reputations by publishing a pamphlet called "Senator MacDougall's Misleading Account of His Visit to Metlakatla, Exposed by the Bishop of Caledonia". I have kept a copy of it to this day to remind myself how evil men can be. His words still burn in my head when I read them.

Duncan read us the pamphlet on a Sunday morning when we had gathered in the Assembly Hall to hear his sermon. He had never been late before, but that morning he was. I was set to go looking for him when he entered the room. He nodded at our greetings but did not smile or speak. The darkness in his face made the gloomy weather outside look bright. Several of us asked what was wrong. He only shook his head and asked us to sit down.

He stood at his usual place at the front of the room, staring down at the pamphlet in his hand. His hand was shaking. He cleared his throat and before saying anything else, he asked the women to take all the children away somewhere they could not hear his words. When they were gone, he told us about the pamphlet and what it said, and that it had been distributed to Whites throughout Victoria. He read each sentence slowly, pausing to hear our reactions before he continued. We watched his face twist with anger and pain as the words left his mouth. When he was finished he simply said, "There it is." He gathered his papers and left the hall.

In the pamphlet, Ridley said Duncan and MacDougall gave us liquor to win our support. He claimed Duncan kept young women in the boarding rooms for his own sexual pleasures and he raped them whenever he wanted. He also said that Duncan whipped those who resisted him in front the town, and whipped others for fun or out of anger. He forced couples to marry against their will, then jailed the husbands so he could molest their wives and force them to perform "dark ceremonies". He added that our men had learned from Duncan to rape our women whenever we wanted to.

The accusations made no sense. There had never been a rape in Metlakatla. Duncan was famous for fighting whisky traders and for banning alcohol from our town. Many Whites had worked with him, some for many years, and no one had ever accused him of these crimes before, not even Ridley who had lived with us for more than three years. Ridley offered no evidence for any of his terrible accusations, but he believed others should believe him because of his position. He was drunk on the poison of his own lies.

Ridley also accused Duncan of stealing money from the missionary society and destroying the record books to hide his crimes. He said Duncan forced Collison to lie about the theft to protect his position, even though Collison worked for Ridley, not Duncan. The pamphlet claimed Duncan was not qualified to be a missionary for he only had a simple education, though he had more schooling than Ridley. The only truthful thing the pamphlet said was that Duncan worked on Sundays. He did, of course. He gave sermons to our congregation.

We sat in shocked silence for a long time. There were tears in our eyes and rage in our hearts. No one spoke but questions screamed inside our heads. How could a man in such an important position be allowed to tell such lies? How could anyone print them? How could he call himself a Christian? Would others believe what he had written? Mostly, we wondered how we should respond to these lies.

Some left the Assembly Hall, but I remained with others to discuss what we could do. Our silence gave way to a multitude of stories of injustices that Ridley had committed. He had stolen our land, divided our town and denied us use of our great church and the Mission House which we had built with our own hands. The Church of England had promised to improve our lives. Instead, they gave us an evil bishop and allowed him to steal or destroy all that we had made. And now there was this pamphlet which proved he had no shred of piety or honour.

Our anger continued to grow in the following days. We pressed the Council to do something to force Ridley to leave. They posted signs around the town stating that our people had created a new Christian Church of Metlakatla and that no other church was allowed in town. It said the buildings that did not belong to the village had to be removed or sold to the people of Metlakatla or they would be taken down. They sent a message to Ridley asking him what he planned to do with his buildings.

Ridley responded to Duncan instead of the Town Council. He threatened to hold him personally responsible for any damage the Church's buildings. The same night, Ridley and his followers stood in front of their buildings with loaded rifles in violation of our town rules. They shouted threats at the Constables who protected our lands. Duncan cautioned them not to react unless they were attacked. The next day he sent a letter to Ridley warning him that he was still the town's Magistrate and that loaded guns were not permitted in the town. He told him not to cause fights or he would press charges.

The tensions remained high. Ridley and his followers guarded their buildings and we guarded ours. We hoped their guns were not loaded but one night we heard a gunshot. People ran from their houses to see what had happened. One of Ridley's men had fired his gun into the sky. The Council wanted him to be charged but Duncan advised us that would do no good. He had broken no White laws and we could not evict him while Ridley was protecting him.

Weeks passed as we waited for the missionary society to react against Ridley's pamphlet of lies. No letter came. The newspapers were filled with hot words supporting either Ridley or Duncan but nothing seemed to come of it. If Indian Commissioner Powell believed Duncan had done these terrible things he would have arrested him and stripped him of his Magistrate's powers, but he did nothing. If the Whites did not believe Ridley, they did nothing to punish him for his lies.

Ridley's pamphlet failed to bring us trouble so he tried to bankrupt our Council. The town's profit came largely from the sale of goods at the store, so Ridley set up a new store on the ground floor of the guest house. He stocked it with the most popular foods and supplies and sold them without profit. The Town Council posted signs around the town asking our people not to shop there. Tom and I complied, but it had been a difficult year. Many families had very little money and they could not resist the lower prices. When some started crossing our fence to shop there, others followed. Soon our store had almost no business.

Tom had a clever idea. He borrowed money from the Town Council and, with the help of many others, we went to Ridley's store. We bought all his supplies and sold them to Duncan for the same price. Our store had new supplies without paying for the shipping fees and Ridley's store had nothing left to sell. We bought Ridley's next shipment too. He was furious and closed his store. Once again, he looked like the fool that he truly was.

Our next crisis was saving our store and keeping the school classes going. Like our great church, the store and schoolhouse were built on our land but with monies from the missionary society. We moved the desks out of the schoolhouse to the Assembly Hall so the students' classes would not be interrupted. We completed the move just in time. Ridley's men marched into the school the next day to throw us out and they found it empty.

We sent a petition to Commissioner Powell, asking him to save our schoolhouse. We told him we had built the school ourselves before Ridley arrived. We told him how much we needed it for our children. Powell decided it belonged to the missionary society for they paid for the materials to build it. Ridley was quick to boast about the news. He announced that it would be used for his new church.

Powell also decided the store belonged to the missionary society, for they had also given us money to build it. We were upset but we honoured his decision. We thought giving the school and the store to Ridley would restore peace in the town, but Ridley did not want peace. He was cruel and only allowed his followers to shop at the store. The rest of us were told to go to Fort Simpson to buy our food and supplies.

We could use the Assembly Hall to worship and hold classes for our children, but we could not live without food or supplies. Fort Simpson was too far away, especially in during the winter storms. It was already in late November and we had no time to build another store. We would not sit quietly and starve to death. Perhaps we did not own the building, but we had bought the supplies inside and we wanted them back.

The Town Council called us to a meeting in the Assembly Hall and we howled our complaints like wounded bears. The Council said it was time to show our anger to Ridley for his sinful and mean-spirited behaviour. Our voices rose and we rose with them. We lit torches and marched through the wet snow and the darkness to the store.

Sam Pritchard broke the lock on the door with an ax and we forced our way inside. We emptied shelves, one by one, passing the goods between us to the door. The women and children waited outside to carry everything back to the Assembly Hall.

Ridley's guards ran to tell the bishop. Ridley rushed from his house in his slippers and housecoat, leading a small band of men towards us. We raised our shovels and axes and blocked them from reaching our women and children. Ridley shouted threats and insults at us but we did not listen. There were hundreds of us and only a few of them. The store was emptied in less than an hour.

Miyana, Ruth and Laura worked with Duncan in the Assembly Hall to pile the supplies along the back wall. He asked our men to guard them until morning when we would set up a new store in a safer location. Many of us volunteered. He made teams of six men to take turns standing guard every hour, but most of us stayed in the hall the whole night. We did not trust Ridley and we were too excited to sleep. It was a proud moment and a time for celebration. The women brought us dry clothing and made us warm drinks. We sat on the school desks, sang songs and told stories until the morning came.

When the store was empty Ridley left, but he returned with Collison and his men the next day. He confronted the few of us who remained on guard. He ordered us to return the supplies immediately or a White gunship would come to destroy our houses. Several men ran to waken the town while Tom went to find Duncan. In a few minutes hundreds of our people had gathered at the Assembly Hall. The children crowded under the eaves to stay dry as the wet snow changed to heavy rain. Our people faced Ridley without weakness or fear.

Tom arrived with Duncan. Ridley cursed wildly when he saw Duncan, but we ignored him. Duncan gathered the Constables and told them to escort the bishop back to his side of the string fence. Ridley screamed defiantly that he would not leave. His men raised their rifles to protect him.

"Anyone who fires a shot will be charged with attempted murder," Duncan cautioned them calmly. Our Constables moved to face Ridley's men. Duncan directed the women and children to move inside the Hall out of the rain but the older boys, who were excited by the threat of a fight, stayed under the eaves to watch.

Ridley's men glanced over at him nervously, but they continued to point their rifles at us. Ridley stared steadfastly at Duncan, poised like a martyr on the bow head of a ship. One of his men held an umbrella over his head though, like the rest of us, he was already wet.

"We are not moving until you and your pack of thieves return every last item of our stock," Ridley barked at Duncan.

"Very well, stand in the rain like as ass if you wish. I hope you'll catch your death of cold," Duncan laughed.

Ridley shook his finger at Duncan and promised that he would be thrown into the jail house instead. He called the rest of us savages and repeated his threat that a White gunship would flatten our houses and teach us proper respect for a bishop.

His insult riled us further. We could not stay silent. This was our war now. We shouted back our own threats and the air was thick with loud and angry words. Our rage surprised Ridley. His face changed to panic. He tried to explain nervously that the missionary society had paid for everything.

"No!" Tom shouted. He pushed his way past the Constables and stood right in front of Ridley. The cold rain dripped down his face but he was hot with anger. "You lie! We cut trees and made boards. We made shelves. We made the roof. You did not pay. You give us only windows, doors and nails!" We cheered behind him in agreement.

He turned his back on Ridley to face us. He shook his fist at the store and shouted at the crowd, "It is not enough to take our food and things from the store. The boards and shelves are ours! We take them too! We leave this stupid man his nails and windows and doors!" The crowd cheered again. I looked at Tom in amazement. At that moment I was the proudest man in Metlakatla.

Tom swung back to face Ridley. Ridley started to utter a threat but Tom raised his axe swiftly. Ridley squealed and leapt back, waving his arms helplessly in front of his face. Ridley's men stepped forward. They pointed their guns at Tom's head. My breath caught in my throat.

Tom turned to the last man on his right. "Move, White man's dog!" he shouted. The man backed away, still pointing his gun at Tom's head. Tom pushed past him as if his rifle was a toy. He marched through the puddles to the store with his axe resting on his shoulder. We all began to cheer. Our men grabbed axes, crowbars and hammers or whatever tools they could find. They ran to follow him and they began to pry off the door and hammer off the boards of the walls.

"No, no, you can't!" Ridley squealed like a child, but his voice was lost in the cheering as our people marched towards the store. Ridley grabbed the rifle from Collison's hands and fired it into the sky. The blast echoed off the great church and then was swallowed by the rain. We paused to look for a moment, but we turned back and continued. Collison was upset with Ridley. He pried his rifle out of Ridley's hands and shouted something angrily into his ear.

Ridley's men stood in the rain watching helpless as we tore the store apart, their guns pointed at the muddy ground as they watched. Ridley shouted that Collison would bear witness to the terrible crime we were committing. He described the horrid punishments we would suffer until his voice failed him. Collison resumed the shouting. Someone brought him a ledger and he said he would record our names so and that charges could be laid against us. He passed the ledger to Ridley while he shouted the names of the men he recognized. Ridley pretended to write them down, though the paper was obviously too wet to write on.

Joseph led us in singing hymns to block out the sound of Collison's shouting. Ridley ordered his men to fire their guns above our heads to frighten us, but they were too wet to fire. His men were wet and cold and tired of being ignored. After an hour they left in defeat to seek warmer shelter.

We worked hard through the rest of the day without slowing. We were soaked to our skins but our hard work kept us warm. The pounding of hammers and the creaking of nails being pried mingled with the sound of our singing and our laughter. Tom and I organized the workers inside. They took the shelves to the Assembly Hall. Others carefully removed the windows without breaking them. First we hauled away the walls, and then the roof and the floor. We tore the frame apart and removed all the nails from the boards. By dinner time the store was gone. The boards were stacked against the wall of the Assembly Hall. We left only the door, four windows and a pile of bent nails in the mud in where the store once stood.

THIRTY
ONE

Ridley was wanted revenge for the destruction of the store. He sent messages to the magistrates in Fort Simpson and Port Essington the next day, claiming Duncan had gone mad and was causing us to riot. He said we were destroying all the buildings in the town. He begged them to save him. The magistrates rushed to Metlakatla, but they saw no riot and no one appeared to be in danger. The magistrate from Port Essington met with Duncan. He was reassured and left the same day without speaking to Ridley.

We had started dismantling the schoolhouse to prevent Ridley from using it for his church. Tom supervised our work as he had done with the store. We worked in teams to remove the windows and other items that belonged to the church. We sang joyfully as we worked. We were still flushed with the excitement from demolishing the store, but this time Ridley and his men were not around to bother or threaten us. We sang, for each time we removed a board or a nail we were closer to being free from Ridley.

The magistrate from Fort Simpson saw what we were doing. He asked us politely to stop until he spoke with Duncan. He spent the rest of the morning in Duncan's office. We waited restlessly in the Assembly House out of the rain. Timothy and the women brought us fresh bread and tea, but no one was in a mood for speaking. We did not want our work to be interrupted.

Duncan and the magistrate came to us in the afternoon. They had agreed we should not to tear the schoolhouse apart until they had spoken to the White government in Victoria. Duncan thought he could convince the White government to give it back to us, and then we would not need to build a new schoolhouse later. We complained loudly, like a fire when water is thrown upon it. We replied that the White government could not be trusted, and Ridley even less so. Neither of them could stop us once the schoolhouse was gone and Ridley might leave if he lost the schoolhouse. The thought of building a new one did not bother us. We would make it bigger and better than before.

But Duncan did not want trouble from Commissioner Powell. He had already agreed to give the school to Ridley. He said we needed win the White government's support first if we did not want to anger them. Removing the store was enough to show Powell that we were angry, he explained. The Town Council agreed with him and told us we should wait for Powell's answer. We were upset but we could not act against our Council, so we laid down our tools.

The magistrate reminded us that Christmas was only three weeks away and it was a time when all Christians must embrace peace and good will. He wanted us to make a truce with Ridley and to forgive him. A truce with Ridley would be a waste of time for he would never honour it, but the magistrate said that the White government would not look kindly on us destroying the school if we would not even try to make a truce.

We were good Christians, not the savages Ridley thought us to be, so we agreed to try. The magistrate also spoke with Ridley and Collison. They promised to make peace if we stopped tearing down the school, but as soon as the magistrate tried to discuss a truce, Ridley began to shout and whine. He accused Duncan of plotting to kill him and refusing to accept Powell's decisions. He said the British navy should be summoned to teach us a lesson instead of making a truce. We answered his words with angry demands that he be arrested for telling his men to threaten us with guns. The magistrate warned both sides to behave. He spoke to us while Collison tried to calm Ridley. After a few minutes, we signed a truce just to be done with the task. We signed it without trust or forgiveness.

The truce did not repair our Christmas Spirit. Ridley taunted us that he had succeeded in saving the school. He complained to Commissioner Powell the same week that he and his followers had no protection. He claimed his wife lived in constant fear. To silence him, Powell gave him the powers of a Magistrate that Duncan had, and he made six of his Ridley's men Constables so that they could arrest us. This only made our situation worse.

Our fragile truce was destroyed by a child, the only one in our town who was filled with Christmas Spirit. On Christmas Day, he marched up and down our shore road singing Christmas carols and banging a toy drum loudly to make the town smile again. It was the drum he banged, not his singing, which caught the attention of other boys. They had purchased the drum together a few months before with another boy who had borrowed money to pay his share. To repay his debt, that boy sold the drum to the father of the child who marched down the street on Christmas Day. The father of the child was one of Ridley's followers.

The other boys had not sold their shares and they wanted their drum back. They asked Collison in October to speak to the boy's father and return their drum. He took their complaint to Ridley, but weeks had passed and Ridley did nothing. So on Christmas Day, the father gave his child the drum as a present. When the other boys saw the child banging their drum, they demanded that he give it back to them. The child knew nothing about their purchase and he refused. Two older brothers of the boys heard their complaints and they took the drum from the child. He went home crying without his drum or his Christmas spirit. That afternoon, Ridley sent his Constables to arrest the two youths who had taken the drum. He used his new Magistrate powers put them in the jail house for a week over Christmas without a hearing and without telling their parents.

The news of them being sent to jail spread quickly and a crowd gathered outside Duncan's office. The families of the boys asked Duncan to intervene but he could do nothing. He feared Ridley might keep them in the jail longer just to defy him. Tom and I set out with several other men to look for Bishop Ridley, not knowing what we would do when we found him. We met him walking with his wife on the road in beside the churchyard.

One of our Constables, Paul Legiac, the nephew of our former Grand Chief and the uncle of one of the boys, confronted Ridley and demanded that he release the two youths over Christmas until a proper hearing was held. Ridley threatened to throw him in the jail for a month if he did not mind his own business. Paul replied we would break open the jail with crowbars if he did not. Soon they were shouting at each other.

Ridley swung his fist at Paul but missed. Two other men stepped up to protect Paul. Ridley swung again and hit them instead and they struck back. One punch caught Ridley's cheek. He screamed loudly and fell to the ground. His screams brought Collison running. He pulled the Bishop away and led the Ridleys back to their house.

Tom and I slipped away while Paul and another Constable argued with Ridley's Constables. We ran to the jail house and freed the two youths before they saw us.

That was Christmas of 1882, our worst Christmas in twenty years. The winter skies were dark and cold and filled with angry winds. Many of us fell sick with colds and fevers from working in the rain. There was no lightness in our hearts. The joy and glory of our Christmas with Bishop Bompas only four years before seemed a lifetime away. The Great Church was boarded up. Its great bell was silent, but its evil Spirit looked down on us and rejoiced.

Our Christmas service was a sad time. It did not feel right to be crowded so tightly into the Assembly Hall. Duncan's words did not soothe us either. He asked us to forgive those who had wronged us, as he did every Christmas, but we could not forgive Bishop Ridley and neither could he. He had no gifts to share with us and no promises of better days to come. Tom and I played with the brass band and we sang hymns with the choir, but there was no joy in our songs. Our hearts were as heavy as the skies above us.

After Bishop Ridley was punched and the youths set free from the jail house, the two sides of Metlakatla did not speak for more than a week. There were no insults or threats, no demands or accusations. We stayed indoors, waiting for the storms to ease and our wounds to heal. Even the Constables on both sides kept back from the property lines so no words would be needed. On New Year's Day, Duncan asked the Members of Council, Constables, Church Elders, firemen and the brass band to gather in the Assembly Hall. We marched slowly along the shore road like a funeral procession. Sam Pritchard had just been elected Chief of the Town Council so he marched at the front. Other Members of the Council were next, followed by Duncan and the Church Elders. Tom and I marched behind them with the brass band and the choir. The Constables and the firemen followed us.

Ridley's followers gathered outside of his residence. Ridley wore his bishop's robes. His wife and the Collison's stood beside him. They were too few to march and they had no brass band or uniforms. Instead, they brought out a small cannon which they fired over our heads every few minutes. At first it shocked us. We stopped playing long enough to hear their laughter. We resumed our music and did not let the cannon interrupt us again. We marched back and forth on the road until we had played all the songs we knew twice. The Ridleys and their followers left before we were finished.

Ridley did not charge Tom and I for freeing the youths, but he laid charges against the two Constables who struck back after he attacked them. Our people stopped his

Constables from arresting them, so he announced from the edge of our string fence that he had sent a plea to Victoria to send gunships to come to his aid. He told us we would all be punished severely. Duncan joked about it to calm our nerves, but we were sure he meant it this time. White Chiefs would answer the call of a bishop who was also a magistrate. We waited anxiously for their gun ships to arrive.

In mid-January, the gun ship Oliver Wolcott arrived in our harbour. Ridley and Collison went with their six Constables to meet it at the dock. People from our side watched from the beach, dressed in our best Sunday clothes as Duncan had advised us to do. The ship's soldiers pointed their guns at us as they approached our dock but when they saw there was no danger, they lowered their guns. Three White Chiefs followed the soldiers down the gangplank. Ridley and Collison shook their hands. Collison was formal and polite, but Ridley gushed and trembled like he was in grave danger. He thanked them loudly for saving his life. I thought at any moment he might fall to his knees and wrap his arms around their legs.

He begged the soldiers, in a voice loud enough for all of us to hear, to prevent us from attacking him as he led them off the dock. He looked at us with panic in his eyes, cowering behind the soldiers as though we were wild animals. The White Chiefs looked puzzled when our brass band played "God Save The Queen" to welcome them. Ridley hurried them along before we could finish.

We parted respectfully as the soldiers and the White Chiefs, with their bushy sideburns and thick mustaches, passed between us. They watched us cautiously as we waved and smiled to them. Our children ran up to greet them, but Ridley swung at them and told them to go away. The Chiefs stared at Ridley for an explanation when the children returned to their mothers crying. He explained that the children might have knives. They stared at him suspiciously, but they said nothing.

The next day the three White Chiefs summoned the Town Council to a meeting in the Assembly Hall. Ridley refused to meet there. He said Duncan's heathens met there to conspire against him. He said it was safer to meet in the schoolhouse but the Town Council complained it would be too cold. The door, the wood stove and several windows had been removed and it blowing snow that day. One of the Chiefs asked why the windows were missing. Ridley shouted over us when we tried to explain.

Another White Chief stopped the argument. He introduced himself as Indian Commissioner Powell, the man who had given the store and schoolhouse to Ridley only a few weeks before. He decided it would be best to meet in the Assembly Hall in spite of Ridley's objections. Powell seemed to be the most important of the three Chiefs. He had a long, serious face and the other two White Chiefs did not question his decisions.

Our women brought hot biscuits and tea. Tea biscuits are like eagle feathers to the White Chiefs and our women were good warriors that day. Ridley warned them that the biscuits were probably poisoned but Commissioner Powell took one and said they tasted quite fine. They began to suspect that Ridley himself was the poison.

Powell started the hearing. He announced that the three Chiefs were here to represent the the Head White Chief, the Premier of British Columbia. He introduced the other two Chiefs, Commissioner Todd, the Police Commissioner who had asked about the schoolhouse, and Commissioner Anderson, the Chief of Fisheries. Powell said Bishop Ridley had asked them to come to Metlakatla because we were destroying his property and threatening his people. He said they had brought soldiers in case there was trouble, but they had no intention of attacking us if there was no reason to.

The accusations angered us and several people began talking at once. Powell stopped us and explained the rules of the hearing. He told us only one person may speak at a time and only with his permission, like in the White courts when our people were put on trial. We hesitated, fearing that this was really such a trial. We did our best to follow their rules.

Ridley and Collison were asked to speak first, for they had summoned the Commissioners. Ridley said our men had attacked a child and stolen his drum and that they had surrounded him and knocked him to the ground. He claimed Paul Legiac had struck him because he did not know the names of other men. Collison was more honest. He had not seen the boys take the drum or the men who punched Ridley. He described how we had torn down the store and ignored Ridley's orders to stop.

Duncan spoke next. He had not seen the fighting either, but he described how Ridley had insulted the Town Council and tried to provoke fights many times. Commissioner Todd asked why we had torn down the store and why Duncan had not stopped us. He explained that Ridley had stolen the supplies we had purchased and he tried to starve us by forbidding us to shop there. He said we had left the windows and doors the missionary society had paid for. We had only taken back the boards that the missionary society had not paid for. He admitted that we had ruined the nails but he said the Town Council would pay for new ones.

Each time Duncan tried to speak Ridley interrupted him, shouting out to the Commissioners that he was lying. When Duncan described why we dismantled the store, Ridley shouted that his plan was to starve his people, which is what Ridley had planned to do to us. Finally Commissioner Anderson warned Ridley that he would have to wait outside the Assembly Hall if he could not obey the rules. After that he was silent, except for a few gasps of disgust that brought angry glares from Commissioner Anderson.

The Commissioners then listened to Tomlinson, Dr. Bluett, Mr. Chantrell, Paul Legiac and the two Constables who had confronted Ridley. They spoke with the youths who had taken the drum and to Tom who had seen the fight. Then they questioned Sam Pritchard, the new Chief of the Town Council, and other men. They heard how Ridley had stolen our buildings and our supplies, how he lied about our people in his pamphlet and how he tried to jail our youths through Christmas week without a hearing. Many others wanted to speak but there was not enough time. The Commissioners adjourned the hearing that evening.

The next morning, we gathered at the Assembly Hall to hear Commissioner Powell read the Commissioners' decisions. The two youths we set free did not have to return to the jail. They said Paul Legiac had done nothing wrong, but the Constable who hit Bishop Ridley was told to pay ten dollars to the Town Council. We took a collection the next Sunday at Duncan's service to pay his fine. We collected more than twenty dollars.

The Commissioners were not as kind to Bishop Ridley. Powell accused Ridley of tricking the White leaders in Victoria into thinking that the troubles at Metlakatla were much worse than they were. The Commissioners, he told him, were summoned at great expense but without good reason. Ridley's troubles were largely his own making, and he provoked trouble by using his new powers as Magistrate unfairly. He warned him he would remove his powers if he misused them again, a warning Duncan had never been given, even after his trials of the whisky traders. Ridley left the Assembly Hall in anger and did not speak with the Commissioners again.

They left the next day for Fort Simpson, and then to Victoria to take their report to the White leaders. They asked the captain of the Oliver Wolcott to stay behind for a few days to be sure there was no more trouble. As soon as they left, Ridley told the captain he and his followers feared for their lives. He asked him to allow his followers to stay on his gun ship for protection. The captain did not believe him, but he offered to take them to Fort Simpson. Ridley called him an ass and marched away in a huff. The Oliver Wolcott left four days later, leaving us to resolve our problems on our own.

In every hard-fought war that drags on, there comes a time when everyone realizes they have lost. Both sides claim victory, whatever the result, but the joys of victory are soon replaced with the greater disappointment that nothing will be as good as it was before. The warriors grow tired. Their flesh is too sore and their hearts too heavy to continue the fight. They step back to rest and clean their sores, knowing there are deeper wounds that may never heal.

Ridley called the gun ship to punish us, but he was threatened and embarrassed instead. After the ship left, Powell surprised us with another gift. He sent a letter to Sir John A. MacDonald, the Prime Minister of all Canada, telling him that either Duncan or Ridley must leave Metlakatla to stop the war between the two sides. Powell spoke in favour of Duncan. He praised his good work and said it would be terrible if he was forced to leave.

Duncan glowed with pride as he read his letter to us at his Sunday sermon. This was proof that we had won the war, he told us. Ridley had been warned and humiliated and he had no choice but to respect us now. We cheered Duncan and we were filled with pride. We sang and paraded through the town with our band and choir again to celebrate our victory. Ridley locked himself in his residence. We saw nothing of him in the days that followed. But he had not been punished or forced to leave. Nothing had really changed. The lines that divided the land and hearts of our town remained.

◇◇◇◇◇◇◇◇◇◇◇◇◇◇◇◇

We prayed every day for God to send Ridley away, but months passed and there was no sign of him leaving. Like a wounded bear, he watched us from a distance and plotted his revenge. We tried to live our lives as though our string fences and Ridley's followers were not there, but we could not relax. We knew at some point the war would resume.

Nothing much was said between us. We did not argue with Ridley's men or challenge them, but there was no peace. The many insults and injustices we had exchanged could not be forgiven or forgotten. We would never get our buildings back while Ridley was still in town. Our saw mill stayed silent most of that year. We did not want to build any new buildings for we fear that they might be taken away from us later.

Our men were disheartened and lethargic. Many who did not work in our cannery left to look for work in Fort Simpson or Port Essington. Tom had no work at the saw mill. He took a job in the cannery, but he did not like it. He complained every night when he returned to our home. He said I had an easy job in Duncan's office and he resented me for that. I was frustrated too, but nothing I said would change Tom's mind. When I tried to spend more time with him to show him my love, but he accused me of pitying him and he became more miserable.

Ridley emerged near the end of summer. He took walks on the beach with his wife in the early mornings. Not long after that, he began to leave his house at other times when the town was busy with activity. The town was curious and full of gossip about his movements. He pretended we were not there, as though we were as invisible as the wind. Some of the town speculated that God had punished him by making him mute or cursing him with a form of blindness, but he was only blinded by his own pride and arrogance.

Before the first snows arrived, he stopped pretending he could not see us and began to stare fearlessly at those who passed him. Some looked away, not wanting to return his challenge, but this only increased his confidence. Some met his challenge but he never backed down. Others tried to greet him with Christian kindness and forgiveness, but he would only raise his nose and turn away without replying, as if he was repulsed by their breath.

No one spoke expected him to leave anymore. Disappointment and anger replaced our fragile peace. He had not accused or insulted us as he did before. He did not yell at Duncan or interfere with the business of the Town Council either, but his disrespectful stares and snubs blew fresh air on the embers of the hatred between us. We knew it would soon grow worse.

Before Christmas, he started to taunt and insult us. His men confronted and threatened those who made shortcuts across church lands. Tom told Duncan we should retaliate so that Ridley would learn to respect us, but Duncan advised him to do nothing. I agreed. The Spirit of the Church was poisoned the hearts of both sides with hatred, but I still had faith that the White God and Jesus would intervene and save our town from the Spirit and Ridley.

Winter passed into spring. The hatred on both sides grew stronger. Each side collected stories about the other side's insults and crimes. These stories were the firewood that fed the fires of our anger. Every sharp word and unpleasant look was retold as something much worse. Forgiveness became unthinkable.

Rumours spread to Victoria too. Senator MacDougall's wife heard White women from Bishop Hills' church saying witnesses had seen Duncan whipping young Tsimshian girls in the town square in front of everyone. Marion Collison said the rumours were true. I once thought the Collisons were good people, but I was now convinced they were as evil as Ridley himself. Senator MacDougall wrote to the missionary society to ask them to tell Ridley and the Collisons to stop spreading lies and apologize to our people. The Society replied that they hoped that everyone would become good Christian friends again, but there was no chance of that.

In the summer of 1884, Ridley secretly requested an official survey of church lands and the missionary society agreed to pay for it. Bishop Cridge learned of the news and sent word to Duncan before the surveyors arrived. Duncan flew into a rage and called for the Town Council to meet. This is it, I told myself. The war had started again.

Thoughts and rumours spread through the town about what would happen after the survey. On Sunday we filled the great church to hear what Duncan would say. He gave us a fiery sermon and warned us about the threat that was coming. His words touched our hearts for we felt the sting of the injustices he described.

"Bishop Ridley has asked for the survey to make the theft of our lands official," he told us. "The missionary society and the Whites in Victoria are jealous of the great cathedral we have built. Instead of giving us credit for our great work, they wish to take it away from us forever. Bishop Ridley wants it for his own self-glorification. He claims the missionary society paid for the church. They paid for some of the supplies but not the timbers or our labour, and they have never paid for your land that this church sits on!"

Duncan said it was our land and we must choose what to do. We all agreed we must do our best to keep what was ours. We had to stop the survey. There were loud arguments in the Town Council meetings about what strategy we should use. Some were prepared to fight to stop it, but others feared the return of the English gun boats. We would first try to reason with the surveyors but beyond that, we could not agree. The tensions were dividing us.

The surveyors arrived with the first frost of autumn. The women had finished collecting summer berries and the leaves of the bushes were already turning red. Ridley and Collison greeted them at the dock. The Town Council, Sam Pritchard, Tom and I and many others were waiting too. We tried to explain to the head surveyor that he did not have the Council's permission to do a survey. Ridley interrupted them and said the surveyor had his permission as the Bishop of the Diocese of Caledonia, and that was all the permission they needed to survey lands that belong to the Church of England.

His words were met with angry words from our men. Ridley's men surrounded the surveyors to protect them from us. Ridley hid behind them too. "You see, dear visitors, these people are extremely dangerous, but no one listens to me," Ridley shouted over the heads of the surveyors. "We live in fear for our lives every day. It is only a matter of time before something terrible tragic will happen!" A few more angry words came from the crowd before we fell silent.

Ridley guided the surveyors to the great cathedral at the top of Mission Point. He told them the Church's property included land beyond the strings and stakes we had set up to mark our territory. The Council called another meeting in the Assembly Hall. We were angry and frightened, but we still disagreed about the best way to stop them. Tom, Joseph, Sam and several others met the surveyors and told them to leave immediately. They did not hurt the survey team, but they frightened them. They were told to leave and they left for Fort Simpson that afternoon.

Stopping the survey was much easier than we expected. The town was jubilant and the threat were gone for a while. The next evening, the Council held another meeting to discuss what we should do next. We agreed that we needed to be firm with Ridley and the government in Victoria about what was ours. We decided that the schoolhouse should be ours, and the Council sent a message to Ridley the next day telling him that we would not let him use it. We no longer cared if Commissioner Powell wanted Ridley to have it.

Ridley begged the White government in Victoria to send protection as he had done before. The new Indian Commissioner, Andrew Elliott, made all of Ridley's men Constables to protect the lands Ridley claimed. We were not too worried. Elliott told us that the government in Victoria would send Commissioners to listen to our complaints as they had done before. We trusted that they would stop Ridley from stealing our lands.

Unfortuantely, the mood of White settlers had changed. The new government of Premier William Smithe sold Indian lands to rich White men who wanted to buy them. He did not negotiate with Indian tribes or pay them for the lands he stole. Indians everywhere became angry and defiant. We were angry with Ridley, but not other Whites. Elliott thought Indians had no right to complain about things being unfair. His Commissioners did not come to hear our concerns. They came to silence us and put fear into our hearts.

We did not understand that. We greeted the Commissioners on the dock with our brass band as we had the last time. As soon as we finished "God Save The Queen", Sam Pritchard stepped forward to offer him his hand and to introduce him to the Town Council, but Elliott would have nothing to do with it. "This is not a social visit," he said, as he and the other two Commissioners pushed past him to follow Ridley up the path to Bishop's residence. We knew then that we did not stand a chance.

THIRTY
TWO

The hearings lasted the next four days. They passed without ceremony. At Ridley's insistence, they were held in the schoolhouse, not the Assembly Hall, in spite of the lack of heat and space. Blankets were nailed over the broken windows and the empty doorway to keep out the wind and a small wood stove was set up near the front of the room.

The Commissioners and their guards took up a quarter of the room. There was not enough room left for all those in town who wished to speak. Sam suggested that the Assembly Hall would be warmer and more people could fit inside to listen, but Elliott did not care. He said this was a hearing, not a theatre. The classroom was soon packed to the doorway. A hundred others waited outside for their turn to speak. We made a canopy of oilskins to give them cover from the rain but it was too windy to provide much protection.

The Commissioners wasted no time giving greetings or explaining why they had come. Theodore Davie, the youngest Commissioner, spoke first before they heard from any of us. He told us we were good people, but we had received bad teachings from some White men who had tricked us into doing bad things. He was interrupted by groans of protest across the room from those who felt he was being unfair.

"Be quiet!" Elliott commanded. "Your disrespect for this Commission will not be tolerated. Anyone who speaks out of turn or makes noise while someone is speaking will wait out in the rain with the others. What Commissioner Davie is saying is of the utmost importance and I would advise everyone to listen closely."

Davie continued. "You have been told that these lands belong to you. This is not true. All lands in Canada belong to the Queen of England, but she has told the governments of Canada to be generous with the Indians who are now in our care. We have set up many reserves on good lands all over British Columbia. Most Indians are satisfied but the people of Metlakatla have been taught by some Whites that this is not good enough. I want to make it very clear that nothing belongs to the Indians anymore. Even the reserves we have given you we can take away at any moment if you do not respect our laws and what we have done for you."

Gasps of surprise and outrage rippled across the room. Elliott issued another stern warning. Some sat in stunned silence, unable to believe what they had just heard. I held my feelings inside and I said nothing. Others could not and they left the room on their own. I wanted to leave too, but Duncan want me to stay. He wanted me to know the enemy. I was grateful Davie's words could not be heard beyond the crowded classroom, for I am sure no good could have come of it.

Elliott's Commissioners had come to condemn Duncan and Metlakatla. They listened to Ridley, who used a full day of their time telling fanciful stories of what we had done to him. White miners, prospectors and cannery managers were brought from the Skeena to testify against Duncan. Few of them had ever met Duncan but they were angry he had stood in their way by trying to protect us. All those who were opposed to Duncan and our people spoke first. Elliott allowed an equal number of to speak in our favour, but hundreds more wanted to speak in favour of us. In this way Elliott prevented most them from speaking.

In the end, it did not matter. The Commissioners only listened to those who spoke against us. Davie interrupted our speakers, accusing us of lying again and again. They listened to those who spoke against us without interrupting, but they accused Tsimshians of repeating words that Duncan had told us to say. To them, we were only clever dogs he had trained to perform fancy tricks.

The Commission gave their report to the White government in Victoria a week before Christmas. It was worse than we had expected. It accused Duncan, Tomlinson and other missionaries of causing unrest and disrespect for White law. It also criticized all other Whites who had spoken as our friends. They said our town had plenty of land for our needs and that our greed had become a dangerous example to other Indian communities. They stated that Metlakatla should be run by Bishop Ridley and our elections and Town Council should be abolished. A survey of church lands would be completed, with force if necessary, and that Duncan and the people of Metlakatla should not expect any further support from the government of British Columbia until these changes had been carried out.

Their report ruined our Christmas. Many were upset that they had not been allowed to speak. Others, like me, knew they would not have listened to us anyway. The White newspapers no longer mentioned the miracle of Metlakatla. They had nothing good to say about us. Twenty years ago, they would not give our people the Smallpox vaccination and they watched us die. They stole our land, our fish and our forests after that, and now they wanted everything else. We had been told we had nothing and we were threatened not to resist their thievery. The land that was ours for a hundred generations had been taken by Whites who had never seen it. We felt more helpless than ever.

Duncan sat at his desk holding his head in his hands after he read the Commissioners' report. He stormed back and forth across his office in pain and frustration for days. He would not look at me and there was no way to comfort him. I feared he had finally been defeated but he was too stubborn to give up, even as the skies grew dark around us.

After a few days, he stopped pacing and returned to his desk. He stayed there, quietly thinking all morning. That afternoon he wrote letters the Bishop Cridge and Senator McDougall in Victoria, sometimes tearing them up and starting over. Finally, he finished them. He addressed and sealed them himself without letting me read them. When he was done he was calm. He even managed a slight smile when he looked at me. My curiosity overcame me.

"Mr. Duncan, what are you going to do?

"I haven't decided yet Jack, but the battle isn't over."

"How can you say that after reading the report? What can we possibly do when they make their decisions without listening to us? How can we keep what we have built when Premier Smithe stops our Town Council and sends you away?" My lips trembling as I voiced my fears.

Duncan looked at me warmly and reassured me. "Their words are only recommendations, Jack, not decisions. We have many enemies in Victoria, it's true, but they don't know what to do with us. Metlakatla is still well-known. Our supporters around the world will cry out in anger if they harm us. Our enemies are afraid of the consequences. Besides, I have been fired already and I am still here. I have committed no crime. They cannot force me to leave."

"Will they try to make us criminals?"

"Of course. White men make laws so they can control people they do not like, but if you are careful not to break their laws they are as helpless as we are."

"But what can we do if they move against us?"

"We will stand our ground and fight them where we can. Hopefully over time we will build new allies."

Duncan was a fierce opponent. He snarled loudly at his enemies in Victoria that spring. He was in no mood for compromise. As our enemies grew, he grew with them. In April, Smithe and the White government voted to give Mission Point and the great church to the missionary society without discussing it with us further. Duncan threatened them with a law suit. The newspapers reported many hot debates in the legislature and eventually they changed their decision. Duncan had saved us again, at least for now. I was filled with admiration for him. Only he knew how to defend our people and I would do anything I could to support him.

Bishop Cridge cautioned him to not sound too proud about his victory. Smithe argued that the federal government should force Duncan to leave Metlakatla. Fortunately, he was not able to convince enough Whites in his government and no letter was sent to Ottawa.

Cridge told Duncan that Smithe had enemies in Victoria too. One of those was John Robson, the Provincial Secretary, and Cridge felt he could become our ally if we spoke with him. Duncan decided it was better that a Tsimshian man speak for us so he sent Sam Pritchard to Victoria. Sam returned with good news in time to join us at the oolichon camps on the Nass. Robson disagreed with Elliott and was willing to work with us.

Senator MacDougall spoke with his friends in Ottawa and he persuaded Duncan that he could make important allies there where Smithe and Ridley had not yet spread their lies. He asked Duncan to make a trip across the country to meet them.

Ridley had become bolder since the Commissioners' report and Duncan did not trust what he would do if he left. Instead of going to Ottawa, he agreed to write to John A. MacDonald, the Prime Minister of Canada, to explain our situation and to ask for his support. His letter said our situation was urgent. Seven hundred people of our town signed a petition, asking the Prime Minister to give Mission Point back to our people so we could pray once again in our great cathedral. Duncan mailed it with his letter at the end of January, and we waited patiently through the spring for a reply.

In the meantime, our situation worsened. Our cannery needed parts. It had been closed since October and there was little other work in town. The saw mill and the carpentry shop had closed and the Town Council was low on money. They could not to collect taxes from families who had no money, and no more money came from England. Our customers in other towns also had no money and had stopped doing business with us. Faith does not feed a hungry family.

Tom was especially restless. He hated being idle. He was also still angry over the Commission's report and he had lost faith in petitions and agreements with White leaders. He spent his days talking with other idle men about how they should fight the Whites to get our church back. Such talk only made him unhappier as his anger grew.

The warmer spring weather was a welcome relief. Our hard work on the Nass took our minds off our troubles. There were still plenty of oolichon, for the Whites did not like the taste of our Little Chiefs, but the salmon run on the Skeena was not so successful. Our catch was small that year. We hoped that work in the cannery would start again and keep our men busy for the summer, but the cannery's generator had failed. The mechanic we paid to come from Victoria to fix it said it would take another two months for a part he needed to come from England.

I feared our people would be discouraged but they found other work that summer. The women dried our salmon catch on the hillside above the cannery and the men hunted like when we were young. Tom, Joseph, my brother George, Paul Legiac and Daniel planned a hunt in the hills east of Tsamsem's Trench. My two nephews, Mary's son Jesse who was almost twenty, and his brother Earl, who had just turned sixteen, went with them. It was Earl's first big hunting trip.

They wanted me to join them. Tom was happier than he had been in months, and Jesse and Earl were so excited. There was no place I would rather be, but Duncan stopped me. He had just received more unsettling news from Victoria.

"I can't afford to let you go right now, Jack. The next two weeks could be very important. Senator McDougall says he has heard that Smithe has contacted Ottawa again and there may be trouble. He has asked John Robson to tell us what is happening. I am expecting a letter to arrive on the next ship and I might need your help."

"How can I help you?" I asked. I meant this as a protest, not an offer.

"I don't know yet, Jack, not until the letter arrives." That was all he would say. I felt so frustrated.

Tom was upset when I told him I could not join the hunting trip. My news threatened his fragile joy. "Why? Tell him you must come with us."

"I am not sure why, Tom. He is expecting something important to happen but he won't tell me what."

"It will be like our hunting trips before we moved to Metlakatla," Tom pleaded with me, "like the time we made love in the tent the morning I shot the bear. You remember?" I nodded with a heavy heart. I stared at the floor, for I could not bear to see the disappointment in his eyes. We were quiet for a minute while we both fought back tears.

Finally I said, "I must stay. Duncan is our only hope."

"Damn you!" he shouted. "What does he need you for? His war with other White men is forever. One week does not matter. You always talk 'Duncan, Duncan, Duncan.' You don't care about me or Jesse or Earl. He has work for you but never for me. You are his pet dog. I will go hunt without you while you wait for Duncan to give you a bone." He slammed the door as he left, before I could say any more.

The next two days passed slowly. My heart was heavy with pain. Tom would not speak or look at me as he prepared for the hunt. A ship arrived from Victoria the day before he left. There was no letter from John Robson but Duncan still would not let me leave with Tom. I waited with the wives on the beach the next morning as the hunters loaded their canoes. Each man gave me a hug and patted my back, except Tom. I kept the brave face of an Elder as I told Jesse and Earl to respect the words of the older men and to remember their prayers. Jesse sensed my pain. He kissed my cheek and promised to bring me back the biggest deer. I felt tears rise in my eyes.

Anne stood beside me. She was there to kiss Jesse goodbye. She was never angry with him for leaving her behind. She loved him purely, like I loved Tom, I told myself, but Tom had a different love for me. He said nothing and would not look at me. I felt a great shame for spoiling the only happy moment he had known that year as he climbed into his canoe without me. I remembered how he had not come to the beach to wish me well when I left for Fort Simpson to find my parents during the Smallpox. He will forgive me after he returns, I told myself to ease my pain.

It was no comfort to work in Duncan's office after their canoes had left. There were only papers to file and the floor to sweep. That did little to distract me from my miserable feelings. I let down Tom, my friends and family for this, I thought with great bitterness. Silently, I prayed to the Lord to bring the important letter that would prove to Tom that I had made the right choice to stay.

My prayers were answered the next morning, but I soon regretted praying for it. A mail bag arrived from Victoria with a letter from the Office of the Provincial Secretary, John Robson. Duncan tore it open hurriedly. I watched as his eyes darted back and forth over the words. I heard him mutter "Dear Lord" as he finished it and for a moment he drifted off into thought.

"What is it, Mr. Duncan?"

"Jack, this is the best news we've received in months!" His face came back to life as he spoke. "Robson says Smithe and his government want to resolve the legal issues over Metlakatla. They are willing to give us title over Mission Point if the federal government in Ottawa asks them to. We might just win this one after all."

I was so excited. It seemed obvious that I would not be needed if Ottawa said yes. I could go searching for the hunting party to tell them the good news.

"But we cannot rest, Jack. We need to convince the Prime Minister to grant us the title," Duncan said with a gleam in his eyes.

"How will we do that?" I asked.

"The way we should have done at the start. I should have listened to Senator McDougall last winter."

"Sir?"

"Pack your bags, Jack. And tell Sam Pritchard to pack his too. We are going to Ottawa to meet Sir John A. McDonald. There's a boat stopping here Friday morning that will take us to Victoria. We have to be on it."

"But Mr. Duncan, I cannot leave now. Tom.... My family has left on the hunting trip and I must be here when they return."

Duncan looked at me with a puzzled expression. "Jack, if your family and friends can go on the hunting trip without you, surely they can manage without you when they are back. You do see how important this trip is, don't you? This could be our best chance to win our church back and stop Victoria from taking our land and our Town Council. Your uncle, Henry Richardson, was Chief of the Council for years. I will speak to him and he will explain to your family how important this trip is."

I had waited for this opportunity to visit the eastern lands for many years, but why did it finally come at such a wrong time? "I don't see how I can be of help in Ottawa, sir."

"The way you always are, Jack, by being yourself. If I go alone I'm just a cranky old missionary who has a personal grudge against the government in Victoria. When you and Sam are with me, they can see I am just representing your people and fighting for your rights. They can see I am doing good for others, not just myself."

"This is not a good time for me."

"Why not? You have no wife or children. No one is counting on you. It is easier for you to come than Sam Pritchard, and I know he will want to come."

"But shouldn't you bring someone else for a change? Some people resent all the things you do for me."

"For a change? Jack, you have never crossed the continent. You have never been on a train, never seen the great deserts, the great plains or the great cities of the east. Haven't you longed to visit other parts of the world since you were a boy, since you saw your first sailing ship? This will be the greatest adventure of your life!" He paused to check my reaction. I must have still looked unhappy. "Besides I am bringing some-one else-Sam. You and Sam are the best examples of the success of my work. You have the best spoken and written English. No one else but the best will do. It is a great honour to be able to represent your people. They will talk about your trip for many generations."

"But …."

"But what, Jack?" He was losing his patience with me and I could think of noth-ing more to say. "It will all turn out well, you'll see. It will only be for a month and you will thank me for the rest of your life. Go on now. I have a lot to do and you're wasting my time."

I walked to Sam Pritchard's house and told him the news. As Duncan predicted, he was excited to go but I was already sick from worry. I told him what I could not tell Duncan, about how upset Tom would be. He told me that Duncan was right, that it was important that I come with them. He was sure Tom loved me enough that he would forgive me when I returned with the good news we would bring, but I was not sure Tom would see things as Sam did.

It was so sudden that I was kept busy with all that needed to be done before we left. The next day passed too quickly and it seemed I would not be ready on time. My sister Mary washed and pressed all my best clothes and Duncan brought me a case to pack them into. "We are not moving away. I am only giving you one steamer trunk," he laughed. I tried to look cheerful though inside I was panicking.

I still tried to think of a way to excuse myself from the trip, or at least to convince Duncan to delay it until Tom returned. Nothing I thought of seemed good enough, so I paid a visit to Timothy. Even he agreed with Duncan.

"Have faith, Little Salmon. There is nothing you can do but let Great Spirit guide you. Tom was angry with you when he left and will still be angry when he returns, even if you stay and wait for him," he told me. "He does not understand how much you have sacrificed for him," he added, "but our people may suffer if you stay, and then Duncan would be angry with you too."

Timothy was right and I always trusted him. I had no choice but to leave with Duncan before Tom returned. I could not leave him a letter for he had never learned to read well. Someone would need to speak to him for me. He was not a close friend of Timothy and Mary would likely scold him and make the situation worse, so before the day was over I went to Laura and told her my story. She saw the concern in my eyes and promised me she would do her best to make it easier for Tom.

The next morning the steamer stopped at Metlakatla on its way down from Fort Simpson to Victoria. The sky was grey and threatening rain as we boarded. Sam and I took our bags to our rooms and then returned to the deck while Duncan went to speak to the captain.

It felt I was in a nightmare, standing on the deck and looking back at the town. My heart screamed for something to happen that would stop us from leaving. Sam nudged me and told me to stop worrying. He was definitely in a good mood. He stretched his arms wide and inhaled the morning air, as though it was different from the air he breathed every day. Metlakatla spread out before us on the hill above the dock like a colourful picture. I was missing it even before we left. It is strange how terrible moments are sometimes filled with such beauty.

Nothing prevented our departure. My heart sank lower as the ship pulled away from the dock and I watch our town shrink away. I watched it as it disappeared, until I could no longer see where the store used to be, the cannery that was closed or the great church boarded up. I felt anxious all the way to Victoria as if I had forgotten to do something important. Now it was too late and I was being carried away like a helpless prisoner. Happy memories of my past trips returned to mock me and make me more miserable. I worried constantly about the hurt Tom would feel when he returned home. I tried to hide my sadness from Sam so I would not spoil his excitement, but I was ill with worry.

Duncan was in good spirits and excited about our big trip. He greeted Sam warmly but he lost his smile him when he saw my woeful face. He was impatient with my sadness and I could not tell him why I was unhappy. He had never had a lover and I doubted if even a lover could have kept him from his mission.

The ship made its usual stops at Port Essington and Bella Coola before spending the night in Fort Rupert's harbour. The next day it continued on to Victoria after stopping in Nanaimo to load coal. We waited overnight in Victoria to board the steamer for San Francisco. Duncan checked Sam and I into a hotel and then went to stay with Bishop Cridge.

The streamer to San Francisco was an American ship. It was larger than the ones that visited Metlakatla. Sam and I climbed to the highest deck to look at the harbour from above. We could see the roofs of the buildings on Government Street above the warehouses along the docks. I felt my first excitement here, on this large ship knowing that I would soon be farther away from home than I had ever been. It was a guilty excitement to be here without Tom.

The ship left the harbour and rounded the south end of the Vancouver Island. It headed north-west with the morning sun on our backs. We followed the long channel that separated the great island on the north side and the land of the Americans to the south. Salish fishermen had once told me about this passage but this was the first time I had seen it. It led to the open sea and the land of the Nootkas who hunt the great whales that follow this coast. I had seen Nootka men in Victoria. They wore ornaments carved from whale bones and rattles on their belts made from the skeletons of men's hands. Their lands belonged to the English now too.

Once our ship reached the open sea it turned south. We passed a Nootka village close to the shore. They still lived in long houses, like the ones we once had in at Gitka'ata and Fort Simpson. Their canoes rested on the sand in front of their houses as ours used to do, but their paint was old and there were no totems by the shore to greet travelers. Perhaps their missionaries had told them totems were evil or maybe, like the Salish, the Nootkas had never had totems. Nootka children stopped their play to wave at us, but no one raced to follow the ship in their canoes as we used to do when I was young.

The steamer kept a good speed and did not slow down during the night. At dawn, the skies were blue and the sea was calm. The only wind was caused by our speed. At midday, the ship turned up the widest river I have ever seen. Duncan told us that it was the Columbia River. This was the land of the Chinook people, who Whites called Flatheads. We followed the river for five hours as it bent south and then west again, until the ship reached a smaller river. We turned into the mouth of that river and soon arrived at a city larger than Victoria, which greeted us on both sides of the river.

This was the White city of Portland. A sign over the dock called it the 'City of Roses'. The ship stayed here all afternoon while some passengers and cargo left the ship and others took their place. Duncan let Sam and I leave the ship to explore the city for an hour but he cautioned us not to buy anything. Our luggage was already full and we needed to save our money for the long trip to Ottawa.

We did not go far anyway, for Portland's streets were muddy. Heavy rains had fallen the week before and the sewers had overflowed. The city did not smell like roses. That evening we watched it from the deck as our ship returned to the sea the way it had come. Our ship turned south again when we reached the sea, but by then it was too dark to see much. The few lights we saw see on the distant shore disappeared into a wall of fog. We returned to our room below deck to escape the chill and we stayed there until morning.

On the second day after leaving Portland, we entered San Francisco harbour. It was late afternoon. Sam and I were excited by the huge harbour and the tall buildings of the city. Surely this must be the largest city in the world, we declared to Duncan. He laughed and said London, where the Queen lives, is much larger. That seemed impossible to us.

We took our baggage off the ship and went looking for a hotel. "This is it," Duncan smiled at us. "From this point we cross the continent on the railway!" He looked back over his shoulder to see our reaction. I was both excited and nervous for I had never been on a train.

Duncan led us through the streets away from the harbour where the hotels were cleaner. He had passed through San Francisco a few times before and he remembered the streets. Drunken sailors from the ships stayed in the hotels near the harbour, he warned us. I had not seen any drunken sailors working on our ship.

Sam and I were amazed by the size of San Francisco. It was much bigger than Portland. The tallest buildings were higher than our own great cathedral. Some were painted different colours and it was cleaner too. The streets and sidewalks were made of stone. There were no open sewers or mud under our feet like in Portland. It did not smell foul.

The largest buildings in Victoria were on the first street next to the docks, but here they grew bigger as we walked further from the harbour. They were packed tightly together. Many had stone carvings and decorations that hung over the sidewalks above us. Sam and I looked at each other and laughed with delight. Duncan smiled at our excitement but he warned us to pay attention so we would not walk into other people around us.

We had only one night in this wonderful city. Duncan said that was just as well. He said it was a city full of sinful bars and prostitution that would try to lure us in. His words did nothing to discourage us from wanting to explore it. Duncan was tired, but he gave us permission to go out if we promised to stay together and not get lost. He told us not to speak to strangers, enter any pubs or go near the harbour. We gave him our word.

We practiced the street names so we could find our hotel again. We followed Battery Street past several pubs and hotels. Sam was restless. He wanted to find something he would remember for the rest of his life. He was not interested in bars and was not a man who would cheat on his wife, but he did not want to explore only one street. He spotted a bluff that rose high above the streets to the north. He decided we should climb it to see the city from above. We followed side streets to the base of the hill. There we found a path that led us to the top.

We sat in a clearing at the edge of the bluff and watched people and carriages move along the streets below us. It was fascinating. The dark shapes of ships floated in the harbour and beyond them I saw the faint lights from the far side of the bay. "If this was a weekend, there would be young lovers up here for sure," Sam said thoughtfully. He missed his wife Catherine, I thought to myself, but at least he was able to say goodbye to her before we left.

It was peaceful and warm. I lay back on the grass and watched the stars. I was thinking how beautiful this place was and that I must take Tom here someday. Suddenly a frightful thing happened. A ghostly claw of immense size reached across the sky above me, only fifty feet above my head. It startled me and I leapt to my feet. It was only streams of fog passing through trees at the top of the hill. It came from behind us, poured over us and flowed down the hillside into the city. Soon the ships in the harbour disappeared and the street lamps looked like smoky fires. The damp air made us shiver so we returned to the hotel.

THIRTY THREE

It was hard to sleep that night. I could not stop thinking about the train we would ride on the next morning. I woke early, even before Duncan came to our room to make sure we were up on time. The train was departing early, so we left without breakfast shortly after sunrise. We carried our bags down to the harbour to catch the ferry across the bay.

Fog sat thick on the water. We could not see where the ferry was going until we neared the far shore. The train station was a short walk from the dock. Here the fog was already lifting. I was afraid and excited. I glanced at Sam and he gave me a big smile. It was a nervous smile like mine.

We waited in the great hall of train station with our bags while Duncan bought our tickets. He warned us not to move until he returned. It was unlike any place I had ever been before. People hurried past us in all directions. Their words and laughter echoed off the high ceilings and walls. I became anxious watching them. Duncan left us alone for a long time and I was afraid our train would leave before he returned. A man in a red uniform came to collect our luggage. Sam thought he was stealing our bags and almost started a fight. Duncan returned just in time. He apologized to the baggage man. Duncan told us he was called a porter.

"You see, this is why you cannot go ahead without me!" Duncan scolded Sam.

Sam's face blushed red. He handed us our tickets. We were thankful that he was there to teach us how to read them. He led us through the station to the platform where our train was waiting. "We still have half an hour before it leaves," he told us. I had worried for nothing.

Duncan climbed on board first to show us it was safe. He beckoned for us to follow him. The man in the red uniform carried our bags and led the way to our cabin. We squeezed between the rows of seats, through the doorways, between the cars and along the narrow corridors while Duncan taught us how to read the numbers on the rooms.

The train felt tight and crowded inside. The ceilings were low. I was afraid we could be trapped inside if anything bad happened, but I said nothing. I did not want to be a timid child.

We arrived at our room. Duncan gave the baggage man a coin and we stowed our bags away. It did not seem crowded or dark once we sat by the large windows. Sam asked Duncan if we could explore the train. "All right, but be back in twenty minutes before the train leaves," he nodded. He opened his Bible and settled into a seat by the window. Sam grabbed me arm and led me into the corridor.

The next car to ours was the dining car. Workers were busy loading the cupboards with food and supplies. They looked at us suspiciously and with some irritation as we squeezed past them. We continued on to the next car and the next. They both had cabins like ours. We stood on a small platform at the end of the last car and paused to watch the porters and passengers on the platform.

"We should return," Sam suggested after a couple minutes. He led us back, but he continued past our cabin to the front of the train as we counted the cars. There were seven cars including ours. The two near the front only had seats and no cabins. There were two more cars beyond them but there was no passageway into them. "I think they are only for the workers. No passengers are getting on," Sam shouted, leaning out from the door.

"Here, you two!" a man in a uniform shouted at us. "How did you get on the train?" He climbed up from the platform and tried to push us out the door.

"No, no!" I stopped him. "We are passengers. We have tickets for New York." I showed him my ticket. My good English seemed to surprise him. He pulled it from my hand and signaled to Sam to pass him his ticket too.

"How did you get these?" he growled at us. I was afraid he would not give them back and he would force us to leave the train.

"Mr. Duncan bought them for us," Sam explained. "He is taking us to Ottawa to meet Mr. MacDonald."

The man in the uniform stared at Sam for a few seconds, as though Sam's words made no sense. "Who is this Mr. Duncan and where is he now?"

"He is a missionary, sir," I answered. "He is reading in Cabin B7." I tried to point to the B7 on my ticket.

The man pulled the ticket away from my finger. He glared at me as if I had done something wrong. Then he seemed to relax. "These tickets only take you as far as Chicago," he told us softly as he handed them back. He was correct. The ticket said Chicago, not New York. I was horrified. How did Duncan make such a mistake?

My reaction amused the man in the uniform. "You need to change trains and buy another ticket when you get to Chicago," he smiled. "I suppose your Mr. Duncan already knows this."

There was a sharp blast of a whistle and someone shouted, "All aboard!"

"You two had better get back to B7. The train is about to leave." The man turned and stuck his head out the door. He blew his whistle twice loudly and signaled something to a man on the platform.

Sam and I hurried back to our cabin as fast as we could. We were not sure what would happen if we did not make it on time. There was a frightening blast of the train's whistle just as we reached our car. We hurried to the seat opposite Duncan. "Good," he said as we sat down. "You better stay here until the conductor comes around to check our tickets."

The train jerked and began to move. I gripped my seat as we rolled out of the station. The houses and streets soon disappeared and we saw only dirt roads and farms. I looked across the corridor and saw we were heading north along the bay. The train moved so slowly at first that I thought we might never reach New York, but once it was beyond the buildings it picked up speed. It went faster and faster. I had never been on anything that moved that fast. Trees and fences flashed past us almost close enough to touch. I pulled away from the window, fearing what would happen if the train hit something that was too close. I could not take my eyes off the passing scenery. I could be watching my death, I thought to myself. Sam was as frightened as I was, especially when he saw a smoke coming from the engine in front. He interrupted Duncan's reading to tell him the train was on fire.

"Yes, I know" he smiled broadly at our childish concerns. "There is always a fire in a train's engine. It heats the water to make steam and the steam turns the wheels to move the train." He closed his Bible and he was our school teacher again. "That is not smoke you see. It is steam. Do you see how it disappears as it cools. Smoke does not disappear that fast." I pressed my face to the window I could see he was right.

"Hello there, you must be Mr. Duncan?" Duncan looked to the door, surprised to hear his name. It was man in the uniform we had met before the train started. "Your tickets, please."

"Jack, Sam, please give the conductor your tickets."

"No worry. I've already checked these two." He smiled at us as he took Duncan's ticket. "They tell me you're on your way to New York."

"Yes, New York and beyond, up to Canada," Duncan answered.

"That's a long trip, sir. There's a change of trains in Chicago, you know."

"Yes, I've made the trip before, thank you," Duncan nodded. The conductor moved on and we went back to watching the scenery.

Duncan suggested it was a good time for breakfast in the dining car. He led us to the car behind. The tables were set with fine silverware and china, like those we had used in Governor Douglas' home. We ordered eggs, potatoes and tea and looked out the window as we ate.

The train climbed onto a great bridge as it crossed a river. I glanced at Sam. He was as frightened as I was as we rose into the sky but neither of us said a word. In no time it rolled down the far side and continued into the hills beyond. What a wonderful road White men have made for this train, I thought. I felt I was seeing a miracle.

Sam and I became used to the speed of the train. We were no longer afraid and we shouted out like young boys whenever we saw something new. We arrived at our first stop, Sacramento, near the middle of the day. Several passengers got off and others climbed on. The train stayed in the station long enough to take on wood and water.

After Sacramento, the train followed a river valley. We returned to the dining car for lunch. The valley grew steeper and soon we were surrounded by forests. After lunch we sat by the window and watched quietly. There was not as much to shout about. We had lived with forests all our lives. The trees here were thinner and shorter than the ones near Metlakatla. Still, the movement held us captive as if we were in a trance. The land became drier until the trees disappeared and the hills became barren and brown. I had heard stories of lands like this beyond the mountains, but I had never seen them.

Duncan ordered tea service to be brought to our room, and later in the evening we went to the dining car for dinner. By then the light was fading. The valleys were cloaked in shadows while the tops of the hills were golden brown in the dying sunlight. The sky was a deep blue without any clouds. It was rarely this clear at home.

The train stopped in a village called Reno for more wood and water.

"This land is called Nevada," Duncan told us. The train started up again and was soon moving swiftly. By the time we were finished our dinner the sky was a pale glow and the hills and trees were only black shapes moving by like Spirits in the night.

We could no longer see the passing land so we closed the window blinds. There was only the rocking and rattling of the train. I was restless. Duncan taught us a card game but even that failed to keep my interest for long. I worried that we were missing the scenery in the dark, but Duncan said we would be riding for several more days and there would be plenty of scenery to entertain us.

I climbed onto the upper bunk bed. I covered myself with a blanket but I could not sleep. The rocking motion and the strange noises of the train kept me awake. I thought again of Tom and how I could explain all the new things I had seen that day. Then I worried he would be too upset to listen to my stories. Eventually I did sleep, but I woke again when the train stopped in the middle of the night. I heard banging sounds and voices of workmen doing something outside but I stayed in my bed.

The next morning we were beyond the mountains. The land was barren of trees or grass. Duncan explained that this was a great desert where it almost never rained. The sun was brilliant and the skies were clear except for small streaks of cloud. The train moved faster now that the land was flat and the path was straight. The speed was less frightening with no trees passing close by the window. The hot sun made our cabin unpleasant and robbed us of our energy. Duncan sat still with his eyes closed while he fanned himself with his book. Sam stared quietly out the window.

Sadness returned to my heart as I looked at the barren lands. I missed the warmth of Tom's arms and I wondered if he would ever forgive me. I pitied myself too. It did me no good to think about either his pain or my own, but it was as impossible not to. I could not change the path I was on or turn the train around. I felt as empty as the desert outside.

The sun declined. The train climbed into new hills and trees appeared in the valleys again. We opened the window wider and the cooler air refreshed us. We ate in the dining car while Duncan told us of the wars between the Whites and the Indians a few years before. This was Indian territory, he told us, though I could not imagine living here. We had seen no one all day, except for two workers at a refill station. He also told stories about his past trips to the east on this same train. He chose the funniest stories, ones that made us laugh, and I felt good again for the first time all day.

The next day we were mostly in the mountains. By evening the land was flatter but it was not as dry as the great desert. At least there were grasses that had turned yellow in the summer heat. We saw our first herd of buffalo in the distance, running at great speed. They were being chased men on horses. Puffs of smoke came from their rifles and we saw two buffalo fall. Sam and I were excited when Duncan thought they might be Indians, but he did not know their name.

On the fourth day, the grasses were green. We passed farms, roads and houses. We saw no one, except for two White farmers riding on carts full of hay. Our train made three stops at stations where passengers boarded the train. All their faces were White. We reached the town of Omaha in mid-morning. Many people boarded here to ride the rest of the way to Chicago.

We reached Chicago that evening. The sun was setting in bright colours of pink and gold that were fading to purples and blues. We collected our bags and followed Duncan through the dirty streets until we found a hotel a few blocks away. Chicago was another great city, even larger than San Francisco, Duncan told us. It was too dark to see and we were too tired to look. Our room was simple with only a desk, two beds, a night stand and a lamp. It smelled of stale smoke. We ate at a restaurant beside the hotel. I felt better after I ate. We returned to our room afterwards. The city seemed to spread on forever in the distance, but it was dark and ugly so we did not go for a walk.

Duncan told us we must sleep right away. Our train to New York would leave at sunrise the next morning. I did not mind. I was grateful to sleep on a bed that was not moving. Duncan slept alone while Sam and I shared the other bed.

We woke sometime in the night to the sound of Duncan's snoring. Sam chuckled and whispered to me that it sounded like a wood saw. I woke again in the middle of the night from a troubling dream. I was back in Metlakatla and Tom was angry and shouting at me. I could not understand what he was saying but his words hurt me anyway. Sam was awake too.

"You were crying," he told me. "Are you all right?"

"Yes. I am not sure why I was crying." My voice was full of pain and I turned away from Sam to hide my pain. He put his arm around me gently and pulled me into his chest. His kindness was reassuring. I fell asleep again to the sound of Duncan's snoring and I slept until Duncan woke us in the morning.

It was still dark. Sam and I were ready to leave in a few minutes for we had packed our bags the night before. We walked to the station in the cool air as the first light gave the clouds a pink glow. The station was already busy. Passengers waited in long lines to buy tickets and vendors walked around selling food and newspapers. I was fully awake with all the noise and excitement.

Duncan had purchased our tickets to New York in San Francisco so we did not need to wait in line. We found our train and our cabin and waited for the other passengers to finish boarding. I checked my pocket watch when the train started to move. It was right on time.

"Is that the same pocket watch you bought in Fort Simpson thirty years ago?" Duncan asked me. I nodded. "You need to change the time. Chicago is two hours ahead of San Francisco."

I was surprised. Did different cities have different times? Duncan chuckled when he saw my puzzled face. "New York is one hour ahead of Chicago, and so is Ottawa. England is five hours ahead of New York." I grinned. Every day I was learning new things, but Duncan already knew them.

The train rolled past the streets of Chicago. The sun was touching the tallest buildings now. The city looked much larger than the night before. Clearly, it was larger than San Francisco. It took much longer to reach the first farms.

There was no desert between Chicago and New York. It was mostly forest and farms. There were more towns too, and many churches and roads. This had been Indian land three generations ago, Duncan told us, but this was White land now. There were no Indian villages. It bothered me that this change happened so quickly. Would our own lands be lost to Whites like this too, I wondered. I felt uneasy but I did not ask Duncan the questions in my mind. I did not want to hear his answers.

This train was slower. There were more stops and more people boarding and leaving each time. By evening, we entered hills that were covered in forests. The train rocked on through the night, its wheels clanking and squealing as it made many turns through the mountains. The next morning it stopped in a small city called Allentown before continuing on to New York.

As we crossed the last river, the first sight of New York astonished me. Its size was greater than anything I had imagined. Sam and I were boys again, saying to each other, "Look at that! Look at that!" There was too much to see, too much to believe, but we saw it with our own eyes. It was delightful, but its great size was frightening too. I knew I could walk for a hundred days and not see it all. One would need to live here to know it. At that moment that idea seemed quite wonderful.

To Duncan, living there was a terrible idea. Big cities have bigger evils, he told us, and New York was the biggest city. It was full of thieves and prostitutes and he decided it was unsafe for us. Sam was disappointed and I was angry. The four hours we waited in the station for the next train were wasted. I wanted to defy Duncan's orders and spend the time exploring, but Sam was too nervous. He said we could not afford to get lost or robbed. Duncan would never leave us on our own later in the trip if we did. He was right. Perhaps we can see more of it on our way home, Sam suggested.

The next day a train took us north and east to Boston. It was an older train with a smaller engine. There were no mountains to climb and it did not need to go as fast for the stations were close together. The scenery was boring so I did not look out the window. I read a book about trains that I had purchased in the station.

The train arrived in Boston in the late afternoon. Most of the passengers got off but we stayed on the train while it rested in the station. Two hours later it left for Portland, Maine. There we left with our luggage to look for a hotel. Our next train would take us north into Canada but it would leave two days later. Our hotel was on the same street as the station. We had our dinner there.

After dinner Sam and I took a walk through the streets. It was a larger city than Victoria but quieter too. There were no sounds of fighting coming from the public houses. There were no drunk men in the street. Duncan said it was a decent town, and decent towns are quiet. There was nothing to do so we returned to the hotel.

Sam was not feeling well the next day so he rested in our hotel room. Duncan was busy working on a proposal to present to John A. MacDonald. It was best to leave him alone so I wandered through the streets, looking at the strange buildings made of brick. The town was neat and orderly, though there was not much to see. I watched men loading ships in the port for a while.

I was happy not to be sitting in a moving train, but the excitement of traveling had faded to weariness. The different styles of buildings no longer mattered. None of the faces that passed me on the sidewalks or on the carriages were friendly. They glanced at me suspiciously and then looked away. Every face was White.

Where had the Indians gone who had lived here before the Whites? A terrible thought crossed my mind. The Whites had driven them away for they only wanted to live with other Whites. Perhaps all Indians would be gone from Victoria too in a few years. Already the Indian camps were gone. What would happen to us after our land was taken away? That was why Duncan was bringing us to Ottawa, to beg to keep our land, but what good would that do if the Whites wanted this to happen?

Duncan and Sam asked why I was quiet when I returned. I told them I was tired. I was telling the truth, but I kept my dark thoughts to myself. The next morning we boarded the Grand Trunk Railway that took us north, away from the sea, through more forests and hills to the shores of another great river. We crossed over it into Montreal, the biggest city in eastern Canada.

Duncan was relieved to leave the United States. We should be happy to be home again, he told us, but Montreal was certainly not our home. It looked like other large

White cities, though its stone buildings looked older. They had strange roofs and iron staircases on the outside that turned in circles as they climbed. People here spoke French, a language I could not speak but I had heard it a few times at Fort Simpson. Now they had to be loyal to the English Queen for they had lost the war.

Queen Victoria was our queen too. Duncan taught us the English had given us their Queen as a gift. Every morning we sang "God Save the Queen" and we promised her our loyalty. But why did we do this? The French had to be loyal for they had lost their war, but we had not fought the English. They did not defeat us. Now they told us our lands and buildings belonged to the English Queen, though she had not paid for them or taken them from us in a fight. Did they think we had lost them because we promised to be loyal to her?   I dared not ask Duncan why we were loyal to the English Queen, but I wondered if he knew we would lose our lands if we promised our loyalty to her? I should not have asked about the French. Again, dark thoughts filled my mind.

The next morning we left Montreal on a train headed west up the river. We got off in a village named Prescott, where we waited in a small station for another train that would take us north to Ottawa. We arrived at our destination in the first week of July. We were tired after so many days of travel. We ate dinner in a restaurant next to our hotel and spent the evening in our room ironing and hanging our best clothes. Duncan wanted us to be ready to meet Prime Minister MacDonald the next day. He was anxious and his mind was busy with many details. He was in no mood to joke or tell stories. It was best not to bother him with the many questions that filled our heads.

The next morning he was cheery and full of energy. Sam and I were excited too. We dressed carefully and combed our hair before going to the restaurant for next door for breakfast.

"I want you to have a good meal in your stomachs," he told us. "We have to wait for a few hours before the Prime Minister is able to meet with us." We both grinned and nodded. We were rested and ready to do our best after coming such a long way.

He led us through the streets of the city. A strong wind blew our hair around. There was nothing we could do but wait until we arrived to straighten ourselves again. We had only been walking a couple minutes when the city buildings disappeared. Across the street on a hill there was a large empty space covered in grass. Beyond it the broad stone walls of the Parliament Buildings rose several floors high. "Wow!" Sam exclaimed.

"Hurry now!" Duncan smiled at us. "You can see more of them later, after we have met with the Prime Minister."

We walked into the big entrance hall. Our footsteps echoed off the walls and the high ceiling as we walked across the tiled floor. Sam and I looked around us in amazement and we laughed like boys again. Duncan asked a man in uniform where we could find the public toilets and he pointed to a sign down a hallway. We straightened our hair in the big mirrors as best as we could.

Duncan followed the directions the man in uniform had given him and we soon found the office of the Prime Minister's office. The Secretary to the Prime Minister looked at Sam and I suspiciously and asked Duncan why he wanted to see the Prime Minister. He sent an assistant away with a message. We sat and waited.

It was a busy office. Men came and went, sometimes in small groups. Most of them wore suits like Senator MacDougall. Some brought bundles of paper and others left messages for the Secretary. Then it fell quiet. The Secretary told us the Prime Minister was in an important meeting and hopefully he would see us before lunch if he got out in time. We grew restless sitting in the same place for hours. Duncan told us not to move around too much or we would crease our good clothes.

We waited all morning. Duncan asked me to stop checking my pocket watch. He said it was rude to look impatient. The air in the office was stale with the smell of old men, old paper and cigars. Finally, the Secretary told Duncan that the Prime Minister would not have time between his meeting and lunch and that he would be gone all afternoon. He suggested we come back tomorrow.

The same thing happened the next day and the day after that. Sam and I grew impatient. We stopped caring if our pants were creased. Duncan was patient but he too looked relieved when the Secretary suggested that he would ask the Deputy Superintendent of Indian Affairs to contact Duncan before he met the Prime Minister, so we would not have to wait in his office every day.

Duncan busied himself in our hotel room. He worked on the details of a proposal for managing the Haida and Tsimshian people that he would present to the Prime Minister. He did not want to be disturbed. Sam and I were free to wander through the town.

I expected that Ottawa would be huge since we had traveled so far to reach it, but it was not much larger than Victoria. The buildings were newer and more orderly than Montreal. Some were made of stone but mostly they were brick. Ottawa was a decent town, like Portland, Maine, so there was nothing much to do. Sam and I walked along the Rideau Canal. We had never seen a canal before. We sat for hours watching small boats go through the locks from the river to the canal. We soon were tired of that. The next day, Sam bought a knife and sat by himself in a park by the river carving pieces of wood into canoes and totems. I found the public library and read the newspapers.

I saw an unusual looking man who was also reading in the library. He had dark brown skin and a blue cloth was wrapped around the top of his head. He gave me a friendly smile and nodded. I asked if he had injured his head.

"Oh heavens no, unless it's from reading too much," he laughed. "This is not a bandage. It is a turban. I wear it for religious reasons."

I apologized for my ignorance. He was equally ignorant about my people but he seemed interested. "If you would like to talk I think we should go for a walk outside. The library staff don't like to hear talking, especially when they see coloured skin." He smiled widely and his head made a strange wobble. We went to a nearby park and sat on a bench in the shade.

His name was Jasbir. He was born India but he lived in England. He had come to Ottawa as an assistant to an English businessman who wanted to sell Indian cloth in Canada. The businessman was meeting with lawyers in Montreal that week.

"I am his office assistant in London. He brought me along to show his buyers that he must know his business because he works with real Indians." I laughed and told him that I was here for the same reason. I told him about Duncan and Metlakatla and about our long trip across the continent to Ottawa. He told me about his travels since he left India and his life in London, which he enjoyed very much. Our stories were quite different but we also had much in common. We were both Indians, though he was from India and I was not. I asked how Whites had mistaken my people for being Indians. We looked nothing like Jasbir.

"The British are not known for their attention to detail," he grinned. He gave his head another wobble. "They are too busy knowing things to learn new ways of thinking. But they have come to rule both of our lands on opposite sides of the globe. They control many other countries too. They boast that the sun never sets on the British Empire. They say her rule is a gift to us. Their kindness has no limits," he chuckled, "but it is best you don't tell them that or they will kill you!" He laughed again. I decided that I liked him very much.

We spent the rest of that afternoon together and several afternoons after that discussing our homes, our travels and our common problem with the English. He told me about his religion and was very interested the beliefs of my people before we knew about the English God. It was good that we are different, he told me, for then we could learn from each other. What good is it to hate others for being different when we cannot all be the same? What good is it to pretend there is only one truth when a man only needs to open his eyes and ears to know it isn't true? These things he taught me.

Jasbir and his English boss left Ottawa a few days later. Before he left, he showed me the biggest story in the White newspapers that month. It was the trial of Louis Riel, the leader of a people who were part Indian and part French called the Metis. He and two Indian leaders had revolted against the Canadian government two months before. Their revolt failed and they were captured. The papers were full of anger and hatred towards the Metis and French speaking people. They wanted Riel to be hanged to death. I remembered seeing an Indian man the Whites had hanged in Victoria years ago and I was saddened.

As I read more, I learned that Prime Minister MacDonald had signed a treaty with the Metis fifteen years before. The treaty promised them land for farming but all the good land was sold to White settlers after that and the Metis got nothing. That is why the Metis revolted. This worried me. Duncan wanted MacDonald to sign an agreement that lands in Metlakatla belonged to the people of Metlakatla, but MacDonald did not keep his promises. He was not a man of honour.

Duncan did not share my concerns, for Riel had fought against the Canadian government with guns. Duncan said violence provokes violence and this was a lesson for our people too. Riel was greatly outnumbered and doomed to fail from the start. For Duncan, Riel's capture was proof that Catholics and the French were fools. He thought the rebellion had nothing to do with his talks with MacDonald, but he had not read the papers. He did not read the shameful things Whites in Ottawa were saying about Indians.

Ten days after we arrived in Ottawa, the Deputy Superintendent of Indian Affairs, Lawrence Vankoughnet, sent a message to Duncan inviting him to meet in. Duncan was delighted. He was in a fine mood before the meeting the next day. He had us press our clothes again and dress with care before we went to Vankoughnet's office. Vankoughnet had a difficult name, but his face was easy to remember. He had soft eyes and the largest sideburns I had ever seen. They brushed against his shoulders when he turned his head. He had a calm, formal manner as he welcomed us into his office. He offered us seats in front of his desk and he looked directly at us and he listened with great care.

Duncan explained our purpose in coming to Ottawa and he introduced us to Vankoughnet as the best examples of our people. Vankoughnet nodded and thanked us both for coming all the way to Ottawa to present our case. He was aware of Duncan's work in Metlakatla and had many words of praise for what we had accomplished. He was especially pleased that Duncan had taught us to be productive.

"I had the same policy myself," he told Duncan. "When the plains Indians begged for the government to help them during their famines I told them they had to work for the food we gave them, even if they were starving. Otherwise I knew they would keep asking and they would grow lazy. I wouldn't have that."

Duncan was encouraged by Vankoughnet's support. He described his plan for managing the Haida and Tsimshian settlements. A superintendent like Vankoughnet would live with us and the Canadian government would pay each working Indian two dollars per year until they became full citizens. Duncan wanted to be our superintendent, though he did not mention this at the time.

Vankoughnet liked his idea of having a management plan. He said he would speak to MacDonald on Duncan's behalf and he was certain a meeting would be set up soon, but he cautioned Duncan not to mention the citizenship issue. "The Riel affair has him a bit on edge. Indians citizenship would be asking too much of him at this point," he insisted.

Two weeks later Duncan received a message at our hotel. MacDonald was available to meet with him in his home two days later to discuss his concerns for Metlakatla. He made no mention of bringing Sam or I, so Duncan felt it was best that we stay behind.

Duncan had a nervous stomach that morning, so Sam and I went to the restaurant by our hotel alone. Sam was deeply disappointed that we were not invited to meet MacDonald. I did not care. We did not speak more than two sentences to Vankoughnet and I felt certain MacDonald would have said nothing to us. I suspected he disliked Indians because of Louis Riel's revolt.

A White man at the table beside ours interrupted our conversation. "It is incredible that they let you eat here with the rest of us. What right do you think you have? Riel's trial starts tomorrow and he hasn't got a chance. He'll be hung by the neck to teach you savages your position in society. You better remember that!" He glared at us defiantly, looking for a fight.

We were shocked by his attack. Sam signaled to the waitress and he complained about what he had said to us. She glanced at the man nervously and apologized to us. She suggested that she would bring our bill. She said we should pay up and leave without a fight.

"This is not right!" Sam exclaimed once we had left the restaurant. "We did nothing wrong. He was trying to start a fight with us." I said nothing. We both knew why we must leave. Whites in Ottawa were hungry for more Riels to hang.

Duncan had a better morning. He met with Sir John A. MacDonald for three hours and returned in a jubilant mood. Their meeting had started off poorly. MacDonald had shocked him by drinking whisky as they talked. Duncan did not dare to say anything. MacDonald seemed to be set against him from the moment they started but as they talked, and the more MacDonald drank, he began to warm to Duncan's ideas.

MacDonald was upset that Victoria had sent him their problem but he knew it had to be settled as soon as possible. The great church and Mission Point should belong to the people of Metlakatla, not the Church of England, he agreed, and he promised to make Duncan the government agent over all the Indians of the northwest coast. Duncan would report directly to Ottawa, not to the Indian Agent in Victoria.

"We have won! We have won!" was all Duncan could say at first. "Wait until Ridley and hears about this! Run to Premier Smithe and lick his wounds in Victoria too, I suspect." But there was no time to rest. He was planning his next step.

"Jack, Sam, I need to buy passage to England as soon as I can. Sir John A. is leaving for London tomorrow and I will need to meet with the Christian Missionary Society as soon as he has spoken to them. I can't wait to see their faces."

"Are we going with you?" Sam asked hopefully.

"I am afraid not. I cannot afford that, and besides, you won't be needed now that MacDonald has given us all that we have asked for." Sam face looked sad. "Don't be disappointed. You two must bring the good news to the people of Metlakatla right away. Sam, I am sure you will want to see Catherine too. I am sure she misses you."

"But how will we get back without you? Who will buy our tickets for us?"

"You can buy your own. It is not that difficult. You saw how I did it at each station." Sam looked alarmed. "I will write out all the instructions for you before I leave," Duncan reassured him.

THIRTY
FOUR

We left Ottawa as suddenly as we had left Metlakatla. I was not disappointed like Sam, but I was angry that Duncan had wasted my time by bringing us along. How I could tell Tom that I had done nothing to help Duncan, but at least we were bringing home good news.

We returned the way we came, through Prescott and Montreal, then to Portland and New York. We had to wait four hours to catch the train to Chicago so we had time to walk around the city. The tall buildings impressed me and still fill my imagination to this day. Sam was still nervous about getting lost or robbed so we only walked a few blocks. I bought more books about America and India at a book store near the station to read on the train.

The train to San Francisco left the same day we arrived in Chicago. We saved money because we did not need a hotel. We had difficulty finding the ticket office for a ship to Victoria, but we found it eventually. We were both relieved to be on the ship heading north.

We used the money we saved by not renting a hotel room in Chicago to stay an extra night in Victoria. We visited Bishop Cridge and Senator McDougall to tell them the good news about Duncan's meeting with MacDonald before we headed home.

Several men were waiting when our ship arrived in Metlakatla. They had come to receive mail and cargo from Victoria. They had no idea Sam and I were on the ship. We climbed onto the dock and they surrounded us with cheers, patted on our heads and shoulders and asked us many questions. We all laughed with delight.

Robert Tomlinson was there too. Duncan had asked him to watch over Metlakatla while he was gone. "What news do you bring us, Jack?" he smiled with anticipation.

"Good news!" I answered.

Sam nodded in agreement. He shook his fists in the air and cried like Duncan, "We have won!"

The men cheered loudly. Tomlinson waited for their voices to die down. "Could you and Sam come with me to Duncan's office before you unpack. I am dying to hear the details of your trip," he smiled. He walked beside us while the others carried our bags.

Tom was waiting at the end of the dock. He looked at me with confusion and hurt on his face. I left Tomlinson's side and approached him. The others stopped and waited.

"I am so glad to see you. I have missed you so much!" I said. I did not wait for him to reply. I threw my arms around his neck and kissed his cheek as I hugged him tightly. "I begged Duncan to bring you with us. He only had enough money for the three of us and he would not wait until you came home from the hunting trip. I had to go with him. He gave me no choice." Tom looked down at his feet. His mouth twisted with pain but he said nothing. "I will talk with you after we meet with Tomlinson."

Tomlinson was anxious to hear my news but I could not think of anything except how to get Tom to forgive me. Tomlinson searched my face with concern. "Come on, let's go," he spoke softly. He put his hand on the back on my neck and led us off the dock. I glanced back at Tom as we walked away. He was staring down at the dock and breathing hard.

Sam and I spent an hour with Tomlinson in Duncan's office. I related the news of Duncan's meetings with Vankoughnet and MacDonald. Tomlinson was thrilled to hear that Mission Point and the St. Paul's Church were ours and that Duncan would be the Indian Agent for all north coast tribes. He asked us if we had enjoyed our adventure and he listened closely as we told our stories. I told him I had met a real Indian in Ottawa. I thought about showing him the books I had bought in New York, but I wanted to show them to Tom first.

Tom was waiting for me in our room. He stared at me defiantly but there was only love in my eyes. He looked away from me. He was still breathing hard.

"Come sit on the bed with me. I have many important things to tell you." I took his wrists and pulled him down onto our bed facing me. He was more nervous than angry now.

I started with the good news, that we had won the war against Ridley. That made him smile for the first time. Then I described our long trip to Ottawa and what each city looked like along the way. Then I told him about meeting Jasbir and what he had taught me. Tom's face changed to sadness again and tears welled in his eyes.

"Tom, I am sorry that we could not go together. I missed you terribly. I cried and prayed for you many times. Sam understood but I could not say anything about my feelings to Duncan. I know it was our plan to travel together and we will someday, just you and me." I squeezed his hands and pulled him into my embrace. I felt his tears on my neck. "Come on, be happy! We have brought back such good news and I have gifts for you too." I showed him the books on New York and India. He looked at me shyly and smiled again. He stood up and started to unpack my bags. I knew then we would be fine and my heart swelled with love for him.

No one asked how Sam or I helped Duncan win our victory. I did not need to make up a lie. Our success was all that mattered. We were heroes. Tomlinson received a letter from Duncan. He was in London waiting for MacDonald to meet with the Christian Missionary Society to break the news that they had lost title to the great church and Mission Point. Ridley heard the news of our success. He withdrew into his home and said nothing. Everyone was hopeful that he would soon pack up and leave.   In late September, six weeks after we returned, terrible news arrived. Ridley marched into our Sunday service in the Assembly Hall and interrupted Tomlinson's sermon. He read a letter from the Christian Missionary Society saying that they had met with Sir John A. MacDonald. He had given the Church of England full ownership of the great church and Mission Point. Duncan was off their payroll and his wages and expense fund for his work at Metlakatla would be used to hire eight new staff for Ridley. He told us that since Duncan had no income, he could not afford to return to Metlakatla. He laughed at the shock and dismay on our faces. There would be big changes coming now that Duncan gone forever, he snarled. He handed the letter to Tomlinson and marched out with his nose in the air.

We could not listen to the Word of God after Ridley left. Some thought Ridley was lying to scare us. Others wanted to see the letter. Tomlinson confirmed it was from the missionary society and he doubted that they would make up such a story. Then some accused Sam and I of lying to hide the bad news. Tomlinson held up his arms and asked for quiet. The room fell silent.

"Sam and Jack are not liars," he reminded the assembly. "Everyone knows that.

arriving from Duncan shortly. In the meantime, I will speak to Senator MacDougall in Victoria and ask him to write to MacDonald for clarification. I am certain there will be a good explanation. We cannot attack each other if something goes wrong. We must stay united and clear about our purpose regardless of whatever happens elsewhere."

Sam and I were no longer heroes. Those who believed Tomlinson thought we were fools instead. Tom was hurt and angry again. He had many questions but I had no answers. Tomlinson wrote to Senator MacDougall as he said he would. While we waited for his answer, a letter arrived from Duncan. He was confused himself, though he knew something had gone terribly wrong. MacDonald had met with him in London. He repeated his promises and said he would meet with him again after speaking to the missionary society. Then Duncan received a letter from MacDonald saying he had left England. He gave no details about his meeting with the missionary society but he said he hoped Duncan would reach a friendly compromise with them.

Our hearts sank. His letter was followed by a letter from Senator MacDougall explaining what had happened. The missionary society had told MacDonald he would lose the support of the Church of England if he denied them ownership of Mission Point. MacDonald needed their support in the coming election. He told MacDougall that he promised Duncan only the position of Indian Agent for Metlakatla and Duncan had refused. He described Duncan as an ambitious man who refused to obey the laws of Canada.

So MacDonald was a liar. He had deceived and betrayed Duncan. My worst fears had come true. Everything sweet had turned sour and our town did not know what to do. Our situation was much worse.

Ridley's new staff arrived in October. He flew a flag of victory above his residence. His men fired off his little cannon and marched around the town carrying banners for the Church of England. He posted an announcement that if Town Council met again they would be arrested. The great church was opened again and we were ordered to attend his sermons every Sunday and accept communion. Those who did not attend would be fined. Those who attended and received communion would be rewarded with a share of those fines.

The Town Council continued to meet in secret in one of the houses. Tomlinson continued to hold separate sermons in the Assembly Hall. Ridley's staff came to note who attended and fines were issued. We all agreed not to pay the fines. The jail was not big enough to hold us all but some of town became discouraged. They feared Duncan would not return and that they would be forced to pay the fines. They changed sides and began to accept communion from Ridley in the cathedral.

Tomlinson counseled us against taking revenge on those who changed sides. He asked Sam to write a letter to Duncan telling him that we were holding firm and waiting for his return. Sam told Duncan that Ridley was holding a lantern for us in one hand and a gun in the other.

Duncan answered Sam's note with a reassuring letter. He promised he would return in the spring. He had met a wealthy American businessman named Henry Wellcome in London. Wellcome was interested in Metlakatla and he had agreed to pay for Duncan's wage and his return trip. Wellcome also wanted to write a book about Duncan's work in Metlakatla. Duncan said he and Wellcome were working on a plan that would free us of Ridley. He would go to Washington with Wellcome to meet American officials before returning home. He could not tell us more at that time.

There was reason to hope again. Duncan never gave up. We had no idea what their plan was, but it was enough to give us faith. We made sure that Ridley heard the rumours that Duncan was returning with the support of a rich American business-man. Ridley was shaken by the news. He insisted that it was a lie, but he could not hide his fear.

Ridley's victory was fading but he stayed his course, adding up fines against us that would never be paid and threatening us with time in jail that would never be served. Some of those who had changed sides came back to us when they heard that Duncan would return. They had not received any rewards for taking communion and they realized Ridley was a liar.

It was a quiet and anxious winter. We waited for news from Duncan and prayed that our hopes for a solution would not be as empty as Ridley's victory. Louis Riel was hanged and the news weighed heavily upon me. The White newspapers rejoiced over his death. Letters replying to their stories spoke hatefully of Indians and the importance of keeping us in our place. I questioned whether there was any purpose in hoping for a solution with Whites.

In early March, most of our town went to the Nass to fish for oolichon. Two men from the Christian Missionary Society arrived in Metlakatla to discuss Mission Point and the great church while we were gone. Two older men who had remained behind canoed to the Nass to tell us of their arrival. Sam, Joseph, Paul Legiac, Daniel, Tom and I returned with them to meet the visitors.

They called a meeting of the sixty people who were not at the oolichon camps. We hoped the men from the missionary society had brought a new compromise but we were disappointed. They only wanted to repeat what the missionary society had already told us. We listened to them for an hour. When they asked if we had questions the room was quiet. Sam stood up and asked for a copy of their presentation so we could study it before meeting again.

The second meeting was held ten days later. Most of the town had returned from the Nass by then. The men from the missionary society were surprised to see the Assembly Hall packed tightly with many people standing at the back and sides of the room. It was a short meeting though. Only Sam responded when they asked for our comments. He told them they had offered us nothing new. The town's concerns had already been presented to the missionary society in several letters and they had been ignored. He said the society was no longer working for the people of Metlakatla and the town wanted them to leave our land forever. His words were greeted with deafening cheers from the rest of us. The two Englishmen were obviously upset as they left the room.

They stayed in Bishop Ridley's home, waiting for Duncan's return. Duncan returned while they waited. The town cheered him at the dock and followed him up the hill to his room. He stopped at the top of the hill to speak to express how happy he was to see us again. He thanked us for showing the world that we have faith in him and for remaining true to our dream. He would share his good news with us soon, he said. Then he asked to speak to Sam and the Town Council in his room.

He looked happy but tired. He told us that he had been many places in the United States, meeting important people and telling them about our wonderful town. He wanted to be sure of the results of his meetings before telling us the outcome. His words excited us but he refused to say anything more. Bishop Cridge and Tomlinson had already warned him about the two men from the missionary society. He asked how the meetings with them went and Sam told him everything.

"You did a wonderful job, Sam. Please let them know that I will be busy for a few days as I have lots of important work to do." He thought for a moment and then added. "Please use exactly those words," he chuckled.

He kept the two missionary society men waiting ten more days before he invited them to his office. They were quite agitated. They demanded Tomlinson to attend but Duncan insisted that Tomlinson was busy with real work. He listened patiently as they expressed their frustrations. After a few minutes he suggested that I did not need to take more notes. They are only repeating old arguments, he said. He smiled at them as their faces flushed red with anger.

The meeting lasted all afternoon but Duncan did not compromise. The Englishmen pushed me out of their way as they left the room. Duncan looked exhausted. "Well, at least that is over. It was a huge waste of time but I doubt they will ever ask me to meet with them again."

They left town the next day. Two weeks later a copy of their report arrived. Duncan read the recommendations but ignored the rest. He let me read it when he was done. The report disagreed with everything Duncan was doing and praised Ridley, saying he was the only one doing good work. It said our people were helpless children unable to speak for themselves and that we were not interested in land ownership issues. Duncan offered the report to the Town Council but they were not interested in reading it either.

"How do men like that lie so easily, Mr. Duncan? How can they pretend they are Christians?" I questioned him.

"I don't know, Jack. It is one of life's great mysteries. But don't forget that the Lord is listening to their lies. Their justifications will mean nothing to Him when they get to Heaven's gates. Just be patient and wait. Justice will triumph in the end."

◇◇◇◇◇◇◇◇◇◇◇◇◇◇◇◇

We waited through the summer for word of Duncan's plan. Tom and I had had a difficult winter after my return from Ottawa but we were growing closer again. Our love was delicate as a wounded bird, but I was certain it would heal and grow strong again. My family was luckier than others in the town. We had joyful news to distract us. There was a hole in the clouds above and the sun shone brightly on us. The Elders of the Eagle and Raven Clans gave their permission for my nephew Jesse Talbot to marry Daniel's daughter, Anne Carter. His parents asked Bishop Cridge to marry them and the plans were set for late September when Cridge would visit Metlakatla.

No one was happier than I was that summer, except for Jesse and Anne. Jesse was my favourite nephew and I was his favourite uncle. By tradition, he was my brother George's heir, not mine, but George did not have time to train him. George was working in Port Essington to support his family as our cannery was still closed. Jesse lived in my house so I had accepted the role as his trainer the past three years as Uncle Gugweelaks had trained me.

Jesse was the future of my Clan as well as the son I never had. Both Tom and I loved him dearly. His joy and curiosity made him a pleasure to teach. The anger and hatred in our divided town never seemed to reach him. His heart was filled with a love for all living things. He could not bear the thought of shooting animals or birds.

His parents, Joseph and my sister Mary, were devout Christians so they never taught him about the Animal Spirits. I did. I taught him that animals surrender to clean and honourable hunters, and they will be reborn when they are treated respectfully. I taught him to thank them for surrendering their bodies. I watched him on his knees as he asked for their forgiveness with tears in his eyes. I cried too, for I had so much to learn from him.

As Jesse grew to be a man his tears stopped but he always thanked the Animal Spirits before touching his kill. It was not just a habit. It was something he felt in his soul he must do. Other young men hunted for skins to trade for White goods, but Jesse would only kill when he needed the meat for food. By his nineteenth year, when he was granted permission to marry Anne, I felt a pride for him greater than I had ever known. Besides being honest and kind by nature, he had grown to be strong and handsome. He had joined the fire brigade the year before to build his strength. He sang with our choir for many years too. He was often asked to lead the others for his voice was as sweet as a songbird.

His marriage to Anne was no surprise. The Spirits had placed them together from the time they could first walk. They thought only of each other. Their youth and passion shone through the darkness of our town and it touched the hearts of everyone around them. We were joyful, for what was meant to be had finally come to pass.

The wedding excited both our families and kept everyone busy. The men and women of the Eagle Clan worked through the summer to make gifts to give to the guests at the wedding party. They helped out because they knew Jesse's father, Joseph, did not belong to a Clan. He could not afford the gifts that were needed to bless their union with strength and happiness. Jennifer, Laura and the women of the Raven Clan kept themselves busy preparing Anne for her wedding day. They were so filled with happiness that a stranger might have thought they were the ones being married.

Jesse saw less of Anne during that time. The preparations took most of her time and the women told her it was bad luck to see her man too often before the marriage. She would soon be his wife but it frightened Jesse to be apart from her so much. They missed each other greatly. In Jesse's eyes, I often saw a lost boy. When the women took Anne to Victoria to have her fitted for a wedding dress made, he came to me with his heart full of troubles.

"Uncle Jack, this waiting is making me crazy. Why does our marriage need so much preparation? Why must they keep me away from Anne so long?"

Anne was Jesse's only close friend. I embraced him and stroked his beautiful hair. "Remember, Jesse, that you are not the only ones getting married. Our Clans are marrying too, through you and Anne, and everyone must be part of the ceremony. Your marriage will make us all stronger and you should be proud of that."

"I can't keep my mind on anything when I am away from her. It feels like a punishment. I know she is sad because she misses me too. Then sometimes I worry that she does not miss me. I would be ashamed if she saw me this way. I feel I am not a worthy husband."

"Do not talk like that. You just need your own preparations to keep you busy. Have you chosen a ring for Anne yet?"

He smiled and pulled his chair closer to mine as if to whisper a secret. "Yes, I know what I am looking for but I haven't found it yet." His eyes sparkled like sunlight on the sea. "Anne loves roses! When we visited Victoria she always stopped to look at every rosebush! I want to buy her a ring with a beautiful rose on it. I want it to be gold, but I think I can only afford silver." I could see that bothered him.

"Perhaps I can help you. I want your wedding to be perfect too."

I knew his answer before he spoke it. "No, Uncle Jack. Thank you, but I must earn it myself without help. This ring is from my soul to hers. You understand, don't you?"

"I do, Jesse. God will reward your pure heart with good fortune if He loves you as much as I do."

He tried to hide his blushing smile. He praised me with his kind, handsome eyes and threw his arms around my neck. "I love you too, Uncle Jack!" His words pounded in my heart like a drum. He asked if I would accompany him to the trading post the next Saturday. "I have some furs to trade and we can see if they have anything rings for sale."

"Of course. It will be fun to go together."

Saturday morning, we paddled his canoe north to Fort Simpson. He could not hold his passion quietly inside any longer. He talked constantly about Anne, the wedding preparations and their plans after their marriage. Duncan had promised him extra shifts at the cannery once it was running again to help him pay for his ring. After a while, he fell quiet and was happy in his thoughts again. I watched his strong, young shoulders as he pulled on his paddle. I was happy in my thoughts too, and I thanked God for blessing me with my nephew.

Jesse had so much love shining in his eyes that morning that I decided to have his picture taken. We stopped a photographer's shop in Fort Simpson on the way to the trading post. He was impatient to shop for a ring, until I told him the photograph was a gift for Ann. I would have copies made for her, our family and Tom and I.

The trading post did not allow Indians to visit on busy Saturdays, but they knew me and they let us in. Jesse looked for a clerk who was free and walked up to him.

"Sir, do you have any wedding rings for sale?"

The clerk grinned at his eager face. "Well son, we don't get much call for them. There aren't many White lasses to marry and your Tsimshian women don't usually go for wedding rings like ours do, but we have a couple. You will be the first to see them." He reached into a drawer and pulled out two small wooden cases. He opened them and set them in front of Jesse.

The smile disappeared from Jesse's face. "Do you have any with roses on them?"

"Roses? Don't get much call for them up here either. No, these are all I have, son. You need a jeweler who can fashion you somethin' special. I'm not sure you could afford that, though."

"I have these furs to sell and I have money I've saved too." The clerk inspected his furs and paid him what they were worth. Jesse opened his money pouch. A bundle of notes and several coins spilled onto the counter.

"Well, that looks like a tidy sum," the clerk chucked. "You might get something nice in silver, but you'll need more than that if you prefer gold. You'd best look for someone in Victoria, lad. There's no jewelers up here." He pushed Jesse's money back to him.

"Put your money away, Jesse" I whispered to him. "Don't show everyone how much you are carrying."

"He's right. You never know who's watching you!" A tall, unshaven man laughed from behind us. "My partner and me sell our gold in Victoria. We're smart enough not to show it 'round here though." His eyes moved from me to Jesse and back again. "Excuse me. The name's Ted and that feller's my partner Will." A man with messy blond hair behind him smiled at us.

The clerk was suspicious. "He's kidding you, lad. There's no gold in these hills."

"Not these hills, fool. We found it this spring in a creek way east of the Nass. Thought we might strike it rich but couldn't find more than a couple ounces. After two months the supplies were running low so we decided to come back and stock up before heading out again. It's not much but we've got enough for a wedding ring. We could sell it to you for much less than you'd pay in a store."

"Really?" Jesse could not hide the excitement in his voice.

The prospector laughed again. "Hey, I was married once. Don't mind helpin' out a young buck who's in love. Besides, I wasn't lookin' forward to the trip down to Victoria just to sell the bit we have. I'm sure we have enough to make a couple pretty earrings too."

"Wow, can you bring it here to Fort Simpson to sell it to me?"

"Sorry, kid. Will here's not feelin' well. He needs to get back to our camp, have a meal and take a rest. Tomorrow we're leaving for Alaska."

"I could go to your camp with you. Uncle Jack, can you wait for me?"

"I don't know if this is a good idea, Jesse. I still need to buy many supplies and we need be home before dark. How long will it take?" I turned to the prospector.

"It's a little over half an hour from here. Your nephew can come with us in our canoe. We'll make the trade and I bring him back by myself. No more than an hour and a half."

"Please, Uncle Jack, it won't take long, I promise."

I did not have the heart to disappoint him. He's a man now, I told myself, and he's bigger than either of these two so he will be safe. "All right, I will finish my shopping and meet you back at the dock in an hour and a half. Don't take any longer or we won't make it back while it is light."

Jesse always kept his promises so when he did not show up at the dock an hour and a half later a great dread grew inside me. I waited another hour, pacing nervously until I could not wait any longer. I climbed into my canoe and paddled in the direction they had gone, away from the trading post and around the point headed east.

The rocks and trees by the shore glowed in the afternoon sun. The air and the sea were strangely calm. I looked for the smoke of the prospectors' campfire but I saw nothing. I paddled for more than half an hour. My heart was pounding like a drum. There must be a good explanation why he had not returned, I thought, but I could not think of one.

I reached the end of the bay. There was no campfire anywhere. Perhaps they did not make a fire. That must be it, I thought. I decided to returned to Fort Simpson, following the shore closely looking for signs of Jesse or the prospectors. My worries were turning into panic. My mind raced with pointless questions that I could not answer. I prayed to God to keep Jesse safe but I was afraid it was too late.

My eyes caught something white moving in the waves of a small cove along the shore. I paddled towards it as fast as I could. I recognized Jesse's shirt. Then I saw it was Jesse floating on his back, rocking against the edge of the rocks.

"No! No! No!" my mind cried in panic as I glided to his side. For a moment I hoped he was still alive. His eyes were open but he was staring at the sky. I jumped into the water and pulled his body into my arms. "Jesse, can you hear me?" He stared but did not answer. He was dead. His skin was already blue and as cold as the sea.

"Jesse, answer me!" I begged. I lifted his head so he could speak but my hand touched something and I froze. The back of his head was crushed in. I felt a hole where his skull should be, the sharp edges of broken bone and spongy softness inside. I dropped his body in shock.

I fainted for a moment and fell into the waves. I coughed and grabbed onto his lifeless body to pull myself up. Somehow I pulled my canoe to the shore and dragged him over beside it. I checked his clothes. His money pouch was gone. I sat there a long time, holding him in my arms and stroking his beautiful face. I wept and I sang to him. I told him I was sorry, that I loved him and I begged him to forgive me. The afternoon passed and the sun was sinking in the west. I said a prayer for him and lifted his broken body into the canoe.

The sun was setting when I reached Fort Simpson. The guard at the fort saw my blood stained clothes and barred me from entering the fort. I pleaded with him. He had me wait at the gate until he brought the Constable. Other concerned Tsimshians gathered around me and asked me questions. I was so cold and my heart so troubled that I could not say much. They brought me a woolen blanket and wrapped it around my shoulders.

They lifted Jesse out of my canoe and carried him to the gate on a plank. The Constable, a Tsimshian man named Luke Harris, arrived and inspected his body. I heard someone say that perhaps I killed him in a fight. Harris asked them to search my canoe for a murder weapon.

Anger replaced my grief and shame. I had spent the afternoon telling myself that his death was my fault, but I would not let the prospectors get away with his murder. I told the Constable what happened. He believed me, but he said we could not look for the prospectors until morning. It was already dark. He would ask me more questions after I ate something and changed my clothes.

A Fort Simpson family took me to their home. They gave me dry clothes and sat me by their stove. I could not eat any food. I sipped the hot tea they brought me but it did not stop my shaking. I sat silently as tears flowed down my cheeks. A small boy came to me and climbed onto my knee to comfort me, just as Jesse used to do when he was small. I sobbed harder.

I returned to the fort an hour later. Harris met me at the gate and took me to a small office. He told me we had to wait for a White officer who was eating dinner with other Whites. Time passed slowly. I grew impatient and asked if the officer knew that my nephew had been murdered. He warned me it was not our place to tell Whites what to do.

Officer Beale arrived a few minutes later. He seemed displeased that he had to hurry away from his dinner for an Indian's murder. He did not listen to my story like Constable Harris had. He asked me instead if Jesse drank whiskey and liked to fight. I thought he had not understood my story, so I tried to repeated it. He stopped me.

No prospectors had visited Fort Simpson recently, he told me. He suggested Jesse was trying to buy whisky and had refused to pay the whisky traders. Young men often try to get away with this, he frowned at me. I could not listen to him speaking about Jesse this way. I became very upset and started shouting at him.

"Calm down, or I will I'll have you thrown out," he barked. When I was quiet he asked, "Did anyone else see these prospectors?"

I mentioned the store clerk. Beale sent Harris to find him. The clerk appeared. He described the prospectors and said they acted suspiciously. Beale inspected Jesse's broken skull and said he had probably been struck by a rock or a hammer from behind. "He probably didn't suffer long," he tried to reassure me. Harris and Beale carried Jesse's body to the storeroom and laid him on the floor. They covered him with a tarp and told me to return in the morning.

I returned to the family that had given me dry clothes. They prepared a bed for me on their kitchen floor near the stove and left me to sleep. I lay there for hours, crying in silence. Late in the night my exhaustion overpowered my grief and I fell asleep.

In the morning I returned to the fort to see Officer Beale. I waited in his office until he was finished his breakfast. I was anxious to help others hunt for the prospectors but Beale shook his head.

"I will spread word up and down the coast for the authorities to watch for them, but I can't send my men out searching. There are hundreds of miles of coastline around here and the killers will certainly be hiding. They could have reached Dundas Island by now or be half way to the Nass. We don't know which way they've headed and we couldn't catch them if we did. There's nothing we can do if they've reached Alaska. We have no jurisdiction there, you know."

"But you cannot let them escape unpunished," I cried.

"It is a very busy time of year, Mr. Campbell. Fort Simpson is crowded with traders and visitors and that always means lots of trouble. I need all the men I have to keep order here. Sooner or later the killers will try to spend your nephew's money and we will catch them. It is better to let them come to us."

"This isn't right! How can you do nothing?"

Beale lost his patience with me. "Speak to Reverend Crosby if you want. Maybe he'll help you round up a search party, though I wouldn't bet on it. Constable Harris will help you carry you nephew's body back to your canoe when you are ready to return home. If our prospectors turn up I will send someone to Metlakatla to find you. That is all for now, Mr. Campbell. Good day." He told Constable Harris to show me out before I could say more.

Harris told me where I could find Reverend Crosby, the Methodist minister who Duncan despised so strongly. It was Sunday morning and Crosby was in the manse behind the church, preparing to give his weekly sermon. He did not appreciate my interruption.

"Yes, who are you? What can I do for you?" he snapped at me as I stood at his doorstep.

"Reverend Crosby, please, my name is Jack Campbell. I need your help and the help of the people of Fort Simpson. My nephew was murdered by prospectors in the east bay yesterday afternoon. They killed him and stole his money."

"What am I supposed to do? There are no prospectors in my congregation. We are decent Christians here."

"No sir, I did not mean he was killed by men from Fort Simpson. I am looking for men who can help me find the killers and bring them to justice. Officer Beale suggested I should ask you for help. He has no free men to help with the search."

"Officer Beale! That Anglican jackass deliberately makes trouble for me. He's not capable of doing his job so he passes his duties on to others. Isn't murder important enough for him either?" He frowned at me as though he was speaking to Officer Beale himself. "Why should we help you search for these killers? What was your nephew doing that made them want to kill him? Was he trying to make a deal with whisky traders?"

"No sir! He was the sweetest and most honest young Christian man. He never drank or gambled and he prayed to God faithfully each day. He was trying to buy gold for a wedding ring. He did not know these prospectors were bad men."

"Ha! Prospectors indeed! The Lord doesn't suffer fools gladly! He won't protect those who can't tell the difference between good and evil. I am here to serve God, not to serve fools. Why don't the people of your village help you? Where are you from?"

"From Metlakatla, sir, both myself and my nephew, but…"

"Metlakatla! You're one of Duncan's. I should've known it. That's why you don't know Sunday is the Lord's Day of rest and why you can't tell good from evil. If you want to be a bloody Anglican instead of a proper Methodist you're a fool to ask for the Lord's protection. Don't blame Him for your misfortunes!" He glared at me with his dark eyes. They invited the Lord to strike me dead.

"Please, Reverend Crosby, if I return to Metlakatla to get help I will lose another day and his killers will escape."

"I suspect they've escaped already, if your story is true. You don't even know which way they have gone, do you?" I shook my head. "You'd better ask your Mr. Duncan to help you. He's a magistrate after all. Too bad they were prospectors. If they were whisky traders Mr. Duncan would send his whole flock out after them." He closed the door in my face without saying goodbye.

I felt like I had a knife in my heart and I wanted to cry. I thought of going from house to house to ask for help, but families were already walking into Reverend Crosby's church in their best Sunday clothes. If I waited until his service was over it would already be too late in the day to form a search party. By the next morning there would be no point to it. As Officer Beale said, my only choice was to wait. It was time to bring Jesse's body home.

Constable Harris helped me move Jesse from the fort to my canoe. The night before he had forgotten to close his eyes before they wrapped him in a tarp. Now his eyelids were stiff and there was no way to shut them. Harris covered Jesse with a white cotton sheet and tucked it around him for the trip home. He hugged me out of kindness before I climbed into my canoe.

The horror of bringing him home to Mary and Joseph filled my thoughts as I paddled south. I must also tell the terrible news to his bride Anne and her parents, Daniel and Jennifer. Their grief would tear me apart. I felt great shame and guilt. I should never have let him go with the prospectors, but I did. I was to blame for his death and I could never forgive myself. I believed no one else would forgive me either. They would also be angry that his killers escaped. My heart was so heavy I knew I would sink like a stone if I fell into the water.

The Spirits of the Sea knew my guilt and they sent a storm to punish me. The North Wind blew hard and the waves grew tall. I paddled with all my strength to keep my canoe from tipping. I did not fear my own death, but I could not let Jesse's body be swallowed by the sea. I would not let his Spirit wander forever lost between our world and Heaven.

His body tossed from side to side in the canoe until the white sheet that covered him tore free. It rose high into the air, as if it was his Spirit flying up to God. Then it fell into the waves that smashed against the rocks near the shore. It was too dangerous to retrieve it. Jesse's frozen eyes looked from side to side as his body rolled with the sea. The bow rode high on a wave and his head bent forward. He looked directly at me and his Spirit saw into my soul. What terrible omen this was, I thought. Was Jesse warning me of danger ahead?

When I reached Metlakatla, there was another great storm of grief and anger as the news of his death spread. Women wailed and the men raged, especially Joseph and George. His brothers Earl and Lester cried openly and I could not console them. My own pain did nothing to soften theirs. Duncan told me not to blame myself but to pray for forgiveness. He was no good at comforting us either. I needed to be held. I turned to Tom, but he too was angry with me and grieving himself. He did not blame me in words but I felt it in his touch.

The storm of grief began to quiet, but then Anne, Mary, Jennifer and Ruth arrived back from their shopping trip to Victoria with Anne's new wedding gown. The grief and horror started over, like a delicate scab that is ripped open. They wept and moaned and tried to comfort each other. There was little I could do to help ease their pain. My dear sister's face grew cold as stone. Her heart closed and I knew it would never open for me again.

Jesse was buried behind the great church the next day, just beyond the lands the now belonged to the Church of England. Most of the town came to his funeral, even the Collisons and some of Bishop Ridley's followers. For a short moment Jesse's beautiful Spirit held back the Spirit of the Church and both sides of the town were brought together to mourn his loss.

THIRTY
FIVE

J esse's coffin was laid into the hole of his grave and Duncan began the funeral service. Just as he started to speak, a message arrived from Officer Beale. Someone in Port Essington heard two men boasting that they had stolen money from an Indian a few days before. He reported them to the magistrate and they were arrested. They had been taken to Fort Simpson and they matched the description the store clerk and I had given to Beale.

The messenger told me I must return to Fort Simpson with him immediately. He was waiting to take to there. I would offend the Spirits to leave during Jesse's funeral but I would offend my friends and relatives if I stayed. I had no choice but to go.

Officer Beale greeted me with a proud smile. "They are whisky traders, not prospectors, Mr. Campbell, and their names are Jake and Harry, not Ted and Will. I arrested them here a year ago but I had to release them because we could not find their whisky. This time we have them though and they won't be released again. The clerk in the trading post has already identified them but I need you to do the same. Constable Harris, please bring them in!"

Harris brought the two men in. Their hands were handcuffed behind their backs. They were definitely the same men Jesse and I had met in the trading post. My eyes burned with hatred, but they stared at the floor instead of me.

"They are the ones who left with Jesse," I told him.

"Are you sure?"

"I am completely sure. That is the man who told us they were prospectors. He said his name was Ted."

Beale waved his hand and Harris led them away. The one who said he was Ted glared at me angrily over his shoulder before Harris pushed him out the door.

"I'm pleased you are so certain. We can't afford any doubts here," Beale said. He leaned towards me and spoke as though we were making plans together. "Our magistrate has agreed to send this case to Victoria to be tried in the highest court of the Province under Judge Begbie, the hanging judge. If they're convicted it will be the last we ever see of them."

He straightened again. "They have refused to sign a confession but the store clerk has signed a statement identifying them. We need you to testify against them in court, Mr. Campbell. You are our best witness because you knew the victim and you found his body. With your testimony I am sure we can convict them. Will you be willing to travel to Victoria to testify two weeks from now, Mr. Campbell?'

"Of course I will go, Mr. Beale. I want them convicted more than anyone."

"Good man. I will give you a letter of reference to show the police. They will find you a place to stay while you are there, but I cannot afford to pay for your way there and back. I am sure your Town Council will help out with your fare if you ask them. I will send a message to Mr. Duncan when the court date has been set."

The message from Beale arrived in a week. The court date was set for mid-September, three weeks later. The Town Council agreed to pay my fare to Victoria and back. I asked them to pay for Tom to go with me. They would have agreed but Duncan was at the meeting.

"Why do you need Tom to go with you?" he asked me. "You know the Council doesn't have much money this year."

"I need a companion with me and Tom has not been to Victoria this year." The Council nodded. They understood my need but they could not explain it to Duncan.

"Nonsense", Duncan answered for them. "We cannot afford two fares. I will ask Senator MacDougall to accompany you to the trial instead. If you need anything he will be glad to help. Tom will have to pay for his own fare if he wants to visit Victoria."

My news did not sit well with Tom. He dearly wanted to sit with me in the courtroom to give me strength. Several times in the past I had gone to Victoria with Duncan when Tom was busy with his work at the saw mill. This year the saw mill was quiet but we could not afford the fare without his wages. When I told him the decision of the Council, he thought I did not want him beside me.

"I do not want to see Victoria. Why did you tell them that? I want to be with you. Go by yourself if you want to be alone! It is your fault Jesse is dead anyway!" He turned away from me in anger. His words stung me deeply. I tried to embrace him and say that I loved him, but he pushed me away. He was impossible to talk to when he was angry.

◇◇◇◇◇◇◇◇◇◇◇◇◇◇◇

I left for Victoria alone two weeks later. Tom was still upset and I was hurt and frightened. I blamed myself that he could not come, but there was nothing more I could do. This was another sign that I was cursed. I prayed to God to bless my trip, but I feared that the Spirit of the Church was stronger.

The trip south was dreadfully slow. It rained steadily and the clouds were low. Sometimes the fog was so thick I could not see the shore. I tried not to think about Tom. I practiced the words I would say in the court, but this did not lighten the weight in my heart.

I had never been to Victoria alone. I looked at it with new eyes with no family or friends to distract me. It had changed greatly since my first visit more than twenty years before. Premier Smithe had sold the Songhee lands to a White businessman and the Songhee sent away without payment for their lands. New White buildings had replaced the houses of their village. Only White faces passed me on the sidewalks. Victoria was becoming like the cities of the East.

I asked several people for directions to the police building before someone answered me. It was early afternoon. I had not eaten lunch, but my stomach was nervous. I decided to show my letter from Officer Beale to the Chief of Police first. I could eat later once I knew where I would stay. I would have the rest of the afternoon to shop for a nice gift for Tom.

The police building was on Government Street next to the court house. When I arrived the officer in charge was busy with other visitors. I waited my turn politely. They left but he did not notice me when I stepped up to the counter. He continued to work on his papers as though I was not there.

"Excuse me please, sir. I need to speak to the Chief of Police."

The officer told me to wait a minute without looking at me and he continued his writing. When he was finished he said nothing. He rose and took his papers to another room. I tried to show the letter to two other officers in the room but they would not look at it. They told me to wait while they served Whites who came in after me.

I waited half an hour before the first officer returned. He was not pleased that I was still waiting. He spoke to me in the most unfriendly manner.

"Why are you here?" he asked, as though I should not be.

"I have a letter from Officer Beale to show the Chief of Police. Are you the Chief?" I thought he must be for he took my letter.

"Who is Officer Beale? Did you do something wrong?" He looked at the letter but did not open it.

"No sir. I have come to Victoria to speak at the trial of two evil White men who killed my nephew. The trial is tomorrow. Officer Beale is at the trading post in Fort Simpson. He told me you will find a place for me to stay."

"Evil White men, eh?" He said this loud enough to get the attention of the other two officers as he turned to look at them. "You've got to watch out for those evil White men!" He turned back to me. "So you have come to put them in jail, have you? Or perhaps to have them hanged? What did your nephew do to them?"

I felt very uncomfortable as though I had offended them. "Please sir, my nephew was a good man. He did nothing to them. They killed him and stole his money. Officer Beale promised that you would give me a place to stay tonight."

"Who is this Officer Beale? Does he think we're some kind of hotel?" I felt the heat of embarrassment and frustration in my face. I said nothing more. "Wait here. I'll speak to the Chief," he said, and he left the room.

When he returned he was smiling and my heart was relieved. "The Chief says we can give you a place to stay if you want." He waited for my answer.

"Yes sir, I do. Thank you very much!"

"Officer Duff, can you please show him to his quarters." He winked at an officer behind him. He nodded towards the door at the back of the room and Duff smiled. I picked up my bag and followed Duff. He led me down a hallway and through another door. Beyond the door there were four jail cells. I stopped when I saw them. A cold panic gripped me.

"Where are you taking me?" I asked.

Officer Duff pulled my bag out of my hand and he pushed me into the first cell. I fell. He locked the door before I could get back on my feet.

"This is not right! Let me out. I have done nothing wrong," I protested.

"What's the matter? You got what you asked for – a free place to stay. It's only for the night. At least you know you won't have a chance to get drunk before the trial tomorrow." Duff laughed as though he had said something clever and turned to go.

"Please, I want to speak to Senator MacDougall or Bishop Cridge."

He laughed. "If they drop by I promise to mention you." He closed the door behind him.

I sat on a cot defeated. There was no one to complain to and I could not escape. Even if I could, Officer Duff had taken my bag with my court clothes. I looked around. There was a small window with bars but it was too high to see out of even when I stood on the cot. I tried to calm myself. Surely Senator MacDougall would come for me before the trial, I thought. I would only be here for one night.

Suddenly I realized I was not alone. I heard someone stir in the farthest cell. He sat up on his cot and stared at me. My breath caught in my throat. He was one of the two whisky traders who had killed Jesse.

"Hey Jake, wake up! It's that Indian from the trading post in Fort Simpson." Jake rolled over and looked at me.

"Well, God be damned! The sewer must have backed up. How did you get in here, Red man? Did you rob someone?" They both laughed hard. Jake stood up to look at me. The one named Harry sat up on the edge of his bed. I was too shocked to speak. They must have known I had come for their trial, but they showed no fear or anger.

Jake fixed his eyes on me. "You've come to rat on us, haven't you? You think they're going to believe what you say, Indian? You better hold your tongue or you'll be as dead as the kid who was with you. We've got a good lawyer and he's going to get us out of here. If you open your mouth we'll come after you."

"I am not afraid. God has seen what you have done. He will strike you both dead!"

"Wooo, he speaks like a real Christian," Jake said to Harry. Harry giggled like a child. Jake turned back to me. This time his voice was full of cruelty. "God doesn't strike anyone dead, you fool, not like I do. Your kid squealed like a pig when I hit him. Had to hit him several times to shut him up. Cost me half his damned money to pay for our lawyer but it was worth it."

His words stabbed at my chest. I had never met anyone so evil. The cell seemed to spin around me. I could not bear to speak or look at them again. I sank back against the wall. The whisky traders returned to their cots. My eyes filled with tears. I prayed to God to hear their confession and bring justice for Jesse and my family.

The afternoon dragged on like an unwanted visitor. The sunlight crept along the wall more slowly than other days. From time to time, the whisky traders shouted insults at me but I refused to answer or to look at them. My stomach screamed with hunger for I had not eaten since breakfast. As the day finally faded, Officer Duff brought us our meals. Jake told Duff to bring me a Bible so that I'd remember not to lie in court. Duff told him to use his mouth to eat or he would take his dinner away. Unfortunately, Duff seemed to dislike me as much as Jake.

I gave up hope that Senator MacDougall would come for me before morning. My prayers had brought me no relief. I was able to sleep once it was dark outside and I heard the whisky traders snoring. I had no blanket or pillow but I wrapped my coat around me and lay down facing the wall.

Officer Duff woke me in the night. He shoved two drunks into my cell.

"I brought you some company, Mr. Campbell. I'd put them in another cell but since you're all named Campbell I thought you'd get along just fine." Duff chuckled over his cleverness as he locked the cell. He had woken the whisky traders too, and they shouted to the drunks to give me a beating. Duff threatened to take away their blankets if they did not stay silent. Then he disappeared again, leaving me with the four of them.

The two young drunks took the beds across from me. The drunkest one lay down and closed his eyes, but the other one sat on his bed and stared at me fiercely. He was a young man with short orange hair. He must have been in many fights in his life for there were scars on his face and his nose looked like it had once been broken.

"What did the copper call you? Mr. Campbell? You can't be a bloody Campbell. You're a stinkin' Indian!" I looked at him in surprise. His face was not mean or evil like the whisky traders, but he was upset.

"Campbell is my baptized name. It is the name I was given by our missionary."

"Jesus! What damn right did he have to give you our name? Is your missionary a Campbell? I bet not. He wouldn't be giving his name away if he was. That name belongs to my Clan. If this was Scotland my family would kill you for stealing our name. My brother and I should teach you a lesson you wouldn't forget, right Thomas?" He looked at his brother, but he was passed out.

"I'm sorry. I didn't know. I am sure he did not mean to offend you."

"Didn't mean to offend me! What the hell are you saying? Your people had their own names, didn't they? What did you do when someone stole your Clan name, eh? I bet you didn't sit back and let them. Bloody high-minded missionaries! Is it fine for them to steal now? And you're a no-good Christian if you're using a stolen name."

I could not answer him. I had never considered that Whites had Clans names too. It was unthinkable to use a name that belonged to another Clan. Before we learned White laws, Clans were allowed to kill someone who did that. Why had Duncan given me this name? My shame burned hot in my cheeks.

The young Scotsman did not wait for my answer. He lay on his cot with his back to me. I laid back too. I prayed softly to Jesus to calm myself. I tried not to think of my many troubles but I found no peace. I was too upset to practice what I would say in the court the next day. I wanted to cry like a child. How I longed for the strength of Tom's arms that night!

The arms of tiredness held me instead and I fell asleep. I dreamed I was at the trial but the Whites accused me, not the whisky traders. The judge asked me to explain why I had stolen a White name and I could say nothing in my defense. My silence angered him and he threw water on me. I woke with a start. Water was hitting my face and there was a terrible smell. The young Scotsman and his brother were relieving themselves on me as I lay on my cot.

"Stop!" I shouted, covering my face with my arms. I sat up quickly. "What are you doing? Are you crazy?"

The Campbell brothers tucked their tsootzes back into their pants and glared at me. They were ready for a fight. "That's what you deserve for stealing our name. Now you smell like a stinking Indian, not a Campbell."

"How dare you! I have done nothing to hurt you. Look what you've done! I must go to court tomorrow to speak at the trial of my nephew's killers but I cannot go like this." I tore off my coat and shirt. They were soaked with urine.

"Don't listen to him," Jake shouted from the far cell. "Indians are killers, not us. We were just protecting ourselves. The bastard's nephew tried to rob us, just like that one stole your name. They're all thieves."

"That's not true! You are murderers! You killed Jesse! You will rot in prison the rest of your lives and burn in Hell after you die!"

"Well now, won't you listen to that? He's a hot one, isn't he?" Jake laughed.

"This will cool him down," said the young Scotsman. He grabbed the pot I had relieved myself in earlier and splashed the urine over my chest and pants. I lost my temper and leapt off the bed at him. The night duty officer had heard my shouts. He entered our cell before the fight started. He cursed at us and moved the two Scotsmen to the next cell. Then he scolded me for fighting and making a mess. The whisky traders laughed with delight.

He left the cell and returned with a pail of soap and water. "You will scrub your cot and the floor clean if you want to leave your cell tomorrow!" he snarled at me. I asked him to bring my bag so I could change my clothes. "Not until your cell is clean," he answered. I did not see him again.

The next morning Duff and two other officers handcuffed the whisky traders and led them away. "Will you let me out now too?" I pleaded, but they ignored me. One of the officers returned to let the Scotsmen out but I was left in my cell for several more hours.

Senator MacDougall arrived early in the afternoon. He pushed past Officer Duff as he unlocked my cell. His face was redder than usual.

"Good Lord, Mr. Campbell, what are you doing here? I have been looking for you everywhere. The trial has started and you are the chief witness. Why are you in this cell?"

"Senator, I am so happy to see you! I brought a letter from Officer Beale in Fort Simpson. He asked the police to find me a place to stay. I thought they would send me to a hotel. I was going to leave you a message but they locked me in here. I have been here since noon yesterday."

"Yes, Mr. Duncan's letter said you would report here first, but I never expected they'd lock you up like a criminal! I was waiting for …" The Senator looked around in disgust. "What is that smell? Did you wet the bed?"

I blushed with embarrassment. "No sir, two Scottish drunks relieved themselves on me last night. The guard made me scrub the cell, not the men who did it. I asked for my bag so that I could change my clothes but they have not brought it to me yet."

"This is outrageous! Where is this man's bag? We need it immediately," he said to Officer Duff.

"I don't remember him having a bag, sir. I can ask the Chief."

"Of course he had a bag. He's come all the way from the north coast. What did it look like, Mr. Campbell?"

I frowned when I heard the name Campbell. "It was a brown leather bag. It has my name on it." Senator MacDougall asked me to wait in the cell and he followed Officer Duff to the front desk. He returned, shaking his head.

"They say you had nothing when you came in. I asked him to look around but they found nothing. What are we going to do? You can't go to court like this."

"But I have to testify, Senator. If I don't they will let the killers go free. They must have my bag. You cannot let them keep it."

"I believe you. They are lying about the bag but I'm afraid there is nothing we can do to prove that at this moment."

"But I cannot go to the courthouse smelling like this. I need to bathe and change my clothes."

"There's no time. Judge Begbie has convened the court for an hour to let me look for you and the hour is almost up." MacDougall checked his watch to be sure. "He might agree to postpone your appearance until tomorrow, but we'd have to request that in front of him in the courtroom. Are you willing to do that?"

He was hoping I would say no. It would embarrass him to bring me to the court smelling of urine but I had no choice.

"Of course. I must try. Jesse's killers cannot go free."

"Very well then," he said with reluctance. "We will try."

He led me along the street and into the court house. People make unpleasant faces and stared at us as we passed. I wished this was a bad dream.

He led me to the courtroom where the trial was happening. He asked me to wait a few feet away as he spoke quietly to the guard at the door. They both looked back at me several times. Then the Senator went into the courtroom alone.

I waited there in the hallway for several minutes. Lawyers and clerks passed by and glared at me with disgust when they smelled my soiled clothes. I felt so ashamed I could not look at them. I bowed my head, closed my eyes and recited a prayer to myself.

"Mr. Campbell," the guard summoned me. He pointed to the Senator who was beckoning me from the door of the courtroom to follow him in.

The court clerk, stood and announced the arrival of Judge Begbie before we were seated. "All rise for the Queen's Court, presided over by Chief Justice Matthew Begbie!" he shouted, and everyone in the room rose to their feet. Judge Begbie entered. He was a tall man with a white beard and dark eyes that scanned the room before he sat down.

"Please be seated," Begbie commanded, and everyone sat. "Senator MacDougall, I see that you have found the witness you went searching for. Mr. Prosecutor, as we are on a tight schedule, could you please ask the witness to take the stand?"

The Prosecutor rose and spoke to the Judge. "Your Honour, if it pleases you, I would like to request a recess until tomorrow morning to allow the witness to wash and change his clothes. He has spent the night in a jail cell and he has had little chance to rest."

"No, Mr. Prosecutor, it doesn't please me. I need to leave for New Westminster tomorrow morning and the testimony cannot be delayed any further. If this trial was important to him he would have stayed out of jail. Please call your witness without further delay."

The Prosecutor hesitated. "Your Honour, Mr. Campbell, the witness, was urinated upon by his cell mates last night and…" The sound of gasps and groans rippled across the courtroom. "…and he is not in a presentable state."

"Silence in the courtroom!" Begbie commanded as he gave the room a stern look.

The foul smell reached his nostrils and he frowned at me. "Mr. Prosecutor, you are quite right. The witness is not presentable. What made you think you could bring him into the Queen's Court stinking of urine?"

"Your Honour, it was not his fault that he spent the night in the jail...." Groans and laughter rippled across the courtroom.

"Silence, please! Mr. Prosecutor, I will have no more of this. We are not here to decide whether the witness should or should not have spent the night in a jail cell. What is clear is that this Court will not suffer the indignity of spending the afternoon smelling this witness's urine while he testifies. Please remove him from the room before the ladies present start fainting from the smell. God forbid, I might faint myself if he's here much longer." Laughter erupted again. Begbie allowed it to continue as the Senator led me out of the room.

"Senator MacDougall, he must let me tell my story. I am the only witness."

"You heard him, Jack. He won't let you and he won't postpone the trial. There's nothing we can do. It's not your fault."

"But Jesse's killers will be set free!" My mind was in a panic. I could not return home without testifying at the trial. Everyone would say it definitely was my fault.

The Senator was right though. There was nothing I could do. He brought me to his home. His housekeeper ran a bath for me and laundered my clothes. I spent the evening in a bathrobe and slept the night in a borrowed nightgown. In the morning I put on my clothes though they were still damp. I visited the police station again. They still claimed they did not have my bag. I bought a ticket for a ship that left for Fort Simpson that afternoon.

Some of my friends and family were kind and forgiving enough not to blame me for Jesse's death but everyone was upset that I had not spoken at his killers' trial. I tried to explain what happened but Mary and Joseph were furious. So were George and Gertie. Daniel and Jennifer Carter said nothing but I could see the hurt and disappointment on their faces. Duncan questioned me about everything. He cursed the police and the judge but even he would not look me in the eye for several days.

The hardest part was that Tom would not forgive me either. He would not even listen to my full explanation. He said I was making excuses. He thought that I was afraid that the White lawyers would say I was responsible for Jesse's death for I let him go alone with the prospectors. Our beds were still tied together but Tom would not hold me as we slept.

A week after I returned, a letter from Senator MacDougall arrived for Duncan. He supported my story and reported that Jesse's murderers were released without punishment. Judge Begbie said there was no reliable evidence against them. Duncan let me read the letter. He told me there was nothing I could do about it now, but he warned me that he had to read it to the congregation the following Sunday. Many people were asking about the outcome of the trial. Everyone was saddened by the news and angrier with me, but no one was sadder or angrier than I was with myself.

I was grateful when the town's attention returned to the fight over our land. Ridley had arranged for a team of surveyors to come to Metlakatla to mark the boundaries of Church of England property and the Metlakatla reservation where our people were allowed to live. Their arrival at the end of September drew everyone's concern. We followed as Ridley led them through the town. In a voice loud enough for all of us to hear, he claimed that Church also owned much of the land beyond our string fences.

The Town Council called a meeting in the Assembly Hall to discuss the situation. The crowd was fearful and angry. Duncan was there but he told us we must decide for ourselves what was to be done. Some suggested court action but most of us believed we would not get a fair hearing in a White court. Joseph, Tom and several younger men said our only solution was to stop them from doing their work. Teams of volunteers agreed to help.

Every night we pulled out the survey team's stakes and every day they started their work over. The head surveyor asked Ridley to assign his men to guard them. That did not stop our men. We made larger teams that Ridley's men could not stop. After a week, the survey team had accomplished nothing, so they summoned a White gun ship. Seven of our men, including Tom, were arrested and held in the jail house until the survey was completed.

We had lost another battle and many of us were discouraged. There seemed no way for us to win. Duncan was not surprised but he was not discouraged either. He called another meeting. It was time to tell us about his plan.

He reminded us that Henry Wellcome had paid for his return to Metlakatla. Wellcome wanted Duncan to move our town out of British Columbia to Alaska, where the White governments in Victoria and Ottawa and the Church of England would not have power over us. We only needed the permission of the American government. Wellcome had many friends in their government. Duncan hoped to win their permission in the following year.

The idea of leaving our town had never crossed our minds. Duncan's suggestion caught us by surprise. Some, like Tom, hated the thought of leaving behind all that we had built in the past twenty-four years. Many thought such a move would be too difficult. We were much older now and at a new place we would not have a saw mill or a carpentry shop to build new houses to shelter everyone. We would need to live in cold, damp tents for at least a year.

Others, like me, thought the idea was wonderful. The sadness, hatred and anger that surrounded us every day was like poison. Our town was the only home we knew but it no longer felt like a home. It would be a bold move, the kind that younger men might make, but we needed to feel younger again.

Duncan asked for a show of hands to see how many of us thought the move would be good and how many preferred to stay and seek for a way to live with Ridley. I raised my hand in support of the move. Tom voted against me. Most of the town voted to stay. The move was a new idea and there were too many questions left to be answered.

Duncan left for Washington the next week. American officials had not agreed to let Metlakatla move to Alaska last summer, but he and Wellcome would work to change their minds over the next few months. If they gave us their permission we would vote again. We could still choose not to move. Whatever we chose then, Duncan would accept our decision and he would stay with us. I remembered my father, Neeshlak, had let our village choose whether to move to Fort Simpson or stay in Gitka'ata. At first we chose to stay but later we changed our minds. I hoped Metlakatla would also have a change of heart when that time came.

Tom became resolute in his decision to oppose the move. He would not discuss it with me, except to say he would not leave everything we had made behind. Perhaps time or other men might change his mind, but I could not.

Duncan's first letter from Washington came the with our Christmas mail a month later. The American Commissioner of Indian Affairs was still doubtful about the move. Duncan and Wellcome had met with the Board of Indian Commissioners, the Indian Rights Association and several churches who were all excited about the idea. They set up a fund-raising drive to help pay for the move, which would save the American government money. He was also helping Wellcome write "The Story of Metlakatla", which would be published in the spring.

News that we were considering a move to Alaska reached Ridley's ears. He was furious. He threatened to excommunicate anyone who followed Duncan to Alaska and we would go to Hell when we died. Sam argued we were already in Hell because of Ridley. The Town Council said Ridley himself was going to Hell so his condemnation would be good news for us in Heaven. Regardless of our response, his threats reminded us that living with him was intolerable. His reaction convinced many who were unsure what to do to support the move.

Two more letters arrived from Duncan that spring. In February, just before we left for the oolichon camps on the Nass, he learned that he and Wellcome had formed a committee of twenty-five prominent business leaders and politicians to support our move to Alaska. The news brought promise of brighter and kinder days ahead, like the approaching summer.

The second letter arrived in March while we were still fishing on the Nass. Duncan said support for the move was growing with American leaders and their lawyers. He and Wellcome had met with the American President, Grover Cleveland, who was like John A. MacDonald but more powerful. The meeting had gone well.

Tom was upset that Duncan spoke about the move as though it was certain to happen, but Duncan predicted the seed he had planted would sprout in our hearts. He was right. As Tomlinson read his letters to our Sunday congregation, the town cheered Duncan's successes. Tom could feel their change of heart and his resolve to stay softened. He did not want to be left behind.

Eventually, Joseph changed Tom's mind. He told him the new town would need many new houses and other buildings and they needed Tom's help. Soon Tom was as excited about the move as his other friends were. He even helped plan how we would dismantle the saw mill and bring it with us.

As our excitement grew, do did Ridley's concern about our leaving. His threats had failed so he tried to persuade us to stay with kindness instead. He expressed his concern for the terrible hardships we would endure without houses, a school or places to meet or pray. His kind words felt strange and false. The first sunny day of spring had arrived. The snows still covered the mountains so beautifully, and the sun seemed to promise that the winter storms would never come again. We could not believe it, and neither could we believe Ridley.

In the first week of April, the Town Council called for a second vote to see how many in the town supported a move to Alaska. This time most of us favoured the move. Tomlinson sent the news of our vote to Duncan. The American government was set to vote and our support for the move would reassure them, Wellcome told Duncan.

After our vote, Dr. Bluett, Sam, Tom, Paul Legiac and Joseph set out to find a place to build the new town. They headed for the islands north of Haida Gwaii on the American side of the border. Two weeks later they returned with good news. There was an excellent site on the west side of Annette Island. Several streams on the island were filled with salmon. One had a steep drop of eight hundred feet perfect for powering a saw mill. It was just as close as our fishing camps on the Nass so our canoes and other small boats could be used for the move.

Duncan returned to Metlakatla with Henry Wellcome in the first week of May. They had come all the way from New York. We received them at our dock like heroes, with our marching band and choir. Everyone was cheering. Old grudges and resentments were forgotten. We had not been this excited in years for our town was starting over.

Wellcome was a slender, friendly and handsome man with sparkling blue eyes. He was about ten years younger than me. He became rich at an early age through his business, Burroughs, Wellcome & Company, selling medicines that were pills instead of liquids. He was delighted to be greeted by our warmth and enthusiasm.

The Town Council, Duncan and many others in the town brought him to visit our carpentry shop, the saw mill and many other buildings. He saw our broken schoolhouse and the place where our store used. He also saw the lines made of wooden stakes and string that divided our town. He gazed in awe at the great church on the far side of the string that had fascinated him with our town for many years.

Wellcome was an excellent speaker, even better than Duncan. He praised our people and our work. He told us he was saddened by what we had lost too, in our struggles with Ridley. He said that never should have happened and that we had his undying support. We cheered him loudly. He apologized, for he needed to return to New York in a couple days, but he left us with the good news that his book, The Story of Metlakatla, had been released the month before. It had become a great success already and it had won the hearts of the American government. They had given their permission for our move just before he and Duncan left New York.

Ridley's warmth disappeared as fast as it had came, once we had decided to move. He threatened to keep anyone who did anything wrong in jail to prevent them from leaving. Duncan advised us to be on our best behaviour until we got to Alaska.

Duncan's suggested that a couple hundred men and women should move right away to start building the new town. They would get ready for the final move the next summer while the rest of the town, including the young and old, could spend the coming winter comfortably in Metlakatla. They would be spared the suffering of living in tents through the winter. His plan made sense but Ridley's threats had changed our hearts. No one wanted to spend more time in Metlakatla while he looked for excuses to jail them. The entire town voted to leave by the end of summer.

Forty men left for Annette Island in early June to clear the land. Tom was chosen to go with them. Duncan asked me to stay behind to help Tomlinson organize the final move in August. He asked us to tear apart the houses so the boards could be used again in the new town. Then he left for Portland to buy supplies for the new town.

It was hectic month when he was gone. The town moved into tents and we began to tear the houses apart. It was like living in tents at the fishing camps, only we would have to live this way for a year in Alaska until the new houses were built. We stored our furniture and other belongings that could not fit in our tents in the Assembly Hall. We had to live without them for now. There was a time when our people had no chairs, clocks and other English things so we told ourselves we could live without them. We would miss them for a while, but we were Tsimshian, not English.

Everyone was in a festive mood in spite of the hardships. We worked hard together, tearing apart the houses and piling the boards on the shore. Canoes filled with the boards and windows left for Annette Island to be stored there until they were needed. Tom would supervise the builders in the new town. I could not be there to work with him but I told myself I was working for him. I felt proud.

Tomlinson worked beside us, hammering the boards off the walls, removing the nails and stacking them on the beach. He was as excited as we were, though he was not coming with us. He preferred small projects over big ones, he explained, and he was also concerned about the Tsimshians who stayed behind. He and his family would return to his mission on the Nass or start a new one somewhere up the Skeena.

Some of Duncan's supporters did not want to move to Alaska, for the new town was on Tlingit land, not Tsimshian. Some would move to Fort Simpson where they had family members. Others moved to Port Essington and others chose to follow Tomlinson, wherever he would go. Laura, her father Jacob and about fifty others would stay for the coming winter. Then they planned to move back to Gitka'ata the following spring.

I was sure the White newspapers in Victoria would rejoice that we were leaving, but they were bitter. They wanted to keep us here like slaves while they denied us rights to our land and our Town Council. They accused Duncan of acting like Moses and filling our heads with false promises. They claimed we were following him blindly like children, as though we had no minds or hearts of our own. They made no mention the evil things Ridley had done to destroy our town.

In early August, Sam returned from Annette Island to tell us it was time to start our move. We greeted his announcement with excited relief. We took down our tents and loaded our canoes. Two days later, the fifty canoes set out for Alaska. Through Sam, Duncan asked me to stay until the move was finished. He would return to inspect our work before the last canoes left Metlakatla.

Duncan also asked us to remove the windows of the great church and the machinery from the saw mill, blacksmith and carpentry shops. He asked us to lock them in the cannery where Ridley could not get them. He would return later with a larger boat to transport them to Annette Island.

Ridley remained silent through most of our preparations. He watched from a distance as the houses came down and we loaded our canoes. He paced back and forth anxiously but he kept his distance. But when we came with our ladders to remove the windows of the great church he came storming towards us shaking his fists.

"You cannot do this, Jack Campbell! I will summon a gun ship if I have to. Those belong to our church. They are property of the Church of England!"

We ignored him and continued our work. We knew no gun ship would come to save a few windows now that we were leaving for Alaska. He glared at us with his hands on his hips as we carried them down to the cannery.

The next day he stopped me as I returned from carrying work tables from the carpentry shop to the cannery. I expected him to start shouting again and I was prepared to take pleasure in ignoring him once more, but his tone had changed.

"Well, Mr. Campbell, you think you have won, don't you?" He spoke calmly and there was a smirk on his face.

"We have left a pile of nails for you, like we did with the store."

"You're feeling smug, aren't you? You think you will soon be free so you don't need to answer me. I have not come for a pile of bent nails or to wish you a safe journey to the Promised Land. There will be no milk or honey there for you, Jack. I will make sure of that. You will pay for what you have done."

"You cannot stop us now, Mr. Ridley. Most of us have left and you can thank only yourself for that. Metlakatla was successful before you came but you have destroyed it with your vanity and selfishness. You are now the Bishop of Nothing and we are leaving you to live with your failure." I looked at his face to see his reaction. He wore a strange smile that bothered me.

"Am I now? And you think you are getting away safely!" He gave an evil chuckle as though he knew a secret. I told myself it was just another game he was playing and I had no reason to be concerned. He had lost the war.

"By the way, where is your partner? I haven't seen him recently."

"Who do you mean?" His question surprised me.

"Tom, of course. You are still together, aren't you?"

I felt shocked and exposed. A fearful dread passed through me. I understood his strange smile and why he had come to speak to me.

"Tom is in Alaska. He is clearing the land and laying out the plan for the new town."

"Is he now? Well, I hope he doesn't encounter any unexpected problems." Ridley sneered at me and then he walked away. He was planning something but I tried to ignore it. It was too late for him to hurt me now, I told myself. Soon I would never see him again.

Duncan arrived two days later with Daniel Carter, Timothy, my brother George and six other men. Sam met them at the dock and showed them what we had stored there and then Duncan climbed the stairs to the town. He was strangely in a foul mood. He did not look at me when I greeted him. He barked at the others to follow him when they stopped to talk to me.

He kept his head down and marched on like a warrior. We had to run to keep up with him. I had seen him like this several times before. I assumed there had been some complications with getting supplies for the new town. We knew better than to talk to him when he was upset and trying to resolve a problem.

"Is there anything you need me to do for you?" I asked him.

"Not now, Jack. I have to talk with Mr. Tomlinson first. Don't go anywhere. Wait outside my office until I call you."

Timothy and Daniel gave me concerned looks. They knew something I did not, but Duncan had told them not to say anything. I waited near his door while he talked to Robert Tomlinson. I heard Tomlinson telling him last minute details of we needed to do. Duncan tried again to convince him to move to Alaska with us, but Tomlinson had plans to build a new mission for those still living in Canada. He did not want Ridley and Crosby to be their only choices for spiritual support.

Tomlinson smiled at me and squeezed my shoulder as he walked past me. He did not look concerned like Timothy or Daniel. Duncan sounded calmer too, so I approached his door.

"Can I come in now, Mr. Duncan?" I asked cautiously.

"Yes, yes," he muttered without looking up. "Please sit down." He pointed to the chair in front of his desk, but he remained standing.

"Jack, do you have anything to tell me?" He tapped a pencil against his fist as he stared out the window.

"About the windows and machinery? We locked everything in the cannery as you instructed," I offered.

"NO! Not about that, for God's sake!" he turned to glare at me. His sudden anger frightened me, but I said nothing. He stepped out from behind his desk and stood facing me. He was breathing deeply to calm himself.

"I received a letter from Mr. Ridley last week. He sent it with one of the canoes that was transporting our lumber." He pulled the letter from his breast pocket and waved it in front of me. "He claims he has recently learned that you and Tom are lovers and that you have lived as lovers behind my back for several years."

He paused to look at my face. I said nothing.

"Of course, I thought this was just another of his insane ploys he has dreamed up to upset me, a last little jab from a pathetic man who has just lost the battle, but it started to make sense. I thought about the many times you wanted Tom to come along when we traveled anywhere. He also said that you have tied your beds together so you could sleep with him. Then I remembered that you had asked for permission for him to move to your house many years ago."

"Sir, I did not want..."

"Others must have known about this, I told myself, so I asked around. I spoke with Joseph and Daniel and several other friends of yours. At first they were silent. They wanted to protect you – protect you! – but I could see in their faces that they knew about your lie. It wasn't news to them! When I pressed them for the truth they admitted that they knew everything. So tell me Jack, in your own words, is this true and how long has it been going on?" His face was red and his eyes were on fire.

"Tom has been my partner since Fort Simpson, before we began English classes with you. I tried to tell you ..."

"WHAT! That was twenty-seven years ago! You deceived me like a fool for all that time? How dare you! Who else knew about your disgusting secret?"

"All the town knows. Everyone who knew us. My family knew too. My father saved Tom from his drunken uncle after Tom's father died, because he knew I loved him. Tom is the only one I have ever loved..."

"That is SICK! That is perverted in the eyes of God! It is as grievous of a sin as any civilized person could imagine. I have spent all my life since I arrived in Fort Simpson twenty-nine years ago trying to save the souls of your people but I keep getting reminded of how little I have accomplished. What made you think you could get away with this?"

"Please, sir, no one meant any harm. We have tried our best to..."

"ENOUGH! You just don't understand, do you? You have made your abominable sin worse by lying about it. Not telling the truth is the same as lying, Jack, and everyone in this town is guilty of lying by not telling me about your evil secret on under my watch. I will make a lesson out of you, Jack, not just for your sake but for their sakes too if they ever want God's forgiveness. I have been thinking about this day and night since I learned the horrible truth. I am glad that you have admitted it openly but that's only a start."

"Mr. Duncan, Tom and I have always supported you. We have been good Christians…"

"No, Jack, you have not. You two have been lying sinners every day while you have been calling yourself Christians. The evil way you have lived is worse than all the good things that you think you have done. None of those good things count for anything when you are so disgusting in the eyes of God. I will not tolerate this anymore. The people of New Metlakatla will learn not to tolerate it either. Do you still want to live with the rest of your people in Alaska, Jack?"

"Of course, sir, I…"

"Fine! If you want to live with us you must stand in shame before them and tell them what you did was very, very wrong. You must promise never to commit these sins again and you must beg their forgiveness for the harm you have done us. You will never speak of your crime after that. It would be terrible if news of this reached the newspapers. We would be ruined. Do you understand that Jack??"

"Yes, sir," I said as I stared at the floor between us. My voice sounded small in my head, like that of a child.

"No-one in the town will be allowed to speak to you or look at you for a month as a punishment for concealing your lies. You will not be allowed to look at them or speak to them either. Is that clear?"

"Yes," I nodded.

"And you must never touch Tom or speak to him again. You must never be in the same room or come within thirty feet of him for as long as you live! I pray to God to strike you dead if you do. Is that understood?" He stood close to me, looking down at me like his angry God, as if he might strike me dead himself.

"No, no, no, NO!" My voice rose in my throat in desperation. "Tamlahk is the only love of my life. We have loved and supported each other through all our troubles since we were boys. I cannot live without him. He is everything to me. I will accept any punishment, but this is too much to ask. I could never forgive myself if I dishonour him."

I cringed upon hearing my own words, expecting Duncan to strike me then, but he just stared at me quietly for a few seconds. He returned to his desk and, without looking at me, he answered calmly, "Very well. I suppose the best you can do is remove yourself from temptation."

He looked up at me. A strange, cruel smile spread across his face. "I have spoken to Tom already. He has admitted his crime and accepted his punishment. He has also promised never to touch you, never to speak to you or to look at you again for the rest of his life. It seems he is not the great lover you thought he was. You are not coming with us to Alaska, Jack. For your own sake, that may be for the best."

I stared at him in disbelief while the pain of his words sank in. The room seemed to fade in front of me. I could not make sense of what had just happened, I was jolted out of my state of shock when he shouted, "What are you waiting for? GET OUT OF HERE!" as he jabbed his finger towards the door.

OLD METLAKATLA

THIRTY SIX

The first rays of the morning sun have lit up the clouds in the western sky. The sea is calm. It gleams brightly as it reflects the yellows and pinks of the clouds. A cool breeze passes over me as I watch the gentle waves lick at the pebbles on the beach.

I do not know how long I have been sitting here. It was dark when I climbed down the stairs with my bag. I could not sleep. I am still not tired, but I cannot shake the sensation that I am dreaming. I do not understand what is happening around me. I can only watch.

The first sounds I hear are the distant voices of the seabirds who are celebrating the morning light. Then come the harsh voices of the ravens and crows, calling out to drive the Ghosts of the Dead back to the Underworld. They are much closer and they seem to be speaking to me. I listen with my arms wrapped around my knees as I sit on the cold sand. I listen, but I do not answer and I do not move. There is nowhere to go.

As the sun rises behind me, over the mountains to the north east, the island on the south side of the channel lights up. The yellows and pinks disappear as the sunlight creeps across the water towards me. The sun catches the steeple of the great church and casts its shadow on the water. I watch as it moves across the row of canoes resting on sand not far from me.

At last I hear the voices of men, the ones who have stayed behind to finish the preparations for the final move to Alaska. I hear their footsteps descending the wooden stairs that lead to the cannery. They carry their tents and clothing in large sacks hung over their shoulders. The first ones pass in front of me. Some glance at me with hesitation, wondering what to do when they see me. Others walk by without looking at me. To them I am already a ghost.

I recognize the approaching voices of Daniel and Joseph. They are talking about the passage to Alaska and wondering if the sea will stay calm. Joseph stares at me, surprised to see me sitting here. His eyes turn back to the beach in front of him. Daniel stops. I see concern for me on his face. He opens his mouth to say something to me, but Duncan's voice barks at him to keep moving.

The men continue on to their canoes. Duncan follows behind the last of them, a shepherd guiding his flock. He glares at me and my bag. He understands I am waiting to be invited to join them. His smile fades and face fills with anger and disgust as he turns away. Once he has reached the canoes I hear him scolding Daniel and warning the others not to speak to me. My heart sinks and a panic grips my heart, but I do not move.

The men make many trips up and down the stairs, bringing bags to fill their canoes. They all ignore me as though I am invisible, everyone except Daniel. He glances at me several times when Duncan is looking away. He tries to speak to me with looks and gestures. He mouths words that are meant to give me hope, I think, but I cannot make out what he is saying. Perhaps I really have become a ghost.

Finally, the canoes are loaded. The men push them into the sea and climb inside once they are off the sand. Only Daniel looks back at me. Duncan orders him to ignore me and concentrate on his paddling. He reminds them there is a full day of travel ahead of them.

They cannot be leaving me, a voice screams inside my head. The panic spreads and tears fill my eyes. I want to cry out to them but I have lost my voice. Their canoes glide silently across the shining water, pulling further and further away from me. I watch in disbelief, my last vision of them blurred by my tears.

I sit in the same position for a long time until my tears finally stop. I am empty and confused. I tell myself they only wanted to scare me, that they will not leave me here to die, but the morning passes and they do not return. I realize they must be half way to Alaska by now, and they are not coming back for me.

I am no longer waiting for their return, but I continue to sit in the same place without moving. I am filled with pain and hopelessness. I do not know what to do next, though whatever I choose to do will not matter.

It is the fierce heat of the midday sun that convinces me to move at last. I am weak and dizzy. I need to find shade. I struggle for my balance under the weight of my bag as I struggle back up to top of the stairs.

The great church grows closer as I climb. I feel the Spirit of the Church watching me through the dark holes of its missing windows. It is smug and vengeful about my demise. It has saved this cruel punishment especially for me, the only one in Metlakatla who is sure of its evil existence.

I cannot bear to look upon it, or for it to look upon me, so I return to the house and the bedroom where Tom I once spent our nights together. I miss him now so strongly, but I wonder if I will ever see him again. There are large holes where the boards that made the sides of our house used to be. Like my life, they have been torn apart.

Strangely, our beds are still here and still tied together. Perhaps Duncan felt they have been tainted by our love and he ordered our men to leave them. Maybe the others left them without telling Duncan, knowing I would need a place to sleep when they were gone. I lie on the bed and pull the pillows tightly to my chest.

I find no peace here. I fall into a restless, dream-like state, but I cannot sleep. Tom seems to speak to me through sheets, crying for me to hold him. Then I remember he has promised Duncan he will never hold me again and my pain begins anew. The wind blows through the holes in the walls to torment me further. I hug the blankets tighter. I do not care if I live or die.

The night passes and the day that follows it. I stay in my broken room a long time, just as I had sat on the beach the day before. Eventually, I leave to get some respite from my troubled dreams. I sit at the top of the hill behind the frames of the houses, out of reach of the shadow of the church. I stare at the harbour. I am still and constant as an old totem, waiting for the canoes to return. They do not return.

I see some of Ridley's men working a few houses away. They are pulling up the stakes and strings that divided our town. It is all their town now. I watch them but they do not seem to see me. Perhaps I am a ghost to them too.

The second night is no better than the first. My dreams are filled with disturbing visions. I watch our canoes paddle away without me again as a panic rises inside me. Tom visits me but he is keeping his promises to Duncan. He won't look at me or touch me. Duncan returns too. He is screaming at me and then he starts to laugh. I realize his laugh is the cruel laugh of the Spirit of the Church, rejoicing in my suffering. Between my dreams I lie awake and cry. By the time daylight arrives again I feel numb. My mind is mercifully silent.

On that second day a boat arrives in the harbour as I am watching from the top of the hill. Several of our men climb onto our dock. I recognize Duncan, Daniel, George, Paul Legiac and others. I see Timothy too. My heart races and fills me with hope. Surely they have come back for me, I tell myself. I grab my bag and climb down the stairs to the shore.

But they have not come for me. They have come to collect the tables, chairs and other furniture from our houses that would not fit into their canoes. I sit on the beach in same spot I waited two days before, but they hurry by without speaking to me. They work silently as they load the boat. I know they are aware of me for their heads are bent in sadness and embarrassment as they pass.

Ridley and Collison descend the stairs to confront Duncan. They demand that he give back the church windows that he will not use in the new town but Duncan refuses.

While they are arguing, Timothy comes to me. He couches down and says, with a look of deep worry, "How are you doing, Little Salmon?"

By this time, I expect everyone to ignore me as they had before, certain that they could not hear the desperate voice that screams to them from inside my head. When I hear Timothy's kind words I begin to sob. The other men stop their work and turn to watch. Their eyes are filled with shame and concern.

"Get back to work!" Duncan shouts at them. He glares at me with contempt, but Timothy ignores him. He continues to hold me and stroke my head with his back to Duncan. For a moment I fear for Timothy's safety, but Duncan marches away as though he cannot bear to look at us.

Timothy pulls away to tell me he must return to the ship.

"No!" I whimper, and I feel my tears rising again.

"It's all right. Just wait here," he quiets me. He hurries to the dock. A couple minutes later he returns with a bag of his belongings.

"I will not leave you here on your own, Little Salmon. I will not abandon you like the others." He sets down his bag and he hugs me again. Then he turns to sit beside me to watch the other men. They pass before us more hurried and determined than before. Duncan's face is filled with anger and the pain of betrayal. This time it is Timothy who has caused his pain. Timothy stares at him with pride and defiance but Duncan does not look back.

A short while later the men finish their work. They climb aboard and the ship moves away from the dock. Timothy keeps his arm around my shoulder. Before the ship is gone from our sight he stands, offers me his hand and leads me to the stairs. We climb to the top and he leads me back to the house.

He is talking to me as though this is any ordinary day. He speaks about the weather and how our men have left the town in such a mess. When we reach the house he chooses a room across the hall from mine and he sets his bags down. I follow him around like a puppy, happy to have him decide for me what I should do.

He asks if I am hungry. Without waiting for my answer he looks through our cupboards, looking for any food left behind. He finds some potatoes and carrots and he fries them in the only pan he can find. The smell of hot food reaches my nostrils and I realized I have eaten nothing in two days.

Once we are finished he suggests I take a nap while he sees what food he can find in the town. There is no longer a store but he will ask around. I do not want to be left alone but the thought of speaking to Ridley's men frightens me. I agree to nap but I cannot sleep. Many dark thoughts pass through my mind as I lie there, and I am filled with sadness and pain again.

Timothy is gone for less than an hour, but it feels much longer to me. The longer he is away the more frightened I become. He returns and finds me terrified and shaking in my bed. I grab his arm and hold onto it for several minutes, but I cannot speak. I can only nod or shake my head when he asks me questions.

Once I am calm again he tells me about his search for food. Ridley's people would not help him. They seemed confused and upset to see him back in the town. He ran into Laura, who was also surprised to see him. She had not heard that I have been left behind by the others. She gives him some her house's food and tells him she will bring him more after she visits the trading post in Fort Simpson.

Laura has also invited us to eat with her and others from Gitka'ata who have not moved to Alaska. Timothy watches my face for my reaction. He sees me withdraw into the covers. "Of course I told her not until you feel better," he reassures me.

That night he sings to me and tells me stories to help me fall asleep. I do not complain that he is treating me like a child. I need him near me. Eventually he accepts this. He climbs into my bed to hold me. I snuggle into the folds of his nightgown and let his arms surround me.

The next day Timothy suggests we move to another house that has not been torn apart. At first I panic at the thought. He strokes my hair while he explains that we will need a warmer, drier place when the rains and cold weather come. He says that I also need to get away from the memories and ghosts that haunt me in this house.

He leads me along the road to the far edge of town, inspecting the houses as we pass. The last few are still complete. We agree on one. It even has a wood stove that is still intact and a table with three chairs. I see that, like me, they were left behind as unfit. They are damaged and wobbly.

There are no beds in the bedrooms so he leads me back to my broken house. He wants me to untie my bed from Tom's and again I start to panic.

"No, no, Little Salmon, you don't want to leave your favourite bed behind, do you?" I shake my head. "You see, this is easy." He pulls me down on the floor beside him and starts to untie a knot. "Now you do this one while I untie the other side."

He slides over to reach the knot by the head of the bed. He begins to sing a favourite song of mine, one everyone knew when we were children. He gets me to sing it with him and soon we are both laughing as we work. We continue to sing as we carry the beds downstairs and up the road to our new house.

And so our new life together begins this way, with song and laughter. I am not alone when he is near. It does not matter that the rest of town is a distance away. The shadow of the great church does not reach us here and I feel safer.

But my problems are not over. Every night I have sad or fearful dreams and I awake crying. Timothy is always there. He brings one of the wobbly chairs upstairs to sit by my bed and watch over me. He sings to me and I relax.

I depend on him for my meals. I never have a suggestion when he asks what we should eat, but he asks me regardless. We find baskets of food on our doorstep. I am not sure whether they are coming from Laura's people or Ridley's. I do not ask.

Timothy asks me to help him repair one of the chairs. Somewhere he has found a hammer, a saw, some glue and nails. I can carve wood, he confides, but I am useless at fixing things. One of the legs needs to be shortened and I use a couple nails to strengthen it so it does not complain when we sit on it. He commends my good work and we sing to celebrate.

I like having work to do and he encourages me. I fix our table and the remaining two chairs. I do not have Tom's talent, but I have learned some skills from him in the past thirty years. I delight in the simple joy of working with wood instead of people. I am happy working alone while Timothy does other errands, but I panic when I finish and he has not yet returned.

Timothy has spread the news that I am willing to repair things and I have become a handy man in the town. The only trained carpenter in town is Ridley himself, Timothy giggles. We laugh at the idea of seeing him doing any work. I am talking with Timothy more now, but I am still shy when others are around. Some men bring things to our house to be fixed. I ask them what needs to be done and tell them what I can fix with as few words as possible.

Timothy has started working too. He is now baking bread for the town in the early mornings as he used to do. The town is grateful, for the bread from Fort Simpson is never fresh. I help him or watch him work if I get anxious alone. Between the two of us, we make enough to repay others for bringing us our food.

One day Laura stops by our house while I am resting upstairs. I want to see her but I do not want to talk so I pretend to sleep. She chats with Timothy softly so not to wake me. I fall asleep and later when I wake I wonder if her visit was a dream.

Timothy tells me Laura has invited us over to have dinner with her daughter Charlotte and a few others of the Gitka'ata group that share her house. I agree, for Timothy will be with me. I listen to Timothy's stories as we eat our meal. He is not afraid to talk or move like a women in front of Laura. This makes her laugh, but she notices how quiet I am.

"I am worried about you," she says, reaching across the table to hold my hand. "You are usually so chatty and happy. Are you OK, Jack?"

"Don't call me that!" The words leap from my mouth with a force that is unfamiliar to me. Laura stares at me in surprise. She glances at Timothy for an explanation. He touches my shoulder and asks me what is wrong. "That is not my name. My name is Gugweelaks. I will not use my English name ever again."

They are not angry with me. In fact, they seem relieved that I have passion inside me. From that evening on, I only use Tsimshian names for our people. Timothy is now Tsangook and Laura is Laguksa once again.

I am changing in other ways too. I am letting my hair grow. I would grow my beard out too, but Tsangook insists that I take care of my appearance. It shows respect for myself and a respect for being alive, he tells me. We sit together by the wood stove in the evenings, combing each other's hair while we tell stories and sing songs together. Happiness is returning to my life like the warm glow of the fire.

One evening it occurs to me that Tsangook has never told me why he chose to leave Alaska to live with me. "Because you needed me, Little Salmon," he answers. "And because I could not accept Duncan as my Chief when he treated you so terribly. You are one of the best men I have ever known. And Duncan has never liked me much. I am too much of a woman for him. There is nothing bad about you or me, but he cannot see that. I saw that I did not belong there with him. Some others felt bad that they stayed in Alaska when I returned to help you, but they have made their choices and so have I. I am happier living here with you. I made the right choice."

His words bring tears to my eyes. He has saved my life by caring of me for the first months after the others left. I am growing stronger and I am finding my voice again, but this would not have happened without him. He is changing too. He seems tired and he struggles when he walks. I have fashioned him a cane, perhaps like the one the first Chief of Gitka'ata used, which he uses wherever he goes.

We take long walks through the town and along the road to the old saw mill to enjoy the autumn air before the snows come. The alder trees and the berry bushes have taken on the colours of rust and blood. Their leaves lie on the ground beneath our feet as we pass. Long grasses and young saplings have sprouted up along the road to the saw mill in the past year. The road yearns to return to its home in the forest that surrounds it.

Signs of decay are spreading through the town as well. The wooden sidewalks are falling apart. In places it is safer to walk through the mud beside them than to risk breaking through the rotting boards. There are potholes filled with rain in the road above the beach. Ridley's men try to keep the gas lights near his residence and the great church working, but several others have died along the road.

Tsangook's sight is growing worse too. With the shorter, darker days, the broken sidewalks and the failing gas lights, if is safer to stay home in the evenings. I am less work for him now. I do not panic anymore, though I am still sad when I think of Tamlahk. Memories of our life together, both good and bad, haunt me now. I wonder if he has suffered like I have and who is taking care of him in Alaska. I still hope he will realize his mistake and return to Metlakatla to live with me.

Ridley's men have broken through the roof of the cannery. They have taken the windows of the great church and they are installing them again. As I pass them working, Ridley's eyes meet mine. He nods at me. He no longer seems hostile or full of contempt. I have seen him watching me from a distance in recent weeks. I wonder what he is thinking. He asks if I would be willing to help his men install the windows. I tell him no. I do not care that he has taken the windows back, but I cannot stand to be near the church.

One morning before the first snows, some of our men return from Alaska. I see their boat arrive in our harbour. Klashwaht, Doolyaks and six younger men climb onto our dock. Duncan is not with them. Klashwaht is giving orders as they unlock the cannery. They see the hole in the roof and that the church windows have been removed. They remove the canning machinery and lay it on the dock.

Ridley confronts them and threatens to send his Constables to arrest them. Klashwaht argues with him as the other men load the equipment onto their boat. While they are busy, Doolyaks runs up the stairs to Mission Point to see if the windows have been installed. I run to meet him near the top of the stairs.

"Jack!" he exclaims. "I am so glad to see you. Everyone has been so worried about you. How are you doing?"

"I am fine, Doolyaks. I am getting better at least. How is Tamlahk? I have not heard a word about him since you moved to Alaska."

"I am afraid he is quite depressed. He keeps to himself a lot now after Duncan shamed him in front of all of us. Duncan has still not forgiven him, even though Tom has received his punishment. He won't let Tom supervise the building of the new town. He has given that job to Joseph." When he mentions Klashwaht's name he glances back at the cannery.

"I cannot let Joseph see me talking to you. He is more Christian than ever now. He is Duncan's eyes and tells Duncan if we break any of his rules. Duncan gave us strict orders not to talk to you on this trip."

At that moment I see Ridley marching back to the stairs and Klashwaht is looking around. Doolyaks clasps my hands and tells me to take care of myself. As he turns away I ask him to tell Tamlahk that I have forgiven him and that I miss him greatly. He tells me he will. Then he runs back to the dock.

Klashwaht's men climb on board their ship before Ridley's Constables can stop them. They pretend to leave but they stop again a mile away. They wade to shore and try to remove the machinery from the saw mill but Ridley's men meet them there. They fire their guns to scare them away before they are able to take anything.

The first storms have arrived with the first deep snows. I wonder how Tamlahk reacted when Doolyaks told him I have forgiven him. No one can send messages in this weather. I imagine he regrets his decision to leave me and he cries himself to sleep every night. I pray that he will overcome his shame and embarrassment and return to me. At other times, I wonder if Duncan has forgiven him and he is doing well again as he supervises the building of the new town. My questions are impossible to answer but they will not stop.

Tsangook is growing weaker and it worries me. He tells me it is nothing, that he is just getting old or feeling a bit sick, but I see the changes from month to month. Our walks are much shorter now, even on the warmer days. He cannot see far. I walk him to the bakery and back each morning and deliver the bread to everyone in the town until he becomes too sick to bake.

He stays inside throughout the winter. As the days grew shorter, we stop visiting Laguksa in the evenings, for he falls on the way home, even with my help. We share midday meals in her house instead, until he no longer feels well enough to go outside. Then Laguksa comes with Charlotte to our house to cook for us and to keep us company. They give us joy whenever they can.

Laguksa and Charlotte are concerned for Tsangook when he does not improve. I begin to fear that he never will. I do not admit this to Laguksa, though I am sure she shares this thought with me.

As the winter progresses I chop wood, cook meals and do all the errands that Tsangook used to do for me. I do the same for others in exchange for food they give us. I sometimes speak to Ridley's people. We never mention our past disagreements or injustices now. Ridley keeps inviting me to hear his sermons in the church on Sundays, but that is one thing I cannot do.

As winter passes and the ice begins to melt, Laguksa, Jaleek and the other Gitka'ata people leave Metlakatla with the others to fish for oolichon on the Nass. I stay behind to care for Tsangook, who now spends much of each day in bed resting. I ask them to tell our people who have moved to Alaska that Tsangook is ill. And if they see Tamlahk they will tell him I want him to move back to Metlakatla to be with me.

Asking them to speak for me upsets me. I do not know what I would say to Tamlahk if he returns or what to think if he does not. I sit by Tsangook's bed and watch him rest as he did for me. He does not panic as I used to do, but I hope my Spirit will convince his to fight to get healthy again. My only concerns are for those who are at the fishing camp and for Tsangook sleeping in his bed. I am the loneliest I have been since the first day I was abandoned.

Laguksa and the others return from the Nass in late March. They did not see Tamlahk but they spoke with others from Alaska. They agreed to take my message to Tamlahk after the camp. They let others know that Tsangook was not doing well. I do not know what to expect. I must wait to see what will happen.

The joy of having Laguka's company again does not last long. She and the rest of our village are making final preparations to return to Gitka'ata. They packed most of their belongings before they left for the Nass and now they are packing the last of what they will take with them. I help them whenever I can, knowing that I will miss them so much when they are gone.

Laguksa is worried for me. She doubts Tsangook will recover and I will have no one to care for me. I can take care of myself and Tsangook, I tell her, but I am worried about the future too. Tsangook will be my only friend after they leave.

"Come with us, Gugweelaks, and bring Tsangook with you. You belong with us. We are your people and we will take care of you," she begs me.

"We cannot," I insist. "Tsangook is too old and too ill to sleep on the ground in a tent. Perhaps when he gets better and you have built new houses we can join you."

She looks at me with resignation in her eyes. She knows I will not come later, even if Tsangook recovers. She knows I am waiting for Tamlahk.

It takes them less than two weeks to finish their preparations. I help them load their canoes at sunrise on the last morning. Jaleek comes to me and grips my shoulders. "You know you are always welcome to come live with us, Gugweelaks." He hugs me and turns away without waiting for my answer. Laguksa, Charlotte and many others hug me and wish me well in turn. Then they climb into their canoes and paddle away. I watch their canoes disppear around the south end of the harbour.

There is a burning pain in my heart as I watch them. The water is calm and the first light of the sun is touching the land. I feel much like I did when the others left for Alaska last summer. Although the Gitka'atans have not forsaken me, I stand like an abandoned child on the sand as my family leaves without me. I have made the right choice, I tell myself, but nothing feels right at this moment.

Caring for Tsangook occupies my mind. I try to find joy again by singing and telling him stories to make him laugh. But he does not laugh easily anymore. He has stomach cramps and fevers and his memory is growing weaker. Sometimes I feel he is not listening to me. I realize at these moments he is fighting the pain and doing his best to conceal it from me.

As the weather begins to warm I take him out as often as he is willing to go. We sit on the retaining wall by the edge of the road, looking at the harbour. He sees only blurs of colour but he loves to listen to the birds sing and to smell the new growth of spring.

One day, as we are sitting in our usual spot, I see the Collisons walking along the road in our direction. We have exchanged polite nods in recent months, but we have not spoken in the past year. I turn back to look at the harbour. I hope they will pass without paying us any mind. Instead, they come over and stand beside us.

"What a lovely spring day!" Marion Collison announces with music in her voice.

"Lovely indeed," echoes Henry Collison.

I nod but offer no reply.

"How are feeling these days, Timothy? We haven't seen much of you this past winter." They must know he has stopped baking, and they have seen him walking with his cane and me leading him because he cannot see.

"I am fine, thank you," he answers them weakly. "I haven't seen much of anything lately but I do enjoy the perfumes of spring."

"Indeed," Mrs. Collison nods. "Good day then," she says and they continue on their way along the road without looking back.

Later that morning, as I tear up the steps of one of the abandoned houses for firewood, Marion Collison sees me and walks up to me.

"Where is Timothy, Jack?" she asks.

"His name is Tsangook and my name is Gugweelaks. We only answer to those names now," I say as I continue with my work.

"Very well. Is Tsangook around?"

"He is sleeping. Why do you ask?"

"Jack, I mean Gugweelaks, I am afraid something might be terribly wrong with him."

"What do you mean?" I feel both anger and fear growing inside of me.

"I am a trained nurse, you know. His blindness is a serious concern. Has he had any other symptoms?"

"What has his blindness got to do with anything else?" Her questions upset me.

"Has he had cramps or fevers or loss of strength in his arms and legs?" She knows his symptoms and what is wrong with him, a voice in my head is telling me, but I am not ready to know.

"What does it matter? I am taking care of him and he is getting better. He just needs rest, that is all!" I hear my voice rising.

"If he has what I think he has, it is called syphilis, and I don't think he will get better again." She looks at me directly, searching my face to see if I understand.

"You are just saying that to hurt me. Haven't you caused my people enough suffering. Will you never stop your evil lies?" I shout at her.

She is quiet for a few seconds. I avoid her eyes. I rip furiously at the steps but the boards resist me. I bash them with my hammer out of frustration. I know she is telling the truth. I feel tears rolling down my cheeks.

"Jack, I am not telling you this to hurt you. I thought maybe I could be of help, just as Duncan was when your people were sick."

I wipe my face with my sleeve and I glance at her. "What can you do to help him? I have tried everything."

"Well, if it is syphilis, it is probably too far along to do much. I might be able to give him something to ease his pain at least."

"That will not help him. He needs to get better. You just want him to die so I will have no one. Your people only want pain and death for my people."

I am sobbing now and I cannot talk further. I gather up my ax and hammer and the few boards I have freed and I walk back to Tsangook without looking at her again.

That night, as I sit beside his bed I watch him struggling against the pain. It is the same almost every night now and there is nothing I can do to help him. He will not even accept the warm tea I bring him. I cannot deny the truth any longer. He is dying and I will lose him soon. I have no idea what I will do if he leaves me, but I realize I would sooner see him pass on instead of suffering like this. A panic I have not known since the autumn grips my heart again. This time there is no one to soothe me. I return to my room, but I cannot sleep.

The next day I go to Marion Collison and I apologize. She is relieved. She sees I am frightened and exhausted. She returns to my house to inspect Tsangook. She asks me many questions and I answer her the best I can, without hope in my heart. She gives him medicine to soften the pain and help him sleep. Then she leads me downstairs to tell me he is dying.

She comes to our house every day now, just as Laguksa used to do before she left for Gitka'ata. She brings a bedpan and clean towels to wipe away the sweat of his fevers. She teaches me how to bathe and move him without causing him too much discomfort. The medicine does the most to comfort him, but she does not have much. She sends me to Fort Simpson to get more while she watches over him.

I have not been to Fort Simpson in more than a year. I think about how strange my life has become over the past year. I feel calmer though. Paddling alone to Fort Simpson has helped to clear my head and to forget my pain. When I arrive I hurry directly to the trading post. It occurs to me as I approach it that I might see Tamlahk there, or maybe some others who have moved to Alaska. My heart starts to race in anticipation.

I look around as soon as I am inside, but I see no one I know. I am disappointed. I walk to the the counter and tell the clerk what I have come for. I show him a list of medicines that Marion has written on a sheet of paper for me. The clerk looks through his supplies and finds most of them.

As I leave the trading post, I run into Doolyaks coming towards me. We are both surprised and elated. We hug each other tightly. He pulls me aside and asks me about Tsangook. I tell him the bad news and he looks horrified. He asks me what I will do when he dies. I do not know.

He has horrible news for me too. My sister Mary fell sick while living in a tent on the beach the past winter. She caught a fever and developed pneumonia. Two weeks later she died. Her death has driven Klashwaht crazy. He has turned to Christianity to hide his pain. He now accuses everyone of breaking God's rules. Duncan's suggestions are the word of God to him now. His son Earl could not bear his rages after losing Jesse and his mother. He has run away. Doolyaks suspects he had fled to the new town of Vancouver to work in a pulp mill.

I am shocked and pained by this news ,but I cannot stop myself from asking about Tamlahk.

"Duncan has forbidden Tom to leave New Metlakatla. He will not let him to go hunting or visit the trading post or the fishing grounds. He fears he will run away and return to you if he does."

"Is he unhappy in Alaska?"

"Yes, he avoids most of us. Either he fears that we have rejected him, like Joseph, or he resents us for obeying Duncan's orders to make him miserable. Others are afraid to comfort him because Duncan will lose his temper if they do. Duncan will only let him do the simple work of labourers. He holds Tom there like a prisoner to punish him."

"Why does he listen to Duncan? If he returns to me we could live as we did before. We would never need to worry about what Duncan thinks again. Please speak to him. Tell him I love him and that I will have no-one if Tsangook dies."

Doolyaks agrees to tell him but he does not know if Tamlahk will return. He will not give me false hopes.

I paddle back to Metlakatla, fighting the rising waves that have come with the afternoon winds. I return to Tsangook's side with the medicine he needs, but medicines that will not cure him. There is nothing Marion or I can do. He continues to grow weaker, but at least he has less pain.

Another six weeks pass. Tamlahk does not return. I lose hope that he ever will. During the long hours by Tsangook's bedside I think of the many times Tamlahk has caused me pain. I once told myself he loves me as much as I love him. Now I doubt this as my anger rises up to bury my pain.

The anger attacks everyone who has hurt me. It accuses Duncan, Ridley, Klashwaht, the White newspapers, Jesse's killers and many others. On his better days, when he is tired of resting, Tsangook sees my anger and pain.

"What is it, Little Salmon?" he questions me.

I feel ashamed that I have caused him concern when he is the one who is dying.

"Why is it, Tsangook, that life is so difficult? Why is there so much suffering? Why do some people hurt others so deeply and then ignore them when they are in pain?"

"Do not give up, my friend. Life is still beautiful and troubles pass like the seasons. The sun will return soon."

"But I need to understand, Tsangook. These questions do not let me have peace. Nothing seems fair. It does not make sense to me."

Tsangook reaches up his feeble arm to wipe my tears with his shawl. "There now, Gugweelaks. Only Great Spirit understands. These questions are too much for our small minds. The only people who pretend to understand are the one who have admitted defeat."

"What?"

"We pretend to understand why we lose but we can only wonder about our successes. Understanding brings no joy, but the mystery of the world does. Leave the hard questions to Great Spirit and accept happiness again."

◇◇◇◇◇◇◇◇◇◇◇◇◇◇◇◇

With those words of wisdom, he fell into a sleep that lasted for a couple hours. When he woke his breathing was hard and his voice was weak. I asked him if there was anything I could do to make him rest more easily.

He nodded but did not say anything. He struggled with great effort for a few seconds before I realized he was trying to remove his shawl.

"Are you too warm? Is that it?" I asked as I pulled it off him and laid it on my lap.

"I want you to wear this so my Spirit will always be with you."

"Are you sure? You might need it later."

There was a twinkle of amusement in his eye. His voice was thin and soft but his words were clear. "You should never refuse a good shawl that is offered to you, Little Salmon."

Those were the last words he spoke. He closed his eyes and tried to rest. His hands clutched the blankets over his chest as though they were his shawl. His breathing was rough and irregular. Two hours later it stopped forever.

THIRTY
SEVEN

Tsangook's death had been approaching for some time, but I was not prepared for it. When it happened a great helplessness consumed me. I shook him and begged him to return to me. When I could not revive him, I lay beside him and hugged his limp body. I sobbed through that evening and through the long night that followed.

I had not cried since Jesse died, not even when I watched Duncan and the others paddle away to Alaska, leaving me behind. I had felt pain and panic, but I could not cry. Later, I felt only despair. I was dead inside and dead men do not cry. Tsangook's love and care had slowly brought me back to life. Now that he was gone I was ready to die again. But this time I did not die. I cried instead. The tears I had denied for so long poured out of me like a flood. I cried for days until I could not cry any more.

Marion Collison found me hugging Tsangook's cold body when she came to check on him the next morning. She pulled me away, set me on a chair and went to find men to help her. After she left I could not sit there looking at him. I climbed back onto his bed and hugged him again. She returned with three men. They wrapped his body in his sheets, still wet from my tears, and took him away. She asked me many questions, but my tears were my only reply.

"I guess this can wait," she said. "When did you eat last?" I could not answer that either. She told me to come with her. I followed her to her home and she prepared me a meal of bread and chicken soup.

I could not focus on anything. My tears flowed silently. I did not wipe them away. My soul had sprung a leak. Henry Collison watched me anxiously, until Marion sent him away. She set up a cot for me in their living room and busied herself with house-work. Later, she noticed I was still awake. She asked me if I wanted to sleep in my own bed and I nodded. She led me back to my room.

"Stay in your bed, not Timothy's." she ordered. She stared at me for a few seconds, wondering if it was safe to leave me. "You aren't going to do anything foolish, are you?"

I looked at her, not knowing what she meant. I wondered if she thought I was going to play with myself as soon as she left. I closed my eyes and pretended to sleep. A few minutes later I heard her soft footsteps creeping down my stairs.

The next morning, I wrapped myself in Timothy's shawl and I felt his Spirit watching over me. Marion arrived and led me back to her home. She made hot cereal and asked me about Tsangook's death as I ate. Tears welled up in my eyes. I dabbed them away as I did my best to answer her.

Tsangook told me he wanted a Tsimshian cremation instead of a Christian buri-al. He wanted to spend eternity with Great Spirit, not a foreign god. The Collisons looked at each other when I told them his request. Henry Collison said he would ask Bishop Ridley. I doubted they would grant his wish. It did not matter. I decided I would do it if they did not.

I sorted through Tsangook's belongings and decided what to keep and what to throw away. He had many dresses that the women in Alaska had given him when they had no space to keep them in their tents. There were hats, gloves and other items too. Shawls were not the only women's clothes he could not refuse, I smiled to myself. I felt his Spirit was with them too. I could not throw them away.

Collison let me know that Ridley would not permit a Tsimshian cremation. Rid-ley remembered losing the fight with Duncan over Tooklan's cremation. Now that Duncan was gone, he would not tolerate another heathen ceremony. A Christian buri-al service would be held for Tsangook behind the great church the next morning.

The Ridleys, the Collisons and the small church congregation were gathered around his grave when I arrived. Ridley already begun the service. His words caught in his throat and his jaw fell open when I approached. He had never seen me dressed so beautifully. I wore Tsangook's favourite white dress and the sun hat he always wore to do his gardening and a veil I had sewn onto it.

Everyone turned to look at me. They all smiled and nodded, except the Ridleys and Collisons. They stared at me in confusion. After a few seconds, their gaze returned to Tsangook's grave. Ridley resumed speaking, hesitantly and distracted. He did not know Tsangook well so he spoke instead about the importance of a Christian burial for a person to receive God's forgiveness. His words were more an explanation or an apology than a sermon.

The Ridleys and Collisons left as soon as the service was over. The others gathered around me to offer their condolences before I retuned to my house. They remembered seeing Tsangook wearing the dress and sun hat and they commented on how beautiful they looked on me. I thanked them.

I spent the following days building a platform behind my house. Marion Collison came by to see how I was managing, and she asked me what it was for. For drying animal furs, I lied. She saw my men's clothing and smiled. She was pleased that I was going hunting again. Hunting is a good activity for a man, she told me. I agreed.

The next week the Collisons left for Haida Gwaii to visit the mission they had started twelve years before. At the same time, most of the town left for the salmon camps on the Skeena. Fewer than a dozen people remained in the village. I had waited for this moment.

Early the next morning, while the first light of the sun glowed softly behind the mountains to the east, I hurried to Tsangook's grave with a wheelbarrow and a shovel. My heart pounded as I dug down through the soft dirt to expose his coffin. I removed the lid and lifted him into the wheelbarrow. I covered him with a tarp and rolled him back to my house. Then I hurried back to fill his grave and pat down the earth. When I was finished, it looked as it had before I disturbed it.

The first rays of sun were shining on the harbour and the shadow of the great church stretched along the road as I ran back towards my house. Soon the Ridleys would finish their breakfast and leave their house for their morning walk.

I washed Tsangook's body and dressed him in his favourite dress. I wrapped him in cedar strings and set him in the wooden box I made for his cremation. I hoisted him onto the platform and piled his belongings around him. On the ground below the platform I prayed to Great Spirit to receive his Spirit and I lit the fire. It quickly consumed the platform. Its smoke surrounded me, stinging my eyes, until a gentle breeze lifted it away from me. The fire roared. Tsangook's body hissed and sizzled as though it was speaking to me. The embers rose high into the morning sky as they carried his Spirit up to the Heavens.

Ridley came rushing over an hour later as the fire was dying. "What are you doing, Jack? You could set the whole town on fire!" His face was a confused mixture of anger and alarm.

"I am burning Tsangook's possessions," I said calmly. "Don't worry. I am watching the fire. I will make sure it is completely cold before I leave it."

He hesitated for a moment before he saw there was no need to panic. He looked at my men's clothes and smiled. He probably thought I had burned all of Tsangook's dresses. He nodded at me and walked back to his residence.

But I had not burned the rest of Tsangook's dresses, shawls and hats. Wearing them each day brought me strength and eased the great burden I had felt for too long. My tears stopped and my heart was calm. I no longer cared what others thought. Tsangook walked with me and I walked with him. It was a woman's walk.

I felt lighter and more peaceful, but I was alone. I floated through each day without purpose. I watched the harbour with the hope that Tamlahk would appear. I wondered what I would do when the autumn rains and the long, chilly nights returned. The Ridleys and Collisons stared at my women's clothes in confusion and embarrassment. They knew I wore them to honour Tsangook. They assumed some day I would stop grieving and return to behaving like a man, so they said nothing.

Our town was now so small that most ships passed us by. Once each week a ship brought our mail on its way to Fort Simpson, but other ships rarely stopped. One day a southbound ship did stop and a passenger got off. From a distance I could see she was a young, slender woman. She stood on the dock looking up at the town. One hand held her bonnet down. Its brims flapped in the breeze like a bird that struggles to fly.

I made my way along the road towards Mission Point to get a better look at her. She met me at the top of the stairs, panting for breath as she hoisted her bags onto the final step. I gasped in surprise.

"Anne! What brings you back to Metlakatla?"

"Uncle Jack, I am so happy to see you! How have you been?" She dropped her bags and threw her arms around me. "Oh, you look so good! Are those Tsangook's clothes? They look lovely on you. And you have grown your hair out too!" She brushed it away from my eyes.

"You are looking lovely too. I am so happy to see you. How are Doolyaks and Yuwahksa?"

"Oh, you are using their Tsimshian names. How sweet of you! But you will have to call me Anne," she giggled. "My parents are fine, thank you. Father is getting older. He cannot do heavy lifting like the younger men but mother still has lots of energy. They send their regards. They have been worried about you."

"I am delighted to see you, but why have you come?"

"Father says Tsangook is dying and I thought you might need help taking care of him."

"I am sorry Anne, but he died a month ago."

"Oh dear," she covered her mouth. "I am too late."

Suddenly I was afraid she would return to Alaska on the next boat now that she did not need to care for Tsangook.

"Are you still living in the same place?" she asked.

"No. Many of the boards were torn off and taken to the new town. I have been tearing off more since then to use for firewood. I live at the end of the road now. Would you like to see it?"

"Yes, of course." She paused to survey the broken houses, the holes in the road and the rotting sidewalks. "Oh Lord, what a mess the town is! We need to fix it up!"

We walked slowly for her luggage was heavy. I asked if she had news of Tamlahk.

"I talk to him whenever I can. So do father and mother, but many others are afraid to. Duncan gets irritable when they do. I don't care though. You and Uncle Tom always loved Jesse and I so much. Jesse's father has been so mean to him. He says Mary's death was God's punishment for keeping your love for Uncle Tom a secret from Duncan. His belief in the Church is so strong now. He thinks everything that goes wrong is God's punishment. No one is Christian enough for him. He scolds all of us and reports everything he sees to Duncan."

"How is Tamlahk doing otherwise?"

"Not well, I'm afraid. He works as a labourer. He made a big mistake staying in Alaska. I told him I was returning to live with you. I asked him to come with me, but he just shook his head. He would not say why."

I fell silent, thinking about the suffering he must be going through. Anne waited a bit before commenting that he could still change his mind. She described what had happened over the past year in the new town. She had cared for Miyana when she fell sick. Many others had fallen ill too from living in tents through the winter beside the chilly beach. Miyana was not the only one who had died.

Klashwaht could not forgive himself or others for her death. He took his anger out on my poor nephew Earl, who was still grieving too. Earl ran away in March. This was news Doolyaks had already told me.

We reached my house and I invited her in. She went from room to room inspecting it. She saw the photograph of Jesse sitting on my dresser in my room. It was the picture that was taken of him in Fort Simpson the day he was murdered. His beautiful smile glowed with joy and love, as hers did when she saw it. "Oh Lord," she cried and held it to her breast. "We have to hang this downstairs where everyone can see it."

Her words made me smile, for she would not return to Alaska. I needed her help more than they did, she told me. She was upset that Duncan and the others had left me behind and by how meanly Tamlahk had been treated since then. She was tired of the hatred and anger she saw in Duncan and Klashwaht. For her, the new town was built on old wounds. She never blamed me for Jesse's death like Klashwaht had. She knew how much I had loved them both.

We quickly settled into a comfortable life together. I gave her my room and I moved to Tsangook's to be closer to his Spirit. She did not judge me for wearing his dresses or acting like a woman. She preferred me that way. To her, they were signs that I was strong and healthy again.

She came to keep me company, not to take care of me, and she came with many talents. She had worked at the fishing camps for several years. She knew how to dry fish, clean meat and collect seabird eggs. She was an excellent cook too, but her true passion was sewing. Marion Collison gave Anne her sewing machine and taught her how to use it. Anne practised every day. Soon women of the town brought her fabrics from Victoria and Fort Simpson and she made curtains or dresses for them. She even learned how to make pants for the men. Her sewing earned us money. Along with money from my repair work, we could afford our meals.

When the stormy weather arrived, she was my companion. We sat together by the wood stove in the evenings when our work was done. I combed her hair and she combed mine, just as Tsangook and I used to do. She sang songs with me and we reminisced about bear watching and other things we did with Tamlahk and Jesse.

She asked me about my life when I was a boy. I shared everything I could remember. I told her about the Hamatsas and the winter ceremonies, about our potlatches and Tsangooks' carvings. What she liked best though were the stories of Tsamsem, Raven and the Animal Spirits. She would lean against me or put her head on my lap and close her eyes. She did not mind if I repeated the same stories on different nights. Each time I added more details. I learned to use different voices for each character and to speak with more passion. With the practice she gave me, I became a better story teller.

I kept to myself before Anne arrived, but she could not live that way. She wanted to be part of the town. She was quick to greet others and give them compliments and encouragement. She did her best to be helpful. There was no room for judgment or resentment in her heart. During the holidays, she organized the women to make feasts. She made the work such fun that even Jane Ridley and Marion Collison joined in. In a kind and gentle way she changed everyone. They all agreed she was a godsend.

I had always loved her dearly, but she had become more beautiful than I had ever imagined. I delighted in our closeness and I could not think of life without her. I was perfectly content. I did not want things to change, but they did. In January I fell ill with a fever. I could not leave my bed for a week. Anne brought my meals, changed my sheets and cooled my skin with wet towels. I saw concern for me in her eyes. I realized she loved me and I thanked Great Spirit for bringing her to me.

As I grew stronger we grew closer than ever. We embraced for long periods without speaking. One evening, when my recovery was no longer in doubt, she told me how frightened she had been that I might die. She told me, with tears in her eyes, that she would have been lost without me. I caressed her and our mouths met. Without a second thought, we made love and held each other until the next morning.

That is how she became my lover. At first it felt strange, like a gift we were not worthy of, but that is always the way gifts from Great Spirit feel, she told me. It would be ungrateful to question such wonderful blessings. I never questioned my attraction to her or whether we should be together. Those answers I knew. The brilliance of her youth fascinated me. When she spoke or when she lay on my lap listening to my stories she gave herself to me as only a young person can. I was her teacher and she was my loving pupil.

But it was more than attraction. Before she came, my heart was filled with so much pain and sadness, so much anger over past injustices, that I could not feel Great Spirit's love. I questioned my reason for living. Anne had lost Jesse, her life's love, and she had nursed my sister until her death. Still she had kept her faith in life. She glowed with joy and kindness as only someone raised on love and respect can. This was the greatest gift her parents had given her. Like a loving parent, I wanted to protect her from the heartbreaks and unfairness of life.

Her body fascinated me too. I was slender and still smooth and firm. Her small, round breasts were lovely to touch. My body had become a stranger to me. It had grown thicker and heavier as I aged. Hair grew in places it had never grown before and it was turning grey. I wondered what attracted her to me. When I was young I pretended to be a cannibal. Now I pretended to be a woman, but Anne had no need to pretend. She moved with such ease and grace. I finally understood why other men spoke so much about their women.

Loving her was easier than it had ever been with Tamlahk. I loved him with all my heart, but he was often a difficult child. How many nights had I spent hugging his back, trying to soothe his rage over something that had upset him? How many times had he refused to speak to me because he was jealous? And now, after betraying me so completely, he kept me waiting for his return. Anne loved me like I loved Tamlahk, generously and without hesitation. She had opened the door to new world and beyond it there was a gentle paradise, so I asked her to marry me.

Others saw we had fallen in love. Our people thought it was natural, that the Spirits had brought us together, but the Ridleys and Collisons could make no sense of it. If I loved Tamlahk how could I love Anne? If a man acts like a woman how could he be drawn to another woman? They thought they knew what should be right, so they thought their eyes must be tricking them. They did not know what to say so, once again, they said nothing.

We joined other Tsimshians in the oolichon camps on the Nass that spring. It was a joyous time away from Whites and the problems in our each of our towns. We stayed with the other Gitka'atans at our old camp at the end of the bay. Neither Duncan nor Ridley were there to separate us.

Doolyaks and Yuwahksa knew Anne and I were lovers and that we wanted to marry. Anne had written to them a few weeks before. They were excited for us. Anne had been so depressed after Jesse's murder that she had no interest in other young men. They had worried as much about me after I Tsangook died. Doolyaks was especially pleased. He joked that his best friend would soon be his son-in-law.

We learned that Laguksa and her people were not able to return to Gitka'ata. The River Spirits at our old town resented that we had abandoned them and they build up sandbars to prevent us from using their beaches again. The Gitka'atans chose a new site for their town, behind an island at the south end of Tsamsem's Trench. They were excited by their new town. They called it Hartley Bay.

Lagusksa was certain the Spirits had blessed us. My Eagle Clan had arranged my marriage to her when I was a boy to build ties with her Raven Clan, and Anne was a Raven. The Spirits had destined me to marry a Raven, she told me. She invited Anne and I to marry in Hartley Bay. It was a wonderful idea, for we both wanted to see the new town.

Klashwaht objected to me being at the fishing camp but the others silenced him immediately, for I had every right to share the fishing grounds with other Tsimshians. He fell into an angry pout and said little to anyone after that. I watched him with forgiveness in my heart. I remembered watching him thirty years before in the same camp, pouting in much the same way.

I had met Tamlahk at the same camp that year. He was not there this time, for Duncan would still not let him to leave Alaska. His absence made me sad. Doolyaks had not told him yet about my engagement to Anne. He might never return to Metlakatla once he knew, but I would not reconsider marrying Anne. If he did find the courage to return, I knew somehow we would find a way for him to live with us.

I did not dwell on Tamlahk for long, for I enjoyed being with my people. In the evenings as we rested around the fire, I told the stories of Tsamsem and the Animal Spirits that I had practised with Anne. My listeners encouraged me to continue. They had not heard our stories in many years. They sat staring at the fire quietly while they listened. My words carried them back to when they were young, to a time before White men taught us that our stories were lies.

Anne and I returned to Metlakatla rested. We made our wedding plans, but we kept them secret from the Collisons and Ridleys. I shared them with Robert Tomlinson though. He came to Metlakatla in April to get the machinery from our saw mill to use at his new mission in Kitwanga. Ridley would not let him take it, even though we were not using it. He was upset but his trip was not wasted. He stopped by my house to see how I was doing. I told him the good news about my engagement to Anne.

Tomlinson was a devout Christian with a temper worse than Duncan's, but he had a kinder and more loving heart. My women's clothing and long hair surprised him but he was more amused than upset. He was also surprised about our engagement. He was full of questions, but our answers convinced him that we were in love. He had good news for us too. Bishop Cridge would ordain him that summer so he had could marry others. We asked if he could marry us at Hartley Bay. He was thrilled that we asked. He would leave Victoria at the end of August and he would stop to marry us on his way home. We confirmed the dates with Laguksa and she organized the people of Hartley Bay to begin preparations. We sent invitations to Doolyaks and Yuhwahksa to give to our friends in Alaska.

In May, Anne and I went to the salmon camp on the Skeena. We invited several people there to our wedding, but we asked them to keep our plans secret from Duncan or he might prevent them from coming. Doolyaks and Yuwahksa sent us a response that they planned a shopping trip to Victoria with other guests from Alaska, making a secret stop in Hartley Bay along their way to attend our wedding.

At the salmon camp, Anne told me she was pregnant. I was astonished and delighted. I had never been so happy. We cuddled in our tent as discussed how best to raise a child. We anticipated its coming like a great adventure, as Tamlahk and I had once dreamed of exploring the world, but this time it was much closer and more certain. We kept it a secret for the moment. I held the joy inside as I told stories about the Animal Spirits around the evening fire. My heart was filled with love for everyone as the happiness Anne and I shared touched those around us. It was most joyful camp ever.

Our wedding preparations occupied our summer. I carved and bought gifts for our guests. Anne made other ones. She made her wedding dress too, though she would not let me see it until our wedding day. Laguksa and her Raven Clan prepared the wedding feast. Our celebration would also show visitors their new town for the first time. The men of Hartley Bay worked hard to complete their houses and a new dock. They planned a great potlatch, like the potlatches my father once hosted, but we had to call it a wedding party instead. The White government had outlawed our potlatches.

Ridley heard about our plans. He was offended that we had not asked him to marry us. I did not want his resentment to ruin our wedding, so I brought him a gift I from Fort Simpson, a diary with blue paper illustrated with flowers. I explained to him that we wanted to be married with our people from Gitka'ata and how excited they were to show us their new town. I did not tell him that Robert Tomlinson would marry us.

Doolyaks and Yuhwahksa stayed with us at Metlakatla the week before the wedding. Anne told them she was pregnant. Their delight added to our excitement. By the end of the week I was exhausted. Thankfully, Doolyaks had paid for our passage south to Hartley Bay on a steam ship so we could rest before the wedding.

We arrived in Hartley Bay two days before our wedding. The new town was small, but it was so fresh and clean. The beach was already filled with the tents of visitors who had arrived before us. Anne and I were given a room for in one of the new houses but we were rarely alone. There was so much to be done. We spend most of the time greeting and talking to the many guests so the others could continue the preparations. I told stories of Gitka'ata in the evenings, the ancient stories of how it came to be, and we shared stories of our lives there when we were children.

Our wedding day was wonderful. Anne looked so lovely in her wedding dress she had worked on for days, and I was proud to stand beside her with everyone watching. My brother Gwashasip represented the Eagle Clan and Jaleek was there as the Chief of Hartley Bay and the Raven Clan. Robert Tomlinson was the only White man, but before he started our marriage ceremony he announced that he was honoured to be part of our Tsimshian celebration.

After the ceremony we shared the great feast and the gift giving. It went on for hours until we could barely keep our eyes open. The next day we spent giving our thanks and saying goodbye to our guests. Doolyaks, Yuhwahksa and the others from Alaska continued south to Victoria. Tomlinson headed north to begin his long journey up the Skeena to Kitwanga. We stayed one more day to catch the mail boat back to Metlakatla.

It was mercifully quiet in Metlakatla. We spent most of the first day sleeping. The second day was just as peaceful but we did our chores. We said little but we smiled a lot.

Anne had began to show she was with a child. She had hidden her pregnancy until our marriage and now she was delighted to show it off. She spoke often with other women who had given birth. Much of what they told she had already heard from Yuwahksa, but she accepted their advice with respect. They would help her raise our child after it was born.

The change in my life over the past year amazed me. I was now married and I would soon be a father. Other men had married and had children, but I had never imagined this for myself. How different it was to be the story teller instead of the listener. I thought about my future. I was forty-eight already. I wondered how old I would be when my child married, or if I would live long enough to see that day.

I had dark thoughts too. I worried that Anne would have a difficult birth. Tamlahk's mother had died giving birth to him and other women had given birth to dead babies. I dared not mention these to Anne. If she shared these fears she never mentioned them to me. Every day I prayed to Great Spirit for an easy birth and a healthy baby. I did not care if it was a boy or a girl.

We spoke only happy thoughts. Anne called to me each time the baby was kicking. Sometimes I sang to it with my mouth beside her belly. "Be careful," she would tease me. "You might scare him." Somehow she knew it would be a boy and I believed her.

She was right, of course. She usually was. Our son was born in late February of 1890, on the first mild day of spring when the snows began to melt quickly. It was a good omen. Great Spirit answered my prayer. Anne was only in labour four hours and our little boy was strong and healthy. We named him Thomas, in honour of Tamlahk.

He opened his eyes on his second day. He stared at the world wide-eyed. I wondered what he thought about this strange world he had come to. I thought of how blessed we were. Anne was tired but calm and happy. I wanted her to rest but she would not stay in bed for long. She was anxious to start making clothes for our little one.

For his first year, we lived only for our little Tommy and each other. We talked about nothing else and no-one seemed to mind. We were delighted by his first laugh and when he started to make noises in a strange language we could not understand. He learned to sit and then crawl, things that every baby learns, but to us these were new. We learned them again through his eyes.

He was a joyful and curious boy. He was not afraid of new things, so we had to be watchful. He would reach for anything, even if it was sharp or hot. His first word was "dada". Perhaps to him it was just a sound, not a word, but we thought he was speaking to me and we were excited. I wanted to teach him everything, but he taught me too. He taught me to believe in miracles and to be grateful for every day we are given. He taught me to become a child too. I was learning about the world for the first time.

I spoke to Tamlahk every day through little Tommy. I shared with him every joy and blessing I felt when I was with my son. I told him he would love his little nephew and that his little nephew would love him too. I believed my love and prayers would somehow travel over the waters to Alaska and reach Tamlahk's heart. I hoped I could entice him to return to Metlakatla this way.

Duncan forbade the people of New Metlakatla to speak to those who remained in Old Metlakatla, but once Tommy was born he could do nothing to stop Doolyaks and Yuwahksa from visiting us. Even he was wise enough not to stand between a child and his grandparents. They brought us news from Alaska and I always asked about Tamlahk. Doolyaks had told him we named little Tommy after him. That brought tears to his eyes, but he would not speak about his feelings to Doolyaks. Each time they prepared to visit us they invited him to come with them. He knew Duncan would never let him to return if he did. There was no need to return, Doolyaks told him, but he would only shake his head and turn away. He must have thought he did not belong here now that I had married Anne.

A couple of months after little Tommy was born, Anne was pregnant again. I was so grateful that Great Spirit wanted to give us more. Anne was pleased too, but she was calmer than I was. She had learned to hold the joy inside. I loved her dearly and admired her strength. Her body was a sacred spring that brought wondrous children into our world. I did not know the words to thank her.

For the first months of Tommy's life, I could not bear to leave him and Anne alone. I missed going to the oolichon and salmon camps. By late summer, when he was learning to sit and crawl, Anne encouraged me to join hunting trips with other men. I objected at first, not wanting to be out of Thomas's sight, but one parent was enough and she was still nursing him.

Once I was in the forest again, I was happy to spend time with the other men. I walked and dressed like a mahanna. I watched over their camp, cut the wood and cooked their meals as Tsangook once did, but I did not satisfy the men in my tent each day as he would. Anne would not have minded but there were too many White men's diseases among our people now. Many other couples could not bear children. I would not risk bringing syphilis or some other disease into my home.

In early January of 1891, Anne gave birth to a beautiful little girl. We gave her the Tsimshian name of my sister, Miyana, and the Christian name Maria. Thomas did not understand why we had a new baby. He looked at her in Anne's arms and wept and screamed out of jealousy. I had to hold him every time Anne held Maria. We taught him that she was his sister and that he too needed to care for her. Our enthusiasm won him over eventually. Within a few months he could say her name. He came to her when she cried and he tried to feed her when he was eating.

When Thomas started to speak, we agreed the children should learn both English and Tsimshian so they would understand both worlds when they were older. Maria needed Anne's attention, so I looked after Thomas. I bathed and fed him each day. I played with him and taught him new words. I loved him as Tamlahk should have been loved when he was a boy. I believed, naively, that I could protect him from the pain and cruelty Tamlahk suffered.

There was no reason to doubt I could when they were babies. We were a happy, loving family and the people of the town loved them too. Doolyaks and Yuwahksa visited us several times each year. They brought them so many toys and picture books that Anne worried they would spoil the children. I disagreed, for children cannot be given too much love.

Thomas and Maria played well together as they grew. Thomas was devoted to her and she trusted him. As I watched they play, I remembered playing with my sister, but Maria did not decide what games they would play as Miyana used to. Anne said they were more like herself and Jesse when they were small. She was right. Thomas was her protector and he tried to teach her everything that I taught him, just as Jesse had looked after Anne.

Marion Collison opened the Metlkatla School for Girls in the fall of 1891, the year that Maria was born. Jane Ridley assisted her. They used the old schoolhouse that had recently been repaired. They only used one classroom, for there were not many young girls in the town. The girls were taught good English manners and to know their place in English society. They also learned reading, writing and basic math, but not the skills they needed to raise a family in a Tsimshian village. Marion Collison and Jane Ridley lacked those some of those skills themselves.

Anne and I wanted Tommy and Maria to grow up to be Tsimshian children. They learned to speak our language as well as they spoke English, even better than Anne, though she was improving too. I taught them our stories of Tsamsem and the Animal Spirits and showed them how to pray to Great Spirit to watch over them.

When they were old enough to climb the hill, they fished with me from our dock or from our canoe. They liked to watch me carving totems from cedar sticks, skinning animals I brought home from my hunts and hanging their furs to dry. They helped Anne gather forest plants, pick berries and gather birds eggs and seaweed from the shore. They helped us plant our garden and they watched Anne prepare our meals. They loved to watch her sew too, especially when she was making things for them. Before they started school, they had learned the alphabet and how to count.

In the summer of 1893, the Collisons moved to the mission at Kincolith on the Nass to work with the Nishka. We never saw them again. The Ridleys were the only Whites left in Metlakatla. Jane Ridley ran the girls school with some help from the village women but Ridley himself did little more than prepare his Sunday sermons and baptize babies and new converts when that was needed.

No one understood why he stayed. He had once told us he could manage our town without our Town Council but he was not able to manage his own life. He still held his nose high and tried to look important, but when the village left for the fishing camps he looked as helpless as an abandoned child. His arrogance had faded. He had not learned to canoe or to shoot a gun in the many years he had lived with us. In spite of his show of superiority, he had accepted that he was only a guest, not our leader.

For this I was grateful. Our town had become Tsimshian again. We no longer had White men deciding everything we should do. I was civil to Ridley, for Anne was popular with the women of the town, but we rarely spoke. He did not ask us to attend his sermons and he no longer seemed to be bothered by my dresses and shawls.

We saw less of Doolyaks and Yuwahksa as the years passed. Doolyaks had heart pains and he could not paddle as far. Yuwahksa stayed to watch over him. We kept in touch with them by writing letters. We met most of our other friends at the fishing camps, but I also wrote letters to Laguksa and Robert Tomlinson several times each year.

In the spring of 1894, when the town was preparing to leave for the salmon camps, Ridley brought a letter to my house. It was from Yuwahksa. It was marked 'important', so he brought it to me directly. He waited to see if he could be of any help. Of course not, I thought to myself. Clearly he was the one who needed help, but he looked so concerned I said nothing.

I tore open the letter, fearing that Doolyaks had fallen ill, but I was not prepared for what I read. Tamlahk had taken his life. His body had been discovered a few days before. One evening after dark, he had slashed open his arms from his wrists to his elbows on a beach near town. He bled to death on the sand before he was found the next morning. The news stunned me. I stumbled backwards and landed clumsily on a kitchen chair.

I read on. Yuwahksa mentioned things about his funeral service and the town's reaction but I could not make sense of any of it. My head spun in confusion. I thought it was not possible, perhaps a mistake or a joke, but Yuwahksa would never tell me this unless it was true.

Ridley looked truly concerned and asked me what was wrong. I could not speak. I read the same words again and again until they began to sink in. A great lump grew in my throat. I cried for Anne while I still could. When she appeared, I stood up and cried, "Tamlahk is dead. He has killed himself." She squealed and threw her arms around me and we sobbed on each other's shoulders.

I did not hear Ridley leave. Over the next few weeks I was not aware of much that went on around me. I remember imagining I was holding Tamlahk in my arms and reassuring him that he was loved and there was no need to take his life. When I accepted that such thoughts were pointless, I called to his Spirit to ask why he had not come to me first. He had not met little Tommy or Maria yet, and we had no chance to say goodbye. He had not let me hug him and tell him how much I loved him. My thoughts and prayers had never reached him, or he did not believe them when they did. For this I blamed myself.

I blamed others too, just to let out my anger and pain. I blamed Duncan and Klashwaht for treating him cruelly. I blamed Ridley for telling Duncan about our love. I blamed the English for believing our love was evil. I was angry with Tamlahk too for not returning to Metlakatla. Seven years had passed since I last saw him. I was angry with myself for letting so much time pass. Why did I not do something when it was clear he would not return? Why did I believe he was managing without me?

My questions had no answers, or at least no answers that could satisfy my broken heart. I asked them over and over without expecting an answer. They summoned up the sweetest memories of him; seeing his beauty for the first time at the fishing camp on the Nass, watching him teach me how to fish for oolichon, him shooting the bear at the hunting camp, making love with him on the floor of the hotel in Victoria, watching him tell Governor Douglas in his broken English how he loved to build things, remembering how he stood up to Ridley and led our men to tear our store apart in the pouring rain. Most of all, I felt his tears on my neck as he whispered "Thank you" in my ear.

Tamlahk's funeral was over by the time I received Yuwahksa's letter. Duncan had refused him a Christian burial for taking his own life. Duncan's cruelty caused him to take his life, but Duncan accepted no blame for his death. Instead, he spoke against Tamlahk at his Sunday service, saying he his death was God's punishment for Tamlahk being a bad Christian. He said he would banish from the town anyone who allowed me to visit his grave. If any faith in a Christian God still lived in my heart by this point of my life, it died with Tamlahk.

THIRTY EIGHT

My anger and sadness were not the worst of my problems. For weeks after Tamlahk's death I would wake in the middle of the night in a panic. In my worse nightmares, I watched Tamlahk slit open his arms. I could not stop him or cry out to him. Anne tried comfort me, but I could not relax. I was shaking and too terrified to close my eyes again. I would sit up and hold my knees until the morning light returned. Some nights I slept without waking, but I was never sure what would happen when I closed my eyes. Sometimes I panicked when I was awake. Just a sad thought about Tamlahk was enough to make the terror return. I felt so unsafe I sometimes wished for my own death.

These memories and my fits of panic held me in a helpless trance for weeks. They drained the strength from my arms and legs. Waves of fear washed over me, threatening to drown me as the tears rolled down my cheeks. Anne was always beside me, giving me her love and strength. She never complained that I had stopped working. Tommy and Maria were concerned for me too. They climbed onto my lap and told me that they loved me. They begged me not to cry. Slowly, as the weeks passed, I taught myself to stop thinking about Tamlahk. My fits of panic slowly faded away. My strength retruned and I became a father and a husband again.

I did not forget Tamlahk but I learned not to dwell on him either. I learned that my life, like every other, is vulnerable. Strength and health are illusions that evaporate when the flames of fear and pain become too hot. My crisis deepened my appreciation for Anne and the children. I wanted to protect them from ever feeling what I had felt, but I knew I could not. I decided to love them as best as I could and to enjoy the time Great Spirit let us to share together.

After that painful spring and summer, the following winter was a happy one. We were close and loving with each other. In the spring, we took Tommy and Maria to the fishing camp on the Nass for the first time, for we could not be separated. It was not safe to fish with them in our boats, so we took the job of chasing away birds that tried to steal our fish from the drying pits. The sticks we used were too heavy for them to use but they had great fun shouting at the birds. To them it was a game. We taught them that they were working, and that working can be fun.

The town received an announcement from the Office of the Indian Commissioner, saying that all children over five years had to attend a White school. We enjoyed teaching Tommy and Maria ourselves, and there was still much we wanted to teach them, but White schools had books and supplies that we did not have. That summer a government official came to Metlakatla to see which children were old enough. Thomas had turned five in February, so we needed to enrol him in September.

The nearest White school was the Thomas Crosby Residential School for Boys in Fort Simpson. We felt lucky that he would be close enough to come home each weekend. He cried at the thought of being away from us all week, but we told him he would like it once he made friends and he saw how much fun it was. We took him to visit the school two weeks before classes started. We found Reverend Crosby in his residence behind his Methodist church. We introduced ourselves.

"Thomas is my first name too!" he smiled at Tommy. "You soon will be living at my school. What do you think about that?" Tommy looked at him suspiciously and clung to my pant leg as he backed away. "A little shy, is he? Well, he'll soon get over that!"

"He has never been away from home before," I explained.

"Well, there will be many others like him. Everything will be fine if he is a good boy."

"He is a lovely boy," Anne replied. "Can he come home on the weekends?"

"This will be his home, but he can visit you on the weekends if you pick him up Friday afternoon and bring him back Sunday afternoon after church. If you cannot pick him up he will stay with us over the weekend too. I wouldn't mind. That way he'll receive a proper Methodist service instead of one of Ridley's."

I looked at Anne. It was best not to mention we did not take him to Ridley's services. Crosby took out a set of keys from his desk and led us to the school. He unlocked the door and led us to the dormitory.

"Thomas is a smart boy. He can count to twenty and he already knows his alphabet. He can read some words, too," Anne told him. Crosby nodded at her. but he said nothing.

"Thomas will sleep with the other boys." We looked around at the rows of bunkbeds that lined the dingy room. "As you can understand with most boys, we need to teach them discipline. They are taught to make their beds properly each morning and to clean their own dishes after each meal. They pray as soon as they get up, before each meal and before going to bed, like proper Christian children. They have Bible study each day as well as math, reading and writing. Most importantly, they learn to take instruction and to obey Christian rules. When he graduates he will be as good as any other Christians and ready to fit into civilized society."

"Will you teach him how to hunt or fish?" I asked. Missionaries rarely could do either.

"Why would we do that? He will be taught how to play football and rugby with the other boys. They provide much better exercise and they teach boys discipline and competition. Those are the skills they need to fit into proper English society, not hunting and fishing."

He looked at us carefully, to see if we dared to challenge him. I looked away. I felt an uneasiness growing inside me, but it would serve no purpose to argue with him.

"One of us could stay in town for the first week to help him settle in," Anne suggested.

"Definitely not! The boys must learn to adjust to school without being coddled. Other boys will make fun of him if he cannot come to class without his mother."

"He's only five," Anne tried to reason with him. Crosby looked at her sternly. He did not want further discussion. He had given his answer.

"Where do the boys come from?" I asked, wanting to change the subject.

"Most of them live in Fort Simpson. They attend day classes and they live with their families in town. Boys who stay in the dormitory come from other villages. Many of them are Nishga from the Nass. Two older boys from Metlakatla stay here too, whom you might know. Is there anything else?" Neither of Anne or I spoke. "Very well then, I can expect you bring Thomas to us day before school begins so he can get settled in. Do not bring him later than that. We do not tolerate lateness here."

We said little on our way home. I saw apprehension in Anne's eyes, but we could not discuss our concerns in front of Tommy. There was little to discuss anyway. Our only option was to send him to another school further away where he would not be able to visit us on weekends, and it would not likely be any better than Crosby's school.

"I don't want to go to school in two weeks," Tommy objected. "I want to stay in Metlakatla."

"You have to go to a White school somewhere, dear," Anne replied. "If you go to school in Fort Simpson you can visit us on weekends. You want that, don't you?"

"That man said that his school would be my home, but my home is in Metlakatla. I want to stay here!"

"You might like it there," I suggested. "You will have lots of other boys to play with. The boys in the dorm will be Nishga, like Uncle Tamlahk, who we named you after." I realized that would mean little to him for he had never met Tamlahk.

"No, I won't," he insisted.

"You are a smart boy. You will do very well. I bet you already know more than the other boys."

There was no point saying more at this time. He needed to get used to the idea, just as we needed to. We tried to sound excited for him, but he saw through our act. He remained doubtful for a while, but as the days passed he acted more bravely, perhaps to reassure us. He said he would teach the other boys the stories of our people that I had always told him, and he said he would learn Nishga too.

We delivered him to Fort Simpson the Sunday before school began, with his bag of clothes and his favourite picture books that he wanted to show the other boys. We brought Maria with us so she could see his school, but girls were not allowed inside, not even to say goodbye. Anne waited outside with her while Tommy and I went inside. He chose his bed and I helped him organize his clothes. He was determined to show me everything was all right, that I had nothing to worry about. I felt reassured. Crosby introduced us to other boys who had arrived. There were still several empty beds, though classes began the next day. I wondered how the boys who did not arrive on time would be punished.

Crosby asked me to leave as soon as Tommy was settled in, so the boys could get ready for their evening meal. It was only mid-afternoon. I think he saw us as bad influences who would interfere with Tommy's education.

Maria was full of questions about Tommy's school. She worried that he would be unhappy without us. She was certainly unhappy without him. We told her he would have lots of fun there and would learn many new things. She counted the days until Friday and made sure we did not forget to pick him up. She was hopping with excitement when Friday arrived. Tommy was happy to see us and he spent most of the weekend playing with his sister.

He was happy enough with his first week. He had played football with the other boys and his teacher was impressed that he already knew his alphabet. His teacher told him in front of his class that he was a smart boy. We were relieved, although we missed him dearly. I wondered if we would have a harder time adjusting to his school than he would.

When he was gone, Maria complained constantly that she had nothing to do. Most of the other girls in town she played with were older. They were enrolled in the girls' school in town, so she decided she wanted to go to school too, just like Thomas. Jane Ridley thought it was a good idea for Maria to start school early. She took her just for the mornings since she was only four and a half.

That arrangement worked well for Anne and I. We had the mornings to ourselves for the first time in five years. It was a sweet time. We spent them talking, laughing, cuddling and making love. We got more work done too. Our afternoons we spent with Maria, teaching her reading and printing or taking her on outings in our canoe when the weather was good.

Tommy spent every weekend with us, but we began to see changes that concerned us. He had less and less to say to us when we asked how his classes were going. He no longer played much with Maria. She was excited about her school and she wanted to tell Tommy about it, but he was not interested. He became withdrawn.

He was a happy, independent boy before school began. Now, instead of playing with Maria, he clung to me. He wanted me to tell him stories while he snuggled next to me during the days, when he used to prefer to be outside. Once I stroked his hair as I told him a story. He hugged me tighter and cried. I asked him what was wrong, but he would not tell me. I thought he was homesick and that it would pass so I let him hug me as much as he wanted to.

His unhappiness grew as the weeks passed. He became defiant and angry, refusing to come to dinner or to help us do simple tasks he once loved to do. He cried and begged us to let him stay home whenever it came time to return on Sunday afternoons. When we asked if he liked school he answered "no", but he did not say more.

His mood affected all of us. Anne and I worried what we should do. He was not adapting to school life. Maria was hurt by his rejection. She refused to come with us to pick him up from school or to drop him off. We had to leave her with other women in the town. She asked us why he was so unhappy. We told her he missed us, but we knew there was something more to it than that.

One Friday at the end of October, he was especially quiet and withdrawn when we picked him up. When we got home, I asked him to help me carry wood into the house but he complained that his hands were too sore. I checked his hands. They were covered with red welts and the skin was broken in two places. I was upset. I asked him what happened and who had done this to him. He backed away from me in fear when he heard the anger in my voice. I realized my mistake and I held him in my arms while he cried. Eventually, he told me his teacher caught him telling a Tsimshian story to the other boys. He took him to Crosby's office and Crosby beat him with a cane.

I was furious and Anne was just as upset. She said I must do something. I told her I would talk to Crosby. I thought about what I would say to Crosby all weekend. I had every right to be angry but as I paddled towards Fort Simpson I was sick from worry. I promised myself I would not lose my temper. When I got to his office, Crosby kept me waiting half an hour while he spoke to the parents of a new boy who had just moved to Fort Simpson. The wait made me more anxious.

He seemed in no hurry to see me after they left. He finally invited me into his office, but he was preoccupied with the paperwork on his desk. He reminded me of Duncan. How ironic, I thought, that they hated each other so much. Without looking up, he asked what I wanted.

"Young Tommy's hands were covered with welts and his skin was broken. They were not even bandaged. He told me you did this to him."

"That's right, Mr. Campbell. I punished him for telling lies."

"My name is Gugweelaks, not Mr. Campbell. What do you mean by that? What could a five-year old boy possibly say that would justify a grown adult beating him so cruelly?"

"We use Christian names here, Mr. Campbell. You had better get used to that, and we have rules here. A boy's schooling needs to teach him to obey the rules of society. We will tolerate nothing less. He was telling foolish stories about some primitive spirit to the other boys. This is a Christian school and the only stories we allow here are Christian ones from the Bible. If you taught him those stories instead of false ones, Mr. Campbell, he would not get in trouble."

"They are Tsimshian stories that have been told by my people longer than England has existed. They are no more lies than your Christian stories. We never beat our children for telling your stories."

"Christian truths, Mr. Campbell, not Indian lies. Your stories keep your people helpless savages while our Christian truths have led us to build the greatest empire in the world. That is the difference. There is no Indian God. It is a sin to tell lies against the true Lord."

"He is only five. Does your God tell you to beat small children with sticks like dogs? Is there no better way to teach him your truths?"

"No, there is no other way. How will he learn what is wrong if he is not properly punished?" Crosby spoke calmly as though he was stating a common fact. "Furthermore, the playground supervisor heard him speaking Tsimshian. That is not permitted either and if I catch him doing it he will be beaten again."

"How can you say that? Many Whites speak two languages. They are not beaten for doing so. Are you punishing children for knowing things that you do not?"

"No, we punish them for speaking savage languages. You better watch your tone with me, Mr. Campbell, or Thomas will not be allowed to visit you on the weekends."

"He is my son. I can remove him from your school!"

"If you do I will report you to the Indian Commissioner. You will be put in jail for breaking the law. Thomas will be given to a White family to raise and you will never see him again. Is that what you want?" Crosby looked at me with contempt in his eyes. White law favoured him, and I was powerless to stop him.

"You cannot do that!" I shouted angrily.

"Yes I can. It has been done many times before. You better think about that."

I could not listen to any more. I turned and walked out of his office and went back to Anne who waited for me outside. She saw that our talk had done no good. What did he say, she asked me, but I could not talk about it until we were back home. I felt Crosby had beaten me like a dog, too. This is how little Thomas has been feeling, I told myself.

I described to Anne everything that Crosby had said to me, once I had control of my emotions. She sat silently for a while, waiting until her thoughts were clear before she spoke.

"If we move Thomas to another school it will likely be just as bad. Whites do not respect our stories or our language anywhere, Gugweelaks, and Thomas will be too far away to visit us on the weekends. If he visits us on the weekends at least we will know how he is doing at the school. We can comfort him and show him we love him. If we teach him not to speak Tsimshian or tell our stories at school perhaps he will not be beaten. It is not good to hide ourselves, but sometimes we must to survive."

"I cannot bear to watch him suffer. It is driving me crazy."

"And I cannot bear to lose him forever. Crosby is telling the truth. They will take him from us if we do not follow their rules. It is not right, but it is our only choice."

It was a truth that hurt to swallow, but it was harder to tell Tommy there was nothing we could do to protect him from Crosby and other Whites. We taught him to recite the rules of the school so he would not be beaten. I stopped telling him our stories and speaking to him in Tsimshian. He could be a Tsimshian boy when he was older, I told myself, when he was old enough to separate our two worlds clearly. Until then, we could only help him to heal the wounds the White school gave him.

Tommy was angry with me. He knew I had spoken with Crosby and now I taught him Crosby's rules. I saw the suspicion in his eyes. I had betrayed him. He went along with our plan, but he held his tears inside and he stopped cuddling with me. My heart broke to feel him pulling away.

Winter arrived without incident. I checked his hands every Friday and there were no new scars. He seemed calmer. He did not cry as often and he did not protest when it was time to return to school. Perhaps my meeting with Crosby had done some good after all. Three times winter storms prevented me from picking him up on Fridays and he spent the weekends at the school. Once I could not to return him safely until Tuesday, but Crosby seemed to understand when I apologized for our lateness.

Finally, it was Christmas and the four of us were a family again. Tommy had fifteen days off from school. He was joyful and affectionate, like before he started school. We were joyful too. We did everything together, cooking, decorating and opening gifts. Our days were filled with laughter. We were all children and it felt timeless, but it lasted only two weeks.

As the time for Tommy to return to school approached, he grew quiet and sullen. Even the new sweater and scarf that Anne had knitted for him to wear at school did not cheer him up. On the morning of his return he clung to me, crying and begging me not to take him back. I felt his fear and anxiety and I almost cried too, but in the end I betrayed him again. I ordered him to be brave and act like a big boy. I told him everything would be all right, even though I knew it would not be.

In the weeks that followed, he cried more and more when he was home. I inspected his hands and his body carefully for signs of beatings, but I found nothing. Still, he was frightened and withdrawn. When I asked him about it, he told me he had seen other boys being beaten for returning to school late or for fighting. One boy accused another of stealing his toy and both boys were beaten, one for stealing and later, when the toy was found, the other boy was beaten for lying. There was nothing I could do to protect him from seeing things happen to other boys.

He had nightmares most nights when he was home. They upset Marie as much as they did Anne and myself. It was worse to learn he had them at school too and that he was beaten for waking the other boys. After that, he refused to cooperate when it was time to get ready for our trip to Fort Simpson. I was so frustrated and angry, I caught myself wanting to strike him and I was horrified with myself. I begged him to cooperate and I told him that I loved him. 'No you don't!' he shouted. That hurt me so deeply I started to cry. He stared at me when he saw my tears. He stopped resisting, but he said nothing to me on the trip back to school.

In mid-February, he caught a cold which became a fever. The fever continued for three days. We were so concerned that I made the trip to Fort Simpson during the coldest week of the winter to bring the doctor to see him. While I was gone, the fever broke. He was thankfully beyond danger when the doctor arrived. He said we had done everything right and that we should continue doing it until he was fully himself. These trips back and forth to Fort Simpson are especially dangerous for children in the winter cold, he reminded us. He agreed to pay Reverend Crosby a visit and explain that he had advised us not to let Tommy return for two weeks.

Tommy could have died. He was not as strong as we thought and teaching him to follow White rules could not protect him. If this was our best option, it was not good enough. We discussed keeping him home for the rest of the year but we were afraid to make things worse. One day, I asked him if other boys cried as much as he did. He nodded. He told me the supervisor of the dormitory touched some of the older boys' tzootzes when they slept. If they started crying he locked them in a closet until they stopped. He told them they would never go home again if they told their parents.

That convinced us to keep Tommy home for the rest of the school year. We would teach him ourselves. I wrote a note in my best English to Reverend Crosby, telling him that Thomas was still fainting and coughing. For the sake of his health and the health of the other boys, we needed to keep him home another month.

At the end of March we received a letter from the school warning us that Thomas would have to start the first year over in September if he missed any more school. I replied that we regretted that Tommy was missing school, but that he might have tuberculosis. Their next note was more sympathetic. They would pray for his good health and they asked us to have the doctor confirm he had tuberculosis. We did not reply, and we heard no more from them before the school year ended.

Tommy recovered completely by early March, but our notes bought us time, as Governor Douglas used to say. He was happier than ever when I told him he would never go to school in Fort Simpson again. He knew I was protecting him and his love for me glowed in his eyes. His birthday celebration that spring was better than Christmas.

I knew we could not keep him at home beyond September if we stayed in Metlakatla. I asked Anne to take the children to Alaska where the Indian Commissioner could not reach them, but she knew Duncan would never let me move there. She wanted our family to stay together.

Our only hope was to disappear. We made a plan to build a cabin in the forest that no one else would know about, a place no one would find. We would stock up supplies so we would not need to visit the trading post. We could not tell anyone, not even the children, for they might mention it in their excitement. All our preparations must be kept a secret. Our one exception was to tell Doolyaks and Yuwahksa so that they would know why we disappeared. They would not know where our cabin was.

In April, I looked for a place to build it. It needed to be close enough to Metlakatla or Fort Simpson in case of emergencies, and away from the trading routes so no one could see us come or go. The islands off the coast were too open to the winter storms, so I searched behind an island to the east of Metlakatla. The mountains around there would shelter us from the worst of the winter storms.

I found a small bay that was hidden behind a rocky headland. From there I could paddle up a stream far enough to be out of view from the bay. I found a gravel beach to pull our canoe onto and a thick patch of berry bushes that could hide a cabin built behind them. The land sloped enough to drain off the autumn rains. The stream would give us fresh water and perhaps some fish.

Anne and I took the children to the salmon camp in May. We dried more salmon than we needed so we could trade for other foods. While others cared for our children by the fire, we planned what we needed to buy and store for the winter. Canned and dried foods would not spoil. We would need extra oil lamps, fuel, blankets and books for the children to read and study with. Anne would knit extra clothing for each of us. I also bought trap lines and fishing nets so we would have fresh meat.

Anne and I were excited and nervous about our daring plan. Talking about it brought us closer together. There was so much to be done we had little time for anything else. I took most of July to clear the land and build the cabin. I left early in the morning before others were awake. If there were others around I waited until they left, or I pretended to canoe towards Fort Simpson. When I bought the lumber from the trading post I covered it with blankets to sneak it past Metlakatla.

I built the cabin ten feet wide and fifteen feet long. It had a peaked roof to keep off the rain and snow, but I did not have the time or skill to add windows. I put in a wood stove and a lean-to against the outside of one wall for storing firewood. I bought a new door for there were no good doors remaining on the abandonned houses in Metlkatla.

In August, officers from the Indian Commissioner's office in Fort Simpson came to see if Thomas was healthy and to make sure we would enroll him in school in September. We brought them to see Thomas. We told them we had kept up his studies at home and we begged them to place him into the second year despite missing four months. The officers said they could not promise us that, but our show convinced them that we wanted him in school.

Thomas was upset. He thought I had betrayed him again, so I told him the truth. I explained I had to fool the White men and I told him how we would hide away in a secret cabin I had built where they could not find us. He was wide-eyed with amazement. He had asked Anne for weeks why I was always away. Now it all made sense to him and he believed me. He was ecstatic, but I had him swear not to tell anyone, not even Maria, so that our plan would not be spoiled.

The rest of the month I transported our canned goods and other supplies to the cabin, always being careful not to be seen. Fortunately, most of the town had left on hunting trips or to shop in Victoria. The weekend before Crosby's school started, we packed our canoe with our last belongings before sunrise and we paddled away to the east.

Maria was full of questions. She had no idea why we had brought her clothes and toys along with Tommy's and why we were headed in the wrong direction. We told her we were going to a secret place where she would need them. That held her interest until we reached our cabin.

Tommy was elated when we arrived. I warned him about bears in the berry bushes or else he would have run ahead of us. Anne organized the children to help carry their clothes and toys the last few feet to the cabin. We sang loudly for the berries were ripe and there could in fact be bears around.

Anne set about organizing the cabin. Most of our supplies were stacked in piles from my previous trips. I had built a bed for the children on one side of the cabin and one for Anne and I on the other side. I had made shelves for the canned goods and boxes for our plates and utensils. I had made other boxes for our clothes too, that also served as seats near the wood stove.

The first two days were an adventure for all of us. The children ran everywhere when they were not busy helping us decide how to set up the cabin. Thomas was proud to be living in the woods away from Crosby's school. He wanted to help me do everything.

Maria's enthusiasm faded when she realized she would not return to the girls' school the following week. She loved her school and she was anxious to start the new year with her friends. When we told her we would stay the rest of the year in the cabin instead of our house in Metlakatla she cried and pouted for hours. We explained that we had to hide Thomas from the White men who would take him away, but that did not console her. Only Thomas could finally convince her how much fun it would be to hide away in the woods.

The first four weeks were fun. The weather was mild, so we were able to leave the door open for fresh air and light. We cut logs to sit on outside while eating our meals. Anne washed and cooked outside and we bathed there too. The children and I fished for salmon in our stream and we picked baskets of berries to eat with our meals. Tommy followed me as I laid our trap lines and he helped me check them each morning. I skinned rabbits we caught in the traps and dried their furs on the slope of the cabin roof. I shot deer and skinned them too. I dug a cache in the ground to bury our meat and I chopped wood and stored it under our lean-to.

We did our work at an easy pace for we had plenty of time for everything. When the sun went down we closed the door to keep in the heat and to keep out the moquitoes. We lit the oil lamp, put wood in our stove and snuggled together under our blankets. I told the children stories or we read their pictures books together. Sometimes we sang English or Tsimshian songs. We were happy. This is the best life one can live, I told myself. I am sure Anne and the children felt then same.

At the end of September, the autumn rains came. They were fun at first too, as they drummed noisily on our roof. Even the first leaks were fun as we hurried to move our boxes of clothes and other things we did not want to get wet. One leak was above the children's bed, which we could not move for it was nailed to the wall. They slept with us in our bed after that. We spent less time outside, though I still needed to check my trap lines and chop wood. We cooked on the top of the wood stove and ate indoors. It was still warm enough to open the door for short period for light and fresh air.

As the rains continued our problems grew. Our meat cache was raided by a bear and another time by a mountain lion. It was hard to hear them with the rain striking our roof, so I fixed a stack of logs over the cache that would make a loud noise if they fell. Our supply of dry firewood was disappearing. I chopped wet wood into small pieces and stacked in one corner of the cabin to help it dry. It was never dry enough to burn well. As the days grew colder we wore our coats inside to keep warm or we stayed under our blankets. We laid blankets on the dry parts of the floor, too, to keep our feet warm.

Winter snows soon replaced the rains. Snow fell for many days, covering the trees and piling up as high as my waist outside our door. The children were delighted, but it was too deep and too cold to play in it for long. It blocked our way and kept us inside. I still struggled through it to check my trap lines. I make marks on the trees so I could find them if they were buried. They rarely yielded catches anymore.

A great silence filled the forest. There was no more tapping of rain on the roof. The water outside froze and the leaks stopped. The meat froze in our cache too, though most animals were sleeping so they no longer bothered us. The snow on our roof kept the cabin warmer but it was too cold to open the door for light or fresh air, even for a few seconds.

Our small cabin became our prison. We reclaimed the spaces the leaks had taken away. We spread our blankets over them to protect our cold feet, but it was always dark in the dim light of our oil lamp and there was little room to move with our laundry and animal furs hanging above us to dry.

The children were unhappy, for they had no place to play. They grew bored and irritable. The few books we brought with us for them to read had lost their charm. Some had became warped and stained with mould by the dampness. My stories and our songs no longer held their attention for long. They fought often and they complained constantly.

Our Christmas was bleak. We had no gifts to give each other and we had run out of ideas of games to play. I caught Anne looking at me from time to time. She was thinking we had made a mistake by coming here. I shared the same thought, but I was not willing to give up yet. It would soon be spring and things would get better.

Sure enough, late January brought a warm spell. Water dripped through our roof again as the ice melted. We did not care. We donned our warm clothes and boots and went outside to play. The sunshine touched our hearts and gave us energy. The children made a game of striking small trees to make the snow on their branches fall on our heads. We threw snowballs at each other and after a brief rest in a snowbank the children followed me to check the traplines.

By the end of the afternoon, when the light was fading from the sky, we returned to the warmth of the cabin. We stripped off our boots and wet clothes and snuggled together under a blanket by the wood stove. We were exhausted, but we were the happiest we had been since we moved to the cabin. I was relieved that spring was coming. The worst of it was over, or so I thought.

The next morning Maria had a sore throat. We kept her in bed, but her sneezing kept her awake. By evening she had a headache and a slight fever. She only wanted warm tea. We kept her in our bed at night in case she got worse. When her fever ended the sickness moved into her chest. By then Thomas had a sore throat. Anne and I fell sick after he did. Our colds settled into our chests too and would not leave us in peace. We were all miserable and unable to sleep much.

I began to doubt myself. I had never felt so old. Life in the woods was too hard for me, but what else could we do. I was not ready to surrender our children to the White schools. I wanted more time to figure out another plan. Anne wanted no more of it. She said I was risking the children's lives. She asked how I would feel if they died. We had our first fight, shouting in front of the children until they began to cry. That silenced us. We said no more for the rest of day. I lay awake, fretting over our situation and listening to the children coughing. No new plan revealed itself to me overnight, so I admitted defeat. We packed our things, bundled up the children as warmly as we could and we paddled back to Metlakatla.

Most of the village was at the oolchon camp when we arrived. Miss Blatter, who had taken over the Metlakatla School for Girls from Jane Ridley, received us. She was also the village nurse and she was furious when she saw how sick our children were. We were not suited to be parents for putting their lives in danger, she scolded us. She set up beds in the drawing room of the Ridley residence to watch over them herself. She would not let them stay with us while they recovered.

She notified the magistrate's office in Fort Simpson. She said we should be arrested for neglecting our children. The magistrate did not agree, but he did tell Reverend Crosby. Officers arrived from the Office of the Indian Commissioner two weeks later to take Thomas and Maria away.

Crosby sent them to Methodist schools that were much further away. Maria was sent to the Kitimaat Indian Residential School for Girls, four hours by canoe beyond Gitka'ata and Thomas was sent the Greenville Mission Boys Boarding School up the Nass farther than I had ever been. In a letter addressed to me, he said he had advised the Greenville School not to allow Thomas to come home again until his education was finished. He would spend his summers at the boarding school while other boys returned to their families. He told them I could not be trusted to care for my son. He made it clear that I would never be allowed to visit him. He did not mention if Maria would be allowed to visit us over the summers.

We did not receive Crosby's letter until the end of May. Until then, Anne clung to the hope of seeing them again. I doubted I ever would. It was almost more than I could bear.

The same vision came to me over and over, sometimes as a nightmare and sometimes as a waking dream that consumed my mind and drove away all other thoughts.

In it Tommy and Maria are being dragged along the road in front of our houses by White truancy officers. The officers keep a tight hold on their wrists to make sure they cannot break away. They are dragged through puddles and over tree roots. When they stumble the officers pull their arms harder to keep them upright.

Maria is crying loudly, calling for Anne. Thomas is led along behind her, crying softly. I am watching them, walking ten feet behind Thomas, close enough to feel his pain but too far away to comfort him. I am carrying his bags. Anne is beside me carrying Maria's bags. Two officers follow close behind us, their hands on their guns, ready to pull them out if we made a move towards the children. Thomas keeps looking back over his shoulder at me, knowing I cannot help him but fearful I will disappear at any moment when if he looks away.

We reach top of the stairs that lead down the hill and along a path to the dock. The officers in front lift the children into their arms, as if they are their own. I want to shout out "They are ours!" but the officer behind me, seeing my restlessness, tells me to keep moving. They carry the children down the stairs as the shadow of the great church falls over us.

Tommy bobs up and down in the officer's arms. He does not look away from me as his tears roll down his cheeks. Maria is looking back too, her eyes red, her face wet with tears and her mouth wide open and bawling. She is crying "Mommy!" as she reaches one arm towards Anne. Anne covers her mouth with her free hand and makes quiet sobbing sounds.

We reach the dock and the first two officers carry the children up the gangway onto their boat. "Please let us hold our children to say goodbye!" Anne calls to them. They ignore her. The other two officers snatch their bags out of our hands and pass them up to the deck. Maria is screaming loudly and now Thomas is crying too. The lead officer signals the others to take them below. The ship's crew unties the lines and raises the gangplank. The ship pulls away from us and moves silently along the passageway to the open sea before turning north to Fort Simpson.

Anne stares out across the water holding her handkerchief to her mouth. My heart is crippled with pain, but I am thinking of what the children are going through. I wonder how they will manage without us, without anyone to love them. Anne and I will survive. We have suffered deeply many times before, but our children have not. They have done nothing wrong, but their punishment will hurt them for the rest of their lives. Their only crime is that they are Tsimshian.

THIRTY
NINE

I remember the summer of 1897 as a cold summer without much sun. It might have been like any other summer to others, but the sun was not comforting to me. The air felt cool and breezes sent shivers through my body.

Perhaps that was because a great fire filled my heart, the same fire that consumed our town a decade before and tore it apart. It was the fire of hatred. I felt it for all White people after my children were taken away. I took my anger out of anyone who approached me, like an animal caught in a trap. I saw no escape, no solution to my pain, so I withdrew inside myself and spoke as little as I could.

Anne must have been in as much pain as I was, but I could not console her. Her presence only reminded me of my own pain. She was as quiet as I was, but her quiet came from sadness, not anger. We still loved each other, but we had nothing to say to each other. We could not talk about our children for there was nothing we could do. We could not ignore what had happened either, for it consumed us.

She was not to blame for what happened, but I could not contain my anger. I spoke harshly to her if she tried to talk to me when I needed to be left alone. It hurt to see tears to her eyes, but I could not apologize or explain my actions when the fire was so strong. It was always strong at that time. She learned to say little to me, even though she needed to talk. It grieves me now when I think about it. I was selfish but unable to change. People tormented by pain cannot give to others.

She tried to understand my anger, but it frightened her. She needed to be comforted. In mid-June we got a letter from Yuwahksa telling us that Doolyaks had suffered a heart attack. He was not doing well and she feared he might not last long. She asked Anne to return to Alaska to help her care for him. Anne would have stayed in my time of crisis, but there was nothing she could do for me, so she left.

She contacted the Kitimaat Residential School and asked them to let Maria return home so she could visit her dying grandfather. Maria arrived with a reminder that she was expected back at school the first week of September, but she would not return. Anne packed Maria and Thomas's belongings and she and Maria left for Alaska in the second week of July.

It was a tearful goodbye. I realized I had given Anne no choice and I would miss her greatly when the fire within me died down. I looked into her eyes and saw there was no fear there. We wept openly and said we would love each other always. In spite of my sadness, I knew it was best that she return to her parents. They could comfort each other and she would have Maria.

My delight in seeing Maria again was replaced by the sadness of losing her forever. At least she would be beyond the reach of truancy officers in New Metlakatla and she would have her mother's love to keep her strong. We promised to write as they boarded the mail ship to Fort Simpson dressed in their Sunday clothes. They waved to me as the boat left the dock.

Anne did write. From Fort Simpson, they caught a boat to Ketchikan, crowded with prospectors rushing to the Klondike gold fields further north. From Ketchikan, they caught a smaller boat to New Metlakatla on Annette Island. Maria was excited by her new home. They joined in the Founders' Day celebration in the first week of August that honoured the tenth anniversary of the town.

Later in August she sent me another letter. Doolyaks had died from a second heart attack. She told me how sad she was about losing him, but she was grateful to Great Spirit for letting her see him before he died. She was also grateful that little Maria had seen him again. She said Maria's company would keep her and Yuwahksa young.

Her letter arrived in a package with two of Tamlahk's shirts. Doolyaks had saved them for me. I had never seen them before. They were shirts he had purchased in Alaska, but I was grateful them for they were his. I held them to my heart to honour his Spirit.

Tamlahk's shirts and the passing of time helped to soften my anger, but not the hatred I felt towards Whites. Hatred took the place of my joy and hope. I prayed to Great Spirit to relieve me of its burden. Fortunately, I rarely saw Whites any more. Ridley and Miss Blatter were now the only two in town, and neither of them spoke to me. I kept to myself as I had when Tsangook died and only spoke with other Tsimshians when I needed to. That way I did not feel the hatred, only a great emptiness that swallowed everything around me.

What little there was left of Metlakatla was as broken as I was. The long row of abandoned houses missing their windows and doors looked haunted. Some had been stripped entirely of their side boards. They stood like skeletons whose flesh had rotted away. Others had collapsed or had been stripped right to the ground. The sidewalks had rotted. The wood that remained was not fit for burning. Bushes replaced them. They pushed up through the ruins of the houses like plants that had overthrown their gardeners.

Closer to Mission Point, the houses that were still occupied looked old too, with their peeling paint and broken steps. No one cared to repair them. Green mould grew on their sides and patches of moss covered their roofs. The road in front of them, where our brass band used to march, was carved and muddied from the rains. Its retaining wall had fallen away in several places. The graveyard behind the church was overgrown. Some of the crosses had been toppled by the roots of saplings and the grass was as tall as the crosses that still stood. The great church cast a dark shadow over everything. It scorned the rest of the town, secure and arrogant on its raised stone platform. "I will still stand here long after the rest of you have gone," it seemed to say. I chose not to care, like others who stayed on. I had nothing to live for. One day I would die, and be forgotten like Metlakatla itself.

Anne's second letter, which brought the news of Doolyaks' death, was so painful it took me two weeks to finish reading. The day I finished it I was sitting on the broken retaining wall by the road and staring down at the harbour, feeling my lowest, when Bishop Ridley approached me.

"A lovely day, isn't it, Jack? Are you enjoying this fine weather?"

"Mmm," I grunted without looking at him.

"How is Anne? How are your children?" He tried to sound interested.

I glared at him, not believing my ears. "Are you pretending not to know? My children have been taken away from me and I will never see them again. Anne took Maria to Alaska so she will never have to suffer in the White schools. Reverend Crosby has sent Thomas up the Nass to the Greenville School with instructions that I must never see him again until he is finished his schooling. He is their prisoner. He cannot visit me on holidays or summers. This how your people treat our people. You tear our families apart and abuse our children. How do you think we feel?"

"I am so sorry, Jack. I never wanted this to happen. You and Anne are good parents."

I was so angry I did not trust what I might say. I looked back to the harbour, hoping that he would leave me alone, but he remained.

"Does Maria have grandparents in Alaska?"

"She has her grandmother, Anne's mother Yuwahksa. Jennifer Carter is what Duncan calls her. Maria's grandfather, Daniel Carter died two weeks ago."

"Oh dear God, I am so sorry to bring up bad news, Jack. Are you alone then? Are your parents still alive somewhere?"

"No, they died of Smallpox thirty-five years ago. Whites like you would not give them the vaccine. Have you ever seen someone die of Smallpox, Mr. Ridley? They get sores that weep puss and blood all over their bodies, even on their eyeballs, and their bodies bleed under their skin until they turn black. That's how I watched my mother die." I wanted to keep going, to describe what Whites never saw when they turned their faces away, but my voice was cracking and I felt like crying.

"Oh Lord, I never knew, Jack. Believe me, if I had been here I would have tried to do all that I could to save her."

"No, you would have done nothing but watch us die. I survived and hundreds other too because Reverend Cridge secretly sent Smallpox medicine from Victoria. Duncan vaccinated us. You would have tried to stop them because you hated both of them. You never cared about our people. You made enemies with us from the day you arrived and you tore apart everything we had created before you came. Then you tore my people apart too, all to satisfy your selfish vanity. Now you have nothing to show for it. Do not tell me you care. I have known you eighteen years and I know you better."

"Please Jack, I know I have been a terribly selfish man most of my life. I see that now and I hate what I have done and the man I have been. I wish I could make it up to you somehow."

It felt good to release my rage. I would have liked to continue but Ridley sounded sincere. There were tears in his eyes.

"I am sorry for saying these things, Mr. Ridley. They have been burning inside me for so long. My heart is so full of pain and I just want to be left alone."

"I know. My heart is filled with pain too. You probably heard that my wife Jane died of a fever last winter, when you were away. I never knew how much I loved her until she was gone. She was all I had and now I have nothing." He sobbed openly. I had never seen him this way. I waited awkwardly until he dried his tears.

"I am sorry for your loss. I know how that feels. I wish I could do something, but I cannot."

"Oh but you can, Jack. I know you can. That is why I came to you today."

"What do you mean? How could I possibly change what has happened?"

"No, what has happened cannot be changed. I know that, but I have watched you for a long time. You are so much stronger than me. When Duncan left you behind I thought that would be the end of you. You seemed so broken, so helpless, but you pulled through, with Timothy's help."

"And why did that happen? It was because of you. How dare you pretend to care now!"

"No, you are right. I behaved like a mean-spirited child at the time, but I was shocked when I saw how you suffered for what I had done. Jane told me I was unfair to you. She said I should apologize but I was too proud, Jack. I have always been so. Oh, I am so ashamed!" He paused to hold back his tears. I thought he would stop there but he continued.

"When Tsangook died I thought that would kill you, but somewhere inside you found the will to keep going. You grew strong again, strong enough to raise a family, and I secretly rejoiced for you. Then Tom killed himself. I was horrified. I knew it was my fault, Jack. I should never have told Duncan about you two. It was as if I had killed Tom with my own hands. I didn't dare try to apologize. I was afraid to make your pain worse. When you disappeared into the woods with your family I prayed every night for you while I was praying for my wife's life. But the Lord took her away from me, Jack. He has left me alone. Perhaps that is my punishment for all my wrongs. Since then I have often wanted to die. I was pleased when you returned safely, but then I watched the truancy officers take your children away. My suffering cannot be as great as yours. I have wanted to reach out to you for so long, but never more than I do now. Is it too much to ask you to forgive me?"

"Yes, it is, probably." I hesitated, not wanting to be cruel. "What is it that you want from me, Mr. Ridley?"

"Oh Jack, please give me a chance. I just need someone to talk to and it must be you."

"Why? Why not talk to someone in your congregation instead?"

"Oh no, I couldn't do that. They expect me to be strong for them, to show them leadership, but I need guidance too. They haven't suffered like you have. Only you can understand my pain and teach me how to keep going. Please help me!" Ridley looked at me as though I could be his saviour.

I stared back at him in confusion. I had not expected this, and I did not know what to say. "I am not sure how I can help you. I ask Great Spirit every day why I have suffered so much. He has not given me any clear answers. I do not know what to do. I hear His voice all around me, but I do not know what He is saying. I think He wants me to listen instead of trying to know."

"Yes! That is how I feel too, but how can I share these thoughts with my congregation? They expect me to know what is right. They don't want me to be listening for answers instead."

"Maybe you are wrong about that. Perhaps your God is trying to teach you a new way."

"You might be right. You see, this is what I mean. You are wise, Jack. You can teach me. Please let me talk with you again in a couple days."

"I suppose so, but you must call me by my Tsimshian name, Gugweelaks."

"Goo-gwee-lax," he sounded my name carefully. "Yes, I will practise it. Thank you!" He flashed a smile that came from his heart, something I had never seen on his face before.

I felt strangely lighter as I watched him walk back to his residence. A smile crept over my face in spite of myself. I realized I needed someone to talk to, too. For the first time, I felt I had things in common I could share with him.

Ridley sought me out almost every day after that to share his thoughts. They were deep thoughts about listening to God and how to become a better man. Each time he was encouraged and enthused by my answers. I suggested he write down his thoughts in a diary as they came to him. He still had the diary I gave him the summer Anne and I were married. He began to use it and, as far as I know, he has done so ever since.

I began to write to Robert Tomlinson again too. I had stopped after my children were taken away, when for my hatred of Whites was too strong. I needed to tell him what had happened with Ridley, though I was not sure myself. He was amazed. Perhaps there is hope for him yet, he told me. He reminded me it takes courage to approach someone after you have wronged them and to beg their forgiveness. But why me, I asked? Why now, when my hatred of Whites is at its strongest? God moves in strange ways, he answered. Ah, just like Great Spirit, I thought to myself.

An even stranger thing happened the next month at the beginning of autumn. I was making my afternoon meal in my kitchen when there was a knock on the door. A slender, muscular White man a few years younger than me stood at my doorway with a large bag slung over his shoulder. He had short orange hair and twinkly blue eyes.

"Does a Jack Campbell live here?" he asked hesitantly, trying to see past me. He had an unmistakable Scottish accent.

"Stuart, is that you?" I gasped, not believing my eyes. "Stuart Sutherland?"

"Jack, my God, it's you! I can't believe it!" His face lit up with a broad smile. I invited him in. "You've made some changes, I see. I didn't recognize you."

"I guess I have," I blushed, not knowing how to explain my appearance. "A lot has happened since we met. That must be.... seventeen years ago."

"I am sure, but it still feels like yesterday at times. I stopped by to see what had become of the town. I heard about the move to Alaska and I thought you would have gone with them. I asked the first man I met about you. He said you are still here and he pointed out your house."

"I was supposed to move, but our missionary learned that Tom and I were lovers. He told me I must promise never to talk to Tom or touch him again. I could not promise him that, so I was left behind."

"Did Tom stay behind with you? Are you still together?" He glanced around for clues of someone living with me.

"No, he made that promise so he went in Alaska without me. I never saw him again."

"Oh my God, Jack, how could he do that? Has he not changed his mind in the past ten years?"

"I think he regretted it, for he was unhappy there. He killed himself three years ago."

"Dear God, I am so sorry! I would never had asked if I had known. What a ghastly thing to happen to you – to both of you, I mean. You must have felt terribly alone."

"There is no need to apologize. So much happened before that and afterwards. I married a woman eight years ago and we had two children before that happened, but I have lost them too. My son Thomas is in a residential school far from here. He is never allowed to visit me, even during the holidays. My wife took our daughter Maria to Alaska this summer so the White schools cannot take her too. She cannot return or we will lose our daughter too. Since July I have been living alone." Stuart's face was deep in thought. "What about you? Where are you living now?"

"Well, nowhere actually. I am between homes, let's say. I decided to make a trip up the coast for old times' sake. I stopped here to see what is left of the town. It looks like a ruin, except for the great church, and it looks so out of place now. An English bloke with a long beard told me where you lived. Is that the bloke you worked for, the bishop who owned the Evangeline?"

"Yes, you must remember him, Bishop Ridley." I laughed. "He has changed a lot too. He calls me Gugweelaks now, not 'boy' any longer. He is becoming a friend, believe it or not."

"Gugweelaks, right. I remember that's your Tsimshian name. I'll use it too from now on."

That was an interesting choice of words, I thought. I saw the huge sack he had brought with him. "Have you come to stay? There's no work here if you still work on ships."

"I'm taking a break from working on ships, Jack. It feels like I've been doing it forever. I became a captain a couple years after we met. I've captained three different ships over the years. I was always lonely though, and there were too many lonely, young sailors working for me. I tried to find a partner, but it was difficult. They were usually ashamed of themselves for loving a man and terrified of being found out. It always ended badly. Finally I met a bonny lad, so bright and fearless. He loved me dearly and I loved him too, but it's impossible to keep secrets on a ship. Rumours started and I had no choice but to fire him to protect us both. He never forgave me. He killed himself a few months later, just like your Tom. I have hated my life since then. I tried to deny the rumours, but no one will hire me anymore. I need to hide away somewhere and start a new life."

His story was sad, but in spite of it I felt a surge of affection. "You are welcome to stay here with me if you want. No one will bother you here."

He smiled, dropped his bag and came in close to me. He slid his arms around my waist and then up my back, pulling me into his chest as he did. His hand slid under my hair and cupped the back of my neck. He pulled my mouth to his and we kissed for a long time. "I am so happy to find you," he said, running his hand across my chest. "Where should I put my bag?" I led him upstairs to my bedroom and we stayed there for the next few hours.

I had not been with a man since I last slept with Tamlahk ten years before. It was also the first time I had been with a White man. I loved touching him. It is strange and wonderful that a woman's body is beautiful for its softness and a man's body for its hardness. Stuart's body was strong from working as a sailor. He had fine orange hair that grew thick on his chest and forearms. Silver hair was sprinkled through his chest hair, through his temples and on the whiskers on his chin. A trail of darker hair led down his stomach to the tangled bush around his tzootz.

My fingers drifted gently over his body. I remembered the orange hair of the store clerk on my first visit to the trading post in Fort Simpson when I was still a boy. I had waited forty years to touch it. It was as lovely as it looked, soft and gentle as a summer breeze.

Stuart lay quietly, watching my eyes as I explored his body. He seemed as grateful to be touched as I was grateful to be touching him. We smiled at each other and laughed every few seconds. We said little else.

Then was a sudden knock on my kitchen door downstairs. "Gooweelax!" a voice shouted out to me. It was Ridley. I held my finger to my lips and gripped Stuart's arm so he would not move or say anything. We lay there quietly for a couple minutes until we were sure he had left.

"Was that our local bishop?" Stuart asked. I nodded.

"Gooweelax?" Stuart imitated him.

"He is trying his best," I said.

"Hopefully not too trying," he chuckled.

Stuart never questioned whether we belonged together. He did not miss his years of traveling either. He had spent that time searching for a home and he was ready to settle down. Metlakatla had what he needed, a peaceful beauty surrounded by nature and isolated from the world of the Whites that had tormented him so much. I asked him once if he missed Scotland. He told me he missed the purple heather on the hills, but he preferred the endless forests of my world.

I wish I had seen as much of the world as he had, but the peace and isolation of our village was enough for me too, now that I had him to share it with. We laughed a lot, like men who had struggled unhappily for years only to find that now the path that lay ahead was a gentle and beautiful one. We never asked how or why it had become easy. We just enjoyed it while it lasted.

We had much in common, but we had our differences too. He did not mind me dressing like a woman. You are the same man underneath, he chuckled. He believed in Christ, but not Christian churches. He was not surprised when I told him there was an evil Spirit living in our cathedral. Christian churches are filled with evil Spirits the world over, he replied. He believed there are many religions but only one God. They are different paths on the same mountain and they all lead to the same summit. I wanted him to know Great Spirit and the lessons of the Animal Spirits. He listened carefully and was never offended, but to him they were only interesting ideas.

He said the best way to find God is through a lover's eyes. I found it uncomfortable when he stared deeply and intensely into mine. I would look away, but he would gently bring my gaze back to his until I learned to trust him. My heart surrendered to his gentle control more than it had ever done before. He taught me to love myself, and that I was worthy of any love I could feel. "Don't worry. You are safe while I am holding you," he said to me.

Stuart adored my smooth skin as much as I loved his orange hair, but nothing excited me more than exciting him. I worked my way down his body from his lips to his nipples, to the long trail of orange fur that led down to the bush of his tzootz, already moist and fragrant with anticipation.

"Oh my God!" he moaned and arched his back in pleasure.

"What's that?" I sat up suddenly.

"What's wrong? Why did you stop?" he asked me sweetly.

"What did you just say?" I frowned at him.

"Huh...," he thought for a second before a smile crossed his face. "I'm sorry. Oh your God," he chuckled.

"That's better," I grinned and went back to what I was doing. I would not surrender completely.

The part of him I loved the most were his blue eyes, which twinkled with light when he looked at me. He loved to make me laugh, to make my eyes twinkle too. His found many things to be funny, even the things that frustrated and infuriated me the most.

"God has a great sense of humour," he laughed. "Parents often find their children amusing when they struggle. That's how God sees us. He won't come to our rescue every time we pray. He wants us to learn to solve our problems. He finds the English especially amusing. They make the same mistakes over and over again and never learn anything." He thought the English were the most arrogant and disrespectful people in the world. I would not disagree with him.

He was eight years younger than me. I asked why he did not want a younger man, but he was tired of them. Young men are like wood fires, he said. Their hearts are easy to light on fire. The flames of their passion roar brightly and their sparks burn everything around them. Then their love dies as fast as it started. Older men burn like coal. They are harder to light and there are fewer flames, but they burn hotter, longer and more steadily. It is easier to trust a love that is hot and steady.

Stuart was open about our love in front or others, in a way he was never able to be before. Others in Metlakatla found our love sweet and amusing. By now, after being discreet about my love with Tamlahk for so many years and then marrying Anne and fathering two children, little I did surprised them.

Ridley was surprised though. He stopped confiding in me. He avoided us when we saw him, or he pretended to be busy. I did not want to face him either. I thought he was upset that I was with a man again, but Stuart was not sure. One day he approached Ridley on his own and asked him if he remembered how he had once worked for him on the Evangeline. Ridley did not recognize him. They joked about how the Evangeline failed to climb the rapids on the Skeena and soon they were chatting like friends. Ridley told him he had stopped chatting with me because he did not want to interfere between Stuart and I. Stuart said he did not mind him meeting with me in the slightest. That was the permission Ridley needed. The next day he knocked on my door again and asked if I had time for a chat. I was relieved that the tension between us was gone.

After that, Ridley came by every few days. Stuart always found something else to do so that we would be alone. Ridley knew that we were lovers but he never asked about it. He did not know how to speak about it. His interest was in spiritual matters anyway. He needed to share his thoughts about God with me, even though I was not a Christian.

He started taking long walks in the forest. He told me he felt the presence of God there, and that gave him peace. The hours he spent surrounded by greenery inspired him to write poetry. He brought his poems to read to me. By this time he had learned to say my Tsimshian name properly and he asked that I call him by his Christian name, William.

I did not keep my love for Stuart a secret from Anne. I needed to tell her about him and how much he meant to me. My love for him did not threaten my love for her, though I worried about telling her. She took my news well. She admitted to feeling guilty for leaving me and she was relieved that I was now with someone who cared about me. Her answer made me love her all the more. I longed to see her and my children again, but that was not possible. Couples often stay together for the sake of their children, but we stayed apart for their protection.

That included Thomas. Men from New Metlakatla went up the Nass in early November and rescued Thomas from the Greenville School. They escaped down the river and over the border to Alaska before they were caught. There was no residential school for young boys in Alaska, so Duncan still taught them himself. As much as I hated Duncan, I was relieved to know this. Maria and Thomas would live with Anne while they went to school and I knew Duncan would not beat or abuse them.

Winter closed in around us. People of our village had learned to stock up on canned foods and dried meats in the fall. Most of the village was older by this time.

We dared not risk the winter storms to get to the trading post and back unless we had to. The cold rain and winds kept us indoors. In the evenings we packed tightly into the reception hall of Ridley's residence, which was warmer and more comfortable than the Assembly Hall. We loved its large fireplace. We shared foods, sang songs and told stories, like we used to do when I was a boy. William loved these gatherings. After Jane died, his home was too large for him, especially during the dark, wet nights of winter.

Stuart was popular at these times. He had learned to entertain others, like all sailors who lived together on crowded ships. His stories about his times at sea were new and fascinating to us. He also had a strong singing voice and he knew many old Scottish songs. He played a fiddle as he sang. Ridley loved his songs more than anyone. He knew some of them too and he did his best to sing along. His voice was not pretty, but he enjoyed himself. No one asked for more than that.

The next spring, I brought Stuart to our oolichon camp at the mouth of the Nass. He loved it. He worked hard beside the others of our village. In the evenings he sang his songs, played his fiddle and told us more stories about his travels around the world. He always had new ones we had never heard. This is what he had always needed, he told me, a place he belonged to, a place where he was accepted and loved. Thank you for bringing me, he said to me. I heard the distant echo of Tamlahk's "thank you's" pulling me back to my youth.

The spring came with the promise of new life. On one of the first warm days, Stuart and I decided to walk to the old saw mill. The road there is a mile long, I told him. This is a road? he chuckled. It was filled with young saplings. There was not even a path anymore, but I could tell the way for the forest on either side was much older and taller. It took us an hour to fight our way there.

The frame of the old mill was still standing, but its boards were cracked and grey. Like an old totem, it had begun its return to the earth. The deck outside was covered with moss and slime. Some of its boards had rotted. We tested each step carefully as we forced our way around the bushes that had sprouted up from below. Inside, the floor was drier but there was a heavy scent of mildew. Two small holes in the roof allowed some light. Pieces of dismantled machinery were piled at one end. They had laid undisturbed for many years. In the dim light, we saw they were badly rusted. On the other side, the bottom half of the old waterwheel had mostly rotted away. The whole place felt haunted. It seemed to ask us to leave it alone.

On the way home, I told Stuart the story of the Salmon Prince. He listened with great interest.

"What a sad and beautiful story," he said once I finished. "There is a great sadness in this land, but it's a beautiful sadness too. Do you believe in reincarnation, Gugweelaks, that we will be born again, not in Heaven but here on this Earth?"

"Yes, if we follow the lessons of the Animal Spirits."

"I hope that doesn't mean I have to eat you when you die," he chuckled. "But I might, you know, if I knew that would bring you back."

"Thank you, but I think it means we need to let go of everything we possess of someone before they can return. People are afraid to let go but they must learn to trust."

"Yes, I think you are right. I guess we will know when the time comes. Hopefully, that will be many years from now."

His comment started me thinking about us. I wondered how much time we had left together. It would feel too short no matter how long that would be. I should not think of this, I told myself. We cannot change what will happen, but the question hung over me like a shadow.

Shadows were long that summer. I received news from Charlotte that Laguksa had died of a stroke. That saddened me greatly, for her life had been hard. She was 63, not young anymore, but she had never seemed like an old woman to me.

The other death that greeted me was my brother Gwashasip's. We had not been close since Jesse's murder. He never forgave me for letting Jesse, his heir, leave the trading post with strangers, and later, for not testifying at his trial. I did not know how to make amends to him. Then he moved to Alaska. He never answered any of my letters. Anne told me about his death in a letter. He slipped off a log while crossing a river on a hunting trip. He drowned before the other men could pull him out. I wrote to his wife Gertie. She was kind enough to write back to me, but it was a simple thank you letter. There was nothing much else to say.

Other than these sad moments, my life with Stuart was peaceful and joyous. He had been living on his savings for the first few months. After the oolichon camp, he accepted work fixing engines and doing other repair work on boats. Sometimes his work took him to Fort Simpson for a few days, since there was not much work on boats in Metlakatla. He was glad to have work to do but he loved being with me more. He had no desire to travel or to be in the company of Whites again. I stayed home too, except for day trips to the trading post in Fort Simpson.

At the end of June, boys from the residential schools returned for the summer. Some left with their familes on trips to Victoria or the new city of Vancouver. Boys who were old enough joined hunting trips, but many of their fathers worked in Fort Simpson or the cannery in Port Essington. Their sons had little to do in the village by themselves. They got into fights and other troubles as boys do when they are bored.

When I had time, I took them out in my canoe. We visited nearby islands to watch bears feeding on crabs on the shore, like Tamlahk and I did with Jesse and Anne when they were small, or we would rest on a beach while I told them stories about Tsamsem and the Animal Spirits. I taught them our dances, how to make bows and arrows to hunt small animals, and spears to catch fish. I also taught them how to carve small totems and we collected birds' eggs for them to take home. I always wore a dress and a shawl and I spoke to them in our language.

They argued with me, for the White schools had taught them our stories were lies and speaking our language was a sin. I told them they needed to know Tsimshian ways, for they belonged to our people. White schools would never teach them the skills and truths they would need to live with us after their schooling was finished.

Some of them found me amusing. They never saw White men wearing dresses or shawls, but they appreciated that I was different. There are many possibilities in Tsimshian life that are forbidden in the world of Whites. They welcomed my lessons like starving children, hungry for the truth and weary of being punished and shamed for being who they were. When summer ended I felt sad because I would not see until next June, but also because I knew they would suffer until then.

I saw less of William in the summer. While I entertained the boys, he wandered in the woods near town speaking to his God. Sometimes I met him coming home from the forest, his eyes glowing with light and his long beard filled with twigs and mosses he had encountered along his way. He was always eager to talk with me. He told me we were blessed to be surrounded by paradise. He was learning to listen and he loved what he heard. It was just the rustling of leaves, the chirping of birds and the sounds of water trickling over stones, but that was how his God spoke to him. He felt Jane's Spirit there too, thanking him for bringing her here, to this magical land so far from England.

He always had poems to read to me, for he never wandered without his diary and a pen. He read to me every poem he ever wrote, but I do not know if they were any good. I have no ear for poetry. Some Whites in Victoria liked them though. His first book of poems was published that fall. It was good to see his face shining with pride in a good way, not the arrogant pride he showed us when he was fighting with Duncan.

He cared less about preaching sermons to his congregation. He confessed to reading some of his poems on Sundays instead of reading from the Bible. What does it matter really, he asked, for he believed his poems came from God, too.

He also cared less about his appearance, since he knew God was only interested in his true self. Some of his congregation were confused and concerned. They politely suggested he should ask the church to send another minister to help with his sermons. That would free up more of his time to be in the forest with God, they explained.

"What a loving congregation I have!" he exclaimed when he told me this. "I think they understand my search for God clearly!"

Although only a hundred people remained in our village, he asked the Church of England for a new minister to help him. He dictated his proposal to me and I wrote it down. His letter said he would like to pass on his deep love of God to a young man who might want to follow in his footsteps. A year later his request was answered. The man who came was John Henry Keen, a jovial, enthusiastic man with a hearty laugh. He was fifty, only a few years younger than William and me. He had worked many years in Masset, translating scriptures for the Haida, so he knew our coast.

Reverend Keen was thrilled to see the great cathedral of Metlakatla. It was still impressive, perhaps more than ever, for it had stayed the same size as our village shrank. I thought he would leave soon after he saw it, for there was not much church work to be done with such a small congregation. He did not mind though. He had other interests to occupy his time. He studied our art with a passion and he collected samples of insects and small animals he found in the forests that surrounded us. Like William, he spent many hours there every week.

How strange the few dozen followers must have looked inside the great church when he gave his first sermon, with rows and rows of empty pews stretching into the distance and the ceiling rising above him as high as the sky. He never complained though. In his first weeks, he organized the men in town into work teams. He worked with them to clean up the graveyard. They straightened the gravestones that had fallen over. They removed the saplings that had sprouted and they cut the grass. They even repaired the broken retaining wall along the road in front of the church.

These changes were small, but they were the first improvements our town had seen in years. Like a spring wind, they inspired other changes. Men began fixing the roofs and entrance steps of their houses and some homes got new coats of paint.

William sat in the pews listening to Keen's sermons for the first few weeks. He was delighted not to have to write his own sermons anymore, and delighted to have the company of another White man who loved the forest as much as he did. He also had more time to write his poetry. He purchased a small tent and camping equipment at the trading post and he began to disappear into the forest for a few days at a time.

I asked him why he remained in Metlakatla. Now that Keen was doing his church work, he could go anywhere he wanted. He told me he loved the great church. He thought of it as his own and he was very proud of it, even if it was empty most of the time. He was under the spell of the Spirit of the Church, as I had often believed. It held him tightly in its grasp, though he was unaware of it. I felt sorry for him but there was nothing I could do to free him. At least for the moment he was happy.

FORTY

S tuart and I had been lovers for two years, but it felt like it had been much longer. We were always together, except when he was working or when I was with William. He knew and understood me better than Tamlahk ever had. He cared for my feelings and attended my needs. We never argued or fought. We laughed instead.

I did not tire of his affections. I listened closely to every word he spoke, for I wanted to be as good to him as he was to me. We came to know each other so well that we often spoke the same words at the same time. Every moment with him was comfortable and joyous. Every day I thanked Great Spirit for teaching me to love again. I did not think much about the future, but I felt grateful that I had someone strong and loving to be with me as I grew older.

After we helped the work teams repair the graveyard behind the church, we decided to paint our house. We chose a bright yellow, for that was the colour of our love, bright and warm like the sun, even when it rained.

It rained harder that fall than in other years. Storms blew over us, one after the other. Our village was a sea of mud. The great church loomed dark and threatening in the gloom. I had strong feelings that bad things were soon to come. We stayed indoors as much as possible to do our repair work. Fortunately, Stuart had chopped a large pile of firewood early in September, enough to last us through the coming winter. In the evenings, we huddled around the fire and talked, or we read to each other. We subscribed to the Daily Colonist from Victoria. The news was old when it arrived, but we were in no hurry. We liked reading stories about other parts of the world.

In the middle of October of that year, 1899, we read that the Boers declared war on the British in South Africa. I had read about the tensions in South Africa before. They had continued for many years. I never understood why and I was not interested. South Africa was far away, even farther than England, and the newspapers were filled with stories of tensions all over the world.

Stuart was interested though. He had sympathy for the Boers. He explained that the British had taken their land away many years ago, so they moved inland to make new nations of their own. The British still threatened them. The papers said they wanted protection for British workers in the Boer mines and they accused the Boers of treating Black people badly. It was strange that the British would care so much about common workers or Black people. Stuart said the truth was that the Boers had found gold and diamonds and the British wanted them.

The papers made jokes about the war. For everyone knew the Boers were nothing against the mighty British Empire. Even Stuart thought they would be crushed in a few weeks, but he was wrong. A week later, the Boers surrounded Mafeking, a town on their western border. Two weeks later they surrounded two other British towns to the south, Ladysmith and Kimberley. The Boers had prepared well. Thousands of British soldiers were killed or captured trying to free these three towns.

Stuart grew concerned as the news worsened. I asked why he was worried. The war was so far away it could not touch us in Metlakatla. My words did not console him. He feared something he dared not speak to me about. His silence made me anxious too, for he had never hidden his concerns from me before. Three days after the third siege began, the newspapers spread panic. They announced that the British Empire would send an army from around the world to fight the Boers. Anyone who had fought on land or who had commanded at sea would be needed to serve the Empire.

When I read this I understood his concern. Why would they need sea captains, I asked him. The fighting was far from the sea. He told me they needed men who had experience commanding other men, like he did. Don't worry, he told me. They would probably use him to run supplies to the front line since he had never been a soldier. Still, I did not want him to go to the far side of the world. I asked if he would offer to go. No, he said he would wait until they came for him.

We did not wait long. A ship heading south from Fort Simpson stopped at our harbour to take him to Victoria two days later. I held back my tears on the dock as we said goodbye. He did his best to sound chipper but I knew he did not want to go. It was not his war.

"Pray to Great Spirit for me," he smiled before he climbed the gangway.

"Be careful," I called to him. It was a strange thing to say, but I could not think of other words.

"I will write to you as often as I can," he called back to me.

I waved to him and watched until his ship disappeared from sight. Then he was gone. Hopefully it will only be for a few months, I told myself, but I feared it might be longer. I felt helpless. A deep and ancient pain filled my heart, one I have felt many times during my life. I thought I would never feel it again, but it had returned. There was nothing I could do but wait and pray.

It was early November. A biting chill in the air filled me with a dread of what would come. I imagined I would not hear from him for several weeks, but his first letter arrived only ten days later. He posted it in Victoria the day before his ship set sail for Africa. He said soldiers of all ages were going with him. The young ones talked nervously and constantly while the older men were mostly silent. He tried to reassure me that he was probably too old to be sent to the front.

His letter did not reassure me. I missed him more than ever. Waiting was a nightmare that I could not wake from. I was already wondering when his next letter would come, knowing I would be more frightened for me once I read it.

I did my best to keep my mind off him. I even searched for William to talk to. Usually he looked for me but now I needed him. He was pleased to listen to my concerns. It put him in a strangely chipper mood I could not appreciate. His advice to me was that I should not worry, but I had no choice but to worry, for I cared about Stuart so much. No other man from our village had gone to the war so no others shared my misery. I found myself wishing I could still talk with Tsangook.

Winter set in. The snows were deep and the winds were fierce. It seemed they understood the torment in my heart. William tried to get me interested in his Christmas celebrations but I could think of nothing but Stuart. Finally, his second letter arrived the week before Christmas. He was in a city called Singapore on the far side of the Pacific. The men of his ship would rest there one day. I searched the globe Stuart had given me on my last birthday and I found Singapore.

He said he missed me as he listened to other men snoring in the ship's hold each night. The ship was crowded. He missed the time when he was a captain and had his own room. Some of the other men looked for prostitutes in Singapore, but he thought only of me.

Already a month had passed since he wrote the letter. By this time he would be in South Africa. Maybe he would be fighting, I worried. It would be a while before I knew. The farther he traveled from me the longer I had to wait for his letters.

The others of Metlakatla missed him, though not as much as I did. They always asked where he was and how he was doing. The women decided to help the soldiers by knitting warm sweaters. They had started several of them before Reverend Keen explained that it would soon be summer in South Africa in a month. They stopped knitting for they were sure the war would be over before their sweaters would be needed.

William came around to check on me every couple of days. He was relieved to see me sad, so he could give me a pep talk. He said "Come on, old boy. Cheer up!" as he patted me on my back. He thought that helped. I pretended it did just to make him stop trying.

I did not attend William's Christmas sermon in the great church, but I did join the villagers in his residence afterwards. How empty it felt without Stuart's stories and his songs. He left his fiddle resting against the wall of our room. When I begged him to come home safely, he joked that he would have to, to get his fiddle. I told him I would not touch it until I saw him again.

Reverend Keen gave us his New Year's blessings in the Assembly Hall. He made a big fuss about this being the first day of a new century. He spoke hopefully, saying this would be a great century of peace and goodwill for all men. He did not bother to make excuses for the war in Africa because, he said, everyone knew it would be over shortly.

It was not short enough, as far as I was concerned. Stuart's next letter did not arrive until the middle of January. He wrote it when they landed in Durban, a day's travel away from the fighting. He was glad to be off the ship, but he still had no idea where he was going to be sent. There was fighting in several places. Troops from India had arrived two months earlier, before the fighting began. He said there were other Indians there too, mostly to work as labourers, stable hands and in the field hospitals.

Another letter arrived as we were mending our nets for the oolichon camp on the Nass. I tore it open anxiously, not knowing what to expect. He was fighting as a common soldier on the front, inland from Durban, where the British troops were trying to break the siege on Ladysmith. They had failed so far and attempts to relieve the other two cities under siege in other parts of the country had also failed. His commander, General Buller, was an arrogant fool. It seemed the war will not be won as easily as we had hoped. The British would not use the Indian soldiers, fearing they might turn their guns against them for invading India. Stuart thought they were probably correct. Indians were carrying the wounded off the battlefields many miles to field hospitals. Many of them were killed trying to save the wounded. They were the real heroes of the war, not the British, he thought. Stuart said his troop was discouraged and not speaking much. They were worried about what would come next.

So was I, but I joined the others at the oolichon camp to keep myself busy. I still worried about him all the time, though. My friends did their best to cheer me when the day's work was over. They sang, danced and told stories around the fire with more enthusiasm than usual. They missed Stuart too. They asked if I knew any Scottish songs or if he had taught me how to play his fiddle. He had tried but I was not a good student of music. I asked Great Spirit to give me another chance.

We finished the oolichon camp in late March. I hurried back to Metakatla. His next letter was waiting for me. He had written the letter in the last week of January. At least I knew he was alive until then, but it gave me more cause to worry. General Buller was still in charge of his troops and they had still not been able to break the siege of Ladysmith. His own men were calling him "General Reverse" because he had retreated after every victory. The newspapers said that thousands of troops had arrived to help him since then and they were getting ready to try again in a few days.

During their last retreat, Stuart was sent with some others to help the Indians carry the wounded across a river. He met their leader, Mr. Gandhi, a small man with a remarkable Spirit. He spoke with Gandhi as they rested on the far side of the river. The stretcher bearers had the hardest job on the battlefield, retrieving the dead and wounded and carrying them to the hospital many miles away. When an Indian was killed by the gunfire while trying to rescue the wounded, another rushed up to take his place. They never complained about their dangerous and difficult work.

Stuart was most impressed with Gandhi. His own troops were more depressed than ever, but Gandhi was cheerful and confident. He had a family in Durban, a wife and three sons with a fourth child on the way with his family. He was only thirty, but he had been married seventeen years. Despite his love for his family, he was glad to be of service, even if it meant putting his own life at great risk. If Indians wish to be full citizens of the British Empire they must contribute to the war effort, he told Stuart.

Gandhi had organized the Indian stretcher carriers without British help. Even so, the British refused his offer of help until they were desperate. They told him Indians were not manly enough to be trusted with jobs that involved strength or danger. He wished to prove them wrong. He said it is best to respond to disrespect and insults with kindness and generosity. Even though he was Hindu, he asked Stuart if he was familiar with the passage in the Bible where Jesus advised his followers to turn the other cheek if they were struck.

What surprised Stuart most was Gandhi's sympathies for the Boers, especially their leaders and their women, who he thought were heroic. No British soldier would dare admit to such feelings. It is rare to meet such a good and honest man, he wrote. Gandhi gave him his address in Durban and asked him to write when he could.

Gandhi's words gave Stuart new hope. I was impressed by him too. Imagine saving the lives of of people who hate you, to show them your strength. Surely that was more powerful than my hatred and bitterness had been. How can someone hate another who saves his life? But were the British truly grateful, I wondered. Did his actions change their hearts?

Several weeks of newspapers also waited for me after the oolichon camp. I searched through them to see what had happened after Stuart wrote his letter. In early March, excited headlines announced that the British had freed Ladysmith and broken the two other sieges. The Boers were retreating. Then I read that 7000 British soldiers had been killed or wounded. I knew that Stuart could be one of them and I felt sick. I promised myself to stop reading the papers.

The weeks passed slowly without another letter. The longer I waited the more I felt certain something terrible had happened. I began to have nightmares. In one dream, I was fighting beside Stuart in a battle. I saw him fall but as I ran to help him the field grew longer and longer, pulling him away from me. I woke up crying. In another dream, I was the one who was shot and he was trying to comfort me. I was certain that at least this last dream could not be a prediction, but my fears still tormented me.

His next letter arrived at the end of April. I was preparing to leave for the salmon camp on the Skeena. It was dated March 4. He is alive, I sighed with relief. He wrote that the battle for Ladysmith lasted two weeks. Many had died but the troops were jubilant when they reached Ladysmith. The people of Ladysmith greeted them with loud cheers and a rousing chorus of "God Save The Queen". They rested there for two days. Stuart was then sent by train to join other troops in another part of the country. He wrote his letter on the train.

Stuart learned that Gandhi and his stretcher bearers were sent home after Ladysmith was freed. The British thanked them and the troops cheered them. Stuart said Gandhi would not get a medal for his bravery. The English only give medals to their own people, but he was happy he was still alive, for many of his workers had died. Stuart planned to write to him from the train.

Stuart missed the boredom of Metlakatla. My life was too anxious to be boring.

Like the sea on a windless day, I looked calm but great currents moved under my surface. I wandered the town restlessly, trying to find peace. The Spirit of the Church mocked me as I passed. It took pleasure in my sadness. Perhaps, I thought, this is why William and Reverend Keen take refuge in the forest.

In early May, two older men brought William to the camp in a canoe. It was his first time at a fishing camp, although he had lived with us for twenty years. Our villagers cheered him and made him feel welcome. He beamed with joy. He had come to bring me another letter from Stuart. I was touched by his kindness. Stuart was now stationed in a town called Bloemfontein. He had been sent there to help capture it, but it fell to the British troops just as Stuart arrived. The Boers had fled the city without a fight. Stuart's new commander wanted to chase after them but his men had to rest. They had drunk bad water that made them sick with high fevers. Stuart said they would rest in Bloemfontein at least four weeks. He told me I could write to him there.

Gandhi had responded to Stuart's letter. Stuart had asked him how he kept such positive feelings in a time of war and where his strength came from. Gandhi said faith keeps him positive. Faith cannot be given, as the British tell us. It is something we must grow into. Real strength is not physical might, but a will that cannot be dominated. He advised Stuart not to lose faith in humanity. A good man is a friend of all living things. A man must know, he added, that he can shake the world in a gentle way.

That idea excited me. I wanted to write to Stuart immediately. William had brought me writing paper and a pen in case I needed them. For the first time I felt he was a real friend. I had not been able to write to him since he left me. I filled my letter with many meaningless things about my life in Metlakatla, but William assured me my boring life would sound like good news to Stuart.

At the end of June, when we returned from the salmon camp, another letter arrived from Bloemfontein dated May 23. Stuart had written it before receiving my letter. His commander had captured Johannesburg in the state of Transvaal. It is close to Pretoria, the capital, and Stuart expected Pretoria itself would fall in a few weeks. Stuart had not gone with them. He stayed behind with other troops to defend Bloemfontein. There was no fighting there but there was still danger. His troops were ordered to always be on guard.

He continued to exchange letters with Gandhi. He asked him how he should behave as an occupying soldier over the Boers. Gandhi told him to treat them with the same respect he would give to a loved family member. Anger and intolerance are the enemies of correct understanding, Gandhi told him. Anger and fear blinds one to the truth and our purpose in this world is to seek the truth. The Boers are upset, for they have been humiliated by the British. It was a mystery to him how some men feel honoured by humiliating their fellow man.

Stuart wanted to follow Gandhi's advice, but he was not sure it was useful in his situation. How could he show love and respect when the Boers he passed in the streets would not look him in the eye? Boers do not want love from the soldiers, he told me, and it was unsettling to know they might try to kill him instead.

Gandhi's words made me think of the war in my own town, and the broken trust that remained. We need to treat everyone like our family, I thought. That is how we heal. His words from the other side of the world, from a man I had not met, filled me with love. I stopped judging and resenting others that summer. I taught the young students who returned from the residential schools not to hold hatred in their hearts for Whites, even if they were beaten and abused. This is the true way of the Shamans, I taught them. It was the clearest path to healing.

Pretoria fell in early June. There was another battle beyond it a week later. The Boers retreated to the far edges of their country and the British closed in on them. There was one last battle in late August. On September 3, the newspapers declared the war was over.

But the war was not over. As soon as the British troops passed, the Boers controlled the land again. The Boer soldiers were invisible to the British, for they looked like everyone else. They met in secret places to plan attacks on railways and bridges. They ambushed British soldiers, who were easy to see in their red uniforms, and they quickly disappeared again. Other Boers hid them, fed them and pretended to know nothing about them. Many trains and bridges were destroyed before the British admitted the war was not over, and that they were losing it.

Stuart was fortunate to stay in Bloemfontein until September. He was safer there, away from the battles and the attacks, but in September the British began to build thousands of blockhouses to protect the railways and bridges. Each blockhouse took three months to build and Stuart was sent with troops to protect the workers who built them. He also helped build fences of barbed wire across the land to make it harder for Boer fighters to travel.

Still the attacks continued. The Boers attacked government buildings and homes of those who helped the British. General Kitchener, a ruthless man who hated the Boers, took charge of the British troops. He ordered his men to burn Boer farms and houses so their fighters had nowhere to hide. They poisoned their water and put their women and children in prison camps. Their husbands and fathers who were captured were sent to prisons in lands far from Africa. When Kitchener was finished, the Boers were destroyed and so were their lands.

Stuart could not believe he was asked to do these things. He told me he would have refused to go to Africa if he knew it would be like this. But it was too late by then. He wrote to Gandhi to ask him what he should do, for his conscience was deeply troubled.

Gandhi said there were causes for which he was prepared to die, but no cause for which he would kill. Burning people's houses and farms, poisoning their wells and sending them to prison camps where they might die is like murdering them, as far as he was concerned. Gandhi's words upset Stuart. Stuart argued that he had to obey his orders or he would be imprisoned himself. He was so troubled and unhappy. He just wanted to feel peace in his life again.

Gandhi apologized for sounding insensitive, but he suggested prison might not be a bad idea. It would be impossible to find happiness in Stuart's situation, he said. Happiness is when what we say and do are in harmony. To believe that something is wrong but to do it anyway is dishonest, Gandhi advised him. You must live as you believe, even though fear will try to stop you. He asked Stuart to listen to his heart and heed its advice instead surrendering to his fears.

Stuart stopped writing to Gandhi for a couple months, for his advice was too difficult to consider. He tried to justify obeying his commanders to me, but I felt the pain and torment in his heart. He was training his eyes not to see and his mind not to understand.

I was as tormented as Stuart. Gandhi's words felt like the truth, but I did not want Stuart to follow his advice if it put him in great danger. I knew he would not escape punishment from the army if he disobeyed his commanders. I wanted him to return to me, so I could not advise him what to do.

I turned to Great Spirit, asking him for guidance. I promised to Him I would try harder to honour the ways of our people and the teachings of the Animal Spirits if He would show me the way out of this crisis. His response came to me as a dream.

In my dream, I was walking on a path by the forest when I felt the Spirits watching me. I was too afraid to continue but I dared not turn my back to return the way I came. I stood without moving as dark shapes slowly came towards me from out of the woods. As they drew nearer, I saw they were Animal Spirits slightly taller than myself. They made no sound as they moved. First I saw Bear, and then Deer, Beaver and Raven. Others followed them – Eagle, Wolf, Frog and others.

Their eyes stayed fixed on me as they approached. I stood tall. I could not defend myself, but I did not fear my death. They gathered around me as if to study me. Bear pointed to path I had just walked and I knew I must return. The Spirits followed me. This time the path led to a beach I did not remember. I paused. Bear pointed the way I must go. They walked with me as I followed the shore, making no footprints where their feet landed.

Suddenly, I was standing before a village. It had painted longhouses, totems and canoes like our villages were when I was a boy. Bear pointed to the largest longhouse that stood in the centre of the row. I left the Spirits and walked to the longhouse. I reached out to pull back the deerskin that covered the door, but it would not move.

"Hello" I cried out. "Is there anyone inside? I want to come in."

A voice answered, "You cannot come in!"

"Why?" I asked. "Are you sick?" I waited a bit but there was no answer, so I asked again.

"You cannot come in!" the voice commanded.

"Why not?" I asked again.

"You are contaminated." It answered. I looked down at my hands and arms and I was shocked. They were covered in red spots that dripped puss. Then I heard laughter. I looked to the top of the hill above the village and I saw the great church of Metlakatla. The evil Spirit of the Church was laughing at me. I woke, tangled in my sweaty sheets and crying.

What kind of message is this, I wondered. It troubled me greatly. I still did not know what to tell Stuart, for it was not about him. I was afraid to ask Great Spirit again in case the next dream would be more terrifying. I would sit with my feelings and let Stuart sit with his, I decided. Hopefully the answers would soon become clear.

By January, Stuart was back in Bloemfontein, supervising food rations for the refugee camp. I was greatly relieved that he was there and not fighting the Boers, but his new assignment was not much easier. British soldiers were on food rations too, and they wanted Stuart to give them some of the Boer rations. They did not like that the Boers in their camps got free food and shelter while they were still hungry. Stuart did not have the heart steal from people who had already lost so much. He made up stories and excuses each time the soldiers asked. He feared if he refused them flatly, he might be attacked or betrayed by his own troops.

The camp was on a field surrounded by a high fence made of barbed wire. It was larger than Fort Simpson, Stuart guessed. He worked outside the fence, organizing and guarding the rations. He did not set foot inside the camp at first. There were very few rations for so many tents. If there were two people in each tent, he did not believe there was enough food or water for all of them.

In the first week of February, during the peak of summer, he was called to his commander's office. His commander wanted to speak to him before giving him a new duty. A woman named Emily Hobhouse had arrived from England. She had come to inspect the refugee camps. "She's an interfering do-gooder, an insufferable complainer and a Boer sympathizer," his commander told him, but he had orders directly from England that she must be allowed to inspect the camps. "Of course, we told her there are only a couple camps set up to house Boer women and children who have asked for our protection, and they are adequately set up with food and water. If she asks about the barbed wire fence, that's for their protection too. Keep her away from worst tents. If she wants to know about other camps, you only know about this one, understood?"

Truthfully, Stuart only knew about the Bloemfontein camp. It was Emily Hobhouse who told him there were forty-four other camps around the country. The army had not fooled her. Stuart said she was a bold woman, serious and full of purpose, with her hair tied back into a tight bun. She was fearless too, so horrified by injustice that she confronted it with no concern for her own safety.

It was a particularly hot day when Stuart first led her through the camp. He did not know what to expect, but it was not what he had imagined. His commander had told him to keep her away from the worst tents, but when Stuart had a close look at them they all looked quite terrible.

The tents were worse inside than they appeared on the outside. At least six people lived in each one, and some had as many as ten. They were so crowded that the women lay on top of each other. The air was thick and hot with countless flies buzzing around and crawling on everything. There was no food, no water, no mattresses on the ground to sleep on, no blankets or fuel for a fire to fight off the cold at night. Many had terrible diseases and everyone was dying of hunger.

There was a medical tent where tired nurses treated the most desperate patients. Hobhouse charged at them in outrage, complaining about the dying children and the lack of blankets, soap, medicine or drinking water, but when she saw the nurses faces she knew they were doing the best they could. The British would not waste supplies on the Boers.

A young Boer woman lay on the first bed inside the tent, naked and barely covered by a sheet in the fierce heat. She was little more than a skeleton. Her feet and head were too large for her shrunken body. Her knees stood out like lumps and her stomach had collapsed in so far that Stuart thought it must be touching her spine. At first, he feared she was dead, but he saw her staring at him with her sunken eyes. He was horrified. She cried out loudly without warning and he almost fainted.

A nurse ran over and tried to steer Hobhouse away. "This one is always a major nuisance. Pay her no mind," she said. "Such a damn moron. She can't even speak English." Hobhouse asked why she was calling out. "She wants her mother," she replied. "She never shuts up about her."

Hobhouse inspected the camp for three days. It was Stuart's duty to follow her everywhere. He could not remember what he saw after the first day. His mind was filled with so much sorrow and pain that the details blurred, but he could not forget the young woman who had called for her mother. He visited the medical tent to check on her the next day, but the bed was empty. She had died in the night.

After those three days, Stuart knew the painful truth. The women and young children were innocent prisoners, starving to death without water, dignity or kindness. He could no longer listen to excuses that the camps were for the good of the Boers. He watched the corpses that were carried out gate on stretchers every morning. Most of them were too small to be adults. Often three or four were piled on one stretcher with no sheet to cover them.

Stuart could not tolerate the soldiers who pressured him to steal their rations after that. He told them about the conditions in the camp, but the soldiers did not care. The sooner they die, the better for us, they replied. That infuriated him. They saw that and they turned against him. Stuart knew he was in trouble. He expected to be called before his superiors any day.

He used what time he had left to write to Gandhi. He told him he knew he must stop helping the British but that he was afraid of what would happen to him when he did. His disobedience would do nothing to stop British cruelty to the Boers. He was sure his efforts would be wasted.

Gandhi answered him with sympathy and concern. He advised Stuart to use love to defend against his fears. Forgive all those who come to hurt you, he advised. Love will make you stronger than your fear of punishment. Only strong men are capable of forgiving, he explained. They have an inner peace that cannot be touched by their enemies. He also believed that all evil must be resisted and that no good effort was ever wasted. He told Stuart that whatever he does may seem insignificant, but it was most important that he stay true to his conscience.

I only heard from Stuart once after that. It was a short and painful letter. His commanding officer had received complaints about Stuart's attitude from the other troops and he had summoned him to his office. He accused him of being a Boer sympathizer. Stuart admitted that he was horrified by what he saw in the camp and that

THIS IS NOT USED

he did sympathize with the innocent woman and children who were dying there. His commander said he must not let his heart get in the way of his duty. Stuart told him it should never be anyone's duty to murder innocent women and children and that he could not continue to be a partner to the army's crimes.

If he had admitted his sympathies and left it at that, perhaps he would have escaped punishment, but Stuart told the truth. It was an unjust war. He was arrested and locked in cell. He was told he would meet with higher commanders in a few weeks and they would give him a dishonourable discharge from the army. One of the soldiers who still liked him agreed to mailed Stuart's letter to me under his name. When I saw it was from someone I did not know, I feared something terrible had happened to Stuart. Instead, I learned nothing had happened yet, but it soon would.

Dear Gugweelaks,

This will alarm you but please stay strong for me. I met with my commander and I told him I can no longer support the war. I have been arrested and jailed. I will find out what my fate will be in a few weeks. I will be discharged from the army, but I am afraid they will not let me return home. They cannot show other soldiers that they can go home by doing what I have done. They will keep me in prison until the war is over and the other soldiers have returned home. Mr. Gandhi's words have given me great comfort and strength. I hope his words will give you strength too. Some day I will return to you, but you must be patient and brave for both of us. More than anything, I regret I will not be able to write to you again or receive your letters. I have already exposed my friend to too much risk by having him send this to you. I love you with all my heart and I pray you will wait for me. I will write to you again as soon they release me.

Stuart

My greatest fear had come to pass. There was nothing I could do. I prayed to Great Spirit for Stuart's safety, but I worried that even He could do nothing. I waited anxiously, knowing I would not hear from him for a long time. I was so anxious I could not sleep. I spoke with William, for I needed to speak my fears out loud. He said little but that he was sad for my suffering and that he would pray for Stuart and me.

I could not go with the others to the fishing camps that spring. I needed to be alone. There was no Uncle Silgitook to keep me company. I wished I could talk to Gandhi, to tell him what happened to Stuart and to ask him what I should do. I read Stuart's letters over and over to remember what he had told Stuart. His instructions were simple to understand but so hard to follow. No-one would punish me. No-one was trying to hurt me. My love for Stuart did not make me strong enough to forgive the British army. What would they care if I did? How could I resist their evil?

Each day, I sat still for hours on the hill above our harbour when the others were at their camps. When they returned, I wandered the forest alone. There was nothing I could say to them. I asked Great Spirit for strength and guidance. The trees swayed in the wind, the light sparkled on the water and the rain splashed in the puddles. He spoke to me through them but I could not decipher His message. Nothing eased the pain in my heart. All I had was hope, and hope is a cruel and cunning beast.

Messages came to me in my dreams, but they did nothing to reassure me. I dreamt I was in the forest, where I had gone to listen to Great Spirit. Sometimes the forest felt safe and at other times I sensed danger. It always grew dark, so dark that I could not see the stars or the shapes of the trees. I became lost and fearful of what would happen.

In one dream, I struggled over fallen logs and through tall ferns to find my way. I saw a small light in the branches in front of me. As I drew closer, I realized, that there were two lights. They were eyes. A cold chill ran up my spine. Suddenly they blinked. Owl screeched and flapped his wings. I turned and ran as fast as I could, but he followed, shaking out the dust and feathers of Death above me. I tripped and fell. The ground disappeared. I fell faster and faster through the cold night air. I woke with a start. My heart was racing and filled with pain, but I was alive.

I worried for days what the message meant. Did something just happen? Was it a prediction or a curse? Was I going to die?

A few weeks later at the end of June, before the village had returned from the salmon camps, a letter arrived from the British Army. My heart sank. I expected it to announce his discharge and prison sentence but instead it told me he was dead. He died of a typhoid fever while in prison awaiting his trial. The postmark on the letter was from May 8, the same week Owl had chased me in my dream. The letter said all charges against Stuart would be dropped and that his belongings would arrive shortly in the mail. The letter did not offer any condolences to those who loved him. The army did not care.

I held the letter for a long time, reading it over and over. I understood the words, but I needed to understand my feelings. I felt a great sadness, for we would never meet again, but I also felt a relief, a strange feeling of certainty. Stuart had reached a place where the British Army could not punish him. His death freed me of waiting for his return and the fear that I might ever see him again.

My life, once filled with pain and worry, was now empty again. My companions were the forest, the sea, the wind and the few people and buildings that were left of our village. The only one that did not belong was the great church. It stood on Mission Hill like a victorious conqueror. Its tall steeple was a sword held high, mocking and scorning the people whose lives it had crushed and enslaved. There was nothing left for its evil Spirit to destroy. It waited only for the last of the town to die.

I sat on the wall along the road that ran in front of our houses, watching as our canoes arrived back from the fishing camp. A week of grieving had passed. My tears, like my words, had dried up. William and Reverend Keen returned from a visit to Haida Gwaii the same week. I showed everyone the letter from the British Army. They offered me their tears and their blessings. I thanked them but I had little else to say. I was in a place of peace where no one could touch me.

A parcel with Stuart's belongings arrived the following week. It contained pieces of clothing, a knife, a picture of me and the pocket watch I had bought in Fort Simpson many years ago. I had given it to him for good luck before he left. I wondered if his Spirit had followed his belongings back to Metlakatla. I held each piece tenderly, but I could not feel him in any of them.

I soon found myself alone again. Keen left for Victoria, to show his collection of forest frogs to a museum. William went with him to meet the bishop there. Most of the others went hunting, went on shopping trips to Vancouver or Victoria or left to visit their relatives in other villages while the weather was good. I did not mind being alone, since I still had no words to say.

I had another dream. It was not frightening this time. I wandered through the forest, following a path that led to a river. I could go no further. I was tired so I sat down at the base of a large tree and rested. A canoe came up the river. It was magic, for it moved against the current without paddles. It shone like silver and seemed to bend from side to side. It stopped on the bank beside me. A handsome man climbed out and walked towards me.

His clothes shone with many colours, as if there was a light inside of him. He walked up to me and offered me his hand and pulled me up to face him. His beautiful smile greeted me.

"I have found you at last," he said. "Please come with me. I have something to show you."

He led me to his canoe and signaled for me to climb in. I did not recognize his face, as beautiful as he was, yet I knew I could trust him. I climbed in and he climbed in behind me. He wrapped his strong arms around me. They too felt familiar.

"Don't be frightened. You are safe while I am holding you," he reassured me. Suddenly, I recognized Stuart's voice and arms. A peace settled over me as I snuggled against his chest. The canoe pulled away from the shore and sped fasted and faster down the river to the sea.

It stopped as night was closing in. We climbed out onto a beach and he led me up the hill to a village above. He stopped and handed me a torch that burned brightly in his hand.

"I must leave you here," he said softly, his eyes glowing with affection. I opened my mouth to beg him not to go, to tell him he must not leave me, but he silenced me with a finger to my lips. His fingertip was sweet and gentle as a kiss. "This will not be the last time you will see me, my love, but first you must do as I have taught you. You must burn all of my belongings in the fire so that I can be reborn." He handed me the parcel that the British army had sent and he pointed to the great church that towered at the top of the hill.

The village disappeared. I sat up in my bed. I felt my face to know if I was still dreaming. I climbed slowly out of my bed and dressed. I put on my coat and stuffed a box of matches in my pocket. I picked up the parcel that had led Stuart's Spirit to me. I paused at the door as I was about to leave. I closed it again and climbed back upstairs. I collected his fiddle, Tamlahk's shirts, Jesse's photograph and Tsangook's dresses and shawls and went back down the stairs.

I was a warm July evening. A soft breeze blew from the north, out over the harbour. I reached Mission Point and the front door of the great church. It was locked. I found a shovel at the back beside the graveyard and I smashed a window beside the door. I threw the parcel, the clothes, the fiddle and the photograph inside and I climbed in after them.

I felt my way to the first oil lamp along the wall and I lit it. Its faint light disappeared into the high vault of the ceiling above, but it was enough light to see what I was doing. I piled what I had brought on the floor. One by one, I took the oil lamps off the walls and smashed them on the floor beside the pile. A cold, threatening chill swirled around me. "It is too late," I said to the Spirit. "You cannot stop me." I stuck a match and tossed it onto the pools of oil.

The fire spread quickly, filling the great hall with a flickering yellow glow. I climbed out the broken window and walked back towards my house. I watched the fire from a distance as it grew and grew. The windows of the great church glowed brighter and brighter, like the eyes of a giant beast filled with rage. It roared and cursed as the windows shattered. Smoke filled the air over Mission Point as flames burst through its great ceiling. They climbed the tall steeple until it became a blazing beacon. The Spirit groaned and cried. Thousands of sparks flew into the night sky, as many as the stars in the skies above them. They flew flying higher and higher, carrying their sacrifice up to Great Spirit.

The steeple and ceiling collapsed inside the walls with a loud crash. The buttresses soon followed, falling onto the stone foundation. The few people still in town came running from their beds when they heard the steeple fall. By then there was nothing they could do to save the church. They spent the rest of the night guarding their houses from the falling embers.

By morning, there was nothing left of the church but charred, smoldering timbers and melted glass. The evil Spirit was gone.

FORTY
ONE

News of the great church burning spread quickly up and down the coast. It was on everyone's lips from New Metlakatla to Victoria. People rushed home from their visits. Men returned from their hunting trips and Reverend Keen and William hurried back from their meetings. They stared at the empty space on Mission Point where it once stood, where only burnt timbers and the stone foundation remained.

Those who live here found it bewildering and hard to believe that their houses and the Assembly Hall were now the tallest buildings. The long shadow the church had cast over everyone and everything was gone. Those who lived elsewhere also came to look at nothing, to see for sure that it was gone. To them, the great church was Metlakatla. Without it, the town itself had vanished.

For a short while, Metlakatla was famous again. Reporters arrived from Victoria to photograph the charred ruins. Newspapers printed stories of how the great church was built with pictures of the opening celebration beside those of the ruins. They mourned its loss as a horrible tragedy, and then quickly forgot about it.

Everyone had a theory about how the fire started. Some claimed that men from New Metlakatla, who had once tried to dismantle our saw mill, had returned thirteen years later to seek revenge for their failure. Anne wrote that many in New Metlakatla believed that was true, but no one admitted to doing it. Some suggested Methodists, under the guidance of Thomas Crosby, started the fire. Others, including those who were woken by the crash, believed that lightning struck the steeple, even though the skies were mostly clear that night. No one suspected it was started by an old man with a box of matches in his pocket.

I could have told them. They would have vented their outrage against me, published my picture, put me on trial and thrown me into a White prison for the rest of my life. I had no fear of that, but they would not be better off for it. They soon grew tired of looking for evidence to back up their stories. With no one to punish, they got on with the task of deciding what to do now that the church was gone.

William felt the loss of the church more than anyone. In his mind it was his church. It was the reason he came to Metlakatla and the reason he stayed through the war with Duncan, after Duncan left and when Jane died. Without it, his position as bishop meant nothing to him. His congregation, as loyal as they were, seemed ridiculously small. He lost interest in giving sermons or communion. He even stopped going to the woods to write poetry.

He complained to me that no one read his poems. They had been published by an Anglican Press that was eager to win his favour, but they had only sold a few copies. Now that his church was gone, those who remembered him in Victoria only spoke of the foolish things he had done while fighting Duncan.

I freed him from the spell of the evil Spirit that held him tightly in its grasp, but it was not a freedom he wanted. We still speak every day but instead of discussing lofty thoughts he speaks of England. He wants to die there. He wonders if he should leave Jane here, in the land she learned to love, or whether he should exhume her body and bring it with him. He fears spending his time in Heaven alone.

Reverend Keen, forever an optimist, organized work teams to clean up the mess after the reporters were gone. They carried the blackened timbers into the forest and used shovels, brooms and wheelbarrows to move the rest out of sight of the town. Stones from the church's foundation were used to make repairs to the retaining wall along the road and to replace the rotting steps that lead down to our dock. He is raising money to build a new church. The town is excited about the project. There are still plenty of stones for a new foundation. Sometimes it takes a great fire before new life can grow again.

The women have been productive too. They are knitting and sewing things to sell in Vancouver and Victoria. One of them made me a ceremonial cape out of a wool blanket. She has stitched a red felt pattern of the Eagle Clan crest on the back and decorated the rest with white buttons that shine like abalone shells. I am wearing it today as I make my way into the forest with my cedar hat and walking stick.

I find a couple burnt timbers that the work teams carried into the forest last summer. Already they are half covered in moss and lichen. Young ferns have taken root on them too. By next year, I will not find them for they will be completely covered. They will shrink as they are eaten away. Forest plants love fallen logs and charcoal.

How arrogant man is to believe that God has made him in His image, and that He has chosen Man above all other beings to be his favourite! Then he builds great churches to congratulate himself. The British believe they are God's choice above all other men. That is why they treat others with such contempt. But our people have behaved no better. Before Christianity, we believed our people were Great Spirit's chosen ones over all other people.

Great Spirit must be laughing at our silliness. We have little respect for what He has created. We are animals like the many others, but lesser animals that use our pride to justify killing each other. The Spirit of the Cannibal crouches in each of our hearts, waiting to spring into battle. One day, we will succeed in killing ourselves off and every other living being will sigh with great relief.

Why is it that we have never understood? It is the forest that Great Spirit created in His image. The forest, with all its many plants and animals, represents Him. When we are gone, and our silliness is over, it will creep forward to reclaim the Earth. It will devour all that Man has built.

This is what I am thinking as I pick my way slowly, deeper and deeper into the woods. I marvel at the peace that surrounds me. Ah yes, this is far lovelier than a British jail cell. Everything is growing again now that spring has returned. Pink flowers, so small and delicate, have sprung up in the moss on the logs and on the forest floor.

It has not rained for three days. I find a log that is almost dry and I sit to rest my tired legs. The forest is less dense here. I look around me at the trees, the hanging mosses and the leaves that tremble above me in the gentle breeze. But mostly the forest is still. The only thing speaks is a small brook that winds through the clearing. I kneel down beside it to take a drink, carefully pushing back my cloak to keep it from falling into the water.

The water is clear as glass. It tastes sweet and clean. I see a white stone on the bottom, round and smooth. It is the perfect size and shape to fit under my tongue, but I have no need for protection today. Sonoqua's eyes are not reflecting in the water. Only my own wrinkled face stares back at me.

The sun has come out. It sparkles on the water, reminding me of my name. I sit on the log again, my back to a tree, and I rest for an hour with my eyes half closed. I think about the many strange things that have happened in my past. How meaningless they seem to me now.

The stillness is broken by a great horned owl, who floats through the air and lands on a branch a few feet in front of me. He blinks slowly, his eyes half open like mine.

"Hello, Mr. Owl," I say softly. "You are still half asleep. You have been sleeping all day, haven't you?" He blinks at me. A ground squirrel pops out of his hole and sees the owl. He stands on his hind legs, bracing his front paws on a log in front of him, and screams a tirade of curses at him. The owl glances at the squirrel with disinterest and looks away again. I have never watched an owl without feeling fear before. His calmness impresses me.

Suddenly, he calls out, "Hoooo ooo." The call is echoed back from a hundred yards away. His mate sails gently over to him and sits on the branch beside him. They are aware of each other, but they do not make a fuss about it. They are like a comfortable couple who have known each other forever. They are exactly the same size. Perhaps they are both males, I smile to myself.

"Hooooo oooo," I call up to him softly. The familiar sound catches his attention. He opens his eyes wide and stretches his neck out to get a closer look at me. He cocks his head from side to side, trying to figure me out. I laugh and bow to him slowly. The couple rests on the branch a few minutes longer. Then they glide away, one a few seconds after the other.

I sit there as the light in the sky begins to fade. Before long I have another visitor. This time it is my old friend Raven. He flies to the same branch where the owls were to inspect me. I nod to him. He hops along the branch and calls out to me. I echo his call and he calls again. He tilts his head this way and that to get a better look at me. He repeats his call. He is trying to warn me, but there is no need. "I know, night is coming," I answer him. "The owls have been here." He tilts his head again and calls one last time before flying away.

The gloom is closing in. I pull my cloak in tightly around me to keep out the chill, but it finds me anyway. I tuck my legs up against my chest and wait. They will be here soon.

The darkness enfolds me. The shapes of the ferns and trees dissolve into the blackness. There is no moon. The light of the stars does not reach me. I could not find my way home now, even if I wanted to.

They have come. I feel their cold touch on my neck and face. I sit very still. There are many of them now, caressing my arms and shoulders and kissing my cheeks. I close my eyes.

"Is that you, mother?" I ask, silently inside my head. "It has been so long. I miss you too." Memlaka's arms pull me to her bossom and I surrender to her embrace. Then she is gone and it is my father, Neeshlak, standing before me, his hands on my shoulders, his eyes looking into mine. I feel his pride for me as I fight back my tears.

And there is Miyana smiling at me. She has forgiven me and she misses me too. Amapaas and Gwashasip are standing behind her, waiting to greet me. How I miss you all! I want to be with you again. I have gone many years without my family.

And now I sense Jesse. Sweet Jesse! His loving arms wrap around me as joyful and enthusiastic as he always was. Doolyaks is there too, with his gentle touch, his big foolish smile and his impressive tzootz. How I miss you, my life long friend! My other friends and relatives have come to greet me too – Laguksa, Hoshieka, Hahkwah, and of course Tsangook! Oh lovely, Tsangook! Have I worn your dresses and shawls well? I wish I had danced in them for you while you were alive. Thank you for all you have taught me!

And now I cannot help myself. My tears flow like a river, for it is Tamlahk standing before me. He is looking down, afraid to look into my eyes. His face is as wet as my own. I see the long scars running down his arms where he cut himself open with his hunting knife. "Dear sweet man, please forgive yourself. I have. I will love you forever," I whisper as I reach out and take his hands. He folds into my chest and hugs me tightly. I hold him for a very long time. Slowly, he pulls away from me with gratitude in his eyes. I see him mouth the words, "Thank you" and he smiles.

A stillness surrounds me. Their hands and lips have moved away. I cannot feel their breath and their faces are beginning to blur. Are they leaving? No, they are parting to let someone else through. He approaches me joyfully.

"Stuart! Bless you for coming!" I hold him too for a long time. When it is time to let go I say to him, "You have met my family and friends. You are in good company, for now they are your family too." He caresses me and flashes his beautiful smile. "Thank you for your kindness and your strength. Thank you for showing me that some White men are more than brothers, and that younger men can be my Elders too. You and the others want me to come with you. I will, but not tonight. When I do, we will share Eternity together, but for now you must be patient." He winks at me with his mischievous blue eyes and fades away into the night.

"Caaw, caaaw!" Raven screams. I wake from my dream. I am still curled up in a ball with my arms around my knees. I take a minute to look at the forest around me. The light is returning to the sky. I breathe in the cool morning air. I slowly straighten my legs and rub my eyes. I stretch out my arms and check my pulse. I am still alive. I thank Great Spirit for holding back the rain all night.

I rest a minute longer before I stand. I brush off the needles and flakes of bark from my cloak to make it clean again. I pick up my walking stick and I look for the best way to go.

Suddenly, I hear a deep, low growl very close to me. I freeze and hold my breath. It changes to a high whine, the kind a Cannibal Spirit makes before he cries "Eat! Eat!"

Ahh, I think to myself. It is just my stomach reminding me I am an animal, like all the others in the forest. I must find my way home and make myself some breakfast. Then I will look for William to see what he has been doing.

ABOUT THE
AUTHOR

Ken Tomilson was a writer, a glass artist, a community-builder, a traveller, and an adventurer. He was beloved for his good humour and gentle wisdom by friends and family around the world. His heart always remained wrapped up in this land, his birthplace: the Northwest Coast of Turtle Island. This book is the great artistic work of his lifetime. Metlakatla came to him as a vision with a demand to be written. Over 15 years, he wrote and re-wrote this love letter to the First Peoples. He completed the novel just as he completed his hero's journey, leaving it as his legacy.

Proceeds from this work will be split evenly between Rainbow Refugee and Out On Screen.

Lightning Source UK Ltd.
Milton Keynes UK
UKHW010952060223
416537UK00007B/1526